BRAIN CHILD

Stephen R. George

ZEBRA BOOKS
KENSINGTON PUBLISHING CORP.

For my wife, Valerie.

ZEBRA BOOKS

are published by

Kensington Publishing Corp.
475 Park Avenue South
New York, NY 10016

First printing: February, 1989

Printed in the United States of America

UNEARTHLY NIGHT

The treatment room was darker than it should have been. The rows of fluorescent bulbs on the ceiling were bright, but their light was being sucked away.

Sucked into a large patch of darkness on the wall behind Celia.

A patch of darkness in which Phylis could discern, like a shadow, the outline of a head. Too large for a human head, she thought.

Out of the darkness two long ropes of shadow began to emerge, pushing into the room like arms.

Celia opened her mouth and screamed.

Behind her, in the blackness, the shadow face appeared to smile, and suddenly its eyes blinked open.

Blazing yellow.

"Dark," Phylis whispered in horror. Then she folded into her own darkness.

CHAPTER ONE

Phylis Reynolds watched in resignation as the late August night lost its balmy comfort, assuming, instead, a crisp edge that compelled the protection of four walls and a roof. In the passenger seat of a three month old, royal blue Buick Regal, just crossing from Minneapolis into St. Paul, she regarded the sudden spatter of rain on the windshield with resentment, as if nature's manners were a personal affront.

"Oh, damn it," she said, sighing. "I thought this would be a perfect night."

The driver of the Regal momentarily took his attention from the glistening freeway and offered his companion a mock pout. Phylis returned the pout for a full second before breaking into a bright smile.

"Paul, you are such a little boy," she said, giggling now in accompaniment to the smile.

Mouth still pouting, but eyes crinkled in good humor, Paul Welch turned his attention back to the road and nodded in agreement. Watching him then, Phylis felt a sudden pang of longing. She studied the smooth lines of his face, which really did look boyish despite his twenty-nine years, and smiled possessively. His raven black hair, combed straight back off his high forehead and tucked neatly behind his ears, gleamed with health. Phylis reached out a slim hand and touched her burgundy nails to his leg.

He again turned away from the road to regard her. "It will be a perfect night. I promise."

"We won't have an outdoor table," Phylis protested feebly.

"But I know the maitre d', and there are some nice tables inside."

Phylis squeezed his thigh to show that she had been joking, and wondered as she did so what the naked flesh beneath the rough fabric of his pants would feel like against her palm. She swallowed, looked away from him and out the window, not trusting herself to speak.

"Besides," Paul said, placing his warm hand over her own and squeezing playfully. "Do you think I'd let our anniversary dinner be ruined by a few drops of rain?"

"Anniversary?"

"Sure." Paul grinned. "It's been two weeks since that fateful first lunch at MacDonalds sent us down this road to destiny."

"Only two weeks? I feel I've known you forever."

"And not bored yet?"

"Not nearly."

Paul turned his attention fully to the road as they approached their exit, but his hand remained protectively over hers. Another barrage of rain spattered against the windshield, and Paul activated the pulse wipers for a single sweep. Phylis turned away from him as if she were gazing out the window, but closed her eyes and focussed on the warmth of his hand upon her own, on the gentle ripple of his thigh muscles beneath her palm as he worked the brake and accelerator pedals.

Please, God, she thought, *let this be the night.*

Dinner at The Terrace was as romantic and wonderful as Paul had promised. The maitre' d' was indeed a friend of Paul's, and Phylis found herself unaccustomedly pampered. They took their time over the entrees, of which Phylis had chosen a New Orleans Cajun chicken dish, and lingered afterwards over a bottle of French, Alsace wine, all the while leaning across the candle lit corner table, talking quietly.

The dining room was well designed for couples such as themselves. The main lighting came from an ornate chandelier, hanging over the central waiter's station, which cast a subdued golden flicker across the tables situated around the perimeter of the cosy room. The only other illumination came from the glass-caged candles at each table. It was very difficult not to be overwhelmed by romance. Or even by lust, Phylis thought, and smiled mischievously.

"What's so funny?" Paul asked, tipping the last few drops of the Alsace into Phylis's glass.

"Nothing. I'm just happy."

Paul shook his head. "That was not a happy smile. That was a cat-who-ate-the-family-budgie smirk."

Phylis laughed aloud, and Paul reached across the table and touched her bare arm. "I'll get another bottle of wine," he said.

Phylis shook her head. "No."

"But ze night, she eez so young," Paul protested.

"Oui," Phylis said. "But ze woman, she doez nod

7

vant ze man to be, how you say? . . . too relaxed."

Paul opened his mouth to say something but closed it again immediately. Phylis squeezed his hand.

"Order us some coffee," she said, pushing her chair away from the table and standing. "I'll be right back."

Phylis stopped at the row of pay-phones outside the powder room. She raked through her purse until she found a quarter, dropped it in the slot, and dialed her home number. The phone rang only twice before it was picked up.

"Susan, it's Phylis."

"Oh, hi, Mrs. Reynolds."

"Everything okay?"

"Fine," Susan said.

"Any trouble with Celia?"

"She stayed up to watch *Night Court,* but I drew the line at *L.A. Law.* She's asleep now."

Phylis chuckled. "She's got you wrapped around her little finger."

"I don't mind. Are you having a good night?"

"Very nice," Phylis said, breaking into a smile even though Susan could not see it. "I just phoned to let you know, we'll be home soon. Leaving here in a few minutes."

"Okay," Susan said. "See you soon."

"Bye." Phylis hung up the phone and closed her purse.

I said "we," she thought. *"We'll" be home soon.*

Still smiling, she pushed open the door and went into the powder room.

She stood in front of the wall mirror, studying herself closely, and touched up her makeup. Afterwards she stepped back to get a full body view. Not bad, she

8

thought. She'd chosen a sky blue summer dress bought a year earlier but worn only once. It fit snugly in all the right places, and was cut just low enough to reveal a touch of what lay beneath without being brazen. Although appearing brazen might not be such a bad idea.

Naughty, she thought.

She stepped back to the counter and ran a brush through her shoulder-length, ash blond hair, teasing the bangs at the front until they looked slightly tousled. She looked her reflection straight in the eyes. For the umpteenth time she wondered if she was going a bit overboard with Paul, but it had been a long time since she'd gone overboard with anybody. Her divorce from Don had been finalized eighteen months ago, and since then her love life had been a desert broken only by the occasional dry mirage. Most of her energy during that time had been channeled into her job as art director of *MPLS Magazine*, a position she'd attained shortly after joining the magazine's staff as layout assistant. Not that she hadn't been trying, romantically that is, but it was so hard when there was Celia to contend with.

The moment the child's name entered her mind she forced it out. Not tonight. Tonight everything was right, everything was perfect.

Paul Welch was the best thing to happen to her in a long, long time. He was one of the stable of freelance writers that contributed to *MPLS*, and six months ago Phylis had worked with him on the presentation of his "Twin cities: 2001" feature. His interest in her had been obvious from the start, but she'd kept a cold, business-like formality between them until, two weeks

9

ago, they'd been forced to share a table at the crowded MacDonalds on east Hennepin Avenue. And surprise, surprise, she had broken down and discovered that she liked him. Very much.

Perhaps the six months of professional distance had set the groundwork for their relationship, for they found themselves instantly at ease with one another, and although Phylis had wanted to go beyond the tentative first stages of physical contact, she had held back because of Celia. But Celia had improved dramatically lately, and Dr. Hammond had said it was time to test some of that progress.

Tonight, Phylis thought. *Definitely, tonight.*

She packed away her makeup case and lipstick, and returned to the dining room. Paul had ordered two coffees, and he was sipping his as she took her seat.

"What's next on the agenda?" he asked, studying her appreciatively over the rim of his cup.

"My place for a night cap?" Phylis said softly, sipping her coffee, gazing into Paul's clear brown eyes.

"Do I finally get to meet your daughter?"

"She'll be sleeping."

"Then we can play chess, or something."

"Or something," Phylis agreed.

Paul's lips curled as he tried to hide a smile. "I'll get the check," he said, and motioned for the waiter.

Phylis leaned across the table and blew into the glass-encased candle. The flame flickered for a moment, then died, and the waxy smelling smoke drifted up to surround them.

The drive back to Phylis's home in West Minneapolis was quiet, disturbed only when Paul asked for directions. Phylis sat as close as she could to the inside edge of the comfortable bucket seat, hand resting on Paul's leg. Once, she used a burgundy nail to trace a circle across the inside thigh of his pants, and Paul tightened his lips stoically and groaned faintly. Phylis smiled, and looked out her window at the glow of the city through the haze of fine rain. The brand new smell of the car made her feel comfortable and at ease.

"Here it is," Phylis said as Paul approached the house. "Three-Oh-Two. Just park in the driveway."

Paul turned into the drive, and the headlights swung a sudden brilliant arc across the front of the bungalow. He stopped the car two feet from the garage door, killing the motor, then the lights.

"Nice place," he said.

"We like it," Phylis said, opening the door and stepping out onto the asphalt. The touch of rain was cool and refreshing, the air smelled of grass and earth. "Watch your step, Paul. Celia may have left a toy on the walk."

The living room curtain parted slightly as they came up the walk, and the front door opened before they reached it, sending a swath of yellow light out onto the rain soaked lawn.

"Thanks, Susan," Phylis said, stepping past the babysitter.

"Hi, Mrs. Reynolds," Susan said. "Hello, Mr. Welch," she added as Paul followed Phylis into the house.

"So, how long were we gone?" Phylis asked, slipping out of her shoes.

"Four and a half hours," Susan said, without glancing at her watch. At sixteen she was a paragon of the all-American, attractive, wholesome-yet-nubile girl-next-door, dressed in faded blue jeans, a Mickey Mouse sweatshirt, and topped with a head of golden blond hair that curled around her ears.

"We'll call it five," Phylis said. "Which makes it fifteen dollars. Okay?" Phylis counted out three fives and handed them to the girl. "Thanks again, Susan, for coming on such short notice."

Susan pocketed the three bills, smiling. "You're welcome. Good night."

She ran down the front path, paused at the street, then sprinted across to her own house, directly opposite. Phylis watched until Susan appeared as a silhouette in her own open door, waving. Phylis waved briefly and closed the door.

"Nice girl," Paul said, pulling off his shoes.

"I don't know what I'd do without her," Phylis said. "Listen, make yourself comfortable. Drinks are in the cabinet by the TV. I'm going to check on Celia."

She left Paul to fend for himself and tiptoed down the carpeted hallway to Celia's room. The door was closed and she opened it carefully, stopping before the point where it would begin to creak. Light from the hallway illuminated the center of the room, but cast the corners in deep shadows. Celia was bundled up to her neck in sheets, mouth slightly open, breathing regularly. Phylis kneeled by the bed and studied her daughter's face. As always, when seeing Celia asleep, a powerful wave of love and protectiveness passed through Phylis, leaving her on the verge of dizziness. She brushed a strand of red hair away from Celia's forehead, then leaned down and kissed the child lightly on the cheek. "Sleep tight, love," she whispered.

She closed the bedroom door, as carefully as she had opened it, and tiptoed back to the living room. Paul had settled himself in a corner of the sofa, jacket off, feet resting on the coffee table. The soft strains of a Peter Gabriel album came from the stereo. Phylis sank gently into the sofa beside him.

"How's Celia?"

"Sound asleep." She looked around and saw that he had no drink. "Do you want anything?"

Paul shook his head and smiled. "I'm fine." Then he leaned closer to Phylis and kissed her on the lips. It began as a normal kiss for them, a delicate touching of lips, but for the first time Phylis opened herself to him. His tongue pushed warmly past her teeth, and her own tongue responded eagerly. When they parted, both of them were breathless.

"I'd forgotten how nice a kiss could be," Phylis said softly, pulling herself closer to Paul.

"You have no idea how long I've wanted to do that," he whispered.

Phylis pushed herself away and studied him with mock seriousness. "How long?"

"Since the moment you told me the first paragraph of my article was not illustratable."

"That long? Surely you can't be satisfied with one kiss," Phylis said huskily.

Paul shook his head and pulled her close again. This time the kiss was longer, deeper, gentler, and Phylis found herself moaning into his mouth. When their lips parted this time he did not pull away, but began to kiss beyond the edge of her mouth, across her cheek, soft lips delicately nibbling at her flesh, until he found the warm hollow of her throat. The wetness of his tongue began to push her towards a passion she had not felt in years.

In response she reached for him, and her hand found his hardness. Now it was Paul's turn to moan. Phylis fumbled with his fly, finally caught it, and drew it down slowly. Paul drew back then, and studied her face carefully.

"Phylis, this . . ."

She touched a burgundy tipped finger to his lips. "I want to," she whispered, and lowered her hand.

"Oh, God," Paul whispered hoarsely.

His own hand traced a line up the inside of Phylis's thigh, stopping at the flimsy material of her panties. He kissed her, caressing her gently through the panties until she was beyond wet, finally pulling the silky material aside to touch her.

Phylis gasped into his neck, and hitched up slightly so that she could press down on his fingers. But as she did so she felt Paul suddenly stiffen and withdraw his hand.

"Darling, what is it?"

He was staring across her shoulder, his face pale. A sudden tremor ran along Phylis's spine as she realized what he was looking at. She heard her daughter's voice before she had turned around.

"Mommy?" Eight year old Celia Reynolds was standing in the living room door, animal cracker nightgown hanging down to her ankles, red hair tousled from sleep, one-eyed teddy bear hugged tightly to her chest.

"Mommy?" Celia asked again, and this time the edge of fear in her voice was pronounced.

"Baby," Phylis whispered, frantically smoothing her dress, knowing what was going to happen next.

Celia looked back and forth between Paul and Phylis, dropped her teddy bear, and began to scream.

CHAPTER TWO

Phylis leapt from the sofa as if it were on fire and ran to Celia. She held the screaming child by the shoulders and shook her. "Baby, it's okay!" she said, her voice frantic with concern. "Celia! Everything is all right!"

But Celia was looking beyond Phylis, at the sofa, where Paul was zipping himself up. The child's eyes were wide with fear, though the scream had toned down to a monotone whimper that seemed to originate somewhere inside of her.

"Is she okay?" Paul asked.

"I think so," Phylis said. "No. I . . . I don't know." Hiding Celia's tear streaked face against her shoulder she turned to Paul. "Maybe you had better go, Paul."

Paul's eyes widened and his mouth opened in surprise. "Go? But—"

"She'll calm down," Phylis said, hugging Celia tighter, and stroking the child's soft red hair. She could feel that her right shoulder was soaked with tears. "But I'll have to stay with her."

"Phylis, we were right in the middle of—"

"Paul!" She cut him off sharply before he could finish, and then, more softly, "There will be other nights."

Paul tucked in his shirt, shaking his head. "I guess I should have expected something like this from you."

"What do you mean?" She was unable to keep a note of hurt from her voice.

Paul walked over to the door, bent over, and began pulling on his shoes. "I heard at the office that you were too hung up on that kid. I should have listened."

"Paul, you . . ." She felt her eyes getting wet, and turned away from his so he would not see.

"I just wish I'd found out before wasting all that money on dinner," he said.

Phylis gasped and turned her head, but he was gone, and the spring loaded door was slowly closing. "Get the hell out of here, you bastard," she said to the empty room.

In her arms, Celia continued to sob.

Phylis stood at the window of Dr. Hammond's fifth floor office waiting room with her arms loosely folded, forehead pressed to the cool plexiglass, watching the traffic on 1st Street below, and the steady flow of pedestrian movement within the glass-walled sky-walks. Behind her, in the room beyond the dark oak door, Celia would be reliving last night's episode, and God only knew what conclusions Dr. Hammond would be drawing. Ironically, it was not Celia's scream that stuck out in Phylis's mind, or even the revealing scene with Paul; it was Celia's teddy bear, dropping to the floor, coming to rest with its single glass eye glaring accusingly up at her. As if even the teddy blamed her.

"Mrs. Reynolds?" Phylis turned at the sound of the receptionist's voice. "Would you care for some coffee?"

17

"No, thank you." Phylis moved away from the window and settled herself in one of the leather-upholstered easy chairs against the wall. For the umpteenth time she let her eyes wander over the numerous prints evenly spaced around the waiting room. All of them were generic, with no sense of personality behind them: simple, uncluttered, and above all cheerful. One represented a meadow, she guessed — green below, blue above. Another might have been sun appearing from behind a cloud — the cloud a bulbous white blob, the sun a circle of yellow. But the prints did not cheer her up.

She pulled a cigarette from her purse, and despite the disapproving glance from the receptionist, lit it, adding to the smokey haze in the room. The cigarette was only half smoked when the oak door swung open, and Celia emerged.

Phylis crushed out the cigarette in the butt-cluttered ashtray that had been empty when she arrived. Celia ran to her and wrapped her thin arms around Phylis's waist. Phylis stroked the child's head.

"Everything okay, darling?"

Celia nodded, then stepped back and looked up at Phylis. "I'm sorry, mommy," she said.

Phylis hugged the child tightly. "Don't be sorry, baby. There's nothing to be sorry about."

Dr. Hammond, who had watched mother and child with no show of emotion, coughed to get Phylis's attention. "I'd like to talk to you, Mrs. Reynolds. Just a couple of minutes. Agnes will look after Celia."

Phylis sat Celia in one of the chairs and handed her one of the magazines from the table, then she followed Dr. Hammond into his office, his inner sanctum, closing the heavy oak door behind her. The contrast between office and waiting room never ceased to effect her. There was no attempt at cheerfulness here, the color scheme being dark and somber, the furnishing heavy and ornate, yet the office put her instantly at ease.

Dr. Hammond added to her feeling of comfort. He was tall and fat, with thinning grey hair that curled around his ears like a comfortable old hat. His watery blue eyes studied her through thick glasses. He was the archetypical father figure, like Orson Welles, and the smell of an exotic pipe tobacco lingering in the air added to this illusion. The room had a homey feel to it. Dr. Hammond seated himself, then motioned for Phylis to do the same.

"You are concerned about what happened last night," he said, the moment Phylis was seated, taking her by surprise.

"Well, yes, of course I'm concerned," Phylis blurted out.

"Of course," Dr. Hammond said, frowning. "The problem is, you may be too concerned, for Celia's good, or for your own."

"Too concerned about my daughter?" She could hardly believe what she was hearing.

Dr. Hammond took a deep breath, then let it out with a hiss. "Mrs. Reynolds, Celia has come through three years of brutal sexual abuse at the hands of her father. I've been seeing her for almost a year and a half now, and it's obvious that she has made some progress in coming to grips with herself."

"But last night—"

"Last night Celia had one of her episodes, yes. She

19

woke from sleep and was confronted, in the safety of her home, with a strange man being intimate with her mother."

Phylis blushed hotly. "But you told me it was time to test her progress," she said softly.

"There's no need to be ashamed of having a man home. You're absolutely right in trying to get your life back on track, and having a man in your life is part of that. But you've got to understand that Celia's reaction was absolutely normal."

"To scream frantically every time she sees a man is normal?"

"Not every time." Dr. Hammond's voice was softer than it had been. "I'm a man, after all, and Celia and I relate quite well. She reacts violently only when she's confronted with such a situation in what she considers a sanctuary. Her own home, for instance. Celia has repressed many of the memories and emotions associated with her father. That is to be expected. Repression is a first line defense of the mind, even more so with children. Celia is facing these repressed memories in nightmares, and they may also manifest themselves in other ways. Screaming, for instance. Or withdrawal. Both of which you've noted in Celia's behaviour."

Phylis raised a hand to her eyes in resignation. "Won't it ever end?"

"Of course it will end," Dr. Hammond said in a conciliatory tone. "As I said, Celia is getting better. She is slowly coming to terms with what happened to her. That process takes time. Perhaps years. As she learns that not all men are like her father, she will become more trusting and accepting of men in general."

"Years?" Phylis suddenly felt hollow.

Dr. Hammond nodded. "Years. But in the meantime Celia is facing another problem, a problem that is drastically affecting her ability to cope with her repressed memories."

Phylis sat up straight, instantly alert. She leaned forward and pierced Dr. Hammond with her gaze. "Can it be corrected?"

Dr. Hammond shrugged. "I don't know. That's up to you."

"Me?" Again, she was shocked.

Dr. Hammond nodded solemnly. He raised one stubby finger to rub the corner of his left eye behind the glasses. "I said earlier that perhaps you were too concerned about Celia's condition. It's obvious that your concern stems mostly from feelings of guilt, and it's those feelings of guilt that are holding Celia back, Mrs. Reynolds."

Phylis did not immediately respond. She could not get the jumble of thoughts and emotions in her mind to return to order. She pushed herself deeper into the plush leather of the easy chair, hands tightly gripping the arm rests. "Guilt?" she said at last.

Dr. Hammond nodded. "For three years Celia came to you and tried to tell you what was happening to her. But you didn't understand, and when you did finally understand, you wouldn't believe." Hammond was leaning forward over his desk, regarding Phylis intently. "The way you reacted was perfectly natural. It is very difficult to accept that one's spouse is doing unspeakable things, especially on the say-so of a child. That is why sexual abuse situations can last so long."

21

"I did fail her," Phylis said softly. Then she sat up and gathered herself. "Whatever guilt I'm feeling is well deserved, Dr. Hammond. It's not Celia's problem."

"Oh, but it is, Mrs. Reynolds," Dr. Hammond said. "You're trying to force Celia to get better in order to alleviate your feelings of guilt. You're not willing to allow her the time she needs. At every sign she may be regressing you panic. In turn, you give Celia the impression that it's all her fault." Dr. Hammond sighed. "She blames herself for what happened last night."

Phylis gasped. "But she can't!"

"I assure you, she does. And I'm afraid the situation is going to get worse. Celia has learned that her father is soon to be released from prison. The knowledge is aggravating her condition."

"Who told her?" Phylis asked in horror.

"Somebody at her day-care center, perhaps, or a friend. Just teasing her, I expect. Children have ways of finding things out, however hard we try to keep them secret. What matters is that Celia's condition may worsen, especially if her father begins legal action to gain visiting rights, or even for custody."

"Oh my God." Suddenly the room seemed to close in on Phylis, and she leaned back in the seat to catch her breath. "What can I do?"

"That's why I asked you in here. I have a proposition to make."

Phylis frowned, sitting at attention again.

"I wouldn't suggest this under normal circumstances," Dr. Hammond said carefully. "But, because there's a chance that Celia may lose all that she's gained through therapy, and for your own sake also, I don't feel I have a choice."

"Dr. Hammond, please, what is it?" Phylis wrung her hands nervously in her lap.

"There's a clinic," Dr. Hammond said. "Lakeview Clinic. It's in-state, a few hours drive away. They're working on an experimental therapy program, audio-neural-cue treatment, and the results have been remarkable. They specialize in emotionally traumatized children. It's a three to four week program, involving on-site habitation, and—"

"How much does it cost?"

"Nothing. Not yet. It's experimental, as I said, and funded entirely through grants."

Phylis pushed herself to the edge of the seat and leaned closer to Dr. Hammond. "Will it help Celia?"

Dr. Hammond shrugged. "Their published results are very encouraging. It might be worth the chance. I just believe that the more advanced Celia is in her recovery, the better her chances at adapting to the imminent release of her father."

"Would they take Celia on?"

"I could find out for you. Take a day or two."

Phylis nodded, grateful. "Please."

When they entered the waiting room again, Celia hopped from her seat and ran to Phylis, hugging her fiercely. "Can we go home now?" Celia asked.

Phylis nodded. She turned away from Dr. Hammond, embarrassed by Celia's show of affection.

In the Datsun, on the way home, Celia was quiet, watching the other cars pass them on the freeway. Phylis was grateful for the silence, and the chance to think about what Dr. Hammond had said. Was she really incapable of waiting for Celia to get better? Was her concern for her daughter simply a manifestation of the guilt she felt? No answers came.

She thought about the experimental therapy Dr. Hammond had suggested. Was her eagerness to try the therapy just another symptom of her guilt? Again, no answer. Anything that might help Celia was worth the chance. Besides, three weeks away from Minneapolis would help them both.

So why, Phylis wondered, had Dr. Hammond been so reticent about suggesting the therapy? It was almost as if he had felt guilty in doing so.

CHAPTER THREE

Two days later, on Friday, Dr. Hammond called Phylis at work. He had talked to the people at Lakeview Clinic, and they were interested in Celia. A representative would be in Minneapolis that evening, and Hammond wanted to give him Phylis's phone number in order to facilitate a preliminary interview. Phylis agreed readily. She did not admit it to Hammond, but she had feared that Celia's would prove too pedestrian a case for the clinic.

The phone call from the Lakeview rep didn't come until close to 7:30 that night, right in the middle of a *Beauty and the Beast* repeat. Celia, who was in love with the beast, Vincent, did not take her eyes from the screen as Phylis rose and answered the phone.

"Mrs. Reynolds?"

"Yes?"

"My name is Dr. Gordon, from Lakeview. I believe you were expecting me to call?" His voice was deep and full of that midwest accent that seems to be, in contrast to some of the country's more pronounced twangs, almost neutral.

"Yes, Dr. Gordon. Is this about the interview?"

"Well, I wouldn't exactly call it an interview. I'd just

25

like to meet you, and Celia. Tonight if I could."

"Tonight?" Phylis pursed her lips, turning worriedly to Celia who was still glued to the set.

"It really won't take long. I just want to introduce myself, and give you directions on how to get to the clinic. I'll come to you, if you give me the address. Just tell Celia that I'm coming. We don't want to get off on the wrong foot."

"But what if she asks why?"

"Tell her the truth."

Phylis gave him the address. He said he'd be there in about half an hour. Phylis returned to the sofa and sat beside Celia. Vincent was holding a dishevelled cab driver by the collar and was growling menacingly into his face.

"Who was that?" Celia did not turn from the television.

"Somebody who's coming over to see you," Phylis said carefully.

"Who?" Now Celia did turn, despite Vincent's prominence on the screen.

"A man. His name is Dr. Gordon."

"Like Dr. Hammond?"

"Just like Dr. Hammond."

Seemingly satisfied, Celia returned her attention to the show. Dr. Gordon arrived fifteen minutes later, not the half hour he had estimated, and he was not what Phylis had expected. On the phone the deepness of his voice had suggested someone of middle age, but she opened the door upon a tall, sun browned, lanky man of about her own age, a grin on his face.

"Mrs. Reynolds? I'm John Gordon." He held out a

large brown hand which Phylis took tentatively in her own. His skin was smooth, dry, and warm. In his open necked cotton shirt, loosely tucked into a baggy pair of white cotton pants, he looked like a beach bum dressed for a night on the town. "May I come in?"

"Oh, yes, I'm sorry." Her voice did not sound as calm as she would have like, and she suddenly realized she had been giving him a rather obvious once over. "You don't look like a doctor."

John Gordon smiled widely, and teeth gleamed bright behind the smile. "That's okay. You don't look like the ragged, overworked mother of an eight year old daughter."

His appreciative gaze, totally open and honest, made Phylis look down with a blush. He stepped past her and into the living room. "You must be Celia," he said, still smiling.

Celia looked at the doctor shyly, and nodded. He didn't look like Dr. Hammond, or any of the other doctors she had ever seen. He didn't look like Trapper John, or even some of the young ones on *St. Elsewhere*. He looked a little like the detective from *Simon And Simon*. This was not her favorite TV show, was not one she was allowed to watch regularly, but on the odd times she had seen the show she had liked the young blonde detective.

He stepped up to her and held out his hand. "I'm John."

Celia placed her own hand within his and shook it solemnly. He didn't really look like a detective either, she thought. "Are you a doctor?"

"Yes, I am," John said. "And what are you?"

"Nothing, yet," Celia said. The silliness of his question exasperated her. It was obvious what she was. "I'm only a girl."

The commercials ended, and the show resumed. "This is my favorite show," Celia said, turning again to the TV. She liked Vincent's ugliness, and recognized his inner beauty. This was a principle she had noticed in real life. At the day-care there was a small boy who's father came to pick him up every night. The boy's father was very ugly. He was fat, and he was bald and his face was scarred and pitted. Celia had recoiled from him the first time she had seen him. But the next day she had noticed how his eyes glowed when he picked up his son, and she had noticed how they tinged with sorrow when the other children backed away from his ugliness. After that she had smiled at him whenever he came to the day-care. He was just like Vincent.

Doctor Gordon plunked into the opposite end of the sofa, as if this were his house and his sofa, and became absorbed in the show. Mommy took the easy chair to the left of the sofa. Celia noticed how her mother's eyes continually moved towards the doctor, that strange sorrowful look flitting across her face. Celia recognized the look, and she knew what her mother was thinking. She was thinking of the doctor as her husband, as Celia's daddy. Of how it would be if this were true. Mommy did that a lot. Celia glanced from the TV to Dr. Gordon, and he smiled at her. She looked away without smiling back. He was not like Vincent. He was nice on the outside, but she could not yet tell about his inside. But Mommy liked him. That she could see.

When the final credits rolled, Celia made a big show of being tired. Mommy looked at her as if she knew she was just acting. "It's late, Mommy. I should be getting to bed."

"I'll come and tuck you in."

"I can do it," Celia said. She turned to Doctor Gordon. "Good night." A shy smile curled her lips.

"Good night, Celia. It was nice to meet you."

Celia nodded. She walked down the hallway to her bedroom, closing out the sound of the TV and the voices of her mother and the doctor. She undressed for bed, folding her clothes neatly across the wooden chair, finally crawling under the sheets with her teddy. She stared at the ceiling, eyes heavy, listening to the muted voices coming from down the hallway.

She knew, of course, why Dr. Gordon was here. He was the same kind of doctor as Dr. Hammond. He would want to talk to her about what she was thinking and feeling. That was okay. Sometimes it helped when she talked to Dr. Hammond. He was a lot like Vincent. He was like a wrinkled Santa Claus on the outside, and he was filled with warm concern. He always wanted to talk about her father, and about the things that made her think about her father.

She rolled over and hugged her teddy tighter, trying to dispell the dark image of her father that popped into her mind. She squeezed her legs tightly together, fighting back a small moan. If the doctors could help make the bad feelings go away then she would see as many of them as her mother wanted. If only they could stop her daddy from coming back, like he had come back the other night when she had woken up. She had seen her mommy on the sofa and her daddy was doing things, just like he used to do to her, and he was looking at her, and his eyes were tiny and black and staring at her, and she had started to scream and scream . . .

But it wasn't really her daddy. It had been Mommy's friend. And Mommy had been upset, and sad, and her friend had gone. If the doctors could stop that from happening again she would see all of them.

Celia breathed deeply, hugged her teddy, and drifted off to sleep.

"Can I get you a drink? Coffee or something?"

John (she could not think of him as Dr. Gordon) shook his head. "No, I'm fine. I really should be going myself. Got a bit of a drive ahead of me."

"Going? Don't you need to know anything about . . . Celia?"

"Mrs. Reynolds. As I said on the phone, I just wanted to meet Celia and yourself. This was not meant to be an interview. As far as we at the clinic are concerned we'd be delighted to have the chance to help Celia. We believe our program would be perfect for her. There's really not much I can tell you about it right now. You'll be given a thorough orientation if you decide to go with us."

"I've already decided that," Phylis said. "I just thought you might want to check us out more thoroughly."

He chuckled. "No. We know all we need to for the moment. Dr. Brand will be in charge of Celia's therapy, and he'll want to talk to you more carefully. I'm what they call the clinic-patient liaison. I'll be spending a lot of time with Celia and yourself, checking on her progress, helping any way I can. The only question I have to ask you is . . . when can you come up?"

Phylis pursed her lips. "Dr. Hammond mentioned that the therapy would take a few weeks. I'd need a week to clear things up at work."

"That sounds fine." He pulled a crumpled envelope from his back pocket and smoothed it out on the coffee table. "Here's a map, and directions. We're about three hours away, if you push it. Four otherwise. You know where Fergus Falls is?"

Phylis nodded.

"We're close," John said. "Would you be able to make it up next Saturday? Leave here in the morning, arrive sometime around noon. That'll give you a day and a half to get used to the place, and we'll get the ball moving on the Monday."

"Sounds great." Phylis said.

John stood. "And bring swimming suits for both Celia and yourself," he said, grinning. "I think you're going to enjoy yourselves." He held out his hand, and this time when she held it Phylis felt her whole body focus itself on the masculine warmth of his touch.

When he had gone she found that she was smiling. She sighed thoughtfully and watched his dark brown Impala coast down the street.

John Gordon drove in silence. He drove with the air-conditioning off, since it clattered incessantly and interfered with his thoughts, and by habit with the radio turned off, since the only classical music FM station in the Twin-cities would waver annoyingly less than ten miles from the cities and fade completely by the time he reached St. Cloud. Besides, he enjoyed the silence. He had left Phylis Reynolds at 8:30. He should be in Lakeview before midnight, but the prospect did not please him.

When he had first arrived at Lakeview, almost six months ago, he had loved the camp. The open air, the lapping water, the lush depth of trees, had been a wonderful change from the dreary grey skies and concrete of Chicago. Two weeks of that idyllic existence had restored his depleted energy, and the presence of Dr. Neville Brand had certainly sharpened his focus on the research that had slowly lost its allure for him over the difficult previous years. But the subsequent six months had produced a deep *need* for the experience of concrete, for the choking smell of exhaust, and for the pressing energy of crowded humans. And Dr. Brand's initial role as mentor had quickly changed to that of impediment. Brand's insistence on following procedures set down by others who knew little, if anything, of the research, and of reporting directly to them, stifled the most interesting aspects of the project. But then again, and this thought assuaged his dissatisfaction, where else could he even remotely touch on the subject that had captured his attention so thoroughly since the time of his doctoral thesis?

He arrived at the Lakeview turn-off just past 11:30,

and switched the headlights to high-beam as he entered the narrow corridor of a road that wound down to the camp. The trees were like walls on either side of the road, so dark they seemed to swallow the illumination from the car's hallogen lamps. An obscuring cloud of dust erupted behind the Impala, and stones clattered against the undercarriage. When he passed the gatehouse of the army-compound the guard, recognizing his car, nodded. John lifted his hand in a perfunctory wave, grunting in disgust. This was the aspect of the project he did not like. The damned interference of Captain Wilkes, a cement-headed army bureaucrat who looked on the research as nothing more than the coddling of inept scientists at play. The contempt was mutual. Ten minutes later he passed through the Lakeview gate.

The cabins were shrouded in darkness, but the main building was lit like a Christmas tree. John swore under his breath. That meant that Brand was still up and about, and likely Margaret Palin. Which meant that despite the lateness of the hour, and the fatigue that was quickly settling upon him, he would be snared into a midnight debriefing. He parked the Impala and walked reluctantly up the stone path and through the glass doors, an aberation amid the rustic, log-cabin look of the building, into the brightly lit reception area. Dr. Brand and Margaret were seated at the reception desk, studying a computer printout that he recognized as the latest audio-emotional topography of the Douglas girl.

"How did it go today, John?" Brand's smile was wide and friendly.

John forced himself into friendly civility. "Good. I got everything done, anyway. And I met with the Reynolds woman and her daughter."

Brand now looked more interested, his dark, hawk-like features assuming that predatory look that had become so familiar over the past months. "What's your initial opinion?"

John shrugged. "What we expected. She fits the profile, except, of course, in the area we discussed. I talked with the girl's psychiatrist, Hammond, and went over her case. The trauma was extended over a period of almost three years, and came to an end when the father was apprehended and jailed. He seems to feel a crisis is approaching because of the father's imminent release from prison. I agree. The girl's recent responses to key stimuli have been dramatic, sometimes violent. The only question is whether the trauma, extended so long, will have produced the required susceptibility to the cues. It's worth a chance."

Brand nodded thoughtfully, tapping a long brown finger against the printout on the desk. Margaret Palin, looking tired, had listened intently to what John had said, and she did not look pleased. She had not agreed to the change in direction the research was taking, especially the idea that future patients might not exactly fit the accepted profile. John smiled at her, but she did not smile back.

"Anything interesting with the Douglas girl?" John asked.

Brand chuckled. "We tried a primal cue session today, using the pattern you isolated from her previous session."

34

"And?"

"Same thing. She fell short. A failure for us, but a cure for the girl. Her mother will be happy."

"It's . . ." He glanced down the corridor. "Still here?"

Brand nodded.

"Can it wait till morning?" John asked hopefully. "I'm pretty tired."

"That would not be a good idea," Margaret said, looking levelly at John. Her wide face was stern. "I've already phoned the compound. They're waiting for you."

John nodded resignedly. "Will I need help?"

Now Margaret smiled grimly. "I sedated it for you."

John stood, yawned, and moved towards the storage room, but Brand motioned for his attention.

"When you're finished, just knock off, John," Brand said. "Tomorrow I'd like you to spend some time with the DeMarch woman. I went over David's initial topgraphy today, and it looks promising."

John nodded. He walked down the corridor, lit only by a single fluorescent bulb at the end, and paused before the storage room. Of all the tasks assigned to him, this was the one he hated most. He opened the door and flicked on the light. The small bundle, covered by a white sheet, lay on top of a metal disecting table. The sheet rose and fell slowly, the thing underneath it breathing deeply and evenly. One corner of the sheet had flipped back, and a small section of pale, glistening flesh was visible. It might have been a finger, or an elongated toe. John flipped the sheet across the exposed appendage and carefully lifted the small bundle. It was not heavy, but felt soft and pulpy against his forearms. Something sharp poked into his ribs. Perhaps a joint.

He carried the bundle down the corridor, and through the reception area. Margaret's eyes followed him slowly, never leaving his face. He smiled at her, then pushed the outside door and walked down the path towards his car. The air was cool and fresh, a light breeze coming off the lake. The trees rustled quietly in the background. He placed the bundle on the front passenger seat, and held it there with one hand as he drove back down the gravel road to the army compound. The guard opened the gate and he drove slowly into the brightly lit courtyard, stopping the car next to the concrete bunker against the back fence. The two guards outside the bunker shifted uneasily on their feet.

John stepped out of the car, smiling. "Got something for you boys," he said, opening the door and lifting out the sheet-covered form.

One of the guards stepped forward, abhorrence evident on his face. "What is it this time, Doc?"

"I haven't looked," John said. He released the bundle, letting it drop to the ground. It landed with a dull thud, and the thing beneath the sheet mewled piteously.

The second guard groaned in disgust, but could not take his eyes from the sheet which was now rippling slowly as the thing beneath it fought off the effects of the sedative.

"You better get it inside," John said. "Before it wakes up."

The first guard nodded, smiling grimly. "We're getting kinda crowded," he said. "When are you smart guys gonna decide what to do with all these things?"

John grinned. "Maybe we can have a barbeque." He got back in the car and turned it slowly around. The two guards were tentatively poking at the bundle on the ground with their rifles. John shook his head, then drove back through the gate and toward Lakeview. As he drove he thought about Phylis Reynolds and her daughter, Celia. He had liked the mother. He had sensed something in her during the short time he had been in the house. Interest, maybe. She was certainly attractive.

For the first time in months he was looking forward to the arrival of a new patient.

CHAPTER FOUR

The following week was a hectic one for Phylis. The people at work were understanding about her need for a leave of absence, and on that score there was no problem, but there was still a lot to wrap up before she could go. She carefully went over every active project with Terry, her assistant, and disposed of the loose ends that came to her attention. In the few quiet moments she managed to steal she found herself dwelling on Paul Welch, and their last scene together. His words were etched in her mind.

But who had told Paul about her? Who in the office would poison him against her just because of her concern for Celia? She found herself regarding her co-workers suspiciously, wondering which smiling face hid the shark's teeth. But the hectic pace of clearing up allowed no time for her suspicion to turn to paranoia. The most awkward moment of the week came when she left the office on Thursday night and almost ran into Paul in the hallway. He had seen her, had taken a step towards her, the intention of speaking with her plain on his face, but she had managed to slip into the elevator just in time to see his shocked look as the doors slid shut. That had been too close. His nearness had brought back every nuance of the humiliation she had felt when he had walked out on her.

Work wasn't the only thing that kept her busy. On Dr. Hammond's insistence she had served a court order against Don, her soon-to-be-released ex-husband, restraining him from contacting either Celia or herself. A confrontation with her father at this time could have a severe effect on Celia, Dr. Hammond said. Phylis was surprised at how easy it was to get the court order, but Dr. Hammond's notarized letter had certainly helped.

Celia, too, felt the strain of the week. The late nights at work resulted in Celia having to remain at the day-care hours longer than usual. Once or twice she was the last child to be picked up. Phylis felt a pang of guilt each morning when she dropped Celia off, but there was nothing to be done about it. Thank goodness it was the summer holidays; school would have compounded the problem.

By the time Friday rolled around both Phylis and Celia were eager for the trip. It would be like a holiday, and one that was sorely needed. Therapy or not, it would be great to get away for awhile.

On Saturday morning Phylis loaded up the yellow Datsun. She fed a cheerful Celia a bowl of Frosted Flakes and a glass of orange juice, while she herself sipped a cup of Maxwell House instant coffee and smoked a cigarette. When they left the house at 9:00, a single white cumulus cloud drifted lazily overhead, but by the time they were out of the Twin-cities area and driving north-west on Interstate 94 the sky was empty.

Celia had her hand out the window, playing airfoil with the wind, her soft red hair swept back off her forehead.

Phylis stopped at the Texaco just past St. Cloud and bought each of them a can of Pepsi, while a spotty-faced young attendant topped up the gas. They left the Interstate at Fergus Falls, just after 12:30. The air was dry and hot, and with both windows open the Datsun reverberated with a throaty roar. It was at these times that Phylis promised herself she would spring for a new Pontiac with air-conditioning.

It took a quarter of an hour to maneuver through the sleepy town of Fergus Falls, but there was no way to access 210 east otherwise. Phylis kept John Gordon's map open on the seat until the two lane blacktop of 210 curved away ahead of them, shimmering from the midday heat. The narrow road wound through a lush landscape of hills and valleys, thick with a mix of deciduous and fir trees, broken periodically by the glitter of small lakes on either side of the road. It really was a beautiful area, Phylis thought. These two weeks might do her as much good as they would Celia.

Half an hour later the town of Battle Lake went by the driver's side window in an eye-blink. Phylis had time to catch a glimpse of a rising main drag, a color-ful waterfront, and a slice of lake.

"Won't be long now, honey," she said.

Celia nodded absently. She was watching the con-stantly changing landscape in awe. It had been four years since Celia had been out of Minneapolis, back when they had used Phylis sister's condo outside of Boulder, Colorado. That would have made Celia just four, and Don would have been with them then. But surely Celia wouldn't remember that trip clearly. Even Phylis had trouble bringing it to mind.

The road began to climb, and suddenly they had a postcard view of the entire west end of Battle Lake, including the town. Sunlight glinted off the water, which looked glass-smooth from up here. The white wakes of boats could be seen clearly, and a smattering of tiny sails. "It's so beautiful," Celia said, and then the road curved away. After that they only caught glimpses of the water through the trees.

As John Gordon's map promised, they came to the gravel road off 210 about twenty minutes past the Battle Lake exit. There was no sign to indicate the road, and Phylis almost drove past it before realizing they were there. Once they turned into the opening, which a partially obscured sign confirmed was Lakeview Road, the dense woods on either side closed in. There was no shoulder, and Phylis wondered what she would do if they met a car coming from the other direction. Crash, she decided with good humor.

About a mile down the road there was a large fenced compound to the right. Three or four squat, woodframe buildings huddled at the center of a gravel courtyard. A few seconds later they came upon the gate, and a large sign that proclaimed:

OTTER TAIL COUNTY
U.S. ARMY RESERVE

The sign was haggard, the letters faded. The barracks looked deserted, but as they passed the gatehouse Phylis spotted the uniformed guard within it, and a few late model cars parked behind one of the buildings. Then they were past it, and there were only the trees on either side of the road. She had time to wonder briefly what an army barracks was doing out in the middle of nowhere, but then the road turned abruptly rougher, and she was forced to concentrate on keeping the car on course.

Celia rolled her window almost all the way up without prompting, as a plume of dust erupted around the Datsun, accompanied by the constant clatter of rocks against the undercarriage and sides. Now I'm glad I don't have a shiny new Pontiac, Phylis thought grimly.

Four miles along, a large timber frame arched over the road. A wooden sign hung from the crossbar:

LAKEVIEW

No mention of clinic, or of psychiatric center. She liked that. The road curved as they passed under the arch, and suddenly Battle Lake stretched before them again, close enough to touch. To the left was a row of cabins, but Phylis drove straight ahead to the main building down by the water.

It was a long structure, looking like the body of a motel, sided to appear like an elongated log cabin. But no log cabin ever had a glass fronted vestibule. She parked the Datsun at the foot of the path and shut down the engine. The glass doors opened and John Gordon emerged, grinning. He was wearing a YMCA T-shirt with a rainbow on the front, blue swimming trunks, and a pair of unlaced white Reeboks.

"Hi!" He greeted them with a wave as he trotted down the path. He leaned against the car and peered in, his tanned face creased in a smile. "You made it."

"Hello, Dr. Gordon," Phylis said, forcing herself to use his title, youthful looks or not.

"Please, just John. Only my mother calls me Dr. Gordon. We try to maintain an air of informality around here."

"Yes, I noticed the sign," Phylis said.

John nodded, then suddenly turned his attention on Celia. "Did you enjoy the trip up here, little lady?"

Celia nodded shyly, looking towards the water. There were a number of boats raised on platforms at the water's edge, and a main dock that extended a good fifty feet into the water.

"I'll tell you what. Why don't I show you to your cabin. Then we can have some lunch, and afterwards we can go for a swim."

Phylis smiled. The thought of slipping into all that cool water was appealing. Celia continued to look out at the lake.

"I detect a silent note of dissent," John muttered. "Okay. How about I show you the cabin, then we go swimming? We can eat later."

"Uh huh!" Celia said eagerly, eyes wide with pleasure.

"I don't know . . ." Phylis began.

"Oh, please, Mommy, please!"

Phylis sighed. "All right. Swimming first."

John opened the back door and pushed in, shoving aside Celia's fat Addidas bag. "I'll guide. You drive," he said.

He directed them to Cabin Three, just out of sight of the main building, but close to the lapping water. Phylis noted that there were cars parked in front of cabins one and two, with a potpourri of towels and swim trunks hanging from a clothes line in front of each. They would not be alone here. John grabbed

43

most of their luggage, leaving only a couple of small bags for Phylis and Celia.

They were following him up to the front porch, Celia in the middle, when a high-pitched squeal came from behind the cabin, and a young boy exploded into view, laughing uproariously. He clamped his laughter the moment he saw the newcomers, and came to a staggering halt.

Phylis almost broke into laughter at the shocked look on his face.

"David!" John greeted him. "I have someone for you to meet."

David walked over confidently, looking only at Celia. He was about Celia's age, Phylis decided, and approximately the same height, but there the similarities ended. While Celia was fair, and almost fragile in appearance, David was dark, and beefy. He was wearing a blue and white striped sailor's T-shirt with a red boat's wheel on the right breast, and beige shorts. His feet were bare and dirty.

"David, this is Celia. And this is Celia's mother, Mrs. Reynolds."

David smiled at Celia and held out a small brown hand. He certainly wasn't a shy little boy, Phylis thought. Celia smiled, but would not take his hand.

"We're going swimming right away," John said. "Want to come with us?"

"Sure," David said, nodding. He turned and ran towards the tree line behind the cabins, but veered at the last moment and disappeared behind Cabin Two. They heard him break into laughter again.

"A wild cat," John said, "but a really nice kid." He stepped into the porch. Celia followed.

But Phylis stopped at the door. She stared intensely at the wall of trees behind the cabin.

David's laughter sounded faintly in the distance.

Phylis smiled nervously and shook her head. The fresh air was making her drunk, she thought. Or being cooped up in the car all day was causing her to have hallucinations. When David had disappeared beyond the edge of the adjacent cabin she had seen—*thought* she had seen—something following the boy's movement, angling after him in the depths of the woods, like some sort of predatory animal.

Phylis suddenly felt silly. It must have been the wind moving the tree branches, she realized with relief, or the sun glinting off leaves.

The thing had certainly not been an animal. It had been too pale for that, and far too large.

CHAPTER FIVE

The front porch was screened on three sides, allowing a breeze to pass through unimpeded, and appeared to serve as the cabin's dining room. A circular picnic table occupied one corner, surrounded by two half-moon benches. The porch led directly into a room that extended the length of the cabin, the left half a living room filled with an odd mixture of furniture, the right half a bright open kitchen area.

"Not exactly the Hilton," John said cheerfully. He carried the bags beyond the living room-kitchen to the rear of the cabin, which was divided into three rooms. A bedroom on either side, and the bathroom in the middle. "Will you be sharing a room?"

"Celia?" Phylis asked.

Celia stuck her head in the smaller bedroom to the left of the bathroom. "I want my own."

"Separate rooms," Phylis said.

"Okay. I'll let you divide the baggage," John said. He placed Phylis's two cases and Celia's Addidas-bag on the floor outside the bathroom. "I'll wait on the porch for you to change."

Phylis picked up her two cases and went into the master bedroom. Though small, it really was quite nice. A queen sized bed took up most of the room, leaving just enough space to edge around it to access the chest of drawers on one side and the vanity on the other. Once she had changed into her swimsuit, Phylis stepped as far back from the vanity as the bed would allow, and studied her form. Not bad, she thought. She had managed to maintain her figure only with great difficulty, especially after Celia was born. The one-piece, green and white swimsuit, bought last year, also did its bit to smooth her lines. She patted her flat stomach and went through to the other bedroom. Celia was still dressed, carefully unpacking her Addidas bag.

"Honey, you can do that later. Dr. Gordon is waiting for us."

Celia nodded distractedly. "This bed is giant, Mommy."

"Well, you'll be able to roll around and not fall out."

Celia giggled.

"Now, hurry up. I'll be out on the porch."

She took a towel, and her cigarettes and lighter. When she stepped onto the porch, John Gordon's eyes widened perceptibly, and she could not help but smile. "The cabin really is lovely," she said quickly, to hide her reaction.

"They're all rather nice," he said. "Not that we had much to do with that. This used to be some sort of resort, but it went belly up. Too many rental cabins around this lake to be competitive."

Phylis sat across the picnic table from John, so that she looked out at the trees. She frowned, remembering her impression of something moving out there. "Are there any animals in the woods?" she asked suddenly.

"You mean, like wild and dangerous types?"

Phylis shrugged. "I thought I saw something moving earlier."

"I suppose it might have been a deer." He glanced over his shoulder at the thick tree growth. "There are one or two of those about. But we've never seen anything more dangerous than that. One of the people from the army post told me they had trouble with a bear a year or so back. But they're a messy bunch, so that's to be expected. Bears love human garbage. You can see that bear hanging on a plaque in their mess hall, just down the road, but it's a sorry looking creature I've heard."

Phylis laughed. She lit a cigarette, and the breeze passing through the porch took the smoke away. "What's the army doing out here anyway?"

"Not much, as far as I can tell, though it used to be an active station. Once in a while they come through our camp to launch a boat, and we let them. They were here long before us, and we try to stay on good terms with them. They come in handy once in a while."

"How?"

"Oh, like moving fallen trees from the road after storms. We get some doozies you know. And keeping the road cleared of snow in the winter. We get a lot of that too, and they have the equipment for it."

The porch door opened and Celia appeared, towel rolled up beneath one arm, red hair poking out from beneath a blue Twins hat. Her blue bikini with white polka dots had been purchased at the same time as Phylis's. Celia's skin was pure white, except for smudges of freckles at her knees and a good splash across her nose.

"Celia, you get right back inside and put on a T-shirt. You know how badly you burn."

"Oh, all right!" She stomped back in, and returned a moment later with a long white T-shirt that hung down to her knees. On the front was a picture of Mr. Spock, and the slogan: SPOCK LIVES!

"That's better," Phylis said.

Outside, Celia walked between Phylis and John, but when John inadvertently brushed against her right shoulder, she gasped and stepped away, going immediately to the other side of her mother.

"Celia!" Phylis scolded, embarrassed by her daughter's reaction, but John touched her arm and shook his head.

Celia gripped Phylis's left hand tightly. John began to whistle, as if nothing had happened. "Can you swim, Celia?" he asked, as they reached the rutted road that led to the main building and the water.

"Uh huh," Celia said. "I took beginners' classes, and I can go across the pool three times."

"That's good. Maybe you could show me —"

"Dr. Gordon!" The voice came from back toward the cabins, and a woman slammed open the door of Cabin One and came running toward them. She was short, and plump, but still quite pretty, Phylis saw, black hair pulled back into a pony tail, wearing a white top and red shorts that made her plumpness seem curvaceous. But as she approached, Phylis could see that the woman was nerve-wracked. Her eyes were red rimmed, as if she had been crying, and her face had that slack, grainy look of sleeplessness.

"Ah, Dora," John said, as she came up to them. "I'd

like you to meet Phylis Reynolds, and her daughter Celia. This is Dora DeMarch, David's . . . mother."

"Hi," Phylis said.

The woman gave Phylis a perfunctory nod, and Celia a suspicious glance, before turning again to John. "It's David. I can't find him. I think he may have wandered into the woods. He . . ."

"Dora."

". . . He was wandering around all morning and—"

"Mrs. DeMarch!" This time he raised his voice enough to get through to her, and she stammered to a halt.

"David's all right," John said.

"But . . ." She could not articulate her concern, seemed almost on the verge of collapse.

John put out a hand to steady her. "We saw David just a few minutes ago. He was fine. I asked him to go swimming with us. He's probably down by the dock."

Dora DeMarch looked past John, down towards the water, squinting her dark eyes against the sun's glare. Suddenly she went slack. John, who was also looking towards the lake, smiled and turned around.

"You see? He even knows enough not to go in the water alone."

Mrs. DeMarch sighed. "I'm sorry." She offered an apologetic smile to John, but would not make eye contact with either Phylis or Celia. She turned and began to walk slowly back to her cabin.

Phylis, John, and Celia, began moving towards the water again. "She seemed so . . . tense," Phylis said, searching for the right word.

"Yes," John agreed. "And that's the biggest part of David's problem."

Phylis waited for more, but there was none forth-coming, and she did not feel it would be proper to pursue the matter. Instead, she asked, "How many patients are here?"

John, who had become momentarily lost in thought, snapped back. "Well, there's Celia, and David, and two other children who you'll likely meet tomorrow."

They were approaching the water now, and John was smiling. "C'mon, let's hit the lake before it dries up."

He pulled off his shirt, dropping it to the grass just above the narrow, pebbly beach, then kicked off his runners, and ran headlong across the sand. The muscles in his back and legs rippled smoothly beneath his bronze skin. David had been standing at the water's edge, and he turned at the sound of John's stampeding approach just in time to be bodily picked up. He laughed in delight. With the boy slung over his shoulder, John continued full speed into the lake, water splashing violently about his thrashing legs, until it became too deep and he toppled over, sending David screaming into the water. Boy and man commenced to splash each other amidst gales of laughter.

Celia, who had witnessed this in silence, suddenly squealed with delight. She dropped her towel, pulled off her shirt, and ran for the water.

Left alone on the grassy ridge, Phylis chuckled. "Off you go, then," she said. She crushed out the cigarette beneath her heel, then kicked off the sandals. She walked carefully across the beach and pushed a toe into the gently lapping water's edge. The sensation was cool and pleasant. Smiling, she took a few steps into the lake, then pushed forward and submerged herself completely. The coolness surrounded her.

She stroked beneath the water, hands brushing the sandy bottom, suddenly realizing that she was very happy. *This is the best you've felt in years,* she thought. She surfaced a few yards from the trio, who were still splashing each other.

"Hello there!" John greeted her, and sent a cascade of water towards her.

It took only a moment for both David and Celia to follow his cue, and before long Phylis found herself surrounded by a constant explosion of water, filled with the joyful screams of children, and her own laughter.

After a while, Phylis and John climbed up on the end of the dock and lay back on the rough wooden planks. The sun dried them in minutes. Celia and David continued to play with each other in the water, swimming occasionally, but mostly splashing with great energy. Phylis rolled onto her stomach and watched the children.

"They seem to like each other," Phylis said.

"Yes, they do," John said softly.

Phylis turned to look at him. He was gazing out at David and Celia with an unreadable expression on his face. "You love the children, don't you?"

He turned to her and smiled, his blue eyes bright. "Yeah, I guess I do."

They continued to watch in silence. Soon, David swam to shore, turned, and waved to them. John waved back. "Your Mom wants to see you!" he shouted.

David ran to his towel, pulled on his shirt, and ran towards the cabins.

"That kid never walks," John said in awe. "Always has to be running."

Celia paddled over to the dock and splashed water over them. Phylis squealed. "Celia!"

"I'm hungry," Celia said with a pout.

John laughed. They went back to the grassy ridge, but only Celia was wet enough to need a towel. She dried herself lightly and pulled on her Spock shirt. Phylis noticed that already the sun had burned a red band across Celia's white shoulders. They began to walk back, but where the path diverged towards the cabins, John stopped.

"You'll find the fridge is well stocked," he said. "I took care of that. If you need anything else, let me know."

"You won't join us?"

"I wish I could. But it's getting on to 3:00, and I have things to do before Dr. Brand returns. I'll drop by later and say hello."

Phylis nodded, but felt disappointed.

"Dr. Brand won't be back until late, so I doubt you'll meet him until tomorrow. We'll go over everything then."

Phylis nodded again.

"Bye, Celia."

"Bye," Celia said.

John walked toward the main building. Phylis watched his retreating form for a moment, then took Celia's hand and began walking toward the cabin. The swimming, the fresh air, and the sun, had drained her. But in a nice way. She sighed dreamily. As they approached the cabin, Celia ran ahead and went inside. Phylis, following, suddenly stopped. She had heard voices.

Looking around, she spotted David DeMarch standing next to the tree line behind Cabin Two. The boy seemed to be gesturing with his arms, as if trying to explain something. Suddenly he turned, saw Phylis, and waved. Phylis waved back, frowning. Who had he been talking to?

David laughed, and ran out of sight behind the cabin. A loud snap came from somewhere deep in the woods, as if something heavy had stepped on a fallen branch. Phylis walked up the path to the cabin and went in.

The snap had been the wind knocking down a branch, she thought. It did not occur to her, until she and Celia were sitting down to lunch, that the wind had died down to nothing while they had been swimming.

CHAPTER SIX

By 8:00, the temperature had dropped considerably from its daytime high, and both Phylis and Celia resorted to sweaters to keep warm. Celia spent most of the evening in front of the television, a first generation RCA monster encased in a heavy imitation teak cabinet, trying to solidify a picture by fiddling with the rabbit ears, but every success was cut short by bursts of static. On the porch, Phylis tried involving herself in the paperback Lawrence Sanders thriller she had brought along, but found her surroundings uncomplimentary for the task. Soon she closed it, cradled her coffee, and watched the sun disappear beyond the trees across the lake.

Around 10:00 John Gordon gave a perfunctory knock on the door and stepped into the cabin. Celia, who was unaccountably moody, would not leave the television and refused to respond to his attempts at conversation. Eventually he sat across from Phylis on the porch.

"She's always like this when she's tired," Phylis tried to explain.

"Either that, or I'm getting too close for her comfort. I started off as a friendly visitor, I may now have achieved the status of intruder." He smiled as he said this, so Phylis did not contradict him. He stayed long enough to have a cup of coffee, then said good night, promising to come by early.

Alone on the porch, Phylis soon began to feel uncomfortable. The darkness beyond the screened walls seemed inpenetrable, almost solid, and the bright light inside the porch made her feel as if she were in a fish bowl. She could see nothing outside except a single light from the main building, a lonely beacon hanging in a pit of nothingness. Fatigue crept in quickly, and after making sure Celia was tucked away, Phylis went to bed herself.

The silence of the deep woods was unnerving. She lay awake for more than an hour, listening intently for any night sounds. The bedroom faced directly into the woods behind the cabin, but the only sound was the gentle hiss of wind passing through branches. Eventually she slept.

She dreamed of the woods, dark, deep, and mysterious, whispering to her. She was running amidst the ancient trees, whipped by branches, scraped by gnarled trunks so that her skin stung painfully, looking for Celia. She could hear Celia's laughter, deeper in the woods, but she could not catch up. From somewhere nearby another sound reached her: a constant, heavy, crashing, as something huge stalked the darkness. Something that did not belong there.

In the morning, Phylis woke first and prepared a quick breakfast of cereal, milk, and juice, for both Celia and herself. When John Gordon arrived with a

56

cheery "Good morning!" Phylis had just finished cleaning up. They walked slowly along the rutted muddy track, enjoying the early morning quiet, and the comfortable warmth of sunlight dappled by trees. It didn't appear as if anybody in the other cabins was up yet.

The main building surprised Phylis. She had expected the inside to reflect something of the ramshackle homeliness of the cabin, but instead found herself in a small, thoroughly modern hospital environment. White tiles gleamed beneath her feet, while pale fluorescent lamps flickered overhead. Somewhere, an air-conditioning unit hummed. The only thing lacking was a stampede of doctors and nurses. The place was empty.

Dr. Brand was expecting them, waiting in a small lounge off the main corridor, and he too was a bit of a surprise. The antithesis of Dr. Hammond, Phylis thought. He was short, a full inch shorter than Phylis, and gaunt. His narrow face was smooth-skinned, but angular, giving him a distinctive hawk-like appearance. His thick brown hair, stylishly cut and neatly combed, might have fallen from the pages of *GQ*. She guessed his age at mid-forties-trying-to-look-mid-thirties. But he was certainly friendly enough, and despite the sterile hospital atmosphere, managed to put Phylis at ease. After chatting idly for a few minutes, engaging both Celia and herself, he got right to the point.

"By now you are wondering exactly what kind of therapy we are offering here," Dr. Brand said.

Phylis, who was sitting beside Celia in one of the plush sofas, smiled nervously. She craved a cigarette, but there were no ashtrays to be seen.

"Audio-neural-cue therapy," Dr. Brand said, "is a

hybrid of the very old, and the very new, though Dr. Gordon insists it remains well within the bounds of traditional psychoanalysis and therapy."

John, who had taken the easy chair across from Phylis, laughed softly.

"You mean, something to do with sounds, and the brain?" Phylis asked.

"Exactly. For hundreds of years artists have said 'A picture is worth a thousand words', and in many senses that is true. But in the case of the human mind, it is not always so. Language, not imagery, is the primary sorting and cataloging method of the brain. Learning it is a built-in ability of the brain, and we begin to do so immediately after birth. A single word can bring to consciousness a thousand images, and a breadth of emotion."

Dr. Brand looked squarely at Phylis, and she felt pinned by his dark eyes. *"Father,* for instance," he said softly.

Phylis managed to conceal her surprised reaction, but Celia perked immediately to attention.

"Word association games are an old favorite of psychiatrists. If you play them fast enough, some startling information about the subject can surface. But up to now, word association has been a little explored avenue in the world of psychotherapy, and the power of language has been largely ignored, especially in a therapeutic capacity. Dr. Gordon and I are rather like pioneers."

John smiled faintly, and offered a self-deprecating shrug.

"You want to play word games with my daughter?"

"In a sense, yes. But very specialized word games,

augmented by some sophisticated equipment and software. Simply, we plan to reduce the emotional weight of specific words, and hence their attendant memories and images."

John suddenly leaned across the table towards Phylis. "Need an ashtray, Phylis?"

Phylis smiled apologetically, nodding. She had been kneading her hands nervously, a sure sign of a nicotine fit. "It's a bad habit, I know."

"There are lots worse," John said. He reached beneath the coffee table and came up with a glass ashtray. Phylis gave him a thankful look, and lit a cigarette. After two puffs she had relaxed considerably. "Please, go on," she said to Dr. Brand.

"The treatment has three stages," Dr. Brand said. "First we must develop what we call an audio-emotional topograph of the subject. The process takes about two days, and allows us to determine which words, images, and memories, are causing irregular emotional responses.

"The second stage is to stop those irregular responses from happening. To do this we must pull the wool over the mind's eye. In effect, we trick the unconscious into believing that the key problem words have no emotional weight. We bypass the maladaptive response circuit. We cut it out completely."

Phylis squinted through a veil of smoke. "Isn't that like brainwashing?"

"Not at all," Brand said calmly. "We don't try to erase memories, or even change them. We just try to control the mind's response to a certain stimulus. And it's all done with word games."

Phylis chuckled, an image of a Dell crossword book

59

flitting through her head. She took another puff on the cigarette. "What about stage three?"

"The third stage involves what we've labelled primal sound cues, and without it the benefits of stage two wear off relatively quickly. You can only trick the mind for so long, before it figures out what's going on. In this stage we go beyond the level of normal cataloging and sorting, that is beyond words and language. We use simple sounds. Sounds that make no sense to the conscious mind, but which are the bedrock of the unconscious structure.

"By presenting certain primal sound cues within the context of a rather complex feedback loop between the subject and our computer, we can alter the subject's deep mental processes to accommodate stage two changes on a long term basis."

Phylis took another puff on her cigarette, then mashed it out in the ashtray. "Will it help Celia?"

"We've yet to run into a non-responsive subject," Brand said.

Knowing she should ask questions, but not sure what, Phylis blurted the only two things that really concerned her. "Is there surgery involved? Will she have to take drugs of any kind?"

Brand glanced at John Gordon, then back to Phylis. "There is a substance involved in the procedure," he said slowly. "But no surgery."

"What do you mean . . . substance?" Phylis was suddenly wary.

"Well, it's not a drug as you define the word. It's an artificial enzyme, catalogued as HG-37, that mimics a substance found naturally in the human brain. Very similar to serotonin, which facilitates neuron firing.

We use it to help with the word associations."

"But what will it do to her?"

"Phylis," John Gordon spoke calmly, leaning across the table towards her. "HG-37 is a harmless enzyme with a half-life in the brain of about three minutes. All it will do is allow Celia to free-associate more readily, and only for a short time. The effect is so small that it's unlikely that either you, or Celia, will notice it at all."

The look of genuine concern on his face calmed Phylis instantly. She nodded. Celia tugged at her sleeve. "What is it, honey?"

"Can we go swimming now?"

Dr. Brand chuckled. "Well, there's not much more I can tell you. Dr. Gordon will be able to answer any further questions you may have. I'd like to start the procedure tomorrow morning, if that's all right with you?"

Phylis nodded. "All right."

John Gordon walked with them back to the cabin. As they passed Cabin Two, Dora DeMarch called and waved. She and David were on the porch eating. She certainly seems in better spirits today, Phylis thought.

David pressed his face up to the screen. "Hi, Celia!" he shouted.

Celia waved, grinning. "Can David come swimming with us?" she asked Phylis.

"We'll see, honey," Phylis said. "We'll have to ask his mommy." As they continued walking, she said to John: "I saw David last night."

"Oh?"

"When we got back from swimming. He was standing behind the cabin, talking to someone in the trees I thought, waving his hands madly. But there was nobody there. When he saw me he ran off."

John chuckled. "You'll see more of that from David. Don't let it bother you. It's part of his therapy."

"Talking to the air is part of his therapy?" Her voice had more edge to it than she had intended.

"All I can tell you is that we've encouraged David's belief in his imaginary playmate. It's helped him a lot."

"Is that wise?" Phylis suddenly remembered her own playmate as a child, Buffy, who had suddenly disappeared around Phylis's fifth birthday. But she had never believed Buffy really existed, had she?

"You should have seen him when he first got here. The difference between then and now is phenomenal." He stopped walking, his facial expression troubled, and put a hand out to touch her elbow. "I understand your curiosity, Phylis, but you really shouldn't concern yourself with David. We sometimes get so caught up in the summer-camp atmosphere at Lakeview, that we tend to forget simple little things. Like doctor-patient confidentiality."

"I'm sorry," Phylis said. "I really didn't mean to pry. Really. It's just that, when I saw David talking to nobody, I also heard a loud noise in the woods."

John frowned, regarding her curiously. "Imaginary friends don't usually make noises."

Phylis blushed. Seeing her reaction, John smiled. "I'm sorry, that was uncalled for." They began to walk again.

"I guess I deserved it," Phylis said. "David's problem is none of my business."

"The woods are full of strange noises," John said.

"Crashes, bangs, even screams sometimes. Inexplicable."

"I guess you're right," Phylis said.

At the cabin John did not come in, but stood outside, leaning against the door frame. Celia ran inside and disappeared into the bathroom.

"Are you coming swimming with us?" Phylis asked.

"I wish I could, but I have to make a run to Fergus Falls. I'll be gone for a few hours. Is there anything you need while I'm over there?"

Phylis glanced through to the kitchen. "A bottle of sunflower oil, a tub of margarine or butter. A jar of jam would be nice." She counted the items off on her fingers. "Celia, can you think of anything we need from town?"

"Frosted Flakes," Celia shouted from the bathroom.

"I'll see what I can do," John said.

Phylis sat on the porch table and watched him walk back to the main building. She lit a cigarette, breathing the smoke deeply. *You are wrong Dr. John Gordon,* she thought. *The woods are not full of strange noises. Only when David is near.*

As if in confirmation, the trees whispered in the wind.

CHAPTER SEVEN

Later that day John dropped by the cabin with a brown paper bag full of groceries. Dora DeMarch and Phylis were sitting on the porch, drinking weak screwdrivers made from Dora's vodka and Phylis's orange juice. Dora, Phylis had decided, was okay, if somewhat uptight. Celia and David were playing together on the scraggly grass in front of the cabin, creating what appeared to be a small city from loose rocks and pebbles. The kids really seemed to like each other, Phylis noted with pleasure.

John placed the bag on the table and sat next to Phylis. "I got what you wanted, and a few extras."

Dora began to fidget the moment John arrived. After finishing her drink, she made her excuses and left. Outside, she grabbed David by the wrist and dragged him toward their cabin. "Time for supper," she explained.

John unpacked the grocery bag. Among the extras was a bottle of red wine, and an assortment of fresh vegetables. "Any plans for supper?"

"Nothing concrete." She'd thought of making a couple of hot dogs for Celia, and cup of soup for herself.

"Then please allow me to prepare some of my famous spaghetti."

"Do you do this for all of Lakeview's patients?"

John gazed at her levelly for a moment. "No, I don't."

Unsure of how to react, but pleased by his admission, Phylis agreed to the offer. She was glad she had. His spaghetti was definitely the best she had ever tasted, and she found she had eaten more than she should have. The wine was a mildly expensive French Beaujolais with a pleasant fruity taste, and afterwards they sipped it slowly as the sun went down. John managed to position the television's rabbit ears so that it produced an acceptable picture, and Celia contented herself by watching Chevy Chase in *European Vacation*, a film she had seen at least twice already.

As the evening wore on, and Phylis became more relaxed, she discovered she was enjoying John's company very much. They did not talk much, but his presence across from her at the table seemed to fill some sort of undefined need. And he, too, seemed pleasantly relaxed.

John shared the last of the wine between them, then leaned across the table towards her. "I have a proposition for you."

"Oh?" She arched her eyebrows.

"Nothing like that," he scolded good humoredly. "It's about tomorrow."

"Ah."

"Dr. Brand will be with Celia most of the day. A full morning, anyway. What happens tomorrow is the equivalent of going to the dentist for an X-ray, he's simply trying to pinpoint where the problem lies. It will be a day, or even two, before we begin to . . . drill, if you'll pardon the expression."

"So?" She sipped her wine.

"So, you're going to have most of the day free. I'm going over to Battle Lake in the morning to pick up some supplies. Would you like to come? I know a fantastic little restaurant on the waterfront where they toss the most amazing salad." He grinned.

Phylis frowned, not liking the idea of leaving Celia alone. John seemed to read her mind. "You won't see Celia, even if you stay. No outside influence allowed. Doctors orders."

"I'll think about it," Phylis said slowly, a smile curling her lips. She sipped her wine.

John Gordon smiled too, and raised his glass in a silent toast.

Phylis slept soundly that night, perhaps aided by the wine, and when she awoke it was light and Celia was already up and setting the porch table for breakfast. Phylis went through and joined her. They ate in silence, as Celia seemed nervous and withdrawn. After breakfast Phylis showered, then dressed. She was applying her makeup before the vanity when she suddenly paused, lipstick barely touching her lower lip. *What are you doing?* She was in the middle of the wilderness, and here she was acting like she was going to a prom! The lipstick she had been about to apply was of a dark shade, and she dropped it back into her makeup case in disgust. She poked around for a moment until she found something lighter. Coral pink. She applied it carefully, then studied herself in the

66

mirror. Better, she thought.

When John Gordon arrived she was sitting on the porch with a coffee, smoking her third cigarette of the day. Celia was also on the porch, reading an "Archie and his Friends" comic.

John held the screen door open and leaned against the frame. "Ready?"

Phylis nodded, crushed out the cigarette, and gulped down the last of the coffee. Celia closed her comic slowly, and turned to John. "Can I take this with me?"

"Sure," John said.

Not looking very happy, Celia rolled up the comic and followed John outside. When Phylis came out, Celia gripped her hand tightly. "Can we go swimming?"

Phylis looked to John. John nodded. "Okay, but later," Phylis said. "After you see the doctor."

Celia nodded stoically, her small face creased in a frown. At the main building a sullen young woman sat at the reception desk flipping through open files. John introduced her as Margaret Palin, who served as nurse, receptionist, and general assistant. Phylis found the buxom, brown-haired Margaret a bit severe and cold, but Celia took to her right away. Holding Celia's hand, Margaret led the child down the hall to the second room before the end. Before entering, Celia looked back once and waved.

"That's it?" Phylis asked, feeling as if she were deserting Celia.

"Actually, you can observe the first part of the session, if you like."

Phylis nodded, relieved. "All right."

The room he took her to was at the end of the hall, adjacent to the room Celia had gone into, and looked into it through a large window on the connecting wall. "It's a mirror on the other side," John explained.

Phylis stood next to the glass and looked through in awe. "My God, it's like a science fiction movie."

Behind her, John Gordon chuckled. "It does look rather imposing, doesn't it?" He stepped closer to her.

In the other room, Celia was lying on a black leather couch, feet towards Phylis and John, looking quite comfortable if somewhat nervous. She kept glancing to her right, where Dr. Brand, in a white smock, was typing something at a microcomputer keyboard nestled in the middle of a bank of equipment. Margaret Palin was applying small electrode pads to Celia's forehead, temples, and palms. Celia watched this operation curiously, but without apparent alarm.

"I'll explain everything," John said. "On the left by Dr. Brand you can see four separate pieces of equipment. That big black box against the wall is our pride and joy, and our only piece of *new* equipment. A Toshiba Digital Audio Synthesizer. State of the art. Basically a very expensive noisemaker. Beside it is the brains of the operation, our VAX mainframe computer. We call it Beverly."

Phylis giggled. "Beverly?"

"My nickname. I knew a Beverly once. She was just like the VAX."

"Cold and calculating?"

"No. A temperamental bitch."

Phylis laughed out loud. John looked at her and smiled. "It's obsolete, but beggars can't be choosers. Beside the VAX is the terminal by which Dr. Brand controls the whole system. And finally, against the other wall, is the telemetry deck by which we monitor Celia via all those wires sticking out of her. Everything is routed through the VAX."

Phylis nodded, impressed despite her usual aloofness to technology. In the treatment room Margaret Palin said something to Celia and smiled. She held up what looked like a fighter pilot's helmet, with a dark metal shield where there should have been glass, and a cable coming out of the top. "What the hell is that?"

"Glorified earphones," John said. "We like to isolate the subject as much as possible, and that's what the shield is for."

Margaret Palin held up a syringe filled with clear liquid and showed it to Celia. Celia nodded bravely and looked away as Margaret tied a tourniquet around her small arm. As Margaret slipped the needle into Celia's flesh, Phylis turned squeamishly away. Then the helmet was fitted in place. Dr. Brand checked his watch.

"It takes about 45 seconds for HG-37 to take effect," John said.

Dr. Brand kept his eyes on his watch, then reached down and tapped the keyboard. Lights flickered across the whole array of equipment. Celia suddenly stiffened, then seemed to relax.

"What's happening?"

"The HG-37 has begun to work," John said. "Dr. Brand has activated the system. At this moment our trusty Toshiba synthesizer is speaking to Celia. As Celia hears each word, she will think about it. As a result of the HG-37 her thoughts will be freer than usual, as will her emotional reactions. The telemetry deck will monitor her heart rate, respiration, palm conductivity, and brain activity, forwarding all readings to the VAX, which will analyze and correlate everything."

"What kind of words is she hearing?" Phylis asked softly.

"At first it will be neutrals. Words with no emotional weight. Until we get a relaxed reading. Then the VAX will drop a key word, an archtype, a word that elicits a roughly equal reaction from most subjects, and we'll monitor the response. This will give us a base line of her primary emotional catalog."

"Why doesn't Dr. Brand just speak to her?" Phylis was frowning. The battery of equipment, her fragile daughter in the midst of it, gave her the shivers.

"Because Celia might react to Dr. Brand, or his voice, or to any number of outside influences. This way we get her reaction to the words alone, because the voice is absolutely neutral, and it is the only thing she can hear. Would you like to hear what she's hearing?"

Phylis looked up sharply. John was smiling faintly, as if amused by her reaction to it all. "Yes, I would," she said.

John reached out to a speaker box below the glass. He twisted a dial, then turned on the speaker. For a moment there was absolute silence, then a voice spoke. It was a voice that was neither masculine nor feminine, neither warm or cold, neither benevolent nor malevolent. It was purely neutral, absolutely calm, and definitely not human. "APPLE," it said, and the word hung in the air like a solitary cloud. Then it was gone. A second later it spoke again. "WINDOW," it said, then more silence. The string of words continued, each spoken in the same calm, almost hypnotic monotone. ". . . DOG . . . CUP . . . PENCIL . . . MILK . . . TABLE . . ." There was no apparent pattern, certainly nothing disturbing about them, and Phylis found herself lulled by the innocuous string. Then, suddenly, a bomb dropped. ". . . MOMMY."

Phylis gasped, bringing her hand to her mouth. In the treatment room, Celia shifted uneasily on the table. Lights flashed on the telemetry reader, and Dr. Brand nodded. Without a break, the voice continued. ". . . FISH . . . CANDLE . . . SCISSORS . . ."

"Turn it off, please," Phylis said, turning away from the glass. She heard the speaker click as John turned it off, then felt his warm hand on her shoulder.

"Are you all right?"

She nodded. "I just found it a bit . . . strange."

"Don't worry. It doesn't go on for long. Maybe half an hour. Then they'll retire to the playroom, and Margaret will observe Celia, and talk to her."

"Why?"

"Well, as I told you, we're dealing with key words right now. Generalities, really. Margaret will try to glean some specifics from Celia. People's names, places, things she likes, things she dislikes. Secondary words. Then we'll go through the process again with those. By tomorrow we'll have our audio-emotional topograph, and we can determine what course to take. Just like taking X-rays."

Phylis nodded distractedly, not really listening. She fumbled in her purse until she found her cigarettes, lit one, and inhaled deeply. "John, are you still going over to Battle Lake?"

"Decided to come?"

She nodded, and took another puff on her cigarette. "Can we go now?"

"Sure," he said, looking rather concerned, and holding the door open for her. "Seen enough?"

"Too much," Phylis said softly. She had not planned on accompanying John to Battle Lake, but seeing Celia in that room had disturbed her. She needed a way to take her mind off it.

You don't want to think about what they're doing to her, she accused herself. *You don't want to think about what you've submitted her to.* She took a final glance into the treatment room, where Celia lay quietly on the couch, and a shiver ran up her spine as she remembered that disembodied, inhuman voice.

CHAPTER EIGHT

They used John's car for the trip to Battle Lake, the Impala having the benefit of serviceable, if somewhat noisy air-conditioning. The army barracks looked deserted when they passed, and Phylis could not even see a guard.

"Must be their day off," she said.

John replied with a grunt. Phylis leaned back in the seat and let the cool air blow over her, watching the trees whip by. Neither of them talked much during the short trip, which suited Phylis fine. Once, she asked him about the patients other than Celia and David, none of whom she had yet seen.

"They're near the end of their therapy program, so we give them a bit more freedom," he said, his eyes unreadable behind dark sunglasses. "They went to Minneapolis for the weekend. They should be back sometime today."

"Why didn't Dora and David go?"

"David's not quite ready."

Phylis dug no deeper, lest she spring the doctor-patient confidentiality trap. They arrived in Battle Lake fifteen minutes later, and Phylis was delighted by the small, lakeside resort town. A smatter of brightly dressed tourists walked on either side of the main street, gazing into the store windows. On each side of the road was a strip of storefronts. On the west was a grocery store, an ice cream parlor, a dress shop, and an appliance repair center. On the other side was the Otter Tail Hotel, a liquor store, and a dim looking bar that advertised COLD COORS LIGHT in flickering neon.

"God, this would be a nice place to live," Phylis said.

"Mostly a summer population," John said as they drove slowly along the road. "Gets a lot of business from Fergus Falls, even Minneapolis, but this is getting on to the end of the season. Not too many who live here all year long. Maybe six hundred. Maybe less."

He parked the car against the curb at the north end of town, overlooking the lake. A few teenagers and children were splashing about inside an area marked off with blue buoys. A frisby skimmed the top of the water. A boat pulling a water skier roared by, just beyond the buoys, sending up a plume of spray that glittered in the sunlight. In the distance, a tapestry of multicolored sails danced on the water. Phylis tried to imagine the lake frozen over, and instead of swimmers she pictured cross-country skiers making tracks along the edge of the lake.

"I could take it all year long," she said.

They went to the grocery store first, where John picked up two bags of mixed supplies, then to a hardware store at the other end of the road. By the time they walked from one end of town to the other it was noon, and John led them to a small, open-air restaurant down at the edge of the lake, overlooking the public dock. The water of Battle Lake stretched invitingly to the horizon.

Lunch was leisurely and slow. Phylis munched her salad, eyes scanning the water constantly for interesting activity. She was looking forward to taking a dip once they got back to Lakeview. A gentle breeze coming off the lake cooled things down to a comfortable level.

"Can you see the clinic from here?" Phylis asked, shielding her eyes to peer across the water.

John followed her gaze. "No. Battle Lake is in the shape of an elongated *S*. We're sitting in the west bay right now, Lakeview is in the east bay, at the opposite end of the *S*. Couple of major points in the way."

Phylis nodded, sipping her wine.

"It's a beautiful boat ride, though, from Lakeview to here," John said. "There are some amazing cabins along the shore. I could show you sometime."

"Celia would enjoy a boat ride."

"But would you?" His gaze was level, and careful.

"Yes, I would," Phylis said, and smiled.

John grinned, and continued to eat his salad. Phylis who was looking beyond him, suddenly found herself being studied by a man, three tables away, who was sitting alone. He looked about fifty, pudgy, wearing a pale blue dress shirt tucked into beige Bermuda shorts. Even from here Phylis could see the sheen of sweat on his round, pale face. His eyes were watery blue, and unabashedly trained on her. She looked away for a moment, but when she looked back he was still staring at her.

"Can we go?" she asked John, feeling uncomfortable under the stranger's scrutiny.

75

He nodded, swallowing the last of his wine, and waved to the waiter for their check. After he paid the bill, Phylis glanced over to the stranger again, but the man had gone. She felt suddenly very foolish. She was glad she had not mentioned it to John; he most certainly would have considered her paranoid.

They walked slowly back to the car. As they drove away, Phylis looked out the passenger window, and froze. The pudgy man was standing in the door of the ice cream parlor, two-scoop cone suspended below his thick lips, and he was staring right at her. She could not turn away. His eyes followed her as the car drove down the road, until finally John turned onto 210. For the second time that day a shiver ran down Phylis's spine, and the car suddenly seemed far too cool.

Approximately two hundred miles to the south, at the Minnesota State Correctional Facility in Stillwater, Phylis's ex-husband Don Reynolds was standing at the release desk, checking through his package of belongings. He was relatively short, five foot eight and a quarter inches to be exact, and the counter was designed to look down on even the tallest of inmates, and so Don found himself reaching up to chest height. He opened the cash envelope, and carefully counted the green bills within. They totaled $4326.00 exactly.

Across the counter, at a higher level, Harry Ward watched Don count the money. The old guard's face wrinkled in concern. "All there?" he asked after Don had finished counting.

Don smiled. "Yeah, all there." He tucked the bills into his wallet and slipped it into his inside breast pocket. It was nice to be back in street clothes again, even if they were the one's he'd worn to court. He looked down at the shiny black leather loafers on his feet and smiled. Real good.

Old Harry Ward stepped down from behind the counter and stood next to him. "Don, I think you've changed since you came here," he said, looking at Don with fatherly concern.

Yeah, I've changed, Don thought. *I'm two fucking years older, my asshole is looser, and I know what cock tastes like.* But all he said was, "Oh?"

"I think you've learned from your mistake. We all make mistakes, son, and you made a real bad one. But a sign of being a good man is being able to learn from mistakes, and I think you've done that."

Don nodded humbly. "You're right," he said. "I know what I did was wrong. I just want to get on with my life." The funny thing was, it wasn't bullshit. He'd fucked up good, and he'd probably screwed up Celia good. He had been angry at first, real angry, but that had diminished over the past year. His dreams of vengeance on Phylis and Celia had become less intense with each passing day. What he had done went beyond what could be forgiven by family loyalty. He had known that all along, really.

"A clean start," Harry said.

"That's right," Don said.

Across the room, Jake Tanner guffawed. In his uniform he had the look of somebody who would be saddled with a nickname like Bull or Moose or Bear, and in fact he looked a lot like Bull from *Night Court,* except dumber, Don thought. Jake didn't need to stand behind a counter to tower over you. He could do that in

77

bare feet. "He's still a fuckin' pervert, Harry," Jake said.

Don looked down at the floor. He could feel the blood rushing to his face, could feel the temperature rising inside. *Just calm down,* he commanded himself. *He isn't worth it!*

"Why don't you give him his going away present," Jake said, grinning stupidly.

Harry frowned, looking down at his hands, as if embarrassed. "Son, I'm sorry to have to do this," he said softly.

Don looked up, now more curious than angry. Harry reached below the counter and brought out a folded sheet of paper. The thing had an official look about it, and suddenly something cold clamped in his guts.

"Go on, give it to him," Jake said.

Harry shook his head sorrowfully, and held out the sheet. Don took the sheet in his hand, and held it for a moment before unfolding it. He began to read it, and behind him, Jake Tanner began to chuckle.

"I'm sorry, son. A man shouldn't have to face this, not when he's just getting back on his feet."

"It's a court order, pervert," Jake said. "Old Harry may think you've changed, but your old lady's got more sense. She ain't taking any chances."

Don was looking down at the court order in his hands, half blind with an emotion he could not identify. The court order alone might not have been enough to push him over the edge, and neither, alone, would Jake's badgering. But together they came as a one two punch that fried a fragile circuit of rationality in Don's mind, a circuit that might otherwise have remained dormant for the rest of his life.

"Do you understand what it says, son?"

Don nodded numbly.

"Don't take it hard, son. Once your family sees how you've changed, they'll give you a chance."

"I just hope they can forgive me," Don whispered. Somewhere in his mind he was amazed that he'd managed to say the words with such feeling.

"They will son, trust me," Harry said, patting his back. "In the meantime, it's my duty to tell you that you're not allowed to go near your wife or daughter. That means not in person, not by phone, and not by mail. Do you understand?"

Don nodded. He folded the court order and slipped it in beside his wallet.

"You want my advice son, you take that cab outside downtown, then you catch a bus straight down to Chicago, or even farther. Don't go anywhere near the Twin-cities."

Don picked up his suitcase and walked over to the door.

"Smart lady, your wife," Jake said.

"Shut up, Jake," Harry said. "Just let him go."

Jake grinned down at him, revealing brown teeth. "Sure, I'll let him go." He unlatched the door, opening it a crack, but when Don stepped forward he closed it again. "See you later, dirtbag," Jake said.

Don pushed the door until it opened, then stepped out into the sunshine. Behind him he heard Jake's laughter, suddenly cut short as the door slammed shut. The cab was waiting in the courtyard and he climbed in.

"Where to, brother?" The black driver said, turning

and grinning.

"I'm not your fucking brother," Don said, slamming the door. The driver turned away, lips tight. "Take me to the bus station, and don't talk."

The driver turned on the meter, and started to drive. Don pulled out the court order and read it again, carefully. It was hot in the car, but not nearly as hot as the rising fire within him. He folded the order and put it away again.

"Fucking cunt," he said.

The driver glanced at him in the mirror, but said nothing. Don looked out the window as downtown Stillwater went by on either side.

He would catch a bus to Chicago. Sure. But not yet. First he was going to Minneapolis, and from there he would work things out. One thing he was sure of. Phylis would pay for this. Divorced or not, she was still his wife, and Celia was his daughter.

And both those fucking cunts would pay.

CHAPTER NINE

The following morning, Celia woke full of energy, and ate two bowls of Frosted Flakes, as Phylis, sipping a cup of instant coffee, looked on in astonishment. After the preliminary session, yesterday, Celia had been jumpy and full of talk, and Phylis had hardly managed to squeeze a word in edgewise as Celia babbled on about Margaret this and Margaret that and my friend Margaret. Why, Phylis wondered, did Margaret seem such a cold fish to me? I'm a bad judge of character, she decided, dismissing an image of Paul Welch from her mind before it could take hold.

It had taken a good hour of swimming before Celia had been ready for supper, and afterwards she had fidgeted nervously before the television. It was a wonder she had ever agreed to go to bed. As Phylis had tucked her in for the night, Celia had looked up at her with those clear green eyes. "Y'know, Mommy, it didn't hurt at all. Not even the 'jection."

"That's good, sweetheart," Phylis said, stroking Celia's soft red hair.

"It's just words!" Celia's voice was filled with wonder.

This morning, Celia was eager to get to the main building, and dragged Phylis most of the way. Margaret Palin greeted them at the reception desk with a cold smile, and Celia ran to her. Phylis felt a sudden pang of jealousy, but extinguished it immediately. The more Celia liked Margaret, the better. It only made things easier.

John Gordon had taken a run to Fergus Falls, Margaret informed her, but Phylis was welcome to observe again, if she wished. Phylis declined. The small, bare, observation room was bad enough with John present, but alone it would be too much for her. Instead, she decided to spend the day on the beach, with the hopes of becoming fully engaged in her book.

Towards noon, Dora DeMarch wandered down to the beach and invited Phylis to her cabin for lunch. David was at the main building, undergoing treatment. Phylis wondered if Celia and David would see each other; they both might enjoy that. Dora seemed morose, but not overly quiet, and as they ate her delicious tuna-salad sandwiches, Phylis listened to David's story.

Dora wasn't David's mother, but his aunt, on his father's side. David's parents had died two years ago in a fire at their house. "David was left all alone. I couldn't let them put him up for adoption. He was family. I know I'm single, but still."

Phylis nodded understandingly, chewing on a mouthful of sandwich.

"David, he blamed himself," Dora continued. "Well, no that's not true. He sort of had an imaginary playmate, you know? And he blamed *it*. He called it Sonny, I think. And after the fire, Sonny would still come around, I guess, and David had these terrible nightmares. Waking up in the middle of the night, screaming and such. Well, the doctors couldn't do nothing, and eventually they recommended here. Sort of a last desperate chance." Dora smiled faintly. "Of course, it wasn't anything to do with David. The fire, I mean. Started in the breaker box in the basement. Some fluke short circuit. But David wouldn't believe it. Not until now, anyway."

"He's getting better?" Phylis asked, not really wanting to know more, but seeing that Dora needed to talk.

"Yeah, I guess. They sort of, you know, encouraged him to become friends with Sonny again. Lots of kids have imaginary playmates, did you know that? But it spooks me. I can hear him talking to it sometimes. And sometimes, I know it's silly, I can almost hear it talking back." She tittered nervously.

It's my turn now, Phylis thought. She wants to hear about Celia, and she expects me to spill all. Fair's fair. But I can't do it. Not yet. Those wounds are too deep. Instead, she said: "I had an imaginary playmate when I was a kid. Her name was Buffy."

"Really?" Dora seemed immensely relieved.

During the course of the afternoon, Phylis met the occupants of Cabins Two and Four, whom Dora dragged down to the beach for introductions. Susan Douglas and Penny Brock were single mothers, of about Phylis's and Dora's age, who had come to Lakeview with their daughters, both of whom were Celia's and David's age. The other thing they all had in common was that the children had suffered a major trauma. Lakeview was the last stop in a string of options.

Both Penny and Susan were near the end of their stay, however, and for this Phylis uttered a silent prayer of thanks. Neither woman could stop talking, and Phylis and Dora exchanged pained glances as the afternoon wore on. Penny's daughter, Candice, and Susan's daughter, Donna, played and splashed at the water's edge, filling the afternoon with screams and laughter. If their mothers had been absent, Phylis would have enjoyed herself.

When Celia finally emerged from the main building, holding the hand of Margaret Palin, Phylis jumped at the chance to excuse herself. Once Celia saw Phylis, she released Margaret's hand, and ran towards her mother.

"Ready for a swim, kiddo?" She did not really want to go back down to the beach, but to refuse would have been unfair to Celia.

But Celia shook her head. "I'm tired."

Phylis put an arm around her daughter's shoulder, and led her back to the cabin. What had happened to all that surplus energy? From the door of the main building Margaret waved, but Celia only managed to flap her arm half-heartedly in response. As well as being thoroughly tired, it seemed, Celia was also not the least bit hungry, and ate a bowl of Frosted Flakes only on Phylis's insistence. Afterwards she retired to the living room and stretched out on the sofa, where she fell immediately asleep. Phylis kneeled at the side of the sofa, stroking Celia's soft red hair, until the child's breathing was deep and even. Then she made herself a pot of tea and returned to the porch. The afternoon with the other mothers had left her too lazy to cook, too lazy, even, to open her book again and begin reading. She'd actually become quite engrossed in it earlier.

Sounds of laughter continued to drift up from the beach, and Phylis sat with her legs stretched out, smoking and sipping tea, until even those sounds desisted. A bank of clouds drifted in from the west, the temperature dropping with their approach, so that by 6:00 the sky had turned dull, and spits of rain were darkening the concrete path.

John Gordon's brown Impala drove up to the cabin just as the rain began to fall in earnest, and he ran from the car with his head bowed from the rain, clutching a brown paper bag to his chest. The porch door slammed shut behind him. "When we get it, we get it good!"

Phylis greeted him with a smile, and found that as soon as she did so she began to feel better. It was as if Celia's fatigue had rubbed off on her, and John's energy was now bringing about a revival. Besides which, she was honestly glad to see him, and happy for company that knew when to keep quiet. "What's in the bag?"

"Supper, if you're interested."

"I am!"

"Great. Then just stay where you are. Don't move a muscle. I'll take care of everything."

Phylis didn't have to be told twice, she relished the thought of being pampered. When John returned from the kitchen with a glass of white wine she graced him with a warm smile.

"Start on this," he said. "Supper will be up soon."

She was halfway through the glass when he returned with a plate of steaming fried chicken, picked up

85

somewhere in Fergus Falls and reheated in the oven. He tossed down a pile of paper napkins, but Phylis had already reached out and picked up a succulent looking breast.

"Mmmmm," she said.

The chicken hit the spot. After the last drumstick was stripped to the bone by Phylis, they sipped wine and listened to the whisper of the trees behind the cabin, watched the sheets of rain dancing on the choppy water of the lake.

"Celia really seemed drained after the session today," Phylis said.

"It was a long day," John agreed. He peered through to the living room, where Celia was turned against the back of the sofa, hugging herself. "I should put her to bed. She'll catch a chill there," he said.

Without thinking, Phylis nodded. John tiptoed over to the dull linoleum, expertly avoiding the creaking spots, leaned over Celia for a moment, then looked back at Phylis, smiling. He silently mouthed: "Sound alseep."

Phylis nodded, and sipped her wine.

As John gently lifted Celia, Phylis felt a pang of emotion. They appeared so much like . . . like father and daughter. The way John looked down into Celia's face, so tenderly, made her long to make him part of her life. Part of *their* life. So immersed was she in this dream, that Celia's suddenly stiffening body did not register with her. It was only the piercing scream that brought Phylis back to earth, but by then it was too late.

She saw that John had paused in alarm at Celia's sudden activity, but he was powerless to avoid the swing of her small hand. John cried out as Celia's nail raked across his eyes, and Celia screamed again. Grunting in pain, John kneeled and carefully put Celia to her feet. Celia's face was twisted in fear and horror.

"Celia!" Phylis yelled.

Celia's head jerked around towards her mother, then she ran to her, sobbing, and buried her face in Phylis's stomach. John held a hand to his face, but Phylis could see the scrape that Celia's sharp nails had inflicted, the blood slowly welling to the surface.

"John, are you all right?"

"Yes, fine. How's Celia?"

Phylis kneeled before the trembling child. "Honey, are you okay?"

Celia snuffled, pouting, and nodded. "I thought I was dreaming. I thought . . ."

Phylis hugged her again, but Celia pushed free and turned to John, eyes red-rimmed, brimming with tears. "I'm sorry Dr. Gordon. I didn't mean it." Her voice trembled, on the verge of breaking, then she ran from Phylis, past John, and disappeared into her bedroom. Phylis moved to follow, but John put out an arm to stop her.

"I'll get going," he said softly.

Phylis looked up into his face, and reached up a hand to delicately touch the inflamed skin around his left eye. "Poor John, are you sure you're okay?"

"Fine. Really."

"I don't know what came over her, she really likes you, I know she does, she—" His sudden touch upon her hand caused her to stop talking, and she realized she had been on the verge of breaking down. "Oh,

God, John, do you think the therapy will help her?"

He reached out both arms and pulled her to him, stroking her hair, holding her tightly against his chest, and she found herself wanting to stay that way, held by him, forever.

"I know it will help. I went over her emotional topograph with Dr. Brand, and we're ready to start working on Celia tomorrow."

Phylis gripped him fiercely, very conscious of the hardness of his body against her own, then pulled away. Her face was streaked with tears, and she left a large stain on his shoulder. "God, I'm sorry, I've ruined your shirt!"

He grinned. "It was worth it. Go and see Celia. I'll come by tomorrow."

Disappointed that he was going, she nodded. But John stopped her again. This time he cupped her chin with both his hands, and Phylis found herself looking into his clear brown eyes, found herself getting lost in them. And suddenly he was leaning over her, and his lips were touching hers. She held him tightly, and opened her mouth to him. His tongue slipped past her lips, and she moaned softly. At last he pulled away, shaking his head.

"I'm sorry. I didn't mean to take advantage like that. It's just—"

This time she reached for him, and with her lips on his, stopped him talking. When they parted, they were both breathless.

"Tomorrow," John said, his voice husky.

Phylis nodded, but said nothing. She was overcome by desire, and had no wish to reveal it further. The downpour had turned to drizzle for a moment, and

John managed to get to his car without getting soaked.

"Tomorrow," Phylis whispered, as the Impala turned and drove towards the main building.

Then, frowning, she went into the bedroom to look after Celia.

CHAPTER TEN

The rain continued, off and on, through the night, and when light slowly crept into the east bay it was grey and somber. A low ceiling of dark clouds scudded over the lake, coming from the west. Phylis delivered Celia to the main building after breakfast, and was met in the reception area by John, Dr. Brand, and Margaret Palin. For the first time since she had met him, John, dressed in a clean white smock, looked like the doctor he claimed to be.

Once Dr. Brand and Margaret had led Celia away, John said, "About last night, I apologize again."

Phylis smiled, reached up, and kissed him gently on the lips. She had intended the kiss to be a mere peck, but it quickly turned into something more. "No apologies needed," she said breathlessly.

"Whew," John said. He looked back along the corridor, then at Phylis again. "I'll bring Celia around to the cabin when we're finished. Maybe all three of us can take a boat over to Battle Lake, for an ice cream cone or something."

"If it clears up," Phylis said.

"It will." John smiled. "Will you be watching today?"

"In your company, or alone?"

"Unfortunately, this stage of the treatment requires the presence of both Dr. Brand, and myself, as well as Margaret. But I'll wave to you through the mirror." He smiled.

Phylis chuckled. "No. That's all right. I have some reading to do."

She spent the morning at the cabin, and thankfully, none of the others ventured forth into the grim day to bother her. Once, she saw a jeep drive into camp, and two young army men in uniform launched a boat from one of the boat elevators at the edge of camp, and rode, laughing, out into the choppy water. The boat rose and fell, rose and fell, crashing from one wave into the next. What they were doing on the lake on a day like today, she did not know, and did not want to know.

The two men returned about an hour later, somewhat subdued by the choppiness of the water. Margaret, who had stepped out of the main building momentarily, waved at them as they raised the boat back onto its platform. Both of them walked over to her, and began to chat. You'd look good in a uniform, Phylis thought of Margaret. Certainly big enough. Then she cut herself off angrily. That's nasty! You're just jealous because Celia likes her.

She returned to her book, and early in the afternoon made herself a cup of tea. The weather did not improve. She heard a car drive up to the main building around 2:00, but assuming it to be another jeep she forced herself not to be nosey. It was not until she heard the crunch of tires in front of the cabin that she looked up, but by then it was too late.

The blue car on the foot of the path looked familiar,

and it took only a moment to place it. Paul Welch's Regal. Panic suddenly gripped Phylis, and she wanted to run, wanted desperately to hide, but there were no handy elevator doors here, no offices to duck into. The car door opened, and Paul Welch stepped out. He was dressed casually, for him, in a light cotton suit, blue shirt, and yellow tie. He smiled when he saw her through the screen, but there was tension there. He walked tentatively up to the door, and knocked twice even though it was open.

"Phylis, hi!" His jovial tone was patently false.

Phylis could not respond. She felt paralyzed. The humiliation of that night, barely three weeks ago, and the words he had spoken to her, burned clearly in her mind.

"Can I come in?"

He took her silence as consent and pushed through the open door. "Nasty weather around here! I almost slid off—"

"What do you want?" She had intended her voice to carry the force of her anger, but instead it trembled, sounding weak and ineffectual.

Paul frowned, seemingly unsure of what he wanted to say, but finally he took a deep breath and focused his attention. "I came to apologize."

"Accepted. Now, please leave."

"Phylis, I—"

"How did you know I was here?"

"I'm a freelance writer. I know how to ask questions." He shrugged, then blushed. "Actually, I asked Terry at the office. You told her. She told me."

Phylis pursed her lips angrily. She should have specified that her whereabouts were to remain a secret.

Better yet, she should not even have told Terry where she was going. But who would have thought that Paul, of all people, would seek her out? Looking at him, she seemed to relive that night, feeling, again, the touch of his hand, his lips, his tongue, and she burned with shame. "Paul, please leave." She felt that at any minute she might burst into tears.

"Listen, please give me a chance to say what I have to say." He was shifting from foot to foot, and his fists were clenching and unclenching to some inner rhythm. The expression on his face was unreadable, but she supposed it might have passed for pained suffering. "I drove four hours, just for this," he said.

Phylis shook her head and stifled a moan. She was trapped, and the only way to get free was to let him talk. Somehow she knew this was true. Let him talk, and then he would leave. She nodded slowly.

"Thank you," he said. He composed himself briefly, then seemed to relax. "What I did, what I said to you that night, was terrible. It was disgusting." His face seemed to confirm his words, twisted in what Phylis could only identify as guilt. "I knew it even as I said those things. I hated myself as I said them. But it's not the first time I've done that sort of thing. I've ruined countless relationships the same way."

"You humiliated me," Phylis said softly. "You hurt me."

Paul nodded, massaging his temples. "I know, I know. All I want, is to ask that you forgive me. And . . ." He paused, running a smooth hand through his black hair. "And give me another chance."

"What?" The shock she felt was so great, that she could think of nothing else to say. So she said it again.

"What?"

"We had the beginning of something good, Phylis," he said defensively. "You know that's true. It was me who screwed it up. I made you believe that sex was all I wanted. I might have even believed it myself. But afterwards . . . I knew it wasn't true. I missed you. I *do* miss you. I want to try again. Give me a chance to prove myself!" He said this last with such emotion, with such a look of pain on his face, that Phylis had to turn away.

"Paul . . ." She did not know what to say.

"I feel responsible for you being here. It was me that set Celia off."

"No. If it hadn't been you, it would have been somebody else."

He shrugged. "But it *was* me, that's the point."

Phylis took a deep breath. "Paul, you've said what you came to say. If that's all, then please go."

"But you haven't answered."

Phylis sighed. "I forgive you. Okay? Apology accepted."

"But what about us? What about another chance?"

"I can't. I don't think it's possible."

"Maybe in time?"

"I don't know," Phylis said, suddenly feeling very confused. "Paul, Celia will be back from her session soon. I don't think you should be here when she comes in."

He nodded in resignation, and a wave of relief surged through Phylis. "What is this place?" Paul asked, cocking his head towards the main building.

"A clinic. For Celia."

"But I've never heard of it." He was frowning.

"It's something new. Experimental."

"Did you check it out before your came? It was all rather sudden, wasn't it?"

Phylis suddenly flushed with anger. "What I do for my child is none of your concern. Now, please go!"

Paul nodded solemnly. "Okay. But think about what I said. Please, call me when you get back. I'm not as bad as you think." He turned slowly, paused in the doorway as if he were going to say something else, then let the door swing close and walked to his car. He seemed to sit there for a long time, regarding her, and when he finally did drive off Phylis sighed with relief.

"Son of a bitch," she muttered. She lit a cigarette and took three deep lungfulls. What right had he to come here looking for forgiveness after what he had done? Yet he had been right. They had seemed on the verge of something really good, until *he* had screwed it up. Again, Phylis suddenly felt confused, and very close to tears.

What about John? Paul was in the past, John was here and now. And Celia really seemed to like him, despite the incident last night, and Celia's feeling definitely had to be taken into account, didn't they? Yes, of course they did. She drew another deep lungfull of smoke from the cigarette, and hissed it out slowly. She *could* forgive, she realized, and that much she would do, but the rest of it was out of the question.

A sudden wind gusted through the porch, and outside, David DeMarch ran past the front of the cabin, his yellow raincoat bright against the grey of the water and sky. He was laughing, arms waving. He disappeared beyond the edge of the cabin, and all she could hear was his laughter. Then, carried by the wind, she heard his voice, as clearly as if he were standing at the door.

"Sonny! Don't!" And then a burst of laughter.

The trees behind the cabin whispered in the wind, and Phylis suddenly felt cold. She rose, intending to make herself another pot of tea. But the shivers, she realized, were not caused by the cold alone.

CHAPTER ELEVEN

Phylis decided not to mention Paul's visit, but it was John who brought up the subject, when, later in the afternoon, he came to the cabin with Celia lagging playfully in tow.

"Hi Mommy!" Despite the steadily advancing black clouds, Celia was back in high spirits. "Can I go out and play with David?"

Phylis turned questioningly to John "Boat ride on, or off?"

He studied the lake, grimacing, as dark swells humped and rolled across the water, turning to noisy waves near to shore. "Maybe tomorrow."

"Okay. Go play with David. But don't go far, don't go near the water, and put on a coat!"

Celia skipped happily into her bedroom, and emerged wearing a purple, knee length Viking raincoat. She ran from the cabin, slamming the porch door, shouting David's name into the wind.

"How did it go today?"

"Very well," John said. "Celia is —" he paused, lips pursed, trying to think of a word — "she's *suited* to the therapy. I think we'll see results very soon."

"That's fantastic!" Suddenly the events of the day

dimmed in comparison to this good news. "I want so much to get our lives back on track." She stood at the sink and poured cold water into the electric kettle. "Some tea?"

"Love some," John said, closing the inner door, and then removing his green raincoat while water dripped to the dull linoleum. The white smock was gone, and he looked handsomely casual in faded blue Levis and a wrinkled, brown plaid shirt. Phylis noted that one of the shirt's pocket buttons was missing, and wished she had brought a needle and thread. *Now that*, she thought, *is definitely a wifely thought!* She turned back to the sink lest he detect something in her look. "Margaret said someone came asking for you earlier," John said slowly, lowering himself into a corner of the sofa.

Phylis clenched her teeth, dropped a tea bag into the Brown Betty, and turned slowly. "Yes. Just somebody from work."

"Long way for a visit," John said. His voice was neutral, and since he was facing away from her she could not read his face.

"His family lives in Fergus Falls," Phylis said, astonished at her alacrity at spontaneous deception.

John grunted. The kettle began to whistle, and Phylis poured the boiling water into the tea pot, splashing some of it on the counter. She transferred the pot, along with two chipped mugs, to a wooden tray on which the words BATTLE LAKE were embossed in an arc over the faded image of a preposterously vicious looking northern pike. She carried the tray to the coffee table. "Cream or sugar?"

John shook his head. She poured him a cup of tea, already looking fairly strong, then sat next to him on the sofa. Their knees, gently touching, made Phylis painfully aware of his presence next to her, but she was still startled when he laid a warm hand on her thigh.

"We should get this up front," he said, looking into her face, lips curved in a pensive smile. "Are we . . . becoming an item?"

"Do you mean, are we becoming involved?"

He sipped his tea and nodded, continuing to study her face. Phylis lay a hand on top of his, pushing her fingers into the spaces between his. "There's definitely something happening," she said carefully, and thought to herself, *Now that, you idiot, is a major league understatement!* "What do you think?"

"I think that I like you. A lot. I like your company, I like kissing you, and I also like Celia. That's a good step beyond the boundaries of normal doctor-patient relationship."

Phylis laughed. "I'll say so!" Then she put down her cup and spoke more seriously. "John, I like you too. I like what's developing between us. I don't know how far it will go, but I'm willing to find out. But let's not rush."

He leaned over and kissed her lightly on the lips. "Deal. And if it's not rushing things too much, I'd like to take you and Celia to Fergus Falls for supper. Just pizza. Sound okay?"

It sounded fabulous. Over the next two days John spent a lot of time with Phylis and Celia. There was no repeat of the previous violent response from Celia, and on Thursday she even fell asleep in John's arms, curled up on the sofa watching television. Phylis regarded this homey tableau with a pang of emotion that brought her close to tears. Eyes glistening, face buried in John's shoulder, she soaked yet another of his shirts.

On Friday an incident occurred that brought home to Phylis just how effective the therapy was, and how far Celia had come in only two days. Celia had fallen asleep on the easy chair, animal cracker nightgown covering everything but her feet, one-eyed teddy bear hugged tightly to her chest. At 10:00 John rose to leave and, leaning into him at the door, Phylis kissed him so passionately that she thought her knees would give way. He, too, quivered in the embrace. At that moment Celia yawned, and her eyes blinked open.

Phylis pulled violently away from John, but Celia only looked up at them and smiled sleepily. It seemed, for a flash, that her eyes widened in surprise, but that response immediately disappeared. "Good night, Dr. Gordon," Celia said, her words slurred by an escaping yawn.

"Good night, Celia," John said, then turned to Phylis and kissed her lightly on the cheek.

"Good night, John," she said softly. Their eyes held for a moment, then he was gone, walking back to the main building.

When Phylis turned around, Celia was already asleep again, small chest rising and falling slowly. The one-eyed teddy looked right at Phylis, but this time its gaze held no malice. Phylis felt happier than she had in years, and she knelt by Celia, stroking the child's hair. Celia's lips turned up in a faint smile as she slept.

"Everything is going to be fine, baby," Phylis said, eyes shining.

On Saturday morning the wind let up and patches

of blue began to show through the clouds, and by 10:00 the lake was glass smooth, and sunlight was streaming through a patchwork sky that was quickly unraveling. John was making a trip into Fergus Falls, but there would be no room for extra bodies on the return trip, he said. That was fine. Phylis felt like doing nothing more than lazing around the beach, and Celia was eager to get back into the water. But before John left, Phylis pulled him close and kissed him. For a moment he was too surprised to respond, but it was not long before his lips moved slowly over hers. Celia, sitting at the porch table, munching a mouthful of Frosted Flakes, looked on in smiling approval.

"Now that's a nice way to start the day," he said.

Dora and David were already at the water when Phylis and Celia marched down, David splashing happily at the foot of the dock, Dora decked out on a towel and smelling of coconut oil. Dora looked up and smiled as Phylis lay out a towel, a look of admiration crossing her face as she regarded Phylis's slim, shapely figure.

"Oh, to have a figure like yours," Dora said wistfully. "I can see why Dr. Gordon is interested."

"Dora!"

"Oh, come on, you can't deny he's fawning all over you. Hell, I just wish it was me. He's so damned good-looking." She laughed loudly. "I wonder what he looks like beneath all those rumpled clothes," she said speculatively.

"Dora!" Phylis exclaimed again, and this time burst into laughter.

The two women lay on the beach, side by side, glistening with suntan oil, while David and Celia shrieked and capered in the water, splashing ceaselessly. As the sun climbed higher, the temperature rose accordingly, and soon Phylis found herself taking the occasional dip to cool off. When she was on her stomach she smoked and read her book, when she was on her back she dozed. Sometime in the early afternoon Dora came out of the water and splashed water on her. Phylis gasped, and leaned up on her elbow.

"I'm heading up to get food and drink. You want to come?"

Phylis shook her head. "Not yet, Dora. I ate a late breakfast." This was a lie, but she did not feel hungry at all.

Dora shrugged, then cupped her hands over her mouth and yelled for David to come along. David whined plaintively, not willing to lose, by default, the perpetual splashing match with Celia.

"I'll look after him, Dora. Go and eat. I'll bring them both up soon."

"Sure?"

"Uh huh."

Dora smiled thankfully, and then trudged up the beach to the grassy ridge. David and Celia commenced their water war again. Phylis smiled, lay back her head, and closed her eyes against the sun. She must have dozed off then, because the next time she opened her eyes she felt thick-headed. But the sun had not advanced much from where it had been, so she could not have been out for long. She rolled to her stomach and reached for her cigarettes, when suddenly it struck her that something was wrong.

It was quiet. Too quiet. She sat up instantly and looked to the water, where David and Celia should have been at war. But David and Celia were gone.

A small moan escaped Phylis's lips, and she jumped to her feet, looking intently down the beach in both directions. She took a deep breath, intending to shout their names, but stopped when she heard the laughter. She let the breath out in a gush. There it was again, back towards the cabin, a mixture of both David's and Celia's voices. She sighed with relief. For a moment there, she had been on the verge of panic.

She walked quickly over the beach and up onto the grass. The moist blades were cool against her bare feet. She could still hear their voices, but where were they? She scanned the row of cabins, stopping only when her eyes had gone past the edge of Number Four, in the distance. More laughter, then suddenly Celia burst into view from behind the cabin, followed by David. Both children stopped, looking back towards the trees. They laughed again, then darted out of sight again.

Phylis began to walk towards the end of the row of cabins, wincing at the stabs of pain as she stepped on rocks and twigs. David and Celia were still out of sight, still giggling. But Phylis felt a chill pass through her. They had been looking towards the woods. The dark woods. The whispering woods. The panic that had dissipated only moments earlier returned in a rush, but this time it's grip was firmer. She began to run.

When she came around the edge of the cabin she could not see the children, only the dark wall of trees. Her chest was heaving, her breath ragged. "Celia! David!"

Laughter again, from somewhere in the woods, and

then David's voice, high and clear: "Sonny!"

Phylis gasped. This time she screamed their names. "David! Celia!" Celia's laughter suddenly stopped. There was a sound of crunching in the trees, and Phylis took a frightened step backwards, then Celia appeared from behind a thick trunk. David came right behind her. The children's faces were pinched in concern, but not from what they had seen in the woods, Phylis realized, but from her panicky yelling.

"Mommy?" Celia walked slowly over to her. "What's the matter?"

Beside Celia, David was looking up at Phylis curiously. Phylis sighed, shaking her head, then chuckled softly. "Nothing, sweetheart. I was just wondering where you were." She felt immensely relieved.

"We were playing," David said, glancing at Celia.

Phylis put her arms around both children and guided them to the front of the cabin. "That's enough playing for now," she said. "Let's go eat. David's mom has made something."

The children grinned, and sprinted ahead. Phylis sighed, shaking her head. What was wrong with her? Why the feelings of panic? She turned and looked into the depths of the wood. *Just trees*, she thought. *Nothing but—*

"Hello." A hand touched her shoulder, and Phylis spun around.

"I'm sorry, I didn't mean to startle you." He took a step backwards at her surprised reaction.

Phylis felt a darkness coming in from the edge of her vision, and a scream bubbled on her lips. She took a frightened step backwards, but came up against the side of the cabin. In sudden horror she realized that she was out of sight of the other cabins.

The man took a step toward her, hands held out in front of him. "Please, don't be frightened," he said, pale faced sheened with sweat.

Phylis pressed a bare white fist to her chin and began to edge away. It had taken only a moment for his face to register, and for her to recognize him. But this did not lessen her terror. He was the same man she had seen at the waterfront restaurant only a few days earlier. The one who had studied her so openly. He reached out a pale hand to touch her.

CHAPTER TWELVE

His flabby white hand hesitated, as if suspended by invisible puppet strings, and it was only a moment before she realized that he was not reaching for her but was, instead, trying to calm her. She looked up at his face and saw that he looked as frightened as she felt. His watery blue eyes were trying to focus on her face, but they darted from side to side, as if he were detecting motion at the corners of his eyes. Sweat had gathered on the ridge above his upper lip, and a nervous tongue now flicked out to clear it.

"Please, don't be frightened!" His voice was hushed, edged with fear, as if he were afraid of being heard by anyone else. "My name is Harold Phelps. *Doctor* Harold Phelps. I used to work here at Lakeview, as Dr. Brand's assistant. I came to talk to you. No, to *warn* you! Please, we must talk."

Phylis slumped against the wall of the cabin, feeling totally drained. Her heart, which had been pounding a mad rhythm against her rib cage, was beginning to slow down, and the fear which had reached up to grip her, from some hitherto unknown dark corner, was now replaced by anger. "Jesus Christ! You shouldn't sneak up on people like that!"

Harold Phelps flinched at her words, and took a step backwards. He was still wearing the beige shorts and blue dress shirt she had first seen him in, though apparently these were a fresh set, and an image of a wardrobe filled with bermuda shorts and blue shirts passed uninvited across her mind. But instead of being amused by it, Phylis found herself unaccountably chilled. "I'm sorry," Harold Phelps said. "I didn't think."

Feeling more in control now, Phylis looked around the edge of the cabin. Celia and David had disappeared into Number Two, safe, and she turned back to Harold Phelps who was peering fearfully into the woods. "What do you want?" Phylis asked.

He turned, startled at the sound of her voice.

And I thought I was nervous!, Phylis thought.

"I saw you at Battle Lake," he said. "At the waterfront, with Dr. Gordon. Remember?"

"I remember. You frightened me then too, just staring like that." Her voice was angry again.

Harold Phelps looked sheepishly at the ground, like a school boy being punished for swearing. "I'm sorry. I really didn't mean to stare. But when I saw you with Dr. Gordon, I couldn't help but wonder if you were the new patient. That was your daughter, with that boy, wasn't it? Celia?"

Phylis frowned, a question tugging at her mind, and suddenly it clicked. "How did you get out here? I didn't see a car."

Harold Phelps pointed farther down the beach. About half a mile south and west, a small boat was pulled up on the beach, at a point that would have been hidden from the main building. "They would

107

have stopped me if I came by car. They don't like me coming here."

"Who would have?"

"The guards. At the army post."

"But they have nothing to do with Lakeview," Phylis said, suddenly getting the strong impression that Harold Phelps was not quite all there. A small voice spoke clearly at the back of her mind: *Be careful, Phylis, he's a loon.*

Harold Phelps looked away from her, into the woods, and as he did so his shoulders hunched protectively, as if he were trying to shrink away from something. "Is there somewhere we can talk, away from . . . do you have a cabin?"

"Yes, but—"

"Please. I won't keep you long. But there are things about Lakeview that I have to tell you."

Phylis studied him carefully for a full ten seconds. He was about her height, but pudgy looking, as if an extra forty pounds (or even more) had been spread evenly over his entire body. His face, though pale and sweaty, looked friendly, and she imagined that if he smiled he would look quite pleasant. But it was his eyes that brought her to a decision: blue, sharp, and totally earnest. He did not appear dangerous.

"Okay, but only for minute," Phylis said. "I just want to get a pair of sandals. My feet are killing me from running over here."

Now Harold Phelps did smile, and Phylis discovered that her impression had been correct; his face suddenly beamed. He followed her to the cabin, staying out of site of the main building, close to the cabins. His furtiveness was almost comical, but Phylis did not

108

laugh. He took a seat at the porch table while Phylis got her sandals, and when she returned he licked his lips. "Could I have a glass of water?"

Phylis let the water run until it was cold, then brought it to him. He sipped it once, paused, then bent his head backwards and drained the glass. He placed the glass firmly on the table. Phylis sat across from him and waited.

"You haven't told me your name," he said.

"Phylis."

"Phylis what?"

She hesitated only momentarily. "Phylis Reynolds."

Harold Phelps nodded, smiling again. "Well, Phylis Reynolds, let me tell you something about yourself, and about your daughter. You are under thirty, and though once married you are now single. You are here for the sake of your lovely daughter who, though normal in most respects, is the victim of a past trauma that she appears incapable of coping with. Lakeview was offered to you as a last resort, and because you love your daughter, and because you want to get on with your life, you decided to come here." He gazed at her levelly across the table, his blue eyes inquisitive but friendly. "Close?"

He's crazy, and he reads minds. Invisible fingers danced across her spine. "How did you know that?"

"I told you, I used to be Dr. Brand's assistant. I just quoted you the optimal subject profile, as worked out by Dr. Brand and myself almost two years ago. I didn't tell you anything specific, just generalities. For instance, I don't know why you're not married any more, or what trauma your daughter experienced. All the patients here fit the same profile, but you know that already, don't you?"

Phylis fumbled a cigarette into her mouth, and once lit she exhaled a plume of grey smoke. *You did know that. You and Dora and Penny and Susan are all alike. You just didn't know you knew it.* "What are you getting at?"

"Just that you didn't choose Lakeview, Lakeview chose you."

Phylis puffed angrily on her cigarette. "Dr. Phelps, or whoever the hell you are, if you have something to say, then please say it. My daughter and my friend are waiting for me."

Phelps appeared taken aback by her outburst, and he ran both hands nervously through his hair before clasping them on top of the table. "When I saw you earlier, you looked like you were frightened of something. Something in the woods."

"What do you mean?" Those invisible fingers played another bar across her back.

"Have you seen something in the woods that doesn't belong there? I think that you have, I can see it in your eyes. You know what I'm talking about."

"If you're trying to frighten me, you're succeeding." His probing had been too close to the truth for comfort, and now she really did feel frightened.

"Not frighten," he said. "I came to *warn* you. You and your daughter are in grave danger. You must leave here before it is too late."

"What the hell are you talking about?" She was becoming exasperated by his cryptic hints.

"Mrs. Reynolds. Phylis. I was relieved of my duties here because I . . . well, among other things, because I began to question the turn our research had taken. Dr. Brand was leading us away from the therapeutic

110

applications we originally mapped out, leading us into much more questionable territory. Other parties began to take an interest in our work. You've seen the army post. Didn't you wonder?"

"John . . . Dr. Gordon told me about the army post," Phylis said angrily. "There's nothing strange about it."

"Please, listen to me. Your daughter is at great risk. You must leave! Don't you understand?" He was leaning across the table, sweating profusely, eyes wide and shining. "They are making monsters here!"

What Phylis now understood, was that it had been a big mistake to talk to Harold Phelps. The veneer of rationality he had shown her earlier had cracked, and something totally chaotic was shining through. Shining brightly through.

"You had better go now," she said softly.

"Please—"

"Go!" She said sharpy. "Go now! Or I'll get Dr. Brand and have you arrested for trespassing!" The threat was an empty one, since both Dr. Brand and John were away from Lakeview, but the tone of her voice was enough. It was as if the plug had been pulled on a great source of power that had been firing up Phelps. He suddenly slumped, defeated, looking exhausted.

"I'm sorry," he said feebly "I got carried away." He stood slowly on wobbly legs, then pulled a sheet of crumpled paper from his shirt pocket. He placed the paper carefully on the table. "This is my number. I'm staying at the Otter Tail Hotel in Battle Lake. If something happens, if . . . well, I may be able to help."

He looked, now, like a frightened little boy, and

Phylis regretted having shouted at him. She walked with him to the door. "Dr. Phelps, I'm grateful for your concern, but I'm sure your worries are unfounded. Celia has gotten a lot better since we've come here."

He looked at her sorrowfully and opened his mouth to say something, then apparently thinking better of it, he closed it again. He smiled grimly. "Good-bye, Mrs. Reynolds."

She watched him walk back to the end of the row of cabins, and then disappear over the ridge that led down to the beach. Phylis walked down towards Dora's cabin. She needed a drink, and hopefully Dora would still have some of that vodka left. Harold Phelp's words were echoing in her head, and when she passed between the cabins, and saw the dark tangle of trees beyond, she whispered to them aloud. "They are making monsters here!"

What had he meant by that? But now something else occurred to her, something that disturbed her more than the words he had said. Why had he approached her, and not one of the others? What was so special about Celia?

She began to walk faster.

CHAPTER THIRTEEN

Dora DeMarch was standing at the kitchen buttering two slices of bread when Phylis entered the cabin. Celia and David, sitting side by side at the porch table and eating what appeared to be grilled cheese sandwiches, looked up when she entered but did not say anything.

"My goodness," Dora said. "You look like you've seen a ghost."

"The kids gave me a scare," Phylis said quickly, relieved that her voice sounded calmer than she had a right to expect.

"Well, come on in. Leave the kids on the porch. Have a seat and I'll fix you a sandwich."

"Actually, I'd like a drink if you've got anything."

Dora grinned. "Never without." She reached to the cupboard above the sink, retrieved the bottle of vodka, and mixed a stiff screwdriver. She handed the drink to Phylis, and then sat in the easy chair with a sandwich balanced on her knee.

Phylis sipped the screwdriver gratefully, and after a second sip began to feel immediately better. The alcohol had a quick effect because of her empty stomach. Crazy or not, Dr. Phelps had frightened her.

"Don't blame Celia for running off," Dora said, munching happily. She used the tip of her tongue to capture a melted dollop of cheese at the corner of her mouth. "It was probably David's idea. Boys will be boys."

"Oh, Celia's not above running off once in a while. It's all right though, they were just playing."

When she finished her sandwich Dora mixed a screwdriver for herself and freshened Phylis's glass, then sinking into the plush easy chair with a sigh, she raised her glass in a toast. "I've had enough fun in the sun for one day. Here's to some fun in the shade."

David and Celia did not complain about being confined to the cabin, since it was much cooler inside, and sat at the porch table playing a procession of board games while Phylis and Dora remained in the living room, drink fixings on hand, talking. When the conversation came around to Lakeview, Phylis's tension returned, and the vodka anesthesia began to wear off quickly.

"Do you find this place to be, well, weird?" Phylis asked, drink suspended halfway between her lap and her mouth.

Dora frowned. "I don't get you."

"Well, I mean, do you think Lakeview is legitimate?"

Dora sipped her screwdriver, which had become less diluted with orange juice as the afternoon progressed, and regarded Phylis curiously. "If you mean, are they helping David, then the answer is yes." She leaned closer to Phylis, her voice suddenly lowering to a whisper. "It's been a long time since he woke screaming."

"Oh, I know that," Phylis said, feeling a bit foolish at what must have seemed like paranoia to Dora. "Celia is getting better too, I can see that. But what about the army barracks just down the road, doesn't that seem a bit strange? And, did it ever occur to you, that all of us . . . you, me, Penny, and Susan, are all in the same boat? We're all single mothers, all about the same age, and our kids are alike too."

"Hey, hey, calm down," Dora said, her face showing concern, and Phylis realized she must have been raising her voice. "I've noticed all those things you mentioned, but so what? David is getting better, and as far as I know Penny and Susan's daughters have improved too. None of us were forced to come here, were we? We can leave any time we want if we don't like it."

Phylis took a deep breath, let it out slowly, and nodded. "I guess you're right. I'm just edgy. Must be the clean air."

"I'll fix that," Dora said, and took Phylis's glass and mixed her another screwdriver, the last few drops of orange juice dripping into the glass to produce what looked like a marginally orange-flavored vodka. When she returned she was grinning. "There's not much point in talking about Penny and Susan anyway. They left last night."

"What are you talking about?" Phylis took the drink, cringing at the strong alcohol smell that drifted up to her.

"Packed their bags and left. Therapy finished, I guess. Looks like it's just you and me now, kid," she took a gulp of her drink. "Those women had mouths that just wouldn't quit!"

Phylis sipped her drink, and the vodka made her

catch her breath. For some reason the knowledge that there were less of them now did not make her feel any better. Damn Phelps and his meddling! He had worked her into a tizzy! She wished that John were here, and even the thought of him made her feel a little better. She took another sip of her drink, managed not to sputter this time, and came to a decision. There was no sense in keeping her concerns bottled up, and when she saw John again she would talk to him about Phelps. He was sure to be able to assuage her fears.

"Well, you look like you're feeling a little better," Dora said.

"I am. Thanks." She raised her drink and smiled.

Don Reynolds arrived in Minneapolis on Monday afternoon, about three hours after his release, and the first thing he did was to book a room at the YMCA just off Hennepin. Well, actually, the *first* thing he had done was to buy a fifth of Canadian Club rye whiskey which he had packed carefully in his case. They were touchy about things like that at the Y, and if he'd gone out later and come back with the bottle they might have questioned him, something he was definitely not in the mood for. Sitting on the window sill of his fourth floor room he drank straight from the bottle, waxing sentimental as he looked out over the narrow slice of the city the window allowed, until he was so drunk that he threw up in the toilet and passed out curled around the pot. He woke on Tuesday feeling like a living bruise and spent fifteen minutes in the shower letting the water roll off him, finally turning it as cold as it would go until he was fully awake. After that he walked over to the bus station and, using $1000 of his cash as a deposit, rented a brand new Ford Taures with 36 miles on the odometer. As he drove away it began to rain and he activated the wipers, losing himself in the rhythmic *whipwhoosh whipwhoosh* as they slashed the water from the glass.

He followed the familiar route to the old neighborhood, and drove by the house twice before parking the Ford at the end of the street, positioned so he could see who was coming and going. Phylis would be at work right now, but he wanted to see her before the confrontation. And brother, this was going to be one motherfucker of a showdown! But Phylis didn't show on Tuesday, and when the house lights flicked on at about 8:00 he figured she must have slipped in the back door. He thought about banging on the door and barging in, but decided against it. He wanted to *see* her first, to get himself worked up. "Fucking bitch, fucking *stupid* bitch." It was still raining, and the clouds seemed even darker than they had earlier.

On Wednesday the same thing happened, and on Thursday he noticed that the girl across the street, Suzie, picked up the mail from Phylis's box and cleared the newspaper from the step, and it occurred to him that maybe Phylis and Celia weren't even at home. This thought started the fires burning a little hotter. He remembered Suzie from before, remembered that she had never liked him and had, in fact, been a little frightened of him. He chuckled at the memory. *If I get you alone now, slut, I'll give you something to be frightened of.* He chuckled.

On Friday he phoned Phylis's work. The girl who answered the phone was so cheerful that Don felt like puking.

"MPLS Magazine, may I help you?"

"I'd like to speak to Phylis Reynolds."

"Uh, Phylis is away for a couple of weeks," the girl said cheerfully. "Would you like to leave a message?"

"When will she back?"

"I'm not sure sir, but if you leave your number I'm sure Ms. Reynolds will be happy to return your call as soon as she's able."

"Mizz? Isn't it Mrs. Reynolds?"

There was a pause. "May I ask who's calling, sir?"

Don hung up. *Fucking stupid bitch!*

That evening, rain pattering on the roof of the Ford, Don's patience was wearing thin, and as he sat chain-smoking unfiltered Camels, a habit he had picked up from his father back in Chicago, he swore continually under his breath. "Fucking bitch, fucking *stupid* bitch . . ." The words were a litany that seemed to calm him in some way, and he was almost unaware that he was speaking at all. At five the slut picked up Phylis's mail and newspaper, and at 8:00 on the nose the timed switch turned on the living room and master bedroom lights. Don grinned, crushed out his ciga-rette in the overflowing ashtray, and lit another. Five minutes later he left the car, crushed the cigarette under his heel, and walked up the street.

He crossed to Phylis side of the street, keeping in the shade of the trees as he walked. It was amazing how much cover simple shadows afforded. When he reached the house he walked quickly up the path, as if he belonged, and then around the side. In the shadows he leaned against the rough stucco and listened. In the distance he could hear traffic, somewhere closer a dog was barking, and from the house next door rock music drifted from a half open window. After a minute he went into the back yard. High fences bordered the houses on either side, and he was effectively screened from observation. Don smiled.

It was a bit more difficult getting in than he had anticipated. He had planned on using his old trick for gaining entry whenever he locked his keys inside, something that happened quite frequently, but after jimmying the outside basement window open with a penknife, he found that the inner window, which used to swing freely, had been been nailed in place.

"Fucking bitch!"

He leaned against the house and, using the toe of his shoe, kicked the wooden edging at the bottom of the inside window. Each time his toe connected Don cringed at the loud thump that echoed through the yard. At the third kick the frame groaned as the nails pulled slightly out, and at the sixth kick the window flew inwards, swinging fully on its hinges. Don kneeled and peered inside.

"Welcome home," he muttered.

As he slid through the opening on his belly, feet first; something sharp caught on his shirt, and he felt a stinging sensation at his belly. When he jumped to the floor the shirt ripped, and blood began to ooze from a deep scratch below his navel. "Shit!" He touched the wound gingerly, but it did not look bad. He remained standing where he was until his eyes became accustomed to the darkness, then studied his surroundings. He was in the laundry room at the back of the basement, but it seemed different than he remembered. In a minute it came to him. The appliances were new, and the walls had been painted. "Busy little bitch."

He climbed the stairs to the main floor, and there again found that changes had been wrought, though nothing major. The house was still the same, basically, and even a lot of the paint was the same. It was just *different,* and it took a few moments before he could put his finger on exactly what those differences were. The realization came as a shock. The difference was that *his* presence was missing. And not just missing in the sense that he wasn't there anymore. Every piece of evidence that he had ever lived here was gone. The print that used to hang above the sofa, the one he and Phylis had picked up in that little flea market in Boulder four years ago, with mountains poking up into a grey sky and the artist's name scrawled in too large letters on the trees in the lower right-hand corner, was gone, and in its place hung a pastel print of a bouquet of flowers. But worse, the little things were gone too. His fish-head ashtray on the coffee table, his worn footstool by the easy chair, his photograph on the wall unit. All gone.

He felt suddenly very, very angry. She had erased him completely. It was as if he had never been, had never lived here, had never been a part of their lives. And the horrible thought occurred to him: *That's the way they want it, Don. They want to forget you. Rub you out!*

In Celia's room he paused for a minute, sitting on the edge of the bed. *My daughter.* He lay on on the bed, face down, and breathed deeply. Her smell was still here, and something moved inside him. For a moment he was close to tears, but he pushed them back and jumped from the bed. He went next to the master bedroom. Phylis's bedroom. The blue walls were now egg-shell white, and the old blue and white striped bed cover had been replaced by a rose quilt adorned with delicate flower patterns. He sat on the edge of the bed, his emotions in turmoil. *Our room. Our bed.*

He opened the drawer in the night table beside the bed, and what he saw made him catch his breath. There was a small cache of books inside the drawer, and he ran his finger over their spines, reading the titles in disbelief. *Emmanuelle. Pleasures Of A Prince. Adventures Of A Victorian Lady. Christina's Desire.* He slammed the drawer shut, blood roaring in his ears. Phylis, that fucking horny bitch! She wants it, he realized. She probably misses it! Or is she getting it? It suddenly struck him that never again would he be able to touch her in that way, and he felt hollow. His anger grew.

In the living room he searched for anything, any clue that might indicate where she had gone, where she had taken Celia, but there was nothing. In the kitchen, however, he found a notepad by the phone, and on the pad, surrounded in typical Phylis doodles, were the words "Lakeview" and "Battle Lake." Under the phone was a folded Mobil map of the state.

Don spread the map on the kitchen table. He sat down and checked the town index, but there was no listing for a Lakeview. There was, however, a listing for Battle Lake. The coordinates were J-12 and, running his fingers along those lines until they intersected, it took only a moment to pinpoint the town. Only a couple of hundred miles to the north. He folded the map and put it back where he had found it, along with the notepad.

Battle Lake. Nice place for a vacation. He tapped

121

his cigarette pack, pulled one out with his lips, lit it with his zippo, and breathed smoke. He would make the drive tomorrow morning. He should arrive before noon.

A sudden picture of Phylis and Celia came to him, and imagining their shocked expressions at seeing him, he chuckled.

Surprise! Surprise! Daddy's here!

CHAPTER FOURTEEN

John Gordon did not return to Lakeview until late on Saturday, and it was not until Sunday morning that Phylis saw him again, which may have been a blessing in disguise since she and Dora had quietly tied one on. Phylis was grim on Sunday morning, despite a clear blue sky that promised a perfect early-September Minnesota day, and her whole body seemed to throb like some giant toothache when she smiled at John. But his returning smile was wide and full of good humor, and leaning against the frame of the open porch door he regarded her with what she could only take as amusement. She had forgotten her resolve to speak to him about Phelps.

"It's funny," John said. "But you look rather a lot like Dora DeMarch this morning, as if you were sisters."

Phylis pouted, and this too caused her head to ache. "Oh, shut up. I need sympathy, not jokes."

John laughed. "Well, at least I don't have to feel guilty about not getting back early yesterday. You and Dora obviously managed to entertain yourselves quite nicely."

"Keep it up and *you'll* be entertaining *yourself* today." She put a cigarette in her mouth and lit it, but even the smoke seemed to taste stale. Nevertheless, she smoked on resolutely.

John came into the porch and sat across from her. "I'm sorry. I promise to be more sympathetic." He patted her hand. "Now, do you think you feel well enough to withstand a boat ride over to Battle Lake?"

"If you drive the boat slowly, I could probably manage," Phylis said, taking a puff on her cigarette.

"I promise. Where's Celia?"

"Down at the beach with David, under orders not to get wet."

John peered down toward the water. "Oh, yes, I see. Celia and David have become fast friends, haven't they?"

"Their mothers too," Phylis said.

"Oh?"

"Do you think you might fit two more in the boat?"

"Dora and David?"

"Uh huh."

"Well, I . . ." He looked mildly disappointed, but covered his reaction with a quick smile. "Sure, it's a good sized boat."

Phylis smiled and placed a hand on top of his. "Thanks, John. I promise we can be alone later. Maybe we can go for a walk when we get back? I'm sure Dora would look after Celia for a short while."

He perked up at this proposition, grinning. "Great! Maybe I can lead you into the deep dark woods."

The thought of *deep dark woods* brought back her previous concern in full force, and she frowned.

"Something wrong?"

Phylis blinked, recovering quickly. "No, nothing wrong. I just remembered I was going to ask you something when I saw you."

"So, ask."

"I had a visitor yesterday, while you were out of camp."

John froze, his face blank. "Your friend from work again?" His voice was cold.

Phylis's eyes widened in shock as she realized how he had interpreted her words. "Oh, no, nothing like that. It was from somebody you know, I think."

Again, John frowned. "Oh?"

"Dr. Harold Phelps," Phylis said, and watched carefully for his reaction.

"Phelps?" His frown had deepened. "What did he want?"

"He came to warn me about Lakeview. He told me that Celia and myself were in great danger." Repeating it now, with John beside her, it all seemed so ridiculous, and she blushed. When John nodded she felt disappointed, and realized she had been hoping he might deny any knowledge of Phelps, as if such a denial might prove that Phelps was nothing but a crank.

"Dr. Phelps used to work here," John said, not looking directly at Phylis. "In fact, I have his old job."

"Yes, he told me that. He said you were making monsters here, and implied that Lakeview was being run by the Army," Phylis said. She took another puff on her cigarette, still watching John.

"Did he frighten you?"

"No, not really." Lie. "More like he *intrigued* me. What could he have meant?"

John shrugged. "Probably nothing." He paused, as if unsure about whether to go on, but continued when it

125

became apparent that Phylis was very interested. "Dr. Phelps was a brilliant man. It was he and Dr. Brand who did all the initial research into mnemonic cues. But Dr. Phelps had a drinking problem, a very bad one, and he was also resentful of Dr. Brand who seemed always to be on the verge of publishing a paper on one thing or another." He chuckled, looking out towards the lake. "When the research began to diverge from the original plan he became convinced that Dr. Brand was trying to usurp him. He also suffered from the delusion that there were monsters of some sort in the woods."

Phylis stiffened. "I saw something in the woods."

"A deer, or some other animal. Not a monster," John said patiently. "But Phelps was convinced. When I first arrived, he was still here. Dr. Brand couldn't bring himself to disengage him. They were good friends, you see. But eventually Dr. Phelps left of his own accord."

"Is he crazy?"

John shook his head. "Not crazy. Maybe a little mixed up. I just hope he didn't frighten you."

"No, but . . . He said the army wouldn't let him drive to camp. He had to come by boat."

John raised an eyebrow. "Another delusion, I'm afraid. Dr. Brand has always welcomed Dr. Phelps into Lakeview."

Phylis studied him for a full five seconds, then took a puff on her cigarette. "Anyway, I thought I should let you know."

"It's good that you did. Phelps can occasionally be a nuisance, but he's never bothered a patient before, or a patient's mother. Dr. Brand will want to know."

Phylis reached out a hand and touched his. "No,

126

please. He didn't really bother me, and he seemed like such a nice man, like he was really worried about Celia and me. He just got me curious."

"Well, I hope I've satisfied your curiosity."

"You have." She squeezed his hand.

"Good." John smiled. "Well, I'll go and prepare the boat, if you'll go and gather the passengers."

Once he had gone, Phylis went through to the bedroom and stood before the vanity mirror. She felt slightly better after talking to John, though the impression lingered that she was being sluffed-off. She ran a brush through her blond hair, which had begun to curl quite naturally around her shoulders since coming here, and then touched up her lightly applied makeup. The terry-cloth shorts and halter top would do for today, since it looked to be rather pleasant. She pirouetted slowly, inspecting herself in the mirror, and decided she looked presentable. Only a close-up revealed the hangover effects. *Honey, you look a lot better than you feel.*

She walked over to Number Two, warmed pleasantly by the dappled sunlight, and found Dora curled up in the easy chair with a glass of orange juice in one hand and a paperback book in the other. The book was a regency romance and the cover showed a love-stricken couple dancing formally but obviously wishing they were embracing more intimately.

"My God, what are you drinking and what are you reading?" Phylis cried in mock horror.

Dora started in surprise, then smiled when she saw Phylis. She held up the glass of orange juice. "This is a virgin," she said. Then, holding up the book, she smiled wickedly. "The heroine of this is about to lose that title."

"Dora, you are incorrigible!"

"I wouldn't throw stones, honey, I saw what you were reading down on the beach," Dora said playfully.

Phylis laughed. "I just came to ask if you'd like to come on a boat ride over to Battle Lake."

"Really? With you and John?" Dora's eyes widened.

"And Celia, and David. Sure, it'll be fun."

"You don't want to be alone?"

"Dora, that book is going to your head. Come on, please. I'd like for you and David to come along."

"Are you sure?"

"Positive. Just finish your juice and come down to the beach. John is getting the boat ready."

Phylis walked slowly down to the water, savoring the sensation of the cool grass poking through the toes of her sandals, a gentle breeze tugging at her hair. Celia and David had joined John at the boat ramp, and were watching, enthralled, as he spun the large wheel that lowered the boat to the water. A pile of flotation vests lay on the sand, along with a freshly painted five-gallon gas tank, and a ragged looking wooden oar. When Dora arrived, wearing the same white top and red shorts she'd had on when Phylis first met her, John handed out vests and helped everybody get into them.

At last John turned the ignition key and the powerful inboard motor puffed to life, sputtering water at the rear, coughing out blue smoke. The smell of burned oil filled the air. Because of the breeze the water towards the middle of the lake was choppy and made for a bumpy ride, the prow slamming from wave to wave like a car with poor suspension on a pot-hole riddled back-road, and Phylis began to feel the effects

128

of her hangover. Everybody else, however, seemed to enjoy the ride, including Dora who squealed with pleasure when spray came over the edge and into her face. Up front, beside John, David and Celia were engaged in a constant shriek as the boat rose and fell. Much to Phylis's relief John finally made for the calmer water closer to shore, and when he turned around to survey his passengers she gave him a grateful smile.

When they came around the point the shoreline suddenly bristled with private docks, and Phylis could catch glimpses of cabins, some of them extraordinarily grandiose, nestled in the protective trees. There were also swimmers close to shore, and even a boat or two leaving a white wake in the water. At about the halfway point they passed a group of people apparently learning how to water ski. Phylis watched as one young man, supported in the water by another man and a woman, was suddenly dragged forward by a ski-boat until he disappeared in a huge wave of his own making. He seemed incapable of stepping up onto the water, and looked more like a log in tow than a human. He was dragged about fifty yards before he lost his grip on the tow line, which shot forward and clipped the tips of his skis with a report like a shotgun blast. The rookie skier collapsed into the water, yelling in dismay, and the boat slowed, turned, and circled back for another try. Phylis looked on sympathetically, while at the front of the boat John exploded into laughter.

It took twenty-five minutes to reach Battle Lake, just a bit longer than by car, and as they approached the public dock John slowed the motor, threw it momentarily into reverse, and edged up to the wooden platform like an expert. When they were all on the dock Phylis looked around curiously. There seemed to be many more people about than she had seen last time she was here.

"Sunday flea market," John explained. "They have it all through the summer months. I think this might be the last one. We can take a look if you want."

"I love garage sales," Dora said.

Phylis didn't mind them either, but a sudden pang from her stomach reminded her that she had not eaten much since Saturday morning.

"How about we get an ice cream cone first?" John suggested, and Phylis had the sudden impression that he had read her mind. Or was it perhaps, she wondered, the synchronicity of prospective lovers?

As they walked to the ice cream parlor Celia gripped Phylis's left hand, while David capered up ahead, and at one point John's fingers delicately touched her own. She slipped her fingers between his and held his hand, and then smiled at the shocked, but pleased expression on his face. Dora gawked in all the windows.

They left the coolness of the ice cream parlor, laden down with ice cream cones and milk shakes, and walked, in the comfortable warmth of midmorning, to the flea market. It was more of a parking lot than a market, really, with tables lined up between haphazardly parked cars, vans, and trucks. Most of the merchandise was junk, but Phylis soon found herself wandering alone between tables, scanning for anything of interest. The air was filled with the smells of hotdogs, country fries, broiling hamburgers, and the distinctive sweetness of cotton candy. It was almost like being on the midway. Once she spotted John and Dora looking over a table full of books, and she wondered if their tastes were similar. The thought made her giggle. Celia and David had parked themselves at a table of comics and toys, and under the watchful eye of the proprietor were oblivious to all else.

At one table, towards the back of the market, Phylis found a box of sunglasses. She picked out a pair that might have been in style ten years earlier, with extra-large lenses and imitation ivory frames, and tried them on. The glasses may have looked silly, but the polaroid glass cut out the glare effectively.

"How much?" She turned, smiling, to the old woman behind the counter.

"Two bucks." The woman looked as if she cared as much about Phylis and the glasses as she did about car crash statistics in California.

Phylis continued to smile, dug out her purse, handed over a five dollar bill, and while waiting for the old woman to make change turned around to look for John. For a moment she was confused, feeling as if she had been dreaming and suddenly kicked awake. The reality around her didn't seem to jibe with the world she expected, but it took a moment for her to pinpoint the anomaly. Staring at her across a table of old electric shavers and curling irons, his dark hair combed forward over a pinched, brown face, was her ex-husband Don. Phylis's quick intake of breath sounded almost like a cough. She dropped her milk shake, heard the dull thud of the container hitting the ground, and felt the sudden cold on her feet.

"You okay, lady?"

Phylis jerked her head around at the old woman's voice. "What?" She felt dizzy and breathless.

"You okay, honey? You look kinda sick."

Phylis grabbed the three one dollar bills extended in the woman's grizzled hand, but when she spun around Don was no longer there. She glanced around frantically. She spotted John at the other side of the small clearing, and darted towards him. She gripped his arm and shook him. "Where's Celia?"

He turned, frowning. "What's wrong?"

"Where's Celia?" Her voice had raised an octave and taken on the glassy edge of panic.

"Over where we left her, with David, at the comics table." He pointed at the tables nearest the road.

Phylis followed his finger, and there was Celia, flipping through a comic, giggling. Phylis moved quickly through the browsing crowd, bumping into hips, knocking shoulders, kicking heels and shins. A litany of curses followed her headlong rush, until finally she kneeled before Celia and hugged the child tightly.

"Mommy?" Celia had dropped her comic in surprise, and now regarded Phylis with solemn childlike concern.

John followed closely behind Phylis, and he kneeled beside her, placing a reassuring hand on her shoulder. "Phylis, what's wrong?"

"I . . ." She looked carefully around the groping, touching, noisy crowd, but could not see Don. He was not there. He was never there. Slowly, with each breath she drew, her panic began to ebb. "I guess I'm not feeling too well," she said, and hearing her own voice she knew the lie sounded hollow, but she could not think of anything else.

The effects of the hangover began to close in again, and so it was not a total lie. Sweat broke out on her brow, and she felt nauseated. At John's insistence they went back to the boat. Phylis held Celia's hand tightly, glancing continuously from side to side, but she did not spot Don again. *Of course not, he wasn't there!*

Once they were in the boat she sighed with relief. She closed her eyes as John pushed the throttle, relishing the rush of cool, calming air that passed across her skin.

Her mind had played a nasty trick on her. Perhaps it was the lack of food, or even overexposure to sun. That could cause hallucinations, couldn't it? Or perhaps she just wasn't used to the abundance of fresh air, and in order to counteract its effect she lit a cigarette, breathing the smoke in deeply.

But she could not quite rid herself of the chill that had gripped the back of her neck.

CHAPTER FIFTEEN

"Good morning, Margaret. Here we are," Phylis said.

"Good morning, Mrs. Reynolds," Margaret said, face stoney. Then, smiling warmly, "And how are you this morning, Celia?"

This was Wednesday, and for the last three days she had had the same conversation with Margaret; the routine never changed.

"Will you be observing today?"

No, I don't think so," Phylis said. She still felt uneasy in the observation room.

The chunky nurse came around to the front of the reception desk and took Celia's hand. "Come along then, Dr. Brand is ready for you."

Celia, who had begun by enjoying the treatment, was now thoroughly bored by the whole procedure, and she turned and waved sullenly to Phylis. Leaning against the counter, Phylis watched Celia and Margaret walk slowly down the hallway. She had not noticed any dramatic improvement in Celia since the treatments had resumed on Monday, but John and Dr. Brand seemed pleased with Celia's progress.

She was about to leave the building when something on the reception desk caught her attention. Margaret's purse lay face down on the desk, open, and Phylis had a clear view of the contents. *Nosey*, she thought, but looked more closely anyway.

Nestled between a vinyl wallet and the blue wrapper of a Maxipad was the checkered butt of a handgun.

She was not much on weaponry, but she recognized this. Her father had owned one just like it. He kept it hidden in a drawer in their bedroom along with assorted other items Phylis was never meant to see, like the poorly photographed sex manual where the female model had looked remarkably like one of her teachers at school, but Phylis had discovered all her parents' secrets at an early age. It was a Colt .45 automatic. She drew a quick breath and stepped away from the counter. Margaret had returned, crepe soles silent on the hallway tiling.

"Everything okay, Mrs. Reynolds?" Margaret took her position behind the counter. She carefully closed her purse, then placed it on the floor by her feet. She smiled at Phylis.

"Yes, everything's fine," Phylis said.

She left the building, frowning, something tugging at her memory, and walked slowly back to her cabin. When it finally clicked she stopped dead in her tracks. The Colt .45 automatic was an armed forces weapon. Her father had managed to keep his after his World War II service. But what was Margaret Palin doing with one?

John would want to hear about this.

* * *

135

After Celia's session, and once Margaret had taken the girl through to the playroom, Brand confronted him with a truth he had been aware of for a long time. John Gordon turned from the telemetry deck, which he had been carefully adjusting, and tried to appear concerned.

"John, you're getting too close to Phylis Reynolds," Brand said slowly, as if choosing his words with great care.

John grunted. "I know." The hell of it was, he wasn't even sure what it was about Phylis Reynolds that attracted him so much. She was attractive, yes, but he'd known many attractive women. Perhaps it was the vulnerability that was so obvious in her, despite her efforts to hide it. "But you're the one who suggested I get closer to her."

"I realize that," Brand said. "I believed, at first, that an emotional tie to the clinic might insure her continued cooperation. But you're taking it too far."

"I told you, I know that."

"Then don't you think it's time to cool things off? Your little relationship could jeopardize this project."

"Don't be ridiculous, Neville. I'm as committed as I ever was. If anything, what's happening between me and Phylis Reynolds is helping the project. There's a lot going on around here that frightens her. I think she might have given up and left already if it wasn't for her interest in me."

Brand considered the suggestion seriously. "You think so?"

"I know so. And that bloody Phelps didn't help anything by approaching her. I told you we should have let Wilkes take care of him."

"And what about you, when you're finished with us. Should I let Wilkes handle you?"

John ignored the remark. "She's also suspicious of David DeMarch. I don't know if she's actually *seen* Sonny yet, but she's sure as hell seen signs of him."

Brand nodded thoughtfully. "That little effort is a dead end, I think. We should consider removing Sonny as soon as possible. It's obvious that David is making no further progress, even with access to the creature."

"I never wanted the fucking thing running around anyway," John said curtly. Brand's idea that David's response to the cues might improve with interaction to Sonny had frightened John. The creature had appeared friendly enough, but it was unpredictable. And what if the kid learned to control it?

"I'll talk to Wilkes. His men can round it up. I also think it's about time for Dora and David to leave. They've outlived their usefulness."

John chuckled. At first it had appeared as if David DeMarch was what they were looking for. His responses to the initial cues had been phenomenal, but had petered off as they entered the primal stage. Now it looked like Celia Reynolds was the new contender. Her initial audio-emotional topograph had revealed an extreme sensitivity to certain negative cues, and during the second stage she had responded extremely well to the therapy. Well enough to convince Phylis not to leave.

"As far as Phylis and myself," John said. "If I back off now she'll be suspicious. She might even pack up and leave. Especially if we're removing Dora De-March. They're friends. I think I should continue to

137

pursue the course I'm on."

Brand stared at him for a long time. "Just don't let your feelings interfere with what you have to do."

"I won't," John said. He turned back to the telemetry deck.

Phylis liked him. He liked her. Nobody was getting hurt. He could end their relationship any time he wanted, he felt sure of that. So why not enjoy it while it lasted?

Her relationship with John Gordon had developed rapidly over the past few days, a fact that bothered Phylis to some extent since she was at a loss to explain it. She liked him, certainly, and granted he always seemed to be there to lean on, like on Sunday after she thought she had seen Don (though she had not yet told John the truth about the incident), and yes, he did really seem to reciprocate her feelings, but . . . Ah, yes, *but* . . . Why did it seem that things were moving too quickly? It was as if their relationship had been planned out in some far away strategy room, like a minor battle in an anonymous war, and regardless of their emotional state they were going to follow the plan, ready or not.

Or was it Celia?

The possibility that she was falling for John merely because Celia liked him troubled her, yet she knew that wasn't the whole truth. She could not so easily discount her own feelings. When she was alone she would bring to mind his wide smile, or the way the corners of his eyes wrinkled when he laughed, or the feel of his warm hand against hers. Sometimes she imagined him standing before her naked, tall, lean, and tanned, and in her mind she would reach out to touch him.

On Wednesday evening Dora agreed to look after Celia, while Phylis and John took the walk she had promised him. There was a narrow foot path behind the main building that wound through the trees and down to the shore some distance from camp, and hand in hand they followed it. The path was overgrown in spots, at one point a renegade bush had somehow bridged the gap from one side to the other, and sometimes footing was difficult because of loose rocks, but they managed nicely. Though the days were warm and sunny, the nights cooled off quickly, and Phylis pressed close to John for warmth. A light breeze skimmed off the lake, rustling the trees, and Phylis found herself experiencing one of those moments when she felt very close to nature. It had happened only twice before, once in the rocky Mountains when Celia was a baby, and once with her father when she had been fourteen and he had taken her fishing. It was the closest thing she had ever had to a mystical experience. Nature seemed to commune with her.

The woods were dark, surrounding them, but with John near she did not care. They came upon a clearing close to the water, at the center of which a large boulder jutted out of the ground at an angle that made it accessible for sitting on, and there they sat, pressed into one another, looking out over the water which the setting sun had turned to a rippling pool of burnished bronze. She almost hated to break the mood by talking, but knew she could not feel fully at ease until her questions were answered.

"Did you know that Margaret Palin has a gun in her purse?"

"So what?" He was looking out across the water, the sun reflected in his eyes, and did not much seem to care.

"Doesn't it seem strange that a nurse would have a gun?"

"Lots of women carry guns. Margaret lives in Fergus Falls. I seem to remember her saying there had been trouble in her neighborhood."

"Not Colt .45 automatics," Phylis said. "It's a cannon."

"Margaret is a big girl."

Phylis pursed her lips. His answers seemed almost rehearsed, but that was a silly thought. Perhaps it was her own reaction that was the strange one, not John's.

John cupped her chin with his hand and turned her face towards him. "Let's not talk about Margaret tonight, okay?" The look in his eyes made her breathing suddenly shallow, and all thoughts of Margaret and her gun fled into the night. Then suddenly his lips were on hers, and she opened her mouth to him. When his hands cupped her breasts she gasped in surprise, but she pulled him closer and sucked harder on his tongue. She squeezed her hand between their bodies and stroked the hard lump between his legs.

He moaned. "Phylis, not here."

"Where?" Her own voice was heavy with desire, and right now she would have lay down willingly on the rock for him.

"My room. Come on."

They walked swiftly back along the path to the

main building where they entered through the front door. The reception area was dark, though a single naked bulb lit the hallway towards the treatment room. John's room was at the opposite end of the building, and it was as messy as a bachelor's room should be. Except this messiness seemed almost planned. The piles of clothes looked carefully placed to produce an air of casual neglect, and the haphazardly piled books had the look of an intricately designed structure. On the surface was chaos, but beneath it all there lay thorough organization. But he did not give her time to follow this line of thought, as his lips suddenly clamped on hers again. When he flipped up the cups of her bra with his thumbs and handled the soft flesh beneath her blouse, she was lost.

The suppressed libido of the last three years crashed into Phylis like a tidal wave, carrying her literally off her feet. She felt her legs give way, and she sank against him. He supported her against the wall, continuing to kiss her lips, his hands now unbuttoning her blouse to expose the flesh beneath. With trembling fingers she unzipped him, then ran her fingers along his erection, smiling when he groaned. John dug into his back pocket, pulled out his wallet, and from it took the small silver package of a condom.

"Well, aren't you the little boy scout," Phylis said, eyebrow cocked, voice husky.

"It's been there two years," he said, grinning. He opened the small package and took a step backwards to put it on.

Phylis held out a hand, smiling wickedly. "Let me."

141

She took the translucent sheath in her fingers and kneeled before him. His penis jutted out like the barrel of a gun, quivering when she placed the condom against its tip, and she held its base with one hand while she gently rolled the condom on with the other. When it had enveloped him completely she leaned forward and took him into her mouth, releasing him again slowly, inch by inch, as his fingers entwined in her hair. When she stood again his face was slack with disbelief.

He waited while she stepped out of her jeans and pulled off the blouse, then stepped towards her and pressed his smooth brown chest against her breasts. The soft hair on his chest tickled her nipples, and she smiled as they kissed. Phylis was wet, and needed no further preliminary touching; she gave her hips a slight upward hitch, guiding him with her hand, and sank onto him. A groan, starting deep in her throat, slipped from her mouth.

That's the sound they make on TV commercials when they bite into a cookie, she thought.

The thought made her want to laugh, but it came out as another groan. John was not an experienced lover, but she did not care. He was a man, and he was inside her, and she used her sharp nails on his buttocks, prodding him to deeper thrusts, gasping every time he slammed her into the wall. When, at last he stiffened, trembling against her, Phylis felt herself begin to explode; a liquid throb that started at her vagina and radiated outwards in waves, shaking her whole body while John's hips spasmed against her inner thighs. Breathing raggedly, face pressed to his neck, she hung onto him like an old shirt.

142

"Phylis, I—"

Phylis raised a finger to her lips. "Shhh. No talking." She wanted to savor his presence silently. The smell of their sex began to fill the room, and soon John softened and slid out of her. During their lovemaking Phylis had kept her eyes open, focused on a tatty looking baseball mitt hanging from the wall over the bed, and she had the sudden thought that she might equate the image with sex for a long time to come.

They dressed slowly and the silence became uncomfortable. *It's like we both feel guilty.* The thought depressed her. *Does it always have to be this way?* She was zipping up her jeans *(covering the evidence)* when John stepped closer to her and turned her to face him.

"Phylis, I don't know if we should have done what we did tonight. Probably not. But I want you to know, I think . . ." He suddenly seemed at a loss for words, and she could sense he was searching for something. "I think I'm falling for you in a big way."

She kissed him tenderly on the lips.

"What we did tonight," he said. "It was like we had to do it in order to go on, do you see what I mean? It was like a stumbling block in our way. Maybe, now, we can really get to know each other."

A woman could fall in love with a man like this, she thought. Feeling a lot better, she hugged him tightly. "That's what I want."

"Me too."

He insisted that he accompany her back to her cabin, and since she did not want to face the darkness alone she agreed. The dark was complete, the cabins seemed like islands of light floating in a black sea, and the woods were impenetrable. It had cooled considerably from early evening, the breeze coming off the water a bit stronger, and Phylis kept her arms crossed over her breast for warmth.

They were halfway between the main building and Dora's cabin when they heard the noise. John must have heard it first, because he suddenly stopped walking. Then Phylis heard it. At first she thought the wind must have toppled a branch from a tree, but the crashing in the wood continued for far too long, and as quickly as it had begun the noise stopped.

"What was that?" Phylis stepped closer to John.

"I don't know," he whispered. They were peering towards the dark line of trees, but they could see nothing. "C'mon, let's get Celia and go back to your cabin."

They had taken a couple of quick steps when the crashing commenced, and suddenly the trees behind them exploded in a fury of snapping branches as something burst into the clearing. Phylis glanced over her shoulder but again could see nothing. John gripped her arm and propelled her forwards. "Run!"

A thin wail split the night behind them, a high wavering note that trembled as it continued, finally ending in a deep moan. The ground around them seemed to shake as they ran, and Phylis felt sure she could hear the *thump! thump! thump!* of heavy pursuit. A scream built in her throat, ready to erupt, when light suddenly speared out of Cabin Two. They were closer than she had thought. Dora's silhouette appeared inside the porch, and as the porch light flicked on Phylis could see that Dora's face was creased in concern. Dora whistled as they stumbled breathlessly up to the cabin.

"Did you hear that?" she said excitedly. "I nearly died!"

Phylis leaned up against the screening, panting for breath. Whatever had been pursuing them was gone. John was pale.

Celia suddenly poked her head around Dora's thick thighs, looking frightened, and ran to Phylis. She hugged Phylis fiercely, then ran to John and gripped his hand. Dora was looking towards the woods, frowning.

"I wonder what it was." Dora's voice was almost a whisper.

"Probably a bear," John said, his breathing returning to normal. "We don't usually see them around here, and I've never heard of one chasing anybody like that. The light must have scared it off."

"Didn't sound like a bear to me," Dora said.

Phylis could see David inside the cabin. The boy was in the bathroom, standing on the pot, looking out the back window at the woods, and as Phylis watched he raised his arm and waved as if to a friend outside. When he turned and saw Phylis he smiled shyly. Phylis tried to smile back, but what appeared on her face was a grimace.

"Listen, Dora, thinks for looking after Celia."

Dora grinned and winked. "You sure you want to walk to your own cabin with a bear out there?"

"I think it's gone now. It will be okay," John said. His eyes flicked expectantly towards the dark trees.

With one arm around Phylis, Celia's hand held in the other, he walked with them back to their cabin.

145

There were no more sounds from the woods. In fact, a total silence had descended. Phylis stood with him at the cabin door and kissed him lightly.

"What was that thing, John?"

"I told you. Probably a bear. I didn't really see it." His voice was cold, and she decided not to press further. "I'll talk to the army boys tomorrow, maybe they can look into it."

Later, Celia refused to sleep alone, but snuggled against Phylis in the master bedroom. In the cold, dark hours of early morning Phylis snapped awake. In the woods something wailed. The same high pitched, trembling moan they had heard earlier.

Like a cry of despair.

Silence returned. Celia shifted restlessly, but did not wake. It was a long time before Phylis got back to sleep.

CHAPTER SIXTEEN

In the morning Phylis woke with a start, squinting her eyes against the sunlight streaming through the bedroom window. How late had she slept? This was the first time the sun had been high enough to wake her. She rolled over and saw the small indentation in the second pillow where Celia's head had rested, but the bed was smooth and empty. Phylis threw off the covers and swung her legs out of bed. "Celia?"

There was no answer. A sudden stab of fear brought back the events of the previous night, and she seemed to hear, echoing in her mind, that mournful wail. "Celia!"

Phylis leapt from the bed and stumbled through to the living room-kitchen area. Celia was on the porch, face pressed to the screen. "Celia!"

Celia turned and regarded her mother curiously. Phylis sighed, a wave of relief passing over her, and she ran a hand through her hair. "I thought you might have run off without breakfast," she said.

"The noises woke me up," Celia said.

"What noises?" Phylis shivered, and hugging herself against the morning's chill she went out on the porch and followed Celia's gaze. Three or four jeeps were parked at odd angles in front of the main building, and a number of soldiers were standing around the glass-fronted entrance. She noticed, alarmed, that they all had guns slung over their shoulders. As she watched, another jeep roared through the gate and came to a squealing stop beside the others. Four more men jumped out, also armed. She could hear their chatter, the occasional burst of laughter.

"What are they doing, Mommy?"

"I don't know, honey," Phylis said, frowning.

The porch door creaked open. "Good morning."

Phylis gasped. "John! You scared the hell out of me!"

"I'm sorry. I thought you saw me coming."

Phylis shook her head. "I was watching the war games out there. All this for a bear?"

John nodded. "Well, yes, but there is another problem." He appeared to be troubled about something.

"Oh?"

"David DeMarch is missing. He ran off into the woods."

"Oh no." Phylis raised a hand to her mouth in shock.

"I'm afraid we'll have to cancel Celia's session for today, if that's okay?"

"Oh, yes, of course." The thought of David running off to the woods gave Phylis the creeps, and the image of him waving at something behind the cabin suddenly flitted through her mind. She imagined, again, the echo of that strange wail. "Poor Dora. She must be frantic."

"Very much so," John said. "I actually came to ask you if you wouldn't mind keeping her company for a

148

while. You two seem to get along well. Just until we get this mess cleaned up."

"Sure. No problem. I'll just get dressed." It suddenly hit home to Phylis that she was wearing nothing but her ratty knee-length nightshirt with the picture of Mickey Mouse on the front. She also lacked even a smidgen of makeup, and her hair was still tousled from sleep. She cringed in horror. "Oh, I must look awful!"

For the first time that morning John smiled. "You look great."

Memories of earlier last night came to Phylis and she blushed warmly. John continued to smile, obviously thinking about the same things, and that only made things worse. "You can tell Dora that we'll be along shortly."

When John had gone Phylis showered quickly, dressed in jeans and a long sleeved sweatshirt with U of M stenciled on the front, and applied her makeup lightly. Holding Celia's hand she walked slowly over to Dora's cabin. The woods were silent, disturbed only by a light breeze that caused the trees to rustle, but she avoided looking into their dark depths lest she see anything. She would die if something moved just as she looked.

Dora was curled into the sofa, feet tucked beneath her rump, sobbing quietly. She looked up as Phylis and Celia entered, and a tremulous smile played across her lips before being vanquished by a sob. Her face was puffed, eyes red-rimmed and wet, and tears streaked her plump cheeks. "Damn it! I'm acting like a baby!"

Phylis sat beside her and put her arms around the

larger woman. "They'll find him, Dora. Don't worry." But her words sounded false.

Dora sobbed into Phylis's shoulder. "Jesus, he's always running off! All the time. I spend half my days wondering if he'll come back alive, and he doesn't seem to care." Her shoulders shook.

"He's a boy," Phylis said, as if that explained everything.

"It wouldn't be so bad," Dora began, then drew in a shuddering breath. "But I keep on thinking about him out there with that *thing*."

"What thing?"

"That *bear!*" She spoke the word as if it were an expletive, then she pulled back from Phylis. "Do you think it is a bear?"

"I guess it must be. They've got the whole damn army out to get it."

Dora sniffed, wiping her eyes. "Yeah. Isn't that strange. I thought the base was deserted."

Phylis frowned. The same thought, though she had not articulated it, had occurred to her earlier. Dora disengaged herself from Phylis and rose shakily to her feet.

"I'm sorry. You must think I'm silly. David always comes back. I shouldn't be worried."

Phylis nodded, relieved that Dora seemed to be calming down, though she was not sure she could have done so herself if the situation were reversed and Celia was the one running around in the woods. "Did he give any indication of why he was running off, or where he might be going?"

Dora shrugged. "I guess he doesn't want to leave. He must like it here."

150

"What do you mean?"

"Well, Dr. Gordon came around this morning. David's treatment is finished. He was going to drive us into the Fergus Falls today, to the bus station. David just ran."

Phylis opened her mouth to speak, but could find no words. *Dora gone?* She found it difficult to imagine life at Lakeview without Dora to keep her company during the day, and suddenly she realized how much she had actually come to like Dora. They had become friends quickly, yes, but she had so *few* friends these days that even fast ones were welcome. "I'm going to miss you," Phylis said softly, her own eyes suddenly wet.

Dora sat down again. "I'll miss you too." They hugged each other, then parted with embarrassed smiles. Phylis thought: *Goddamned emotional females!*

Celia, who had spent the last few minutes watching the activities of the soldiers, came back into the living room with a look of grievous concern on her small face. "I'm hungry," she said.

Dora sprang to her feet. "Oh my gosh. I haven't been very thoughtful, have I? You two just sit tight for a few minutes and I'll whip up something good. Pancakes sound okay?"

"Mmmm hmmm," Celia said, nodding.

"Dora, why don't *you* sit down. I can fix something."

Dora motioned for Phylis to remain seated. "No, please, let me. I need something to keep me occupied."

While Dora busied herself making breakfast, Phylis picked up the book Dora had been reading the other

151

day, and began to flip through it while she smoked a cigarette. By the time breakfast was ready, the smell of pancake batter and coffee filling the small cabin, she was a chapter and a half into the book and reluctant to put it down.

"I'll be damned. You like it." Dora said, bringing through a tray laden with a steaming plate of pancakes, a bottle of maple syrup, and eating utensils.

Phylis dropped the romance. "It's . . ."

"Oh, come on, Phylis, I saw your face."

Phylis laughed. "Oh, all right. It started well, anyway."

As they ate breakfast the two woman talked about the books they had read recently, and Phylis discovered that other than Dora's penchant for soppy romances their tastes were similar. Afterwards, Celia flipped through a pile of David's comics, most of which fell into the super-hero vs. super-villain category, and somehow managed to keep herself entertained. Phylis delved further into Dora's book. The only thing that stopped her from becoming totally engrossed in the quick-witted, humorous, story was the fact that Dora was fidgeting nervously, constantly peering outside.

Toward lunch time Celia stood, stretched, and began to stalk. "Can we go out for awhile, Mommy?"

Phylis sighed. "I don't think so, Celia. We should stay here and keep Dora company."

But Dora closed her book and grinned. "Actually, I could use a bit of fresh air myself. Why don't we all go for a walk?"

When they were outside Phylis was glad she had worn jeans and a long-sleeved top. Although it was mostly sunny, a cool breeze swept the trees, and a menacing ring of clouds circled the lake. As they walked along the path to the main building Phylis held tightly to Celia's hand, while Dora scanned the trees with great concentration.

The jeeps were still parked in the gravel yard in front of the main building, but most of the men who had been there earlier were now gone. Into the woods to look for David and the bear, Phylis presumed. There were two soldiers standing beside one of the jeeps, and in the jeep an officer was running his finger over an open map and seemed to be explaining something. The soldiers leaned closer, nodding. The front door of the main building opened and Dr. Gordon and Dr. Brand emerged, talking animatedly, and behind them came Margaret Palin, holding onto a clipboard. When John saw Phylis he smiled and angled over.

"How are things going?" His face held a worried expression.

"Have you found David yet?" Dora asked.

"Why don't we ask Captain Wilkes," John said, and led them over to the jeep.

Captain Wilkes was a robust man, about Dr. Brand's age, with rosy cheeks and a stout middle that looked to be about as hard as granite. Dr. Brand and Margaret were leaning over the door of the jeep and studying the map on Wilkes lap.

"Captain Wilkes, Mrs. Demarch was asking about her son."

Wilkes glanced from Phylis to Dora and back again, and Phylis suddenly felt very uncomfortable under his scrutiny.

"Have you found him?" Dora asked. The reserved facade she had built up through the morning was beginning to show cracks.

"Oh, yes, we've *found* the lad," Wilkes said, smiling grimly.

"You have?" Dora's face brightened.

"We just can't *catch* him!" Wilkes looked disgusted. "He seems intent on evading my men. But I promise you, it won't be long before we lay our hands on the little son-of-a . . . the, er, little rascal."

"What about the bear?" Phylis asked.

"Oh, yes, the bear," Wilkes said softly, now turning his attention to Phylis. "Well, apparently it's heading for the ridge just west of here. Far away from the boy, I assure you. He's in no danger. But I have some of my men tracking it. Bloody things can be a nuisance. Why, a couple of years back we had one sniffing around our compound. I got *that* bastard myself."

Dora slumped with relief, and Phylis put an arm around her. "Thank God," Dora said. She was close to tears.

Dr. Brand looked over at Phylis with a stern gaze. "Mrs. Reynolds, may I suggest that you take Mrs. DeMarch back to her cabin and wait there for further word."

Phylis stared right back. She did not like being treated like a child. "We're out for a walk. You can find us down by the lake."

Dr. Brand's face froze, and he appeared ready to say something more when Phylis saw the almost imperceptible nod that John gave him. "That's fine," he finally said, his voice tightly controlled.

Margaret Palin impaled Phylis with an icy glare.

154

John came over to them and put an arm around Dora's shoulder. "David's all right. This is some sort of game for him, that's all."

Dora nodded. John smiled at Phylis and winked, and she smiled back. She turned and saw Celia over by the jeep, looking up at Captain Wilkes.

"You better run along, son, before your mother misses you."

Celia frowned angrily. "I'm a girl!"

"Celia!"

Celia turned at her mother's voice and trotted over. "He thought I was a boy," she said petulantly.

Phylis chuckled and ruffled Celia's short, red hair. John kneeled by her. "You look like a very pretty young lady to me."

Celia smiled shyly and looked away. "Thanks," Phylis mouthed silently, then: "Later?" She raised her eyebrows.

John nodded, smiling, then walked back to the jeep. The two soldiers were staring at Phylis with open curiosity on their faces, but Wilkes said something and they looked quickly away. Frowning, Phylis took Celia's hand and walked with Dora down to the beach.

They were not long down at the water, certainly no more than half an hour, when John's shout came down to them. "Phylis! Dora!"

Celia, who was in the middle of throwing a skipper out into the water, dropped the flat stone and ran to Phylis. Dora was already on her feet and running up to the main building. Holding Celia's hand, Phylis hurried after her. When they came over the ridge Phylis saw the soldier emerge from the trees at the

155

side of the main building, and even from here could see that his rugged face was scratched and sweaty. But David Demarch was held in his arms.

"David!" Dora cried, running towards them.

The soldier lowered David, and the boy ran to Dora and into her arms. Phylis and Celia walked slowly up to Captain Wilkes's jeep. Dora was hugging David furiously, lips pressed into the boy's short black hair, whispering his name over and over as if it were a protective spell. "David, David, David . . ."

The soldier who had carried David from the trees unslung his gun and slumped, exhausted, against the jeep. "Well done, Field," Wilkes said.

"He almost got away again," Field said hoarsely, wiping the back of his hand across his sweaty forehead.

"Any sign of . . ." Wilkes began, but Field shook his head curtly.

Phylis felt almost as relieved as Dora at seeing David, and she kneeled beside him and stroked the boy's hair. "Where did you go, David?"

David pulled away from Dora. He was pouting. "I just wanted to say good-bye," he said, then looked over at the trees.

Goose bumps rose on Phylis's neck. *Say good-bye to what?*

Suddenly there was shouting from deep in the woods, and a man screamed. Another man shouted. Wilkes pushed himself to a standing position in the jeep. Phylis jumped to her feet and looked towards the trees.

When the piercing wail began she shivered, and raised her hands to cover her ears. But there was no need. Three shots rang out in quick succession, echoing through the trees, and the wail abruptly stopped. Silence pressed down on the clearing.

David DeMarch took a step away from Dora, his face creased in anguish. "Sonny!" he cried. Then he burst into tears.

CHAPTER SEVENTEEN

Phylis looked on in disbelief as David squirmed violently in Dora's arms. His small voice, muffled against her shoulder, was filled with despair. "Sonny! Sonny!" the hackles on the back of Phylis's neck rose.

"David, be quiet," Dora said harshly. But David continued to squirm, trying to twist out of her grasp, the noises emerging from his mouth now inarticulate grunts and cries. Dora, blushing with embarrassment, looked around the small clearing with pleading eyes.

Dr. Brand mumbled something to Margaret Palin, but Phylis could not hear what was said. Margaret nodded and ran up the path to the main building. Even amidst the turmoil Phylis noticed that Margaret's wide backside did not jiggle beneath the pink fabric of her uniform. *Muscle.* Then: *from sitting at a desk?* Margaret returned momentarily with a syringe. She handed it to Dr. Brand, then looked down at David with what could only be disgust. With casual precision Dr. Brand squeezed a few drops of liquid from the point of the needle and turned to Dora.

"A mild sedative. He's been through a lot. This

will calm him down."

Dora nodded, then looked at Phylis with questioning eyes that seemed to ask, *what else can I do?*

After the injection was administered David immediately became quiet. He ceased moving, his arms slowly losing their violent rhythm, but kept his head on Dora's shoulder. Soon his small body was wracked with sobs. John Gordon placed a comforting hand on Dora's shoulder. "Dora, we can delay your departure until tomorrow. Give David a chance to rest."

Dora shook her head and looked up at him. "No. I think it might be better if David left here as soon as possible. I'm sure there must be a bus from Fergus Falls leaving to Minneapolis sometime this afternoon or evening."

"Are you positive?"

Dora nodded, laying her head on David's bobbing shoulder. "It would be better."

Phylis felt a tug at her sleeve and looked down into Celia's worried face. "Is David okay?"

"I think so, honey. I think maybe David was frightened after being lost in the woods."

"Did they kill Sonny?" Celia asked.

Phylis's muscles clenched in her gut and she kneeled down beside Celia and studied the child's face carefully. "Celia, have you ever seen Sonny?"

Celia looked past Phylis at David and Dora, her expression one of deep concern. Phylis repeated her question and Celia blinked. "No, but David told me about him."

Phylis sighed with relief. What would she have done if Celia had said yes?

"Did they kill Sonny?" Celia asked again.

"No, Celia. They shot a bear, because it was dangerous."

This seemed to satisfy Celia. She nodded distractedly and looked away towards the water.

Captain Wilkes was grinning, looking down at David with amusement. Phylis felt a sudden stab of anger at him. *Bastard.*

"All's well that ends well," Wilkes said.

John stepped up to the jeep and shook Wilkes's hand. "Thanks again for your help, Captain."

"A little excitement never hurt anybody," Wilkes said, rubbing his hands together.

"Bears around camp are a bit more excitement than we like, I'm afraid," John said. He turned to Phylis and winked.

"Do you want the carcass?" Wilkes asked.

"Carcass?"

"The bear carcass. Probably a nice skin. Make a fine rug. Or a trophy."

"No, that all right. Hang it in your mess with the last intruder."

Phylis felt the sudden desire to contradict John. She wanted to see the bear, to see its carcass, to touch the three bullet holes in its hide.

"You want to see it, Phylis?" John asked, and again she had the impression he'd been reading her mind.

"No, that's okay." Despite her thoughts, she didn't really want to look at the dead animal. *Poor bear.*

John came over and squeezed her hand. His eyes looked tenderly into her own. "You okay?"

"Uh huh." She was feeling depressed, but now that

160

he was beside her she did feel better. She forced a smile.

John crouched and poked Celia playfully in the ribs. Celia giggled. "And you, little lady, missed your appointment this morning." Celia giggled again and pressed closer to Phylis's hip. "Do you know what that means?"

"Nope."

"It means I'm going to have to buy you an ice cream cone tomorrow. Is that punishment enough?"

"Okay."

One by one soldiers were beginning to emerge from the bushes, and as the jeeps filled they followed Wilkes down the road to the army compound, disappearing in plumes of gravel-dust beyond Lakeview's gate, until finally there was only a single jeep remaining. Dora was standing now, hanging onto David's hand. David, though calm, seemed slightly off kilter, as if he were drunk, or seeing something that nobody else could see.

Phylis reached up and pecked John on the lips. "I'll see you later, okay?" He blinked, surprised. "I'm going to help Dora for a little while." He nodded, his eyes understanding, then followed Dr. Brand and Margaret into the main building.

"What a nightmare," Dora said. She would not make eye contact with Phylis.

Phylis squeezed her hand. "Come on. I'll help you pack."

As they walked back to Dora's cabin, two young soldiers emerged from the trees at the side of the main building and went to the remaining jeep. Their faces were sweaty, and one of them had a bloody scratch across his right cheek. They were laughing, but nervously, and Phylis thought it was the laughter of men who have recently been terrified and somehow lived to tell about it.

An hour later they had finished packing Dora's things into two large cases, and were sitting in the living room drinking very strong coffee. David and Celia were playing Monopoly on the coffee table, and although Celia was losing badly she was enjoying herself. David had recovered from his initial dopiness, but despite the slackening effect of the sedative he had not returned to his agitated state. When Dora had told him they would be leaving shortly he had actually seemed relieved. Outside, the distant ring of clouds was tightening, cooling things off. It looked like rain was imminent.

"You look so glum," Dora said to Phylis over the rim of her coffee mug.

Phylis exhaled a cloud of smoke and tried to smile, but the fact was that *glum* was exactly the way she felt. "I don't like the idea of being alone here."

"There will be others coming. There always are."

"But I'll still be alone." She took another drag on her cigarette, then gulped some coffee with a grimace. She picked up Dora's book and dropped it back to the sofa. "How will I ever finish this now?"

Dora laughed. "Keep it."

This did not make Phylis feel any better, but she smiled anyway. "Thanks."

There was a knock at the porch door and John Gordon stuck his head in. "All set, Dora?"

"Yep. Any time."

"I called the station at Fergus Falls. There's a Greyhound for the Twin-cities leaving at 4:30. If we leave now we can make it in good time."

"Just give me a minute."

"I'll be in the car." The door slammed shut behind him.

"I'd try not to lose him, if I were you," Dora said, smiling impishly.

Phylis blushed. "I'll try not to." It was hard to get offended by talk like that from Dora, she was just so damned open about everything.

Phylis picked up one of the cases, Dora the other. "Come on, David," Dora said. At the car John took the cases and lifted them easily into the trunk.

"Want to come for the ride?" he asked Phylis.

"No. I hate good-byes. Especially long ones at air-ports and stations." She hugged Dora, then stepped back. "Bye, bye, David."

"Bye," David said, climbing into the back seat.

"Listen," Dora said. "My address and phone num-ber are in the back of that book. If you want—"

"I'll return it," Phylis said.

"Well, if you want. Maybe we could see each other sometime. I mean, the kids really like each other."

"I'll come to see *you*," Phylis said.

Dora nodded, her eyes suddenly wet. She got into the front of the car and closed the door. The Impala roared to life and rolled away. Celia waved. "Bye, David!"

Phylis watched the car as it passed through the main gate, and it seemed that she could see, a mo-ment before the obscuring plume of gravel dust exploded into the air, David's face pressed to the glass, looking forlornly into the woods.

Phylis tidied up the remnants of breakfast and coffee, then closed up Dora's cabin. Somebody would have to clear out all the food, unless there was to be another patient very soon. Although she had said to Dora that a new patient would still leave her alone, she hoped now that the camp would fill up quickly. There's a big difference between being *lonely* and being *alone,* she thought. John could keep her from being lonely, but only a new patient could keep her from the other.

By the time she was finished the wind had died to nothing and the puffy grey clouds hung immobile overhead like an air-brushed ceiling. The lake was glass smooth. *The calm before the storm?*

She had planned on waiting in their cabin for John to return, but instead she stopped at the foot of Dora's path. "You hungry, kiddo?"

"Nope." Celia was holding her hand, looking towards the trees.

Phylis frowned thoughtfully, then came to a decision. "Come on." She led Celia towards the main building.

Margaret Palin looked up from the reception desk as Phylis and Celia entered. The look on her face was anything but welcoming.

"Dr. Gordon isn't back yet," Margaret said, her voice very suggestive.

"That's okay," Phylis said. "I just want to use a phone."

That galvanized Margaret. She sat up straight and her eyes widened. "A phone?"

Phylis looked around and saw the pay phone in the corner of the waiting lounge. It had probably been there when the place was a motel. "I can use the pay phone," she said pleasantly. "Thanks."

Margaret's face tensed. "May I ask whom you're calling?"

Phylis turned, smiling. "You may ask, but I'll never tell." She had intentionally spoken in a playful tone. Something about Margaret's demeanor suggested that to do otherwise would invite trouble. "Celia, stay and talk with Margaret for a minute."

Celia grinned. She had obviously planned on doing just that. Margaret glanced at Phylis, her face expressing an emotion that was somewhere between anger and exasperation. Phylis turned away. *What is it with that woman?* She dialed *0* and was connected to the Fergus Falls exchange. She asked the operator to charge the call to her account number, and then gave the number she was calling. The phone rang three times before it was answered.

"MPLS Magazine, may I help you?" Penny's voice was as cheerful as ever, and the sound of it sent a flood of emotion through Phylis that she could hardly comprehend. It was as if she had been isolated in the wilderness for years, and had suddenly heard the voice of civilization, the voice of home. She could almost sense the bustle of the office behind Penny, and beyond that the constant chatter of the city itself. "Hello?" Penny said, and Phylis realized that she had not yet responded.

"Penny? This is Phylis Reynolds."

165

Pause. "Ms. Reynolds? Are you back?" Phylis smiled. Penny had insisted on calling her "Mizz" since the divorce. "Guys go for Ms.," she had said.

"No, not back yet," Phylis said. "But I need you to do something for me."

"Sure. What?"

"If Paul Welch is there, I want you to get him on the line."

"Paul? Hmmmm." Over the phone she could hear Penny flipping through some papers. "Yeah, he's around somewhere. Will you hold while I find him?"

"Yes." There was a click, and the strain of some soupy music drifted over the line. It took her a moment to recognize the tune. It was "The Sound of Music" in strings, completely de-balled. She looked over at the reception desk. Celia was yapping cheerfully, but Margaret was scowling at Phylis. Phylis smiled and waved. *Bitch*.

The line suddenly clicked and Phylis feared she'd been cut off. Then it clicked again. "Phylis?"

"Paul?"

"Yes! How are you? Where are you?"

"Please, just listen for a minute. I need a very big favor, if your willing."

There was no delay. "You know I'm willing."

I know, she thought. *I'm using you. This is as bad as what you did to me*. "It's about what you said. You asked me if I knew anything about this place, about Lakeview. Remember? Well, I don't. I didn't even think about it before taking Celia here. Now, I know this is a nuisance, and if you don't want to do it then just tell me and I'll understand."

"You haven't told me what it is you want yet," he

said patiently.

Phylis lowered her voice. "Could you dig up some information on this place for me?"

"Sure, whatever you want. I might even get a story out of it."

Phylis chuckled. Paul could get a story out of anything. "Okay. It's called Lakeview Clinic, I think, or it might be Lakeview Research Center, or something like that. I'm not sure. It's run by a guy called Dr. Neville Brand," she spoke slowly so he could take notes. "He's assisted by Dr. John Gordon. They've both published papers on various subjects. They're doing research into something they call audio-neural-cue therapy, or mnemonic cue therapy, or maybe even primal sound therapy."

"Sounds weird."

"They tell me it's basically glorified word association games. But I'd like to know more. Oh, and maybe if you can find something on Dr. Harold Phelps. I'd appreciate it."

"I'll get on it right away," he said, then paused. "Is everything all right out there?"

"Sure. I'm just curious."

He paused again, then his voice suddenly lowered. "Have you thought about the other things I said?"

"You're forgiven."

"Not that. About us?"

"Paul, it's too soon." *Liar!*

"Okay. No pressure. You want me to bring what I find out to you?"

"No, just phone." She read him the number off the payphone. "Leave a message and I'll call back. We're supposed to be here another couple of weeks. Paul, I have to go. I really appreciate it."

"Bye," he said.

She hung up, then turned to face Margaret who was still glaring at her. Phylis smiled brightly.

"Everything okay?" Margaret asked.

"Just dandy," Phylis said.

When they got outside Phylis was startled by the change in the weather. They had been in the building less than fifteen minutes but the lake was now choppy under a gusting wind, and the grey clouds had blackened ominously and were moving swiftly eastward.

"Mommy! Mommy! It's going to rain!" Celia's voice was raised in a shriek of delight.

Phylis cringed under the violent sky. She had never understood Celia's joy at the explosive outbursts of nature. They started back towards the cabin, but as they came abreast of Number One Phylis paused and looked towards the woods. Wasn't that where the bear had burst out after them the other night? There were broken branches scattered about on the scraggly grass. What the hell, she thought, curiosity winning out over her concern about the weather.

Pulling Celia after her she walked to the edge of the tree line. This was it. Something had barged through the bushes here, breaking branches in its charge. The swath of destruction seemed very wide, almost four feet from side to side. Did bears get that fat? She glanced upward, her breath suddenly catching in her throat. Twelve feet up there were snapped branches hanging by tattered threads of bark.

Bears don't grow that tall.

The ground around her feet seem soft and moist, and struck by a thought she looked down. At first she could see nothing, but about six feet into the trees she saw a single print embedded in a patch of half dry mud.

"Oh my God."

A drop of rain splashed her cheek. Then another. Behind her, over the lake, a camera flashed. Lightning. The dull rumble of thunder rattled the air.

She continued to peer into the darkening woods. About six feet beyond the first print she saw another. Her heart hammered in her chest. Each print was roughly circular, about a foot in diameter, edged on one side by three smaller indentations. *Toes?*

The rain began to patter around them. The cold water made her gasp, and she seemed to come out of a daze. Holding Celia's hand she ran for the cabin. Lightning flickered in the distance.

Bear, hell, she thought.

She had never seen a bear big enough to leave prints like that. They looked more like the print an elephant might leave. But there were no elephants running free in Minnesota, were there? But, of course, she knew an elephant hadn't left those tracks.

There wasn't an elephant in the world that walked on only two feet.

CHAPTER EIGHTEEN

When they got back to the cabin Phylis dried
Celia's dripping hair with a Disneyland towel. The
rain had exploded from the sky after the first few
tentative drops, and now it hammered against the
roof and slashed the window of the small cabin with
astonishing intensity. Although it was still a few
hours until dusk the advancing clouds had brought a
darkness of their own and they were forced to turn
on the lights. The lake was a roiling jungle of waves
that seemed to jump and move in all directions,
frozen periodically by the strobe of lightning. At
those instants Phylis could see the full extent of the
cloud cover, the way the darkness above moved and
twisted, and her heart froze. Even Celia, who so
loved a storm, was taken aback by the ferocity of
this particular outburst of nature, and after a few
minutes of keen observation from the porch she retired to the living room with an anxious expression
on her face.

It was crazy, but the discovery of the strange
prints at the edge of the wood had not frightened
Phylis, and instead she felt a sense of resolve pos-
sessing her, a strong desire to get to the bottom of

this mystery.

But you should be scared, sister, she thought. *The feets that sank those holes was made for squashing.*

Though not frightened she had badly needed a drink, and it was with some relief that she discovered, tucked into a corner of the cupboard above the sink, the remnants of the Beaujolais John had brought over last week. There was enough for a glass and a half. The wine tasted somehow harsher and slightly thicker than it had when originally opened, but she managed to drain the last of it without difficulty. After a quick dinner of frozen turkey pie, at which Celia valiantly poked her fork without eating more than a mouthful, they sat together in the sofa to wait out the storm.

When the arc of a car's headlights splashed across the wall Phylis rose and went to the porch. John's brown Impala rolled to a stop beside her yellow Datsun and the lights cut out. John was peering through the windshield, face distorted by sheets of water. He waved and grinned.

"He'll get all wet," Celia said. She stood beside Phylis, face pressed to the screen.

John seemed to be waiting for a break in the downpour, but when it became obvious that no such break was coming he made a bolt for the cabin. He slammed through the porch door, shaking water from his hair. "Boy oh boy. I told you . . ."

". . . you get some doozies around here," Phylis finished for him, smiling.

"That's right." He brushed water from his windbreaker.

171

"Dora and David get away alright?"

"Sure," he wiped water from his face and unzipped the light jacket. "But I almost didn't make it back here. Couldn't see a darned thing in the rain."

"Poor John," Phylis said. She went into the kitchen and put on a pot of coffee. "Might as well just sit around with us, unless you've got other plans," she called through.

But John was already sitting on the sofa. When the coffee was ready she poured two cups and brought him one. Celia was sitting beside John, and Phylis was amused to see that her breathing was slow and regular. Asleep. John accepted the coffee, careful not to nudge Celia with his elbow.

"I guess the day was too exciting for her," he said softly, sipping the coffee. He smiled appreciatively.

"For me too," Phylis said.

"Oh?"

She had tried working out an approach to telling him about the tracks that would not make her sound crazy, but of course there was no way to do that, was there? Direct is best, she thought.

"I found something in the woods after you'd gone," Phylis said. She sipped her coffee.

John had been in the process of raising his cup for another sip, but the cup halted just below his chin. His brown eyes focussed full on her, but she could not read what was behind them. "Oh? What did you find?" His words were careful, as if he really did not want to know.

"I found tracks. At the place where we were chased the other night."

"Bear tracks, you mean?" He finished the upward lift of the cup and sipped the coffee.

"I don't think so. Some other kind of prints. They were too large to be bear tracks."

"You'd be surprised at how large bears can grow," he said, chuckling, as if he could now dismiss her finding.

"How large?"

"What?" She had caught him off guard.

"How large can they grow?"

He blinked. "Well, I don't really know. *Fairly* large."

"Twelve feet tall?"

"Twelve—" He suddenly seemed wary and Phylis did not like the look that passed across his face, but it was gone so quickly that afterwards she was not sure she had seen it at all. It was the look of somebody trapped. "That's a bit too tall," he said, again carefully understated.

"I found prints about a foot wide," Phylis said, holding up her hands to show him. "And the trees were damaged very high up around the path the thing had taken, as if it just knocked things down as it moved."

He studied the circle her hands formed, and then reached out and held her wrist. He gently lowered her arm. "Phylis, is it possible you imagined what you saw?"

Phylis blinked, a sudden stab of fury burning behind her eyes. "God damn it, John, don't use that condescending tone with me! I know what I saw!"

"Okay, okay." He jerked his hand back as if he'd

been burned, and his expression turned to one of hurt confusion.

Phylis suddenly felt guilty at her outburst. What she was saying must sound very strange. Worse, it probably sounded totally paranoid. "I'm sorry. I didn't mean to snap." She reached out and took his hand, squeezing gently.

"I'm sorry too," he said. "I didn't mean to sound like I didn't believe you. It's just that . . . well, they did shoot a bear over on the ridge. And there hasn't been any trouble since then."

Since David left, you mean, she thought. "Are you sure it was a bear?"

"That's what Wilkes said."

"But did you see it?"

"No, but—"

"Then it might have been something else."

He looked at her levelly before speaking again. "You could be right. There's a way to find out."

"How's that?"

"We'll drive to the compound tomorrow and ask Wilkes to show us the carcass. He did offer."

The simplicity of his suggestion caught her by surprise. "Well—"

"And you could show me your tracks. Hell, for all I know there is *something* lurking around the woods."

"Something?"

"Some animal. A large one." He shrugged.

Phylis suddenly felt a surge of tenderness for him. He was trying so damned hard to be supportive, yet she was acting as if *he* were the one trying to hide something. She suddenly felt ashamed. "The rain

174

will have washed the tracks away," she said.

"There might be others."

"I suppose I also could have exaggerated their size in my mind," Phylis said slowly. "It was a strange day, and the clouds were making things dark." She suddenly felt confused, not at all sure what she had seen.

"Phylis, don't"—he reached out and touched her cheek—"don't try to convince yourself one way or the other. That's too easy. Tomorrow we'll look and see what we can find. Okay?"

She held his hand against her cheek, and then kissed his palm. "Okay." She continued to kiss his hand, then began to use her tongue to probe the soft flesh between his fingers. John moaned. Phylis felt warmth spreading from her abdomen through her groin. Since their first night of passion they had kissed, and touched, but had refrained from going further, as if afraid that to do so might somehow jeopardize what they had. But now her desire was rising again. *I need this,* she thought. *I need him.*

Between them, Celia stirred in her sleep. Phylis let go of John's hand and nodded at Celia. "If we put her to bed we'll be alone," she whispered.

John's face was flushed. He nodded.

When he picked up Celia and cradled her in his arms Phylis had a sudden sense of deja vu.

Just like last time.

But when Celia's body suddenly stiffened, she knew this time that the treatment would take effect; Celia might yawn, or smile, or even go back to sleep, but she would do no more than that. So it

175

came as a great shock to Phylis when Celia's eyes snapped open in terror. When Celia's scream rent the air Phylis gasped and dropped both coffee mugs. The mugs smashed on the floor, sending the warm, dark liquid over Phylis's legs and across the linoleum. John reacted quickly. He lowered Celia immediately and stepped out of the swing of her small arm. For a moment this ugly tableau was frozen, as if in some terrible 3-D photograph, and then Celia sobbed and threw herself at John, hugging him fiercely.

"I'm sorry! I'm sorry! I didn't mean it!" Her voice was hysterical, wavering uncontrollably.

John kneeled and stroked her hair. "It's okay, Celia. It's okay."

Phylis snapped out of her stupefied paralysis and rushed to Celia. She held the child tightly. "Oh, baby, are you all right?"

Celia nodded, yawning. "Sleepy."

Phylis led Celia to her bedroom, and after changing her into her animal cracker nightgown she tucked Celia in. Sleep came immediately, and Celia's small face relaxed, Phylis kissed Celia's smooth, warm forehead, overcome with love. When she returned to the living room she found John sitting on the sofa, looking very thoughtful. Phylis plunked in next to him and sighed. "I thought it was all over," she said. "What happened?"

John squeezed her hand. "We told you at the beginning that the benefits of stage two were only temporary. Her condition is like a photograph that's been developed without going through the fixer.

Soon it fades to black."

"Is she ready for the next step?"

"I think so. That's for Dr. Brand to decide. But I think we could test her tomorrow, perhaps even commence the primal-sound treatment as soon as Monday."

Phylis nodded. Five minutes ago she had been ready for passionate love, now the heat had gone. But she could not . . . *would* not disappoint John. She reached for him and kissed him gently on the lips, probing with her tongue. Suddenly she felt his arms around her, but instead of pulling her closer he was pushing her away. The look on his face was of concern.

"Phylis . . . I won't say I don't want you right now, because I do. Very much. But I think we should wait. For Celia's sake." The words seemed to come out with great effort, and with even greater effort he rose to his feet.

Phylis looked up at him in awe. In one moment her feeling for him had jumped from *fond affection* to something very close to *love*. He pulled her to her feet and kissed her, and she responded fully. "We'll have our night together, don't worry," he said hoarsely.

She watched him run to his car, pelted by rain, and waved as the Impala turned and drove towards the main building, water splashing up around its wheels.

Honey, you are falling like a ton of bricks!

She smiled.

Outside, the rain continued to fall like bullets. A

sudden flash of lightning revealed the lake, alive with large swells. The lightning flashed again, and this time her attention was drawn to the trees. They swayed in the brief moment of light. Swayed invitingly.

Come in and discover our mysteries.

She turned away from the lush, inviting darkness, and returned, shivering, to the warmth of the cabin.

CHAPTER NINETEEN

On Friday, after completing a second audio-emotional topograph of Celia, Dr. Brand concurred with John's opinion that they proceed with the primal-sound-cue stage of the treatment. When Phylis brought Celia to the main building on Monday morning a slate grey sky pressed low over the lake, making the woods look more black than green. The forecast was for occasional sun and a significant warming. Phylis hoped it would happen soon. The weekend weather had depressed her and Margaret Palin's icy demeanor did nothing to cheer her up.

"Will you be observing this morning?" Margaret had already come to the front of the reception desk to lead Celia away.

"Yes, I think I will," Phylis said, more from a desire to somehow change the predictable routine than to actually observe the proceedings. Besides, Dora was gone. What else was there to do?

Margaret stopped in mid-stride. "You'll be alone. Dr. Gordon's presence is required for the procedure."

This attempt by Margaret at dissuasion only served to firm Phylis's resolve. "That's fine," she said, smiling tightly. "I could use a little solitude."

Margaret nodded curtly and led Celia down the hall. Celia turned and smiled at Phylis before disappearing into the treatment room. When she entered the observation room Phylis felt a slight chill spread over her neck, the memory of the synthesizer voice suddenly coming back to her. Through the glass she watched as Celia hiked herself onto the couch, pushing back against the headrest to find a comfortable position. Dr. Brand was typing something at the terminal's keyboard while John was bent over the telemetry unit looking grim. They seemed to be speaking to each other, but only in curt, short sentences. When Margaret approached John and said something to him he glanced through the glass at Phylis. He can't see me, she thought, it's a mirror on the other side. But she felt uncomfortable. John said something to Brand and then left the room. A moment later he came into the observation room. He was smiling.

"Margaret tells me you want to watch," he said.

Phylis glanced sharply through the glass at Margaret who was talking to Celia. *Meddling bitch!* "Is there something wrong with that?"

"Certainly not!" He leaned closer to her and kissed her warmly on the lips, lingering much longer than was necessary for a good-morning kiss.

"Hello to you too," Phylis said.

He grinned and again leaned closer. "Another?"

"Not unless you want to start something I'll have to finish." She blocked his advance with her forearm and smiled lasciviously.

"Promise?"

Phylis chuckled. "Celia asked me to ask you when you're going to keep *your* promise and buy her an ice cream cone." The change of subject was crude but effective.

John's face went blank. Then he slapped his forehead. "Jesus, I forgot." He looked at Celia through the glass, his face softening affectionately. "Well, we should be finished here by early afternoon. We could go over to Battle Lake later, if you want."

"Celia will make you a friend for life."

He turned to Phylis and stared into her eyes. "I hope so."

His deep brown eyes made her swoon, filling her with the desire to lean into him and be held, but she backed away. What he had said needed some kind of response, but what she did not know. Again, she felt the rush of events moving too quickly. Needing to fill the silence she said, "Uh, can I listen in again?"

"I wouldn't recommend it," he said quickly.

"Why not?"

"We're dealing with primal sounds at this stage. They're quite psycho-active and you might not appreciate the effect."

"Psycho-active?" She had heard of psycho-active drugs, like marijuana and LSD, but sounds?

"I mean, they can elicit a very strong emotional responses. Stronger than you might expect."

"Sounds?" She said the word softly.

"We were using *words* last time, Phylis, spoken and understood at a conscious level. This time we're using *sounds* aimed directly at the unconscious."

"Yes, but not aimed at me. I don't see . . ."

He took a sudden step towards her, his face twisted in rage. "You stupid bitch!"

Phylis stumbled away from him, hand jerking to her

mouth. *What had he called her?*

But he was smiling again. "See? Those were just words, and you exhibited a pronounced emotional response."

Phylis was suddenly furious at John, and at herself for having reacted to what was now obviously a demonstration. "You just called me a bitch!"

He stepped into the circle of her arms and held her close to his chest despite her angry struggles. "I could just as easily have said, *I love you*." He kissed her gently on the lips.

Phylis stopped struggling. She felt like a puppet being jerked around by a master who's hands were engaged in a war with each other. Had that been another demonstration?

"Now, admittedly we'll be using sounds aimed specifically at Celia, but certain sounds are common to all of our psyches. They can have a much more profound effect than the words I just used."

"Okay. I get the point. I won't listen."

He kissed her again. "It's for your own good."

When he left she found that she was shaking like a leaf. Had he meant what he'd said? *I love you*. With a trembling hand she fumbled a cigarette to her mouth and lit it. She inhaled the smoke deeply into her lungs, hissing it out slowly. Or had he merely been giving a further demonstration of the power of words?

Damn it! He had her acting like a silly school girl.

The trouble was, she was beginning to like it. "Falling in love is a disease that gets worse as it progresses." As a teenager she'd had a friend, Mary Fillmon, who used to say that. Mary had always exhibited symptoms of the disease, while Phylis had somehow been immune.

But now she was showing all the signs of a thorough infection.

In the treatment room everything looked ready. John and Margaret were looking expectantly at Dr. Brand. He suddenly nodded his head and Margaret leaned over Celia. She touched the syringe full of HG-37 to Celia's arm, finding a vein with practiced ease, and smiled slightly as she slid the needle into Celia's flesh. Phylis winced. But Celia didn't even blink. Jesus, Phylis thought, she's getting used to this kind of torture. Margaret slid the earphone helmet into place and stepped back.

A lump rose in Phylis's throat. Celia looked helpless sitting there, fragile. From her neck down she was a little girl, her pale hands folded across her stomach, her blue dress slightly rumpled about her hips, her knees showing the perpetual smudges of freckles. But her head was the gleaming faceless mask of a robot. For a moment she imagined Celia as an evil hybrid of flesh and machine and she took a hard drag on her cigarette to rid herself of the image. The hot smoke burned her throat and mouth.

Dr. Brand checked his watch, nodded to John, then tapped the keyboard of the terminal. The bank of equipment flashed to life like some multi-million dollar home-stereo prototype. John and Dr. Brand immediately became occupied in making adjustments to the complicated equipment.

At first Celia seemed oblivious to the sudden burst of electronic life, but soon her hands began to knead one another, her heels clicked rhythmically together, and suddenly, without warning, she spasmed as if a bolt of electricity had sizzled through her. Her small body arched off the couch, vibrating like a high tension wire, then crashed back to the padded surface.

"Oh my God," Phylis whispered.

What am I letting them do to you?

Margaret Palin bent over Celia, her face creased with concern. She looked up and said something to Dr. Brand. Brand turned, frowned, then shook his head. John, who had been staring at the telemetry deck in disbelief, was now looking over at Celia with open wonder on his face.

Phylis pressed close to the glass, almost touching it, hands rigid and white against the lower sill. Her thoughts were in turmoil, but one phrase echoed through her head until she was not sure if she had spoken it out loud.

What are they doing to my baby?

Despite John's warning, motherly instincts flaring to life like a huge engine suddenly given full throttle, she reached out and turned the knob that activated the speaker box.

At first all she could hear was a low rumble. Soon, however, her mind tuned itself to what she was hearing, and the background hiss began to change its form. It was like being at a party where everybody was talking at the same time, she thought. Information overload. *Nothing makes sense.* But soon she became aware of a pattern, or a *beat* within the steady noise. It was like the slow, subdued plunking of a bass guitar, or the thick, steady thump of a kettle drum, and yet it was also like a voice shouting to be heard above a roaring surf. And that voice was hauntingly familiar, she thought.

She strained to hear it, strained to focus herself on what it was saying, only marginally aware that each time it spoke Celia's small body threw itself into a quivering arch above the couch.

What was it saying? It wasn't even a voice, really. Just a sound. A sound she had heard before. She cocked her head and listened carefully. The beat came, the voice spoke.

A gurgle, inarticulate and feeble. She felt her own mouth trying to form around the sound, but the beat was gone. Phylis frowned in consternation. Where had she heard it before? It was on the tip of her tongue. The crescendo came again, Celia's body spasmed.

This time Phylis's lips moved, and a sound emerged from her mouth, a distorted echo of what was emerging from the speaker box, but recognizable. *I've said that before.* The knowledge came with such surety that she could not deny it. But what did it mean? The sound, hardly capable of being spoken at all, was certainly not a *word*. There was no dictionary definition for it, she was sure of that. But even so, vague memories, disturbing and frightening, were rising within her.

The beat came again. And this time it clicked. The wavering sound seemed to pop up in her mind like a thick, sticky bubble. No wonder it had been hard to remember! She had been trying to impose a linguistic interpretation on something . . . *primal.* It was like saying "whack" to signify a hand hitting a face, or "slam" for a baseball bat connecting with the ball, or "blam" for the firing of a gun. A sound, never meant to be articulated as a word. Sometimes you got close, sometimes you missed.

In her normal voice she said: "Daahg."

Then: *Where have I heard that before?*

The memory came at her in a rush of images that left her reeling on her feet, breathless and dizzy. It was as if her mind suddenly came unmoored and began to drift, to wander freely. She was no longer standing in the observation room, no longer even within the body to which she had grown accustomed, but instead had returned to an earlier time, to a much smaller body, a much less coordinated body, and this new room was one she would come to know well as she grew older. But in the memory, so much like a dream, she had no language to express *bedroom*. She was only six weeks old, and this was her new world.

There were shadows and shapes that moved across her field of vision and when they passed she forgot they ever existed. They were just gone, until they returned. There were pale things that wriggled in front of her, and she was only vaguely aware that they might actually be *part* of her, but it would be a long time before she learned to call them *hands* and feet.

Mostly there was the hunger, and there was the Big Warmth that would appear before her and surround her with its smell and fill her mouth with its flesh so that she could suck and feed. It would be many months before she would utter the word *Mama,* but even now her baby's mind understood her relationship to the Big Warmth. There was also the other Big One, but she knew less of it. It would surround her sometimes, but it would not feed her, and it could not provide the comfort she craved. Her life revolved around these things. She gauged time only by her hunger and the appearance of the feeding flesh.

186

But there were also the sounds.

She had suckled, and now she verged on the other world, the dark sleep world. The Big Warmth had held her until she was very close to the darkness, and she had hardly noticed its departure. But something made her eyes snap open. Her baby's face registered fear. The world was darkness. Vague shapes drifted before her eyes.

And she knew she was not alone.

It came to her in the dark, as it always did, and huddled somewhere just beyond her sight. Her wide eyes searched the darkness and found nothing. But she knew, as only a baby can know, that it was in the room with her. It was waiting for her to slip into the other world, and then it would have her. A noise bubbled in her throat, a tiny wail of fear that would mean nothing to anyone who heard it, but which expressed all her horror and fear and misery. The sound was not a word, but for the baby it was a name for the thing that came to her room.

"Daahg." A baby's gurgle. A *name*, in the adult word she would later occupy, that would be stripped of its reality, and most of its horror, and used merely to indicate the physical state most closely resembling the real thing. *Dark*.

And even as her tiny mouth released the sound the blazing yellow eyes blinked open and she began to scream, and scream, and scream, until an eternity later the Big Warmth came and took the darkness away. For a while.

Phylis snapped back with a gasp that jolted her body painfully. The observation room seemed to shimmer around her, as if *this* were the memory and the other

187

place was reality.

My God, what's happening to me?

The treatment room was darker than it should have been. The rows of fluorescent bulbs on the ceiling were bright, but their light was being sucked away.

Sucked into a large patch of darkness on the wall behind Celia.

A patch of darkness in which Phylis could discern, like a shadow, the outline of a head. Too large for a human head, she thought.

Too large for bear tracks.

Out of the darkness two long ropes of shadow began to emerge, pushing into the room like arms.

Celia opened her mouth and screamed.

Behind her, in the blackness, the shadow face appeared to smile, and suddenly its eyes blinked open.

Blazing yellow.

"Dark," Phylis whispered in horror. Then she folded into her own darkness.

CHAPTER TWENTY

Phylis woke gagging, nose burning from smelling salts. She sputtered, coughed, tried to push the horrible odor away, and finally bolted upright as a spasm of nausea swept through her. John's voice came to her from down a long tunnel, echoing, getting louder, until suddenly the world shifted and slipped back into place.

"Phylis, are you all right?"

Phylis blinked, everything coming back into focus. She was sitting on the floor of the observation room, the linoleum cool beneath her palms, and John was leaning over her, his brown face looking worried. Her head throbbed painfully. "Oh, God," she muttered, placing one hand against her forehead. Everything began to come back in a rush. "Where's Celia? What happened in there?"

"Whoa!" John put an arm across her shoulder to stop her from getting up. "You jump around like that and you'll faint again."

Margaret Palin was looking scornfully down at her, but somehow Margaret didn't seem important just now. She turned to John and keeping her voice calm she asked: "What happened in there?"

"Nothing. Everything was fine."

She could hardly believe what she had heard. "Bullshit," she muttered, and this time brushed off his hand as he tried to support her. She stood, wavering on her feet, fighting the sudden dizziness. The fluorescent bulbs above strobed annoyingly, aggravating the pain in her head, but in a moment she began to feel better. "I saw that . . . thing!" She turned angrily to John.

His eyes widened in confusion. "What thing?"

What was the matter with him? He had been right there in the room with Celia, he must have seen it. She wanted to grab him and shake him and make him admit it, but when she looked through the glass, she could see that Celia lay comfortably on the couch, groggy but apparently well. Dr. Brand was standing beside her, talking, smiling, talking again.

"I thought I saw . . ." What *had* she seen? The whole thing had taken on the dimensions of a nightmare. When John touched her arm she twirled in surprise.

He drew his hand away, then laid it gently on her arm again. "Did you listen in?"

Phylis blushed. "I was worried," she said in a small guilty voice. The memory of Celia galvanized in a trembling arch above the couch was indelibly etched in her mind.

"I told you, those sounds are *very* psycho-active."

"It didn't happen in my head," Phylis said quickly, turning away from him. "I saw something in that room." She suddenly felt confused and angry, but

190

unsure where her anger should be directed. Were they lying to her? Trying to hide something from her? If so, why? But when she turned again to face John his face was lined not with deception, but with concern.

"Phylis, nothing happened. The session went well."

Phylis lowered her head. She felt exhausted, close to breaking into tears. Could she possibly have been hallucinating? Nothing like this had happened to her before. She had always been so levelheaded. Even in university when she had dabbled occasionally with drugs she had been aware, always, that what she was experiencing was drug induced. She had never fallen for a hallucination. Not until now anyway.

John was holding out his hand towards her, palm up, and she saw there were two little yellow pills nestled against the brown skin. She blinked, then looked up at him.

"These are sedatives. I want you to go back to your cabin. Take one of them. It will help you relax, but it won't knock you out. You can read, or sit outside. You can take the second one if you need it."

She opened her mouth to argue but he put a finger to her lips. "Please, Phylis. You're strung out." His eyes were tender, almost pleading, and she could not bring herself to square off against him. She took the pills from his hand. "Oh, all right," she said.

He smiled. "And let Margaret walk you back to

your cabin, okay? I don't want you fainting again."

"Can't you come?" The thought of being escorted by Margaret was not appealing.

"I have to go over the results of the session with Dr. Brand. I'll bring Celia around when we're finished, okay?"

Phylis nodded reluctantly, feeling very foolish, like a school girl who had upchucked after her first drink. And she certainly wasn't getting any sympathy from Margaret. On the contrary, she seemed to sense disdain and hostility coming from the other woman, and this made her feel worse. Margaret was ice cool and in control, while Phylis had just demonstrated that she was foolish and weak.

In the treatment room Celia was giggling, covering her mouth with her hand, and Dr. Brand was smiling pleasantly. *Like nothing happened.* But something else caught Phylis's eye. To the left of the couch, on the wall behind Celia's head, there were faint streaks in the paint. Like claw marks. They had not been there before. Or had they? If she said something John was sure to have an explanation. He seemed to have a lot of those.

Damn it, don't become paranoid!

She turned away, disgusted at herself, and left the observation room followed by Margaret. John squeezed her hand affectionately before turning into the treatment room, and she forced herself to give him a warm smile. Walking down the hallway she was extremely conscious of Margaret's proximity behind her, as if the other woman were some sort of guard or attendant. As they entered the reception area Phylis stopped, blinking in surprise. An OUT OF ORDER sign was taped to the pay phone. She stared at it a full five seconds before turning to Margaret in alarm.

"The phone. It was working a couple of days ago," she said.

Margaret shrugged. "They'll be sending somebody down this week to repair it, but we don't sit high on their priority list." She smiled sympathetically.

A sudden chill spread across Phylis's neck. How would Paul Welch manage to call her now? It suddenly seemed very important that she be able to contact somebody on the outside. With the pay-phone out of order she was effectively cut off, like a prisoner. *Maybe it was broken on purpose.* The suspicion came and sat on her chest like a hundred pound weight and she suddenly felt short of breath. She leaned against the reception counter for support and placed her black purse on top of it. When she peered over the edge of the counter she could see the beige phone on the corner of the desk.

"I'd like to use your phone, Margaret, if that's okay. I've got a call to make."

Margaret's lips tightened and she regarded Phylis appraisingly. "I'm sorry, but that phone is not for personal use."

Phylis felt something tighten in her gut. Not anger, and not fear, but something that made her lips curl up in a smile. A look of indecision played across Margaret's flat, pale features. "Margaret, I have a call to make. I want to make it *now*, and I want to make it privately. Either you leave me alone for a few minutes to make my call or I'm taking Celia and we're getting the hell out of this place. Now that might be fine with you, but I doubt it will sit well with Dr. Brand or Dr. Gordon."

Margaret's face froze. Something dangerous came to life behind her small eyes but was immediately smothered. She reached over the counter, picked up the phone, and placed it gently in front of Phylis. Her smile was not pleasant.

"Thank you," Phylis said.

Margaret turned and walked quickly back down the hallway to the treatment room. Phylis felt elated, her sense of weakness and inferiority shrinking quickly. That was one woman she didn't want to meet in a dark alley. She opened her purse, rummaged briefly, and pulled out a crumpled piece of paper. She spread the paper on the counter, picked up the receiver and dialed the hastily scrawled number. The phone rang six times before it was answered by a grating female voice.

"Room 216," Phylis said. After the connection was made the phone rang another four times.

The voice that finally answered was soft and tired sounding. *Weary,* Phylis thought. "Hello?"

Phylis cupped the mouthpiece and kept her voice low. "Dr. Phelps?"

Silence. Then a tentative, "Yes?"

"This is Phylis Reynolds, over at Lakeview. You came to see me a while ago."

Another pause, this one longer. "What is it?" The voice was sharper.

"You said I should call you if . . . if something

happened. Well, I think something has happened. And I'd like to talk to you about it."

"Can you talk now?"

Down the hallway John and Margaret emerged from the treatment room and began walking towards the reception area, their footsteps loud on the gleaming linoleum. "No. Not now. But I'll try to come into Battle Lake later today. I have to go now." She did not wait for his reply, but gently laid the receiver back in its cradle. When John and Margaret turned the corner she was clipping her purse closed, and she smiled at them. "All done," she said.

John's eyes moved from her face to the phone then back again. He smiled. "Sorry about the payphone. I told Margaret earlier to let you use the desk phone if you needed it, but she was worried about your agitated state. If you need to use it again please feel free to do so."

She gaped at him in astonishment, her ideas of being cut off and held prisoner now a lot of foolish claptrap. *Girl*, she thought, *you really are becoming paranoid.*

"I didn't mean to snap at Margaret," she said, now embarrassed at the outburst she had initially been proud of. "I guess I *was* a bit agitated."

Margaret smiled. "I understand, Mrs. Reynolds." Somehow the smile did not quite make it.

"I do feel better now, though," Phylis said, looking at John. "I think I might take a ride into Battle Lake if you're going to be busy with Celia for a while."

"Sure," John nodded. "Enjoy yourself. There's a couple of interesting knickknack stores if you're looking for souvenirs."

Phylis nodded, relieved. John stepped closer to her, and even though Margaret was looking on he kissed her thoroughly. She felt herself melt into his arms, and all her suspicions melted with her.

"I didn't tell you earlier," he said once they had parted. "But Captain Wilkes has invited us down to see the prime specimen his men bagged. He apologized for not being able to accommodate us earlier, but any time we want he'll be happy to receive us. He still says the thing is ours."

Phylis blinked. She had forgotten about the bear, but John's words brought it back with a twinge of unease. She remembered the tracks in the woods. Though she had taken John out to see them on Friday morning the rain had done a good job of cleaning everything up. Even the hanging branches had been knocked down by wind and rain. Had she also imagined the tracks? No, and she was sure they had not been made by a bear. "How about later this afternoon? When I'm back and you're finished."

"Fine," he said. Then he squeezed her hand. "Got to run. Have fun." He walked away, his footsteps echoing in the empty hallway.

Phylis smiled at Margaret, even more embarrassed now that they were alone. "I can get back myself," Phylis said.

"If you're sure." Margaret said.

Phylis nodded. "Thanks anyway."

Outside the fresh air made her feel better. Whether she had imagined everything in the observation room or not, *something* had happened, and she wanted to know what it had been. Her earlier panic had put her on the verge of grabbing Celia and running, of forgetting the therapy and heading straight back to Minneapolis. But that initial panic was gone and another, more rational urge had taken its place. *You're here for Celia,* she told herself. *Don't fail her again!*

To her left, as she walked, the woods were quiet as death.

CHAPTER TWENTY-ONE

Dust exploded around the Datsun as she passed through Lakeview's gate and hit the dry gravel. She lit a cigarette and breathed smoke, opening the window slightly to let it out. The forecasters had been right about the weather. The clouds had slowly cleared and now the temperature was rising, heralding the arrival of an idyllic early September Minnesota afternoon. She'd changed into shorts and a pastel-colored blouse at the cabin, and now her thighs were sticking wetly to the vinyl seat. When she passed the army compound five minutes later she did a double take; the gravel courtyard was a maze of green Jeeps and other vehicles. The place had been deserted two weeks ago! The guard in the gate-shack nodded to her as she drove by, as if he knew her, and she wondered if he was one of the men who had been in the camp the day David was missing.

It was a great relief when she finally turned the small car onto the blacktop of 210 and could loosen her white-knuckled grip on the steering wheel. The trees zoomed by in a green collage, and once or twice she glimpsed the glitter of the lake through the thick foliage. The road cut a winding ribbon through the gentle hills. When she turned into Battle Lake she was mildy surprised to see the town veritably empty, a sharp contrast to the colorful activity during the last two trips. But it was Monday, the weekenders were back to the concrete city, and the regulars weren't prone to wandering like tourists. She found a parking spot right in front of the ice cream parlor.

The Otter-Tail Hotel was a two story woodframe structure that had been one of the first buildings erected in the town, though it was getting a lot less use these days than it had twenty, or even ten years ago. The bar still did pretty good business though, from weekenders as well as regulars. Although it was not air-conditioned an ornate brass-trimmed overhead fan did a good job of circulating the lobby air. The desk clerk was a stooped woman who looked about eighty years old and not nearly ready for the grave. She looked up as Phylis entered the lobby, her tiny dark eyes giving the younger woman a thorough appraisal before deciding, with an expert's eye, that Phylis was not a paying customer and likely never would be.

Phylis climbed the creaking wooden stairs to the second floor where the sharp tang of pine-scented disinfectant filled the air. An old man who might have been the twin of the desk clerk was mopping the hallway floor. It looked spotless to Phylis. His grey-headed mop left great glistening streaks on the dry wood. He did not look up as Phylis walked by, but stopped moving the mop until she was out of reach.

She knocked on the door of 216. She waited ten seconds then knocked again. When the door swung open she took an involuntary step backwards, hissing out air she had unknowingly held in her lungs. Harold Phelps's eyes widened when he saw her, and then he smiled. She noticed at once that he was not wearing the bermuda shorts and blue dress shirt, but a baggy pair of green corduroy pants and a white short-sleeved shirt buttoned up to the neck. For that she felt relieved.

"Well, I really didn't think you'd come until tomorrow," he said. "Come in, please."

The room was spartan, containing only the single bed (neatly made), a straight backed wooden chair that might have been antique, and a squat chest of drawers with a mirror backing it. There were no pictures on the green walls, no cover on the single light-bulb, and the curtains on the window overlooking the street were bleak. Perhaps the hotel was frequented by hunters in the fall, Phylis speculated, and that type of person might enjoy this austerity. But for herself she thought she'd go nuts in a day or two. She wondered how Phelps had managed to stay here so long. A thick, almost sweet odor permeated the small room.

"You said on the phone that something had happened," Phelps said. In this environment he showed none of the nervousness, or fear, that he had exuded on their first meeting. He seemed more curi-

200

ous than anything, and his blue eyes gleamed sharply. He motioned for Phylis to sit on the edge of the bed and she did so.

"Mind if I smoke?" She took her cigarettes and lighter from her purse.

"Please do," Phelps said. He handed her an ashtray from the windowsill. It was filled with dark ash but no butts. He was pipe smoker, Phylis thought, identifying the sweet pungent odor she had sensed upon entering the room. She lit a cigarette and took two deep lungfuls of smoke.

"I'm not sure how to begin," she said, exhaling small puffs of smoke with each word. "I feel so silly now. I mean, it's probably nothing." It was only the fact that he had approached her earlier that allowed her to continue, for once she heard her voice talking and the things it said she knew that anyone other than Phelps would have thought her crazy. Even so, her face blushed hotly as she spoke. She told him of the noises in the woods, of David De-March's strange behavior, of the thing that had chased her, of the three shots and David's hysterical response, and of the tracks she had found. Finally she told him of the morning's events, of the sounds, and of what she had seen.

He listened carefully, his blue eyes gleaming, once or twice stopping her to clarify a point, and after she was finished he frowned deeply. She did not know what she had expected his reaction to be, but she was immensely relieved that he did not start laughing. In fact, he seemed to take it more seriously than Phylis did herself. Her cigarette had burned down and she lit another, adding to the smokey haze in the room.

"What exactly do you want from me?" Phelps asked, his voice calm and even.

"I'm not sure," Phylis said slowly. She had been frightened so badly this morning and he had seemed the only person she could turn to. "When I called you this morning I was positive that something had happened, something strange, maybe even dangerous. I guess I hoped you could help me sort it out. But now . . ."

"Now you're not sure," Phelps said, his thick lips turning into a smile that was at once friendly and mocking. It was a father's smile, Phylis thought. "You now think that perhaps Dr. Gordon is right and the primal sounds you heard precipitated a hallucination."

Phylis shrugged. "I guess so."

"You may even feel that all your fears and suspicions are unfounded," Phelps said, the smile still there.

Phylis nodded again, smiling now herself. Phelps's smile disappeared as if it had been sliced off his face. "Nothing could be farther from the truth," he said.

Phylis found herself locked on his blue eyes, unable to look away. She took a drag on the cigarette and finally managed to look down into her lap.

Phelps sighed. He had been sitting in the wooden chair, facing Phylis, but now he stood and leaned his pudgy body against the window frame and looked out into the street. "I'm going to tell you a few things," he said. "And then I'll give you some advice." He turned so that his rump was supported by the window sill and crossed his arms. "What do you know about the audio-neural-cue treatment?"

"Just what Dr. Brand told me. They change the emotional weight of words, and so the emotional weight of the memories that go along with them."

"That's the good part," Phelps said. "I was Dr. Brand's assistant for five years, working continuously on audio-cues. I even helped him develop the actual therapy. We had some marvelous results to begin with, especially with traumatized children. We managed to eliminate nonadaptive responses completely in most cases. Unfortunately, most of our results were short-lived. Many of our initial subjects reverted to their original states, some even worse than when they had started."

"They told me all that," Phylis said. "That's why they finish off with the primal sounds."

Phelps smiled, but it was a humorless thing. "Ah, yes, the primal-sound-cues. That was a late development. Dr. Brand and I were stumped for a long time by our inability to produce long lasting results. But two years ago Brand stumbled upon the work of a brilliant young psychologist named Timothy Heslap. Heslap had done some outstanding audio-neural research, but unlike us he was not using words. He called them primal sounds. Heslap's work was brilliant, though he was not so much interested in therapy as he was in the construction of a new model of the human mind. He managed to develop a model of unconscious structure that assimilated most of Freudian theory and went beyond it. You're familiar with Freud's model of the mind?"

"A little," Phylis said, trying to dredge up her old university psychology courses. "Uh, let's see. Conscious, pre-conscious, and unconscious. All our behavior explained as the interaction between animal desires, social mores, and conscience. Id, ego, and superego."

Phelps chuckled. " 'A' plus, my dear. Simply put, but basically correct. The favorite analogy is of an iceberg. The tip floating above the water is conscious thought, while the bulk of the berg below the water is the unconscious mind."

Phylis nodded, smiling. Her psychology professor had used the same illustration.

"The common ground of most mind models is this: they assume that each human mind in an isolated effect. You are you, I am me, separate and distinct. Heslap's model is similar, but with one major difference. He postulates a level *below* the unconscious. Forget the iceberg, and think instead of a group of small islands surrounded by the sea. On the surface they are isolated, but really they are the tips of mountains that extend far below the water. If you go down far enough you can see that they emerge from the same sea bed. They are joined."

Phylis blinked, trying to comprehend this new model.

"Heslap called this sea bed Nether. The common ground of all minds. He tended to think of Nether as a dumping ground for all the things the conscious and unconscious could not assimilate. A mental garbage ground for humanity. He even expressed the opinion that Nether might actually be a *place,* just a different aspect of our own reality."

"I don't quite see where this is taking us," Phylis said, but had the funny sensation that she *did*, in fact, see, and that she did not want to see any more.

"As I said, Heslap wasn't interested in therapy, and Dr. Brand was not interested in new models of the mind. All Brand saw was that the primal sounds could be used to modify the audio-neural treatment. Using Heslap's primal sounds we managed to stablize the under-structure of the work we did at the conscious and unconscious levels. You see, the primal sounds work almost exclusively in the domain of Nether. They hardly affect the unconscious or conscious mind at all. At last we were able to achieve long lasting effects."

Phelps was sweating now, and tiny rivulets dripped down the side of his face and neck, to gather at the tight collar of the shirt. He ran a pale hand through his hair. "Our research advanced quite rapidly after that. We discovered that by augmenting the level of certain neuro-transmitters found naturally in the brain we could enhance the effect of the therapy. We tried many with mixed results. One of the substances we tried was a synthetic enzyme developed at the University of Illinois. It was originally involved in research for enhancing vision, and Dr. Brand managed to procure a sample."

"HG-37," Phylis said softly.

Phelps nodded. "Yes. The only member of the HG synth-enzymes that is psycho-active by the way. We tried HG-37 on a young subject, let's call her Marsha, and according to our interim audio-neural topographs the therapy was astonishingly effective. Everything went well until . . ." Phelps paused and began stuffing a pipe with tobacco, seemingly incapable of talking at the same time.

"Until what?" Phylis said impatiently.

He borrowed Phylis's lighter, sucking the flame into the bowl until smoke billowed thickly into the room. He held the pipe stem with his teeth. "Everything went well until we got to the primal-sound stage of the treatment. Did you know that Heslap originally labeled them primal *keys?*"

Phylis shook her head. *Keys open doors,* she thought.

"We were near the end of the treatment when . . . something appeared in the room with us. One moment we were watching Marsha, the next moment there was something crawling out from under the bed. About the size of a large cat, or small dog, but it was like nothing we'd ever seen before. It seemed misshapen, almost *mutated,* like the caricature of a particularly nasty cat. We shut down the equipment, but the thing was still there. It didn't seem dangerous. It actually liked our attention, like a pet or something. But when Marsha saw it she became hysterical. It was the cat from her dreams, she told us. The cat that had attacked her when she was a baby, climbing into her crib to scratch at her face."

Phylis suddenly felt light-headed.

"But it wasn't a nightmare. It was real," Phelps said.

"This is crazy," Phylis said. She could not believe what Phelps had been saying. "Things just can't *appear!*"

"No, they can't," Phelps agreed. "But they can walk through doors."

Phylis stabbed him with her gaze. "Doors that primal keys open?"

Phelps nodded. "Nether is as real as this world around us, and the only doors are the human mind."

Phylis shuddered. "This is insane." She should get up and walk out right now, just get out in the sunshine and clean this shit out of her system. There was no way in the world that any of this could be true. No way . . .

"We were ecstatic," Phelps said. "This was *the* major scientific breakthrough of the century, and in a science that had been ridiculed from the moment of its inception. But we did not know how to proceed. At least, I didn't know. But Brand said this was a chance for us do some real research, to get some *real* backing. And he found it for us. The Defense

207

Department. Some weird secretive wing into very off-the-wall projects. They were intrigued. They were more than intrigued, they were *excited*. They saw *potential*. They wanted us to bring more things out of Nether. We complied. It was easy. Finally they wanted us to start bringing out *specific* things, a particular type of creature. Something that had weapons potential."

"Oh my God," Phylis said.

"This was more difficult," Phelps said. "Our subjects so far had managed to bring through relatively insignificant creatures. It was as if their mind's could not open the door wide enough. We began to look for the right kind of subjects. Children with traumas in the near past seemed to produce the best results, and again our research advanced. One day we brought out this thing . . . it was a man, I suppose, or at least it looked like a man. As much like a man as the first thing had looked like a cat. But it was different. It attacked and killed one of our nurses. We couldn't control it, and it escaped. By this time we had moved to Lakeview and it was no problem for the army to hunt it down."

Phylis was shaking her head, not wanting to hear any more, not wanting to know how Celia fitted in.

"That's when I wanted to stop it," Phelps said. "But Brand wouldn't. He kept saying that what we were doing might be bad now, but it would lead to good. I didn't think so. I began to have nightmares. I began to drink . . ."

Phelps looked down at his pale hands, then up at

Phylis again. He smiled. "Eventually Dr. Brand found it necessary to bring in another assistant. Dr. Gordon. A very nice young man, really, quite willing to follow orders. After a while I left Lakeview, and I came here. I wanted to be near. I knew what was going on, I knew what they were trying to bring through. I thought, at first, that I could stop it. But it looks like it's gone past that now."

"What do you mean?" The fear in her voice was obvious.

"They wanted something that was not based on reality, something *completely* Nether. A baby's imaginary monster, what could be less real?"

"But what can it do?"

Phelps shrugged. "I don't know. I have no idea."

Phylis was shaking her head in dismay. "Why *us?* Why Celia?"

"When you arrived at Lakeview with your daughter I knew something was going on," Phelps said. "After three days, more men arrived at the compound. It was is if they were getting ready for something. Something big. I assumed your daughter's preliminary audio-emotional topographs must have indicated she had . . . potential. I had to warn you, but—"

Phylis put out a hand to stop him from going any further. "Dr. Phelps. None of this makes sense. Celia is getting *better!* I can see it."

"I never said the therapy wasn't effective. But they're using you. Whatever has happened has happened, it can't be changed. But you must take your daughter and leave Lakeview immediately. Leave now. Just go and forget this place."

Phylis shook her head. He was repeating to her the same panicked thoughts she had fought off earlier. "I can't do that. I'm here for my daughter, to help get her better. Once before, I hurt her by *not* acting when I should have. This time I can't let my knee-jerk fear reaction push me into acting too quickly and taking Celia away from the only thing that's been able to help her."

"But you must! They'll keep using you until they get what they want!"

"I won't. I can't believe everything you've told me, Dr. Phelps. It's . . . too far out. If I did, I'd have to believe that a man I've come to like, and trust very much, has been lying to me. I *am* going to try and find out what's going on here. But I won't leave until I do. There's too much at stake."

Phelps pushed violently away from the window, waving his pipe at her, but suddenly his twisted features softened like a balloon losing its air. "I'm sorry, I . . ." He turned to the window, shaking his head. "You must do as you think best. But please consider this. What if they won't let you leave later?"

Phylis stood slowly. "I'll deal with that when it comes."

"It may have come now," Phelps said.

Frowning, Phylis went to the window and followed his gaze. In the street an army Jeep was parked two vehicles away from the Datsun. The two men in it were licking at ice cream cones. They looked up at Phelps's window, then quickly turned away.

"Coincidence," Phylis said, but did not believe it.

"You won't leave?"

"I can't. For Celia."

"I wish I could change your mind," Phelps said. "But if you need help, if there's anything I can do . . ."

Phylis nodded. She walked to the door and opened it, but before leaving she turned and saw Phelps staring out the window, shaking his head sadly.

CHAPTER TWENTY-TWO

When Phylis got back to Lakeview John and Celia were down at the dock playing in the water. She parked the Datsun at the main building and walked slowly across the cool grass and down to the beach, warm sunlight playing across her skin. The clouds had broken up even more since she had left for Battle Lake, until now only a few fluffy renegades remained in the sky, hardly a danger to the sun which had just passed its zenith.

"Hi guys!" She waved as she stepped off the grassy ridge and into the sand.

Celia jumped halfway out of the water and squealed. "Hi Mommy!"

John turned and grinned. "Hi Mommy," he said, and his smile turned into something very suggestive.

Seeing John, Phylis remembered Phelps appraisal of him: *A very nice young man, really, quite willing to follow orders.* But whose orders?

Celia came running up the beach, her pumping legs churning the water into froth. She was wearing only her blue bikini with the white polka dots and Phylis could see, even before Celia was completely out of the water, that the skin of her shoulders had

212

turned alarmingly red. "Celia, you know better than to stay out in the sun without a T-shirt! Look at your shoulders. You're going to have a nasty sunburn now."

"I forgot," Celia said, not looking up at her mother.

John strolled slowly up to them, water dripping from his lean body. "Actually, I was the one who forgot. Blame me. I plead guilty."

Phylis sighed and put her hands on her hips in exasperation. "I don't know which of you is more of a child," she said.

Both Celia and John giggled. John raised his eyebrows. "Have a good trip?"

Phylis tried not to let her feelings show on her face. What Harold Phelps had told her had run through her mind during the drive back, but she still hadn't been able to accept or deny any of it. *Something* was going on at Lakeview, of that she was certain, but what it was she could not say. Could she trust John Gordon? She wanted to, with all her heart. They were *lovers* for God's sake, and that relationship implied a lot of trust and honesty. Didn't it? If he was lying to her, or trying to hide something from her, she'd be able to tell. She was sure of that.

All those thoughts ran through her head the moment after John spoke, her features trembling on the verge of a troubled frown, and she managed to smile finally. "It was relaxing."

John smiled. "Ready to inspect the grizzly of Otter Tail County?" he said ghoulishly, raising his hands like claws and baring his teeth.

213

He looked so silly that Phylis had to giggle.

"I want to see the bear, I want to see the bear!" Celia yelled.

"All right, but put on a shirt!" Phylis said.

As they walked back to the cabin John's fingers slipped into hers and she held his hand tightly. The day was bright, the wind whispered gently through the trees, and all her suspicions seemed foolish. Light of day can destroy any conspiracy, Phylis thought.

"How did it go . . . after I left?" she asked.

"Celia is showing marked improvement," John said after a pause. "We did a quick map after the session and we're seeing a dramatic stabilizing of her emotional responses."

"Which means?"

"Which means you won't be here much longer," John said, squeezing her hand. There was a slight tone of sadness in his voice. "I think a couple of more sessions will about do it."

"And after we leave?" The question was one that had been growing in the back of Phylis's mind like a tumor. How far would this relationship go? The trees trembled in the gentle breeze, their green leaves seeming to change color as the wind altered their angle to the sun. The thought of going back to the concrete and stink of Minneapolis, which she had always thought of as *clean*, was not appealing.

"Minneapolis is a four hour drive," John said, "Three for me. That is, if you wanted to continue . . ." His words trailed off into silence.

Phylis squeezed his hand. "I want to," she whispered.

Up ahead Celia threw open the door of the cabin and disappeared inside. John tugged Phylis's hand and began walking more quickly. "C'mon. Let's check out your monster."

"Dr. Gordon," Captain Wilkes said gruffly, looking up from his desk. He smiled widely, his red lips splitting to reveal a set of large, square, perfectly white teeth. Then, more softly and with a slight tip of his head, "Mrs. Reynolds." He did not even deign to acknowledge Celia who stood by Phylis with her hand nestled within her mother's.

Wilkes office reflected the rugged appearance of the man, the cluttered desk obviously belonging to someone who did not care much for organization, who stayed in his office only out of necessity. On the wall behind him was a map of Minnesota, Battle Lake carefully marked with a red pin. The only other decoration was a department store oil painting of a mountain scene in winter. Phylis decided that she liked the office about as much as she liked Wilkes — not at all.

"We thought we'd come down and have a look at the creature that has been terrorizing our camp," John said. "Curiosity has gotten the better of us."

Wilkes grunted and stood up. In the confined space of the small office he looked even larger than Phylis remembered, his shoulders jutting squarely out from his neck, chest protruding like a heavily ribbed barrel. His twinkling grey eyes seemed to rest on Phylis for an unnecessarily long time and, again, she began to squirm under the scrutiny.

215

What was it about the man that made her feel so uncomfortable? It was as if he regarded her as some sort of specimen, and not as a human at all. When he came around the desk towards them Phylis took an involuntary step backwards, then blushed when it became obvious that he had noticed. But the corners of his mouth only twitched in an amused smile.

"Come along then, and I'll show you the sorry beast!"

They followed him out of the barracks and into the courtyard. He led them through the maze of Jeeps and cars to a small building, more of a shack really, against the fence at the north end of the compound. The trees surrounding the compound stirred restlessly in the breeze, but the air in the compound seemed stagnant and still. Phylis had the distinct impression that it was hotter here than down at Lakeview. Their passage across the gravel court yard stirred a cloud of dust that hung immobile, like a poison gas. Celia tugged at Phylis's hand, and when Phylis looked down Celia's eyes were wide with wonder. She gestured to the rows of green vehicles. "Is this a war, Mommy?"

Phylis shook her head. "Not yet, honey."

The door to the shack was padlocked and Wilkes opened it with one of the keys on the chain hanging from his belt. She'd read somewhere that men who displayed keyrings on their belts were insecure about their masculinity, or possibly latently homosexual, but for some reason Phylis didn't think this was the case with Wilkes. He probably wore it on his belt because, as he might put it, he *liked* the fucking thing on his belt thank you very much. He flicked a switch just inside the doorway and a hundred watt bulb blazed in the darkness. They followed him through the doorway.

It was some sort of storage shed for junk, Phylis thought. There were boxes piled against the wooden walls, some so tattered they looked like they'd been there for years. Seeing her gaze Wilkes said, "Old files. Unlike the private sector we have to keep our records forever." He chuckled again. "Last year I asked for permission to destroy our old files. I mean the really old ones, like more than twenty years old. They said, 'Sure, just make photocopies of everything you throw away.'" He laughed uproariously at his own joke.

On the hardwood floor at the center of the shack a canvas tarp covered something bulky. A thick smell rose from the floor, like rotten meat. Phylis bit down on a gag. Celia pinched her nose. "Pee-you!" she said.

Wilkes kicked the edge of the tarp and flipped it off to reveal the bear beneath. Phylis looked down in disbelief. The creature lay on its side in a gruesome parody of a fetus, hairy arms crossed over one another, large diamond shaped head cocked at a weird angle as if trying to listen to some far-away noise, mouth gaping to reveal rows of large teeth. The bear looked a lot like a large dog, Phylis thought, but it was a poor looking thing with patchy and dull fur, and she could even see ribs poking through the sagging skin of its chest. Black blood dripped from its open mouth to a glistening pool on the hardwood floor. There were three surgically precise holes in the bear's chest forming a crude triangle about two inches on a side, the flesh around them bruised and puffy. The black eyes were open and staring. Phylis had the impression they could see her. She imagined her image forming on the back of the dead eyes, like a photograph, and she shivered.

"Poor thing," Phylis said.

Wilkes grunted. "Piss poorest specimen of a brown bear I've ever laid eyes on," he agreed, misunderstanding her. "Would have stuffed the bastard but hell, I'd be embarrassed to have it hanging around."

"Bears are noble animals," John said, staring down at the carcass. "I mean, *usually* they are. It's a shame they have to encroach on man's domain."

"Maybe we're the ones encroaching on the bear's domain," Phylis said.

John did not reply, but Wilkes chuckled softly.

Celia crouched down and touched a finger to the bear's nose. Phylis jerked her back in disgust. "Celia, don't touch it. It's dead." Celia continued to stare.

Phylis estimated the length of the carcass to be about five feet. At best. A sudden image of the tattered branches twelve feet up the trunks of the trees flashed through her mind and she shook her head. She bent over and studied the rear paws. Though wide and flat they did not look at all like the tracks she had found. This animal looked pitiful in death, and she imagined that neither would it have been an impressive sight alive.

Looking down on it she shook her head slowly.

"Sonny," she said. The word emerged as a whisper.

"Silly, that's not Sonny," Celia said, as if her mother should know better.

Phylis regarded her daughter curiously but did not say anything more.

Wilkes grunted again. "I take it you don't want this flea-bitten bag of bones," he said, and smiled when John shook his head. "Good. Then I can get rid of the damned thing." He ushered them out into the bright sunlight.

Phylis frowned thoughtfully. This bear had not made the tracks she had found. She was certain. She took a deep breath of the clean air, glad to be out of the confines of the shack with its thick, dusty smell of death and decay.

"Captain," she said, turning as Wilkes closed the shack and locked it. "I was wondering, why have so many men moved in here during the past week or two? It was almost empty when I arrived."

Wilkes looked at her with a frown creasing his wide face. "Never empty," he said. "Government property. Always got to keep a minimum staff for upkeep. But we're coming up to autumn now, and this is a good place for exercises. No better training ground than the northern wilds of Minnesota!" He was grinning, but when he saw that Phylis was not smiling his grin faded. "Actually, Mam, we're preparing for our annual winter exercise. But don't worry, we never interfere with the operation of Lakeview."

John nodded in agreement.

"Where are the men now?" Phylis asked, scanning the deserted compound.

"Got 'em out on a day hike," Wilkes said, but did not elaborate.

He walked them back through the files of Jeeps to John's Impala parked next to the gate house, and as they approached it a squat cement bunker came into view behind the main barracks. Phylis had seen it earlier, when they had arrived, but had paid it no heed. Two armed men stood at attention outside the door. Phylis could see that the only windows on the small building were barred, and the door appeared to be made from iron.

"Our own little jail-house," Wilkes said, his voice almost a bark. "Sometimes it takes more than a walk in the woods to calm down the wild ones."

Phylis nodded uneasily, but something else was bothering her. As John turned the Impala onto the gravel road and headed back towards Lakeview she stole a final glance towards the cement bunker. The two man outside were supposedly guarding comrades who had misbehaved.

So why, she wondered, were they armed?

And why did they look so frightened?

CHAPTER TWENTY-THREE

Don Reynolds could not believe his luck.

It had been a week and a day ago that he'd arrived in Battle Lake, this pissant little shithole of a town squatting on the edge of a lake like a piece of dogshit next to a puddle. That first day it looked like he'd blown everything. He'd been browsing through that idiotic little flea market when he turned around and bumped noses with Phylis. He'd almost dropped a load in his pants. He wanted to meet her, yeah, but not like that, not out in the open with everybody watching. He wanted a private meeting, something in the quiet of night.

Her face had frozen when she'd spotted him, frozen in fear, and it was only blind good fortune that the rickety old bag had taken Phylis's attention away from him and allowed him to duck away behind a table piled high with paintings. He watched her through the spaces between the moon eyed children and dogs. She couldn't see him. She thought she'd been dreaming. Fucking hallucinating. He wanted to laugh. But he only smiled, watching her panic. Fucking stupid bitch, thinking she could run away from him.

He'd felt a twist of something else in his guts when she'd met up with the tall, brown man, but he'd fought that down. It was something that made him want to go up to her right then and have it out. But that would be no good. He wouldn't be able to do all that he wanted. So instead he'd stayed hidden, clenching and unclenching his fists.

And then he'd seen Celia. His heart had stopped. She'd grown since he'd last seen her, grown a lot. She wasn't a *baby* any more. She was a *girl* now. Her hair was longer, fuller, more . . . sexy. His breathing became ragged when he saw her, and he became hard.

He'd wanted to follow them in his car, and when they went to the dock and took off in that boat he'd been angry. Seething. He stood on the dock watching as the small boat disappeared across the lake beyond the point. There was no way to tell where it had gone. Even from here he could see that the lake was surrounded in cabins. They could have gone to any one.

He returned to his room at the Otter Tail Hotel. If Phylis had come into town once, she would come in again. And when she did he'd be waiting.

He hated the week he spent in Battle Lake. Hated it with a passion. He felt like going for drives sometimes, or renting a boat and going out on the water, but if he did that and Phylis came into town he'd miss her and he wasn't going to chance that. To make things worse the weather was piss poor, going from battering rain one day to blistering heat the next. He hated it. And so he spent most of his time in the hotel bar, looking out the window between the glowing lines of the neon Coors sign, waiting.

And finally Phylis had shown up.

Don was sitting in the bar sipping on a cold Strohs beer when the yellow Datsun rolled up to the ice cream parlor across the street. He sipped the beer slowly, watching carefully as Phylis emerged from the Datsun, her long legs glistening in the sun. Damn, she was a good looking bitch. He remembered fondly their first years together. It had been good then. Very good. Until Celia came along.

But Celia wasn't with her today. Phylis came across the street to the hotel, and Don turned his head away from the window lest she spot him. She went straight into the lobby of the hotel without a glance at the bar, and he heard her sandals slapping on the wooden stairs as she climbed. Who was she visiting? He had been here a week and he recognized almost everybody on sight. There were a couple of old-timers on the main floor, flea-bitten old men who spent their time on the dock fishing, and there was that pasty faced city fella on the second floor, two doors down from Don. Could that be who she was visiting? He couldn't imagine who else.

He finished the beer and went outside. His car was parked about twenty yards behind the Datsun, with four other cars parked between. She would never see him if he just sat there. With the car running and air-conditioning cranked up full he smoked unfiltered camels and studied the hotel. On the second floor he spotted the city fella in 216, leaning against the window. He seemed to be gesticulating with his hands, talking to somebody. Phylis? Where else could she be? Or was there maybe some young stud stashed in one of those rooms, and was she maybe humping him like crazy right now? He thought of the books he'd found in her bed-table drawer and anger suddenly welled in him. *Fucking bitch!*

Half an hour later the man in the window stepped away, then came back a moment later and looked into the street. Don sank into the seat trying to hide, but the man did not look toward the Ford. His pale face was looking across at the ice cream parlor. And suddenly Phylis was standing beside him at the window, following his gaze.

Don chuckled. Should have been more careful, bitch. I know where you are, and this time you have no boat to make good your escape. *Make good your escape.* That was a term they'd used well down at Stillwater. "Hey, Frank, when ya gonna make good your escape?" Or, "I hear tell Jody down in C-block made good his escape." Well, this time there'd be no escape for Phylis.

It wasn't long before Phylis came out of the hotel. She looked worried, he thought, and glanced nervously at an army Jeep in which two young soldiers sat licking at their ice cream cones. Or was that maybe lust on her face? Jesus Christ, couldn't she get enough? He'd seen the army boys drive up only a few minutes after Phylis, and they'd been sitting there ever since. It was like they too had been waiting for her.

The Datsun roared to life, spewing out a cloud of

smoke, then turned into the street and drove up to the highway. The Jeep waited a moment, then followed. Cigarette clamped between his lips, smiling faintly, Don put the Ford into gear and followed both cars.

The Datsun turned east on 210, quickly gathering speed. The Jeep waited until the Datsun had a good lead then followed. Don shook his head. What the fuck was going on here? After the Jeep had turned he followed at a reasonable distance. A fucking convoy, he thought.

Twenty minutes later the Datsun slowed and turned onto a narrow little road that looked like it might double back towards the lake, and the Jeep followed. Don stopped the Ford on the shoulder before the turn off, watching the clouds of gravel dust that were drifting in the air. Sunlight shining through the trees cut bright highlights in the choking dust, like stage lights in a smoke filled bar. Once the dust began to settle he turned onto the road and followed.

About a mile down the road he passed an army compound on the right, crawling with Jeeps, and he saw the two men who'd been following Phylis talking with a large guy in an officer's uniform. A guard at the gate followed the Ford as it passed, his black eyes unreadable. Don kept driving. None of their fucking business where he was going. He hadn't spotted Phylis's Datsun in the compound so that meant she had come this way. The remnants of the dust in the air confirmed that opinion.

A few miles later he slowed as a sign arched over

the road ahead. LAKEVIEW, it said. Nothing more. *Lakeview what?* He slowed the car and parked it. There had been no turn offs, no where else to go, so this was where she had to be.

He got out of the car and walked a few yards closer to the sign until he had a view of the clearing beyond. There was a large building down by the water, sort of like a motel except there was no sign. To the left were the row of cabins. Phylis's Datsun was parked in front of the large building, and down by the water he could see her, partially hidden by a small ridge. The lake glittered in the distance. Suddenly he heard Celia's voice, and then a man's voice, laughing, and he backed away so that he was hidden by the trees. Soon Celia came running over the ridge, followed closely by Phylis and the same tall brown dude that had been with her at Battle Lake. But now they were holding hands.

Don clamped his lips tight, fire growing in his gut. *The fucking, slutty bitch!* He watched as they walked along the row of cabins, and grinned as he saw them enter the third one along the row. Cabin Three.

He lit a cigarette and returned to the car. The sun was high and bright and the temperature had been rising steadily since morning. Don undid the top two buttons of his shirt. It was daylight now, but it would be dark tonight. Dark enough to do what he wanted.

He started the Ford, turned it quickly, and drove back along the gravel road towards the highway. Less than half an hour later he was sitting back at the Otter Tail Hotel's bar. The bartender's name was Lou, and he was wearing a plain white T-shirt tucked into baggy, faded blue jeans.

"Beer?"

Don shook his head. "Rye. Canadian Club."

"Don't got no Canadian Club."

"You got *any* rye for Christ's sake?"

"Got Five Star."

"Okay, then give me Five Star."

Lou nodded his grizzled head, pulled a bottle from a high shelf and poured a carefully measured shot into a glass. "Anything in it?"

"Neat." Don took the glass, held it to his lips, and tipped the burning liquid down his throat.

He grimaced then grinned and placed the glass on the counter. "One more."

Lou complied. Although Don spent most of his time in the bar he had never talked much with Lou. Neither he nor the bartender were big talkers. But now he had a question and likely Lou would have the answer.

"What's that place on the other side of the lake," Don asked, sipping his second rye.

"Other side of the lake?" Lou echoed, looking towards the east wall as if he could see across the water. "Well, there's the old army barracks. Ain't been used much for years."

"Oh?" He didn't mention that he'd seen a hundred million Jeeps sitting in the compound. "Anything else? A motel or something?"

Lou frowned, leaning his flabby white arms on the counter. "Was a motel once," he said. "A motel and cabins. Run by old Henry Turner and his wife Mabel. But that closed down a few years back. I think the state bought it up and gave it to some clinic."

"Clinic?" The glass of rye was suspended below his lips.

"For kids. Like a camp, except for *strange* kids." Lou grinned, twirling a finger at his temple and crossing his eyes. "You wanna go there?"

Don scoffed and looked away. When Lou shuffled to the end of the bar to polish glasses, Don let his mind ponder the situation. A clinic? Phylis had taken Celia, his daughter, to some wacked-out fucking clinic on the edge of the world? Why? He tossed back the rest of the shot and swallowed it with a gulp.

Well, it didn't matter any how. Celia wouldn't be staying there much longer. He was getting her out. *Making good her escape.*

Tonight.

CHAPTER TWENTY-FOUR

The visit to the army compound had disturbed Phylis much more than she cared to reveal at the time, and it was only Wilkes's presence that had stopped her from blurting all her suspicions and fears. *Not in front of this man.* And so she'd hemmed and hawed and accepted his answers as if nothing was wrong. It was only when John dropped them off at the cabin that her thoughts settled, only then that she took the time to think things through.

She sat at the porch table with a large glass of Pepsi and a cigarette, lulled by the glitter of the lake and the comfortable rustle of the trees.

Captain Wilkes's bear had not left the tracks she had found. She did not doubt that the bear had been shot somewhere in the woods, poor thing, but it was not the creature that had stalked her and John that night. She was beginning to believe that Harold Phelps might be saner than he appeared. David De-March seemed to believe the creature in the woods was Sonny, his imaginary playmate, but could it have been something, as Phelps suggested, that had walked out of Nether? David had not been frightened of the creature, whatever Sonny was, and had seemed to consider it a friend. But the thing Phylis had seen emerging from the wall behind Celia had not been friendly. Definitely not.

Celia came through and slammed a pile of comics on the porch table, and then began to flip through the brightly colored covers for something she hadn't read too often. Phylis had refrained from questioning Celia about the morning session, afraid of how the child might react, but now she knew that she must. Had she been afraid of the answers Celia might give? She drew hard on her cigarette, leaving the question unanswered.

"Celia, how did things go in your session this morning?"

Celia shrugged, eyes scanning the first page of a *Love Stories* comic. "Okay, I guess."

"Do you remember any of it?"

"Uh huh." She flipped the page.

Best to come right to the point, Phylis thought. "I was watching the session," she said.

Celia looked up, frowning. "I didn't see you."

"Did you see the mirror on the wall?"

Celia nodded, and suddenly her green eyes widened in understanding. "Oh! Is that like the mirror in Batman where you can see through it from the other side?"

"Yup," Phylis said.

Celia seemed delighted with this news. "Wow." She returned her attention to the comic.

"Do you want to know what I saw?"

Did she imagine it or did Celia suddenly stiffen? The child's grip on her comic seemed too tight, the paper on the verge of tearing beneath her fingers. She looked up at Phylis with a strange look on her face, as if resigned to the fact that Phylis was going to reveal what she saw. Celia nodded slowly.

"I saw . . . I *thought* I saw something coming out of the wall behind you," Phylis said. She tried to smile.

Celia looked very serious now. "What did it look like?" Her voice was soft, hushed, as if speaking of something terrible.

"It was dark. Like a shadow," Phylis said, the memory coming back without effort. "It had long arms. And yellow eyes."

Celia gasped. She looked at her mother in dismay. "I thought I was dreaming because of the sounds."

"I used to dream about it too, when I was just a baby," Phylis said.

Celia nodded fiercely. "The sounds made me think I was a baby again, and I remembered the thing . . ." Her words trailed off and her frown deepened.

"Dark" Phylis said, reflectively and even using the word as a name made a shiver run up her back.

Celia jerked back to attention, eyes wide. "Was I dreaming, Mommy? Was it in the room?"

"I don't know, honey. Dr. Gordon and Margaret were there too and they didn't see anything."

Celia turned back to her comic, but now she was obviously troubled. She stared at the page for a long time before turning it. Phylis, too, was troubled.

Dark had been a nightmare from her own childhood, the nameless, faceless, yellow-eyed beast that lurked at the bottom of her crib, waiting for her to go to sleep. How could Celia have had the same dream? Unless Phelps was right about the common unconscious. Nether.

The sun was dipping into the lake when John arrived to prepare dinner as he had promised. Phylis was still sitting at the porch table, now on her third glass of Pepsi and umpteenth cigarette. She had almost finished the book. Celia had retired to the living room with her comics. As John came into the porch Phylis put out a hand to stop him from entering the cabin.

"John, I need to talk with you."

"Can you do it as I work my gourmet magic?" He grinned.

Phylis shook her head. "Outside." She turned and called through to Celia. "Honey, John and I are going to sit outside for a minute."

"Okay," Celia said.

John frowned. "Sounds serious?"

"It is."

They went outside and sat on a small wooden bench against the front of the porch, leaning back against the warm wood, heads pressed into the screening. The setting sun had turned the lake to gold. It was a postcard view. Phylis had spent a long time that afternoon planning her approach. She did not want to confront John with accusations that he was a liar or had been hiding things from her. Their relationship would not stand up to an attack like

232

that. Besides, she did not believe that was true. She could not believe it. But in order for them to continue together she had to tell him all that she knew, all that she suspected.

"I saw Harold Phelps when I was in Battle Lake this morning," she said.

"Phelps?" He spat the name.

"I told him everything that happened since I came to Lakeview. I told him about the session this morning and about the thing I saw."

"What did he say?" Curiosity had overcome his disgust.

"He told me about the audio-neural therapy. Everything. He explained about the lower level of unconscious, the joined level. Nether. He also told me about the things that come come out of Nether during the primal-cue stage of the treatment."

"The things that come out of Nether?"

"Things like David DeMarch's imaginary playmate. Sonny. The one that chased us that night and left those tracks I found. He also told me about the Defense Department funding."

John turned to face her, his mouth hanging open in a surprised O. "You think David's playmate is real because of those tracks you found?"

"Not just that. There are lots of little things. Like the way the army is pouring into this area like something big is going down. Like the way Wilkes is guarding something in that bunker of his, something that has the two guards outside looking very frightened. And especially like that thing I saw this morning."

233

"But I told you, the primal sounds are very psycho-active. They can induce hallucinations."

"The same hallucination in mother and child?"

John turned his head sharply. "Celia saw it too?"

"She thought she was dreaming."

John pursed his lips and tugged at his chin with his fingers. "Phylis, I didn't see anything this morning. I've never seen anything like what you're talking about. I do know that we're dealing with a radically different therapy, despite my protests to the contrary, and we haven't begun to scratch the surface of its potential. But —"

"Was Phelps telling the truth? About Nether?"

John shrugged. "Timothy Heslap was, *is* a brilliant clinical psychologist. Granted, we have borrowed from his research to augment our own. His primal sound research helped us jump a barrier that had blocked Dr. Brand for a long time. But that doesn't mean we subscribe to all his theories. His "common unconscious" model of the human mind is widely disputed."

"Where does your funding come from?"

"I . . . I don't know. That's Dr. Brand's area. I'm just the hired help." He suddenly laughed nervously. "Why this third degree?"

Phylis drew a deep breath, then sighed it out. "John, I can't discount everything I've seen and heard. I know I'm not crazy, and I know there's something going on here, and it's centered around Celia." She paused and looked directly at him. "I'm not sure I want her to stay for another session. I'm thinking of packing up and leaving."

John blanched. "Don't do that. Celia is making marvelous progress. To take her away now, before we're sure that she's completely well, could be a big mistake."

"Knowing all I've told you, do you think it's wiser to stay here?"

John groaned. He reached out and grasped both Phylis's hands in his own. "Look, what you've said is very disturbing, and I can understand the way you feel. I can even see where your suspicions are coming from. But don't do anything rash. Let me look into it. I'll do a bit of checking. Hell, maybe Harold Phelps is right and I've had my head stuck up my ass for the last six months. But let me check it out before you run away with Celia." His intense expression softened. "Do you think I'd let anything happen to her, or to you? You've got to know how I feel about the both of you."

Phylis took another deep breath and her whole body seemed to relax. "I know how you feel. I hope you know how we feel about you. But there's been some strange stuff happening, and I can't ignore it any longer."

"I'll look into it. I promise. I'll even go behind Dr. Brand's back and sneak a look at some of Margaret's files. If I see anything weird, anything at all that's not quite right, I'll drive you back to Minneapolis myself. I won't let anything happen to you or Celia."

She leaned closer and kissed him. "Thanks, John. I feel better knowing your on our side."

He squeezed her hand. "C'mon. Let me make you some dinner. I, ze masder chef ov Baddle Lake's east

235

bay, vill aztonish you wizz my culinary experteez!"

Phylis giggled and allowed herself to be dragged back into the cabin. She felt better. Relieved. If there was something going on John would find out. She trusted him in that. But somehow she felt as if she'd been pulled off the mark, her attention somehow diverted from something important.

At least, while he's here we're safe, she thought.

But as the night closed in and the darkness bore down like a vice, squeezing away the last of the light, she began to wonder. The weird regression she'd experienced while observing Celia's session had surfaced a lot of her baby memories, and one of them seemed to clamor for attention. It was a truth that she'd been constantly aware of as a baby, she realized, a truth that neatly divided the day from the night and shaped her baby life:

Only at night does the dark come out.

CHAPTER TWENTY-FIVE

Four miles down the gravel road somebody else was also lamenting the fall of darkness. His name was Bobby Kemp, and at 23 years old he was, in his own estimation, a paragon of military perfection: an inch and a half below six feet tall, compact, muscular, and lean, he had the look of a particularly nasty predator. His partner in sentry duty at the bunker was Thomas Webber, who though of milder temperment was of similar appearance and demeanor.

The darkness seemed to close in around the compound like a thick blanket, blocking out everything. The trees were a high black wall against the slightly less dense darkness of the sky above. There was no moon tonight, and the stars, though numerous, looked very lonely up there, cold and terribly isolate. Just like us, Bobby thought, stealing a glance at Tommy. Tommy was the kind of guy who took every order like it was his sacred duty, a privilege to perform. Hell, he even seemed to *like* standing out here in the dark, despite the heavy presence of the bunker behind his back and the things inside it.

At the best of times Bobby liked sentry duty about as much as he liked puking his guts out after a binge, but up here in the dark woods of Minnesota it was worse. He wondered sometimes why he'd ever asked for transfer to a special duty squad. *Special duty* my ass, he thought. Stuck out here in the middle of fucking (its Saturday night so lets *really* cut loose and buy a six pack of Molson Canadian) Minnesota, and worse yet assigned to sentry duty by Captain "hike till your balls shrivel" Wilkes.

Bobby had imagined special duty would be a bit more adventurous than this. Shit, he'd heard the stories about the assassinations, the abductions, the break-ins, the secret agent stuff. Special duty was supposed to be *special,* man, not this backwoods hush hush bullshit. He'd been here two weeks and he still didn't know what was going on, not really, and the little bit that he did know was making him nervous as hell. "Our concern," Wilkes had said, "is the clinic just down the road. Our assignment is to keep a lid on anything that happens here. This is a clean-up squad, boys, and you might not like what you have to clean up." Well, Wilkes had been right about that. Whatever was going on at that clinic was not right. Bobby didn't exactly believe in God, or the Bible, or any of that stuff his Aunts in Pennsylvania were so hot-shit about. What he did have a grip on was "The Laws Of Nature," and what those laws said was "Big eats small; strong conquers weak," but most of all they said "Don't fuck with mother nature." Well, hell, down the road they were doing a whole lot more than just fucking around with the old broad. They were getting her knocked-up on a regular basis and having her spurt forth all sorts of things that should never have seen the light of day.

Like the things in the bunker.

Bobby didn't know where the things came from, or where they would be going when the bunker became too crowded (like last fucking week, baby), or even what the things were exactly. He just knew that they shouldn't have been alive. Period. But Wilkes was as tight-mouthed as he was tight-assed and no explanations had been given and Bobby would bet his big six inches that none were forthcoming. Even during the scare last week everything had been tight. "Do your job, don't ask questions." Yeah, right. The dude from the clinic had been by, Bobby had seen him, and afterwards Wilkes had been on some kind of action high for days.

Operation Bear-Hunt he'd called it. But Bobby had seen what had been hauled in, and it sure as fuck hadn't been a bear. Bobby was glad he hadn't been in the group that found the thing, 'cause sure as shit he would have froze and got his ass killed. It was bad enough *seeing* these things, but *killing* them was something else entirely. Guns just didn't seem adequate somehow. But thankfully he'd been assigned to one of the teams ordered to track down the kid. The little boy. Bobby was aware that the kid was connected in some way to the other thing, but he wasn't sure just what that connection was. Wilkes had been adamant on one point: "Keep them apart. Immobilize the thing out there, and get the kid back to that camp. But don't let them get together!" The way Wilkes spoke Bobby got the feeling that if the kid and the thing got together there would be a reaction like an atomic explosion. Or something equally as bad. Whatever it was, he didn't want to find out.

There were things in the bunker that had been there long before Bobby arrived, things that the clinic dude had hauled down and given to Wilkes for disposal. Into the bunker they went. He'd never really got a good look at any of them, but he could imagine. His imagination was pretty good for things like that. One of the things he hated about sentry duty was that you could hear things moving behind your back, inside the bunker. Dry rustling sounds, pig squeals, wet squelches, deep throat groans. Nightmare, secret-swamp sounds. Fuel for the imagination. As if the fire needed fuel.

Now Wilkes was going on about the little girl at the clinic like she was some sort of fucking superhero. Shit, the kid must have been all of seven years old, but Wilkes was talking like she was the next best thing to the fucking neutron bomb. What the hell was the army coming to?

Bobby unbuttoned the chest pocket of his jacket and dug out the crumpled pack of Camels. He stuck one between his dry lips and lit it, sucking back the smoke like it was some sort of euphoria inducing drug. He didn't offer one to Tommy. Tommy didn't smoke. Tommy didn't drink. Tommy was a good little soldier.

"Better put it out, Kemp. No smoking on duty." Tommy's Texas drawl was enough to make you want to puke. He pronounced duty as *dooodee*.

"Y'all bedda quit ya smokin," Bobby drawled in imitation, chuckling.

"Wilkes said—"

240

"Fuck Wilkes," Bobby said, grinning around the cigarette.

"*They* smell it," Tommy said, his voice hushed now. "They get riled up. Put it out."

Ah, fuck, Bobby thought. The pussy was right about that, and even now he could hear the sudden shifting inside the bunker, the stealthy movements of fleshy mass seeking out the smoke from the cigarette. Like leaches to blood. But hell, he needed the smoke. He took a deep drag, then another, and then crushed the butt out against the stock of his M-16. He stuffed it into his pocket. If Wilkes found the butt his ass was fried.

Tommy lapsed back into silence. He's fucking *concentrating* on being a sentry, Bobby thought in disgust. Do it right. He bit down on a chuckle and grunted instead, but Tommy didn't seem to notice.

Bobby checked his watch.

The time was 11:34.

He thought: *Twenty-six more minutes of this shit.*

Tommy suddenly shifted on his feet and brought the sleek form of his M-16 down so that it aimed into the darkness. "Did you hear that?"

"What?" Bobby said, bringing his own gun into position. He hadn't heard anything. Or had he?

"Listen. I heard it. A shuffle or something."

Bobby cocked his head and listened. All he heard was absolute silence. The wind had died to nothing and not even the trees were stirring. The barracks were quiet too, only the single dim light showing in the doorway.

"I think you've been fucked in the ear once too often," Bobby said in disgust, relaxing his grip on the

M-16.

Then he heard it. A shuffle, to the right, towards the western edge of the compound, as if something had moved slowly. Something very large, Bobby thought. He brought the M-16 down again.

Tommy took a step away from the bunker, squaring himself against the direction of the noise. Bobby heard the sudden *snick* of the safety coming off, and he did the same to his own gun. It was so dark that he could not even see the fence in the direction of the sound.

It took a moment for that fact to sink in, and another before he realized what was wrong with that observation.

There were two mercury-halogen lamps in the compound, one by the main gate and the other at the side of the main barracks, and the light they cast glittered off the fence around the entire perimeter of the compound.

The entire perimeter of the compound.

Bobby let his eyes slowly track along the fence, a dimly illuminated geometric pattern that stretched from the gatehouse beyond the barracks where it was blocked from view by the building, resuming again beyond the edge of the bunker until . . .

It stopped.

Blocked off. By something dark.

A patch of darkness blocked out about thirty feet of fence, and it also extended upwards, and upwards, merging with the blackness of the trees in the background. Yet higher still the blackness rose, into the relative brightness of the night sky. He craned his neck to peer higher, to encompass the outline that formed a dark hump against the glittering stars.

"Who goes there?" Tommy said, his voice a hoarse whisper in the night.

Bobby was holding his breath. His heart was hammering in his chest like some ancient combustion engine about to seize. *It's about the size of a three story building,* he thought.

But it's blocking the fence.

Which means that . . .

. . . whatever it is . . .

. . . it's inside the compound.

Bobby had been looking upward, as if in rapture, and it was only Tommy's frantic backward stumbling that brought his gaze down again. Tommy tripped over his own boots and fell at Bobby's feet, white face upwards in a rigor mortis gaze of mortal terror.

Bobby heard a sound like a paper cup being stepped on.

THWUMP

And a shape articulated itself out of the darkness and moved towards them. The shape came closer, growing larger, until it was towering over him by a good three feet. Like a man, wet leather skin, coal lump eyes. Behind the shape the darkness loomed like an impossibly large shadow. The thing before them seemed to extend out of the darkness like an appendage. Bobby looked up into the leering face. It looked down upon him with an emotion that looked agonizingly like love, as if it *knew* him. Intimately. Somehow that was the most frightening thing of all.

"Bobby," it said, and reached out two huge meaty arms to grab both Tommy and himself.

He thought: *I know that thing.* Something inside

Bobby, something hidden for so long he had believed it never existed, quivered in terrible recognition.

The pale form that held them in its grip suddenly darkened, as if crossed by a shadow, and the monstrous shape behind it collapsed upon itself and stood before them.

Where the man-shape had been there was now a patch of blackness. And Bobby knew what was going to happen next, because it had happened before, years before, in the darkness of his room, his nursery, when the darkness had lurked in the corners, waiting until little baby Bobby got close to sleep so it could . . .

. . . open its eyes.

Blazing yellow.

A sound bubbled up from the deepest, darkest regions of Bobby Kemp's mind, the mind that was now somehow shrinking into itself, and he was astonished to hear the same sound emerge from Tommy Webber's insanely twisted lips. But how could Tommy have known? This was *my* monster, Bobby thought. My—

Daahg. A feeble gurgle from the back of the throat, a baby's name for a nameless horror.

Somewhere inside him the sounds started to bubble, to raise to consciousness, and he was a baby again, but in a man's body, looking up at the huge, dark face. And suddenly he was being pushed towards Tommy Webber, pushed *into* Tommy Webber, and he perceived at the corner of his eyes that their flesh was *melting* together, like molten wax, and it was almost funny to see the look of insane horror on Tommy's face because, hey kids, it was the same look

244

that was carved into his own. All he could do was look up into the huge, pale face.

His dying fingers squeezed reflexively on the trigger of the M-16. Two shots split the silence, but to Bobby they seemed muted, unimportant. He thought: *it wants to open the bunker.* But now, even that unimaginable occurrence, seemed unimportant.

His sanity departed like a bullet from the muzzle of a .44 magnum pistol, unstoppable, and Bobby felt himself sinking back into the depths of his own mind, back down the deep tunnel that opened for him.

The thought suddenly came to him as he slid down that warm, inviting tunnel: *This is where it came from!.* He knew beyond doubt that he was right.

The darkness zoomed up to meet him. Bobby thought: *At least it's over. Dying isn't so bad.*

And then he was through.

Into the other place.

The dark place, where creatures Bobby had no name for slithered and crawled.

The place that, until now, had lurked safely beyond the edge of his consciousness, beyond his comprehension.

It had been there all along. Always.

And Bobby Kemp knew he had been wrong. The horror was not over yet.

Oh God, please, no God, please . . .

It was just beginning.

Don Reynolds turned the Ford off the black-top of 210 and onto the narrow gravel of Lakeview Road. He cut the headlights and rolled the car to a slow stop. The moment the lights died the darkness imploded around the car as if it had been waiting. The moonless sky would complicate the task of navigating the tight little road, but the lights were too risky. His approach, at least, had to be secret.

The dash clock read 11:42. He lit an unfiltered Camel, sucking the smoke into his lungs, then turned down the rheostat that controlled the brightness of the dash. For a moment he felt disoriented, as if he were floating in a black velvet bag, his only points of reference the disembodied green figures of the clock and the tiny red slashes of the speedometer. He closed his eyes and breathed deeply. When he opened them again the disorientation had passed, and soon his night vision cut in. The sky above assumed a navy blue hue, speckled with tiny pinpricks of light, while the trees on either side of the car remained unfathomably black. The gravel road was a ghostly trail curving into the darkness ahead. He put the car in gear and slowly, ever so slowly, moved along the road.

Five minutes later he detected a faint glow against the trees ahead. The army compound. He muttered a foul curse and drew heavily on the cigarette. The compound, of course, would be lit, and there would be a guard in the gatehouse. What were his chances of slipping by unnoticed?

A fat fucking zero, that's what.

He was not sure of the connection between the army compound and the clinic, but his gut instinct told him there was one. The two guys in the Jeep had definitely been following Phylis, and they had taken pains not to be spotted. Would they have something to say if he drove past them with his lights out? Running dark was a sure sign of ill intentions. But hell, coming in like a fucking Christmas tree would be worse.

His hand hovered over the rheostat for a full five seconds before he pulled it back. He'd take his chances with the dark. His foot pressed harder on the accelerator as he approached the illuminated stretch of road bordering the compound, and when he hit the edge of the fence he was going just over 35 miles per hour. A dangerous speed in the dark.

But his stealth was unnecessary. There was some sort of commotion in the compound. The gatehouse door was hanging open and a full unit of half-clothed men was clustered around a squat building at the rear fence. Something glistened wetly on the ground between their legs. None of the military boys even glanced his way as the Ford rolled by, and then the compound was behind him and the darkness closed in again. He chuckled hoarsely. That had been easy. He sucked greedily on the cigarette and continued to drive.

He had slowed to round a bend, following the gentle ghostly curve of the road, when the deer stood up at the edge of the trees.

"What the fuck . . ."

The pale shape glimmered against the backdrop of trees. It was small for a deer, perhaps a doe, but as he passed by he saw that he had been wrong. The thing had four legs, yes, but it's head had been . . . Don frowned. For a moment the head had appeared to be human. He had seen thick lips hanging slackly open and a fleshy brow leaning on dark eyes. But that was impossible. A trick of the darkness. He glanced in the rear-view mirror but of course could see nothing.

He shook his head and continued to drive, again concentrating on the road and the task at hand. As he drove his lips turned up in a tight smile. He was still smiling when the shape loped into the path of the car. Even if the headlights had been on he would not have been able to stop in time, and as it was he hardly caught a glimmer of movement before he saw the pale shape rise above the hood and heard, with a sudden sinking feeling in his belly, the crunch of metal into flesh. Something thudded on the hood of the car and rolled off onto the road. Don slammed on the brakes.

"Jesus, Mary!"

He pulled the lever into park and leaned against the steering wheel. His lungs dragged air down his throat in short, ragged gasps, double timing to the beat of his heart.

"Jesus, Mary!"

In the rear-view mirror he could see the lump, a whiter shade against the paleness of the road, and he knew with sickening certainty that it was a man. He opened the door of the car, his head swimming with the shock of the collision, and wobbled on the gravel. The car hadn't sustained much damage but the thing in the road didn't look so lucky. He walked slowly towards it, eyes widening in shock as he drew closer, whole face slackening with disbelief when he finally stood over it.

It was not a man.

"Oh, fuck," Don Reynolds whispered.

He had assumed the thing had been a man because in the moment of collision, when time had frozen, he had seen the face suspended in the frame of the windshield, shock and pain etched on its pale features. But now he could see the body below the human face.

The first thing that popped into Don's mind was: *chicken*.

The thing looked like an immense plucked chicken with a human head. Where the head should have extended into a neck and then smoothly into shoulders there was instead a sagging fleshy bag that folded over the thing's chest. The shoulders were raised high, as if hunched, almost higher than the head, and the arms that unfolded from them were thin and flat, like skin stretched over a rigid framework of bones, ending in obscenely smooth knobs of skin. The torso bulged with muscles at the chest, but narrowed to a twist of ropy flesh at the waist. There were no genitals, at least that he could discern, and the legs were huge hocks that ended in claws the size of dinner plates, each one protruding two razor sharp prongs at the front and a single vicious meat hook at the rear.

"Jesus, Mary . . ."

Don kneeled and tentatively reached out a hand to touch the thing's neck. The flesh beneath his palm was cold as ice. There was no pulse. A foot long gash on the left breast opened on the pulpy mass of unfamiliar entrails and the gleaming ragged edge of a snapped bone. No blood leaked from the wound.

Whatever it was, it was dead.

He stood and ran a hand through his hair. From

what nightmare had this thing walked?

He walked back to the still running car. To his right, in the darkness of the trees, there was a crash, followed by a howl of anguish. The howl had not come from a human voice, Don knew, but neither had it come from the mouth of an animal. He saw a flash of white within the darkness as something very large blundered through the trees. Don's heart hammered in his chest and terror gripped him like a huge hand.

He slammed the door of the car and put it in gear. A plume of dust rose behind the Ford as he continued on to Lakeview. To his credit he had forgotten his original plan of confrontation. His thoughts, if he had paused to study them, were more of fatherly concern than he would have believed possible. There was something in the woods. Something weird. His daughter was at a clinic. A clinic in the woods. The concepts bumped together in his mind, trying to join, and though he could not discern the exact relationship between them he knew that there was one. His plan of action was simple: he was getting Celia out of here. For her own good.

Ten minutes later the Lakeview sign arched over the road. Don cut the engine and coasted to a stop in neutral. Once out of the car he paused and listened carefully. Whatever creatures he had seen in the woods were still a couple of miles away, but they were coming closer. He knew that instinctively. They were not here yet, which meant he had some time, but they would get here soon enough.

He crouched at the base of the sign and studied the clearing. Cabin Three was the only one showing lights. He began to edge nearer, staying close to the tree line. As he drew abreast of the cabin the inside door opened. Don stopped in mid-stride, breath held tightly. A man stepped onto the porch then stopped and turned. Phylis stepped out of the door and into his arms. Don watched as his wife kissed the tall, lean stranger. The kiss continued for an unreasonably long time. Don set his mouth in a tight line, holding back the words that wanted to come out. Instead he let them echo inside his head. *Fucking bitch, fucking slutty bitch!*

Finally the kiss ended. A few soft words were spoken. The man began to walk back towards the long building at the other end of the clearing. Phylis watched him go, then went back inside.

Don smiled.

He crouched silently, the dark trees yawning behind him like an immense mouth. He listened to the gentle lapping of the water against the dock and to the very faint rustle of wind in the trees.

He waited three minutes.

Then he stood, grinning, and walked towards the cabin.

CHAPTER TWENTY-SIX

Phylis felt a pang of disappointment at John's insistence on leaving. When Celia had gone to bed she had made it plain that she was romantically inclined, and although he had responded in kind at first, his enthusiasm had tapered considerably as the night progressed. It was almost as if he did not intend to touch her again until he proved the good intentions of Lakeview Clinic.

Her suspicions had hurt him, she realized, but after talking with him she had felt greatly relieved. He had not jumped to defend himself, which was a good sign, but had instead listened carefully, and had agreed to check into her story. If there was something strange going on at Lakeview, then John Gordon was not part of it. She was sure of that.

She watched his form fade into the darkness as he walked back to the main building, the light from the cabin casting a glistening sheen across his back. The ache in her groin began to ebb, and with it the disappointment. There would be other nights.

She closed the door and returned to the sofa. The cabin smelled pleasantly of the chicken paprika John had cooked for supper. The man had many hidden talents. Though it was past midnight she was not tired. She lit a cigarette and picked up her book.

When the knock sounded at the cabin door she sat to attention, then placed the book spread open on the coffee table and smiled. Perhaps her feminine charms had managed to cut through the macho veneer John had erected around himself. She crushed out the cigarette, brushed her blouse smooth, then went to the door and opened it.

"Hello, cunt."

His fist caught her on the right cheek and she stumbled backwards and fell to the floor, knocking the back of her head. Stars danced before her eyes.

Don stepped into the cabin and closed the door. He turned to her, smiling.

Her thoughts were caught in a whirl wind of confusion: *It's Don, he found us, it's Don, Oh God, he found us* . . .

Don stepped towards her and pulled her to her feet. He looked exactly as she remembered him, the same pinched face, the same scowl, the same close cropped black hair. But now, perhaps, there was a harassed look to the small eyes, she thought. He still looked dangerous.

"Don, please, you shouldn't have come here."

He pushed her toward the sofa and toppled her into it. He reached into his rear pocket and pulled out a folded sheet of paper.

"I got your invitation," he said.

Phylis recognized the court order. "Celia's psychiatrist said we should do it. He said Celia might not be able to handle seeing you."

"Not handle seeing her daddy?" He grinned. "That doesn't sound very friendly."

He dropped the court order on the coffee table and spun around. Energy seemed to push at his seams, keeping him in motion. He began to pace in front of her, gazing at her constantly. What was he going to do? Surely there was nothing he *could* do. Not out here, in the middle of nowhere.

"What the hell is this place?"

"It's a clinic."

"I know its a fucking clinic you stupid bitch. But what the hell *is* it?"

"It's . . . experimental. It's for Celia." She found herself suddenly very calm, almost as if she were an observer, and not stuck smack in the middle of this volatile situation.

"What does she need it for?"

"Because of what you did to her," Phylis said. She could hardly believe she'd confronted him with it, but again she felt distant from the situation, as if she were not directly involved.

"What I did?" He scowled down at her. "You mean showing her a little affection?"

"I mean using her to fulfill your perverse desires. I mean sexually abusing her. A little girl who couldn't defend herself." Her eyes began to scan for a weapon she might use against him, and she realized at that moment that she was in some sort of shocked state of heightened awareness.

254

At this moment I am very, very dangerous.

She knew that was true. But would Don know it?

Her words hit him hard and he flinched at each one. He shook his head. "I was gonna leave you alone," he said slowly. "But this . . ." He nodded at the court order. "This is just *asking* for it." He leaned down so that his face was close to her. "Know what I mean?"

Phylis said nothing. What could she say? Out of the corner of her eye she detected the movement, but not soon enough to avoid the fist that caught her the right cheek. Pain exploded in her head and she fell sideways to the sofa. But the stars quickly disappeared, and the pain instantly dulled to a manageable throb. She sat up again and stared at him coldly.

"You shouldn't have brought her here," he said, standing upright again. "There's something weird about this place. There's *things* running around in the woods."

Though she understood what he had said she did not respond. She had to keep him talking until she found an opportunity to act. "I had to bring her here. She was getting worse. She couldn't cope. The doctor said that she knew you were getting out soon, and that was aggravating her condition."

"Where is she?"

"She's at the main building," the lie came without a pause. "The therapy won't be finished until tomorrow."

The sounds of sheets rustling came from the small bedroom. Don smiled. He pulled Phylis upright and smiled into her face. "You sure she isn't here some-place?"

"She—"

His fist plowed into her sternum and the air in her lungs exploded outwards in a cough. The pain of the punches to her face had been nothing to this new hollowness that blossomed within her chest and stomach. Blind with pain she collapsed into the sofa gasping for breath.

"Lie to me again, cunt, and I'll rip your fucking lungs out."

Phylis gasped raggedly, heaving in lungfulls of air. She nodded.

"Who's the guy?"

She looked up questioningly.

"The asshole who left here a few minutes ago. I saw you with him at Battle Lake."

Her eyes widened. She *had* seen him that day! She almost wanted to laugh. "He's . . . a . . . friend," she said between gasps.

"You fucking him?"

She shook her head. Her breathing was returning to normal but her chest ached badly. Whatever else happened, she would have nasty bruises.

"I'm taking Celia out of here."

Phylis held up her hand. "Don, no. Her therapy is almost finished."

"Fuck the therapy! She doesn't need it! This is all bullshit! Once she sees me again she'll be all right."

"You'll scare her."

He shook his head. "Listen, I know what I did

before wasn't smart. I know that. But I'm different now. You shouldn't have tried to keep me away, everything would have been fine." He seemed on the verge of tears, and his voice had taken on a child-like petulancy. "Once she sees me she'll know."

"You can't take her."

He leaned over and hauled her to her feet again. "I *can* take her!" He pulled back his fist for another punch, then paused. His face went slack with surprise.

"Celia?"

Phylis groaned in dismay. She turned and saw Celia standing between the bedrooms, hand buried beneath her chin, lips slightly pouted. Don was focussed on Celia, his eyes wide.

Phylis felt as if a thousand volts of electricity had exploded into her body, smashing through from head to foot. She jammed her knee into Don's groin with such force that he jumped off his feet. When he buckled forward, air hissing from his mouth, she grabbed his hair, lifted his head, and slammed the butt of her palm into his nose. Blood spilled from his nostrils and he fell backwards across the coffee table and crashed to the floor.

"Celia, run! Run and get Dr. Gordon! Hurry!"

She did not wait to see how Celia responded, but threw herself at Don. Her mind was a complete blank. She was acting totally on instinct. She fell on top of her fallen husband and began to batter at his blood soaked face with her balled fists. He lay immobile for a few seconds, head rocking from side to side under the barrage of blows, and then he rolled over and threw her from him. Panic seized Phylis. She screamed and jumped at him again, biting into his cheek. She felt the flesh separate beneath her teeth, and spat out the chunk of meat in her mouth.

Don screamed, his face now bloody and torn. His fists swung wildly, once of them clipping Phylis on the point of the chin. Her head snapped backwards and she dropped to the floor like a bag of potatoes. She groaned, blackness wavering at the edge of her vision. Don stood over her, hand clutched to his ruined cheek. His eyes were wild.

"You bit me! You fucking bitch!" he kicked her in the stomach.

"Daddy."

Don twirled around. Celia was still standing between the bedrooms. Phylis managed to sit up, lights blazing behind her eyes, her stomach a throbbing mass of pain.

"Oh, Celia, no—" Phylis whispered.

"Please don't hit Mommy any more," Celia said.

Don stared at her silently; his breathing slowly became more shallow. Blood flowed from between his fingers, soaking his shirt.

"Baby," he said hoarsely.

"Please, Daddy," Celia said.

Phylis felt all the fight drain out of her. The distance she had somehow managed to put between herself and the situation vanished in a flash and the pain flowed in to take its place. She groaned in despair. She had failed Celia again.

Don took a step towards Celia. "I'm taking you away from here," he said.

"I can't go," Celia said.

"I'm your daddy," Don said more harshly. "I can take you."

"You were hitting Mommy," Celia said, brushing a strand of red hair off her forehead.

"Mommy was hitting me too," Don said defensively. "But I'm taking Mommy too. I'm taking both of you away from here."

He looked down at Phylis and smiled. She did not even have the energy to grunt.

"Mommy, I can't go," Celia said plaintively.

"Honey, we have to do what your daddy says," Phylis said, her voice a small thing squeezed by pain. There was no choice now. They would have to go with him, somehow protect themselves from him, and escape when the opportunity presented itself. The priority now was to stay alive, and the way Don was behaving that was going to be difficult.

"But I *can't*," Celia said. "It told me it wanted me to stay."

Phylis frowned. "Who told you?"

"*It* told me. You *know*." She frowned at Phylis in exasperation.

Phylis shook her head. She could not deal with this now. "Honey, we have to go."

"But it won't let me!"

Don took a step towards Celia, then turned and stared angrily at Phylis. "You see what this place is doing to her?" He turned to Celia again. "What

259

thing, baby?"

"The monster," Celia said. "The . . . the *Dark*."

Don stared at her silently for a few seconds, then turned again to Phylis. His face was now troubled. "We're getting the fuck out of here. If you make so much as a peep I'll break your neck."

Phylis nodded.

Don went to the bathroom and came back with the Disneyland towel pressed to his cheek. Already blood was seeping through the fabric. He looked at Phylis with child-like accusation, and for a moment she actually felt guilty about biting him. He just wanted to see his kid, she thought. But she stopped herself quickly. That was not all he had wanted. He always wanted more.

"Let's go," he said.

"Let Celia get a coat," Phylis said.

"No. I've got a car. She won't need a coat. C'mon, baby."

He herded them out the door, holding tightly to Celia's hand, his other hand coiled in Phylis's hair. At least Celia isn't screaming her head off, Phylis thought. The therapy, if nothing else, seemed to have cut to the root of the problem.

They stayed behind the cabins, close to the trees. The darkness was like a solid thing, impenetrable and very spooky.

"Where are we going?" Phylis whispered.

"Shut up. My car is by the sign."

Phylis frowned. They were behind Cabin One now. The sign should have been visible. Even in the dark she could still make out the outlines of objects. But the sign, and even the road, seemed cloaked in a darkness more solid than all the rest. After a few more steps even Don began to notice and he slowed considerably.

"What the hell."

"It's the monster," Celia whispered.

"Celia, shhhh," Phylis said.

"What the hell," Don repeated.

They had stopped completely now. Don's grip on her hair loosened and she managed to raise her head and get a good look at what lay ahead. The slab of pure darkness was like a hill directly in front of them, a hill that rose against the lighter backdrop of trees to finally obscure the stars at its apex. Within the peak of the hill two bright yellow stars gleamed.

Not stars, Phylis realized. *Eyes!*

"Oh, my, God." She fell to her knees.

Celia stepped closer to Phylis and hugged her. "It's the monster." Celia whispered.

Don took another step towards the darkness. A sound like two large hands clapping together echoed through the trees.

THWUMP

Something began to walk out of the darkness, as if a curtain had parted. It was roughly man-shaped, and waddled towards them as if it had trouble handling its bulk. The darkness loomed behind it like the mouth of a huge cave. As the thing approached, Phylis whimpered and hugged Celia tightly to her breast. The creature was three times the height of a

261

man and as wide as a small car. It walked on legs like tree stumps, but oddly metallic looking. It's torso was bright yellow, though in the darkness it looked almost orange. She could see faded numbers painted on its chest.

This is a dream.

Don stood as if frozen, head slowly cocking as the thing drew closer. On top of the torso a huge white face rested. It looked down at Don. Flabby white flesh hung like moist dough from the contours of a squarish skull. Yellow eyes gleamed brightly. Curlicues of dark hair mottled its heavy brow. Thick red lips smiled.

"Hello, Donald," the thing said. It's voice was a thick liquid sound squeezed from a rotting dead body.

Don turned to Phylis, his face registering confusion. "What is it?" he whispered hoarsely.

Whatever you don't want it to be. Phylis thought.

"No," Don said, taking a step backwards.

Two huge hands, like the claws of some unlikely industrial waldo reached out and grabbed his shoulders. The claws pinched tightly and the crack of breaking bones filled the darkness. Don screamed.

Phylis shuddered, moaning, and hugged Celia tighter. She did not want to look, but she could not stop. Don's arms hung useless at his sides as the thing pulled him closer, lifting him off the ground.

The yellow torso began to shift and a panel lifted up on its gut to reveal a metallic looking funnel. A red and a green button popped out of the yellow flesh, like day-glo tumors.

And suddenly Phylis recognized the thing.

The city workers in Minneapolis called it "The Mouth" because it chewed up thick branches and spat out wood chips and sawdust. Once a year a small army of the machines were dragged through the city behind trucks, chewing up the branches from the trimmed trees. But the thing before her was a mutant version, a conglomeration of metal and inhuman flesh. Like something out of a child's imagination, an anthropomorphized nightmare machine.

The memory came to her of the first happy year of their marriage, of Don running out of the house one sunny July morning and shouting at the workmen to turn the fucking thing off. While she did not like the scream of the machine herself, she could not understand his reaction. But when he told her, she had understood. As a child of four he had watched the workmen clearing the piles of branches from the boulevard in front of his father's Chicago home. He had watched, horrified, as one clump of branches was dragged towards the spinning rotor. A squirrel was trapped in the nest of branches, it piteous cries inaudible over the scream of the blades. The branches were thrown into the maw, squirrel included, and four year old Don Reynolds watched in horror as a spray of woodchips, blood, and fur, splattered the rear of the truck. He had run into the house and thrown up.

The mutant Mouth standing before them now suddenly began to whine, and inside the metallic maw the glittering blades began to spin. As the blades picked up momentum the sound was like a jet engine, filling the night. Don began to squirm, his legs kicking wildly, his head shaking frantically. Even over the whine of the machine Phylis could hear his screams.

Whatever you don't want it to be.

Then the arms of the creature bent and slowly began to push Don's face towards the blades. Don's fingers scrabbled frantically at the edge of the funnel, desperately trying to stop his movement towards the blades, but his arms were too badly twisted by the mechanical claws. Phylis could not watch.

But she could hear . . .

Don's wavering scream of fear and horror, powered by a lifetime of nightmares that began that horrible afternoon in Chicago . . .

The jet engine whine of the blades, the sudden change in pitch like a chainsaw binding in wood. . .

And she could feel . . .

The sudden patter of warm wetness on her hands and neck, and a heavier plop on her forearm.

She opened her eyes. It was raining blood and globs of flesh.

A piece of wrinkled skin, bloody at the edges, slid from her arm.

She screamed.

The whine of the blades stopped. The waldo arms released what was left of Don's body, everything from the chest down, and it fell twitching to the ground. Don's arms fell separately, the shoulders minced off by the machine.

The body stood on wobbling legs for a moment, as

if still live but slightly drunk, a misshapen dwarf, then keeled over with a dull wet thud.

The arms continued to twitch for a few seconds, the fingers still desperately clawing the bloody grass.

Phylis screamed again.

The creature took a step backward, then another, then became engulfed in the blackness. The hill began to recede, to merge with the background of trees until it had disappeared within them. Was it her imagination or did she really see two blinking yellow eyes moving through the woods?

The sign was visible again. And Don's car.

Phylis held tightly to Celia, both mother and child now crying. Phylis hardly noticed the lights of the main building flaring to life, or the sudden shouts that filled night. When John Gordon appeared beside her she fell sobbing into his arms, then backed off as he retched and vomited violently.

Then she and Celia were being led back to the cabin and the night was filled with bright lights, the roar of Jeeps, and the frightened shouts of men.

CHAPTER TWENTY-SEVEN

Captain Wilkes had a look in his eye that stated, very plainly, that anybody who got in his way at this moment would be fucked over so badly they just might die. John Gordon studied Wilkes carefully, for the first time feeling a small amount of respect for the man. When all hell had broken loose, Wilkes had been there to clean it up. And now he was taking control. The only person in the room who greeted this fact with pleasure was Margaret Palin, who leaned against the wall of Wilkes's office with a supercilious look on her face that made John want to strangle her. Brand fidgeted nervously, content to let the captain run with the ball until the mess was cleared up.

"You white-smocked little scientific fuckers make me want to puke," Wilkes hissed, slamming his open hands on his desk. "Why wasn't I informed that you brought something through that met our specifications?" His small bright eyes focussed on Brand.

Dr. Brand sighed. "Because, Captain, we didn't

know we had brought it through."

Wilkes glared at him in disbelief, then turned to Margaret. Margaret nodded quickly. "There was no indication that the Reynolds girl had responded at all to the primal cues," Margaret said. "There was certainly no physical manifestation. It's quite unusual for a subject to respond during the first session."

"She surprised you, did she?" Wilkes grinned coldly.

In more ways than one, John thought. He did not mention that the telemetry readings showed a flat line during Celia's primal session, an indication that she'd locked into Nether, unheard of for the first session. So why had there been no indication of a manifestation?

"Phylis Reynolds told me she saw something coming out of the wall in the treatment room," he said to Wilkes. "But none of us saw it."

Wilkes looked back and forth between Margaret, Brand, and John, the disgust plainly evident on his face. "This thing you didn't see, came to the compound tonight and opened the bunker. In the process it killed two of my men. Melted them together. On top of that it minced up some poor fucker at your camp. I think I'm safe in saying that the project has been compromised. And this is what I've reported to Virginia."

Brand looked up sharply, concern deeply etched in his gaunt face.

"Unfortunately, they don't share my view that we close down immediately," Brand said. "They've authorized me to audit a demonstration. You either prove to me this project has potential, by tomorrow, or we're out of here."

John shook his head. "You can't push us like that."

Wilkes grinned. "I can. I am."

John started to protest, but Brand held out his hand. "I think we can effectively demonstrate the potential we are working with."

Wilkes nodded uneasily. "In the meantime, I want to know what that thing is."

"We don't know," John said. "We were working with a cue we isolated in all the other subjects, something that seems to be common to all of them. It seemed to represent a childhood monster."

"No, no," Brand interrupted. "Not *a* monster, not *the* monster. Simply, *Monster*. It's the concept behind all monsters. The form, if you will, that all fears and imaginary monsters are based upon. It has no correlative in the real world. It is simply Monster, personified. Your monster would be different from mine, as mine would be different from Margaret's, or from John's."

"Jesus Christ," Wilkes said softly. "Can it be controlled?"

"We've had no trouble with anything else we've brought through," Brand said.

Wilkes nodded. "Okay. I'll have my men clean up the mess we've got outside. Tomorrow I'll have them hunt down the things from the bunker. Will there be any trouble from the Reynolds woman?"

"I'm sure there will," Brand said. "Is there any way

we can force her to stay?"

"I don't want to force her. We're not in a position where she needs to be eliminated. Not yet. I don't want another Louisiana horror. I'll think of something to keep her here. An accident of some sort."

John and Brand left Margaret in the office with Wilkes and went out to the courtyard. The outside air was cool and refreshing, and John took in a few good lungfuls to calm himself.

"Things are going crazy, Neville," he said.

Brand nodded. "We're being pushed too fast. And that creature was a surprise. We weren't ready for it."

"What kind of demonstration can we give?" John said. "I have a feeling we're going to be shut down."

"No. We won't. You saw Celia's readings. She's amazingly responsive. Maybe even responsive enough for a breakthrough."

John turned sharply. "You can't be serious."

Brand smiled. "Not full-fledged, of course. Just a little something to demonstrate the potential we're dealing with. Nothing to be frightened about."

John turned away, and looked up at the stars. For the first time since joining the project he felt things were wrong. And despite what Brand said, he was frightened. Very frightened.

Phylis woke with a small cry trembling on her lips. She sat upright and furiously blinked back the veil of sleep. Last night's nightmarish events rushed back like a train through a tunnel and left her rocking on the edge of the bed. Her face throbbed painfully and felt thick beneath her fingers. The flesh around her right eye was swollen, but not enough to restrict her vision. Her stomach and chest sent jolts of pain reverberating through her body at every move, and yet nothing seemed broken. Thank God for small mercies, she thought. She leaned over and nudged Celia's pale shoulder. "You awake?"

Celia groaned and pulled the blankets closer to her chin. She nudged again. "You awake, honey?"

This time the groan was longer. Celia rolled languorously to her other side and smiled at Phylis, her mouth fighting against a yawn. Then the smile disappeared and her eyes opened wide, her small body stiffened as if she had been probed by a very cold instrument, and she sat bolt upright. "It wasn't a dream, was it?" Celia said.

"Nope. Not unless we both had it."

Celia's mouth dropped and she fell back on the pillow, her red hair fanned out across the blue fabric. "Daddy was here. But it got him."

Celia's simplistic recounting of last night's horror gave Phylis the shivers, and she nodded slowly.

"It *told* me it wouldn't let me leave. He wouldn't listen," Celia said.

Phylis pressed her soles against the cold linoleum. "Don't think about it, sweetie." She stood and stretched, wincing at the resulting creaks and pops from her joints. "Get up now, and get dressed. We're going to get out of here."

"But . . ." Celia's eyes widened in fear.

"Don't worry," Phylis said. "It's daylight."

Celia seemed on the verge of panic, but after a moment her features softened and her little face nodded solemnly. "It only comes in the dark." She stated the fact as if she were reading from a text book.

"Right."

Celia swung herself out of bed and marched resolutely through to her bedroom. The sounds of rummaging came through the walls. Phylis chose a comfortable plaid shirt to go with her designer jeans, the contrast between the softness of the shirt and the roughness of the denim providing a strange sense of security. These were *home* clothes, for lazing around the living room, or clearing up the kitchen, and once she was in them she began to feel better.

"Should I pack my things?" Celia's voice was muffled by the bathroom walls.

"Don't bother. John will send it to us."

Celia's footsteps sounded softly along the hallway and then her face peered in through the half open door. She was wearing her navy blue sundress and her red hair was neatly combed, pulled back from her forehead. Her face still looked worried.

"What about my comics?"

Phylis pulled the brush quickly through her own ash blonde hair. "Okay, bring your comics."

"And teddy?"

"Sure. Teddy too. But hurry, sweetie. We've got to get going."

Celia did not move. When Phylis glanced at her

271

Celia was still watching her carefully. "What is it honey?"

"Are we running away?"

No. We're just leaving before somebody else gets hurt."

"Are we going to tell Dr. Gordon?"

Phylis pursed her lips. She'd been thinking the same thing herself. Informing John about their departure would necessitate going into the main building. In the end everybody would know, but she was not yet prepared to deal with their reactions.

"We'll call John when we get home and tell him to come and see us. We don't want to waste time this morning."

Celia nodded, seemingly satisfied, and went back to her bedroom.

Phylis lit a cigarette and breathed the smoke hungrily. Sunlight streamed through the bedroom window and gave life to the roiling dust motes and smoke in the air, but it also revealed clearly the state of her face. The skin on her right cheek was red and spotty, as if it had been rubbed with sandpaper, but the swelling around her eye was not as bad as it felt. She applied a thin veneer of makeup, enough to reduce her new battered look, and just enough to show that she was not running in panic. She stepped back to appraise herself. Not bad for somebody who just had the shit kicked out of them.

Celia was waiting in the kitchen with her pink Addidas bag at her feet and her one-eyed teddy under her arm.

272

"All ready?"

Celia nodded. "Yup."

"Then let's get out of here."

"Aren't we going to have breakfast?"

"Not yet. I saw a MacDonalds in Fergus Falls, right off the main road, we can stop there. You can have pancakes if you want."

Celia tossed her Addidas bag in the rear seat then snapped her seatbelt. Phylis latched the cabin door from the outside then climbed into the Datsun. She stepped on the gas pedal and turned the key. The engine turned four times but did not cough to life. The smell of gasoline came into the passenger compartment.

"Oh, shit."

"What's wrong?" Celia asked.

"I flooded it."

She cursed herself silently. She put her foot on the gas pedal then pulled the choke lever all the way out. *Just wait*, she thought, *don't panic; let the gas evaporate*. She counted a very long thirty seconds in her head then turned the key again. The engine turned three times then coughed to life in a gout of blue smoke.

Celia pinched her nose. "Yech."

"You like the smell of cigarettes better?"

Celia nodded, nose still pinched. Phylis dug out her cigarettes, lit one, then opened her window to let the smoke out. "Let's go home," she said.

She put the Datsun in gear and moved it into the rutted path that led to the road. The car sounded

273

terribly loud in the morning silence. The echoes coming back from the trees sounded louder than the engine itself. The lake glittered invitingly in the early morning sunshine. As they passed Cabin One Phylis could not stop herself from looking at the small clearing before the trees, but what was left of Don's body had been removed. The grass was still dark with blood, and slivers of flesh littered the surrounding area. She groaned. Celia would not look out the window.

Thank God we didn't eat breakfast.

The site of Don's demise produced no emotion in Phylis, only a cold lump of nausea in her stomach and a strong sense of conviction: *it had not been a dream.*

As the Datsun passed under the wooden Lakeview sign Phylis felt like a traitor. Was she allowing her panic to destroy Celia's only chance at a normal life? But the answer had to be "no." She had come here for Celia, and now she was leaving for Celia. I'm acting *for* her, she thought, not *against* her.

The trees arching over the gravel road produced the illusion of being inside some sort of natural cathedral. Sunlight glinted through the leaves, cutting swirling swaths through the dust raised by the car. At one point Phylis slowed as they passed a green tarp spread over a large lump at the side of the road. She contemplated, for a very brief moment, stopping the car and pulling back the edges of the green canvas to see what lay beneath. But fear erupted in her mind. What if it was Don's body?

What if it had been dragged out here until something could be done with it? She had no wish to face those remains. Not now, not ever. She pressed harder on the gas pedal and wished the gravel would end. The trees to either side of the road were dark and lush, and from the corner of her eye she fancied she detected the occasional burst of pale movement. Even Celia strained at her seat belt to peer into the woods. Phylis wanted desperately to be on the smooth black-top of 210 and heading for Fergus Falls and then home.

Five minutes later she turned a bend in the road and brought the Datsun to a shuddering stop. The army compound was situated about a half mile ahead, and she had intended to drive by at full speed as if nothing were wrong. But now a blockade was stretched across the road, replete with flashing yellow lights. Two soldiers stood at attention in front of the barricade with rifles held across their chests. Behind them, a hundred yards away, a group of six soldiers clustered around a tanker-truck jack-knifed across the road. One of the two at the barricade stepped towards the car and Phylis noticed for the first time that he was wearing a small mask over the lower half of his face. The sharp smell of gasoline was thick in the air and Phylis felt a pang of nausea.

She rolled down her window.

"What happened?" Her voice was quiet.

The young soldier leaned against the driver's side of the car and peered in at her. His face was gaunt and pale, spotted with acne. A small line of white

275

scar tissue bisected his left eyebrow. His small blue eyes regarded her curiously. "Bit of an accident," he said, voice slightly muffled by the mask. "We were getting our delivery of fuel when the tanker knifed. Now we got a spill. You won't be able to pass."

Phylis felt her face go white. "We want to leave right now," she said quietly.

The soldier stepped back. "I'm sorry, but—"

"Where's Captain Wilkes?"

The soldier blinked. "He's—"

"Get him." Her voice had taken on a very sharp edge. As an afterthought she added: "Please."

The soldier stared at her for a moment, weighing the authority of her words, trying to decide how seriously he needed to take this woman and her child. Finally he nodded and walked towards the group of men around the sprawled tanker. He returned with another man in tow. Phylis recognized the barrel chest immediately. Captain Wilkes crouched down and smiled through the open window. He pulled down his mask and rivulets of sweat spilled down his red face and neck.

"Mrs. Reynolds," he said. "Sorry for any inconvenience, but there's nothing we can do."

"My daughter and I have to leave here right now," she said as calmly as she could.

Wilkes glanced over at Celia and smiled nervously. "I'm sorry, really, I am, but there's nothing I can do. We're working as quickly as we can to clean up this bloody mess, but we've got a spill of two or three thousand gallons of high octane fuel. Just running

276

into the ditch. It's not an easy job."

Phylis glared out at him. "And I suppose you must be tired after the action last night."

He frowned. "You mean the accident at Lakeview?"

Phylis laughed coldly. "Accident hell. My ex-husband was chewed to pieces."

He nodded solemnly. "Yes, we think it may have been—"

"Please, don't even suggest it might have been a bear," Phylis said. "We both know what it was."

He frowned again and glanced at Celia. Phylis suddenly recognized the look on his face. It was fear. He was scared of Celia.

"I don't really know anything about the clinic's business," he said at last. "But I know my own. You can't get through here. Not yet. If you return to your camp I'll let you know when it's safe."

Phylis's lips tightened into a white line. She was furious, but she was helpless. If she spoke now she would spit and hiss like a cat. Wilkes would like that. She rolled up the window and turned away from him. She backed up the car in three moves, then roared back along the road towards Lakeview.

Phylis stood in the reception area of the main building and listened for signs of life. Somebody was obviously up, but where were they? All the overhead fluorescents were flickering and a portable radio at the reception desk was tuned to an AM station in

Fergus Falls. Paul McCartney wailed about living and letting die. *Exactly the way I feel*, Phylis thought.

She picked up the phone and placed it carefully on the counter. What if there was no dial tone? The thought made her pause. Finally she shook her head and picked up the receiver. The dial tone buzzed loud and strong. She spread the crumpled sheet before her and dialed the number.

"Otter Tail Hotel."

"Room 216, please."

There was a brief pause before the ringing started. It rang four times. "Oh, please answer, please be there," Phylis muttered. It rang another four times before it clicked.

"Hello?" The voice was groggy and thick.

"Dr. Phelps?"

"It's eight o'clock in the morning," Phelps complained.

"This is Phylis Reynolds."

There was another pause, and Phylis could almost picture him sitting to attention in bed. "What is it?" Now his voice was alert.

"Something happened last night," Phylis said. "A man was killed. There's something here . . . the thing I told you about. It wants my daughter to stay. We tried to leave this morning, but there was an accident at the army post, the road was blocked, and we couldn't—

"What do you mean it wants your daughter to stay?"

"It *told* her."

278

There was a long silence. "The road is blocked?"

"Yes."

"I could—" His voice suddenly stopped.

"Dr. Phelps?"

Silence. The line was dead. Phylis moaned in anger and slammed the receiver back in its hook. She waited a moment then picked it up again. Still dead. "Damn!"

Had she told him enough? She had to assume that she had. He knew what was going on, and what he didn't know he could figure out. His last sentence had been cut short, but Phylis finished it in her own mind. *I could . . . come and get you by boat.* She closed her eyes to calm herself.

Outside, the sun had risen above the tree line and was warm against her skin. But across the lake she could see the dark line of a cloud bank on the horizon. The wind was coming from the west. It gently nudged the lake water into small waves.

She walked slowly back to the cabin where she had left Celia. There was nothing to do but wait.

The morning silence was broken by a snapping of branches to her left. Phylis stopped short, hand clasped to her mouth. Another snapped branch.

Then the trees by the road parted and a pale shape stepped into the sunlight. It was as tall as a man, but most of its height consisted of a tripod formation of spindly legs. Atop the legs rested what looked like play dough moulded into the shape of a wide mouth. On top of the mouth two large blue eyes blinked against the sun.

The mouth smiled to reveal two rows of glistening black teeth.

Then the thing bounded toward her.

CHAPTER TWENTY-EIGHT

After Phylis phoned him on Thursday, Paul Welch felt unaccountably elated, as if he were a teenager getting a phone call from the school beauty. His palms had sweated as he talked to her. But most of all he felt relieved. He'd embarrassed himself by his earlier actions, like a boor, an insensitive fool, and it had taken him a couple of days after the incident to realize how much Phylis Reynolds was coming to mean to him, and then the horror at what he had done set in. How could he have been such an idiot? Her phone call from Lakeview had made one thing clear: she was giving him a chance to make up for it. He certainly didn't deserve such a chance, but he was going to make the most of it. If Phylis wanted to know everything about Lakeview, then he would dig it up for her.

On Friday he called the State Psychiatric Board and inquired about Doctors Brand, Gordon, and Phelps. The results of the inquiry had disturbed him. Neither Brand nor Gordon appeared in the registry, which meant they were not licensed to practice in

Minnesota. Phelps was listed as a clinical psychologist, not a psychiatrist. The board had no record at all of Lakeview Clinic, by that or any other name, and they suggested he check with state and federal grant regulators. If Lakeview was a research site it would not need to be licensed as a clinic or a hospital. But Paul had another idea. He visited Phylis's office at *MPLS Magazine* and flipped through her rolodex. There were listenings for two doctors: Dr. G. Anderson, and Dr. M. Hammond. The white pages listed Anderson as a family practitioner, but had no listing for Hammond. He checked the yellow pages under Psychiatric Counselling and found Hammond's name and number.

But when he phoned, the doctor was uncooperative.

"I *told* her it was experimental," he said to Paul defensively. "She was under no illusion that she was entering an accredited psychiatric institution."

"She knows that, Doctor. But she asked me to find out more about the place. I was hoping you could help."

"No, I'm sorry, I can't. If Mrs. Reynolds should come to me herself I shall gladly give her all the information I have."

End interview.

The Minnesota Scientific Endowment and Grant Commission was more helpful. The receptionist was a middle aged woman who amply filled the pink angora sweater she wore. Her face was pleasant and her manner was professional. The tag on her sweater said her name was Pat Winters.

"I'm a writer for *MPLS Magazine*," Paul explained. "I'm doing an article on public expenditure for psychiatric research and I was wondering if you'd be able to help me track down the funding for a specific clinic." He unleashed upon her the full force of his ice melting smile.

She smiled back. "You could be a housewife from Anoka and I'd help you," she said. "It's public information."

Paul reduced the intensity of his smile to formally friendly. The fact that he was spending most of a Friday afternoon for his research had not left him in the best of moods, but Pat Winters' attitude made the effort more palatable. "The clinic I'm researching is called Lakeview. Think you'll have them listed?"

"If they're getting public money, they're listed."

She typed something at her terminal and waited. A moment later a few lines of information scrolled onto the screen. Pat Winters frowned. "Not state funded," she muttered, and typed something else. This time she smiled brightly when the information popped up. "Here it is. Lakeview Clinic. Battle Lake, Minnesota. Federally funded."

"By who?"

She ran her finger down the screen. "Pandora Foundation."

"What's that?"

"Well, let's take a look." She typed some more into

283

the terminal and a moment later the screen lit up. This time she frowned. "That's odd." She typed some more, still frowning.

"What is it?"

She pursed her lips, then raised her eyebrows. "Ah, I see."

"What?"

"U.S. Defense Department. No other information available."

"Doesn't it say what they're being funded for?"

She smiled grimly. "Not here it doesn't."

He thanked her, left the building, and drove down to the main branch of the public library. It took two hours to dig out the articles by Brand and Gordon, and two rolls of quarters to photocopy the ones he found interesting. Both Dr. Brand and Dr. Gordon had published extensively, Gordon recently, but Brand voluminously over the past 20 years. Most of Gordon's work, and certainly the last few years of Brand's, had a similar focus: sound, as it related to memory, information processing, and emotion.

One of the more intriguing pieces was by Brand in the January 1985 issue of *Psychological Bulletin* entitled "Trauma Manifestation in Mnemonic Therapy." Though most of the article was technical, the gist came across quite clearly. In case studies Brand had documented *physical* manifestations of past trauma during therapy sessions, including bad skin rashes, hair losses, and in one case the growth of a large benign tumor on the subject's wrist. Brand compared the results with the effects of deep hypnosis where certain subjects reacted accordingly to suggestions that they had been burned, frozen, or hit.

In the March 1987 issue of *The American Journal of Parapsychology*, a decidedly quackish newsletter, Dr.'s Brand and Gordon collaborated on an article entitled "Doorways in the Mind: Suppressed Trauma and Physical Projections". The piece was, again, technical, but the conclusions were succinct: under certain conditions, most notably while during mnemonic therapy, suppressed trauma could result in the projection of objects *outside* the subject's body. As in, *POOF*, here is the creature that has been giving you nightmares. It was no wonder that none of the respectable journals had carried the article. Either Brand and Gordon had flipped, or they had stumbled across something that nobody wanted anything to do with. After March 1987 he could not find any published work by either doctor. It was as if they had disappeared, or stopped working. But more than likely that was the time that Lakeview had opened its doors.

By Tuesday at 11:00 A.M. he'd had his fill of research and was ready to call Phylis. The only thing still bothering him was the funding of Lakeview, the apparent secretiveness of the Pandora Foundation. On impulse he phoned his contact at the governor's office.

"Terry, it's Paul Welch. *MPLS Magazine*."

There was a long pause. "Paul. You need an interview with the governor?" The was no sense of play-fulness, or joking in the voice.

Paul chuckled anyway, and lit a cigarette. "Nope. This is personal. I need a favor."

Another pause. When Terry Haber spoke again his voice was markedly subdued. "What do you need, Paul?"

"I've got a friend who's out at a place called Lake-view. She asked me to dig up some information on the place. I tried. I found out it's a research project funded by the Pandora Foundation. You know any-thing about it?"

"Not off the top of my head. Give me half an hour, I'll get back to you."

"Appreciate it, Terry."

"Buddy, you know we owe you, and we'll still owe you after this."

Paul hung up, smiling. Two years ago he had been witness to a stunning outburst of drunken revelry by the governor of Minnesota, and the precipitation of an incident that to most men would have been slightly embarrassing, but which to the governor of a state could have been career ending. More out of a sense of empathy than compassion Paul had not writ-ten the incident up. Why ruin a man's life for a drunken mistake? Nobody had been hurt. The gover-nor's secretary, Terry Haber, had expressed thanks on the governor's behalf. Favors were due, and this was the first time he'd tried to collect.

Paul took a drag on the cigarette then crushed it

out in disgust, only half smoked. Damn it! He was trying to ration himself to four a day and that was number two already. He poured himself a cup of coffee and continued to skim through the articles. Outside, the weather took a turn for the worse. Dark clouds came scudding in from the west and began spitting on the ground. Inside, Paul turned on the lights so he could see. Damned unpredictable Minnesota Septembers.

Half an hour later the phone rang.

"Paul, it's Terry."

"What you got for me?"

There was a heavy silence, and when Terry finally spoke his voice was hushed and worried. "Listen, whatever reason you think you've got for digging into the Pandora Foundation's business it's not good enough. Get off it right now."

"What are you talking about? I told you, I've got a friend out there, with her kid."

"Paul, what I'm going to tell you is not for public consumption. It stays with you, okay?"

"I understand."

"The Pandora Foundation is some weird offshoot of the Defense Department. They support a lot of stuff, most of it pretty strange. Some of it very strange. Science fictiony stuff. Anything with weapons potential. Know what I'm saying?"

"I think so."

"We're talking about augmented chimps for jungle warfare, biologically redesigned humans for space exploration, tanks with human brains. Like, these guys take Stephen King seriously. They were involved in that fiasco down in Louisiana last year where they found sixteen dead kids with their brains literally fried out."

"What the hell are they doing in Minnesota?"

"You got me. I didn't know about it until you told me. They don't exactly advertise. But if you've got people out there, my advice is to get them out. Quickly, and with no fuss. You'd be doing them a big favor."

"You think—"

"Paul, I've said too much already. Just take my advice."

"Thanks, Terry." He hung up.

Lightning flickered across the sky and lit up the inside of the apartment. What the hell had Phylis gotten herself involved in?

He unfolded the sheet of paper with the number she had given him and dialed. There was some clicking and shifting as the call was routed, and finally it rang. It rang twice before the operator cut in. "That number is out of order."

Goose bumps rose on Paul's neck. "There might be another number," he said quickly. "Could you check it for me? It's a place called Lakeview Clinic, on the Battle Lake exchange."

The operator sighed. The tone of her voice said she dealt with too many civs who thought they were telecommunications experts. There was some buzzing and clicking and then her voice was back on the line. "I'm sorry, sir, but that number is out of order too."

"Isn't that unusual?"

"Not this week. We've had some storms. If there's trouble, it should be repaired by tomorrow."

He hung up. Now what? He relit the cigarette he had half-smoked earlier and sucked in the foul tasting smoke. He had found out enough to want to get Phylis and Celia away from the clinic, but there was no way to get through to them. Why had Phylis called him in the first place? They were not exactly close friends, and she had not been overly communicative last time he had seen her. He doubted the call had been expressly to give him a chance to redeem himself. No. Something must have happened to make her suspicious, suspicious enough to want to know more.

He smoked greedily, staring out the window. The phones were down. Probably an accident, but maybe not. There was no way to contact her.

That left one option. It was just past noon. If he pushed it he could make Battle Lake by 3:00.

He dug his rain coat out of the closet and pulled it on. At the apartment door he paused, then returned to the bedroom. From the bottom drawer of his bedside table he pulled a grey-blue, snob-nosed Smith & Wesson .38 caliber police special in a blue nylon holster. The gun was registered in his name, but the only time he had taken it from the apartment was for target practice. He was not a good shot.

289

There was a small yellow box of ammunition beneath a tatty pair of underwear, and he dropped both gun and bullets into the pockets of his coat.

The weight of the gun and ammo banged against his hip as he bounded down the stairs, and the premonition came to him so suddenly it almost made him stop:

Before the day was over he would need them.

CHAPTER TWENTY-NINE

Never before in her life had Phylis reacted with such a gut-action, non-thinking, knee-jerk reflex. The fleshy tripod took a step (or two . . . it was hard to follow the movement of the three spindly legs) toward her and she was running, legs pounding, heart hammering, mouth gaping open to suck back oxygen, toward the cabin. A scream hung unborn on her lips, not enough reserve air in her system to push it out. Behind her the three horse-hoof feet of the tripod smacked into the dirt and grass as it came *clip-clip-CLOP* after her. She hit the outer screen door of the porch at full stride, smashing her elbow painfully against the wooden frame and ripping a corner of the screen as she barged through. Before the screen door had stopped clattering in its frame she was inside the cabin proper and slamming the door.

"Mommy?" Celia was curled up in the sofa with her one-eyed teddy and a comic book, eyes wide in shock at Phylis's thundering entrance.

Phylis held a finger to her lips. "Shhh, honey," she whispered, forcing her lungs to slow their furious panting so that she could form the words. Her heart continued to hammer. She edged over to the living room window and peered out through the screening of the porch. Where was it? Had the damn thing run off into the trees?

The tripod wheeled into the frame of the outer screened window and stopped. Two big baby blues blinked at her. The wide lips curled up in a smile. Black teeth glistened.

"Oh, Jesus," Phylis muttered and ducked away from the window.

"What's *that?*" Celia said, jumping from the sofa.

"Stay away from the window, Celia."

"But what is it?"

"I don't know." Phylis latched the inner door and tested it. The light wood rattled against its frame. She cursed the poor construction of the cabin. If the thing wanted in, it would get in; that much was obvious.

Celia remained standing at the window looking outside. The tripod stared back at her, still smiling.

"Celia, I told you to stay away from the window!" She grabbed the child by the elbow and yanked her out of view.

"Ooooow!" Celia held her elbow and pouted.

Phylis kneeled and hugged Celia tightly. "I'm sorry, baby, but we don't know what that thing is. We don't want it getting mad at us."

"But it was smiling."

"Sharks smile too," Phylis said, cringing at the

292

thought of the tripod's black serrated teeth.

"Oh, Mommy, shark's don't smile!"

Celia tugged herself loose but did not move back to the window. Phylis stuck her head beyond the edge of the window and blinked. The creature was gone. She heard the muted *clip-clip-clop* of its hooves as it moved around the cabin. Celia's eyes followed the sound around the perimeter of the walls.

"What's it doing?"

Phylis shrugged. "I don't know, honey."

A tentative scratching came from the bathroom at the rear of the cabin. Before Phylis could stop her, Celia darted towards the sound. "Look!" Celia squealed in delight.

The grinning mouth and blinking blue eyes were framed in the bathroom window.

"Oh God." Phylis barged past Celia and into the bathroom. The window was open and the creature's pale face was pressed up against the screen. Phylis stood on the pot and swung the window closed. The tripod mewled like a puppy, cocking its head at an odd angle. The smile disappeared slightly. Phylis paused. The thing certainly didn't seem dangerous. Curious, perhaps. She opened the inside window again and the inhuman face outside brightened noticeably.

"Hello," Phylis said.

The blue eyes, each about the size of her head, blinked once. Then the huge face, which appeared to be mostly mouth, began to move excitedly back and forth on its spindly legs. Like it's wagging its tail, Phylis thought. The creature became a blur of motion.

"Stop!" Phylis said.

The creature froze as if caught in a camera's flash. It blinked. Celia who had followed Phylis into the bathroom tugged at the bottom of her mother's jeans. "See, I told you it was smiling."

Phylis stepped off the pot. "It seems okay. But don't get it excited. We don't know what it will do."

She guided Celia back into the living room and into the sofa where she took a seat next to her. In a moment the tripod came clip clopping to the front of the cabin and peered in the living room window at them.

"What should we call it?" Celia asked, staring out at the creature.

"I don't think it has a name, honey," Phylis said, calmer now but still flabbergasted at the thing outside.

"*Legs,*" Celia said. "Can I call it Legs?"

Phylis chuckled at the appropriateness of the title.

"Can we take Legs with us when we go?"

"No!" Phylis said sternly. And then more softly: "Legs has to stay here. This is where he lives."

Celia looked petulantly at Legs, and Legs looked petulantly back. "When are we leaving?"

"We have to wait for Dr. Gordon," Phylis said. *Or Phelps,* she thought. *Whoever gets here first.*

"Where is he?"

"I don't know, honey, I don't know."

An hour later Legs was still standing outside the living room window, immobile but for the occasional blink. Celia had taken to waving at the creature periodically, and when she did so Legs's lips would turn upwards in a wider smile. Legs seemed content to stand and watch. During that hour other shapes emerged from the woods, some barely poking their misshapen heads into the sunlight, others stepping boldly into the clearing. None were the same as Legs. Some were roughly man shaped, others not even closely resembling anything Phylis had seen. The only common factor seemed to be their paleness, as if they had spent their entire lives in darkness.

Creatures from Nether, Phylis thought in awe.

They hobbled and crawled and hopped and trotted with no apparent guidance, thankfully staying away from the cabin. Legs ignored the newcomers and they ignored him. The woods echoed with their strange noises.

"Where did they all come from?" Celia asked, following the movement of the pale shapes against the edge of the tree line.

"Down the road somewhere," Phylis said, and an image of the army bunker suddenly appeared in her mind.

At noon Phylis made a couple of grilled cheese sandwiches for each of them and they sat in silence eating the food. The day's early promise faded, and now a ring of dark clouds edged the lake. Phylis watched the advancing front warily. A storm on top of the current weirdness would be too much. Not to mention the fact that it might make the lake unnavigable.

Please, Dr. Phelps, come and get us!

By 1:00 the clouds were close and the wind had picked up. There was still no sign of John, or Dr. Brand. Even Margaret Palin would have been a welcome sight. Anything to signal a return to normalcy. And something else was beginning to make Phylis edgy: the faint smell of gasoline was now evident in the air. Celia, who had managed to occupy herself with her comics, was becoming irritable as the day wore on.

At 1:30 Phylis sat to attention. For a moment she had heard . . . There it was again! A faint buzz, now audible, now gone. Celia heard it too and dropped her comic.

"It's a boat," Celia said, looking up at Phylis.

Phylis crushed out the cigarette she had been smoking and went to the living room window. The window afforded only a narrow view of the lake, but in the distance, rising and falling on the wind-chopped water, was a small boat.

"Phelps," Phylis whispered.

The buzz of the approaching boat also attracted the attention of the pale creatures wandering at the edge of the woods. One by one the things began to move down to the beach to await the arrival of the noise-maker. Legs turned momentarily to study the approaching boat, but did not leave his position in front of the living room window. Phelps ignored his motley audience and beached his craft without delay, running as close to the shore as possible before lifting the motor and gliding in. There must have been eight or nine of the strange creatures, all of varying shapes and sizes, gathered around the landing. For a moment Phylis felt seized by panic as Phelps's form disappeared behind the wall of pale flesh, and she sighed with relief when the wall parted and Phelps came marching through. He seemed to be talking to the creatures, gesticulating wildly with his arms. They did not follow as he marched across the beach and over the ridge, but remained at the boat. Whatever the things were, they seemed to have at lest some level of intelligence.

Phelps was again wearing his beige bermuda shorts and a blue dress-shirt, but Phylis was so glad to see him that she did not mind. Legs turned as Phelps approached. The tripod shuffled and Legs moved closer to the doctor. Phelps slowed and stopped about ten yards from the cabin. Legs stepped closer, large head bent forward. Phylis held her breath. Phelps did not seem worried and he began talking to the creature.

"That's a nice monster, nice boy, come to daddy, nice monster . . ." His soft words drifted through the porch and into the cabin.

Legs took two more steps and was upon Phelps. The grinning lips pressed against Phelps head, then

297

Legs backed off.

Sniffing him! Phylis realized, *Like a dog.*

Phelps smiled and marched past. Legs did not follow the doctor into the porch, but resumed his position at the living room window. Once he was inside the cabin Phelps closed the door and leaned against it, panting.

"Where did they all come from?" His voice was hoarse.

"They appeared an hour or so ago," Phylis said. "I think they might have come from the army compound. These are the things you were talking about? From Nether?"

Phelps nodded. "They've been busier than I imagined out here," he said.

Celia pressed against the back of Phylis's legs, poking her head around her mother's thighs to view Phelps. Phelps kneeled, smiling.

"You must be Celia," he said.

"Celia," Phylis said. "This is Dr. Phelps. He's a friend."

"Do you know Dr. Gordon?" Celia asked.

Phelps nodded. "Yes."

"He's my mommy's friend too," Celia said.

Phylis blushed, but Phelps ignored the comment. "From your phone call this morning I gathered you wanted to get out of here. Ready to leave now?"

Phylis nodded, paused, then shook her head. "I . . . I should try and find John, tell him we're leaving."

Phelps looked at her for a long five seconds. "Mrs. Reynolds, somebody cut the line as we were talking earlier. I doubt it was an accident. That means they did not want you talking to me, and they certainly won't like it that I've come out to get you."

"But who?"

"Phelps shrugged. "Brand. Gordon. The army. Who knows."

Phylis shook her head. "No. John's on our side. I talked to him. I have to find him before we go."

Phelps was silent again.

"It won't take long," Phylis said.

"How long?"

"Maybe fifteen minutes. Maybe half an hour. The farthest he could be is the army compound."

"Mrs. Reynolds, let's leave right now. You can see that something is going on here. Why take chances?"

"John Gordon has been good to us. Maybe he's in danger too."

Phelps pursed his lips. He sighed, obviously not believing her explanation. Finally he shrugged in resignation. "Okay. I'll come with you."

Phylis shook her head. "Just stay here with Celia. I don't want her out there with those things. If I'm not back in, say, forty-five minutes, just get her out of here. Take her to Battle Lake. I'll get in touch later."

"Mommy!" Celia cried. "You can't leave me!"

"No, sweetie, I won't." She kneeled and hugged Celia. "You'll be oaky with Dr. Phelps. I'll go and find John. Then we can leave."

She did not wait for further argument. Legs took a few steps towards her as she came out of the cabin, but backed off when she climbed into the Datsun. The sudden roar of the car's engine attracted the attention of the creatures at the beach, but by the time they had focussed on her she was already moving towards the main building. In the rear view mirror she could see Phelps and Celia in the living room window, and Legs, like some alien monstrosity, standing guard over them.

She left the Datsun running when she ran into the main building. She checked every room. There was nobody there. John's room was as messy as ever, but there was no sign of him. Exasperated she returned to the Datsun. A small voice in her head clamored for attention:

Go back to the cabin, it said, *get Celia and Phelps, and get the hell out of here!*

She shut it out. She needed to find John.

"Romantic fool," she muttered.

She put the Datsun in gear and drove through the gate and towards the army compound. A small cloud of dust rose around the car. Spits of rain splashed the windshield. "Jesus," she hissed.

She activated the wipers. Soon the rain was coming down heavily and she was forced to slow down, the ragged wipers of the Datsun inadequate for the squall. The combination of heavy rain, dark clouds, and the overhanging branches produced the illusion of darkness.

It only comes out in the dark, she thought uneasily.

The smell of gasoline became sharper as she drove until it began to make her feel nauseated. In the ditch to her left she could see rain drops splashing into the fluid already there. The water would carry the gasoline even further, she realized.

By the time she saw the huge pale shape looming in the center of the road it was too late. She slammed on the brakes and the Datsun swerved in a huge arc. The thing in the road filled the windshield, then stepped aside. *Pillsbury Dough Boy!* The thought passed through Phylis's mind like a bullet.

Then the road disappeared and the towering, dark, inviting trees filled her vision. She managed a small scream before her head cracked into the windshield, and then the darkness flooded in to take her.

CHAPTER THIRTY

The storm followed Paul Welch like a nightmare. It came out of the southwest on dark thundering wings and overtook him just before St. Cloud, passing overhead in a roar. Scalpel thin slices of lightning spilled pale luminescence on the bulbous underbelly of the clouds. Fat pebbles of water began to crash into the windshield. He activated the Regal's wipers at full speed and the world cleared and faded in rhythm to the squeaking rubber arcs.

One effect of the storm was that it slowed him down considerably. Though Interstate 94 westbound was not busy, especially on a dreary Tuesday afternoon, the rain was so heavy that he ran into a wave of cars thirty miles from Fergus Falls. That thirty miles took almost an hour to drive, and after Fergus Falls the blacktop of 210 was worse. The rain fell in obscuring sheets that blended the road neatly into the grass on either side of it. It was almost 4:00 when he came to the turnoff for Lakeview.

He slowed the Regal and stopped. A barricade stretched across the narrow opening, two yellow warning lights flashing at either side. Two soldiers in long black rain-slicks, gleaming like freshly spilled oil, stood in front of it. The warning lights reflected from their coats like the beating of warm hearts.

Paul opened his window. "What's going on?"

One of the soldiers stepped across the road and stood by the car, rain spattering off his rain-slick into Paul's face. The soldier was about Paul's age, though sharper edged. He looked like a dripping version of the Marlboro man.

"Sorry, sir, road's closed temporarily."

"I'm here to pick up a couple of people from the clinic down there," Paul said.

The black rain-slick shrugged anonymously. "Gotta tanker jack-knifed about a mile down the road. Big gas spill. Road's blocked."

"When did this happen?"

"This morning, sir," the soldier said. "Should have it cleared up by tomorrow sometime."

Paul grunted. He tried to look down the road but the soldier shifted to block his view.

"I'll try tomorrow," Paul said.

"You do that," the soldier said.

Paul swung the Regal around and drove slowly back along 210 towards Battle Lake. Wind buffeted the car on every bend in the road. He lit cigarette number three and smoked it as he drove, opening

303

his window a quarter inch to let the smoke out.

Well, he'd given it a shot. He'd tried. He'd come up here, but he'd been blocked. He could try again tomorrow.

Tomorrow will be too late.

The certainty of the thought hit him like a fist. Phylis and Celia were in danger. Every freelance dig-em-up-and-find-the-bones-in-the-closet writer's instinct in his body was screaming like a tooth under the dentist's drill. Something was going on at Lakeview, and it was coming to a head. If he came back tomorrow he'd find Phylis and Celia dead, brains fried like those kids down in Louisiana, with logical explanations flying through the air like spitballs.

At the Battle Lake turn off he slowed the car and parked. Time to consider his options.

The easiest would be to drive back to the Twincities and wait it out. He could come back up tomorrow and find whatever there was to find. Hell, maybe the tingling he felt was the electricity from the storm. Phylis and Celia were probably sitting in their cabin right now having a good old time. When he showed up tomorrow they'd think he was crazy for driving all that way.

Bullshit.

The other option was to continue with his original plan. The road was blocked, but Lakeview sat on the lake and could be accessed via the water. He leaned forward and peered up at the black, roiling

304

sky. The lake would be difficult. But he knew, knew beyond doubt, that the tingling was not from the storm. His body had detected a story, the infallible bullshit detector had started beeping the minute that soldier had stepped towards him. There might not be a tomorrow for Phylis and Celia.

He put the Regal in gear, drove into Battle Lake, and parked down by the waterfront. The small town seemed deserted. There was hardly a car in the street. In the ice cream parlor he could see a few people sitting around a table looking curiously over at him, but he ignored them. He buttoned up his raincoat, made sure the gun and ammo were secure in his pocket, and walked down to the dock. The lake was bad. It was worse than bad, it was a nightmare. Three foot waves crashed into the wooden dock and the four boats tied to the public platform clattered and banged against their tether-posts.

A hundred yards down the peer a sign swung in the wind.

BOB'S BOAT BONANZA

The wooden sign was attached to a small shack, a single light burning in the storm's darkness. Smoke rose from the blackened pipe-chimney protruding from the roof, drifting upwards a scant fifteen feet before being dissipated by the wind. Paul shielded his eyes from the driven rain and walked towards the shack.

The wooden door was open and he stepped into

the bright warmth inside. A wiry old man was hunched over a card table with a glass held before him and a half-full bottle of Wild Turkey at his elbow. He was flipping through the August *Penthouse*. He raised his grizzled face as Paul entered and slowly closed the magazine.

"Whatcha want?"

"You're Bob?"

"Shore. Whatcha want, I said?"

Paul pulled back the hood of his coat and smiled. The shack was small, about the size of his bathroom back in the city, and with Paul inside it the room was definitely crowded. A small wood-burning stove beside the table was open, and inside it flames licked greedily against a freshly added log. The air was redolent of burning sap.

"I need to rent a boat," Paul said.

"Ain't ya seen the weather?"

"I know. But it's an emergency."

"I ain't puttin my boats out in weather like this," Bob said.

"I can pay."

The small grey eyes studied Paul from head to foot. "How much?"

"What's the daily rental?"

"Thirty for the day. Plus damage deposit. But like I said, I ain't puttin a boat out today."

"I need something fairly large, fairly stable, with a big motor. Not one of the nine-fives."

306

"Ain't 'cha listenin? I said no boat today."

"I'll buy one."

The small wizened faced studied him again. Even the wrinkles in the ruddy skin could not hide the disdain. The glass raised and the half inch of bourbon inside disappeared in a single gulp. "What kind of 'mergency you got, boy?"

"I have two friends trapped at the other side of the lake in a . . . cabin. The road is blocked."

The old man nodded. He carefully poured himself two fingers of bourbon, bent to look at the amber liquid closely, then added another finger. He pulled a blackened poker from a hook at the side of the table and adjusted the logs in the stove. The flames licked higher. Then he turned to Paul again. "I got a sixteen foot aluminum tub with fiber glass reinforced seams outfitted with an Evinrude twenty-five horse outboard. That suit you?"

"It'll take three people?"

"Shore. But look at the water, boy. You'd need the Queen 'Lizabeth for a safe ride in water like that."

"How much?"

"I can let you have her for fifteen hundred. 'Cause she's kind of old." Then he smiled and quickly added: "But she's good."

Paul nodded. "You'll take American Express?"

"Shore. Don't leave home without it." He grinned, grabbing the card out of Paul's fingers.

He filled in the slip, then used the phone to check

307

the transaction. In very neat letters he wrote the authorization code at the top of the form then handed it to Paul to sign.

"C'mon, I'll introduce you to your new berth." Bob pulled on a ratty old green waterproof poncho and stepped out into the storm. Paul followed. The outside air was bone-cutting cold in contrast to the cozy warmth of the shack. They walked to the very last boat in a row of rickety looking aluminum hulls that had been drawn out of the water and locked into place on the wooden dock.

"Here she is," Bob said.

The boat was old. Very old. The reinforced seams were actually fiber glass spot repairs made over the years. The twenty-five horse Evinrude was an early model, the paint so badly faded and chipped that the lettering was indecipherable. The prop looked as if it had been hammered back into shape too many times to count.

"Don't you worry about the way she looks," Bob said. "I seen this old girl out in worse weather than this. You just gotta be careful."

"How much gas will I need to get there and back?"

Bob frowned, holding his chin with two dark fingers. "I'm gonna throw in two five gallon tanks with the deal. That should do you." He disappeared into a small shed at the end of the dock. When he reemerged a few moments later he was stooped almost

308

to the ground, a battered gas tank in either hand.

Paul took one of the tanks and placed it in the boat. He connected the fuel hose from the motor to the nozzle on the tank. Bob leaned over and placed the other tank at the front of the boat.

"Make it more stable," Bob explained.

With Bob's help it was fairly easy lowering the boat into the water. The launch area was protected from the worst of the waves by two concrete abutments on either side. Paul climbed into the boat. He pulled the cord on the motor and it snarled to life, blue smoke belching up from beneath the water.

He smiled. He had been worried about the motor.

"Just hold on a sec, boy," Bob said. The old man disappeared back inside the small shed, then came out again with three life jackets that had obviously seen better days. He tossed them into the boat with Paul. "You gonna need these in this kind of weather."

Paul nodded gratefully. "Thanks."

"These friends of yours. They a woman and a young girly?"

Paul blinked, staring up at Bob in astonishment. "How did you know."

Bob smiled revealing a row of crooked brown teeth. "She's got a couple friends, that woman. You're the second today come for a boat to run over there."

Paul frowned but did not otherwise respond. He

flipped the motor into reverse and backed out of the launch bay. The moment he was in clear water the small boat began to rock violently on the waves. He glanced once more at Bob, who was looking down at him with a scornful damn-fool-city-boys-don't-know-bad-water-from-good look, then put the motor in gear and turned to open water. The prow crashed noisily through the waves, sounding like a tin pail being smashed against a tree. The rivets in the prow's center seam rattled ominously but appeared to hold well enough. Rain lashed mercilessly into Paul's face as he guided the boat towards the first point.

Soon he was able to anticipate the rhythm of rise-fall-crash as the boat sped over the steep waves, and his rump rose and fell accordingly on the rough wooden seat, making the ride a bit easier. When he rounded the point the lake gaped in front of him, a roiling black surface swept by grey sheets of rain. He headed towards the south shore where the swells seemed smaller. The orange life jackets jumped in the bottom of the boat as if they were alive. The black sky moved steadily northwest punctuated by occasional flashes of lightning that seemed to freeze the lake at its worst moments.

He wondered who the other person had been who had chanced the dangerous waters to get to Phylis and Celia, but no answers came. He set his lips in a tight line and continued to guide the boat, but the

task was made more difficult by the premonition
that seemed stronger with every yard he travelled:

It's already too late.

CHAPTER THIRTY-ONE

Phylis regained consciousness slowly, cataloging the growing number of aches and pains in her body, finally blinking awake to a reality she had hoped was only a bad dream. Outside, the rain had stopped but the sky was very dark. She pushed herself away from the steering wheel, pressed painfully into her rib cage, and attempted to sit up straight. Her head throbbed. She gingerly touched her forehead, wincing at the exquisite lance of pain. In the rear-view mirror she could see the gash just below her hair line, now crusted with black blood. At least it had stopped bleeding.

She glanced at her watch. It was past 5:00. The significance of the time eluded her for a few moments, and she stared blankly at the face of the watch, but when she finally realized what the numbers were telling her she gasped.

She had been unconscious for more than three hours!

Which meant Phelps would have left with Celia, leaving her alone.

But for the things in the woods.

She scrambled in panic from the Datsun and found herself knee-deep in slime. The car had come to rest in the shallow ditch at the west side of the road, front bumper bent around the smooth trunk of a towering spruce, rear wheels invisible beneath the dirty water.

"Shit!"

She lifted her legs high and splashed to the edge and up the slippery grass bank to the gravel of the road. The Datsun was stuck for good. It would require a tow truck to get it out, and no guarantees it would start after that. Damn, how could she have crashed at a time like this?

The memory flashed through her head in a montage of quick shots. Passing under the Lakeview sign . . . the spatter of heavy rain on the windshield, too much for the ragged wipers . . . the sudden lumbering body in the road, a mass of bulging pale flesh, like the Michelin Tire Man.

But there was no sign of the creature now. No sign of anything, or anybody, just the dark trees swaying in the wind skimming off the lake. The sky was a flat black ceiling pressing low; if she looked closely, she could detect movement in the clouds. Luckily the rain had stopped. A downpour now would make her situation unbearable. Despite the rain, however, gasoline fumes still clogged the air. If

313

she had crashed on the other side of the road, where most of the gasoline had spilled into the ditch, she might now be considering her situation from inside a thick black layer of charred skin. She cringed thinking about it.

Phylis took a deep breath, ignoring the gasoline stench, and began marching back towards Lakeview.

She had driven farther than she remembered; it took a good five minutes to reach the sign. She paused by one of the wooden posts. Voices drifted from the clearing beyond, and when she stepped closer she saw the two soldiers outside the front door of the main building, talking quietly, rifles held ready across their chests. She slowly edged into the shadows at the side of the road. Three Jeeps littered the parking area, along with John's Impala. It hadn't been there earlier. That meant John, and the Jeeps, had arrived *after* her crash.

So why hadn't they stopped?

They could not have missed the bright yellow Datsun marooned at the side of the road, even in the downpour. Or could they? She shivered, the wind cutting through her thin plaid shirt.

She hugged the tree line and worked her way towards the cabin, keeping out of sight of the soldiers. She ducked below the edge of the porch window and shuffled along the front of the cabin, almost tripping over the body lying prone before the porch door. It was Legs. She studied the crumpled body, feeling unaccountably sorry for the creature.

314

There were numerous gaping wounds in the monstrous head. Bullet holes. One of the bright blue eyes was open, the other a shattered mass of soppy flesh. The three legs, so graceful and agile in life, were now bent at odd angles. One of them was broken in two or three places, snapped like a small branch, hanging together by strings of skin.

She muffled a groan and entered the cabin, carefully closing the screen door so it would not squeak or bang.

The cabin was empty. She checked both bedrooms and the bathroom. No sign of Celia, or Phelps, and thankfully no sign of a struggle. In the living room she paused, frowning, not sure what had caught her attention. Then she spotted it, and icy fingers of panic stroked her neck. Celia's one-eyed teddy was nestled in a corner of the sofa, staring blindly into the living room. Celia would never have deserted teddy. Not for anything.

Phylis moved to the living room window, and carefully peered around the edge. Though the clouds were dark, almost black, there was still enough residual light to see clearly. The lake moved restlessly under fingers of wind, and Phelps's small boat still rested on the beach.

Damn! They hadn't gotten away!

For a moment she felt rage at Phelps, and she held it at bay only with strong effort. If they hadn't gotten away it wasn't Phelps's fault. Damn it. The man had risked his life on the rough lake to get over here. Something must have happened.

Again she glanced at the main building, its lights bright under the dark sky.

Think logically, don't panic.

They missed you on the road. It was raining hard, that was quite possible. The accident had happened on a curve, and they would have had to look very carefully to see the Datsun. Okay, so they missed you. It was obvious that Celia and Phelps were still somewhere in Lakeview, most logically at the main building, and she could not stay hidden forever. One way or another she had to confront the situation.

Once she made up her mind it was easy. She made as much noise as possible leaving the cabin, slamming the screen door and kicking her feet in the gravel as she walked. The soldiers spotted her immediately and their rifles came unglued from their chests.

What if they shoot me?

The thought came like a bolt of lightning and almost froze her. The thought of dying out here in the middle of nowhere, with nobody to hear about it, frightened her badly. But she managed to keep walking, a smile pasted onto her face, until she was at the foot of the stone path that led up to the glass doors. Both young soldiers took a menacing step towards her.

"Halt!"

"It's only me," Phylis said, relieved that her voice

was calmer than she felt. "Have you seen Dr. Gordon?"

"What do you want?"

"I'm looking for my daughter. I had an accident on the road. I thought they might be inside." She took another step towards the doorway.

Both guns came up, aimed in her direction. "Stop."

"You don't understand," still smiling. "I think my daughter's inside, and I want to see her."

"Nobody's allowed inside."

Their voices were bland, emotionless, matching the blank, shell-shocked looks on their faces. Phylis frowned, unsure how to continue. She had made up her mind to march forward when the glass door behind the soldiers opened, and John Gordon stepped out.

"It's all right, you can let her through."

"John, thank God!"

She ran to him sobbing with relief, and threw her arms around him. She pressed her face into his chest, hugging him tightly. She had never been so glad to see anybody in her life. But he did not hug back. After a moment Phylis stepped away. John was staring down at her, his face a mask of neutrality.

"So, you're okay," he said.

"I had an accident."

"Yes, we saw the car."

His flat statement strangled her fragile sense of relief. *He knew.*

317

"Where's Celia?" Phylis whispered.

"Inside."

"And Dr. Phelps?"

John smiled hearing Phelps name. "He's here too. Come on."

She followed him into the building. The two soldiers stepped apart, not bothering to hide the look of distaste on their faces, and followed closely. *They want to kill me,* Phylis realized in horror.

John walked down the hallway to the treatment room. Phylis moved quickly to keep up.

"John, what's going on here?"

"Nothing," he said.

She reached out and grabbed his arm, spinning him around. "John, please, tell me what's happening."

Anger tightened his features, then the careful neutral look returned immediately. He shook his head slowly. "It's almost over, Phylis."

He turned and continued walking. Phylis shook her head in confusion, and followed. He held the door of the observation room for her.

"You're alive," Captain Wilkes said, smiling.

The two soldiers stepped past Phylis and assumed positions on either side of Wilkes. Harold Phelps, sitting in a straight-backed wooden chair in the center of the room hands cuffed behind him, smiled as Phylis entered. She felt her features slacken in surprise.

"Captain Wilkes, I demand an explanation," Phylis

said, forcing her voice to carry a note of indignation.

Wilkes laughed. "Come on in. You're just in time for the demonstration."

Phylis moved closer to Wilkes. In the treatment room Celia was strapped to the black couch, head pressed back into a white pillow. Her face was puffed from crying, eyes red rimmed. Dr. Brand was bent over the computer console, while Margaret Palin sat beside Celia, talking softly to the child. Phylis stepped closer to the glass. Wilkes grabbed her arm and pulled her back.

"What are you doing to my daughter?" Phylis whispered.

"Don't be naive, Mrs. Reynolds," Wilkes said. "You already know the purpose of this institution, or at least have made some accurate guesses. I know Dr. Phelps has been talking to you."

"She knows nothing," Phelps said. "Let her and the child go."

Wilkes chuckled. "They know enough. But that's not the point. We have here," he nodded at Celia, "the finest subject the project has yet encountered."

Phylis's mind was suddenly a maelstrom of confusion. It was all too much. She sagged against the wall, her eyes filling with tears. "John, please, help us." It was the only thing she could think of saying; he was the only one she could turn to.

John, leaning against the door, frowned. "Sorry."

"But what about . . . us?"

"I like you a lot. None of that was planned."

She turned away, choking back a sob. "If you're looking for your weapon, it's already out," she said.

"Weapon?"

"The creature you were trying to bring through," Phylis said, turning to him again. "The one that killed my husband."

John nodded. "An interesting by-product of our research, but not its focus."

Phylis turned to Phelps, eyes questioning.

"I'm afraid I was mistaken about that," Phelps said. "They're after something bigger. Something a lot more dangerous. I've been trying to tell them that the creature they brought through is after the very same thing. It wants Celia to stay."

Phylis shook her head in confusion, then nodded slowly. "Yes, but . . . what same thing is it after?"

"It's a possibility we discussed early in our research," Phelps said, speaking directly to Phylis. "But something we never considered very seriously. A breakthrough. An uncontrolled eruption of Nether. An open door."

"Not uncontrolled, Dr. Phelps," John said. "We're always in control here."

Phelps chuckled. "This whole project is out of control. That's obvious. And this creature you brought through, this creature you so blithely shrug off as if it were a puppy, is the cause of all your troubles. It attacked the army compound and released all your past failures for a reason. Are you so

320

blind you can't see a diversion when it jumps out at you? It's trying to take the attention away from itself. It *wants* a breakthrough, Gordon. It wants to be able to move freely between Nether and here. All the evidence points that way."

"Shut up, Phelps," Wilkes said. "I've got Dr. Gordon's and Dr. Brand's assurance that the demonstration will be under control."

"Once the door is open, Captain, it's very hard to close," Phelps said.

"It's only a kid's mind, for Christ's sake," Wilkes said angrily. "We can shut it down any time we want. This creature you're talking about is nowhere in sight. We have nothing to worry about."

"You're wrong," Phylis said. "It's here now."

"What?"

"It's waiting," Phylis said. "It can come out anytime it wants."

Wilkes chuckled. Phelps glanced nervously around. The two soldiers shifted restlessly on their feet.

"You better hope it doesn't interfere," Wilkes said, turning to Phylis. "Because *Lieutenant* Palin has her finger on a switch that will shut this whole project down."

In the treatment room Margaret Palin placed the speaker helmet over Celia's head and pressed it firmly in place. She held the syringe to Celia's arm, pushed the needle into the freckled flesh, and injected the clear solution. Then she reached behind

321

her and pulled up the dark shape of a .45 calibre service automatic. She pumped it once, loading a shell into the chamber, nodded to Dr. Brand, and pressed the muzzle of the gun to the side of Celia's helmet.

Phylis held her breath.

"That's unnecessary," John said softly.

Wilkes nodded. "I hope so. We'll see. But there's one sure-fire method of closing the door we're about to open," he said, smiling. "And that's to blow your daughter's brains out, Mrs. Reynolds."

CHAPTER THIRTY-TWO

The storm eased up as he came around the second point, the hard driven rain changing slowly to a cool mist that tingled on the skin. Paul Welch sighed with relief. There had been moments during the past forty-five minutes when he regretted his decision to approach Lakeview by water, when the small boat had seemed ready to break to pieces on the angry swells, when the wind had seemed so strong he thought he was actually moving *backwards,* and when the driven sheets of rain had blinded him. But this sudden break gave him hope. He was more than halfway there. He chanced a glance behind him and could see the grey sheets hanging from the clouds, sweeping across the distant trees and into the water, like an impossibly long line of dirty laundry blowing in the wind. Ahead of him the east shore was also obscured by the ravages of the storm. A jagged arc of lightning split the sky, blinding him momentarily with its intensity, and a clap of thunder exploded in the clouds. Even the jumping water seemed to cringe from the sound.

"Use it while you've got it," Paul muttered to himself, guiding the boat closer to the shore. Beyond the point the water appeared to be almost glass smooth. It would not be long before this pocket of quiet passed and the full force of the storm resumed, but if he was lucky he would be almost at Lakeview by then.

When the boat hit the smoother, shallower water near shore, it picked up speed instantly. The prow lifted proudly, the motor assumed a constant throaty gurgle, and the rickety aluminum tub actually managed to hydrofoil across the water. Paul smiled. That was better. The trees whipped by in a blur of brown and green as he squinted his eyes into the mist and wind.

He traveled in fifteen minutes what it had taken forty-five minutes to come in the storm. The eastern shore drew closer, became better defined, and finally resolved into discrete images of trees, grassy banks, and pebbled beaches. He had estimated Lakeview's location at the very eastern bay of the lake, and as he approached the slight point that preceded the deep bite in the shore, he slowed the engine. The boat growled and sank in the water. When he rounded the rocky point, a miniature peninsula of boulders topped by leaning pine trees, the clinic came into view. In the dusk-like darkness of the storm the enclave of cabins looked decidedly sinister. The main building was a bank of bright lights, a sharp outline against the backdrop of trees, while the darker cabins peeled off to the right like a curled tail. A dim light leaked from the cabin he recognized as Phylis's

Paul rounded the point, keeping close to shore, and approached the clinic's beach slowly. The dark outline of a dock defined itself as he drew closer, and then he saw the other boat, dragged hastily onto the beach. Whoever had come ahead of him was still here.

He cut the engine and drifted in to shore, using the chewed end of a paddle to push the boat closer, until the prow hissed against sand and finally crunched to a stop. He hopped into the knee-deep water and pulled the boat halfway out of the water. It was too heavy to drag farther. He glanced at the other boat and hissed in disgust. Old Bob had done a number on his predecessor. The little tub, a twelve foot junker powered by a ragged nine-point-five horse Mercury outboard, made his sixteen footer look like a yacht. It must have taken hours to get across the lake in that thing.

Paul sniffed the air, frowning. Below the fresh smell of rain and trees and earth there was another, sharper, more pungent odor. Gasoline. The air stunk of it, a metallic tang that bit into the nostrils. Well, the soldiers hadn't been lying about that, at least.

He unzipped the pocket of his rain coat and pulled out the reassuring bulk of the Smith & Wesson .38, and with his other hand retrieved the box of shells. He emptied the box into his palm. There were only five. Jesus. He'd never really kept track of the gun, or its ammo.

He shrugged and loaded the five bullets. Five was better than none, and let's hope to God there was no need to use even one. He tossed the empty box to the beach. With the gun hanging limply in his right hand, he marched up across the small ridge and towards the dim light of Phylis's cabin.

Phylis backed away from the observation window, not quite believing the scene playing out around her. It had the unreal feeling of a dream, a nightmare from which she could not escape. In the treatment room Celia lay immobile on the black couch, firmly strapped in place, while Margaret Palin, *Lieutenant* Margaret Palin, she corrected herself, held a gun to the child's head.

"Shooting the girl would not be a good idea," Harold Phelps said, leaning sideway so he could see past Wilkes and Phylis.

"Only if it's necessary," Wilkes said gruffly, not looking around. "We're not monsters," he said more softly, turning to face Phylis.

"That's not what I mean," Phelps continued. "If you do actually manage to produce a breakthrough, killing the girl is the last thing you want to do."

Now Wilkes turned to face the doctor. "Why?"

"You need her mind to open the door," Phelps

said. "And you also need her to close it again."

Wilkes stared at the handcuffed man angrily, then turned to John Gordon. "What's he talking about?"

John shrugged. "Speculation. We don't know enough about the process yet. But I agree with him, it would be unwise to shoot the girl."

Wilkes's small black eyes focused on John like twin lasers. "Are you sure you're ready for this demonstration?"

"Everything is under control, Captain. You've disbelieved from the very start that our research had any value. Now we're going to prove you wrong. It's unfortunate that we've been put in this position so soon, but we must make the best of the situation."

Wilkes grunted, turning back to the observing glass. He leaned forward and pressed the intercom button. "Lieutenant Palin."

Margaret turned to face the glass.

"Under no circumstances is the girl to be harmed," Wilkes said.

"But, sir—"

"Under no circumstances," Wilkes repeated.

Margaret nodded curtly and took the gun from Celia's head. Phylis sighed, a small whimper passing her lips. She turned to John and gave him a small look of gratitude. Wilkes shook his head. "I hope you boys know what you're doing," he said.

Dr. Phelps continued to lean to his left. "Dr. Gordon, how are you precipitating the breakthrough?"

John ran a hand through his hair. He continued

to study Celia through the glass. "Feed back loop," he said softly, not turning to face Phelps. "We start at her zero mnemonic response value and let the Vax handle the rest. No pattern of attack. The synthesizer will feed her whatever she wants to. hear. Under the effect of the HG-37 compound she won't be able to fight it, in fact she'll reflexively seek the most powerful cues."

"You bloody fools," Phelps muttered hoarsely.

Phylis heard the conversation as if down a long tunnel, none of it making any sense. Celia was in danger, that's all that mattered.

You've failed her again. The small voice within her spoke in an accusing tone. It was her own voice.

In the treatment room Celia's small legs began to vibrate as if a current of electricity had passed through her.

"It's started," John said.

"How long will it take?" Wilkes asked.

"We don't know. She's very responsive, so probably not very long. Dr. Brand is ready to initiate a shutdown sequence the moment we achieve breakthrough."

"I want to *see* this breakthrough," Wilkes said.

John did not respond. He pursed his lips and focussed on Celia. Phylis fought back the whimper that started to emerge from her throat as Celia's small body strained within her bonds. If she had not been strapped down her body would have arched above the couch, just as it had done in the earlier session. When the creature, the darkness, had appeared in the room. Phylis shivered at the memory.

Phelps had said the creature *wanted* a breakthrough. Then where was it? Why wasn't it here, waiting, watching? She glanced furtively around, eyes seeking the dark corners where the shadows seemed to congregate. The same shadows that had lurked at the bottom of her crib when she was a baby.

Phylis closed her eyes. *Crazy thoughts. Keep them away.*

When she opened her eyes again the room seemed dimmer, as if one of the fluorescent bulbs had burned out, but when she looked up she could see that all of them were flickering madly. But now the shadows in the corners seemed even darker than they had earlier, deeper, as if they opened onto some vacuous, unfathomable darkness behind the reality of the room.

She shivered. Nobody else had noticed. Phelps continued to strain in the seat, trying to see into the observation room. John's eyes were trained intently on Celia, watching for the imminent breakthrough. Wilkes seemed frozen, enthralled with the action in the treatment room, where Celia's small body writhed beneath her bonds. The two soldiers were the only ones who seemed nervous. They shifted uneasily on their feet, their hands kneading the hardness of their rifles, eyes flickering from the scene in the other room to the darkness solidifying around

329

them.

"Look at that," Wilkes muttered, stepping closer to the glass.

A flickering diamond of light, like a phosphene flash against closed eyelids, played across the pale wall behind Celia's spasming body. The flicker widened, another appeared, then another, until the diamond was about a yard across. It's edges were as clearly defined as if a pathologist's scalpel had cut them in dead flesh. Within the boundary of the glimmering light pale shapes writhed, moved, twisted, none identifiable.

"Jesus Christ," Wilkes said softly. "Is this it?"

"The beginning," John said.

"Stop it now," Phelps hissed from behind them. "Initiate the shutdown, Dr. Gordon."

John shook his head, hypnotized by what was happening on the wall behind Celia.

Phylis turned away. The shadows in the room were more pronounced. In the corner behind Phelps the shadow was so dark it looked like a bottle of ink had been spilled on white paper. *Wasn't the wall visible when we came in?*

Phelps, noticing her concern, turned and glanced at the corner. When he turned, his face was white as death. "I think we've got company," he said softly.

Wilkes turned to him. He noticed the deepening shadows in the room immediately, and his face stiffened. "Dr. Gordon . . ."

John turned, and the inky shadow spilled farther

into the room.

"What . . ." John muttered.

The sound of the scream caused them all to turn at once. Celia was rigid, as if locked in the clasp of death. Her small mouth opened and another scream emerged, filled with terror. The diamond behind her expanded like a balloon, filling the wall, growing into the roof and beyond it, the area within its perimeter a sea of flickering shapes.

"Celia!" Phylis screamed.

Though the child could not possibly hear her through the observation glass, Celia's head rose from the white pillow, and the blank glass of the audio helmet seemed to focus on her. Celia's mouth opened again, and this time she wailed in despair, the wail increasing in volume, wavering, until it formed into a word that cut into Phylis's heart.

"Moooommmmmyyyyyy!"

And then the darkness solidified. It poured from the corners of the observation room and the treatment room like some liquid piece of deep space, surrounding them completely, blocking off all light.

In the solid, impenetrable blackness that surrounded her, Phylis could not see the others. But she could hear them: Wilkes's ragged breathing, the frantic shuffling of the two soldiers as they scrambled to bring their weapons to bear on an enemy that was everywhere and nowhere, the faint whimper of Phelps struggling against his handcuffs, the deep breathing of John as he tried to assimilate what was happening.

Most of all there was her own whimper, finally bubbling up from her throat, growing in intensity as it continued. Because she knew what was going to happen next, remembered it from the nights in the crib when the darkness had crowded the corners of her nursery.

The yellow eyes opened, like lanterns in fog, impossibly huge in the darkness. Below them the shadows curled into what could only be a smile.

Phylis screamed.

CHAPTER THIRTY-THREE

Paul studied the creature on the ground with a mixture of curiosity and disgust. It appeared almost to be a gigantic three-legged, daddy-long-legs spider. The three legs were twisted like licorice sticks, one of them so badly broken that shards of bone were protruding in jagged points from the papery skin. The pale flesh of the body, or the head, or whatever the hell it was, was pockmarked with ragged holes. *Bullet holes.* Most of the body looked like a mouth, a mouth twisted in shock and pain. Whatever the thing was, it just *shouldn't have been,* should not have existed, *could* not have existed. He shook his head. The words he had read only the day before came back to him: "In some cases suppressed trauma may result in the projection of objects outside the subject's body."

"Shit," he muttered.

He entered the cabin tentatively, but his stealth was unnecessary. There was nobody there, and neither was there any sign of further violence. Phylis's rusting yellow Datsun was gone.

Outside, he studiously avoided looking at the creature lying crumpled by the porch door, and walked towards the main building. He could see that there were a number of cars parked out front, including a couple of army Jeeps. Why not? It's a defense department project.

What had Phylis gotten herself involved in? A pang of guilt jumped up to assail him. It had been his thoughtless actions that had precipitated the incident that resulted in Phylis coming here. A large drop of rain splattered on his cheek, then another. He glanced across the lake, groaning as he saw the sheets of rain sweeping off the water towards shore. He swore softly under his breath. At least the respite had lasted long enough for him to get here. Holding the gun tightly he walked faster.

He was less than fifty yards from the main building when the howl erupted from the woods to his right. He stopped in midstep, gun at the ready. The trees rustled noisily and a pale shape burst from the bushes and ran towards him. Paul frowned. The creature, scampering towards him on four misshapen legs, looked like a dog: a pale, fleshy, hairless, vicious looking Boxer. The sound coming from its toothy mouth was more of a human whine than a dog's growl, and it sent shivers up his spine. He pointed the gun.

"Stop!"

The dog-thing skidded to a halt fifteen yards away, large black teeth exposed in what might have been a grin. "Go away," Paul hissed.

The dog whined and its grin widened. The whine changed to a definite growl. A deep-throat, angry, chew-you-to-bits growl. It pounced forward.

Paul squeezed the trigger. The gun clapped loudly, and a small round hole appeared in the dog's side. It collapsed, whining, legs shaking. In a moment it stopped moving. The shot continued to echo through the clearing.

Paul felt another pang of guilt. Jesus, it had only been a dog. Maybe it had been somebody's pet, for Christ's sake. But he knew that was not true. This creature had come from the same place the thing at the cabin had come from. He walked closer and touched it with his toe. The body seemed flabby, boneless. It was dead. He shivered in disgust and continued on towards the main building. The shot had not aroused attention, unusual in itself, but he kept the gun ready. Four shots left.

He opened the door and listened. There were voices coming from down the hallway to his left, muted by distance and doors. He did not recognize Phylis's or Celia's voice. He stepped inside, letting the door swing shut, and the sound of the rain and wind disappeared. Paul pulled down his hood.

Where the hell was everybody?

He stepped farther into the reception area. The white floor tiling was streaked with mud and water.

335

Somebody had come this way only a short while ago. He glanced to his right and saw the payphone in the corner, the OUT OF ORDER sign hanging loosely from the receiver. So it *had* been down. Maybe purposely so. He followed the wet streaks on the floor.

He had taken two tentative steps down the corridor when he heard the scream. A child's voice, filled with terror.

A cold, hard knot tightened in his stomach.

A shout: "Celia!" Phylis's voice.

The scream came again, this time turning to a word: "Mommy!" A long, drawn out wail.

It seemed, as the last scream echoed into silence, that the darkness at the end of the hallway deepened, became more pronounced. Paul held the gun tightly. His instinct was to run, break open the doors, force his way in. But that might spell disaster for all of them. He edged forward, gun held out, closer to the deepening darkness.

Phylis's scream trailed into nothing, swallowed by the darkness. The yellow eyes pierced her, drew closer. The darkness swirled about her, a mad whirlpool of shadow. She heard sounds, breathing, a wooden chair moving on tile. Then a ragged scream from behind her, from where Phelps had been cuffed to his chair.

"Gordon! What the hell is going on?" That was

Wilkes's voice.

She heard the metallic clicks of the soldiers' guns, their panicked breathing. Suddenly two loud explosions filled the room, and for a moment the nightmare tableau was illuminated in the harsh glare of the guns' powder flashes. Wilkes's face was a mask of terror, mouth hanging open; Phelps strained at his cuffs, neck corded with effort, beads of sweat clinging to his pale forehead; John backed against the door, eyes wide in horror, mouth open in a silent O of surprise.

The observation window exploded in a storm of glass splinters as the bullets smashed through. From the darkness of the treatment room she could hear Dr. Brand whimpering, and Margaret's quick, ragged breathing.

"Celia!" Phylis shouted the name into the darkness.

"Mommy!" Celia's voice was an orchestra of terror and fear, turned up to full volume.

Phylis held her hand out in front of her, feeling for the smashed opening of the glass. Her hand slid on the bottom of the sill, and she winced as a sliver of glass slicked into her palm. She drew back and her hip rubbed against the control box for the speaker. Static filled the room, the same static that Celia would be hearing inside her helmet. And behind the static, behind the insane babble of noises that filled the darkness, there was another sound.

Phylis paused, heart hammering in her chest.

The noise from the speaker filled her head, primal sound, the sound that Celia's panicked mind was striving for, the noise the Vax controlled synthesizer was dutifully producing. A sound that Phylis's own baby mouth had screamed in panic and terror so many years ago.

"MAAAMAAA!"

BIG WARMTH

A sound that brought relief from the leering darkness that had lurked at the bottom of the crib so many years ago.

She sensed, rather than saw or heard, the heavy, sluggish movement from the treatment room.

The speaker continued to fill both rooms with its noise, the sound that Celia's mind, freed by the HG-37, was eager to hear.

"MAAAMMMAAAA!"

Mama. Mommy. Big Warmth. Safety. Food. Protection.

The concepts threw her mind into a flurry of emotion and memory.

The darkness wavered, and the fluorescent lights above flickered through, as if they were obscured by smoke. In the treatment room the outline of the huge glittering diamond glowed faintly, and within the outline something moved. Something very big.

The darkness coalesced into a large lump beside her, yellow eyes blazing angrily. Icy tendrils wrapped themselves around Phylis, huge dark fingers, squeezing, and she felt herself lifted from the ground. She screamed. Then she was flying through the air, through the broken observation window. She crashed at the foot of the couch, right arm buckling painfully behind her. For a moment her vision filled with pulsating red, but she fought back against the tide of faintness.

The room was brighter now. In the observation room she could see the large blob of darkness, almost man-shaped, yellow eyes peering through at her. What might have been arms reached out to either side of the creature, and suddenly John and Wilkes were dragged together in front of the darkness. Wilkes's mouth opened to scream but no sound emerged. John's eyes were wide in astonished disbelief. Dr. Phelps, arched above his confining chair, arms rigid behind him, as if he were caught in the throes of a fatal heart attack.

Again, Phylis sensed something large moving in the treatment room, a familiar presence.

Big One. Big Warmth. Mama.

A large amorphous blob of light passed across her, obscuring the shattered glass of the observation room, and then passed through. The dark seemed to tremble, wavered at its edges like a mirage, as if the blob of light had physically affected it. And Phylis finally understood.

The only thing that had saved her from the darkness as a baby, was the presence of her mother. The Big Warmth that came when she screamed in baby terror, flooding her nursery with light and safety.

And now, reacting to the presence of the darkness around her, Celia had called for the same thing. Except Celia was filled with HG-37 and hooked into Nether. And from nether came the only thing she knew of that could defeat the darkness and take it away.

Mama. Big warmth.

She watched, filled with a mixture of horror and awe, as the darkness and the light began to twirl around each other. Within the tornado she caught glimpses of John and Wilkes, then Phelps, and soon, as the tornado intensified, the screaming faces of the two young soldiers who had become inadvertently drawn into the nightmare vortex. Beside her, Margaret Palin drew herself to her feet, fumbling for her service .45. Dr. Brand was bent over the computer console, typing furiously, glancing in horror over his shoulder.

But he was not looking at the battle in the other room. He was looking behind Phylis, at the wall behind Celia. Phylis turned slowly, not wanting to look, knowing what she would see.

The diamond now extended beyond the room, beyond the walls on either side, beyond the floor. A glittering doorway to another world. To Nether. The common unconscious world of humanity. The dumping ground of the mind.

Pale shapes, some horribly familiar like the faded memories of a nightmare, others unidentifiable, capered beyond the doorway, ready to spill into the room, a neverending torrent that would fill the world. Waves of light and darkness rippled across the writhing mass, illuminating and shadowing in apparent random patterns. Phylis could not look away. She recognized, in the twirling shapes before her, something of herself, some secret memories hidden beyond her grasp. Inside her mind she sensed the mirror of what she was looking at, somewhere deep where she could not normally reach, now awakened and rising.

She opened her mouth to scream her protest.

Then the door to the treatment room opened, and Paul Welch stepped through.

CHAPTER THIRTY-FOUR

It was a nightmare of Spielbergian proportions, special effects courtesy of George Lucas.

For one brief moment his mind denied what his eyes were seeing, as most minds will do when faced with the impossible, and then he acted purely on instinct. Phylis was lying on the ground, right arm buckled behind her, face smeared with blood, gazing up at him in wonder. On the couch behind her a small body was strapped, head encased in a metallic helmet. *Celia.* Beside the girl a buxom young woman, dark hair swept off her forehead in severe lines, was raising a gun. He saw all these things in less than a second, registering each without emotion. He saw the dark-haired man in a white smock bent over a computer console at the other side of the room and dismissed his presence immediately — non-threatening. What was important, what galvanized him to instant action, was the dark-haired

342

woman raising her gun and pressing it to Celia's metal encased head.

His hand swung up and he fired a single shot. It caught the woman in the forehead and she jerked to rigid attention. Her arm swung upwards in death's reflex and the large handgun fired once. The bullet missed Celia, but the man by the computer straightened, then collapsed, a bright red hole in the center of his white back.

"Paul!"

Phylis was trying to push herself to a standing position. For the moment Paul ignored her. His mind still registered danger. Behind Celia a world of madness swirled, a portal open on a Salvador Dali vision of hell. He turned away from it, refusing to see, knowing that if he looked any longer his mind would fold in on itself, drawing him down to some dark, inescapable hole. This room opened on another, separated by an opening that had once contained glass. The other room was a huge blender filled with essence of light, essence of darkness, and a few human bodies thrown in for flavor.

"Paul!" Phylis was kneeling now.

He crouched down beside her, unable to speak.

"The computer," she hissed. "Shut down sequence!"

He stepped over her to the bank of equipment, making sure he did not step on the crumpled form of the dead man in the smock. The terminal he had been typing at showed a dark green screen. In the upper left hand corner four words blinked:.

INITIATE SHUT DOWN? [RETURN].

His right hand jabbed out and hit the return key. The screen went blank.

The noises that had filled the room with their background chatter stopped for a moment, and then resumed. But these noises were different. Calmer. He forced himself not to listen, realizing that the noises were coaxing him to passivity. He went back to Phylis, keeping his eyes away from the madness behind her.

"Okay. What now?" He had to shout above the surf-like roar that filled both rooms.

"We have to wait," Phylis said. "For the door to close." She jerked her head at the hellish scene behind Celia's prone form.

In the other room the tornado of light and darkness began to slow, became instead an image of grappling monsters. Light and dark. A comic book vision of the battle between good and evil, and between the two forms the trapped faces of five men, twisted in terror and fear, one of them somehow tied to a seat. The pulsating light moved towards the opening, pulling the men with it, pushing through the frame of broken glass. Paul edged back, dragging Phylis away from the foot of the couch. The light was winning the battle. It encompassed the darkness, encompassed the five men, drew them through the shattered opening, towards the mael-strom in the wall.

The opening was smaller now. He could see its boundaries, pushing at the edges of the walls, like a rear screen projection from an old movie. Celia's body on the couch was the only point of stillness in the picture.

Phoney, he thought.

Above the bed, partially obscuring Celia, the blob of light moved closer to the shrinking opening. Within the mass, the five men seemed to be held in some stupendous grip, limbs thrashing but otherwise incapable of movement. Phylis managed to loosen his grip and reached up towards the figures.

"Dr. Phelps!" Her pale hand disappeared into the glow.

Paul leaned forward, renewed his grip, and pulled her away. The figure tied into the chair seemed to respond to Phylis's cry. For a moment his stiff features relaxed, almost into confusion, and then the rigor mortis-like grimace returned. It was a look of eagerness, Paul thought, as if he *wanted* to be dragged into the hell beyond the wall. Phylis turned away, pressing her face into his chest.

"He tried to help us," she sobbed. "He came in the boat."

Paul held tightly to Phylis, frightened she might reach again for the twirling blob. Above the bed, the maelstrom paused, pulsating, then pushed through into the constantly shifting landscape beyond. The light and darkness separated, hovered for a moment, then merged with the background. Now, against the roiling backdrop, the five men could be seen, outlined as if in silhouette, dark struggling shapes bobbing on a sea of madness.

Their screams were terrible to hear. One voice seemed to reach out, a cry of terror and despair:

"Phylis! For God's sake, Phylis!"

"John . . ." Phylis whispered, then turned her eyes away.

Then the screams turned full volume, lost coherency, lost all trace of humanity, as they merged into a pure sound of terror.

Paul closed his eyes. He tried to close his ears. But the screams went on, and on, and on.

When, at last, he opened his eyes agin, the twirling mass of shapes had reduced to the size of a small painting, hanging askew above the bed, shrinking as he watched, shrinking, until only three glittering points of light remained on the wall. Then two. One. Gone, as if there had never been an opening.

Silence filled the room. A palpable, solid presence.

"Jesus Christ," Paul said, and meant it with all his heart. His voice was a small thing, wavering, unsure.

Phylis worked herself to her feet. Tears were

streaming down her face. She bent over Celia and pulled the helmet from the child's head. Celia's green eyes blinked up at her mother.

"Mommy?"

Phylis bent over the cowering child and hugged her fiercely. Her face winced in pain.

"I think I broke my arm," Phylis said, turning to Paul. "Can you take her?"

Paul nodded numbly. He picked up Celia in his arms, and the little girl hugged him tightly, burying her face in his neck.

"I brought a boat," Paul said. "The road's blocked."

Phylis nodded. "Let's go."

Phylis followed Paul blindly. Her mind was numb, incapable of contemplating what she had just seen. In the reception area Paul stopped, looking outside.

"It's raining bad. The wind has picked up. It's going to be a rough ride."

"Doesn't matter," Phylis said. "We've got to get out of here. There are things in the woods."

Paul looked at her a moment, and then he nodded. Phylis sighed. She could not have argued at that point. If he'd said they should stay she would have broken down and cried, and cried, and maybe never have come back to the real world.

"Paul, do you have a lighter?"

He frowned. "A lighter?" Holding Celia with one hand he patted his pockets until he produced a small yellow Bic.

Phylis took it from his trembling fingers. "Go to the beach. I'll be there in a minute."

He paused, obviously not liking the look in her eyes. "Phylis. There's a big gasoline spill outside."

She nodded. "Go."

His gaze lingered on her for a moment, and then he pushed out into the wind and rain and began trotting towards the beach. Phylis went to the reception desk. From the garbage she pulled a sheet of paper and lit with the Bic. After it was burning she dropped it back into the metal container. In a moment flames sprang high from the can, licking at the bottom of the reception desk. She stepped back, watching. Soon the bottom of the desk began to burn, smoke billowing into the reception area. Phylis dropped the lighter and ran.

Paul was waiting at the beach. Celia was lying in the bottom of the boat, a life jacket draped over her small arms.

"Get in," Paul said.

But as Phylis approached the boat Celia sat rigidly at attention and stared at her. "Mommy. My teddy."

The words were small and feeble, but they carried a power that Phylis could hardly comprehend. She locked eyes with Celia for a long second. To leave

348

teddy was an unthinkable act, one that would be tantamount to saying that things were not all right, that they never would be.

"Paul, start the boat. I'll be back in a minute."

He opened his mouth to object, but one look at the expression on Phylis's face shut him up. He nodded.

Phylis turned and ran back toward the cabin. Her feet slipped continually on the wet grass, and once her foot slid into a gopher hole sending her sprawling to the ground. But she was moving on instinct. *Impulse engines only, Captain.* She scrambled to her feet and moved onward.

She studiously avoided looking at the sprawled body of Legs, and smacked open the screen door with her shoulder. Celia's teddy was propped up in the corner of the sofa. She picked it up. But there was something else. Something else she needed. It took a moment, but finally it came to her. Dora's book was on the kitchen counter. She grabbed it and stuffed it down the front of her jeans.

When she stepped through the porch door and out onto the path she knew it was all over. All hope disappeared in a rush of air from her mouth.

The creature stood less than an arm's length from her, a mountain of pale flesh, towering above her. Her head craned back on her neck and she looked up at its face, a bulbous mass of play dough, grinned down at her. Lips the size of her forearms

349

split into a grim.

"Da-vid?" Its voice was thick, yet melodious. Tiny black eyes stared down at her.

"Sonny," Phylis whispered.

"David?" The voice, a child's voice, though deeper than any man's voice she had ever heard, carried the weight of infinite sorrow.

"David's gone," Phylis said.

"David?"

She stepped past it, shoulder brushing against one huge thigh, and ran toward the water. She glanced back and saw that Sonny had not moved. The creature was looking toward her, its immense face twisted in grief. Phylis ran. To her right, the glass vestibule of the main building popped open in a spray of glass, sounding like a hundred wine glasses breaking on a linoleum floor, followed by a deep *WHOOSH* sound. A tongue of flame darted out of the building. For a moment she thought it would recede. But the tongue of flame extended, elongated, curling blue at its edges, and suddenly a tendril of flame leapt from the ground and darted towards the road. The gasoline. A wave of warmth passed over her neck, and a sudden blast of scorched air sent her rolling onto the beach.

Suddenly Paul was standing over her, lifting her by the good arm, hauling her toward the boat. Somehow she had managed to hang onto teddy. The sharp edge of Dora's book cut into her belly. She climbed over the cold metal edge of the boat, sitting down hard. Paul pushed the prow, grunting, until sand grated beneath the hull and the boat drifted free. He hopped in, climbing over Celia, placing his warm hand on Phylis's shoulder for support, until he was sitting by the motor. He pulled the cord once and the motor sputtered to life, gurgling blue smoke like a water borne version of the Datsun.

She lifted Celia with her good arm, hugging the child tightly. Celia, in turn, pulled teddy close to her face. The boat crashed violently through the waves, rocked by the wind. Rain came down like bullets, driven so hard that she could not face forward.

Phylis turned, looking past Paul's evenly tanned face. He smiled at her, then concentrated on guiding the boat. Lightning flickered overhead. Phylis looked past Paul, towards the receding shore. The main building was a torch, leaping up to the sky. Flames spilled out of the windows, adding black smoke to the already black sky, and a wall of flame extended back into the woods. Already she could see some of the trees burning. Soon she could not even discern the outline of the main building, only the bright yellow of the flames.

As she watched, a pale shape lumbered down to the beach. It stood on the grassy ridge, silhouetted against the brightness of the burning building. A faint wail came across the water, then was carried away by the wind.

"Sonny," Phylis muttered, remembering the beginning of the nightmare.

Then they rounded the first point and Lakeview disappeared behind the dark line of trees, but she could still see the orange glow against the underbelly of the clouds.

She watched the glow for a long time, hugging Celia, as the small boat crashed into the darkening night.

EVERYMAN, I will go with thee,

and be thy guide,

In thy most need to go by thy side

GOTTHOLD EPHRAIM LESSING

Born in 1729 in Upper Lusatia. Educated
at Leipzig University. Visited England,
and afterwards lived in Berlin and Leipzig.
Travelled to Italy, 1772. Died in 1781.

Laocoön
Nathan the Wise
Minna von Barnhelm

EDITED BY
WILLIAM A. STEEL

DENT: LONDON
EVERYMAN'S LIBRARY
DUTTON: NEW YORK

NO. *843*

INTRODUCTION

A feature in the story of German literature which all its critics have remarked is the rapidity of its development in the course of the eighteenth century, and the astonishing contrast between the opening and the closing decades of the period. The second half of the century witnessed the outburst of splendour in Goethe and Schiller and Kant, and showed Germany keeping step with England and France. The fertilising influences of the Renaissance had reached Germany late, for in England the Elizabethan age had come, and flourished in full luxuriance, and Milton had followed his greater predecessor, whilst in Germany poetry, drama and literature generally still remained a poverty-stricken and almost negligible product.

There were special reasons for this retardation. Early in the seventeenth century the curse of war had brooded heavily over Europe, with particular darkness over Germany—for thirty years the cock-pit where was fought out the fateful struggle between the Catholic South and the Protestant North. On both sides the armies were mercenaries, and their marches to and fro were marches of military locusts, devouring and destroying everywhere. Nor was it merely material desolation that resulted; the springs of intellectual and spiritual activity also were choked in the universal debacle. The war was over by 1648, but a prolonged period was required for complete recovery.

Another hindrance to the advance of German letters was the absence of national unity, the want of an acknowledged centre of the national life. Berlin, Leipzig, Hamburg, all contended for the central place, at least in the production of books and in theatrical enterprise; and thus an advantage was lost which England and France enjoyed by their great capitals. It is also worth remarking that whatever furtherance for intellectual activities can be looked for from men in the high places of society was conspicuously wanting. The King himself, the great Frederick, besides being almost exclusively absorbed by the interests of his army, was cold not only to German literature but even to the German language. He liked to speak French and to have Frenchmen about him. There is nothing blameworthy in Frederick's preference. Who is there that does not prefer lightness, clarity and grace to heaviness and clumsiness? If we criticise the mistaken notions of French dramatists of those days, their bondage to ancient rules and examples, let us at the same time freely acknowledge their merits. Lessing himself confesses that he owed much to them, acknowledging a particular obligation to Diderot, as the man who has taken so great a share in forming his taste. " Be this what it may," he writes, " I know that without Diderot's example and doctrines it would have taken a quite different direction." Frederick's preference for French writers, then, can be easily understood, yet the natural consequence of his attitude was undoubtedly to chill and discourage German authors and to undermine their efforts. Frederick's real service was in a different field; he brought to Germany a natural self-consciousness and self-confidence which it had hitherto lacked.

When, moreover, German literature began once more to show signs of vitality and renewal, the leaders who undertook its superintendence were unfortunately unequal to the task. They wanted the natural genius which the great business demanded, and they followed mistaken paths. For some time before Lessing's birth in 1729, the outstanding literary figure was Gottsched, dictator for a generation in German letters, implicitly obeyed by all who wrote. The praise cannot be withheld from him of labouring indefatigably to stir up amongst aspiring men the ambition to write well; but by all accounts we have of him his place was distinctly in the second class, a man pedantical and essentially prosaic, without the gift of critical discernment. This was characteristically shown in the book he issued for the guidance of poets—*Kritische Dichtkunst für die Deutschen*, a volume of precepts and rules from which none must deviate. Lessing quietly laughs at Gottsched's classification of a collection of poems he published—1st class, poems addressed to Royal personages; 2nd, those addressed to counts, noble people, and such-like; 3rd, friendly lyrics! It was idle to look for inspiration to Gottsched: rules and precepts may furnish useful warnings against grave blunders, but they also can easily become bonds and fetters. The worst of his counsel was that he directed his disciples to wrong models and false ideals; they were instructed to imitate the French in their artificial and pseudo-classic drama, in short, to imitate what was itself an imitation. There could be only one result—originality and independence were discountenanced, and the denial of freedom led to lifeless and uninspired performances. To rely on a code of rules, or even on patterns drawn from Greek perfection, was a mistake. A wiser counsel by far is embodied in the old poet's words—" *Look in thy heart, and write!* "

No wonder, then, that under tuition like Gottsched's the field of German poetry and drama took on the aspect of Ezekiel's vision, a valley of dry bones. It had, however, now not long to wait for an inspiring breath to restore it to life and vigour, to bring flesh again on the dry bones, and set it on its feet, standing up boldly in freedom and self-reliance. After a faint dawn of day in Klopstock's poem *Der Messias*, a rather ineffectual echo of Milton's *Paradise Lost*, the full sunlight broke on the desolate scene from the genius of Lessing. His was the life-giving spirit. No qualifications were lacking to him for the task. From his early boyhood he was a student and lover of books, and he speedily acquired a knowledge of Greek and Roman literature that was extraordinarily wide and exact, as a thousand passages in *Laocoön* bear witness. His faultless taste was early formed, and his native gifts, a keen analytic intellect and instinctive justness of judgment, made him the perfect critic. No better plan of education could have been framed for him than to be permitted to browse in the library at home, and to be taught the rudiments of learning by his father, who did this work so thoroughly that young Lessing, entering at the age of twelve the " Prince's School " in Meissen, immediately took a foremost place among his fellows. " Tasks which others find too hard," wrote the rector to the father, " are child's play to him."

The design of Lessing's parents was that he should follow his father's profession. This was entirely contrary to his own inclinations. It was only after years of painful struggle, in which he had to endure much misunderstanding and censure of the bitterest kind, that he could enter upon his chosen career as a dramatist and journalist. His father and mother were puritans of the straitest sect, with a fanatical fear and hatred of the stage, an attitude which even now is not unknown amongst ourselves, especially in provincial places. Indirectly, no doubt, the narrow-mindedness and persecution of which he was so intimate a witness were a stimulus to Lessing in the frequent controversies of his career, in which he was always a champion of freedom and tolerance. With his characteristic tenacity he held to his own choice.

Parenthetically, it may be remarked how great a part of Lessing's energy was expended in controversy : not only on dramatic or purely literary questions, though these drew volume after volume from him, but on theology and philosophy, which largely engaged his pen for years together. It was labour he delighted in, for he was a born controversialist. His keen wit, his stores of exact and many-sided knowledge, gave him a peculiar advantage in these contests, and he enjoyed the still greater advantage that he contended only for truth, when his opponents were more concerned for orthodoxy. The enemies he chiefly loved to assail were bigotry, narrow-mindedness, and pretension. When Lessing began in earnest his efforts to raise German literature and drama to a higher level, he followed his favourite method of controversy and chose for an object of attack, Gottsched, the literary dictator, as the embodiment of the principles and practice that were hindering the advance.

" Our tragedies were full of nonsense, bombast, filth, and the wit of the mob. Our comedies consisted of disguises and enchantments, and blows were their wittiest ideas. To see this corruption it was not necessary to be the finest and greatest spirit. And Herr Gottsched was not the first who saw it ; he was only the first who had confidence in his own power to remove it. And how did he set to work ? He understood a little French, and began to translate ; everyone who could rhyme and understand ' *Oui, monsieur,*' he encouraged also to translate. . . . If the masterpieces of Shakespeare, with some modest changes, had been translated, I am convinced that better consequences would have followed than could follow from acquaintance with Corneille and Racine. . . .

For genius can only be kindled by genius; and most easily by a genius which seems to have to thank nature for everything and does not frighten us away by the tedious perfections of art." [1]

We have here one out of many proofs of Lessing's acquaintance with and sympathetic appreciation of the English dramatic writers. The drama is, of course, his chief interest, but his knowledge of other departments of our literature extended beyond it. In an article contributed to a quarterly magazine projected in Berlin he has the following on an effort by some of his friends to imitate the essays of the English *Spectator* :—
" You know who were the first authors in this kind of literature—men wanting neither in wit, thought, scholarship nor knowledge of the world—Englishmen who, in the greatest calm, and in easy circumstances, could study with attention whatever influences the spirit and manners of the nation. But who are their imitators among us ? For the most part, young witlings, who had scarce mastered the German language." [2]

The first really notable dramatic work of Lessing was a prose tragedy, *Miss Sara Sampson*, in which the influence of English models was immediately traced, and which was forthwith pronounced a novel type—a " *bürgerliches Trauerspiel* " it was styled, or " tragedy of common life." This piece had, therefore, an importance in the history of the German theatre beyond its intrinsic literary or theatrical value; it marked the beginning of an epoch, and became the favourite type on the German stage. From the day of its production the regard of German playwrights was turned not to France but to England. Lessing had written successful comedies when scarcely out of his boyhood, but *Miss Sara Sampson* made him known to the nation and to foreign critics. It also confirmed Lessing in the choice of dramatic writing as his proper sphere. More triumphant successes were soon to follow. It was in the three well-known dramas—*Emilia Galotti, Minna von Barnhelm,* and *Nathan der Weise*—that Lessing reached his highest level.

It is perhaps the last-named that is best known, but each of the three is worthy of his genius. *Emilia Galotti* is a tragedy on the lines of the story of Roman Virginia, most poignantly

[1] Sime's *Lessing*, Vol. I. p. 181.   [2] *Ibid.*, p. 127.

affecting, well-constructed for stage purposes (eminently
bühnen-fähig as the Germans say), but almost too painful for
popular acceptance. *Minna von Barnhelm* is the best of
German comedies, all critics agree; it is a story of military life
in the Frederician time, full of humour and good-humour,
touched here and there, but only slightly, with the German
weakness of over-sentimentality, and having the great merit of
being as enjoyable to-day as when it was first produced. This
in itself is a testimony to the human quality of it. The
characterisation is superbly worked out, every figure an un-
mistakable personality. It is still frequently staged. *Nathan der
Weise* is more properly a dramatic poem than a stage play, an
eloquent plea for *tolerance*, and embodying much of the earnest
thought of Lessing upon subjects lying nearest to his heart.
These two plays, along with the famous essay in literary
criticism, *Laocoön*, are the fragments of Lessing's immense
production presented in this little volume of translations.
The *Laocoön* is too large and too multifarious for any attempt
at detailed description in this brief preface. In its own
department of literary criticism it is authoritative, and one
of the acknowledged classics of the world.

Before closing these introductory words something should
be said of the personal fortunes of Lessing. He was born in
1729 in Kamenz, a small town in the kingdom of Saxony,
where his father was Pastor Primarius, or chief pastor, of the
place. His short life of fifty-two years, ending in 1781 in
Brunswick, was a record of incessant and ill-rewarded labour,
vexed perpetually by care and poverty. He quickly gained
his wide reputation as a critic and dramatist, and his work,
especially his excellent dramatic pieces, ought to have brought
him at least the means of comfortable living, if not a fortune.
So far from this was his experience that, at the close, what he
possessed did not suffice to cover the expenses of his funeral.
One secret of his troubles was the constant demands upon
him for help made by the poor pastor's large family at home,
whose members thought that a man so distinguished as their
famous brother must have an income corresponding, whereas
he was frequently himself in the most desperate straits. Until
1776, when he was forty-seven, he was not in a position to
marry. His wife, Eva König, to whom he had been greatly
attached for many years, was the widow of a manufacturer in

Vienna. It was the happiest of unions, but even here ill-luck
pursued him, for his wife lived only one year after marriage,
dying in childbirth.

Lessing's days were few and full of trouble; they were full
also of most fruitful labour. After two centuries his fame
continues, based firmly on his dramatic poems, and even more
securely on his critical writings, which the world will not
willingly let die.

W. A. STEEL.

SELECT BIBLIOGRAPHY

COLLECTED WORKS. The most important of these is edited by K. Lach-
mann, the *Sämmtliche Schriften* appearing in 13 vols. in Berlin, 1838–40; in
12 vols. in Leipzig, 1853–7; reissued by F. Muncker in 23 vols., 1886–1924.

PLAYS. *Die Alte Jungfer*, a comedy in 3 acts, 1749; *Philotas*, a tragedy
in 1 act, 1759; *Der Misogyne*, a comedy in 2 acts, 1762; *Der Junge Gelehrte
in der Einbildung*, a comedy in 1 act, 1764; *Minna von Barnhelm*, a comedy
in 5 acts, 1767; trans. into English by J. J. Johnstone as *The Disbanded
Officer*, 1786; anonymously as *The School for Honour*, 1799; by Fanny
Holcroft, 1806; by W. E. Wrankmore, 1858; by Major-General P. Maxwell,
1899; by E. U. Ouless as *The Way of Honour*, 1929. *Emilia Galotti*, a
tragedy in 5 acts, 1772, trans. into English by B. Thompson, 1801; by Fanny
Holcroft, 1805; by C. L. Lewes, 1867. *Miss Sara Sampson*, first bourgeois
tragedy of the German stage, in 5 acts, 1772; *Nathan der Weise*, dramatic
poem, in 5 acts, 1779; the most widely translated of all Lessing's works,
trans. into English by R. E. Raspe, 1781; by Wm Taylor of Norwich, 1791;
by A. Reid, 1860; by E. Frothingham, 2nd ed., 1868; by Andrew Wood,
1877; by E. K. Corbett, 1883; by R. D. Boylan, 1888; by W. Jacks, 1894;
by Major-General P. Maxwell, 1895. *Faust*, 1836; *Der Schatz*, comedy in
1 act, 1877.

MISCELLANEOUS WORKS. *Ein Vade Mecum für den Herrn Samuel Gotthold
Lange*, a criticism of Lange's trans. of Horace, etc., 1754; *Pope ein Meta-
physiker*, in collaboration with Moses Mendelssohn, 1755; *Fabeln*, 1759;
trans. by J. Richardson, 1773; anonymously in 1825, 1829, 1845, 1860;
selected Fables ed. by Carl Heath, 1907; *Laokoon*, 1766, followed by numerous other editions in Germany; trans. by W. Ross, 1836; by E. C. Beasley,
1853, revised edition, 1883; by Sir R. Phillimore, 1874, other editions, 1905,
1910; by E. Frothingham, 1874. *Briefe Antiquarischen Inhalts*, 1768;
Hamburgische Dramaturgie, theatrical criticisms, 1769; selections edited by
G. Waterhouse, 1926; *Kleinigkeiten*, a volume of poems, 1769; *Wie die Alten
den Tod gebildet*, an important essay, 1769; *Berengarius Turonensis*, 1770;
Zur Geschichte und Litteratur, 3 vols., 1773–81; *Eine Parabel*, a reply to the
criticisms of Pastor Goetze, 1778; *Ernst und Falk*, 1778–1870; trans. as
Lessing's Masonic Dialogues, by the Rev. A. Cohen, 1927. *Die Erziehung
des Menschengeschlechts*, 1780; trans. as *The Education of the Human Race*,
by F. W. Robertson, 1858; latest edition, 1927. *Fragmente des Wolfen-
buttel'schen ungenannten*, a rationalistic attack on Christianity, 1784; *Leben
des Sophokles*, 1790.

LETTERS. *Freundschaftlicher Briefwechsel zwischen G. E. Lessing und seiner Frau*, 1789; *Gelehrter Briefwechsel zwischen ihm, J. J. Reisse und Moses Mendelssohn*, 1789 and 1820; *Briefwechsel mit seinen Bruder K. G. Lessing*, 1795; *Briefwechsel mit Frau W. Gleim*, 1757–79, 1795; *Briefwechsel zwischen Lessing und seiner Frau*, 1870.

BIOGRAPHIES. In German the most important are those by C. G. Lessing, 1793; by T. W. Danzel, 1850–4, 2nd ed., 1880; by A. Stahr, 1859; trans. into English by E. P. Evans, 1866; by J. H. J. Dünster, 1882; by Erich Schmidt, 1884, 3rd ed., 1909; by A. W. Ernst, 1903.

In English there are Lives by James Sime, New York, 1877; by Helen Zimmern, 1878; by T. W. H. Rolleston, with a bibliography by J. P. Anderson, 1889. See also Wilhelm Todt: *Lessing in England, 1767–1850*, 1912.

CONTENTS

LAOCOÖN

OR

THE LIMITS OF PAINTING AND POETRY:

WITH INCIDENTAL ILLUSTRATIONS ON VARIOUS
POINTS IN THE HISTORY OF ANCIENT ART

"Ὕλη καὶ τρόποις μιμήσεως διαφέρουσι
(Πλουτ. ποτ. Ἀθ. κατὰ Π. ἢ κατὰ Σ. ἐνδ.)

PREFACE

THE first who likened painting and poetry to each other must have been a man of delicate perception, who found that both arts affected him in a similar manner. Both, he realised, present to us appearance as reality, absent things as present; both deceive, and the deceit of either is pleasing.

A second sought to penetrate to the essence of the pleasure, and discovered that in both it flows from one source. Beauty, the conception of which we at first derive from bodily objects, has general rules which can be applied to various things : to actions, to thoughts, as well as to forms.

A third, who reflected on the value and the application of these general rules, observed that some of them were predominant rather in painting, others rather in poetry; that, therefore, in the latter poetry could help out painting, in the former painting help out poetry, with illustrations and examples.

The first was the amateur; the second the philosopher; the third the critic.

The two former could not easily make a false use either of their feeling or of their conclusions. But in the remarks of the critic, on the other hand, almost everything depends on the justice of their application to the individual case; and, where there have been fifty witty to one clear-eyed critic, it would have been a miracle if this application had at all times been made with the circumspection needful to hold the balance true between the two arts.

Supposing that Apelles and Protogenes in their lost treatises upon painting confirmed and illustrated the rules of the same by the already settled rules of poetry, then one can certainly believe it must have been done with the moderation and exactitude with which we still find Aristotle, Cicero, Horace, Quintilian, in their writings, applying the principles and practice of painting to eloquence and poetry. It is the prerogative of the ancients, in everything to do neither too much nor too little.

But we moderns in several things have considered ourselves

their betters, when we transformed their pleasant little bye-ways to highroads, even if the shorter and safer highroads shrink again to footpaths as they lead us through the wilds.

The startling antithesis of the Greek Voltaire, that painting is a dumb poetry, and poetry a vocal painting, certainly was not to be found in any manual. It was a sudden inspiration, such as Simonides had more than once; the true element in it is so illuminating that we are inclined to ignore what in it is false or doubtful.

Nevertheless, the ancients did not ignore it. Rather, whilst they confined the claim of Simonides solely to the effect of the two arts, they did not omit to point out that, notwithstanding the complete similarity of this effect, they were yet distinct, both in their subjects and in the manner of their imitation (ὕλη καὶ τρόποις μιμήσεως).

But entirely as if no such difference existed, many of our most recent critics have drawn from that correspondence between painting and poetry the crudest conclusions in the world. Now they force poetry into the narrower bounds of painting; and again, they propose to painting to fill the whole wide sphere of poetry. Everything that is right for the one is to be granted to the other also; everything which in the one pleases or displeases is necessarily to please or displease in the other; and, obsessed by this notion, they utter in the most confident tone the shallowest judgments; and we see them, in dealing with the works of poets and painters beyond reproach, making it a fault if they deviate from one another, and casting blame now on this side and now on that, according as they themselves have a taste for poetry or for painting.

Indeed, this newer criticism has in part seduced the virtuosos themselves. It has engendered in poetry the rage for description, and in painting the rage for allegorising, in the effort to turn the former into a speaking picture without really knowing what she can and should paint, and to turn the latter into a silent poem without considering in what measure she can express general concepts and not at the same time depart from her vocation and become a freakish kind of writing.

To counteract this false taste and these ill-founded judgments is the primary object of the pages that follow. They have come together incidentally, according to the order of my reading, instead of being built up by a methodical development of general principles. They are, therefore, rather unordered *collectanea* for a book than themselves a book.

Yet I flatter myself that even as such they are not wholly to be despised. Of systematic books there is no lack amongst us Germans. Out of a few assumed definitions to deduce most logically whatever we will—this we can manage as well as any nation in the world.

Baumgarten confessed that for a great part of the examples in his *Æsthetics* he was indebted to Gesner's Dictionary. If my argument is not as conclusive as Baumgarten's, at all events my examples will taste more of the original sources.

As I started, as it were, from Laocoön and return to him several times, I have desired to give him a share in the superscription. Some other little digressions concerning various points in the history of ancient art contribute less to my purpose, and they only stand here because I cannot hope ever to find for them a more suitable place.

I would further remind the reader that under the name of Painting I include the plastic arts in general, and am not prepared to maintain that under the name of Poetry I may not have had some regard also to the other arts whose method of imitation is progressive.

I

THE general distinguishing excellence of the Greek master-pieces in painting and sculpture Herr Winckelmann places in a noble simplicity and quiet greatness, both in arrangement and in expression. " Just as the depths of the sea," he says, " always remain quiet, however the surface may rage, in like manner the expression in the figures of the Greek artists shows under all passions a great and steadfast soul.

" This soul is depicted in the countenance of the Laocoön, and not in the countenance alone, under the most violent sufferings. The pain which discovers itself in every muscle and sinew of the body, and which, without regarding the face and other parts, one seems almost oneself to feel from the painfully contracted abdomen alone—this pain, I say, yet expresses itself in the countenance and in the entire attitude without passion. He raises no agonising cry, as Virgil sings of his Laocoön; the opening of the mouth does not permit it : much rather is it an oppressed and weary sigh, as Sadolet describes it. The pain of the body and the greatness of the soul are by the whole build of the figure distributed and, as it were, weighed out in equal parts. Laocoön suffers, but he suffers like the Philoctetes of Sophocles : his misery touches us to the soul; but we should like to be able to endure misery as this great man endures it.

" The expression of so great a soul goes far beyond the fashioning which beautiful Nature gives. The artist must have felt in himself the strength of spirit which he impressed upon the marble. Greece had artist and philosopher in one person, and more than one Metrodorus. Wisdom stretched out her hand to Art and breathed more than common souls into the figures that she wrought," etc., etc.

The remark which is fundamental here—that the pain does not show itself in the countenance of Laocoön with the passion which one would expect from its violence—is perfectly just. This, too, is incontestable, that even in this very point in which a sciolist might judge the artist to have come short of Nature

6

and not to have reached the true pathos of the pain : that just here, I say, his wisdom has shone out with especial brightness.

Only in the reason which Winckelmann gives for this wisdom, and in the universality of the rule which he deduces from this reason, I venture to be of a different opinion.

I confess that the disapproving side-glance which he casts on Virgil at first took me rather aback ; and, next to that, the comparison with Philoctetes. I will make this my starting-point, and write down my thoughts just in the order in which they come.

"Laocoön suffers like the Philoctetes of Sophocles." How, then, does the latter suffer? It is singular that his suffering has left with us such different impressions—the complaints, the outcry, the wild curses, with which his pain filled the camp and disturbed the sacrifices and all the sacred functions, resounded no less terribly through the desert island, as it was in part they that banished him thither. What sounds of anger, of lamentation, of despair, by which even the poet in his imitation made the theatre resound ! People have found the third act of this drama disproportionately short compared with the rest. From this one gathers, say the critics, that the ancient dramatists considered an equal length of acts as of small consequence. That, indeed, I believe ; but in this question I should prefer to base myself upon another example than this. The piteous outcries, the whimpering, the broken ἆ, ἆ, φεῦ, ἀτταταῖ, ὤμοι, μοι ! the whole long lines full of παπα, παπα, of which this act consists and which must have been declaimed with quite other hesitations and drawings-out of utterance than are needful in a connected speech, doubtless made this act last pretty well as long in the presentation as the others. On paper it appears to the reader far shorter than it would to the listeners.

To cry out is the natural expression of bodily pain. Homer's wounded warriors not seldom fall to the ground with cries. Venus scratched screams loudly ; not in order that she may be shown as the soft goddess of pleasure, but rather that suffering Nature may have her rights. For even the iron Mars, when he feels the spear of Diomede, screams so horribly, like ten thousand raging warriors at once, that both hosts are terrified.

However high in other respects Homer raises his heroes above Nature, they yet ever remain faithful to her when it comes to the point of feeling pain and injury, and to the utterance of this feeling by cries, or tears, or abusive language.

By their deeds they are creatures of a superior order, by their sensibilities mere men.

I am well aware that we Europeans of a wiser posterity know better how to control our mouth and our eyes. Politeness and dignity forbid cries and tears. The active fortitude of the first rude ages has with us been transformed into the fortitude of endurance. Yet even our own ancestors were greater in the latter than in the former. Our ancestors, however, were barbarians. To conceal all pains, to face the stroke of death with unaltered eye, to die smiling under the teeth of vipers, to bewail neither his sin nor the loss of his dearest friend, are the marks of the ancient Northern hero. Palnatoko gave his Jomsburgers the command to fear nothing nor once to utter the word fear.

Not so the Greek! He both felt and feared; he uttered his pain and his trouble; he was ashamed of no human weaknesses; but none must hold him back on the way to honour or from the fulfilment of duty. What with the barbarian sprang from savagery and hardness, was wrought in him by principle. With him heroism was like the hidden sparks in the flint, which sleep quietly so long as no outward force awakes them, and take from the stone neither its clearness nor its coldness. With the barbarian, heroism was a bright devouring flame, which raged continually and consumed, or at least darkened, every other good quality in him. When Homer leads out the Trojans to battle with wild outcries, and the Greeks, on the other hand, in resolute silence, the commentators remark with justice that the poet in this wishes to depict those as barbarians and these as civilised people. I am surprised that they have not remarked in another passage a similar characteristic contrast. The opposing hosts have concluded a truce; they are busy with the burning of their dead, which on neither side takes place without hot tears : δάκρυα θερμὰ χέοντες. But Priam forbids his Trojans to weep; οὐδ' εἴα κλαίειν Πρίαμος μέγας. He forbids them to weep, says the Dacier, because he dreads that they will weaken themselves too much and return to battle on the morrow with less courage. Good! But I ask, Why must Priam dread this? Why does not Agamemnon, too, give his Greeks the same command? The sense of the poet goes deeper. He would teach us that only the civilised Greek can at the same time weep and be brave, whilst the uncivilised Trojan in order to be so must first stifle all human feeling. Νεμεσσῶμαί γε μὲν οὐδὲν κλαίειν, in another place, he puts in the mouth of the understanding son of wise Nestor.

It is worthy of remark that amongst the few tragedies that have come down to us from antiquity two pieces are to be found in which bodily pain is not the smallest part of the calamity that befalls the suffering hero : there is, besides the Philoctetes, the dying Hercules. And even the latter Sophocles represents complaining, whining, weeping and crying aloud. Thanks to our polite neighbours, those masters of the becoming, to-day a whimpering Philoctetes, a screaming Hercules, would be the most laughable, the most unendurable persons on the stage. It is true one of their latest dramatists has ventured on Philoctetes. But would he venture to show them the true Philoctetes ?

Amongst the lost dramas of Sophocles is numbered even a " Laocoön." Would that Fate had only granted us this Laocoön also ! From the slight references made to it by some ancient grammarians it is not easy to gather how the theme was handled. Of one thing I feel sure : that the poet will not have depicted Laocoön as more of a stoic than Philoctetes and Hercules. All stoicism is untheatrical, and our pity is always proportionate to the suffering which the interesting subject expresses. If we see him bear his misery with greatness of soul, then indeed this greatness of soul will excite our admiration, but admiration is a cold emotion, whose passive wonder excludes every other warmer passion as well as every other more significant representation.

And now I come to the inference I wish to draw. If it is true that outcries on the feeling of bodily pain, especially according to the ancient Greek way of thinking, can quite well consist with a great soul; then the expression of such a soul cannot be the reason why, nevertheless, the artist in his marble refuses to imitate this crying : there must be other grounds why he deviates here from his rival, the poet, who expresses this crying with obvious intention.

II

Whether it be fable or history that Love prompted the first attempt in the plastic arts, it is at least certain that she was never weary of lending her guiding hand to the ancient masters. For if painting, as the art which imitates bodies on plane sur-

faces, is now generally practised with an unlimited range of
subject, certainly the wise Greek set her much straiter bounds,
and confined her solely to the imitation of beautiful bodies.
His artist portrayed nothing but the beautiful; even the
ordinary beautiful, beauty of inferior kinds, was for him only
an occasional theme, an exercise, a recreation. In his work
the perfection of the subject itself must give delight; he was
too great to demand of those who beheld it that they should
content themselves with the bare, cold pleasure arising from
a well-caught likeness or from the daring of a clever effort;
in his art nothing was dearer to him, and to his thinking nothing
nobler, than the ultimate purpose of art.

" Who will wish to paint you, when no one wishes to see
you?" says an old epigrammatist concerning an extremely
misshapen man. Many a more modern artist would say, " Be
you as misshapen as is possible, I will paint you nevertheless.
Though, indeed, no one may wish to see you, people will still
wish to see my picture; not in so far as it represents you, but
in so far as it is a demonstration of my art, which knows how
to make so good a likeness of such a monster."

To be sure, with pitiful dexterities that are not ennobled
by the worth of their subjects, the propensity to such rank
boasting is too natural for the Greeks to have escaped without their Pauson, their Pyreicus. They had them; but they
did strict justice upon them. Pauson, who confined himself
entirely to the beauty of vulgar things and whose lower taste
delighted most in the faulty and ugly in human shape, lived in
the most sordid poverty. And Pyreicus, who painted, with
all the diligence of a Dutch artist, nothing but barbers' shops,
filthy factories, donkeys and cabbages, as if that kind of thing
had so much charm in Nature and were so rarely to be seen,
got the nickname of the rhyparograph, the dirt-painter, although
the luxurious rich weighed his works against gold, to help out
their merit by this imaginary value.

The magistrates themselves considered it not unworthy of
their attention to keep the artist by force in his proper sphere.
The law of the Thebans, which commanded him in his imitation
to add to beauty, and forbade under penalties the exaggeration
of the ugly, is well known. It was no law against the bungler,
as it is usually, and even by Junius, considered. It condemned
the Greek " Ghezzi "; the unworthy artifice of achieving likeness by exaggeration of the uglier parts of the original : in a
word, caricature.

Indeed, it was direct from the spirit of the Beautiful that the law of the Hellanodiken proceeded. Every Olympian victor received a statue; but only to the three-times victor was an Iconian statue awarded. Of mediocre portraits there ought not to be too many amongst works of art. For although even a portrait admits of an ideal, still the likeness must be the first consideration; it is the ideal of a certain man, not the ideal of a man.

We laugh when we hear that with the ancients even the arts were subject to municipal laws. But we are not always right when we laugh. Unquestionably the laws must not usurp power over the sciences, for the ultimate purpose of the sciences is truth. Truth is a necessity of the soul; and it is nothing but tyranny to offer her the slightest violence in satisfying this essential need. The ultimate purpose of the arts, on the other hand, is pleasure, and pleasure can be dispensed with. So, of course, it may depend on the law-giver what kind of pleasure, and in what measure any kind of it, he will permit. The plastic arts in particular, beyond the unfailing influence they exert on the character of a nation, are capable of an effect that demands the close supervision of the law. When beautiful men fashioned beautiful statues, these in their turn affected them, and the State had beautiful statues in part to thank for beautiful citizens. With us the tender, imaginative power of mothers appears to express itself only in monsters.

From this point of view I believe that in certain ancient legends, which men cast aside without hesitation as lies, something of truth may be recognised. The mothers of Aristomenes, of Aristodamas, of Alexander the Great, of Scipio, of Augustus, of Galerius, all dreamed in their pregnancy that they had to do with a serpent. The serpent was a symbol of deity, and the beautiful statues and pictures of a Bacchus, an Apollo, a Mercury and a Hercules were seldom without a serpent. The honest women had by day feasted their eyes on the god, and the bewildering dream called up the image of the reptile. Thus I save the dream, and surrender the interpretation which the pride of their sons and the shamelessness of flatterers gave it. For there must certainly be a reason why the adulterous phantasy was never anything but a serpent.

Here, however, I am going off the line. I merely wished to establish the fact that with the ancients beauty was the supreme law of the plastic arts. And this being established, it necessarily follows that all else after which also the plastic arts might strive, if it were inconsistent with beauty must wholly yield to her, and if it were consistent with beauty must at least be subordinate.

I will dwell a little longer on *expression*. There are passions and degrees of passion which express themselves in the countenance by the most hideous grimaces, and put the whole frame into such violent postures that all the beautiful lines are lost which define it in a quieter condition. From these, therefore, the ancient artists either abstained wholly or reduced them to lower degrees in which they were capable of a measure of beauty. Rage and despair disfigured none of their works. I dare maintain that they never depicted a Fury.

Wrath they reduced to sternness : with the poet it was an angry Jupiter who sent forth his lightnings; with the artist the god was calmly grave.

Lamentation was toned down to sadness. And where this softening could not take place, where lamentation would have been just as deforming as belittling—what then did Timanthes? His picture of Iphigenia's sacrifice, in which he imparted to all the company the peculiar degree of sadness befitting them individually, but veiled the father's face, which should have shown the supreme degree, is well known, and many nice things have been said about it. He had, says one, so exhausted himself in sorrowful countenances that he despaired of being able to give the father one yet more grief-stricken. He confessed thereby, says another, that the pain of a father in such events is beyond all expression. I, for my part, see here neither the impotence of the artist nor the impotence of art. With the degree of emotion the traces of it are correspondingly heightened in the countenance; the highest degree is accompanied by the most decided traces of all, and nothing is easier for the artist than to exhibit them. But Timanthes knew the limits which the Graces set to his art. He knew that such misery as fell to Agamemnon's lot as a father expresses itself by distortions which are at all times ugly. So far as beauty and dignity could be united with the expression of sorrow, so far he carried it. He might have been willing to omit the ugliness had he been willing to mitigate the sorrow; but as his composition did not admit of both, what else remained to him but to veil it? What he dared not paint he left to be guessed. In a word, this veiling was a sacrifice which the artist offered to Beauty. It is an example, not how one should force expression beyond the bounds of art, but rather how one must subject it to the first law of art, the law of Beauty.

And if we now refer this to the Laocoön, the motive for which I am looking becomes evident. The master was striving after the highest beauty, under the given circumstances of bodily pain. This, in its full deforming violence, it was not possible to unite with that. He was obliged, therefore, to abate, to lower it, to tone down cries to sighing; not because cries betrayed an ignoble soul, but because they disfigure the face in an unpleasing manner. Let one only, in imagination, open wide the mouth in Laocoön, and judge! Let him shriek, and see! It was a form that inspired pity because it showed beauty and pain together; now it has become an ugly, a loathsome form, from which one gladly turns away one's face, because the aspect of pain excites discomfort without the beauty of the suffering subject changing this discomfort into the sweet feeling of compassion.

The mere wide opening of the mouth—apart from the fact that the other parts of the face are thereby violently and unpleasantly distorted—is a blot in painting and a fault in sculpture which has the most untoward effect possible. Montfaucon showed little taste when he passed off an old, bearded head with widespread mouth for an oracle-pronouncing Jupiter. Must a god shriek when he unveils the future? Would a pleasing contour of the mouth make his speech suspicious? I do not even believe Valerius, that Ajax in the imaginary picture of Timanthes should have cried aloud. Far inferior artists, in times when art was already degraded, never once allow the wildest barbarians, when, under the victor's sword, terror and mortal anguish seize them, to open the mouth to shrieking-point.

Certain it is that this reduction of extremest physical pain to a lower degree of feeling is apparent in several works of ancient art. The suffering Hercules in the poisoned garment, from the hand of an unknown ancient master, was not the Sophoclean who shrieked so horribly that the Locrian cliffs and the Euboean headlands resounded. It was more sad than wild. The Philoctetes of Pythagoras Leontinus appeared to impart his pain to the beholder, an effect which the slightest trace of the horrible would have prevented. Some may ask where I have learnt that this master made a statue of Philoctetes? From a passage of Pliny which ought not to have awaited my emendation, so manifestly forged or garbled is it.

III

But, as we have already seen, Art in these later days has been assigned far wider boundaries. Let her imitative hand, folks say, stretch out to the whole of visible Nature, of which the Beautiful is only a small part. Let fidelity and truth of expression be her first law, and as Nature herself at all times sacrifices beauty to higher purposes, so also must the artist subordinate it to his general aim and yield to it no further than fidelity of expression permits. Enough, if by truth and faithful expression an ugliness of Nature be transformed into a beauty of Art.

Granted that one would willingly, to begin with, leave these conceptions uncontested in their worth or worthlessness, ought not other considerations quite independent of them to be examined—namely, why the artist is obliged to set bounds to expression and never to choose for it the supreme moment of an action?

The fact that the material limits of Art confine her imitative effort to one single moment will, I believe, lead us to similar conclusions.

If the artist can never, in presence of ever-changing Nature, choose and use more than one single moment, and the painter in particular can use this single moment only from one point of vision; if, again, their works are made not merely to be seen, but to be considered, to be long and repeatedly contemplated, then it is certain that that single moment, and the single viewpoint of that moment, can never be chosen too significantly. Now that alone is significant and fruitful which gives free play to the imagination. The more we see, the more must we be able to add by thinking. The more we add thereto by thinking, so much the more can we believe ourselves to see. In the whole gamut of an emotion, however, there is no moment less advantageous than its topmost note. Beyond it there is nothing further, and to show us the uttermost is to tie the wings of fancy and oblige her, as she cannot rise above the sensuous impression, to busy herself with weaker pictures below it, the visible fullness of expression acting as a frontier which she dare not transgress. When, therefore, Laocoön sighs, the imagination can hear him shriek; but if he shrieks, then she cannot mount a step higher from this representation, nor, again, descend a step lower without seeing him in a more tolerable and consequently more uninteresting condition. She hears him only groan, or she sees him already dead.

Further. As this single moment receives from Art an unchangeable continuance, it must not express anything which thought is obliged to consider transitory. All phenomena of whose very essence, according to our conceptions, it is that they break out suddenly and as suddenly vanish, that what they are they can be only for a moment—all such phenomena, whether agreeable or terrible, do, by the permanence which Art bestows, put on an aspect so abhorrent to Nature that at every repeated view of them the impression becomes weaker, until at last the whole thing inspires us with horror or loathing. La Mettrie, who had himself painted and engraved as a second Democritus, laughs only the first time that one sees him. View him often, and from a philosopher he becomes a fool, and the laugh becomes a grin. So, too, with cries. The violent pain which presses out the cry either speedily relaxes or it destroys the sufferer. If, again, the most patient and resolute man cries aloud, still he does not cry out without intermission. And just this unintermitting aspect in the material imitations of Art it is which would make his cries an effeminate or a childish weakness. This at least the artist of the Laocoön had to avoid, if cries had not been themselves damaging to beauty, and if even it had been permitted to his art to depict suffering without beauty.

Among the ancient painters Timomachus seems to have chosen by preference themes of the extremest emotion. His frenzied Ajax, his Medea the child-murderess, were famous pictures. But from the descriptions we have of them it clearly appears that he understood excellently well, and knew how to combine, that point where the beholder does not so much see the uttermost as reach it by added thought, and that appearance with which we do not join the idea of the transitory so necessarily that the prolongation of the same in Art must displease us. Medea he had not taken at the moment in which she actually murders the children, but some moments earlier, when motherly love still battles with jealousy. We foresee the end of the fight. We tremble beforehand, about to see Medea at her cruel deed, and our imagination goes out far beyond everything that the painter could show us in this terrible moment. But for this very reason we are so little troubled by the continued indecision of Medea, as Art presents it, that rather we devoutly wish it had so continued in Nature

itself, that the struggle of passions had never been decided, or
had at least endured long enough for time and reflection to
weaken rage and assure the victory to motherly feeling. To
Timomachus, moreover, this wisdom of his brought great and
manifold tributes, and raised him far above another unknown
painter who had been misguided enough to represent Medea
in the height of her rage, and thus to give to this transient
extreme of frenzy a permanence that revolts all Nature. The
poet who blames him on this account remarks, very sensibly,
addressing the picture itself : " Dost thou, then, thirst perpetually for the blood of thy children ? Is there constantly a
new Jason, always a new Creusa here, to embitter thee for
evermore ? To the devil with thee, even in picture ! " he adds,
with angry disgust.

Of the Frenzied Ajax of Timomachus we can judge by Philos-
tratus' account. Ajax appeared not as he rages amongst the
herds and binds and slays oxen and goats for his enemies.
Rather, the master showed him when, after these mad-heroic
deeds, he sits exhausted and is meditating self-destruction.
And that is actually the Frenzied Ajax; not because just then
he rages, but because one sees that he has raged, because one
perceives the greatness of his frenzy most vividly by the despair
and shame which he himself now feels over it. One sees the
storm in the wreckage and corpses it has cast upon the shore.

IV

Glancing at the reasons adduced why the artist of the Laocoön
was obliged to observe restraint in the expression of physical
pain, I find that they are entirely drawn from the peculiar
nature of Art and its necessary limits and requirements. Hardly,
therefore, could any one of them be made applicable to poetry.

Without inquiring here how far the poet can succeed in
depicting physical beauty, so much at least is undeniable, that,
as the whole immeasurable realm of perfection lies open to his
imitative skill, this visible veil, under which perfection becomes
beauty, can be only one of the smallest means by which he
undertakes to interest us in his subject. Often he neglects this
means entirely, being assured that if his hero has won our good-
will, then his nobler qualities either so engage us that we do
not think at all of the bodily form, or, if we think of it, so pre-
possess us that we do, on their very account, attribute to him,

if not a beautiful one, yet at any rate one that is not uncomely. At least, with every single line which is not expressly intended for the eye he will still take this sense into consideration. When Virgil's Laocoön cries aloud, to whom does it occur then that a wide mouth is needful for a cry, and that this must be ugly? Enough, that *clamores horrendos ad sidera tollit* is an excellent feature for the hearing, whatever it might be for the vision. Whosoever demands here a beautiful picture, for him the poet has entirely failed of his intention.

In the next place, nothing requires the poet to concentrate his picture on one single moment. He takes up each of his actions, as he likes, from its very origin and conducts it through all possible modifications to its final close. Every one of these modifications, which would cost the artist an entire separate canvas or marble-block, costs the poet a single line; and if this line, taken in itself, would have misled the hearer's imagination, it was either so prepared for by what preceded, or so modified and supplemented by what followed, that it loses its separate impression, and in its proper connection produces the most admirable effect in the world. Were it therefore actually unbecoming to a man to cry out in the extremity of pain, what damage can this trifling and transient impropriety do in our eyes to one whose other virtues have already taken us captive? Virgil's Laocoön shrieks aloud, but this shrieking Laocoön we already know and love as the wisest of patriots and the most affectionate of fathers. We refer his cries not to his character but purely to his unendurable suffering. It is this alone we hear in his cries, and the poet could make it sensible to us only through them. Who shall blame him then, and not much rather confess that, if the artist does well not to permit Laocoön to cry aloud, the poet does equally well in permitting him?

But Virgil here is merely a narrative poet. Can the dramatic poet be included with him in this justification? It is a different impression which is made by the narration of any man's cries from that which is made by the cries themselves. The drama, which is intended for the living artistry of the actor, might on this very ground be held more strictly to the laws of material painting. In him we do not merely suppose that we see and hear a shrieking Philoctetes; we hear and see him actually shriek. The closer the actor comes to Nature in this, the more sensibly must our eyes and ears be offended; for it is undeniable that they are so in Nature when we hear such loud and violent utterances of pain. Besides, physical pain does not generally excite that degree of sympathy which other evils awaken.   Our imagination is not able to distinguish enough in it for the mere sight of it to call out something like an equivalent feeling in ourselves. Sophocles could, therefore, easily have overstepped a propriety not merely capricious, but founded in the very essence of our feelings, if he allowed Philoctetes and Hercules thus to whine and weep, thus to shriek and bellow. The by-standers could not possibly take so much share in their suffering as these unmeasured outbursts seem to demand. They will appear to us spectators comparatively cold, and yet we cannot well regard their sympathy otherwise than as the measure of our own. Let us add that the actor can only with difficulty, if at all, carry the representation of physical pain to the point of illusion ; and who knows whether the later dramatic poets are not rather to be commended than to be blamed, in that they have either avoided this rock entirely or only sailed round it with the lightest of skiffs ?

How many a thing would appear irrefragable in theory if genius had not succeeded in proving the contrary by actual achievement ! None of these considerations is unfounded, and yet Philoctetes remains one of the masterpieces of the stage. For some of them do not really touch Sophocles, and by treating the rest with contempt he has attained beauties of which the timid critic without this example would never dream. The following notes deal with this point in fuller detail.

1. How wonderfully has the poet known how to strengthen and enlarge the idea of the physical pain ! He chose a wound —(for even the circumstances of the story one can contemplate as if they had depended on choice, in so far, that is to say, as he chose the whole story just because of the advantages the circumstances of it afforded him)—he chose, I say, a wound and not an inward malady, because a more vivid representation can be made of the former than of the latter, however painful this may be. The mysterious inward burning which consumed Meleager when his mother sacrificed him in mortal fire to her sisterly rage would therefore be less theatrical than a wound. And this wound was a divine judgment. A supernatural venom raged within without ceasing, and only an unusually severe attack of pain had its set time, after which the unhappy man fell ever into a narcotic sleep in which his exhausted nature must recover itself to be able to enter anew on the selfsame way of suffering. Chateaubrun represents him merely as wounded

by the poisoned arrow of a Trojan. What of extraordinary can so commonplace an accident promise? To such every warrior in the ancient battles was exposed; how did it come about that only with Philoctetes had it such terrible consequences? A natural poison that works nine whole years without killing is, besides, more improbable by far than all the mythical miraculous with which the Greek has furnished it.

2. But however great and terrible he made the bodily pains of his hero, he yet was in no doubt that they were insufficient in themselves to excite any notable degree of sympathy. He combined them, therefore, with other evils, which likewise, regarded in themselves, could not particularly move us, but which by this combination received just as melancholy a tinge as in their turn they imparted to the bodily pains. These evils were—a total deprivation of human society, hunger, and all the inconveniences of life to which in such deprivations one is exposed under an inclement sky. Let us conceive of a man in these circumstances, but give him health, and capacities, and industry, and we have a Robinson Crusoe who makes little demand upon our compassion, although otherwise his fate is not exactly a matter of indifference. For we are rarely so satisfied with human society that the repose which we enjoy when wanting it might not appear very charming, particularly under the representation which flatters every individual, that he can learn gradually to dispense with outside assistance. On the other hand, give a man the most painful, incurable malady, but at the same time conceive him surrounded by agreeable friends who let him want for nothing, who soften his affliction as far as lies in their power, and to whom he may unreservedly wail and lament; unquestionably we shall have pity for him, but this pity does not last, in the end we shrug our shoulders and recommend him patience. Only when both cases come together, when the lonely man has an enfeebled body, when others help the sick man just as little as he can help himself, and his complainings fly away in the desert air; then, indeed, we behold all the misery that can afflict human nature close over the unfortunate one, and every fleeting thought in which we conceive ourselves in his place awakens shuddering and horror. We perceive nothing before us but despair in its most dreadful form, and no pity is stronger, none more melts the whole soul than that which is mingled with representations of despair. Of this kind is the pity which we feel for Philoctetes, and feel most strongly at that moment when we see him deprived

of his bow, the one thing that might preserve him his wretched life. Oh, the Frenchman, who had neither the understanding to reflect on this nor the heart to feel it ! Or, if he had, was small enough to sacrifice all this to the pitiful taste of his countrymen. Chateaubrun gives Philoctetes society. He lets a young Princess come to him in the desert island. Nor is she alone, for she has her governess with her ; a thing of which I know not whether the Princess or the poet had the greater need. The whole excellent play with the bow he set quite aside. Instead of it he gives us the play of beautiful eyes. Certainly to young French heroes bow and arrow would have appeared a great joke. On the other hand, nothing is more serious than the anger of beautiful eyes. The Greek torments us with the dreadful apprehension that poor Philoctetes must remain on the desert island without his bow, and perish miserably. The Frenchman knows a surer way to our hearts : he makes us fear the son of Achilles must retire without his Princess. At the time the Parisian critics proclaimed this a triumphing over the ancients, and one of them proposed to call Chateaubrun's piece " *La Difficulté vaincue.*"

3. After the general effect let us consider the individual scenes, in which Philoctetes is no longer the forsaken invalid ; in which he has hope of speedily leaving the comfortless wilderness behind and of once more reaching his own kingdom ; in which, therefore, the painful wound is his sole calamity. He whimpers, he cries aloud, he goes through the most frightful convulsions. To this behaviour it is that the reproach of offended propriety is particularly addressed. It is an Englishman who utters this reproach ; a man, therefore, whom we should not easily suspect of a false delicacy. As we have already hinted, he gives a very good reason for the reproach. All feelings and passions, he says, with which others can only slightly sympathise, are offensive when they are expressed too violently. " For this reason there is nothing more unbecoming and more unworthy of a man than when he cannot bear pain, even the most violent, with patience, but weeps and cries aloud. Of course we may feel sympathy with bodily pain. When we see that any one is about to get a blow on the arm or the shin-bone, and when the blow actually falls, in a certain measure we feel it as truly as he whom it strikes. At the same time, however, it is certain that the trouble we thus experience amounts to very little ; if the person struck, therefore, sets up a violent outcry, we do not fail to despise him, because we are

not at all in the mind to cry out with so much violence." (Adam Smith, *Theory of the Moral Sentiments*, Part I, sect. 2, chap. i, p. 41, London, 1761.) Nothing is more fallacious than general laws for human feelings. The web of them is so fine-spun and so intricate that it is hardly possible for the most careful speculation to take up a single thread by itself and follow it through all the threads that cross it. And supposing it possible, what is the use of it? There does not exist in Nature a single unmixed feeling; along with every one of them there arise a thousand others simultaneously, the very smallest of which completely alters the first, so that exceptions on exceptions spring up which reduce at last the supposed general law itself to the mere experience of a few individual cases. We despise him, says the Englishman, whom we hear shriek aloud under bodily pain. No; not always, nor at first; not when we see that the sufferer makes every effort to suppress it; not when we know him otherwise as a man of fortitude; still less when we see him even in his suffering give proof of his fortitude, when we see that the pain can indeed force cries from him, but can compel him to nothing further—that he will rather submit to the longer endurance of this pain than change his opinions or his resolves in the slightest, even if he might hope by such a change to end his agony. And all this we find in Philoctetes. With the ancient Greeks moral greatness consisted in just as unchanging a love to friends as an unalterable hatred to enemies. This greatness Philoctetes maintains in all his torments. His pain has not so dried his eyes that they can spare no tears for the fate of his old friends. His pain has not made him so pliable that, to be rid of it, he will forgive his enemies and allow himself willingly to be used for their selfish purposes. And this rock of a man ought the Athenians to have despised because the surges that could not shake him made him give forth a cry? I confess that in the philosophy of Cicero, generally speaking, I find little taste; and least of all in that second book of his Tusculan Disputations, where he pours out his notions about the endurance of bodily pain. One might almost think he wanted to train a gladiator, he declaims so passionately against the outward expression of pain. In this alone does he seem to find a want of fortitude, without considering that it is frequently anything but voluntary, whilst true bravery can only be shown in voluntary actions. In Sophocles he hears Philoctetes merely complain and cry aloud, and overlooks utterly his otherwise steadfast bearing. Where save here could he have found the opportunity for his rhetorical outburst against the poets? "They would make us weaklings, showing us as they do the bravest of men lamenting and bewailing themselves." They must bewail themselves, for a theatre is not an arena. The condemned or venal gladiator it behoved to do and suffer everything with decorum. No complaining word must be heard from him, nor painful grimace be seen. For as his wounds and his death were to delight the spectators, Art must learn to conceal all feeling. The least utterance of it would have aroused compassion, and compassion often excited would have speedily brought an end to these icily gruesome spectacles. But what here it was not desired to excite is the one object of the tragic stage, and demands therefore an exactly opposite demeanour. Its heroes must show feeling, must utter their pain, and let Nature work in them undisguisedly. If they betray restraint and training, they leave our hearts cold, and pugilists in the cothurnus could at best only excite astonishment. This designation would befit all the persons of the so-called Seneca tragedies, and I firmly believe that the gladiatorial plays were the principal reason why the Romans in tragedy remained so far below the mediocre. To disown human nature was the lesson the spectators learned in the bloody amphitheatre, where certainly a Ctesias might study his art, but never a Sophocles. The tragic genius, accustomed to these artistic death scenes, necessarily sank into bombast and rodomontade. But just as little as such rodomontade could inspire true heroism, could the laments of Philoctetes make men weak. The complaints are those of a man, but the actions those of a hero. Both together make the human hero, who is neither soft nor hardened, but appears now the one and now the other, according as Nature at one time, and duty and principle at another, demand. He is the highest that Wisdom can produce and Art imitate.

4. It is not enough that Sophocles has secured his sensitive Philoctetes against contempt; he has also wisely taken precautions against all else that might, according to the Englishman's remark, be urged against him. For if we certainly do not always despise him who cries aloud in bodily pain, still it is indisputable that we do not feel so much sympathy for him as these outcries seem to demand. How, then, shall all those comport themselves who have to do with the shrieking Philoctetes? Shall they affect to be deeply moved? That is against nature. Shall they show themselves as cold and as

disconcerted as we are really accustomed to be in such cases? That would produce for the spectator the most unpleasant dissonance. But, as we have said, against this Sophocles has taken precautions. In this way, namely, that the secondary persons have an interest of their own; that the impression which the cries of Philoctetes make on them is not the one thing that occupies them, and the spectator's attention is not so much drawn to the disproportion of their sympathy with these cries, but rather to the change which arises or should arise in their disposition and attitude from sympathy, be it as weak or as strong as it may. Neoptolemus and his company have deceived the unhappy Philoctetes; they recognise into what despair their betrayal will plunge him; and now, before their eyes, a terrible accident befalls him. If this accident is not enough to arouse any particular feeling of sympathy within them, it still will move them to repent, to have regard to a misery so great, and indispose them to add to it by treachery. This is what the spectator expects, and his expectations are not disappointed by the noble-minded Neoptolemus. Philoctetes mastering his pain would have maintained Neoptolemus in his dissimulation. Philoctetes, whom his pain renders incapable of dissimulation, however imperatively necessary it may seem to him, so that his future fellow-travellers may not too soon regret their promise to take him with them; Philoctetes, who is nature itself, brings Neoptolemus, too, back to his own nature. This conversion is admirable, and so much the more touching as it is entirely wrought by humane feeling. With the Frenchman, on the contrary, beautiful eyes have their share in it. But I will say no more of this burlesque. Of the same artifice—namely, to join to the pity which bodily pain should arouse another emotion in the onlookers—Sophocles availed himself on another occasion : in the *Trachiniae*. The agony of Hercules is no enfeebling agony, it drives him to frenzy in which he pants for nothing but revenge. He had already, in his rage, seized Lichas and dashed him to pieces upon the rocks. The chorus is of women; so much the more naturally must fear and horror overwhelm them. This, and the expectant doubt whether yet a god will hasten to the help of Hercules, or Hercules succumb to the calamity, form here the real general interest, mingled merely with a slight tinge of sympathy. As soon as the issue is determined by the oracle, Hercules becomes quiet, and admiration of his final steadfast resolution takes the place of all other feelings. But in comparing the suffering Hercules with the suffering Philoctetes, one must never forget that the former is a demigod and the latter only a man. The man is not for a moment ashamed of his lamentations; but the demigod is ashamed that his mortal part has prevailed so far over the immortal that he must weep and whimper like a girl. We moderns do not believe in demigods, but our smallest hero we expect to feel and act as a demigod.

Whether an actor can bring the cries and grimaces of pain to the point of illusion I will not venture either to assert or to deny. If I found that our actors could not, then I should first like to know whether it would be impossible also to a Garrick; and if even he did not succeed, I should still be able to suppose a perfection in the stage-business and declamation of the ancients of which we to-day have no conception.

V

There are some learned students of antiquity who regard the Laocoön group as indeed a work of Greek masters, but of the time of the Emperors, because they believe that the Laocoön of Virgil served as its model. Of the older scholars who are of this opinion I will name only Bartholomew Marliani, and of the modern, Montfaucon. They doubtless found so close an agreement between the work of art and the poet's description that they thought it impossible that the two should have lighted by chance upon identical details such as are far from offering themselves unsought. At the same time their presumption is that if it be a question of the honour of the invention and first conception, the probability is incomparably greater that it belongs rather to the poet than to the artist.

Only they appear to have forgotten that a third case is possible. For it may be that the poet has as little imitated the artist as the artist has the poet, and that both have drawn from an identical source older than either. According to Macrobius, this more ancient source might have been Pisander. For when the works of this Greek poet were still extant, it was a matter of common knowledge, *pueris decantatum*, that the Roman had not so much imitated as faithfully translated from him the whole of the Capture and Destruction of Ilium, his entire Second Book. Now, therefore, if Pisander had been Virgil's predecessor also in the story of Laocoön, then the

Greek artists needed not to learn their lesson from a Latin poet, and the surmise as to their era is based upon nothing.

All the same, were I obliged to maintain the opinion of Marliani and Montfaucon, I should suggest to them the following way out. Pisander's poems are lost; how the story of Laocoön was told by him no one can say with certainty; but it is probable that it was with the same details of which we still find traces in the Greek writers. Now, these do not agree in the least with Virgil's narrative, and the Roman poet must have recast the Greek legend as he thought best. His manner of telling the tale of Laocoön is his own invention; consequently, if the artists in their representation are in harmony with him, it is almost a certainty that they followed him and wrought according to his pattern.

In Quintus Calaber, indeed, Laocoön displays a similar suspicion of the Wooden Horse as in Virgil; but the wrath of Minerva which he thereby draws upon himself expresses itself quite differently. The earth trembles under the warning Trojan; horror and dread seize him; a burning pain rages in his eyes; his brain reels; he raves; he goes blind. Only when, though blind, he ceases not to urge the burning of the Wooden Horse, does Minerva send two terrible dragons, and these attack only the children of Laocoön. In vain they stretch out their hands to their father; the poor blind man cannot help them; they are torn in pieces, and the serpent glides away into the earth. To Laocoön himself they do nothing; and that this account was not peculiar to Quintus, but must rather have been universally accepted, is proved by a passage in Lycophron, where these serpents bear the epithet " child-eaters."

If, however, this account had been universally received amongst the Greeks, the Greek artists in that case would hardly have been bold enough to deviate from it, and it would hardly have happened that they should deviate from it in precisely the same way as a Roman poet did if they had not known this poet, if perhaps they had not actually had the express commission to follow his lead. On this point, I think, we must insist if we would defend Marliani and Montfaucon. Virgil is the first and only one who describes the father as well as the children destroyed by the serpents; the sculptors do this likewise, while yet as Greeks they ought not : therefore it is probable that they did it at the prompting of Virgil.

I quite understand how far this probability falls short of

historical certainty. But as I do not intend to draw any historical conclusions from it, I yet believe at least that it can stand as a hypothesis which the critic in forming his views may take into account. Proven or not proven, that the sculptors followed Virgil in their works, I will assume it merely to see how in that case they did follow him. Concerning the outcries, I have already explained my opinion. Perhaps a further comparison may lead us to observations not less instructive.

The idea of binding the father with his two sons into one group by the deadly serpents is unquestionably a very happy one, evincing an uncommonly graphic fancy. To whom is it to be assigned? The poet, or the artist? Montfaucon refuses to find it in the poet. But Montfaucon, as I think, has not read him with sufficient attention.

> . . . *Illi agmine certo*
> *Laocoönta petunt, et primum parva duorum*
> *Corpora natorum serpens amplexus uterque*
> *Implicat et miseros morsu depascitur artus.*
> *Post ipsum, auxilio subeuntem ac tela ferentem,*
> *Corripiunt, spirisque ligant ingentibus. . . .*

The poet has depicted the serpents as of a marvellous length. They have enfolded the boys, and when the father comes to their aid, seize him also (*corripiunt*). From their size they could not at once uncoil themselves from the boys; there must therefore be a moment in which they had attacked the father with their heads and foreparts, while they still with their other parts enveloped the children. This moment is required in the development of the poetic picture; the poet makes it sufficiently felt; only the time had not yet been reached for finishing the picture. That the ancient commentators actually realised this appears to be shown by a passage in Dentatus. How much less would it escape the artists in whose understanding eyes everything that can advantage them stands out so quickly and so plainly.

In the coils themselves with which the poet's fancy sees the serpents entwine Laocoön, he very carefully avoids the arms, in order to leave the hands their freedom.

> *Ille simul manibus tendit divellere nodos.*

In this the artists must necessarily follow him. Nothing gives more life and expression than the movement of the hands; in emotion especially the most speaking countenance without it is insignificant. Arms fast bound to the body by the coils of the serpents would have spread frost and death over the whole group. For this reason we see them, in the chief figure as well as in the secondary figures, in full activity, and busiest there where for the moment there is the most violent anguish.

Further, too, the artists, in view of the convolutions of the serpents, found nothing that could be more advantageously borrowed from the poet than this movement of the arms. Virgil makes the serpents wind themselves doubly about the body and doubly about the neck of Laocoön, with their heads elevated above him.

> *Bis medium amplexi, bis collo squamea circum*
> *Terga dati, superant capite et cervicibus altis.*

This picture satisfies the imagination completely; the noblest parts are compressed to suffocation, and the poison goes straight to the face. Nevertheless, it was not a picture for artists, who want to exhibit the effects of the pain and the poison in the bodily frame. For in order to make these visible the chief parts must be as free as possible, and no external pressure whatever must be exercised upon them which could alter and weaken the play of the suffering nerves and straining muscles. The double coil of the serpents would have concealed the whole body, so that the painful contraction of the abdomen, which is so expressive, would have remained invisible. What one would still have perceived of the body, over, or under, or between the coils would have appeared under pressures and swellings caused not by the inward pain, but by the external burden. The neck so many times encircled would have spoiled completely the pyramidal tapering of the group which is so agreeable to the eye; and the pointed serpent heads standing out into the air from this swollen bulk would have made so abrupt a break in proportion that the form of the whole would have been repulsive in the extreme. There are doubtless draughtsmen who would nevertheless have been unintelligent enough to follow the poet slavishly. But what would have come of that, we can, to name no other instances, understand from a drawing of Francis Cleyn, which can be looked on only with disgust. (This occurs in the splendid edition of Dryden's English Virgil.) The ancient sculptors perceived at a glance that their art demanded an entire modification. They removed all the serpent coils from neck and body to thighs and feet. Here these coils, without injuring the expression, could cover

and press as much as was needful.   Here they aroused at once
the idea of retarded flight and of a kind of immobility which
is exceedingly advantageous to the artistic permanence of a
single posture.

I know not how it has come about that the critics have
passed over in perfect silence this distinction, which is exhibited
so plainly in the coilings of the serpents, between the work of
art and the poet's description.   It exalts the artistic wisdom
of the work just as much as the other which they mention,
which, however, they do not venture to praise, but rather seek
to excuse.   I mean the difference in the draping of the subject.
Virgil's Laocoön is in his priestly vestments, but in the group
appears, with both his sons, completely naked.   I am told
there are people who find something preposterous in representing a prince, a priest, unclothed, at the altar of sacrifice.
And to these people connoisseurs of art reply, in all seriousness,
that certainly it is an offence against custom, but that the
artists were compelled to it, because they could not give their
figures any suitable attire.   Sculpture, say they, cannot imitate
any kind of cloth; thick folds would make a bad effect.   Of
two embarrassments, therefore, they had chosen the smaller,
and were willing rather to offend against truth than to incur
the risk of blame for their draperies.   If the ancient artists
would laugh at the objection, I really cannot tell what they
would have said about the answer.   One cannot degrade Art
further than by such a defence.   For, granted that sculpture
could imitate the different materials just as well as painting,
should then Laocoön necessarily have been clothed?   Should
we lose nothing by this draping?   Has a costume, the work of
slavish hands, just as much beauty as the work of the Eternal
Wisdom, an organised body?   Does it demand the same
faculties, is it equally meritorious, does it bring the same honour,
to imitate the former as to imitate the latter?   Do our eyes
only wish to be deceived, and is it all the same to them with
what they are deceived?

With the poet a dress is no dress; it conceals nothing; our
imagination sees through it at all times.   Let Laocoön in
Virgil have it or lack it, his suffering in every part of his body
is, to the imagination, an evil equally visible.   The brow is
bound about for her with the priestly fillet, but it is not veiled.
Indeed, it does not only not hinder, this fillet, it even strengthens
yet more the conception that we form of the sufferer's misfortunes.

Perfusus sanie vittas atroque veneno.

His priestly dignity helps him not a whit; the very symbol which secures him everywhere respect and veneration is soaked and defiled by the deadly venom.

But this accessory idea the artist had to sacrifice if the main work were not to suffer damage. Besides, had he left to Laocoön only this fillet, the expression would in consequence have been much weakened. The brow would have been partly covered, and the brow is the seat of expression. So, just as in that other particular, the shriek, he sacrificed expression to beauty, in the same way here he sacrificed custom to expression. Generally speaking, custom, in the view of the ancients, was a matter of little consequence. They felt that the highest aim of Art pointed to dispensing with the customary altogether. Beauty is this highest aim; necessity invented clothing, and what has Art to do with necessity? I grant you there is also a beauty of drapery; but what is it compared with the beauty of the human form? And will he who is able to reach the higher content himself with the lower? I am much afraid that the most finished master in draperies shows by that very dexterity in what it is he is lacking.

VI

My hypothesis—that the artists imitated the poet—does not redound to their disparagement. On the contrary, this imitation sets their wisdom in the fairest light. They followed the poet without allowing themselves to be misled by him in the slightest. They had a pattern, but as they had to transpose this pattern from one art into another, they found opportunity enough to think for themselves. And these thoughts of theirs, which are manifest in their deviation from their model, prove that they were just as great in their art as he in his own.

And now I will reverse the hypothesis and suppose the poet to have imitated the artists. There are scholars who maintain this supposition to be the truth. Whether they had historical grounds for that, I do not know. But when they found the work of art so superlatively beautiful, they could not persuade themselves that it might belong to a late period. It must be of the age when Art was in its perfect flower, because it deserved to be of that age.

It has been shown that, admirable as Virgil's picture is, there are yet various features of it which the artists could not use. The statement thus admits of being reduced to this, that

a good poetic description must also yield a good actual painting, and that the poet has only so far described well when
the artist can follow him in every feature. One is inclined to
presume this restricted sense, even before seeing it confirmed
by examples; merely from consideration of the wider sphere
of poetry, from the boundless field of our imagination, and
from the spiritual nature of the pictures, which can stand side
by side in the greatest multitude and variety without one
obscuring or damaging another, just as the things themselves
would do or the natural signs of the same within the narrow
bounds of space and time.

But if the less cannot include the greater, the greater can
contain the less. This is my point—if not, every feature
which the descriptive poet uses can be used with like effect
on the canvas or in the marble. Might perhaps every feature
of which the artist avails himself prove equally effective in the
work of the poet? Unquestionably; for what we find beautiful
in a work of art is not found beautiful by the eye, but by our
imagination through the eye. The picture in question may
therefore be called up again in our imagination by arbitrary or
natural signs, and thus also may arise at any time the corresponding pleasure, although not in corresponding degree.

This, however, being admitted, I must confess that to my
mind the hypothesis that Virgil imitated the artists is far less
conceivable than the contrary supposition. If the artists
followed the poet, I can account for their deviations. They
were obliged to deviate, because the selfsame features as the
poet delineated would have occasioned them difficulties such as
do not embarrass the poet. But what should make the poet
deviate? If he had followed the group in every detail would
he not, all the same, have presented to us an admirable picture?
I can conceive quite well how his fancy, working on its own
account, might suggest one feature and another; but the
reasons why his imagination should think that beautiful features,
already before his eyes, ought to be transformed into those
other features—such reasons, I confess, never dawn upon me.

It even seems to me that if Virgil had had the group as his
pattern he could scarcely have refrained from permitting the
union together, as it were in a knot, of the three bodies to be
at least conjectured. It was too vivid not to catch his eye,
and he would have appreciated its excellent effect too keenly
not to give it yet more prominence in his description. As I
have said, the time was not yet arrived to finish this picture

of the entwined group. No; but a single word more would perhaps have given to it, in the shadow where the poet had to leave it, a very obvious impression. What the artist was able to discover without this word, the poet, if he had seen it in the artist's work, would not have left unspoken.

The artist had the most compelling reasons not to let the suffering of Laocoön break out into a cry. But if the poet had had before him the so touching union of pain and beauty in the work of art, what could have so imperatively obliged him to leave completely unsuggested the idea of manly dignity and great-hearted endurance which arises from this union of pain and beauty, and all at once to shock us with the terrible outcries of Laocoön? Richardson says, "Virgil's Laocoön must shriek, because the poet desires to arouse not so much pity for him as terror and horror in the ranks of the Trojans." I grant, although Richardson seems not to have considered it, that the poet does not make the description in his own person, but lets Æneas make it, and this, too, in the presence of Dido, to whose compassion Æneas could never enough appeal. It is not, however, the shriek that surprises me, but the absence of any gradation leading up to the cry, a gradation that the work of art would naturally have shown the poet to be needful, if, as we have supposed, he had had it for a pattern. Richardson adds, "The story of Laocoön should lead up merely to the pathetic description of the final ruin; the poet, therefore, has not thought fit to make it more interesting, in order not to waste upon the misfortune of a single citizen the attention which should be wholly fixed on Troy's last dreadful night." Only, this sets out the affair as one to be regarded from a painter's point of view, from which it cannot be contemplated at all. The calamity of Laocoön and the Destruction of the City are not with the poet pictures set side by side; the two together do not make a great whole which the eye either should or could take in at a glance; and only in such a case would it be needful to arrange that our eyes should fall rather upon Laocoön than upon the burning city. The two descriptions follow each other successively, and I do not see what disadvantage it could bring to the second, how greatly soever the preceding one had moved us. That could only be, if the second in itself were not sufficiently touching.

Still less reason would the poet have had to alter the coiling of the serpents. In the work of art they leave the hands busy and bind the feet. This disposition pleases the eye, and it is a living picture that is left by it in the imagination. It is so clear and pure that it can be presented almost as effectively by words as by actual material means.

> . . . *Micat alter, et ipsum*
> *Laocoönta petit, totumque infraque supraque*
> *Implicat et rabido tandem ferit ilia morsu*
>
> *At serpens lapsu crebro redeunte subintrat*
> *Lubricus, intortoque ligat genua infima nodo.*

These are the lines of Sadolet, which would, no doubt, have come from Virgil with a more picturesque power if a visible pattern had fired his fancy, and which would in that case certainly have been better than what he now gives us in their place :—

> *Bis medium amplexi, bis collo squamea circum*
> *Terga dati, superant capite et cervicibus altis.*

These details, certainly, fill the imagination ; but she must not rest in them, she must not endeavour to make an end here ; she must see now only the serpents and now only Laocoön, she must try to represent to herself what kind of figure is made by the two together. As soon as she sinks to this the Virgilian picture begins to dissatisfy, and she finds it in the highest degree unpictorial.

If, however, the changes which Virgil had made in the pattern set before him had not been unsuccessful, they would yet be merely arbitrary. One imitates in order to resemble. Can resemblance be preserved when alterations are made needlessly ? Rather, when this is done, the design obviously is—not to be like, and therefore not to imitate.

Not the whole, some may object, but perhaps this part and that. Good ! But what, then, are these single parts that agree in the description and in the work of art so exactly that the poet might seem to have borrowed them from the latter ? The father, the children, the serpents—all these the story furnished to the poet as well as to the artists. Excepting the story itself, they agree in nothing beyond the one point that they bind father and children in a single serpent-knot. But the suggestion of this arose from the altered detail, that the selfsame calamity overtook the father and the children. This alteration, as has already been pointed out, Virgil appears to have introduced ; for the Greek legend says something quite different. Consequently, when, in view of that common binding by the serpent coils, there certainly was imitation on one side or the other, it is easier to suppose it on the artist's side than on that of the poet. In all else the one deviates from the other; only with the distinction that, if it is the artist who has made these deviations, the design of imitating the poet can still persist, the aim and the limitations of his art obliging him thereto; if, on the other hand, it is the poet who is supposed to have imitated the artist, then all the deviations referred to are an evidence against the supposed imitation, and those who, notwithstanding, maintain it, can mean nothing further by it than that the work of art is older than the poetic description.

VII

When one says that the artist imitates the poet, or that the poet imitates the artist, this is capable of two interpretations. Either the one makes the work of the other the actual subject of his imitation, or they have both the same subject and the one borrows from the other the style and fashion of the imitation. When Virgil describes the shield of Æneas, it is in the first of these senses that he imitates the artist who made it. The work of art itself, not that which is represented upon it, is the subject of his imitation, and although certainly he describes at the same time what one sees represented thereon, yet he describes it only as a part of the shield, and not the thing itself. If Virgil, on the other hand, had imitated the Laocoön group, this would be an imitation of the second kind. For he would not have imitated the group, but what the group represents, and only the characteristics of his imitation would have been borrowed from it. In the first imitation the poet is original, in the second he is a copyist. The former is a part of the general imitation which constitutes the essence of his art, and he works as genius, whether his subject be a work of other arts or of Nature. The latter, on the contrary, degrades him wholly from his dignity; instead of the things themselves, he imitates the imitations of them, and gives us cold recollections of features from another's genius in place of original features of his own.

When, however, poet and artist, as not seldom happens, view the subjects that they have in common from an identical standpoint, it can hardly fail that there should be agreement in many particulars without implying the slightest degree of imitation or common aim between them. These agreements

in contemporaneous artists and poets, concerning things
that are no longer extant, may contribute to reciprocal illustration; but to attempt to establish such illustration by finding
design in what was mere accident, and especially to attribute to
the poet in every trifle a reference to this statue or that painting,
is to render him a very equivocal service.   And not to him alone,
but to the reader also, for whom the most beautiful passage is
thereby made, if God will, very intelligible, but at the same
time admirably frigid.

   This is the purpose, and the error, of a famous English work.
Spence wrote his *Polymetis* with much classical erudition and a
very intimate acquaintance with the surviving works of ancient
art.   His design of explaining by these the Roman poets, and,
on the other hand, of deriving from the poets elucidations for
ancient works of art hitherto unexplained, he often accomplished
very happily.   But nevertheless I contend that his book is
altogether intolerable to any reader of taste.

   It is natural that, when Valerius Flaccus describes the Winged
Lightning upon the Roman shields—

> *Nec primus radios, miles Romane, corusci*
> *Fulminis et rutilas scutis diffuderis alas,*

this description becomes to me far clearer when I perceive the
representation of such a shield upon an ancient monument.   It
may be that Mars, hovering exactly as Addison fancied he
saw him hovering, over the head of Rhea upon a coin, was
also represented by the ancient armourers on shields and helmets,
and that Juvenal had such a shield or helmet in mind when he
alluded to it in a single word which, until Addison, remained a
riddle for all the commentators.   For my part, I think that the
passage of Ovid where the exhausted Cephalus calls to the
cooling breezes :

> *Aura . . . venias. . .*
> *Meque juves, intresque sinus, gratissima, nostros !*

and his Procris takes this Aura for the name of a rival—that to
me, I say, this passage appears more natural when I gather
from the works of ancient artists that they actually personified
the soft breezes and worshipped a kind of female sylphs under
the name of Aurae.   I grant you, that when Juvenal styles a
distinguished good-for-nothing a Hermes-statue, one could
hardly find the likeness in the comparison without seeing such
a statue, without knowing that it is a miserable pillar, which

bears merely the head, or at most the torso, of the god, and, because we perceive thereon neither hands nor feet, awakens the conception of slothfulness. Illustrations of this sort are not to be despised, although, in fact, they are neither always necessary nor always adequate. The poet had the work of art in view as a thing existing for itself, and not as an imitation; or with both artist and poet certain conceptions of an identical kind were taken for granted, in consequence of which a further agreement in their representations must appear, from which, again, we can reason back to the generally accepted nature of these conceptions.

But when Tibullus describes the form of Apollo, as he appeared to him in a dream—the most beautiful of youths, his temples bound about with the modest laurel; Syrian odours exhaling from the golden hair that flows about his neck; a gleaming white and rosy red mingled on the whole body, as on the tender cheek of the bride as she is led to her beloved—why must these features be borrowed from famous old pictures? Echion's *nova nupta verecundia notabilis* may have been seen in Rome, may have been copied a thousand times. Had then the bridal blush itself vanished from the world? Since the painter had seen it, was it no larger to be seen by a poet save in the painter's imitation? Or if another poet speaks of the exhausted Vulcan, or calls his face heated before the forge a red and fiery countenance, must he needs learn first from the work of a painter that labour wearies and heat reddens? Or when Lucretius describes the changes of the seasons and causes them to pass before us in their natural order with the entire succession of their effects in earth and sky, was Lucretius an ephemeron? Had he not lived through a whole year himself to witness all these transformations, but must depict them after a procession in which their statues were carried around? Must he first learn from these statues the old poetic artifice whereby abstract notions are turned into actual beings? Or Virgil's *pontem indignatus Araxes*, that splendid poetic picture of a stream overflowing its banks and tearing down the bridge thrown over it, does it not lose all its beauty if the poet is there alluding merely to a work of art in which this river-god is represented as actually breaking down a bridge? What do we want with these commentaries which in the clearest passages supplant the poet in order to let the suggestion of an artist glimmer through?

I lament that so useful a book as *Polymetis* might otherwise have been has, by reason of this tasteless crotchet of foisting

upon the ancient poets in place of their own proper fancy an
acquaintance with another's, been made so offensive and so
much more damaging to the classic authors than the watery
expositions of the shallowest philologist could ever have been.
I regret yet more that in this matter Spence should have been
preceded by Addison himself, who, from a passionate desire to
exalt the works of ancient art into a means of interpretation,
has just as little distinguished between the cases in which it is
becoming in a poet to imitate the artist and those in which it is
disparaging.

VIII

Of the likeness which poetry and painting bear to each other
Spence has the most singular conceptions possible. He believes
the two arts in ancient times to have been so closely united that
they always went hand in hand, that the poet constantly kept
the painter in view, and the painter the poet. That poetry is
the more comprehensive art, that beauties are at her command
which painting can never attain, that she may frequently have
reason to prefer unpicturesque beauties to picturesque—of this
he does not appear to have a notion, and therefore the smallest
difference which he detects between poets and artists of the
old world puts him in a difficulty, and he resorts to the most
extraordinary subterfuges to escape from his embarrassment.

The ancient poets generally endow Bacchus with horns. It
is quite wonderful, then, says Spence, that we find these horns
so seldom on his statues. He lights on this explanation and on
that : on the uncertainty of the antiquaries, on the smallness
of the horns themselves, which might have crept into conceal-
ment under the grapes and ivy-leaves, the unfailing head-
covering of the god. He winds about and about the true reason
without ever suspecting it. The horns of Bacchus were not
natural horns, such as we see on the fauns and satyrs. They
were but a garnishment of the brow, which he could assume
and lay aside at will.

> *Tibi, cum sine cornibus adstas,*
> *Virgineum caput est—*

so runs the solemn invocation of Bacchus in Ovid. He could
thus show himself also without horns, and did so when he
would appear in his virginal beauty. The artists certainly
would also wish so to represent him, and would therefore avoid

every less pleasing adjunct. Such an adjunct the horns would
have been if attached to the diadem, as we may see them on a
head in the royal cabinet at Berlin. Such an adjunct was the
diadem itself, hiding the beautiful brow, and for this reason it
occurs on the statues of Bacchus just as rarely as the horns,
although indeed it was dispensed with just as often by the
poets, both in the representations of Bacchus and in those of
his great progenitor. The horns and the diadem prompted the
poet's allusions to the deeds and the character of the god; to
the artist, on the contrary, they were hindrances to the exhibi-
tion of greater beauties, and if Bacchus, as I believe, for that
very reason had the surname *Biformis*, Δίμορφος, because he
could show himself in a fair and in a terrible aspect, then it
was quite natural for the artists greatly to prefer that one of
his forms which best answered the purpose of their art.

Minerva and Juno in the Roman poets often dart forth
lightning. " Then why not also in their images? " asks Spence.
He replies, " It was an especial privilege of these two goddesses, the grounds of which were perhaps only to be learned in
the Samothracian mysteries; artists, moreover, were regarded
by the ancient Romans as common people, were therefore seldom
admitted to those mysteries, and so doubtless knew nothing of
them, and what they did not know they could not depict."
I might in return ask Spence, Did these common people work
out their own notions, or work at the command of more distinguished persons who might have been instructed in the
mysteries? Were artists among the Greeks regarded with a
like contempt? Were the Roman artists not for the greater
part born Greeks? And so on.

Statius and Valerius Flaccus depict an angry Venus, and with
features so terrible that at the moment we should rather take
her for one of the Furies than for the Goddess of Love. Spence
looks round in vain amongst the works of ancient art for such
a Venus. And what is his conclusion? That more is permitted to the poet than to the sculptor or the painter? That
is the conclusion he ought to have drawn, but he has accepted
the principle once for all, that in a poetic description nothing is
good which would be unsuitable to be represented in a painting
or a statue. Consequently, the poets must have erred. " Statius
and Valerius belong to an age when Roman poetry was in its
decline. They show in this particular also their corrupt taste
and their faulty judgment. With the poets of a better time
one will not find these offences against graphic expression."

To speak in this way betrays a very poor faculty of dis-
crimination. All the same, I do not intend to take up the
cudgels for either Statius or Valerius, but will confine myself
to but one general observation. The gods and sacred persons,
as the artist represents them, are not entirely the same beings
which the poet knows. With the artist they are personified
abstractions which must constantly retain the selfsame characterisation, if they are to be recognisable. With the poet, on
the other hand, they are actual persons who live and act, who
possess beyond their general character other qualities and
emotions, which will stand out above it according to occasion
and circumstance. Venus to the sculptor is nothing but Love ;
he must therefore endow her with the modest, blushful beauty
and all the gracious charms that delight us in beloved objects
and that we therefore combine in the abstract conception of
Love. Deviate however slightly from this ideal, and we shall
fail to recognise the picture. Beauty, but with more majesty
than modesty, is at once no Venus, but a Juno. Charms, but
commanding, masculine, rather than gracious charms, give us a
Minerva in place of a Venus. In reality, an angry Venus, a
Venus moved by revenge and rage, is to the sculptor a contradiction in terms ; for Love as Love is never angry, never
revengeful. To the poet, on the other hand, Venus certainly is
Love, but she is more : she is the Goddess of Love, who beyond
this character has an individuality of her own, and consequently
must be just as capable of the impulse of aversion as of inclination. What wonder, then, that to him she blazes in rage or
anger, especially when it is injured love that so transforms her ?
Certainly it is true that the artist also in composition may
just as well as the poet introduce Venus or any other divinity,
out of her character, as a being actually living and acting.
But in that case her actions must at least not contradict her
character, even if they are not direct consequences of it. Venus
commits to her son's charge her divine weapons ; this action
the artist can represent as well as the poet. Here nothing
hinders him from giving to Venus all the grace and beauty that
appertain to her as the Goddess of Love ; rather, indeed, will
she thereby be so much the more recognisable in his work. But
when Venus would avenge herself on her contemners, the men
of Lemnos ; when in magnified and savage form, with stained
cheeks and disordered hair, she seizes the torch, throws around
her a black vesture and stormily plunges down on a gloomy
cloud ; surely that is not a moment for the artist, because in

such a moment he cannot by any means make her distinguishable. It is purely a moment for the poet, since to him the
privilege is granted of so closely and exactly uniting with it
another aspect, in which the goddess is wholly Venus, that we
do not lose sight of her even in the Fury. This Flaccus does :

> *Neque enim alma videri*
> *Jam timet, aut tereti crinem subnectitur auro*
> *Sidereos diffusa sinus. Eadem effera et ingens*
> *Et maculis suffecta genas, primumque sonantem*
> *Virginibus Stygiis nigramque simillima pallam.*

Statius does just the same :

> *Illa Paphon veterem centumque altaria linquens,*
> *Nec vultu nec crine prior, solvisse jugalem*
> *Ceston et Idalias procul ablegasse volucres*
> *Fertur. Erant certe, media qui noctis in umbra*
> *Divam alios ignes majoraque tela gerentem*
> *Tartarias inter thalamis volitasse sorores*
> *Vulgarent : utque implicitis arcana domorum*
> *Anguibus et sacra formidine cuncta replevit*
> *Limina.—*

Or we might say, to the poet alone belongs the art of depicting
with negative traits, and by mixing them with positive to bring
two images into one. No longer the gracious Venus, no longer
the hair fastened with golden clasps, floated about by no azure
vesture, but without her girdle, armed with other flames, with
greater arrows, companioned by like Furies. But because the
artist is obliged to dispense with such an artifice, must the poet
too in his turn abstain from using it ? If painting will be the
sister of poesy, let not the younger forbid to the elder all the
garniture and bravery which she herself cannot put on.

IX

If in individual cases we wish to compare the painter and
the poet with one another, the first and most important point
is to observe whether both of them have had complete freedom,
whether they have, in the absence of any outward compulsion,
been able to aim at the highest effect of their art.

Religion was often an outward compulsion of this kind for
the ancient artist. His work, designed for reverence and worship, could not always be as perfect as if he had had a single
eye to the pleasure of the beholder. Superstition overloaded
the gods with symbols, and the most beautiful of them were

not everywhere worshipped for their beauty. In his temple at Lemnos, from which the pious Hypsipyle rescued her father under the shape of the god, Bacchus stood horned, and so doubtless he appeared in all his temples, for the horns were a symbol that indicated his essential nature. Only the free artist who wrought his Bacchus for no holy shrine left this symbol out; and if amongst the statues of him still extant we find all without horns, this is perhaps a proof that they are not of the consecrated forms in which he was actually worshipped. Apart from this, it is highly probable that it was upon these last that the rage of the pious iconoclasts in the first centuries of Christianity chiefly fell, their fury sparing only here and there a work of art which had not been defiled by idolatrous worship.

As, however, works of both kinds are still found amongst antiquities in excavation, I should like the name of " works of art " to be reserved for those alone in which the artist could show himself actually as artist, in which beauty has been his first and last object. All the rest, in which too evident traces of religious ritual appear, are unworthy of the name, because Art here has not wrought on her own account, but has been an auxiliary of religion, looking in the material representations which she made of it more to the significant than to the beautiful; although I do not mean by this that she did not often put great significance into the beauty, or, out of indulgence to the art and finer taste of the age, remitted her attention to the former so much that the latter alone might appear to predominate.

If we make no such distinction, then the connoisseur and the antiquary will be constantly at strife because they do not understand each other. If the former, with his insight into the aims of art, contends that this or that work was never made by the ancient artist—that is to say, not as artist, not voluntarily— then the latter will assert that neither religion nor any other cause lying outside the region of art has caused the artist to make it—the artist, that is to say, as workman. He will suppose that he can refute the connoisseur with the first figure that comes to hand, which the other without scruple, but to the great annoyance of the learned world, will condemn to the rubbish-heap once more from which it has been drawn.

Yet, on the other hand, it is possible to exaggerate the influence of religion upon art. Spence affords a singular example of that tendency. He found that Vesta was not worshipped in her temple under any personal image, and this he deemed enough to warrant the conclusion that no statues of this goddess ever existed, and that every one so considered really represented not Vesta, but a vestal. Strange inference! Did the artist, then, lose his right to personify a being to whom the poets give a distinct personality, whom they make the daughter of Saturnus and Ops, whom they expose to the danger of ill-usage at the hands of Priapus, and all else they relate of her—did he lose his right, I ask, to personify this being in his own way, because she was worshipped in one temple merely under the symbol of fire? For Spence here falls into this further error: that what Ovid says only of a certain temple of Vesta—namely, of that at Rome—he extends to all temples of the goddess without distinction and to her worship in general. She was not everywhere worshipped as she was worshipped in this temple at Rome, nor even in Italy itself before Numa built it. Numa desired to see no divinity represented in human or animal form; and without doubt the reform which he introduced in the service of Vesta consisted in this, that he banished from it all personal representation. Ovid himself teaches us that before Numa's time there were statues of Vesta in her temple, which when her priestess Sylvia became a mother raised their maiden hands in shame before their eyes. That even in the temples which the goddess had in the Roman provinces outside the city her worship was not wholly of the kind which Numa prescribed, various ancient inscriptions appear to prove, where mention is made of a " Pontificus Vestae." At Corinth also there was a temple of Vesta without any statues, with a mere altar whereon offerings were made to the goddess. But had the Greeks therefore no statues of Vesta? At Athens there was one in the Prytaneum, beside the statue of Peace. The people of Iasos boasted of one, which stood in their city under the open sky, that neither snow nor rain fell upon it. Pliny mentions a sitting figure from the hand of Scopas which in his time was to be seen in the Servilian Gardens at Rome. Granted that it is difficult for us now to distinguish a mere vestal from Vesta herself, does this prove that the ancients could not distinguish them, or indeed did not wish to distinguish them? Notoriously, certain characteristics indicate rather the one than the other. Only in the hands of the goddess can we expect to find the sceptre, the torch, the palladium. The tympanum which Codinus associates with her belongs to her perhaps only as the Earth, or Codinus did not recognise very well what he saw.

X

I notice another expression of surprise in Spence which shows plainly how little he can have reflected on the limits of Poetry and Painting. "As for what concerns the Muses in general," he says, "it is certainly singular that the poets are so sparing in the description of them—more sparing by far than we should expect with goddesses to whom they owe such great obligations."

What is this, but to wonder that when the poets speak of them they do not use the dumb language of the painter? Urania is for the poets the Muse of Astronomy; from her name, from her functions, we recognise her office. The artist in order to make it distinguishable must exhibit her with a pointer and a celestial globe; this wand, this celestial globe, this attitude of hers are his alphabet from which he helps us to put together the name Urania. But when the poet would say that Urania had long ago foretold his death by the stars:

Ipsa diu positis letum praedixerat astris Urania.—

why should he, thinking of the painter, add thereto, Urania, the pointer in her hand, the celestial globe before her? Would it not be as if a man who can and may speak aloud should at the same time still make use of the signs which the mutes in the Turk's seraglio have invented for lack of utterance?

The very same surprise Spence again expresses concerning the personified moralities, or those divinities whom the ancients set over the virtues and the conduct of human life. "It is worthy of remark," says he, "that the Roman poets say far less of the best of these personified moralities than we should expect. The artists in this respect are much richer, and he who would learn the particular aspect and attire of each need only consult the coins of the Roman Emperors : the poets speak of these beings frequently, indeed, as of persons; in general, however, they say very little of their attributes, their attire and the rest of their outward appearance."

When the poet personifies abstract qualities, these are sufficiently characterised by their names and by what they do. To the artist these means are wanting. He must therefore attach symbols to his personifications by which they can be distinguished. By these symbols, because they are something different and mean something different, they become allegorical figures. A woman with a bridle in her hand; another leaning on a pillar, are in art allegorical beings. But Temperance and Steadfastness are to the poet allegorical beings, and merely personified abstractions. The symbols, in the artist's representation, necessity has invented. For in no other way can he make plain what this or that figure signifies. But what the artist is driven to by necessity, why should the poet force on himself when no such necessity is laid upon him?

What surprises Spence so much deserves to be prescribed to the poets as a law. They must not make painting's indigence the rule of their wealth. They must not regard the means which Art has invented in order to follow poetry as if they were perfections which they have reason to envy. When the artist adorns a figure with symbols, he raises a mere figure to a superior being. But when the poet makes use of these plastic bedizenments, he makes of a superior being a mere lay-figure.

And just as this rule is authenticated by its observance amongst the ancient poets, so is its deliberate violation a favourite weakness amongst their successors. All their creatures of imagination go in masquerade, and those who understand this masquerade best generally understand least the chief thing of all, which is to let their creatures act and to distinguish and characterise them by their actions.

Yet amongst the attributes with which the artists distinguish their abstract personalities there is one sort which is more susceptible and more worthy of poetic employment. I mean those which properly have nothing allegorical in their nature, but are to be regarded as implements of which the beings to whom they are assigned would or might make use when acting as real persons. The bridle in the hand of Temperance, the pillar on which Steadfastness leans, are purely allegorical, and thus of no use to the poet. The scales in the hand of Justice are certainly less purely allegorical, because the right use of the scales is really a part of justice. But the lyre or flute in the hand of a Muse, the spear in the hand of Mars, hammer and tongs in the hands of Vulcan, are not symbols at all, but mere instruments, without which these beings could not effect the achievements we ascribe to them. Of this kind are the attributes which the ancient poets did sometimes weave into their descriptions, and which I on that ground, distinguishing them from the allegorical, would call the poetic. The latter signify the thing itself, the former only some likeness of it.

XI

Count Caylus, again, appears to require that the poet shall embellish the creatures of his imagination with allegorical attributes. The Count was more at home with painting than with poetry. In the work, neverthless, where he expresses this requirement I have found the suggestion of more important considerations, the most essential of which, for the better judging of them, I will mention here.

The artist, according to the Count's view, should make himself very thoroughly acquainted with the greatest of descriptive poets, with Homer, with this " second Nature." He shows him what rich and still unused material for most admirable pictures is offered by the story handled by the Greek, and how much more perfect his delineations will prove the more closely he clings to the very smallest circumstances noticed by the poet.

Now in this proposition we see a mingling of the two kinds of imitation which we have separated above. The painter is not only to imitate what the poet has imitated, but he is further to imitate it with the self-same features; he is to use the poet not as narrator only, but as poet.

This second species of imitation, however, which detracts so much from the poet's merit, why is it not equally disparaging to the artist? If before Homer such a succession of pictures as Count Caylus cites from his pages had been extant, and we were aware that the poet had based his work on them, would he not lose unspeakably in our estimation? How comes it that we withdraw from the artist no whit of our esteem even though he does nothing more than translate the words of the poet into figures and colours?

The reason appears to be this. With the artist we deem the execution more difficult than the invention; with the poet, again, it is the contrary, and we deem the execution, as compared with the invention, the lighter task. Had Virgil taken from the sculptured group the entangling of Laocoön and his children, the merit in his picture which we consider the greater and the harder of attainment would be lost, and only the smaller would remain. For to shape this entangling by the power of imagination is far more important than to express it in words. Had, on the other hand, the artist borrowed this entangling from the poet, he would still, in our minds, retain sufficient merit, although the merit of invention is withdrawn. For expression in marble is more difficult by far than expression in words; and when we weigh invention and representation against each other we are always inclined to abate our demands on the artist for the one, in proportion to the excess we feel that we have received of the other.

There are two cases in which it is a greater merit for the artist to copy Nature through the medium of the poet's imitation than without it. The painter who represents a lovely landscape according to the description of a Thomson has done more than he who copies it direct from Nature. The latter has his model before him; the former must first of all strain his imagination to the point that enables him to see it before him. The one makes a thing of beauty out of lively sensuous impressions, the other from weak and wavering descriptions of arbitary signs.

But natural as the readiness may be to abate in our demands on the artist for the particular merit of invention, it is equally so on his part, for like reasons, to be indifferent to it. For when he sees that invention can never become his more shining merit, that his greatest praise depends on execution, it becomes all one to him whether the former is old or new, used once or times without number, and whether it belongs to himself or to another. He remains within the narrow range of a few designs, become familiar both to him and to everybody, and directs his inventive faculty merely to changes in the already known and to new combinations of old subjects. That, too, is actually the idea which the manuals of painting connect with the word *Invention.* For although certainly they divide into the pictorial and the poetic, yet the poetic is not made to consist in the production of the design itself, but purely in the arrangement or the expression. It is invention, but not invention of the whole, only of separate parts and their position in relation to each other. It is invention, but of that lower type which Horace recommended to his tragic poet :

> . . . *Tuque*
> *Rectius Iliacum carmen deducis in actus*
> *Quam si proferres ignota indictaque primus.*

Recommended, I say, but not commanded. Recommended, as easier for him, more fitting, more advantageous; but not commanded as better and nobler in itself.

In fact the poet has a great advantage who treats a well-known story and familiar characters. A hundred indifferent trifles which otherwise would be indispensable to the under-

standing of the whole he can pass by; and the more quickly
he becomes intelligible to his hearers, the more quickly he can
interest them. This advantage the painter also has if his theme
is not strange to us, if we make out at the first glance the purpose and meaning of his entire composition, if we at once not
merely see his characters speaking, but hear also what they
speak. It is on the first glance that the main effect depends,
and if this forces on us troublesome reflection and conjecture,
our inclination to be moved grows cold; in order to be avenged
on the unintelligible artist, we harden ourselves against the
expression, and woe betide him if he has sacrificed beauty to
expression ! We then find nothing whatever that can charm us
to tarry before his work; what we see does not please us; and
what we are to think concerning it we are left uninstructed.

Now let us consider these two things together; first, that the
invention or novelty of the theme is far from being the principal
thing that we desire of the painter; secondly, that a well-known
theme furthers and facilitates the effect of his art; and I judge
that the reason why he so seldom attempts new themes we
need not, with Count Caylus, seek in his convenience, his ignor-
ance, or the difficulty of the mechanical part of art, demanding
all his time and diligence; but we shall find it more deeply
founded, and it may be that what at first appears to be the
limitations of art and the spoiling of our pleasure we shall be
inclined to praise as a restraint wise in itself and useful to
ourselves. Nor am I afraid that experience will confute me.
The painters will thank the Count for his goodwill, but hardly
follow his counsels so generally as he expects. If they should,
in another hundred years a new Caylus would be wanted who
should bring again to remembrance the old themes and re-
conduct the artist into the field where others before him have
gathered immortal laurels. Or do we desire that the public
shall be as learned as the connoisseur with his books? That to
the public all scenes of history or fable which might suggest a
beautiful picture shall become known and familiar? I grant
that the artists would have done better if since Raphael's day
they had made Homer instead of Ovid their manual. But as
that in fact has not happened, let us leave the public in their
old rut, and not make their pleasure harder to attain than a
pleasure must be in order to be what it should.

Protogenes had painted the mother of Aristotle. I don't
know how much the philosopher paid him for the picture.
But, either instead of payment or in addition thereto, he gave

him counsel that was worth more than the payment. For I cannot imagine that his counsel was a mere flattery. But chiefly because he considered the need of art—to be intelligible— he advised him to paint the achievements of Alexander, achievements of which at that time all the world was speaking, and of which he could foresee that they would be memorable also to posterity. Yet Protogenes had not discernment enough to follow this counsel; *impetus animi*, says Pliny, *et quaedam artis libido*, a certain arrogance of art, a certain lust for the strange and the unknown, attracted him to quite other subjects. He preferred to paint the story of a Jalysus, of a Cydippe and the like, of which to-day one cannot even guess what they represented.

XII

Homer treats of a twofold order of beings and actions : visible and invisible. This distinction it is not possible for painting to suggest; with it all is visible, and visible in one particular way. When, therefore, Count Caylus lets the pictures of the invisible actions run on in unbroken sequence with the visible ; when in the pictures of mingled actions, in which visible and invisible things take part, he does not, and perhaps cannot, suggest how the latter, which only we who contemplate the picture should discover therein, are so to be introduced that the persons in the picture do not see them, or at least must appear not necessarily to see them; it is inevitable that the entire composition, as well as many a separate portion of it, becomes confused, inconceivable, and self-contradictory.

Yet, with the book in one's hand, there might be some remedy for this error. The worst of it is simply this, that by the abrogation of the difference between the visible and invisible things all the characteristic features are at once lost by which the higher are raised above the inferior species. For example, when at last the divided gods come to blows among themselves over the fate of the Trojans, the whole struggle passes with the poet invisibly, and this invisibility permits the imagination to enlarge the stage, and leaves it free play to conceive the persons of the gods and their actions as great, and elevated as far above common humanity as ever it pleases. But painting must assume a visible stage the various necessary parts of which become the scale for the persons acting on it, a scale which the eye has immediately before it, and whose disproportion, as regards the higher beings, turns these higher beings, who were so great in the poet's delineation, into sheer monsters on the canvas of the artist.

Minerva, on whom in this struggle Mars ventures the first assault, steps back and snatches up from the ground with powerful hand a black, rough, massive stone, which in ancient days many hands of men together had rolled thither as a land-mark—

'Η δ' ἀναχασσαμένη λίθον εἵλετο χειρὶ παχείῃ,
Κείμενον ἐν πεδίῳ, μέλανατρηχύν τε μέγαν τε,
Τὸν δ' ἄνδρες πρότεροι θέσαν ἔμμεναι οὖρον ἀρούρης.

In order to estimate adequately the size of this stone, let us bear in mind that Homer makes his heroes as strong again as the strongest men of his time, and represents these, too, as far excelled in strength by the men whom Nestor had known in his youth. Now, I ask, if Minerva flings a stone which not one man, but several men of Nestor's youth had set for a landmark, if Minerva flings such a stone at Mars, of what stature is the goddess to be? If her stature is in proportion to the size of the stone, the marvellous vanishes. A man who is three times bigger than I must naturally also be able to fling a three-times bigger stone. But if the stature of the goddess is not in keeping with the size of the stone, there is imported into the picture an obvious improbability, the offence of which is not removed by the cold reflection that a goddess must have superhuman strength. Where I see a greater effect I would also see a greater instrument. And Mars, struck down by this mighty stone—

'Επτὰ δ' ἔπεσχε πέλεθρα . . .

covered seven hides of land. It is impossible that the painter can give the god this monstrous bulk. Yet if he does not, then Mars does not lie upon the ground, not the Homeric Mars, but only a common warrior.

Longinus remarks that it often appeared to him as if Homer wished to elevate his men to gods and to degrade his gods to men. Painting carries out this degradation. In painting everything vanishes completely which with the poet sets the gods yet higher than godlike men. Stature, strength, swiftness—of which Homer has in store a higher and more wonderful degree for his gods than he bestows on his most pre-eminent heroes—

must in picture sink down to the common measure of humanity, and Jupiter and Agamemnon, Apollo and Achilles, Ajax and Mars, become the same kind of beings, to be recognised no otherwise than by stipulated outward signs.

The means of which painting makes use to indicate that in her compositions this or that must be regarded as invisible, is a thin cloud in which she covers it from the view of the persons concerned. This cloud seems to have been borrowed from Homer himself. For when in the tumult of the battle one of the greater heroes comes into danger from which only heavenly power can deliver him, the poet causes him to be enveloped by the tutelary deity in a thick cloud or in actual night, and thus to be withdrawn from the place; as Paris was by Venus, Idäus by Neptune, Hector by Apollo. And this mist, this cloud Caylus never forgets heartily to commend to the artist when he is sketching for him a picture of such events. But who does not perceive that with the poet the enveloping in mist and darkness is nothing but a poetical way of saying invisible? It has, on this account, always surprised me to find this poetical expression realised and an actual cloud introduced into the picture, behind which the hero, as behind a screen, stands hidden from his enemy. That was not the poet's intention. That is to transgress the limits of painting; for this cloud is here a true hieroglyph, a mere symbolic sign, that does not make the rescued hero invisible, but calls out to the beholder, "You must regard him as invisible to you." This is no better than the inscribed labels which issue from the mouths of the persons in ancient Gothic pictures.

It is true Homer makes Achilles, when Apollo snatches away Hector from him, strike yet three times at the thick vapour with his spear: τρὶς δ' ἠέρα τύψε βαθεῖαν. But even that, in the poet's language, means no more than that Achilles became so enraged that he struck yet thrice before he noticed that he no longer had his foe in front of him. An actual mist Achilles did not see, and the whole artifice by which the gods made things invisible consisted not at all in the cloud, but in the swift snatching. Only, in order to show at the same time that no human eye could follow the body thus snatched away, the poet first of all envelops it beforehand in vapour; not that instead of the body withdrawn a fog was seen, but that whatever is under fog we think of as not visible. Therefore at times he inverts the order of things, and, instead of making the object invisible, causes the subject to be struck with blindness. Thus

Neptune darkens the eyes of Achilles to save Æneas from his murderous hands, removing him in a moment from out the tumult of the rearguard. In fact, however, the eyes of Achilles are here just as little darkened as in the other case the withdrawn heroes were enveloped in fog; the poet merely adds the one thing and the other, in order thereby to make more perceptible the extreme swiftness of the withdrawal which we call the vanishing.

The Homeric mist, however, the painters have made their own not merely in the cases where Homer himself uses or would have used it—in actual invisibilities or vanishings—but everywhere when the beholder is to recognise something in the picture which the persons in it, either altogether or in part, do not recognise. Minerva became visible to Achilles alone when she held him back from assaulting Agamemnon. " To express this," says Caylus, " I know no other way than to veil her in a cloud from the rest of the council." This is quite contrary to the spirit of the poet. To be invisible is the natural condition of his gods : no blinding, no cutting-off of the light, was needed in order that they should not be seen, but an illumination, a heightening of mortal vision, was necessary if they were to be seen. It is not enough, therefore, that the cloud is an arbitrary and unnatural sign with the painters; this arbitrary sign has not at all the positive significance which it might have as such, for they use it as frequently to make the visible invisible as they do the reverse.

XIII

If Homer's works were entirely lost, and nothing was left of his *Iliad* and *Odyssey* save a succession of pictures such as Caylus has suggested might be drawn from them, should we from these pictures, even from the hand of the most perfect master, be able to form the conception we now have, I do not say of the poet's whole endowment, but even of his pictorial talent alone ? Let us try the experiment with the first passage that occurs to us—the picture of the pestilence. What do we perceive on the canvas of the artist ? Dead corpses, flaming funeral pyres, dying men busy with the dead, the angry god upon a cloud letting fly his arrows. The greatest riches of this picture is, compared with the poet, mere poverty. For if we were to replace Homer from the picture, what could we make him say? "Then did Apollo become enraged and shot his arrows amongst the Grecian host. Many Greeks died and their corpses were burned." Now let us turn to Homer himself :—

Βῆ δὲ κατ' Οὐλύμποιο καρήνων | χωόμενος κῆρ, |
Τόξ' ὤμοισιν ἔχων | ἀμφηρεφέα τε φαρέτρην·
Ἔκλαγξαν δ' ἄρ' ὀϊστοὶ ἐπ' ὤμων χωομένοιο,
Αὐτοῦ κινηθέντος· ὁ δ' ἤϊε νυκτὶ ἐοικώς |.
Ἕζετ' ἔπειτ' ἀπάνευθε νεῶν, μετὰ | δ' ἰὸν ἕηκε·
Δεινὴ δὲ κλαγγὴ γένετ' ἀργυρέοιο βιοῖο·
Οὐρῆας μὲν πρῶτον ἐπῴχετο | καὶ κύνας ἀργούς,
Αὐτὰρ ἔπειτ' αὐτοῖσι | βέλος ἐχεπευκὲς ἐφιεὶς
Βάλλ'· αἰεὶ δὲ πυραὶ | νεκύων | καίοντο θαμειαί.

Just as far as life is above painting, the poet here is above the painter. With his bow and quiver the enraged Apollo descends from the rocky peak of Olympus. I do not merely see him descend, I hear him. At every step the arrows rattle about the shoulders of the wrathful god. He glides along like night. And now he sits opposite the ships—fearfully twangs the silver bow—he darts the first arrow at the mules and dogs. And then, with a more poisonous shaft, he strikes the men themselves; and everywhere without cessation break into flame the corpse-encumbered pyres. The musical painting which we hear in the words of the poet it is not possible to translate into another language. It is just as impossible to gather it from the material picture, although it is only a very trivial advantage which the poetic picture possesses. The chief advantage is that what the material painting drawn from him exhibits the poet leads us up to through a whole gallery of pictures.

But, then, perhaps the pestilence is not an advantageous subject for painting. Here is another having more charms for the eye—the gods taking counsel together over their wine. A golden palace open to the sky, arbitrary groups of the most beautiful and the most worshipful forms, their cups in their hands, waited on by Hebe, the image of eternal youth. What architecture, what masses of light and shade, what contrasts, what manifold expression! Where can I begin, and where leave off, to feast my eyes? If the painter so enchants me, how much more will the poet! I turn to his pages, and find— that I am deceived. Four simple lines only, such as might serve for the inscription of a picture; the material for a picture is there, but they themselves do not make a picture :—

Οἱ δὲ θεοὶ πὰρ Ζηνὶ καθήμενοι ἠγορόωντο
Χρυσέῳ ἐν δαπέδῳ, μετὰ δέ σφισι πότνια Ἥβη
Νέκταρ ἐῳνοχόει· τοὶ δὲ χρυσέοις δεπάεσσι
Δειδέχατ᾽ ἀλλήλους, Τρώων πόλιν εἰσορόωντες.

This an Apollonius or an even more mediocre poet would have
said equally well; and Homer here stands just as far below the
painter as in the former case the painter stood below him.

Yet more, Caylus finds in the whole of the Fourth Book of the
Iliad no other picture, not one, than in these four lines. " However much," he remarks, " the Fourth Book is marked by
manifold encouragements to the attempt, owing to the abundance of brilliant and contrasted characters and to the art with
which the poet shows us the entire multitude whom he will set
in action—yet it is perfectly unusable for painting." He might
have added, Rich as it is otherwise in that which we call poetic
picture. For truly these are for number and perfection as
remarkable as in any other Book. Where is there a more
finished or more striking picture than that of Pandarus, as, on
the incitement of Minerva, he breaks the truce and lets fly his
arrow at Menelaus? Or that of the approach of the Grecian
host? Or that of the two-sided, simultaneous onset? Or
that of Ulysses' deed by which he avenges the death of his
Leucus?

What, then, follows from the fact that not a few of the finest
descriptions in Homer afford no picture for the artist, and that
the artist can draw pictures from him where he himself has
none? That those which he has and the artist can use would
be very poverty-stricken pictures if they did not show more
than can be shown by the artist? What else do they, but give
a negative to my former question? That from the material
paintings for which the poems of Homer provide the subjects,
however numerous they may be and however excellent, nothing
can be concluded as to the pictorial talent of the poet.

                             XIV

But if it is so, and if one poem may yield very happy results
for the painter yet itself be not pictorial; if, again, another in
its turn may be very pictorial and yet offer nothing to the
painter; this is enough to dispose of Count Caylus' notion,
which would make this kind of utility the criterion or test of
the poets and settle their rank by the number of pictures which

they provide for the artist. Far be it from us, even if only by our silence, to allow this notion to gain the authority of a rule. Milton would fall the first innocent sacrifice to it. For it seems really that the contemptuous verdict which Caylus passes upon him was not mere national prejudice, but rather a consequence of his supposed principle. " The loss of sight," he says, " may well be the nearest resemblance Milton bore to Homer." True, Milton can fill no galleries. But if, so long as I had the bodily eye, its sphere must also be the sphere of my inward eye, then would I, in order to be free of this limitation, set a great value on the loss of the former. The *Paradise Lost* is not less the first epic poem since Homer on the ground of its providing few pictures, than the *Leidensgeschichte Christi* is a poem because we can hardly put the point of a needle into it without touching a passage that might have employed a multitude of the greatest artists. The Evangelists relate the facts with all the dry simplicity possible, and the artist uses the manifold parts of the story without their having shown on their side the smallest spark of pictorial genius. There are paintable and unpaintable facts, and the historian can relate the most paintable in just as unpictorial a fashion as the poet can represent the least paintable pictorially.

We are merely misled by the ambiguity of words if we take the matter otherwise. A poetic picture is not necessarily that which can be transmuted into a material painting; but every feature, every combination of features by means of which the poet makes his subject so perceptible that we are more clearly conscious of this subject than of his words is called pictorial, is styled a picture, because it brings us nearer to the degree of illusion of which the material painting is specially capable and which can most readily and most easily be drawn from the material painting.

XV

Now the poet, as experience shows, can raise to this degree of illusion the representations even of other than visible objects. Consequently the artist must necessarily be denied whole classes of pictures in which the poet has the advantage over him. Dryden's Ode on St. Cecilia's Day is full of musical pictures that cannot be touched by the paint-brush. But I will not lose myself in instances of the kind, from which in the end we learn nothing more than that colours are not tones and that eyes are not ears.

I will confine myself to the pictures of purely visible objects which are common to the poet and the painter. How comes it that many poetical pictures of this kind cannot be used by the painter, and, *vice versa*, many actual pictures lose the best part of their effect in the hands of the poet?

Examples may help us. I repeat it—the picture of Pandarus in the Fourth Book of the *Iliad* is one of the most finished and most striking in all Homer. From the seizing of the bow to the very flight of the arrow every moment is depicted, and all these moments are kept so close together, and yet so distinctly separate, that if we did not know how a bow was to be managed we might learn it from this picture alone. Pandarus draws forth his bow, fixes the bowstring, opens his quiver, chooses a yet unused, well-feathered shaft, sets the arrow on the string, draws back both string and arrow down to the notch, the string is brought near to his breast and the iron head of the arrow to the bow; back flies the great bent bow with a twang, the bowstring whirs, off springs the arrow flying eager for its mark.

This admirable picture Caylus cannot have overlooked. What, then, did he find in it to render it incapable of employing his artist? And for what reason did he consider fitter for this purpose the assembly of the carousing gods in council? In the one, as in the other, we find visible subjects, and what more does the poet want than visible subjects in order to fill his canvas? The solution of the problem must be this. Although both subjects, as being visible, are alike capable of actual painting, yet there exists the essential distinction between them, that the former is a visible continuous action, the different parts of which occur step by step in succession of time, the latter, on the other hand, is a visible arrested action, the different parts of which develop side by side in space. But now, if painting, in virtue of her signs or the methods of her imitation, which she can combine only in space, must wholly renounce time, then continuous actions as such cannot be reckoned amongst her subjects; but she must content herself with actions set side by side, or with mere bodies which by their attitudes can be supposed an action. Poetry, on the other hand——

XVI

But I will turn to the foundations and try to argue the matter from first principles.

My conclusion is this. If it is true that painting employs in its imitations quite other means or signs than poetry employs, the former—that is to say, figures and colours in space—but the latter articulate sounds in time; as, unquestionably, the signs used must have a definite relation to the thing signified, it follows that signs arranged together side by side can express only subjects which, or the various parts of which, exist thus side by side, whilst signs which succeed each other can express only subjects which, or the various parts of which, succeed each other.

Subjects which, or the various parts of which, exist side by side, may be called *bodies*. Consequently, bodies with their visible properties form the proper subjects of painting.

Subjects which or the various parts of which succeed each other may in general be called *actions*. Consequently, actions form the proper subjects of poetry.

Yet all bodies exist not in space alone, but also in time. They continue, and may appear differently at every moment and stand in different relations. Every one of these momentary appearances and combinations is the effect of one preceding and can be the cause of one following, and accordingly be likewise the central point of an action. Consequently, painting can also imitate actions, but only by way of suggestion through bodies.

On the other hand, actions cannot subsist for themselves, but must attach to certain things or persons. Now in so far as these things are bodies or are regarded as bodies, poetry too depicts bodies, but only by way of suggestion through actions.

Painting, in her co-existing compositions, can use only one single moment of the action, and must therefore choose the most pregnant, from which what precedes and follows will be most easily apprehended.

Just in the same manner poetry also can use, in her continuous imitations, only one single property of the bodies, and must therefore choose that one which calls up the most living picture of the body on that side from which she is regarding it. Here, indeed, we find the origin of the rule which insists on the unity and consistency of descriptive epithets, and on economy in the delineations of bodily subjects.

This is a dry chain of reasoning, and I should put less trust in it if I did not find it completely confirmed by Homer's practice, or if, rather, it were not Homer's practice itself which had led me to it. Only by these principles can the great manner of the Greeks be settled and explained, and its rightness established against the opposite manner of so many modern poets, who would emulate the painter in a department where they must necessarily be outdone by him.

Homer, I find, paints nothing but continuous actions, and all bodies, all single things, he paints only by their share in those actions, and in general only by one feature. What wonder, then, that the painter, where Homer himself paints, finds little or nothing for him to do, his harvest arising only there where the story brings together a multitude of beautiful bodies, in beautiful attitudes, in a place favourable to art, the poet himself painting these bodies, attitudes, places, just as little as he chooses? Let the reader run through the whole succession of pictures piece by piece, as Caylus suggests, and he will discover in every one of them evidence for our contention.

Here, then, I leave the Count, who wishes to make the painter's palette the touchstone of the poet, that I may expound in closer detail the manner of Homer.

For one thing, I say, Homer commonly names one feature only. A ship is to him now the black ship, now the hollow ship, now the swift ship, at most the well-rowed black ship. Beyond that he does not enter on a picture of the ship. But certainly of the navigating, the putting to sea, the disembarking of the ship, he makes a detailed picture, one from which the painter must make five or six separate pictures if he would get it in its entirety upon his canvas.

If indeed special circumstances compel Homer to fix our glance for a while on some single corporeal object, in spite of this no picture is made of it which the painter could follow with his brush; for Homer knows how, by innumerable artifices, to set this object in a succession of moments, at each of which it assumes a different appearance, and in the last of which the painter must await it in order to show us, fully arisen, what in the poet we see arising. For instance, if Homer wishes to let us see the chariot of Juno, then Hebe must put it together piece by piece before our eyes. We see the wheels, the axles, the seat, the pole and straps and traces, not so much as it is when complete, but as it comes together under the hands of Hebe. On the wheels alone does the poet expend more than one feature,

showing us the brazen spokes, the golden rims, the tires of
bronze, the silver hub, in fullest detail. We might suggest that
as there were more wheels than one, so in the description just
as much more time must be given to them as their separate
putting-on would actually itself require.

> Ἥβη δ' ἀμφ' ὀχέεσσι θοῶς βάλε καμπύλα κύκλα,
> Χάλκεα ὀκτάκνημα, σιδηρέῳ ἄξονι ἀμφίς.
> Τῶν ἦ τοι χρυσέη ἴτυς ἄφθιτος, αὐτὰρ ὕπερθε
> Χάλκε' ἐπίσσωτρα προσαρηρότα, θαῦμα ἰδέσθαι·
> Πλῆμναι δ' ἀργύρου εἰσὶ περίδρομοι ἀμφοτέρωθεν·
> Δίφρος δὲ χρυσέοισι καὶ ἀργυρέοισιν ἱμᾶσιν
> Ἐντέταται, δοιαὶ δὲ περίδρομοι ἄντυγές εἰσι.
> Τοῦ δ' ἐξ ἀργύρεος ῥυμὸς πέλεν· αὐτὰρ ἐπ' ἄκρῳ
> Δῆσε χρύσειον καλὸν ζυγόν, ἐν δὲ λέπαδνα
> Κάλ' ἔβαλε χρύσεια.

If Homer would show us how Agamemnon was dressed, then
the King must put on his whole attire piece by piece before our
eyes: the soft undervest, the great mantle, the fine laced boots,
the sword; and now he is ready and grasps the sceptre. We
see the attire as the poet paints the action of attiring; another
would have described the garments down to the smallest ribbon,
and we should have seen nothing of the action.

> Μαλακὸν δ' ἔνδυνε χιτῶνα,
> Καλὸν νηγάτεον, περὶ δὲ μέγα βάλλετο φᾶρος·
> Ποσσὶ δ' ὑπὸ λιπαροῖσιν ἐδήσατο καλὰ πέδιλα,
> Ἀμφὶ δ' ἄρ' ὤμοισιν βάλετο ξίφος ἀργυρόηλον·
> Εἵλετο δὲ σκῆπτρον πατρώϊον, ἄφθιτον αἰεί.

And of this sceptre which here is called merely the paternal,
ancestral sceptre, as in another place he calls a similar one
merely χρυσείοις ἥλοισι πεπαρμένον—that is, the sceptre
mounted with studs of gold—if, I say, of this mighty sceptre
we are to have a fuller and exacter picture, what, then, does
Homer? Does he paint for us, besides the golden nails, the
wood also and the carved knob? Perhaps he might if the
description were intended for a book of heraldry, so that in
after times one like to it might be made precisely to pattern.
And yet I am certain that many a modern poet would have
made just such a heraldic description, with the naïve idea that
he has himself so painted it because the painter may possibly
follow him. But what does Homer care how far he leaves the

painter behind? Instead of an image he gives us the story of the sceptre : first, it is being wrought by Vulcan; then it gleams in the hands of Jupiter; again, it marks the office of Mercury; once more, it is the marshal's baton of the warlike Pelops, and yet again, the shepherd's crook of peace-loving Atreus.

Σκῆπτρον ἔχων, τὸ μὲν Ἥφαιστος κάμε τεύχων.

Ἥφαιστος μὲν δῶκε Διὶ Κρονίωνι ἄνακτι,
Αὐτὰρ ἄρα Ζεὺς δῶκε διακτόρῳ ἀργεϊφόντῃ·
Ἑρμείας δὲ ἄναξ δῶκεν Πέλοπι πληξίππῳ,
Αὐτὰρ ὁ αὖτε Πέλοψ δῶκ' Ἀτρεϊ, ποιμένι λαῶν·
Ἀτρεὺς δὲ θνήσκων ἔλιπεν πολύαρνι Θυέστῃ,
Αὐτὰρ ὁ αὖτε Θυέστ' Ἀγαμέμνονι λεῖπε φορῆναι,
Πολλῇσιν νήσοισι καὶ Ἄργεϊ παντὶ ἀνάσσειν.

And so in the end I know this sceptre better than if a painter had laid it before my eyes or a second Vulcan delivered it into my hands. It would not surprise me if I found that one of the old commentators of Homer had admired this passage as the most perfect allegory of the origin, progress, establishment, and hereditary succession of the royal power amongst mankind. True, I should smile if I were to read that Vulcan, the maker of this sceptre, as fire, as the most indispensable thing for the preservation of mankind, represented in general the satisfaction of those wants which moved the first men to subject themselves to the rule of an individual monarch; that the first king, a son of Time (Ζεὺς Κρονίων), was an honest ancient who wished to share his power with, or wholly transfer it to, a wise and eloquent man, a Mercury (διακτόρῳ ἀργεϊφόντῃ); that the wily orator, at the time when the infant State was threatened by foreign foes, resigned his supreme power to the bravest warrior (Πέλοπι πληξίππῳ); that the brave warrior, when he had quelled the aggressors and made the realm secure, was able to hand it over to his son, who, as a peace-loving ruler, as a benevolent shepherd of his people (ποιμὴν λαῶν), made them acquainted with luxury and abundance, whereby after his death the wealthiest of his relations (πολύαρνι Θυέστῃ) had the way opened to him for attracting to himself by presents and bribes that which hitherto only confidence had conferred and which merit had considered more a burden than an honour, and to secure it to his family for the future as a kind of purchased estate. I should smile, but nevertheless should be confirmed in my esteem for the poet to whom so much meaning can be

attributed.—This, however, is a digression, and I am now
regarding the story of the sceptre merely as an artifice to make
us tarry over the one particular object without being drawn
into the tedious description of its parts. Even when Achilles
swears by his sceptre to avenge the contempt with which
Agamemnon has treated him, Homer gives us the history of
this sceptre. We see it growing green upon the mountains, the
axe cutting it from the trunk, stripping it of leaves and bark
and making it fit to serve the judges of the people for a symbol
of their godlike dignity.

Ναὶ μὰ τόδε σκῆπτρον, τὸ μὲν οὔ ποτε φύλλα καὶ ὄζους
Φύσει, ἐπεὶ δὴ πρῶτα τομὴν ἐν ὄρεσσι λέλοιπεν,
Οὐδ' ἀναθηλήσει· περὶ γάρ ῥά ἑ χαλκὸς ἔλεψε
Φύλλα τε καὶ φλοιόν· νῦν αὖτέ μιν υἶες Ἀχαιῶν
Ἐν παλάμῃς φορέουσι δικασπόλοι, οἵ τε θέμιστας
Πρὸς Διὸς εἰρύαται . . . .

It was not so much incumbent upon Homer to depict two
staves of different material and shape as to furnish us with a
symbol of the difference in the powers of which these staves
were the sign. The former a work of Vulcan, the latter carved
by an unknown hand in the mountains; the former the ancient
property of a noble house, the latter intended for any fist that
can grasp it; the former extended by a monarch over all Argos
and many an isle besides, the latter borne by any one out of the
midst of the Grecian hosts, one to whom with others the guarding
of the laws had been committed. Such was actually the distance that separated Agamemnon from Achilles, a distance
which Achilles himself, in all the blindness of his wrath, could
not help admitting.

Yet not in those cases alone where Homer combines with his
descriptions this kind of ulterior purpose, but even where he
has to do with nothing but the picture, he will distribute this
picture in a sort of story of the object, in order to let its parts,
which we see side by side in Nature, follow in his painting after
each other and as it were keep step with the flow of the narrative.
For instance, he would paint for us the bow of Pandarus—a
bow of horn, of such and such a length, well polished, and
mounted with gold plate at the extremities. How does he
manage it? Does he count out before us all these properties
dryly one after the other? Not at all; that would be to sketch,
to make a copy of such a bow, but not to paint it. He begins

with the chase of the deer, from the horns of which the bow
was made; Pandarus had waylaid and killed it amongst the
crags; the horns were of extraordinary length, and so he destined
them for a bow; they are wrought, the maker joins them,
mounts them, polishes them. And thus, as we have already
said, with the poet we see arising what with the painter we
can only see as already arisen.

> Τόξον ἐΰξοον ἰξάλου αἰγὸς
> Ἀγρίου, ὅν ῥά ποτ’ αὐτὸς ὑπὸ στέρνοιο τυχήσας
> Πέτρης ἐκβαίνοντα δεδεγμένος ἐν προδοκῇσι,
> Βεβλήκει πρὸς στῆθος· ὁ δ’ ὕπτιος ἔμπεσε πέτρῃ.
> Τοῦ κέρα ἐκ κεφαλῆς ἑκκαιδεκάδωρα πεφύκει·
> Καὶ τὰ μὲν ἀσκήσας κεραοξόος ἥραρε τέκτων,
> Πᾶν δ’ εὖ λειήνας χρυσέην ἐπέθηκε κορώνην.

I should never have done, if I were to cite all the instances of
this kind. A multitude of them will occur to everyone who
knows his Homer.

XVII

But, some will object, the signs or characters which poetry
employs are not solely such as succeed each other; they may be
also arbitrary; and, as arbitrary signs, they are certainly
capable of representing bodies just as they exist in space. We
find instances of this in Homer himself, for we have only to
remember his Shield of Achilles in order to have the most
decisive example in how detailed and yet poetical a manner
some single thing can be depicted, with its various parts side
by side.

I will reply to this twofold objection. I call it twofold,
because a just conclusion must prevail even without examples,
and, on the other hand, the example of Homer weighs with
me even if I know not how to justify it by any argument. It
is true, as the signs of speech are arbitrary, so it is perfectly
possible that by it we can make the parts of a body follow each
other just as truly as in actuality they are found existing side
by side. Only this is a property of speech and its signs in
general, but not in so far as it suits best the purposes of poetry.
The poet is not concerned merely to be intelligible, his representations should not merely be clear and plain, though this
may satisfy the prose writer. He desires rather to make the

ideas awakened by him within us living things, so that for the
moment we realise the true sensuous impressions of the objects
he describes, and cease in this moment of illusion to be conscious
of the means—namely, his words—which he employs for his
purpose. This is the substance of what we have already said
of the poetic picture. But the poet should always paint; and
now let us see how far bodies with their parts set side by side are
suitable for this kind of painting.

How do we arrive at the distinct representation of a thing in
space? First we regard its parts singly, then the combination
of these parts, and finally the whole. Our senses perform these
various operations with so astonishing a swiftness that they
seem to us but one, and this swiftness is imperatively necessary
if we are to arrive at a conception of the whole, which is nothing
more than the result of the conceptions of the parts and their
combination. Provided, then, the poet leads us in the most
beautiful order from one part of the object to another; provided he knows also how to make the combination of those
parts equally clear—how much time does he need for that?
What the eye sees at a glance, he counts out to us gradually,
with a perceptible slowness, and often it happens that when we
come to the last feature we have already forgotten the first.
Nevertheless, we have to frame a whole from those features;
to the eye the parts beheld remain constantly present, and it
can run over them again and again; for the ear, on the contrary,
the parts heard are lost if they do not abide in the memory.
And if they so abide, what trouble, what effort it costs to renew
their impressions, all of them in their due order, so vividly, to
think of them together with even a moderate swiftness, and thus
to arrive at an eventual conception of the whole. Let us try
it by an example which may be called a masterpiece of its
kind :—

> Dort ragt das hohe Haupt vom edeln Enziane
> Weit übern niedern Chor der Pöbelkräuter hin,
> Ein ganzes Blumenvolk dient unter seiner Fahne,
> Sein blauer Bruder selbst dückt sich und ehret ihn.
> Der Blumen helles Gold, in Strahlen umgebogen,
> Thürmt sich am Stengel auf, und krönt sein grau Gewand,
> Der Blätter glattes Weiss, mit tiefem Grün durchzogen,
> Strahlt von dem bunten Blitz von feuchtem Diamant.
> Gerechtestes Gesetz ! dass Kraft sich Zier vermähle,
> In einem schönen Leib wohnt eine schöne Seele.
>   Hier kriecht ein niedrig Kraut, gleich einem grauen Nebel,
> Dem die Natur sein Blatt im Kreuze hingelegt ;

Die holde Blume zeigt die zwei vergöldten Schnäbel,
Die ein von Amethyst gebildter Vogel trägt.
Dort wirft ein glänzend Blatt, in Finger ausgekerbet,
Auf einen hellen Bach den grünen Wiederschein ;
Der Blumen zarten Schnee, den matter Purpur färbet,
Schliesst ein gestreifter Stern in weisse Strahlen ein.
Smaragd und Rosen blühn auch auf zertretner Heide,
Und Felsen decken sich mit einem Purpurkleide.

Here are weeds and flowers which the learned poet paints
with much art and fidelity to Nature. Paints, but without
any illusion whatever. I will not say that out of this picture
he who has never seen these weeds and flowers can make no
idea of them, or as good as none. It may be that all poetic
pictures require some preliminary acquaintance with their
subjects. Neither will I deny that for one who possesses such
an acquaintance here the poet may not have awakened a more
vivid idea of some parts. I only ask him, How does it stand
with the conception of the whole? If this also is to be more
vivid, then no single parts must stand out, but the higher light
must appear divided equally amongst them all, our imagination
must be able to run over them all with equal swiftness, in order
to unite in one from them that which in Nature we see united
in one. Is this the case here? And is not the case rather, as
one has expressed it, " that the most perfect drawing of a
painter must be entirely lifeless and dark compared with this
poetic portrayal "? It remains infinitely below that which
lines and colours on canvas can express, and the critic who
bestows on it this exaggerated praise must have regarded it
from an utterly false point of view : he must have looked
rather at the ornaments which the poet has woven into it, at
the heightening of the subject above the mere vegetative life,
at the development of the inner perfection to which the outward
beauty serves merely as a shell, than at the beauty itself and at
the degree of life and resemblance in the picture which the
painter and which the poet can assure to us from it. Nevertheless, it amounts here purely to the latter, and whoever says
that the mere lines :—

Der Blumen helles Gold, in Strahlen umgebogen,
Thürmt sich am Stengel auf, und krönt sein grün Gewand,
Der Blätter glattes Weiss, mit tiefem Grün durchzogen,
Strahlt von dem bunten Blitz von feuchtem Diamant,

—that these lines in respect of their impression can compete
with the imitation of a Huysum, can never have interrogated
his feelings, or must be deliberately denying them. They may,

indeed, if we have the flower itself in our hands, be recited concerning it with excellent effect; but in themselves alone they say little or nothing. I hear in every word the toiling poet, and am far enough from seeing the thing itself.

Once more, then; I do not deny to speech in general the power of portraying a bodily whole by its parts : speech can do so, because its signs or characters, although they follow one another consecutively, are nevertheless arbitrary signs; but I do deny it to speech as the medium of poetry, because such verbal delineations of bodies fail of the illusion on which poetry particularly depends, and this illusion, I contend, must fail them for the reason that the *co-existence* of the physical object comes into collision with the *consecutiveness* of speech, and the former being resolved into the latter, the dismemberment of the whole into its parts is certainly made easier, but the final reunion of those parts into a whole is made uncommonly difficult and not seldom impossible.

Wherever, then, illusion does not come into the question, where one has only to do with the understanding of one's readers and appeals only to plain and as far as possible complete conceptions, those delineations of bodies (which we have excluded from poetry) may quite well find their place, and not the prosewriter alone, but the dogmatic poet (for where he dogmatises he is not a poet) can employ them with much advantage. So Virgil, for instance, in his poem on agriculture, delineates a cow suitable for breeding from :—

> . . . *Optima torvae*
> *Forma bovis, cui turpe caput, cui plurima cervix,*
> *Et crurum tenus a mento palearia pendent ;*
> *Tum longo nullus lateri modus : omnia magna,*
> *Pes etiam, et camuris hirtae sub cornibus aures.*
> *Nec mihi displiceat maculis insignis et albo,*
> *Aut juga detrectans interdumque aspera cornu*
> *Et faciem tauro propior, quaeque ardua tota,*
> *Et gradiens ima verrit vestigia cauda.*

Or a beautiful foal :—

> . . . *Illi ardua cervix*
> *Argutumque caput, brevis alvus, obesaque terga,*
> *Luxuriatque toris animosum pectus, etc.*

For who does not see that here the poet is concerned rather with the setting forth of the parts than with the whole? He wants to reckon up for us the characteristics of a fine foal and of a well-formed cow, in order to enable us, when we have more or less taken note of these, to judge of the excellence of the one or the other; whether, however, all these characteristics can be easily gathered together into one living picture or not, that might be to him a matter of indifference.

Beyond such performances as these, the detailed pictures of physical objects, barring the above-mentioned Homeric artifice of changing the Co-existing into an actual Successive, has always been recognised by the best judges as a frigid kind of sport for which little or nothing of genius is demanded. " When the poetic dabbler," says Horace, " can do nothing more, he begins to paint a hedge, an altar, a brook winding through pleasant meads, a brawling stream, or a rainbow :—

> . . . Lucus et ara Dianae
> Et properantis aquae per amoenos ambitus agros,
> Aut flumen Rhenum, aut pluvius describitur arcus."

Pope, who was a masculine man, looked back on the pictorial efforts of his poetic childhood with great contempt. He expressly required that whosoever would not unworthily bear the name of poet should as early as possible renounce the lust for description, and declared a merely descriptive poem to be a dinner of nothing but soup. Of Herr von Kleist I can avow that he was far from proud of his " Spring " : had he lived longer, he would have given it an entirely different shape. He thought of putting some design into it, and mused on means by which that multitude of pictures which he seemed to have snatched haphazard, now here, now there, from the limitless field of rejuvenated Nature, might be made to arise in a natural order before his eyes and follow each other in a natural succession. He would at the same time have done what Marmontel, doubtless on the occasion of his Eclogues, recommended to several German poets; from a series of pictures but sparingly interspersed with sensations he would have made a succession of sensations but sparingly interspersed with pictures.

XVIII

And yet may not Homer himself sometimes have lapsed into these frigid delineations of physical objects?

I will hope that there are only a few passages to which in this case appeal can be made; and I am assured that even these few are of such a kind as rather to confirm the rule from which they seem to be exceptions. It still holds good; succession in

time is the sphere of the poet, as space is that of the painter.
To bring two necessarily distant points of time into one and
the same picture, as Fr. Mazzuoli has done with the Rape of the
Sabine Women and their reconciling their husbands to their
kinsfolk, or as Titian with the whole story of the Prodigal Son,
his dissolute life, his misery, and his repentance, is nothing but
an invasion of the poet's sphere by the painter, which good
taste can never sanction. The several parts or things which
in Nature I must needs take in at a glance if they are to produce
a whole—to reckon these up one by one to the reader, in order
to form for him a picture of the whole, is nothing but an invasion
of the painter's sphere by the poet, who expends thereby a
great deal of imagination to no purpose. Still, as two friendly,
reasonable neighbours will not at all permit that one of them
shall make too free with the most intimate concerns of the
other, yet will exercise in things of less importance a mutual
forbearance and on either side condone trifling interferences
with one's strict rights to which circumstances may give occasion,
so it is with Painting and Poetry.

It is unnecessary here for my purpose to point out that in
great historical pictures the single moment is almost always
amplified to some extent, and that there is perhaps no single
composition very rich in figures where every figure has completely the movement and posture which at the moment of the
main action it ought to have; one is earlier, another later, than
historical truth would require. This is a liberty which the
master must make good by certain niceties of arrangement, by
the employment or the withdrawal of his *personæ*, such as will
permit them to take a greater or a smaller share in what is
passing at the moment. Let me here avail myself of but one
remark which Herr Mengs has made concerning the drapery of
Raphael. " All folds," he says, " have with him their reasons,
it may be from their own weight or by the pulling of the limbs.
We can often see from them how they have been at an earlier
moment; even in this Raphael seeks significance. One sees
from the folds whether a leg or an arm, before the moment
depicted, has stood in front or behind, whether the limb has
moved from curvature to extension, or after being stretched
out is now bending." It is undeniable that the artist in this
case brings two different moments into one. For as the foot
which has rested behind and now moves forward is immediately
followed by the part of the dress resting upon it, unless the dress
be of very stiff material and for that very reason is altogether

inconvenient to paint, so there is no moment in which the dress makes a fold different in the slightest from that which the present position of the limb demands; but if we permit it to make another fold, then we have the previous moment of the dress and the present moment of the limb. Nevertheless, who will be so particular with the artist who finds his advantage in showing us these two moments together? Who will not rather praise him for having the intelligence and the courage to commit a fault so trifling in order to attain a greater perfection of expression?

The poet is entitled to equal indulgence. His progressive imitation properly allows him to touch but one single side, one single property of his physical subject at a time. But if the happy construction of his language permits him to do this with a single word, why should he not also venture now and then to add a second such word? Why not even, if it is worth the trouble, a third? Or, indeed, perhaps a fourth? I have said that to Homer a ship was either the black ship, or the hollow ship, or the swift ship, or at most the well-rowed black ship. This is to be understood of his manner in general. Here and there a passage occurs where he adds the third descriptive epithet: Καμπύλα κύκλα, χάλκεα, ὀκτάκνημα, round, brazen, eight-spoked wheels. Even the fourth: ἀσπίδα πάντοσε ἴσην, καλήν, χαλκείην, ἐξήλατον, a completely polished, beautiful, brazen, chased shield. Who will blame him for that? Who will not rather owe him thanks for this little exuberance, when he feels what an excellent effect it may have in a suitable place?

I am unwilling, however, to argue the poet's or the painter's proper justification from the simile I have employed, of the two friendly neighbours. A mere simile proves and justifies nothing. But they must be justified in this way: just as in the one case, with the painter, the two distinct moments touch each other so closely and immediately that they may without offence count as but one, so also in the other case, with the poet, the several strokes for the different parts and properties in space succeed each other so quickly, in such a crowded moment, that we can believe we hear all of them at once.

And in this, I may remark, his splendid language served Homer marvellously. It allowed him not merely all possible freedom in the combining and heaping-up of epithets, but it had, too, for their heaped-up epithets an order so happy as quite to remedy the disadvantage arising from the suspension of their application. In one or several of these facilities the

modern languages are universally lacking. Those, like the
French, which, to give an example, for καμπύλα κύκλα,
χάλκεα, ὀκτάκνημα, must use the circumlocution "the round
wheels which were of brass and had eight spokes," express the
sense, but destroy the picture. The sense, moreover, is here
nothing, and the picture everything; and the former without
the latter makes the most vivid poet the most tedious babbler—
a fate that has frequently befallen our good Homer under the
pen of the conscientious Madame Dacier. Our German tongue,
again, can, it is true, generally translate the Homeric epithets
by epithets equivalent and just as terse, but in the advantageous
order of them it cannot match the Greek. We say, indeed,
" Die runden, ehernen, achtspeichigten "; but " Räder " trails
behind. Who does not feel that three different predicates,
before we know the subject, can make but a vague and confused picture? The Greek joins the subject and the first predi-
cate immediately, and lets the others follow after; he says,
" Runde Räder, eherne, achtspeichigte." So we know at once of
what he is speaking, and are made acquainted, in consonance
with the natural order of thought, first with the thing and then
with its accidents. This advantage our language does not
possess. Or, shall I say, possesses it and can only very seldom
use it without ambiguity? The two things are one. For when
we would place the epithets after, they must stand in statu
absoluto ; we must say, " Runde Räder, ehern und achtspeichigt."
But in this status our adjectives are exactly like adverbs, and
must, if we attach them as such to the next verb which is pre-
dicated of the thing, produce a meaning not seldom wholly
false, and, at best, invariably ambiguous.

But here I am dwelling on trifles, and seem to have forgotten
the Shield—Achilles' Shield, that famous picture in respect of
which especially Homer was from of old regarded as a teacher
of painting. A shield, people will say—that is surely a single
physical object, the description of which and its parts ranged
side by side is not permissible to a poet? And this particular
Shield, in its material, in its form, in all the figures that covered
the vast surface of it, Homer has described in more than a
hundred splendid verses, with such exactness and detail that
it has been easy for modern artists to make a replica of it alike
in every feature.

To this special objection I reply, that I have replied to it
already. Homer, that is to say, paints the Shield not as a
finished and complete thing, but as a thing in process. Here

once more he has availed himself of the famous artifice, turning the *co-existing* of his design into a *consecutive*, and thereby making of the tedious painting of a physical object the living picture of an action. We see not the Shield, but the divine artificer at work upon it. He steps up with hammer and tongs to his anvil, and after he has forged the plates from the rough ore, the pictures which he has selected for its adornment stand out one after another before our eyes under his artistic chiseling. Nor do we lose sight of him again until all is finished. When it is complete, we are amazed at the work, but it is with the believing amazement of an eye-witness who has seen it in the making.

The same cannot be said of the Shield of Æneas in Virgil. The Roman poet either did not realise the subtlety of his model here, or the things that he wanted to put upon his Shield appeared to him to be of a kind that could not well admit of being shown in execution. They were prophecies, which could not have been uttered by the god in our presence as plainly as the poet afterwards expounds them. Prophecies, as such, demand an obscurer language, in which the actual names of persons yet-to-be may not fitly be pronounced. Yet these veritable names, to all appearance, were the most important things of all to the poet and courtier. If, however, this excuses him, it does not remove the unhappy effect of his deviation from the Homeric way. Readers of any delicacy of taste will justify me here. The preparations which Vulcan makes for his labour are almost the same in Virgil as in Homer. But instead of what we see in Homer—that is to say, not merely the preparations for the work, but also the work itself—Virgil after he has given us a general view of the busy god with his Cyclops :—

> *Ingentem clypeum informant. . . .*
> *. . . Alii ventosis follibus auras*
> *Accipiunt redduntque, alii stridentia tingunt*
> *Aera lacu. Gemit impositis incudibus antrum.*
> *Illi inter sese multa vi brachia tollunt*
> *In numerum, versantque tenaci forcipe massam—*

drops the curtain at once and transports us to another scene, bringing us gradually into the valley where Venus arrives at Æneas' side with the armour that has meanwhile been completed. She leans the weapons against the trunk of an oak-tree, and when the hero has sufficiently gazed at, and admired, and touched and tested them, the description of the pictures on the Shield begins, and, with the everlasting: " Here is," " and

there is," " near by stands," and " not far off one sees," becomes
so frigid and tedious that all the poetic ornament which Virgil
could give it was needed to prevent us finding it unendurable.
Moreover, as this picture is not drawn by Æneas as one who
rejoices in the mere figures and knows nothing of their significance :—

> . . . *rerumque ignarus imagine gaudet ;*

nor even by Venus, although conceivably she must know just
as much of the future fortunes of her dear grandchildren as the
obliging goodman; but proceeds from the poet's own mouth,
the progress of the action meanwhile is obviously at a standstill.
No single one of his characters takes any share in it; nor does
anything represented on the Shield have any influence, even the
smallest, on what is to follow; the witty courtier shines out
everywhere, trimming up his matter with every kind of flattering
allusion, but not the great genius, depending on the proper
inner vitality of his work and despising all extraneous expedients
for lending it interest. The Shield of Æneas is consequently a
sheer interpolation, simply and only intended to flatter the
national pride of the Romans, a foreign tributary which the
poet leads into his main stream in order to give it a livelier
motion. The Shield of Achilles, on the other hand, is a rich
natural outgrowth of the fertile soil from which it springs; for
a Shield had to be made, and as the needful thing never comes
bare and without grace from the hands of the divinity, the
Shield had also to be embellished. But the art was, to treat
these embellishments merely as such, to inweave them into the
stuff, in order to show them to us only by means of the latter;
and this could only be done by Homer's method. Homer lets
Vulcan elaborate ornaments because he is to make a Shield
that is worthy of himself. Virgil, on the other hand, appears to
let him make the Shield for the sake of its ornaments, considering them important enough to be particularly described,
after the Shield itself has long been finished.

XIX

The objections which the elder Scaliger, Perrault, Terrasson,
and others make to the Shield in Homer are well known.
Equally well known is the reply which Dacier, Boivin, and
Pope made to them. In my judgment, however, the latter go
too far, and, relying on their good cause, introduce arguments

that are not only indefensible, but contribute little to the poet's
justification.

In order to meet the main objection—that Homer has crowded
the Shield with a multitude of figures such as could not possibly
find room within its circumference—Boivin undertook to have
it drawn, with a note of the necessary dimensions.   His notion
of the various concentric circles is very ingenious, although the
words of the poet give not the slightest suggestion of it, whilst,
furthermore, not a trace of proof is to be found that the ancients
possessed shields divided off in this manner.   Seeing that
Homer himself calls it σάκος πάντοσε δεδαιδαλμένον—a shield
artfully wrought upon all sides—I would rather, in order to
reserve more room, have taken in aid the concave surface; for
it is well known that the ancient artists did not leave this
vacant, as the Shield of Minerva by Phidias proves.   Yet it
was not even enough for Boivin to decline availing himself of
this advantage; he further increased without necessity the
representations themselves for which he was obliged to provide
room in the space thus diminished by half, separating into two
or three distinct pictures what in the poet is obviously a single
picture only.   I know very well what moved him to do so, but
it ought not to have moved him; instead of troubling himself
to give satisfaction to the demands of his opponents, he should
have shown them that their demands were illegitimate.

I shall be able to make my meaning clearer by an example.
When Homer says of the one City :—

> Λαοὶ δ' εἰν ἀγορῇ ἔσαν ἀθρόοι· ἔνθα δὲ νεῖκος
> 'Ωρώρει, δύο δ' ἄνδρες ἐνείκεον εἵνεκα ποινῆς
> 'Ανδρὸς ἀποφθιμένου· ὁ μὲν εὔχετο πάντ' ἀποδοῦναι
> Δήμῳ πιφαύσκων, ὁ δ' ἀναίνετο μηδὲν ἑλέσθαι·
> "Αμφω δ' ἱέσθην ἐπὶ ἴστορι πεῖραρ ἑλέσθαι.
> Λαοὶ δ' ἀμφοτέροισιν ἐπήπυον, ἀμφὶς ἀρωγοί·
> Κήρυκες δ' ἄρα λαὸν ἐρήτυον· οἱ δὲ γέροντες
> "Ηατ' ἐπὶ ξεστοῖσι λίθοις ἱερῷ ἐνὶ κύκλῳ,
> Σκῆπτρα δὲ κηρύκων ἐν χέρσ' ἔχον ἠεροφώνων·
> Τοῖσιν ἔπειτ' ἤϊσσον, ἀμοιβηδὶς δὲ δίκαζον.
> Κεῖτο δ' ἄρ' ἐν μέσσοισι δύω χρυσοῖο τάλαντα—

he is not then, in my view, trying to sketch more than a single
picture—the picture of a public lawsuit on the questionable
satisfaction of a heavy fine for the striking of a death-blow.
The artist who would carry out this sketch cannot in any single

effort avail himself of more than a single moment of the same; either the moment of the arraignment, or of the examination of witnesses, or of the sentence, or whatever other moment, before or after, he considers the most suitable. This single moment he makes as pregnant as possible, and endows it with all the illusions which art commands (art, rather than poetry) in the representation of visible objects. Surpassed so greatly on this side, what can the poet who is to paint this very design in words, and has no wish entirely to suffer shipwreck—what can he do but in like manner avail himself of his own peculiar advantages? And what are these? The liberty to enlarge on what has preceded and what follows the single moment of the work of art, and the power thus to show us not only that which the artist has shown, but also that which he can only leave us to guess. By this liberty and this power alone the poet draws level with the artist, and their works are then likest to each other when the effect of each is equally vivid; and not when the one conveys to the soul through the ear neither more nor less than the other can represent to the eye. This is the principle that should have guided Boivin in judging this passage in Homer; he would then not so much have made distinct pictures out of it as have observed in it distinct moments of time. True, he could not well have united in a single picture all that Homer tells us; the accusation and the defence, the production of witnesses, the acclamations of the divided people, the effort of the heralds to allay the tumult, and the decisions of the judge, are things which follow each other and cannot subsist side by side. Yet what, in the language of the schools, was not *actu* contained in the picture lay in it *virtute*, and the only true way of copying in words a material painting is this—to unite the latter with the actually visible, and refuse to be bound by the limits of art, within which the poet can indeed reckon up the *data* for a picture, but never produce the picture itself.

Just so is it when Boivin divides the picture of the besieged city into three different tableaux. He might just as well have divided it into twelve as into three. For as he did not at all grasp the spirit of the poet, and required him to be subject to the unities of the material painting, he might have found far more violations of these unities, so that it had almost been necessary to assign to every separate stroke of the poet a separate section of the Shield. But, in my opinion, Homer has not altogether more than ten distinct pictures upon the entire Shield, every one of which he introduces with the phrases ἐν μὲν ἔτευξε,

or ἐν δὲ ποίησε, *or* ἐν δ' ἐτίθει, *or* ἐν δὲ ποίκιλλε 'Αμφιγυήεις.
Where these introductory words do not occur one has no right
to suppose a separate picture; on the contrary, all which they
unite must be regarded as a single picture to which there is
merely wanting the arbitrary concentration in a single point of
time—a thing the poet was in nowise constrained to indicate.
Much rather, had he indicated it, had he confined himself
strictly to it, had he not admitted the smallest feature which in
the actual execution could not be combined with it—in a word,
had he managed the matter exactly as his critics demand, it is
true that then these gentlemen would have found nothing to
set down against him, but indeed neither would a man of taste
have found anything to admire.

Pope was not only pleased with Boivin's plan of dividing and
designing, but thought of doing something else of his own, by
now further showing that each of these dismembered pictures
was planned according to the strictest rules of painting as it
is practised to-day. Contrast, perspective, the three unities—
all these he found observed in the best manner possible. And
this, although he certainly was well aware that, according to
the testimony of quite trustworthy witnesses, painting in the
time of the Trojan War was still in its cradle, so that either
Homer must, by virtue of his god-like genius, not so much
have adhered to what painting then or in his own time could
perform, as, rather, to have divined what painting in general
was capable of performing; or even those witnesses themselves
cannot be so trustworthy that they should be preferred to the
ocular demonstration of the artistic Shield itself. The former
anyone may believe who will; of the latter at least no one can
be persuaded who knows something more of the history of art
than the mere data of historians. For, that painting in Homer's
day was still in its infancy, he believes not merely because a
Pliny or such another says so, but above all because he judges
from the works of art which the ancients esteemed that many
centuries later they had not got much further; he knows, for
instance, that the paintings of Polygnotus are far from standing
the test which Pope believes would be passed by the pictures
on the Shield of Homer. The two great works at Delphi of
the master just mentioned, of which Pausanias has left us so
circumstantial a description, are obviously without any perspective. This division of the art was entirely unknown to the
ancients, and what Pope adduces in order to prove that Homer
had already some conception of it, proves nothing more than

that Pope's own conception of it was extremely imperfect. "Homer," he says, "can have been no stranger to perspective, because he expressly mentions the distance of one object from another. He remarks, for instance, that the spies were set a little further off than the other figures, and that the oak-tree under which the meal was prepared for the reapers stood apart. What he says of the valley dotted over with flocks and cottages and stables is manifestly the description of a wide region seen in perspective. A general argument on the point may also certainly be drawn from the multitude of figures on the Shield, which could not all be represented in their full size; from which, therefore, we may unquestionably conclude that the art of reducing by perspective was in that age already well known." The mere observation of the optical experience that a thing appears smaller at a distance than close at hand, is far indeed from giving perspective to a picture. Perspective demands a single viewpoint, a definite natural field of vision, and it was this that was wanting in ancient paintings. The base in the pictures of Polygnotus was not horizontal, but towards the background raised so prodigiously that the figures which should appear to stand behind one another appeared to stand above one another. And if this arrangement of the different figures and their groups were general, as may be inferred from the ancient bas-reliefs, where the hindmost always stand higher than the foremost and look over their heads, then it is natural that we should take it for granted also in Homer's description, and not separate them unnecessarily from those of his pictures that can be combined in one picture. The twofold scene of the peaceful city through whose streets went the joyous crowd of a wedding-party, whilst in the market-place a great lawsuit was being decided, demands according to this no twofold picture, and Homer certainly was able to consider it a single one, representing to himself the entire city from so high a point of vision that it gave him a free and simultaneous prospect both of the streets and the market-place.

I am of opinion that the knowledge of true perspective in painting was only arrived at incidentally in the painting of scenery, and also that when this was already in its perfection, it yet cannot have been so easy to apply its rules to a single canvas, seeing that we still find in later paintings amongst the antiquities of Herculaneum many and diverse faults of perspective such as we should nowadays hardly forgive to a schoolboy.

But I absolve myself from the trouble of collecting my scattered notes concerning a point on which I may hope to receive the fullest satisfaction in Herr Winckelmann's promised history of art.

XX

I rather turn gladly to my own road, if a rambler can be said to have a road.

What I have said of physical objects in general is even more pertinent to beautiful physical objects. Physical beauty arises from the harmonious effect of manifold parts that can be taken in at one view. It demands also that these parts shall subsist side by side; and as things whose parts subsist side by side are the proper subject of painting, so it, and it alone, can imitate physical beauty. The poet, who can only show the elements of beauty one after another, in succession, does on that very account forbear altogether the description of physical beauty, as beauty. He recognises that those elements, arranged in succession, cannot possibly have the effect which they have when placed side by side; that the concentrating gaze which we would direct upon them immediately after their enumeration still affords us no harmonious picture; that it passes the human imagination to represent to itself what kind of effect this mouth, and this nose, and these eyes together have if one cannot recall from Nature or art a similar composition of such features.

Here, too, Homer is the pattern of all patterns. He says: "Nireus was beautiful; Achilles was more beautiful still; Helen possessed a divine beauty." But nowhere does he enter upon the more circumstantial delineation of those beauties. For all that, the poem is based on the beauty of Helen. How greatly would a modern poet have luxuriated in the theme!

True, a certain Constantinus Manasses tried to adorn his bald chronicle with a picture of Helen. I must thank him for the attempt. For really I should hardly know where else I could get hold of an example from which it might more obviously appear how foolish it is to venture something which Homer has so wisely forborne. When I read in him, for example :—

Ἦν ἡ γυνὴ περικαλλής, εὔοφρυς, εὐχρουστάτη,
Εὐπάρειος, εὐπρόσωπος, βοῶπις, χιονόχρους,
Ἑλικοβλέφαρος, ἁβρά, χαρίτων γέμον ἄλσος,
Λευκοβραχίων, τρυφερά, κάλλος ἄντικρυς ἔμπνουν,

Τὸ πρόσωπον κατάλευκον, ἡ παρειὰ ῥοδόχρους,
Τὸ πρόσωπον ἐπίχαρι, τὸ βλέφαρον ὡραῖον,
Κάλλος ἀνεπιτήδευτον, ἀβάπτιστον, αὐτόχρουν,
Ἔβαπτε τὴν λευκότητα ῥοδόχροια πυρίνη,
Ὡς εἴ τις τὸν ἐλέφαντα βάψει λαμπρᾷ πορφύρᾳ.
Δειρὴ μακρά, κατάλευκος, ὅθεν ἐμυθουργήθη
Κυκνογενῆ τὴν εὔοπτον Ἑλένην χρηματίζειν—

then I imagine I see stones rolling up a mountain, from which
at the top a splendid picture is to be constructed, the stones,
however, all rolling down of themselves on the other side.
What kind of picture does it leave behind—this torrent of
words? What was Helen like, then? Will not, if a thousand
men read this, every man of the thousand make for himself his
own conception of her?

Still, it is certain the political verses of a monk are not poetry.
Let us therefore hear Ariosto, when he describes his enchanting
Alcina :—

> Di persona era tanto ben formata,
> Quanto mai finger san pittori industri :
> Con bionda chioma, lunga e annodata,
> Oro non è, che piu risplenda, e lustri,
> Spargeasi per la guancia delicata
> Misto color di rose e di ligustri
> Di terso avorio era la fronte lieta,
> Che lo spazio finia con giusta meta.
>
> Sotto due negri, e sottilissimi archi
> Son due negri occhi, anzi due chiari soli,
> Pietosi à riguardar, à mover parchi,
> Intorno à cui par ch' Amor scherzi, e voli,
> E ch' indi tutta la faretra scarchi,
> E che visibilmente i cori involi.
> Quindi il naso per mezo il viso scende
> Che non trova l'invidia ove l'emende.
>
> Sotto quel sta, quasi fra due valette,
> La bocca sparsa di natio cinabro,
> Quivi due filze son di perle elette,
> Che chiude, ed apre un bello e dolce labro ;
> Quindi escon le cortesi parolette,
> Da render molle ogni cor rozo e scabro ;
> Quivi si forma quel soave riso
> Ch' apre a sua posta in terra il paradiso.
>
> Bianca neve è il bel collo, e'l petto latte,
> Il collo è tondo, il petto colmo e largo ;
> Due pome acerbe, e pur d'avorio fatte,
> Vengono e van, come onda al primo margo,

Quando piacevole aura il mar combatte.
Non potria l'altre parti veder Argo,
Ben si può guidicar, che corrisponde,
A quel ch' appar di fuor, quel che s'asconde.

Mostran le braccia sua misura giusta,
Et la candida man spesso si vede,
Lunghetta alquanto, e di larghezza angusta,
Dove nè nodo appar, nè vena eccede.
Si vede al fin de la persona augusta
Il breve, asciutto e ritondetto piede.
Gli angelici sembianti nati in cielo
Non si ponno celar sotto alcun velo.

Milton says of the building of Pandemonium : " Some praised
the work, others the master of the work." The praise of the
one, then, is not always the praise of the other. A work of
art may deserve all applause while nothing very special redounds
from it to the credit of the artist. On the other hand, an artist
may justly claim our admiration even when his work does not
completely satisfy us. If we do not forget this, quite contra-
dictory verdicts may often be reconciled. The present case is
an instance. Dolce in his dialogue on Painting puts in Aretino's
mouth an extravagant eulogy of Ariosto on the strength of
these stanzas just cited; and I, on the contrary, choose them
as an example of a picture that is no picture. We are both
right. Dolce admires in it the knowledge which the poet displays of physical beauty; but I look merely to the effect which
this knowledge, expressed in words, produces on my imagination. Dolce argues, from that knowledge, that good poets are
also good painters; and I, from the effect, that what painters
can by line and colour best express can only be badly expressed
by words. Dolce commends Ariosto's delineation to all painters
as the most perfect model of a beautiful woman; and I commend it to all poets as the most instructive warning against
attempting even more unfortunately what failed in the hands
of an Ariosto. It may be that, when Ariosto says :—

Di persona era tanto ben formata,
Quanto mai finger san pittori industri—

he proves thereby that he perfectly understood the theory of
proportions as only the most diligent artist can gather it from
Nature and from antiquity. He may, who knows? in the
mere words :—

Spargeasi per la guancia delicata
Misto color di rose e di ligustri—

show himself the most perfect of colourists, a very Titian.
One might also, from the fact that he only compares Alcina's
hair with gold but does not call it golden hair, argue as cogently
that he disapproves the use of actual gold in laying on the
colour.   One may even find in his " descending nose " :—

> *Quindi il naso per mezo il viso scende—*

the profile of those ancient Greek noses, copied also by Roman
artists from the Greeks.   What good is all this erudition and
insight to us his readers who want to have the picture of a
beautiful woman, who want to feel something of the soft excitement of the blood which accompanies the actual sight of beauty?
If the poet is aware what conditions constitute a beautiful
form, do we too, therefore, share his knowledge?   And if we
did also know it, does he here make us aware of those conditions?   Or does he in the least lighten for us the difficulty
of recalling them in a vividly perceptible manner?   A brow in
its most graceful lines and limits :—

> *. . . la fronte*
> *Che lo spazio finia con giusta meta ;*

a rose in which envy itself can find nothing to improve :—

> *Che non trova l'invidia, ove l'emende ;*

a hand somewhat long and rather slender :—

> *Lunghetta alquanto, e di larghezza angusta :*

what kind of picture do we gather from these general formulas?
In the mouth of a drawing-master who is calling his pupils'
attention to the beauties of the school model they might perhaps be useful; for by a glance at the model they perceive the
pleasing lines of the delightful brow, the exquisite modelling
of the nose, the slenderness of the dainty hand.   But in the
poet I see nothing, and feel with vexation how vain is my best
effort to see what he is describing.
    In this particular, where Virgil can best imitate Homer by
forbearing action altogether, Virgil, too, has been rather happy.
His Dido also is to him nothing further than *pulcherrima Dido.*
If indeed he describes anything of her more circumstantially, it
is her rich jewelry, her splendid attire :—

> *Tandem progreditur . . .*
> *Sidoniam picto chlamydem circumdata limbo :*
> *Cui pharetra ex auro, crines nodantur in aurum,*
> *Aurea purpuream subnectit fibula vestem.*

If we on that account would apply to him what the ancient
artist said to a pupil who had painted a Helen in elaborate
finery—" As you are not able to paint her beautiful, you have
painted her rich "—then Virgil would answer, " It is no fault
of mine that I cannot paint her beautiful; the blame rests on
the limits of my art; be mine the praise, to have remained
within those limits."

I must not forget here the two songs of Anacreon in which
he analyses for us the beauty of his beloved and of his Bathyllus.
The turn he gives it there makes everything right. He imagines
a painter before him, and sets him to work under his eye. So,
he says, fashion me the hair, so the brow, so the eyes, so the
mouth, so neck and bosom, so the hips and hands ! Of what
the artist can put together only part by part the poet can
only set a copy in the same way. His purpose is not that we
shall recognise and feel in this verbal instruction of the painter
the whole beauty of the beloved subject; he himself feels the
insufficiency of the verbal expression, and for this very reason
calls to his aid the expressive power of art, the illusion of which
he so greatly heightens that the whole song appears to be more
a hymn to Art than to his beloved. He does not see the image,
he sees herself and believes that she is just about to open her
lips in speech :—

> Ἀπέχει βλέπω γὰρ αὐτήν,
> Τάχα, κηρέ, καὶ λαλήσεις.

In the sketch, too, of Bathyllus the praise of the beautiful boy
is so inwoven with praise of art and the artist that it is doubtful
for whose honour Anacreon really intended the poem. He
collects the most beautiful parts from various paintings in
which the particular beauty of these parts was its characteristic
feature; the neck he takes from an Adonis, breast and hands
from a Mercury, the hips from a Pollux, the abdomen from a
Bacchus; till he sees the whole Bathyllus in a perfect Apollo :—

> Μετὰ δὲ πρόσωπον ἔστω,
> Τὸν Ἀδώνιδος παρελθών,
> Ἐλεφάντινος τράχηλος·
> Μεταμάζιον δὲ ποίει
> Διδύμας τε χεῖρας Ἑρμοῦ,
> Πολυδεύκεος δὲ μηρούς,
> Διονυσίην δὲ νηδὺν . . .
> Τὸν Ἀπόλλωνα δὲ τοῦτον
> Καθελὼν ποίει Βάθυλλον.

Similarly also Lucian does not know how to give us a conception of the beauty of Panthea except by reference to the finest female statues of ancient artists. And what is this but to confess that language by itself is here powerless, that poetry stammers and eloquence is dumb where Art does not in some measure serve them as interpreter?

XXI

But does not Poetry lose too much if we take from her all pictures of physical beauty? Who wishes to do so? If we seek to close to her one single road, on which she hopes to achieve such pictures by following in the footsteps of a sister art, where she stumbles painfully without ever attaining the same goal, do we, then, at the same time close to her every other road, where Art in her turn can but follow at a distance?

Even Homer, who with evident intention refrains from all piecemeal delineation of physical beauties, from whom we can scarcely once learn in passing that Helen had white arms and beautiful hair—even he knows how, nevertheless, to give us such a conception of her beauty as far outpasses all that Art in this respect can offer. Let us recall the passage where Helen steps into the assembly of the Elders of the Trojan people. The venerable old men looked on her, and one said to the other :—

> Οὐ νέμεσις Τρῶας καὶ ἐϋκνήμιδας Ἀχαιοὺς
> Τοιῆδ' ἀμφὶ γυναικὶ πολὺν χρόνον ἄλγεα πάσχειν·
> Αἰνῶς ἀθανάτῃσι θεῆς εἰς ὦπα ἔοικεν.

What can convey a more vivid idea of Beauty than to have frigid age confessing her well worth the war that has cost so much blood and so many tears? What Homer could not describe in its component parts, he makes us feel in its working. Paint us, then, poet, the satisfaction, the affection, the love, the delight, which beauty produces, and you have painted beauty itself. Who can imagine as ill-favoured the beloved object of Sappho, the very sight of whom she confesses robbed her of her senses and her reason? Who does not fancy he beholds with his own eyes the fairest, most perfect form, as soon as he sympathises with the feeling which nothing but such a form can awaken? Not because Ovid shows us the beautiful body of his Lesbia part by part :—

Quos humeros, quales vidi tetigique lacertos !
Forma papillarum quam fuit apta premi !
Quam castigato planus sub pectore venter !
Quantum et quale latus ! quam juvenile femur !—

but because he does so with the voluptuous intoxication in which it is so easy to awaken our longing, we imagine ourselves enjoying the same sight of exquisite beauty which he enjoyed.

Another way in which poetry in its turn overtakes art in delineation of physical beauty is by transmuting beauty into charm. Charm is beauty in motion, and just for that reason less suitable to the painter than to the poet. The painter can only help us to guess the motion, but in fact his figures are motionless. Consequently grace with him is turned into grimace. But in poetry it remains what it is—a transitory beauty which we want to see again and again. It comes and goes; and as we can generally recall a movement more easily and more vividly than mere forms and colours, charm can in such a case work more powerfully on us than beauty. All that still pleases and touches us in the picture of Alcina is charm. The impression her eyes make does not come from the fact that they are dark and passionate, but rather that they :—

Pietosi à riguardar, à mover parchi—

look round her graciously and are gentle rather than flashing in their glances; that Love flutters about them and from them empties all his quiver. Her mouth delights us, not because lips tinted with cinnabar enclose two rows of choicest pearls; but because there the lovely smile is shaped which in itself seems to open up an earthly paradise; because from it the friendly words come forth that soften the most savage breast. Her bosom enchants us, less because milk and ivory and apples typify its whiteness and delicate forms than because we see it softly rise and fall, like the waves at the margin of the shore when a playful zephyr contends with the ocean :—

Due pome acerbi, e pur d'avorio fatte
Vengono e van, come onda al primo margo,
Quando piacevole aura il mar combatte.

I am sure such features of charm by themselves, condensed into one or two stanzas, will do more than all the five into which Ariosto has spun them out, inweaving them with frigid details of the fair form, far too erudite for our appreciation.

Even Anacreon himself would rather fall into the apparent

impropriety of demanding impossibilities from the painter than leave the picture of his beloved untouched with charm :—

Τρυφεροῦ δ' ἔσω γενείου,
Περὶ λυγδίνῳ τραχήλῳ
Χάριτες πέτοιντο πᾶσαι.

Her chin of softness, her neck of marble—let all the Graces hover round them, he bids the artist. And how? In the exact and literal sense? That is not capable of any pictorial realisation. The painter could give the chin the most exquisite curve, the prettiest dimple, *Amoris digitulo impressum* (for the ἔσω appears to me to signify a dimple); he could give the neck the most beautiful carnation; but he can do no more. The turning of this fair neck, the play of the muscles, by which that dimple is now more visible, now less, the peculiar charm, all are beyond his powers. The poet said the utmost by which his art could make beauty real to us, so that the painter also might strive for the utmost expression in his art. A fresh example of the principle already affirmed—that the poet even when he speaks of works of art is not bound in his descriptions to confine himself within the limits of art.

XXII

Zeuxis painted a Helen and had the courage to set under it those famous lines of Homer in which the enchanted Elders confess their emotions. Never were painting and poetry drawn into a more equal contest. The victory remained undecided, and both deserved to be crowned. For, just as the wise poet showed beauty merely in its effect, which he felt he could not delineate in its component parts, so did the no less wise painter show us beauty by nothing else than its component parts and hold it unbecoming to his art to resort to any other method. His picture consisted in the single figure of Helen, standing in naked beauty. For it is probable that it was the very Helen which he painted for her of Crotona.

Let us compare with this, for wonder's sake, the painting which Caylus sketches from Homer's lines for the benefit of a modern artist : " Helen, covered with a white veil, appears in the midst of an assemblage of old men, in whose ranks Priam also is to be found, recognisable by the signs of his royal dignity. It must be the artist's business to make evident to us the triumph of beauty in the eager gaze and in the expression of amazed admiration on the faces of the sober greybeards. The scene is by one of the gates of the city. The background of the painting thus can lose itself in the open sky or against the city's lofty walls; the former were the bolder conception, but one is as fitting as the other."

Let us imagine this picture carried out by the greatest master of our time and place it against the work of Zeuxis. Which will show the real triumph of beauty? That in which I myself feel it, or this where I must argue it from the grimaces of the susceptible greybeards? *Turpe senilis amor;* a lustful look makes the most venerable countenance ridiculous; an old man who betrays youthful passions is really a loathsome object. This objection cannot be made to the Homeric elders; for the emotion they feel is a momentary spark which their wisdom extinguishes immediately; intended only to do honour to Helen, but not to disgrace themselves. They confess their feeling and forthwith add :—

> Ἀλλὰ καὶ ὥς, τοίη περ ἐοῦσ', ἐν νηυσὶ νεέσθω,
> Μηδ' ἡμῖν τεκέεσσί τ' ὀπίσσω πῆμα λίποιτο.

Without this resolution they would be old coxcombs, what, indeed, they appear in the picture of Caylus. And on what, then, do they direct their greedy glances? On a masked and veiled figure ! That is Helen, is it? Inconceivable to me how Caylus here can leave the veil. Homer, indeed, gives it her expressly :—

> Αὐτίκα δ' ἀργεννῇσι καλυψαμένη ὀθόνῃσιν
> 'Ωρμᾶτ' ἐκ θαλάμοιο . . .

but it is to cross the streets in it; and if indeed with Homer the elders already betray their admiration before she appears to have again taken off or thrown back the veil, it was not then the first time the old men saw her; their confession therefore might not arise from the present momentary view: they may have already often felt what on this occasion they first confessed themselves to feel. In the painting nothing like this occurs. If I see here enchanted old men, I wish at the same time to see what it is that charms them; and I am surprised in the extreme when I perceive nothing further than, as we have said, a masked and veiled figure on which they are passionately gazing. What is here of Helen? Her white veil and something of her well-proportioned outline so far as outline can become

visible beneath raiment. Yet perhaps it was not the Count's
intention that her face should be covered, and he names the
veil merely as a part of her attire. If this is so—his words,
indeed, are hardly capable of such an interpretation : " *Hélène
couverte d'un voile blanc* "—then another surprise awaits me;
he is so particular in commending to the artist the expression
on the faces of the elders, but on the beauty of Helen's face he
does not expend a syllable. This modest beauty, in her eyes
the dewy shimmer of a remorseful tear, approaching timidly !
What ! Is supreme beauty something so familiar to our artists
that they do not need to be reminded of it ? Or is expression
more than beauty ? And are we in pictures, too, accustomed,
as on the stage, to let the homeliest actress pass for a charming
princess, if only her prince declares warmly enough the love he
bears her ?

In truth, Caylus' picture would bear the same relation to
that of Zeuxis as burlesque does to the loftiest poetry.

Homer was, without doubt, read in former times more
diligently than to-day. Yet one finds ever so many pictures
unmentioned which the ancient artists would have drawn from
his pages. Only of the poet's hint at particular physical
beauties they do appear to have made diligent use; these they
did paint, and in such subjects alone, they understood well
enough, it was granted them to compete with the poet. Besides
Helen, Zeuxis also painted Penelope, and the Diana of Apelles was
the Homeric Diana in company of her nymphs. I may here
call to mind that the passage of Pliny in which the latter is
mentioned requires an emendation.* But to paint actions
from Homer simply because they offer a rich composition,
excellent contrasts, artistic lights, seemed to the ancient artists
not to be their *métier*, nor could it be so long as art remained
within the narrower limits of her own high vocation. Instead,
they nourished themselves on the spirit of the poet; they
filled their imagination with his most exalted characteristics;
the fire of his enthusiasm kindled their own; they saw and

---

* Pliny says of the Apelles : *Fecit et Dianam sacrificantium virginum
choro mixtam : quibus vicisse Homeri versus videtur id ipsum describentis.*
Nothing can be better deserved than this eulogy. Beautiful nymphs
about a beautiful goddess who stands out above them with a brow of
majesty make a sketch which is fitter for painting than for poetry. The
sacrificantium, though, is to me very doubtful. What does the goddess
amid sacrificial vestals ? And is this the occupation which Homer gives
to the playmates of Diana ? Not at all ! they wander with her through
the woods and hills, they hunt, they sport, they dance.

felt like him; and so their works became copies of the Homeric, not in the relation of a portrait to its original, but in that of a son to his father—like, yet different. The resemblance often lies only in a single feature, the rest having amongst them all nothing alike except that they harmonise with the resembling feature in the one case as well as in the other.

As, moreover, the Homeric masterpieces in poetry were older than any masterpiece of art, as Homer had observed Nature with a painter's eye earlier than a Phidias or an Apelles, it is not to be wondered at that various observations of particular use to them the artists found already made in Homer before they themselves had had the opportunity of making them in Nature. These they eagerly seized on, in order to imitate Nature through Homer. Phidias confessed that the lines :—

ʾΗ, καὶ κυανέῃσιν ἐπ᾽ ὀφρύσι νεῦσε Κρονίων·
᾽Αμβρόσιαι δ᾽ ἄρα χαῖται ἐπερρώσαντο ἄνακτος
Κρατὸς ἀπ᾽ ἀθανάτοιο· μέγαν δ᾽ ἐλέλιξεν Ὄλυμπον

served him as a model in his Olympian Jupiter, and that only by their aid did he achieve a divine countenance, *propemodum ex ipso cœlo petitum*. Whosoever considers this to mean nothing more than that the fancy of the artist was fired by the poet's exalted picture, and thereby became capable of representations just as exalted—he, it seems to me, overlooks the most essential point, and contents himself with something quite general where, for a far more complete satisfaction, something very special is demanded. In my view Phidias confesses here also that in this passage he first noticed how much expression lies in the eyebrows, *quanta pars animi* is shown in them. Perhaps also it induced him to devote more attention to the hair, in order to express in some measure what Homer means by "ambrosial" locks. For it is certain that the ancient artists before the days of Phidias little understood what was significant and speaking in the countenance, and almost invariably neglected the hair. Even Myron was faulty in both these particulars, as Pliny has remarked, and after him Pythagoras Leontinus was the first who distinguished himself by the elegance of coiffure. What Phidias learned from Homer, other artists learned from the works of Phidias.

Another example of this kind I may specify which has always very much pleased me. Let us recall what Hogarth has noted concerning the Apollo Belvidere. "This Apollo," he says,

" and the Antinous are both to be seen in the same palace at
Rome. If, however, the Antinous fills the spectator with
admiration, the Apollo amazes him, and, indeed, as travellers
have remarked, by an aspect above humanity which usually
they are not capable of describing. And this effect, they say,
is all the more wonderful because when one examines it, the
disproportionate in it is obvious even to a common eye. One
of the best sculptors we have in England, who recently went
there on purpose to see this statue, corroborated what has just
been said, and in particular that the feet and legs in relation
to the upper part are too long and too broad. And Andreas
Sacchi, one of the greatest Italian painters, seems to have been
of the same opinion, otherwise he would hardly (in a famous
picture now in England) have given to his Apollo, crowning the
musician Pasquilini, exactly the proportions of Antinous, seeing
that in other respects it appears to be actually a copy of the
Apollo. Although we frequently see in very great works some
small part handled carelessly, this cannot be the case here.
For in a beautiful statue correct proportion is one of the most
essential beauties. We must conclude, therefore, that these
limbs must have been purposely lengthened, otherwise it would
have been easy to avoid it.   If we therefore examine the
beauties of this figure thoroughly, we shall with reason conclude that what we have hitherto considered indescribably
excellent in its general aspect has proceeded from that which
appeared to be a fault in one of its parts " (Hogarth, *Analysis
of Beauty*).   All this is very illuminating, and I will add that
in fact Homer has felt it and has pointed out that it gives a
stately appearance, arising purely from this addition of size
in the measurements of feet and legs. For when Antenor
would compare the figure of Ulysses with that of Menelaus, he
makes him say :—

Στάντων μὲν Μενέλαος ὑπείρεχεν εὐρέας ὤμους,
Ἄμφω δ᾽ ἑζομένω γεραρώτερος ἦεν Ὀδυσσεύς.

(" When both stood, then Menelaus stood the higher with his
broad shoulders ; but when both sat, Ulysses was the statelier.")
As Ulysses therefore gained stateliness in sitting, which Menelaus
in sitting lost, the proportion is easy to determine which the
upper body had in each to feet and legs. Ulysses was the
larger in the proportions of the former, Menelaus in the proportions of the latter.

XXIII

A single defective part can destroy the harmonious working
of many parts towards beauty. Yet the object does not necessarily therefore become ugly. Even ugliness demands several
defective parts which likewise must be seen at one view if we
are to feel by it the contrary of that with which beauty inspires
us.

Accordingly, ugliness also in its essential nature would not
be a reproach to poetry; and yet Homer has depicted the
extremest ugliness in Thersites, and depicted it, moreover, in
its elements set side by side. Why was that permitted to him
with ugliness which in the case of beauty he renounced with so
fine a discernment? Is the effect of ugliness not just as much
hindered by the successive enumeration of its elements as the
effect of beauty is nullified by the like enumeration of its elements? To be sure it is, but herein lies also Homer's justification. Just because ugliness becomes in the poet's delineation
a less repulsive vision of physical imperfection, and so far as
effect is concerned ceases as it were to be ugliness, it becomes
usable to the poet; and what he cannot use for its own sake,
he uses as an ingredient in order to produce or intensify certain
mixed states of feeling with which he must entertain us in
default of feelings purely pleasurable.

These mixed feelings are awakened by the laughable and the
terrible. Homer makes Thersites ugly in order to make him
laughable. It is not, however, merely by his ugliness that he
becomes so; for ugliness is imperfection and for the laughable
a contrast is required of perfection and imperfection. This is
the declaration of my friend Mendelssohn, to which I should
like to add that this contrast must not be too sharp or too
glaring, that the *opposita* (to continue in painter's language)
must be of the kind that can melt into each other. The wise
and honest Æsop, even if one assigns him the ugliness of Thersites, does not thereby become laughable. It was a ridiculous
monastic whim to wish the τέλειον of his instructive tales transferred to his own person by the help of its deformity. For
a misshapen body and a beautiful soul are like oil and vinegar,
which, even when they are thoroughly mixed, still remain completely separated to the palate. They afford us no *tertium
quid ;* the body excites disgust, the soul satisfaction, each its
own for itself. Only when the misshapen body is at the same

time frail and sickly, when it hinders the soul in her operations, when it becomes the source of hurtful prepossessions against her—then indeed disgust and satisfaction mingle and flow together, but the new apparition arising therefrom is not laughter, but pity, and the object which we otherwise should merely have esteemed becomes interesting. The misshapen and sickly Pope must have been far more interesting to his friends than the sound and handsome Wycherley.—But, however little would Thersites have been made laughable by mere ugliness, just as little would he have become laughable without it. The ugliness; the harmony of this ugliness with his character; the contradiction which both make to the idea he entertains of his own importance; the harmless effect of his malicious chatter, humiliating only to himself—all must work together to this end. The last-named particular is the οὐ φθαρτικόν which Aristotle makes indispensable to the laughable; just as also my friend makes it a necessary condition that such contrast must be of no moment and must interest us but little. For let us only suppose that Thersites' malicious belittling of Agamemnon had come to cost him dear, that instead of a couple of bloody weals he must pay for it with his life—then certainly we should cease to laugh at him. For this monster of a man is yet a man, whose destruction will always seem a greater evil than all his frailties and vices. This we can learn by experience if we read his end in Quintus Calaber. Achilles laments having killed Penthesilea; the beautiful woman in her blood, so bravely poured out, commands the esteem and pity of the hero, and esteem and pity turn to love. But the slanderous Thersites makes that love a crime. He declaims against the lewdness that betrays even the most valiant man to folly :—

> . . . Ἥτ᾽ ἄφρονα φῶτα τίθησι
> Καὶ πινυτόν περ ἐόντα. . . .

Achilles gets into a rage, and without replying a word strikes him so roughly between cheek and ear that teeth and blood and soul together gush from his throat. Horrible unspeakably! The passionate, murderous Achilles becomes more hateful to me than the spiteful, snarling Thersites; the jubilant cry which the Greeks raise over the deed offends me. I take part with Diomede, who draws his sword forthwith to avenge his kinsman on the murderer : for I feel, too, that Thersites is my kinsman, a human being.

But grant only that Thersites' incitements had broken out in sedition, that the mutinous people had actually taken ship and traitorously forsaken their captains, that the captains had thus fallen into the hands of a revengeful enemy, and that a divine judgment had brought utter destruction to both fleet and people : in such a case how would the ugliness of Thersites appear? If harmless ugliness can be laughable, a mischievous ugliness is always terrible. I do not know how to illustrate this better than by a couple of excellent passages of Shakspeare. Edmund, the bastard son of Earl Gloucester in *King Lear*, is no less a villain than Richard, Duke of Gloucester, who paved his way by the most detestable crimes to the throne which he ascended under the name of Richard III. How comes it, then, that the former excites far less shuddering and horror than the latter? When I hear the Bastard say :—

> Thou, Nature, art my goddess, to thy law
> My services are bound; wherefore should I
> Stand in the plague of custom, and permit
> The curiosity of nations to deprive me,
> For that I am some twelve or fourteen moonshines
> Lag of a brother? Why bastard? Wherefore base?
> When my dimensions are as well compact,
> My mind as generous, and my shape as true
> As honest Madam's issue? Why brand they thus
> With base? with baseness? bastardy! base, base!
> Who in the lusty stealth of Nature take
> More composition and fierce quality
> Than doth, within a dull, stale, tired bed,
> Go to creating a whole tribe of fops
> Got 'tween asleep and wake?—

in this I hear a devil, but I see him in the form of an angel of light. When, on the other hand, I hear the Duke of Gloucester say :—

> But I, that am not shaped for sportive tricks
> Nor made to court an amorous looking-glass,
> I, that am rudely stamped and want Love's majesty,
> To strut before a wanton ambling nymph;
> I, that am curtailed of this fair proportion,
> Cheated of feature by dissembling Nature,
> Deformed, unfinished, sent before my time
> Into this breathing world scarce half made up,
> And that so lamely and unfashionably
> That dogs bark at me as I halt by them;
> Why, I (in this weak piping time of peace)
> Have no delight to pass away the time;
> Unless to spy my shadow in the sun
> And descant on my own deformity.

And therefore, since I cannot prove a lover
To entertain these fair, well-spoken days,
I am determined to prove a villain !

then I hear a devil and see a devil in a shape that only the
Devil should have.

XXIV

It is thus the poet uses the ugliness of forms; what use of
them is permitted to the painter? Painting, as imitative
dexterity, can express ugliness; but painting, as beautiful art,
will not express it. To her, as the former, all visible objects
belong; but, as the latter, she confines herself solely to those
visible objects which awaken agreeable sensations.

But do not even the disagreeable sensations please in the
imitation of them? Not all. A sagacious critic has already
made the remark concerning the sensation of disgust. "The
representations of fear," he says, "of sadness, of terror, of
pity and so on, can only excite discomfort in so far as we take
the evil to be actual. These, therefore, can be resolved into
pleasant sensations by the recollection that it is but an artistic
deceit. The unpleasant sensation of disgust, however, in
virtue of the laws of the imagination, ensues on the mere representation in the mind whether the subject be considered as
actual or not. Of what use is it, therefore, to the offended
soul if Art thus betrays herself by a surrender to imitation?
Her discomfort arose not from the foreboding that the evil was
actual but from the mere presentation of the same, and this *is*
actual. The sensations of disgust are therefore always nature,
never imitation."

The same principle holds good of the ugliness of forms. This
ugliness offends our sight, is repugnant to our taste for order
and harmony, and awakens aversion without respect to the
actual existence of the subject in which we perceive it. We
do not want to see Thersites, either in Nature or in picture,
and if in fact his picture displeases us less, this happens not for
the reason that the ugliness of his form ceases in the imitation
to be ugliness, but because we have the power of abstracting
our attention from this ugliness and satisfying ourselves merely
with the art of the painter. Yet even this satisfaction will
every moment be interrupted by the reflection how ill the art
has been bestowed, and this reflection will seldom fail to be
accompanied by contempt for the artist.

Aristotle suggests another reason why things on which we look in Nature with repugnance do yet afford us pleasure even in the most faithful copy—namely, the universal curiosity of mankind. We are glad if we either can learn from the copy τί ἕκαστον, what anything is, or if we can conclude from it ὅτι οὗτος ἐκεῖνος, that it is this or that. But even from this there follows no advantage to ugliness in imitation. The pleasure that arises from the satisfaction of our curiosity is momentary, and merely accidental to the subject from which it arises; the dissatisfaction, on the contrary, that accompanies the sight of ugliness is permanent, and essential to the subject that excites it. How, then, can the former balance the latter? Still less can the momentary agreeable amusement which the showing of a likeness gives us overcome the disagreeable effect of ugliness. The more closely I compare the ugly copy with the ugly original, the more do I expose myself to this effect, so that the pleasure of comparison vanishes very quickly, and there remains to me nothing more than the untoward impression of the twofold ugliness. To judge by the examples given by Aristotle, it appears as if he himself had been unwilling to reckon the ugliness of forms as amongst the unpleasing subjects which might yet please in imitation. These subjects are corpses and ravening beasts. Ravening wild beasts excite terror even though they are not ugly; and this terror, and not their ugliness, it is that is resolved into pleasant sensations by imitation. So, too, with corpses : the keener feeling of pity, the terrible reminder of our own annihilation it is that makes a corpse in Nature a repulsive subject to us; in the imitation, however, that pity loses its sharper edge by the conviction of the illusion, and from the fatal reminder an alloy of flattering circumstances can either entirely divert us, or unite so inseparably with it that we seem to find in it more of the desirable than the terrible.

As, therefore, the ugliness of forms cannot by and for itself be a theme of painting as fine art, because the feeling which it excites, while unpleasing, is not of that sort of unpleasing sensations which may be transformed into pleasing ones by imitation; yet the question might still be asked whether it could not to painting as well as to poetry be useful as an ingredient, for the intensifying of other sensations. May painting, then, avail itself of ugly forms for the arriving at the laughable and the terrible?

I will not venture to give this question a point-blank negative.

It is undeniable that harmless ugliness can even in painting be made laughable, especially when there is combined with it an affectation of charm and dignity. It is just as incontestable that mischievous ugliness does in painting, just as in Nature, excite horror, and that this laughable and this horrible element, which in themselves are mingled feelings, attain by imitation a new degree of offensiveness or of pleasure.

I must at the same time point out that, nevertheless, painting is not here completely in the same case with poetry. In poetry, as I have already remarked, the ugliness of forms does by the transmutation of their co-existing parts into successive parts lose its unpleasant effect almost entirely; from this point of view it ceases, as it were, to be ugliness, and can therefore ally itself more intimately with other appearances in order to produce a new and distinct effect. In painting, on the contrary, the ugliness has all its forces at hand, and works almost as strongly as in Nature itself. Consequently, harmless ugliness cannot well remain laughable for long; the unpleasant sensation gains the upper hand, and what was farcical to begin with becomes later merely disgusting. Nor is it otherwise with mischievous ugliness; the terrible is gradually lost and the monstrous remains alone and unchangeable.

Keeping this in view, Count Caylus was perfectly right to leave the episode of Thersites out of the list of his Homeric pictures. But are we therefore right, too, in wishing them cut out of Homer's own work? I am sorry to find that a scholar of otherwise just and fine taste is of this opinion. A fuller exposition of my own views on the matter I postpone to another opportunity.

XXV

The second distinction also, which the critic just named draws between disgust and other unpleasant emotions of the soul, is concerned with the aversion awakened within us by the ugliness of physical forms.

" Other unpleasant emotions," he says, " can often, apart from imitation and in Nature itself, gratify the mind, inasmuch as they never excite unmixed aversion, but in every case mingle their bitterness with pleasure. Our fear is seldom denuded of all hope; terror animates all our powers to evade the danger; anger is bound up with the desire to avenge ourselves, as sadness is with the agreeable representation of the happiness that preceded it, whilst pity is inseparable from the tender feelings of love and affection. The soul is permitted to dwell now on the pleasurable, and now on the afflicting, parts of an emotion, and to make for itself a mixture of pleasure and its opposite which is more attractive than pleasure without admixture. Only a very little attention to what goes on within is needed to observe frequent instances of the kind; what else would account for the fact that to the angry man his anger, to the melancholy man his dejection, is dearer than any pleasing representations by which it is sought to quiet or cheer him? Quite otherwise is it in the case of disgust and the feelings associated with it. In that the soul recognises no noticeable admixture of pleasure. Distaste gains the upper hand, and there is therefore no situation that we can imagine either in Nature or in imitation in which the mind would not recoil with repugnance from such representations."

Perfectly true ! but as the critic himself recognises yet other sensations akin to disgust which likewise produce nothing but aversion, what can be nearer akin to it than the feeling of the ugly in physical forms? This sensation also is, in Nature, without the slightest admixture of delight, and as it is just as little capable of it in imitation, so there is no situation in the latter in which the mind would not recoil with repugnance from the representation of it.

Indeed, this repugnance, if I have studied my feelings with sufficient care, is wholly of the nature of disgust. The sensation which accompanies ugliness of form is disgust, only somewhat fainter in degree. This conflicts, indeed, with another note of the critic, according to which he thinks that only the *blind* senses—taste, smell, and touch—are sensitive to disgust. " The two former," he says, " by an excessive sweetness and the third by an excessive softness of bodies that do not sufficiently resist the fibres that touch them. Such objects then become unendurable even to sight, but merely through the association of ideas that recall to us the repugnance to which they give rise in the taste, or smell, or touch. For, properly speaking, there are no objects of disgust for the vision." Yet, in my opinion, things of the kind can be named. A scar in the face, a hare-lip, a flattened nose with prominent nostrils, an entire absence of eyebrows, are uglinesses which are not offensive either to smell, taste, or touch. At the same time it is certain that these things produce a sensation that certainly comes much nearer to disgust than what we feel at sight of other deformities of body

—a crooked foot, or a high shoulder; the more delicate our temperament, the more do they cause us those inward sensations that precede sickness. Only, these sensations very soon disappear, and actual sickness can scarcely result; the reason of which is certainly to be found in this fact, that they are objects of sight, which simultaneously perceives in them and with them a multitude of circumstances through the pleasant presentation of which those unpleasing things are so tempered and obscured that they can have no noticeable effect on the body. The blind senses, on the other hand—taste, smell, and touch—cannot, when they are affected by something unpleasant, likewise take cognisance of such other circumstances; the disagreeable, consequently, works by itself and in its whole energy, and cannot but be accompanied in the body by a far more violent shock.

Moreover, the disgusting is related to imitation in precisely the same way as the ugly. Indeed, as its unpleasant effect is more violent, it can even less than the ugly be made in and for itself a subject either of poetry or painting. Only because it also is greatly modified by verbal expression, I venture still to contend that the poet might be able to use at least some features of disgust as an ingredient for the mingled sensations of which we have spoken, which he intensifies so successfully by what is ugly.

The disgusting can add to the laughable; or representations of dignity and decorum, set in contrast with the disgusting, become laughable. Instances of this kind abound in Aristophanes. The weasel occurs to me which interrupted the good Socrates in his astronomical observations :—

ΜΑΘ. Πρώην δέ γε γνώμην μεγάλην ἀφηρέθη
  'Ὑπ' ἀσκαλαβώτου. ΣΤ. Τίνα τρόπον ; κάτειπέ μοι.
ΜΑΘ. Ζητοῦντος αὐτοῦ τῆς σελήνης τὰς ὁδοὺς
  Καὶ τὰς περιφοράς, εἶτ' ἄνω κεχηνότος
  Ἀπὸ τῆς ὀροφῆς νύκτωρ γαλεώτης κατέχεσεν.
ΣΤ. Ἥσθην γαλεώτῃ καταχέσαντι Σωκράτους.

Suppose that not to be disgusting which falls into his open mouth, and the laughable vanishes. The drollest strokes of this kind occur in the Hottentot tale, Tquassouw and Knoninquaiha in the *Connoisseur*, an English weekly magazine full of humour, ascribed to Lord Chesterfield. Everyone knows how filthy the Hottentots are and how many things they consider beautiful and elegant and sacred which with us awaken disgust and aversion. A flattened cartilage of a nose, flabby breasts hanging down to the navel, the whole body smeared with a cosmetic of goat's fat and soot gone rotten in the sun, the hair dripping with grease, arms and legs bound about with fresh entrails—let one think of this as the object of an ardent, reverent, tender love; let one hear this uttered in the exalted language of gravity and admiration and refrain from laughter!

With the terrible it seems possible for the disgusting to be still more intimately mingled. What we call the horrible is nothing but the disgusting and terrible in one. Longinus, it is true, is displeased with the τῆς ἐκ μὲν ῥινῶν μύξαι ῥέον in Hesiod's description of melancholy; but, in my opinion, not so much because it is a disgusting trait as because it is merely a disgusting trait contributing nothing to the terrible. For the long nails extending beyond the fingers (μακροὶ δ᾿ ὄνυχες χείρεσσιν ὑπῆσαν) he does not appear to find fault with. Yet long nails are not less disgusting than a running nose. But the long nails are at the same time terrible, for it is they that lacerate the cheeks until the blood runs down upon the ground :—

> . . . Ἐκ δὲ παρειῶν
> Αἷμ᾿ ἀπελείβετ᾿ ἔραζε. . . .

A running nose, on the contrary, is nothing more than a running nose, and I only advise Melancholy to keep her mouth closed. Let one read in Sophocles the description of the vacant, barren den of the unhappy Philoctetes. There is nothing to be seen of the necessaries or the conveniences of life beyond a trodden matting of withered leaves, a misshapen bowl of wood, and a fireplace. The whole wealth of the sick, forsaken man! How does the poet complete the sad and fearful picture? With an addition of disgust. " Ha ! " exclaims Neoptolemus, recoiling, —" torn rags drying in the wind, full of blood and matter ! "

> ΝΕ. Ὁρῶ κενὴν οἴκησιν, ἀνθρώπων δίχα.
> ΟΔ. Οὐδ᾿ ἔνδον οἰκοποιός ἐστί τις τροφή ;
> ΝΕ. Στιπτή γε φυλλὰς ὡς ἐναυλίζοντί τῳ.
> ΟΔ. Τὰ δ᾿ ἄλλ᾿ ἔρημα, κοὐδέν ἐσθ᾿ ὑπόστεγον ;
> ΝΕ. Αὐτόξυλόν γ᾿ ἔκπωμα, φλαυρουργοῦ τινὸς
>   Τεχνήματ᾿ ἀνδρός, καὶ πυρεῖ᾿ ὁμοῦ τάδε.
> ΟΔ. Κείνου τὸ θησαύρισμα σημαίνεις τόδε.
> ΝΕ. Ἰοὺ ἰού· καὶ ταῦτά γ᾿ ἄλλα θάλπεται
>   Ῥάκη, ραρείας του νοσηλείας πλέα.

And, similarly, in Homer dead Hector, dragged along, his
countenance disfigured with blood and dust and clotted hair :

> *Squalentem barbam et concretos sanguine crines*

(as Virgil expresses it), a disgusting object, but all the more
terrible on that account and all the more moving. Who can
think of the torture of Marsyas in Ovid without a sensation of
disgust?

> *Clamanti cutis est summos derepta per artus,*
> *Nec quidquam nisi vulnus erat. Cruor undique manat,*
> *Detectique patent nervi, trepidaeque sine ulla*
> *Pelle micant venae : salientia viscera possis*
> *Et perlucentes numerare in pectore fibras.*

But who does not feel at the same time that the disgusting is
here in place? It makes the terrible horrible; and the horrible
itself in Nature, when our pity is engaged, is not wholly disagreeable; how much less in the imitation! I will not heap
up instances. But one thing I must still note : that there is a
variety of the terrible, the poet's way to which stands open
simply and solely through the disgusting—this is the terrible
of *hunger*. Even in common life it is impossible to express the
extremity of hunger otherwise than by the narration of all the
innutritious, unwholesome, and especially all the loathsome
things, with which the appetite must be appeased. As the
imitation can awaken in us nothing of the feeling of hunger
itself, it resorts to another unpleasant feeling which in the case
of the fiercest hunger we recognise as the smaller of two great
evils. This feeling it seeks to excite within us in order that
we may from the discomfort conclude how fearful must be that
other discomfort under which this becomes of no account.
Ovid says of the oread whom Ceres sent off to starve :—

> *Hanc (Famem) procul ut vidit. . . .*
> *. . . Refert mandata deae, paulumque morata,*
> *Quanquam aberat longe, quanquam modo venerat illuc,*
> *Visa tamen sensisse Famem. . . .*

An unnatural exaggeration! The sight of one who hungers,
were it even Hunger herself, has not this infectious power;
pity and horror and disgust it may make us feel, but not hunger.
This horror Ovid has not spared us in his picture of famine,
and in the hunger of Erysichthon, both in his description and
that of Callimachus, the loathsome features are the strongest.
After Erysichthon had devoured everything, not sparing even
the beast which his mother had reared to be a burnt-offering

for Vesta, Callimachus makes him fall upon horses and cats, and beg upon the streets for the crusts and filthy fragments from strange tables :—

Καὶ τὰν βῶν ἔφαγεν, τὰν Ἑστία ἔτρεφε μάτηρ,
Καὶ τὸν ἀεθλοφόρον καὶ τὸν πολεμήϊον ἵππον,
Καὶ τὰν αἴλουρον, τὰν ἔτρεμε θηρία μικκά—
Καὶ τόθ' ὁ τῶ βασιλῆος ἐνὶ τριόδοισι καθῆστο
Αἰτίζων ἀκόλως τε καὶ ἔκβολα λύματα δαιτός—

And Ovid makes him finally put his teeth into his own limbs, to nourish his body with his own flesh :—

Vis tamen illa mali postquam consumpserat omnem
Materiam. . . .
Ipse suos artus lacero divellere morsu
Coepit, et infelix minuendo corpus alebat.

For that very reason were the repulsive Harpies made so noisome, so filthy, that the hunger which their snatching of the viands was to produce should be so much more terrible.   Listen to the lament of Phineus in Apollonius :—

Τυτθὸν δ' ἦν ἄρα δή ποτ' ἐδητύος ἄμμι λίπωσι,
Πνεῖ τόδε μυδαλέον τε καὶ οὐ τλητὸν μένος ὀδμῆς.
Οὔ κέ τις οὐδὲ μίνυνθα βροτῶν ἄνσχοιτο πελάσσας
Οὐδ' εἴ οἱ ἀδάμαντος ἐληλαμένον κέαρ εἴη.
Ἀλλά με πικρὴ δῆτά κε δαιτὸς ἐπίσχει ἀνάγκη
Μίμνειν, καὶ μίμνοντα κακῇ ἐν γαστέρι θέσθαι.

I would from this point of view gladly excuse the loathsome introduction of the Harpies in Virgil ; but it is no actual present hunger which they cause, but only an impending one which they prophesy, and, furthermore, the whole prophecy is resolved in the end into a play upon words. Dante, too, prepares us not only for the story of the starvation of Ugolino by the most loathsome and horrible situation in which he places him in hell with his aforetime persecutor ; but the starvation itself also is not without elements of disgust, which more particularly over-comes us at the point where the sons offer themselves as food to their father.   There is in a drama of Beaumont and Fletcher a passage which I might cite here in place of all other examples were I not obliged to think it somewhat overdone.

I turn to the question of disgusting subjects in painting. If it were quite incontestable that, properly speaking, there are no disgusting subjects whatever for sight, of which it might be

assumed that painting, as fine art, would refuse them : all the
same, she must avoid disgusting subjects in general, because
the association of ideas makes them disgusting to sight also.
Pardenone in a picture of Christ's burial makes one of the
onlookers hold his nose. Richardson condemns this on the
ground that Christ was not yet so long dead that His body
could have suffered corruption. In the Resurrection of Lazarus,
on the other hand, he thinks it might be permitted to the painter
to show by such an indication what the story expressly asserts—
that his body was already corrupt. In my view this representation is unendurable in this case also; for not only the
actual stench, but the mere idea of it awakens disgust. We
flee offensive places even if we have actually a catarrh. Yet
painting accepts the disgusting not for disgust's sake : she
accepts it, as poetry does, in order to intensify by it the laughable and the terrible. But at her own risk ! What, however,
I have in this case noted of the ugly holds yet more certainly of
the disgusting. It loses in a *visible* imitation incomparably less
of its effect than in an *audible* one; and therefore can mingle
less intimately with the laughable and terrible elements in the
former case than in the latter; as soon as the first surprise is
past, as soon as the first eager glance is satisfied, it isolates
itself in its turn completely and lies there in all its crudeness.

XXVI

Herr Winckelmann's *History of Ancient Art* has been issued.
I will not venture a step further until I have read that work.
To reason too nicely about art from mere general conceptions
may lead to vagaries that sooner or later one will find confuted
in works of art. The ancients, too, knew the bonds that unite
poetry and painting, and they will not have drawn them tighter
than is advantageous to both. What their artists did will
teach me what artists in general ought to do ; and where such
a man carries before us the torch of history, speculation can
follow boldly.

We usually dip here and there in an important work before
we begin to read it seriously. My curiosity was above all things
to learn the author's opinion of the Laocoön—not, indeed, of the
art of the work, of which he has already spoken elsewhere, but
rather of its age. On that point to which party does he adhere ?
To those who believe Virgil to have had the group before his

eyes, or to those who think the artists followed the poet in their work? It is very much to my liking that he is entirely silent regarding a mutual imitation. Where is the absolute necessity for that? It is not at all impossible that the resemblances between the sculpture and the poetic picture, which we have been considering, are accidental and not intentional resemblances; and that the one was so little the model of the other that they need not even have had the same kind of model before them. Nevertheless, had he supposed such an imitation to be evident, he would certainly have had to declare for the former. For he is satisfied that the Laocoön dates from the times in which art among the Greeks attained the summit of its perfection—from the time, that is to say, of Alexander the Great.

"The kind Fate," he says, "which has still kept watch over the arts, even in their destruction, has preserved for the whole world's admiration a work from this age of art, as an evidence of the truth of history regarding the splendour of so many vanished masterpieces. Laocoön with his two sons, wrought by Agesander, Apollodorus, and Athenodorus of Rhodes, is in all probability of this age, although one cannot positively determine the date, or, as some have done, declare the Olympiad in which these artists flourished."

In a note he adds: "Pliny says not a word of the time in which Agesander and his assistants in this work lived; Maffei, however, in his treatise on *Ancient Sculpture*, makes out that they flourished in the 88th Olympiad, and to this decision some others, including Richardson, have subscribed. But Maffei, in my view, has taken an Athenodorus among the pupils of Polycletus for one of our artists, and as Polycletus flourished in the 87th Olympiad, his supposed pupil has been placed an Olympiad later; other grounds Maffei can have none."

Quite certainly he could have no other; but why does Herr Winckelmann rest satisfied with merely adducing this supposed reason of Maffei's? Does it confute itself? Not quite; for although certainly it is not supported by any other evidence, still it surely makes a little probability for itself when one cannot otherwise show that Athenodorus, Polycletus' pupil, and Athenodorus, the assistant of Agesander and Polydorus, cannot possibly have been one and the same person. Fortunately this can be shown, even from the place of their nativity. The first Athenodorus, according to the express testimony of Pausanias, was from Klitor in Arcadia; the other, on the contrary, as Pliny testifies, was born in Rhodes.

Herr Winckelmann cannot have had any object in passing by without completely confuting, by adducing this circumstance, the allegation of Maffei. Much rather must the grounds which, with his undoubted knowledge, he deduces from the artistic quality of the work have appeared to him weighty ; for he did not trouble himself whether or not the opinion of Maffei had still any probability. He recognises without hesitation in the Laocoön too many of the *argutiæ* which were peculiar to Lysippus, with which this master first enriched art, to allow of its being considered a work of earlier date.

Yet even if it is proved that the Laocoön cannot be older than Lysippus, is it also proved, then, that it must be of about his time, and cannot possibly be a much later work ? If I overlook altogether the ages in which Greek art down to the commencement of the Roman monarchy by turns raised its head high and by turns sank again, why might not Laocoön have been a happy fruit of the rivalry which the wasteful luxury of the first emperors must have excited amongst the artists ? Why might not Agesander and his assistants have been the contemporaries of a Strongylion, an Arcesilaus, a Pasiteles, a Posidonius, a Diogenes ? Did not the works of these masters share the esteem bestowed on the best which art had then produced ? And if undoubted works from their hands were yet extant but the period of their authors unknown, and were no conclusions to be drawn from anything but their art, what divine inspiration is to guard the critic from placing them in the very times which Herr Winckelmann deems alone worthy of the Laocoön ?

It is true Pliny does not expressly note the time in which the artists of the Laocoön lived. Yet if I had to argue from the entire context of the passage whether he desires to reckon them with the ancient or with the modern artists, I confess that I seem to discover in it a greater probability for the latter. Let who will, decide it.

After Pliny has spoken in considerable detail of the oldest and greatest masters in sculpture—of Phidias, of Praxiteles, of Scopas—and thereupon has named the rest (especially some whose works were to be seen in Rome) without any chronological order, he continues in the following strain : *Nec multo plurium fama est, quorundam claritati in operibus eximiis obstante numero artificum quoniam nec unus occupat gloriam, nec plures pariter nuncupari possunt, sicut in Laocoonte, qui est in Titi imperatoris domo, opus omnibus et picturae et statuariae artis praeponendum. Ex uno lapide eum et liberos draconumque mirabiles nexus de*

consilii sententia fecere summi artifices, Agesander et Polydorus et
Athenodorus Rhodii. Similiter Palatinas domus Cæsarum re-
plevere probatissimis signis Craterus cum Pythodoro, Polydectes
cum Hermolao, Pythodorus alius cum Artemone, et singularis
Aphrodisius Trallianus. Agrippae Pantheum decoravit Diogenes
Atheniensis, et caryatides in columnis templi ejus probantur inter
pauca operum : sicut in fastigio posita signa, sed propter alti-
tudinem loci minus celebrata.

Of all the artists named in this passage Diogenes of Athens is
the one whose date is most indubitably determined. He
decorated the Pantheon of Agrippa ; he lived, therefore, in the
time of Augustus. But if we consider the words of Pliny more
carefully, I believe we shall find the time of Craterus and Pythodorus, of Polydectes and Hermolaus, the second Pythodorus
and Artemon as well as Aphrodisius Trallianus, just as incon-
testably settled. He says of them : *Palatinas domus Caesarum*
replevere probatissimis signis. I ask, Can this mean no more
than that the palaces of the Caesars were full of these excellent
works ? in the sense, that is, that the Emperors sought them
in all quarters and had them set up in their dwellings ? Surely
not ; they must have wrought these works expressly for these
palaces of the Emperors and must have lived in that age. That
there were late artists who wrought only in Italy may surely
be concluded from the fact that one finds them mentioned
nowhere else. Had they wrought in Greece in earlier times
Pausanias would have seen one or other of their works and
have preserved a record of them for us. A certain Pythodorus
he does indeed allude to, but Harduin is quite wrong in taking
him for the Pythodorus named by Pliny. For Pausanias
mentions the statue of Juno from the studio of the former,
which he saw at Coronea in Boeotia, ἄγαλμα ἀρχαῖον, which
appellation he bestows only on the works of those masters who
lived in the most primitive and rudest periods of art, long before
a Phidias and a Praxiteles. And with works of that sort certainly
the Emperors would not have decorated their palaces. Still
less weight attaches to the further supposition of Harduin, that
Artemon is perhaps the painter of the same name whom Pliny
mentions in another place. Identity of name offers only a very
slight probability, which is far indeed from warranting us in
doing violence to the natural interpretation of a genuine passage.

If consequently it is beyond any doubt that Craterus and
Pythodorus, that Polydectes and Hermolaus with the rest lived
in the age of the Emperors, whose palaces they filled with their

splendid works; then in my opinion one can assign no other age to these artists either whose names Pliny passes over along with theirs with a mere *similiter*. And these are the masters of the Laocoön. Let us only consider it : if Agesander, Polydorus, and Athenodorus were masters as ancient as Herr Winckelmann takes them to be, how improper were it not for a writer with whom precision of expression is no trifling matter, if he must spring at one bound from them to the most recent masters and make this spring as if it were but an ordinary step !

Yet some may object that this *similiter* refers not to the relationship in respect of period, but to some other circumstance which these masters may have had in common. Pliny, that is to say, may be speaking of such artists as worked in association, and on account of this association remained less well known than they merited. For as no one can appropriate to himself alone the honour of the joint work, and to name on every occasion all who had a share in it would be too long-winded (*quoniam nec unus occupat gloriam, nec plures pariter nuncupari possunt*); in this way their collective names would be neglected. This may have happened to the artists of the Laocoön, as to so many other masters whom the emperors employed for their palaces.

This I grant. But even then it is highly probable that Pliny is speaking here only of later artists who worked in association. For if he had desired to speak also of more ancient masters, why should he have mentioned the artists of the Laocoön only? Why not others also? An Onatas and a Calliteles ; a Timokles and Timarchides, or the sons of this Timarchides, from whose hands a jointly-wrought Jupiter existed in Rome. Herr Winckelmann himself says that one might make a long list of this kind of ancient works which had more than one father. And should Pliny have bethought him only of the single Agesander, Polydorus, and Athenodorus, if he did not wish expressly to confine himself to the most recent times?

If, moreover, a conjecture becomes so much the more prob-able the more and greater the difficulties that can be explained by it, then certainly this one—that the artists of the Laocoön lived under the first Emperors—is so in a very high degree. For had they wrought in Greece at the period in which Herr Winckelmann places them, had the Laocoön itself in earlier days stood in Greece, then the complete silence which the Greeks observed concerning such a work (*opus omnibus et picturae et statuariae artis praeponendum*) is extremely surprising.

It must be extremely surprising if masters so great had wrought nothing else or if Pausanias had never come across their other works in all Greece, no more than the Laocoön itself. In Rome, on the other hand, the greatest masterpiece could remain hidden for a long time, and even had the Laocoön been already finished under Augustus, it need not therefore appear singular that it is Pliny who first makes mention of it; Pliny first, and last. For let us only recall what he says of a *Venus* of Scopas that stood in a temple of Mars at Rome, *quemcunque alium locum nobilitatura. Romae quidem magnitudo operum eam obliterat, ac magni officiorum negotiorumque acervi omnes a contemplatione talium abducunt: quoniam otiosorum et in magno loci silentio apta admiratio talis est.*

Those who would gladly see in the Laocoön group an imitation of the Virgilian Laocoön will accept with satisfaction what I have said above. Yet another conjecture has occurred to me which they might not much disapprove. Perhaps (so they may think) it was Asinius Pollio who had the Laocoön of Virgil wrought out by Greek artists. Pollio was a particular friend of the poet, outlived the poet, and appears even to have written a book of his own about the *Æneid*. For where else than in a work of his own concerning that poem can the detached notes so properly have stood which Servius cites from him? Pollio was at once a lover and a connoisseur of art, possessed a rich collection of the most splendid works of the older masters, employed the artists of his own time to make new ones, and with the taste which he showed in his choice so bold a composition as the Laocoön was completely in keeping: *ut fuit acris vehementiae sic quoque spectari monumenta sua voluit.* Nevertheless, as the collection of Pollio in Pliny's time, when Laocoön stood in the palace of Titus, appears to have been undispersed and all collected in one special Gallery, this conjecture of mine might in its turn lose something of its probability. And why could not Titus himself have done what we wish to ascribe to Pollio?

XXVII

In this view that the artists of the Laocoön flourished under the first Emperors, and at any rate cannot be so old as Herr Winckelmann makes out, I am confirmed by a little piece of news which he himself now for the first time makes public. It is this :—

At Nettuno, formerly Antium, the Cardinal Alexander
Albani in the year 1717 discovered, in a great vault which lay
under the sea, a vase made of the dark-grey marble now called
" Vigio," in which the group is inserted and upon which stands
the following inscription :—

ΑΘΑΝΟΔΩΡΟΣ   ΑΓΗΣΑΝΔΡΟΥ
ΡΟΔΙΟΣ   ΕΠΟΙΗΣΕ

" ' Athanodorus, son of Agesander of Rhodes, made this.'
We learn from this inscription that father and son wrought on
Laocoön, and presumably Apollodorus (Polydorus) was also
Agesander's son ; for this Athanodorus can be no other than he
whom Pliny names.   Further, this inscription proves that more
works of art than merely three, as Pliny asserts, have been found
on which the artists have set ' made ' in the perfect tense, that
is to say, ἐποίησε, *fecit ;* he informs us that the other artists
out of modesty expressed themselves in the imperfect tense,
ἐποίει, *faciebat.*"

In all this Herr Winckelmann will find but little to contradict
the supposition that the Athanodorus of this inscription can
be no other than he of whom Pliny makes mention amongst
the artists of the Laocoön.   Athanodorus and Athenodorus,
moreover, is but one name ; for the Rhodians used the Dorian
dialect.   But concerning what he further infers from it I have
something to say.   First, that Athenodorus was a son of Agesander may pass : it is very probable, only not incontestable.
For it is well known that there were old artists who, instead of
naming themselves from their fathers, preferred to be called
after their teachers.   What Pliny says of the " brothers "
Apollonius and Tauriscus is hardly susceptible of any other
interpretation.

But how ?   This inscription—shall it, then, confute Pliny's
allegation that not more than three works of art have been
found the makers of which made themselves known in the
perfect tense (instead of ἐποίει, by ἐποίησε)?   This inscription !   Why are we to learn for the first time from it what we
might have gathered long before from many others ?   Have we
not already found upon the statue of Germanicus " Κλεομένης
ἐποίησε "?   on the so-called *Deification* of Homer " Ἀρχέλαος
ἐποίησε "?   on the famous vase at Gaeta " Σαλπίων ἐποίησε,"
and so on ?

Herr Winckelmann may say : " Who knows this better than
I ?   But "—he will add—" so much the worse for Pliny !   His

allegation is then so much the oftener contradicted, so much the more certainly refuted."

Not quite ! For how, if Herr Winckelmann makes Pliny say more than he actually wants to say? and if, therefore, the examples cited confute not Pliny's assertion, but merely the surplusage which Herr Winckelmann has imported into it? And so it is in reality. I must cite the whole passage. Pliny in his dedicatory epistle to Titus wants to speak of his work with the modesty of a man who is best aware how far it falls short of perfection. He finds one noteworthy instance of such modesty among the Greeks whose boastful book-titles, large in promises (*inscriptiones propter quas vadimonium deseri possit*), he rather makes game of, and says : *Et ne in totum videar Graecos insectari, ex illis nos velim intelligi pingendi fingendique conditoribus, quos in libellis his invenies, absoluta opera, et illa quoque quae mirando non satiamur, pendenti titulo inscripsisse : ut* APELLES FACIEBAT, *aut* POLYCLETUS; *tanquam inchoata semper arte et imperfecta ; ut contra judiciorum varietates superesset artifici regressus ad veniam, velut emendaturo quidquid desideraretur, si non esset interceptus. Quare plenum verecundiae illud est, quod omnia opera tanquam novissima inscripsere, et tanquam singulis fato adempti. Tria non amplius, ut opinor, absolute traduntur inscripta* ILLE FECIT *quae suis locis reddam : quo apparuit, summam artis securitatem auctori placuisse, et ob id magna invidia fuere omnia ea.* I would ask particular attention to Pliny's words : *pingendi fingendique conditoribus.* Pliny does not say that the custom of acknowledging one's work in the imperfect tense was universal or had been observed by all artists at all times; he says expressly that only the first old masters—those creators of the plastic arts, *pingendi fingendique conditores,* an Apelles, a Polycletus and their contemporaries—had had this wise modesty; and as he names these only, he thereby intimates by silence, but plainly enough, that their successors, especially in the more recent periods, had manifested more self-confidence.

But taking this for granted, as one must, the inscription here mentioned of one only of the three artists of the Laocoön may be perfectly accurate, and it may nevertheless be true that, as Pliny says, only about three works were extant in the inscriptions of which their authors made use of the perfect tense— that is to say, among the older works from the time of Apelles, Polycletus, Nicias, Lysippus. But, then, it cannot be accurate that Athenodorus and his assistants were contemporaries of

Apelles and Lysippus, as Herr Winckelmann would make them.
We must argue rather : if it is true that amongst the works of
the older artists, Apelles, Polycletus and the rest of this class,
there were only about three in whose inscriptions the perfect
tense was employed ; if it is true that Pliny has himself specified
these three works, then Athenodorus, who is author of none of
these three works, and who nevertheless uses the perfect tense
upon his works, cannot belong to those old artists : he cannot
be the contemporary of Apelles and Lysippus, but must be
assigned to a later period.

In short, I believe it might be taken as a quite trustworthy
criterion that all artists who used the ἐποίησε have flourished
long after the times of Alexander the Great and shortly before
or under the Emperors. Of Cleomenes it is unquestionable;
of Archelaus it is in a high degree probable ; and of Salpion at
any rate the contrary can in no way be shown. And so of the
rest, Athenodorus not excepted.

Herr Winckelmann may himself be judge in the matter.
But I protest at once in anticipation against the contrary
proposition. If all artists who used the ἐποίησε belong to the
later schools, it does not follow that all who used the ἐποίει
belong to the earlier. Among the later artists it may be that
some actually possessed this modesty, which so well becomes a
great man, and that others affected to possess it.

XXVIII

After the Laocoön, on no point was I more curious than on
what Herr Winckelmann might have to say of the so-called
Borghese Gladiator. I fancy I have made a discovery about
this statue on which I pique myself as much as one can about
discoveries of the kind. I was already apprehensive that Herr
Winckelmann would have anticipated me in it. But I find
nothing of the sort in his book, and if anything could make me
distrustful of its correctness it would be just this, that my
apprehension has not been justified. " Some   people," says
Herr Winckelmann, " make of this statue a Discobolus—that is,
one who is throwing the discus or a metal quoit, which was also
the opinion of the celebrated Herr von Stosch in a letter to me,
without, I imagine, a sufficient consideration of the posture in
which this kind of figure should be placed. For a man who is
about to throw something must withdraw his body backwards,

and when the throw is being made his weight rests on his right leg, while the other is free; but here the posture is just the opposite. The whole figure is thrown forward, and rests on the left leg, the right being behind and outstretched to the utmost. The right arm of the statue is new, and in the hand a piece of a javelin has been placed; on the left arm one sees the strap of a shield which he has been holding. If one considers that the head and the eyes are directed upwards and that the figure appears to guard itself with the shield against something coming from above, one might with more justification take this statue as a representation of a soldier who has particularly distinguished himself in a perilous situation : on public gladiators the honour of a statue was presumably never bestowed among the Greeks, and this work appears to be older than the introduction of gladiators amongst them."

There could not be a juster conclusion. This statue is just as little of a gladiator as it is of a quoit-player; it is really the representation of a warrior who distinguished himself in such a posture at some moment of danger. But as Herr Winckelmann guessed this so happily, why did he not go further? How is it that the very warrior did not occur to him, who in this very posture averted the complete defeat of an army and to whom his grateful country erected a statue in the identical posture? In one word, the statue is Chabrias.

The proof of this is the following passage of Nepos in the life of this general : *Hic quoque in summis habitus est ducibus; resque multas memoria dignas gessit. Sed ex his elucet maxime inventum ejus in proelio, quod apud Thebas fecit, quum Boeotiis subsidio venisset. Namque in eo victoriae fidente summo duce Agesilao, fugatis jam ab eo conductitiis catervis, reliquam phalangem loco vetuit cedere, obnixoque genu scuto projectaque hasta impetum excipere hostium docuit. Id novum Agesilaus contuens, progredi non est ausus, suosque jam incurrentes tuba revocavit. Hoc usque eo tota Graecia fama celebratum est, ut illo statu Chabrias sibi statuam fieri voluerit, quae publice ei ab Atheniensibus in foro constituta est. Ex quo factum est, ut postea athletae ceterique artifices his statibus in statuis ponendis uterentur, in quibus victoriam essent adepti.*

I know people will still hesitate a moment to give me their assent, but I hope, too, really for only a moment. The posture of Chabrias seems to me to be perfectly identical with that of the Borghese statue. The forward-thrown spear, *projecta hasta*, is common to both, but the *obnixo genu scuto* the commentators explain by *obnixo in scutum, obfirmato genu ad scutum :* Chabrias showed his men how they should firmly prop the shield by the knee and behind it receive the enemy—the statue, on the contrary, holds the shield high. But how if the commentators were mistaken? How if the words *obnixo genu scuto* were not to be associated, and one must rather read *obnixo genu* by itself, and *scuto* by itself or along with the immediately following *projectaque hasta ?* One needs but a single comma and the resemblance is at once as perfect as possible. The statue is a soldier, *qui obnixo genu, scuto projectaque hasta impetum hostis excipit ;* it shows what Chabrias did, and is the statue of Chabrias. That the comma is actually required is shown by the *que* attached to *projecta*, for if *obnixo genu scuto* were to be read together it would be superfluous, as, indeed, for that reason it is omitted in some editions.

With the high antiquity which would thus be attributable to this statue the form of the letters in the artist's inscription found upon it perfectly agrees, and Herr Winckelmann himself has concluded from the same that it is the most ancient of the existing statues in Rome on which the artist has acknowledged the authorship. I leave it to his penetrating glance whether he has noticed any other point of art that would conflict with my view. Should he honour it with his concurrence, then I might flatter myself that I had furnished a rather better example how happily the classic writers are illustrated by the works of ancient art, and these in their turn by them, than is to be found in all Spence's folio.

XXIX

Herr Winckelmann brings to his work a limitless erudition and an exact and all-embracing knowledge of art, and has yet at the same time wrought with the noble confidence of the ancient artists, who devoted all their diligence to their main subject, and, as for subsidiary matters, treated them with an apparently deliberate negligence or handed them over entirely to the first comer. It is no small merit to have fallen only into such errors as anyone might have avoided. They strike one on the first cursory perusal, and if they are to be noticed at all, it must be merely with a view to remind certain people who imagine nobody has eyes but themselves that they do not require to be noticed.

In his treatises on the Imitation of the Greek masterpieces

Herr Winckelmann has already been more than once misled by Junius. Junius is a very insidious writer; his whole work is a Cento, and as he is always trying to speak in the words of the ancients, he not seldom applies passages from them to painting which in their proper place treat of anything rather than painting. When, for example, Herr Winckelmann wishes to teach us that the highest in art just as little as in poetry is to be reached by the mere imitation of Nature, that both poet and painter must choose the impossible that is probable rather than the merely possible, he adds : " The ' possibility and truth ' which Longinus demands from a painter in opposition to the ' incredible ' of the poet can quite well exist alongside of it." But this postscript would be better away, for it shows the two greatest critics in a disagreement that is wholly without grounds. It is not true that Longinus ever said such a thing. He says something similar of eloquence and poetry, but by no means of poetry and painting. Ὡς δ' ἕτερόν τι ἡ ῥητορικὴ φαντασία βούλεται, καὶ ἕτερον ἡ παρὰ ποιηταῖς, οὐκ ἂν λάθοι σε, he writes to his Terentian ; οὐδ' ὅτι τῆς μὲν ἐν ποιήσει τέλος ἐστὶν ἔκπληξις, τῆς δ' ἐν λόγοις ἐνάργεια. And again,—Οὐ μὴν ἀλλὰ τὰ μὲν παρὰ τοῖς ποιηταῖς μυθικωτέραν ἔχει τὴν ὑπερέκπτωσιν καὶ πάντη τὸ πιστὸν ὑπεραίρουσαν· τῆς δὲ ῥητορικῆς φαντασίας κάλλιστον ἀεὶ τὸ ἔμπρακτον καὶ ἐναλῆθες. Only Junius here edges in " painting " instead of " eloquence," and it was in Junius, and not in Longinus, that Herr Winckelmann read : Praesertim cum Poeticae phantasiae finis sit ἔκπληξις, Pictoriae vero ἐνάργεια. Καὶ τὰ μὲν παρὰ τοῖς ποιηταῖς, ut loquitur idem Longinus, and so on. Very good ; Longinus' words indeed, but not Longinus' meaning !

The same thing must have happened to him in the following observation :—

" All actions," he says, " and postures of the Greek figures that are not marked with the character of wisdom, but were overpassionate and wild, fell into a fault which the ancient artists called Parenthyrsus." The ancient artists ? That could only be shown from Junius. The Parenthyrsus was a technical term in rhetoric, and perhaps, as the passage in Longinus appears to indicate, only to be found in Theodorus.

Τούτῳ παράκειται τρίτον τι κακίας εἶδος ἐν τοῖς παθητικοῖς, ὅπερ ὁ Θεόδωρος παρένθυρσον ἐκάλει. ἔστι δὲ πάθος ἄκαιρον καὶ κενόν, ἔνθα μὴ δεῖ πάθους· ἢ ἄμετρον, ἔνθα μέτριον δεῖ. Indeed I really doubt whether this word can be applied to painting at all. For in eloquence and poetry there is a kind of pathos that can be carried as high as possible without becoming Parenthyrsus, and only the highest pathos in the wrong place is Parenthyrsus. In painting, however, the highest pathos would be Parenthyrsus always, well as it might be excused by the circumstances of the person who expresses it.

To all appearance, then, various inaccuracies also in his *History of Art* have arisen simply from the fact that Herr Winckelmann has in his haste taken counsel with Junius only, and not with the originals themselves. For example, when he tries to show by instances that with the Greeks everything excellent in all kinds of art and work was particularly esteemed, and the best workman in the most insignificant department of labour could make his name illustrious, he introduces amongst other things the following : " We know the name of a maker of very exact balances or weighing-machines—he was called Parthenius." Herr Winckelmann can only have read the words of Juvenal, to which he here appeals, *lances Parthenio factas,* in the catalogue of Junius. For had he referred to Juvenal himself, he would not have been misled by the ambiguity of the word *lanx,* but would at once have recognised from the context that the poet did not mean scales or balances, but plates and dishes. Juvenal is at the moment praising Catullus because in a dangerous storm at sea he acted like the beaver which bites away its own flesh in order to escape with its life, and caused his costliest things to be thrown into the sea, in order not along with them to sink with the ship. These treasures he describes, and says amongst other things :—

> *Ille nec argentum dubitabat mittere, lances*
> *Parthenio factas, urnae cratera capacem*
> *Et dignum sitiente Pholo vel conjuge Fusci.*
> *Adde et bascaudas et mille escaria, multum*
> *Caelati, biberat quo callidus emtor Olynthi.*

Lances, which stand here amongst goblets and kettles, what else can they be but plates and dishes ? And what does Juvenal mean to say but this, that Catullus caused to be thrown overboard all his table silver, amongst which were dishes of chased work by Parthenius ? *Parthenius,* says the ancient commentator, *caelatoris nomen.* But when Grangaeus in his notes on this name adds, " *sculptor, de quo Plinius,*" he must only have written this as a good guess ; for Pliny mentions no artist of this name.

" Yes," continues Herr Winckelmann, " even the name of the saddler, as we should call him, has been preserved who made Ajax's leathern shield." This, too, he cannot have taken from the source to which he refers his reader, the Life of Homer by Herodotus. For here, certainly, the lines from the *Iliad* are cited in which the poet assigns the name of Tychius to this worker in leather; but it is at the same time expressly stated that in reality a leather-worker of Homer's acquaintance bore this name, to which he wished to show friendship and gratitude by inserting it in his poem : Ἀπέδωκε δὲ χάριν καὶ Τυχίῳ τῷ σκυτεῖ, ὃς ἐδέξατο αὐτὸν ἐν τῷ Νέῳ Τείχει προσελθόντα πρὸς τὸ σκυτεῖον, ἐν τοῖς ἔπεσι καταζεύξας ἐν τῇ Ἰλιάδι τοῖσδε.

> Αἴας δ' ἐγγύθεν ἦλθε, φέρων σάκος ἠΰτε πύργον,
> Χάλκεον, ἑπταβόειον, ὅ οἱ Τυχίος κάμε τεύχων,
> Σκυτοτόμων ὄχ' ἄριστος, Ὕλῃ ἔνι οἰκία ναίων.

It is therefore precisely the opposite of what Herr Winckelmann avers; the name of the saddler who had made the shield of Ajax was already in Homer's time so completely forgotten that the poet took the liberty of inserting an altogether different name in place of it.

Various other minor errors are mere slips of memory, or relate to things which he introduces merely by way of incidental illustration. For instance, it was Hercules, and not Bacchus, of whom Parrhasius boasted that he had appeared to him in the form in which he painted him.

Tauriscus was not a man of Rhodes, but of Tralles in Lydia.

The *Antigone* is not the first tragedy of Sophocles. But I refrain from gathering together a heap of such trifles. It could not, of course, appear censoriousness; but whoever knows my high esteem for Herr Winckelmann might take it for fastidiousness.

NATHAN THE WISE
A DRAMATIC POEM IN FIVE ACTS

BY

GOTTHOLD EPHRAIM LESSING

PERSONS

Sultan Saladin.
Sittah, his sister.
Nathan, a rich Jew in Jerusalem.
Recha, his adopted daughter.
Daja, a Christian, but in the house
    of the Jew as companion to Recha.
A young Knight Templar.
A Dervish. (Al-Hafi)
The Patriarch of Jerusalem.
A Friar.
An Emir, with various Mamelukes of Saladin.

ACT I—Scene I

Scene : *Apartment in Nathan's house*

Nathan returning from a journey. To him Daja

Daja. 'Tis he ! 'tis Nathan ! Now may God be praised
  That you at last, at last return again.
Nathan. Yes, Daja; God be praised ! But why *at last*?
  Have I then hoped for earlier home-coming?
  And was it in my power? Think ! Babylon
  By such a road as I perforce must follow,
  Now left, now right, is from Jerusalem
  At least two hundred leagues; and then my task,
  To gather in the debts the merchants owed me,
  Was scarce a business to make for speed,
  'Tis no such off-hand matter.
Daja.   Nathan, Nathan,
  How wretched meanwhile all things might have been
  To greet you on return ! Your house. . . .
Nathan.   On fire !
  So much I've heard already; now God grant
  That this is all the evil I must hear of !
Daja. So near it was to burning to the ground.
Nathan. Then, Daja, we had built another house;
  And one to suit us better.
Daja.   True enough !
  Yet Recha by a hair's breadth only 'scaped
  Of burning with it.
Nathan.   Burning? Recha? She?
  That no one told me. Then indeed no house
  I should have wanted more. My Recha burned,
  Within a hair's breadth !—Ha ! she is, in truth !
  Has actually perished ! Say the word !
  Out with it ! Kill me, torture me no longer—
  Yes, yes, she was burned with it.
Daja.   Were it so,
  Would it be from my lips that you would hear it?

113

Nathan. Why do you fright me, then? O Recha mine!
  My Recha!
Daja.   Yours? Your Recha call you her?
Nathan. How should I ever disaccustom me
  To call this child my own?
Daja.   Do you name all
  That you possess with only so much right
  Your own?
Nathan.   Nothing with greater! Everything
  I else possess Nature and Fortune's grace
  Rained down on me. This property alone
  I owe to virtue.
Daja.   At how dear a rate
  You make me pay for your pure goodness, Nathan!
  If goodness, with such purpose exercised,
  Can be called goodness!
Nathan.   Such a purpose, say you?
  What, then?
Daja.   My conscience . . .
Nathan.   Daja, first of all,
  Listen and hear me tell . . .
Daja.   My conscience, I . . .
Nathan. What a rare stuff I bought in Babylon,
  Tasteful and worthy of you, so rich and fine,
  Even for Recha I scarce have brought a finer.
Daja. What use? For, Nathan, I must tell you freely
  My conscience will no longer be deceived.
Nathan. And how the bracelets, and the golden chain,
  The ear-rings and the brooch will pleasure you,
  Which in Damascus booths I rummaged out;
  Ask me to show them.
Daja.   Ever 'twas your way!
  Only at ease when giving costly gifts!
Nathan. Be you as glad to take as I to give—
  Nor speak of them!
Daja.   Nor speak! Nathan, who doubts
  That you are honour's self, great-heartedness?
  And yet . . .
Nathan.   And yet—am but a Jew—is't not
  What would you say?
Daja.   Nathan, what I would say
  You know far better.
Nathan.   Well, no words

Daja.   I'm dumb.
  What God may see herein deserving doom
  And which I cannot alter or prevent—
  Cannot, I say—come on you !
Nathan.   Come on me !—
  But now where is she ? Where lies hid ? O Daja,
  Are you deceiving me ? Does she not know
  That I am come ?
Daja.   That ask I you, her father !
  The fright still quivers in her every nerve,
  Whate'er her fancy shapes is only fire,
  Nothing but fire. In sleep her spirit wakes,
  And sleeps in waking ; now an animal,
  And now more than an angel.
Nathan.   Dear my child !
  What are we human creatures !
Daja.   Long she lay
  This morning with closed eyes, and was as dead.
  Sudden she started up and cried, " O hearken !
  My father's camels come : I hear their tread,
  I hear his gentle voice ! "—as suddenly
  Her eye grew dim again, and so her head,
  Her arm's support withdrawn, dropped on the pillow.
  I, out at gate ! and there beheld your face !
  What wonder ! her whole soul was every hour
  With you, with you alone—and him.
Nathan.   With him ?
  What him ?
Daja.   With him who saved her from the fire.
Nathan. Saved her ! Who was he ? Who ? And where is he ?
  Who saved for me my Recha ? Tell me, who ?
Daja. 'Twas a young Templar Knight whom just before,
  Brought here a prisoner, Saladin set free.
Nathan. A Templar ! What ! Whom Saladin let live ?
  And did no meaner miracle suffice
  To save my Recha ? God !
Daja.   No. Without him
  Venturing once more his new-won life, she perished !
Nathan. Where is he, Daja, this heroic man ?
  Where is he ? Come and lead me to his feet.
  But first you gave him, not reserving aught,
  The treasure I had left you ? Gave him all ?
  Promised him more—much more ?
  E **843**

Daja.   Alas ! we could not.

Nathan. Not?   Not?

Daja. He came, and no one knows from whence;
    He went, no one knew whither.   Without word,
    Led by his ear alone, with fore-spread mantle,
    Boldly through flame and smoke he sought the voice
    That called to us for help.   We gave him lost,
    When suddenly from out the smoke and flame he stood,
    In his strong arm holding her high.   Unmoved
    And cold before our sobbed-out thanks, he set
    His prize down gently, thrid the crowd, and vanished !

Nathan. Vanished !   But not for ever, I will hope.

Daja. When the first days were past we saw him go,
    Under the palm-trees walking up and down,
    Yonder, that shade the Holy Sepulchre.
    With trembling I approached him, spoke my thanks,
    Besought, entreated, conjured him but once
    To see the gentle girl who could not rest
    Until her thanks were wept out at his feet.

Nathan. Well?

Daja.   Vain, in vain !   To our entreaty deaf,
    He poured even bitter mockery on me . . .

Nathan. Till you were frighted from him . . .

Daja.   No, in truth !
    For I assailed him every day anew;
    And every day endured new mockery.
    What did I not bear from him !   What had not
    Willingly borne !   But many days now past
    He comes no more to seek the palm-trees' shade
    Girdling the quiet grave of the Redeemer;
    And no man knows where now he lives retired—
    You are amazed !   You ponder !

Nathan.   I but think
    What feeling this in such a soul as Recha's
    Surely begets.   To find herself disdained
    By one proven worthy of so high regard;
    So driven away, and still to be so drawn;
    A long contention sets of heart and head,
    Whether misanthropy shall win the day
    Or melancholy; often neither wins,
    And fantasy that mixes in the strife
    Makes of us dreamers in whom, ill exchange !
    The head acts heart, and heart acts head by turns;

The latter is, if I have not misread her,
My Recha's case : she dreams.

Daja.   She's dutiful,
And all love-worthy !

Nathan.   Still she dreams, she dreams !

Daja. One special crotchet—may we dare to call it ?—
She cherishes. 'Tis that her Templar Knight
Can be no earthly creature, born of woman ;
One of the angels rather, whose sweet guard
She trusted in from her blest infancy,
Flew from his veil wherein even in the fire
He hovered round her, took the Templar's form
To save her—do not smile ! Who knows ? who knows ?
Even if we smile, we'll leave her this illusion
In which the Jew, the Christian, and the Muslim
Are joined in one—surely a blessed dream !

Nathan. Even to me 'tis blessed ! Go, brave Daja ;
See what she does ; if I can speak with her—
This wondrous angel-guardian then I'll find,
And if it pleases him still here below
To play the pilgrim, still his knightly part
To fill, sure I shall find and bring him hither.

Daja. You undertake things harder than you know.

Nathan. Then the sweet dream to actuality
More sweet will yield its place, for, trust me, Daja,
To men a human creature is more dear
Than any angel, so you will not grieve
To see this angel-mania exorcised.

Daja. You are so good, and yet you are so wicked !
I go—but listen, see !—here Recha comes.

Scene II

Recha, and the foregoing

Recha. Home safe and sound, my father, home once more ?
I feared 'twas but your voice sent to announce you.
But come ; no hills, or wastes, or rivers part
Us now ; we breathe within the self-same walls.
Why haste you not your Recha to embrace ?
Poor Recha ! who meanwhile was burned with fire,
Almost, but almost only : Shudder not
It is a horrid death, to die in fire !

Nathan. My child, my darling child!
Recha.   And you must over
  Euphrates, Tigris, Jordan; over who knows
  What waters? O how often have I trembled
  For you, before the fire came close to me!
  Since then I think to die in water were
  Refreshment, comfort, safety; but in truth
  You did not drown, nor did I die in fire—
  Let us be glad and lift our heart to God.
  He bore you and the vessel on the wings
  Of His *invisible* angel-host across
  The treacherous rivers. He too gave the sign
  To my good angel that he *visibly*
  On his white wing should bear me through the fire.
Nathan. (White wing! Ah, yes, the Templar's fore-spread
      cloak.)
Recha. Visibly, visibly, should bear me through
  The scorching flame, safe covered by his wing;
  Thus I have seen an angel face to face,
  And *my own* angel.
Nathan.   Recha were worthy that,
  And would in him see nought more beautiful
  Than he in her.
Recha [*smiling*].   Whom flatter you, my Father?
  The angel, or yourself?
Nathan.   Yet, had a man,
  Even such as Nature gives us every day,
  Done you this service, he must then appear
  To you an angel. Yea, he must and would.
Recha. No, not that kind of angel; no! a real,
  An actual angel he! Have not yourself
  Taught me 'tis possible that angels are,
  That God for good to them that love Him can
  Work wonders? And I love Him.
Nathan.   He loves you,
  And works for such as you His hourly wonders;
  Ay, has indeed from all eternity
  Wrought them.
Recha.   I love to hear that doctrine.
Nathan.   How?
  That it would sound so natural, commonplace;
  If a mere Knight had saved you, were it then
  Less miracle? Chief miracle it is

That the true miracles become to us
So commonplace, so everyday.   Without
This universal miracle could it be
That thinking men should use the word like children,
Who only gape and stare upon what's strange,
And think what's newest is most wonderful.

Daja. [*To Nathan.*] O will you, Nathan, with such subtleties
Break her now o'er-stretched brain?

Nathan. Hear me !   For Recha
Were it not miracle enough to find
Her saved by one whom first a miracle
Must himself save?   Yea, no small miracle !
For what man ever heard that Saladin
Spared a Knight Templar's blood? or such a Knight
Did ever ask or hope that he should spare him,
Or offered more for freedom than the belt
Carrying his weapon, or at most his sword?

Recha. My father, that proves all, and argues clear
It was no Templar, but the semblance only,
For if no captive Templar ever came
Into Jerusalem but to certain death;
Nor any such was ever granted freedom
To walk Jerusalem streets, then how could one
Spring up at midnight for my rescue?

Nathan.   See !
She argues well.   You, Daja, answer her.
You tell me he came here a prisoner;
Then doubtless you know more.

Daja.   Well, yes; I know
What common rumour says—that Saladin
Showed mercy to him for his dear resemblance
To a child-brother Saladin had loved.
Yet as full twenty years have run their course
Since the boy died—his name I know not what;
He dwelt, I know not where—the story seems
An idle tale strange and incredible !

Nathan. Nay, Daja, why were this incredible?
Is it rejected only to make room
For things less credible, as happens oft?
Why should not Saladin, who loves his race,
As all men know, have had in younger years
A brother whom he specially beloved?
Was 't never known two faces should be like?

Can an old passion not return again?
Like causes, do they not work like effects?
Since when?   Tell me, what's here incredible?
Ah, my wise Daja, it were then no more
A miracle; *your* miracles alone,
Demand, or shall I say deserve, belief?

Daja. You mock.

Nathan.   But first you mocked at me.   Yet, Recha,
Even so your great deliverance remains
A miracle and possible alone
To Him who by weak threads can turn—His sport
If not His mockery—the stern resolves
And deep-laid plans of monarchs.

Recha.   O my father !
My father, if I err, you know I err
Unwillingly.

Nathan.   Nay, more, you wish to learn :
But see !   A brow so moulded or so arched;
Bridge of a nose, this way or that way shaped;
Eyebrows that on a blunt or sharper ridge
Rest full or pencilled delicate, a line,
A bend, a fold, an angle, or a mole,
Or what else, on some Western countenance,
And you escape the fire, in Asia !
Were that no wonder, miracle-hungry folk?
Why trouble, then, an angel?

Daja.   Why, what harm—
Nathan, if I may speak—what, after all,
What harm to wish an angel for a saviour
Rather than man?   For so one feels the First
Ineffable Cause of one's salvation drawn
Much closer.

Nathan.   Pride, mere pride !   The iron pot
Wants silver tongs to draw her from the furnace,
That she may dream she's made of silver too.
Pah ! ask you what's the harm?   Then, I would ask,
What profit?   " That's to feel God so much nearer "—
Your thought—is folly, if not blasphemy.
The thought is harmful, does the soul a mischief.
Come, hear me for a moment.   To this being
Who saved you, be he angel or but man,
Would you not render service in return
With a glad heart, repaying what you might?

How then and what, if angel?   What of service,
Say what great service can you do for him?
Thank him, you'll say, and sigh to him or pray,
Dissolve in rapturous tears before him, fast,
Give alms and celebrate his Festival.
All nothing!   For methinks thereby far more
Yourself and your dear neighbours gain than he.
Your fasting will not fatten him, your expense
Not make him rich, nor will your rapturous worship
Add to his glory, nor your faith in him
Make him a mightier angel.   Is't not so?
But, if a human creature!

Daja.   Certainly,
I know a human creature's needs had given
More opportunity to serve; God knows
How ready we were for it!   But he wished,
He needed, nothing; in himself content,
And with himself at peace as only angels
Are or can be.

Recha.   At last, when he quite vanished . . .

Nathan. Vanished!   How mean you, vanished?   Shown himself
Under the palms no more?   Then, did you make
More eager search elsewhere?

Daja.   We did not.   No!

Nathan. No, Daja, no?   But thereof may come sorrow!
Fond dreamers!   Should your angel now be sick?

Recha. Sick!

Daja.   Sick!   O say not so!

Recha.   What shuddering
Strikes my heart dead!   Feel, Daja, this cold brow—
So warm it was, and suddenly 'tis ice!

Nathan. He is a Frank, a stranger to our clime;
He's young; unused to hunger and to vigil,
And heavy labours laid upon him now.

Recha. Sick!

Daja. Nathan means only it were possible.

Nathan. Well, there he lies!   Without a friend, or gold
To buy friends for him.

Recha.   Father, O this heart!

Nathan. No tendance, counsel none, nor friendly talk,
The spoil of pain, perhaps of death, he lies!

Recha. Where? where?

Nathan.   He who for one he had not seen
  Nor ever knew—enough, a fellow creature—
  Plunged in the fire . . .
Daja.   O spare her, spare her, Nathan !
Nathan. Who would not nearer come or further know
  What he had saved, to spare himself the thanks.
Daja. O pity her, Nathan !
Nathan.   Further, who desires not
  To see her more, unless again to save—
  Enough—a fellow creature.
Daja.   Cease, and look !
Nathan. He on his bed of death, nor comfort hath
  But memory of this deed !
Daja.   O Nathan, cease !
  You kill her !
Nathan.   Him you killed, or might have killed.
  Recha ! My Recha ! this is medicine,
  Not poison that I bring.   Come to yourself !
  He lives, mayhap is not even sick !
Recha.   In truth?
  Not dead?   Not sick?
Nathan.   Not dead; for sure, not dead !
  For God rewards good deeds, even here rewards them.
  But come !   I need not teach you what you know :
  How easier far is dreaming pious dreams
  Than acting bravely; how a worthless creature
  Will dream fine dreams, in order to escape—
  (Though oft his object's hidden from himself)—
  Some serviceable labour.
Recha.   Ah, my father !
  Never again leave Recha to herself !
  May it not be that he is only gone
  Upon a journey?
Nathan.   Yes, without a doubt.
  I see, below, a Mussulman who scans
  With searching gaze my camels and their load.
  Who is he?   Know you him?
Daja.   It is your dervish.
Nathan. Who?
Daja. Why, your chess-companion—your dervish !
Nathan. Al-Hafi !   my Al-Hafi?
Daja.   Purse-bearer
  To the Sultan now.

Nathan.   Al-Hafi !   Are you dreaming ?
　　'Tis he ! in truth, 'tis he !   He comes this way—
　　In with you, quick !   And now what shall I hear ?

SCENE III

Nathan and the Dervish

Dervish. Do not be startled, open your eyes wide !
Nathan. Is't you ?   Or is it not ?   In silk attire,
　　A dervish !
Dervish.   Well, why not ?   Can nought be made
　　Out of a dervish, nothing ?   Tell me why ?
Nathan. O much, no doubt !   But I have ever thought
　　The true, the genuine dervish, would refuse
　　To be aught else than dervish.
Dervish.   By the prophet !
　　That I'm no genuine dervish may be true.
　　Yet when one must—
Nathan.   What !   *must*—a dervish *must* ?
　　No man needs must, and shall a dervish, then ?
　　What must he ?
Dervish.   What a true man asks of him
　　And he sees clear is right ; that must a dervish !
Nathan. By Heaven, thou speak'st the truth.   Come hither,
　　　man,
　　Let me embrace thee.   Thou art still my friend ?
Dervish. Dost thou not ask first what I am become ?
Nathan. Despite what thou'rt become !
Dervish.   But might I not
　　Be now a fellow of State whose friendship were
　　To thee inopportune, a burden ?
Nathan.   If thy heart
　　Is Dervish still, I'll trust it.   For State office,
　　That's but a garment !
Dervish.   Which still must be regarded ;
　　What think you ?   Now advise me—at your court
　　What should I be ?
Nathan.   A Dervish, nothing more.
　　Yet later, very probably, a cook.
Dervish. And thus with you unlearn my handicraft ?
　　Just cook !   Not waiter also ?   Now confess
　　Saladin knows me better—I am made
　　　*E 843

His Keeper of the Treasure.
Nathan.   Thou? By him?
Dervish. The smaller Treasure, be it understood;
   The chief, that of his House, his father guards.
Nathan. His House is large.
Dervish.   And larger than thou thinkest,
   For every beggar is a member of it.
Nathan. Yet Saladin so hates the beggar tribe—
Dervish. That root and branch he means to blot them out,
   Though in the attempt himself become a beggar.
Nathan. Bravo! That mean I; Saladin, well done!
Dervish. And beggar he is now, in spite of one!
   For every sunset sees his treasury
   Emptier than empty. For however full
   The morning's flood, the ebb comes ere midday.
Nathan. By channels drained, alike impossible
   To fill or close.
Dervish.   You hit the bull's eye there.
Nathan. I know it.
Dervish.   Truly, it is little good for princes,
   Vultures to be among the carcases;
   But ten times less when they are carcases
   Among the vultures.
Nathan.   Not yet that, my dervish.
   Not that!
Dervish.   Your speech is wisdom, sir. Now come
   What will you give to have my place from me?
Nathan. What does your place bring in?
Dervish.   To me? Not much.
   To you it would be wondrous profitable.
   For were the Treasure at ebb, as oft it is—
   Then you would raise your sluices; make advances
   And take in usury whatever pleased you.
Nathan. With interest on interest again?
Dervish. Ev'n so!
Nathan.   Until my capital were interest
   And nothing more.
Dervish.   Is that no lure for you?
   Divorce then, nothing else, is what remains
   To us two friends and our past happiness!
   For verily I reckoned much on you.
Nathan. Verily? Reckoned! How?
Dervish.   That you would help me carry

My office with all honour, and offer me
An ever-open treasury.　You tremble.
Nathan. Well, let us understand each other.　Here
Is room for difference.　Thou, my friend, art thou.
Al-Hafi, dervish, to my uttermost
Is welcome, but Al-Hafi, Saladin's
Attorney—why, to him—
Dervish.　　　　　　　　Ah !　I guessed right.
Thou would'st be kind if prudence should allow,
Prudent and sage.　But patience !　Thou would'st make
Of one Al-Hafi two ; but presently
Those two **may** separate.　See this robe of honour
Saladin gave me, look before it fades
And turns to rags, such as may clothe a dervish,
Hangs on a nail in old Jerusalem,
And I am by the Ganges, where barefoot
I lightly tread the hot sand with my teachers.
Nathan. That would be like you !
Dervish.　　　　　　　And play chess with them.
Nathan. Your chiefest joy !
Dervish.　　　　　　　Think only, what seduced me !
That I should be no more a beggar, rather
Might play the rich man 'mongst the beggars, might
Perchance, hey presto !　change the richest beggar
Into a poor rich man ?
Nathan.　　　　　　No, no ; not that !
Dervish. No, something more absurd !　For the first time
Flattery trapped me, the good-hearted fancy
Of Saladin it was that overcame me.
Nathan. What fancy ?
Dervish.　　　　　　" Only a beggar could interpret
The soul of beggars, only a beggar learn
How rightly to give alms.　Your predecessor,"
So said he, " was too cold by half, too rough ;
When he did give, he gave ungraciously ;
Blustered enquiry of the wretch he gave to ;
Not satisfied to know the need, must learn
First how the need arose, and then weighed out
According to the cause, a stingy dole.
But not so will Al-Hafi !　Nor in him
Will Saladin appear unkindly kind.
Al-Hafi is not as choked pipes that yield
In mud and foam what they received so pure,

The limpid waters. No; Al-Hafi thinks,
Al-Hafi feels as I do." Such the tune
The fowler's pleasing pipe played in mine ear
Till the bullfinch was netted. O a fool !
Fool of a fool am I !

Nathan.   Gently, my Dervish,
Gently !

Dervish.   Eh, what ! Were it not foolery
To tread men underfoot by scores of thousands,
Starve, rob, enslave, lash, stab and crucify them,
Then to a handful play philanthropist?
Were it not foolery to ape the mercy
Of the All-Highest, Who sends sun and rain
Alike upon the evil and the good,
On wilderness and pasture, to ape this
And not to have the overflowing riches
Of the Almighty? What ! were it not folly. . . ,

Nathan. No more, Al-Hafi, cease !

Dervish.   Nay, of my share
In this wild folly let me question you.
Were it not foolish in these fooleries
To note the good side only, and be partner
For the good's sake in folly? Answer me !

Nathan. Al-Hafi, ask you counsel? Hear it, then ;
Make haste, return into the wilderness !
With men you might, dehumanised, forget,
Unlearn to be a man.

Dervish.   This fear I too.
Farewell !   [*Exit.*

Nathan. What ! what ! so fast away? Dost then imagine
The desert will take wings? Would he but wait
And hearken to a friend ! Ho ! ho ! Al-Hafi !
He's gone ; and I so wished to question him
About our Templar.   In all likelihood
He knows him.

Scene IV

Enter Daja hastily.   Nathan

Daja. Nathan ! Nathan !

Nathan.   Well, how now?

Daja. He has appeared again ! He has returned !

Nathan. Who, Daja? who has come again?
Daja.   He! He!
Nathan. Well, he! But who? Why name him simply " he "?
  That's not becoming, even if he is an angel.
Daja. He's pacing up and down amongst the palms,
  And plucks as he goes by dates from the boughs.
Nathan. And eating?—and a Templar?
Daja.   Why torment me?
  Her eager looks through the close-column'd palms
  Divined him ere they saw, and fixedly
  Now follow him. She begs, beseeches you
  Without delay to seek him there. O hasten!
  She from her window casement will make sign
  Which way he turns, nearer or further off.
  Hasten!
Nathan.   What, travel-stained, just as I lighted
  From off the camel? Were that well? Go thou
  In haste to him; tell him of my return.
  For think, the worthy man has but declined
  Entering my doors in absence of the host,
  And will come readily when he invites him.
  Go, tell him I invite him heartily.
Daja. Utterly vain! He will not; one word says it—
  He darkens not the door of any Jew.
Nathan. Then go, if nothing more, to follow him:
  Keep him in sight; your eyes accompany him.
  I follow straight.   [*Nathan goes in, and Daja out.*

SCENE V

SCENE: *An open space with palm-trees, amongst which the
    Templar walks up and down. A friar follows him at some
    distance on one side, seeming as if he would address him.*

Templar. He follows me as once before; and look,
  See how he peers behind his hands! Good brother,
  Should I perhaps say " Father "? Is it so?
Friar. " Brother," not more; lay-brother at your service.
Templar. Well, brother, if one self had anything!
  But, as God lives, I have not—
Friar.   None the less
  Warm thanks, and God give thee a thousandfold
  What thou wouldst joy to give. The will, the will

Makes givers, not the gift.   Neither for alms
Was I sent after thee.
Templar.   Yet, thou wert sent?
Friar. Yes, from the cloister.
Templar.   Where I even now
Had hoped to find a simple pilgrim-meal?
Friar. The table was already laid; come only,
Come back, my lord, with me.
Templar.   Whither?   And why?
I have not eaten flesh for many a day;
What matters it?   I find the dates are ripe.
Friar. Nay, let my lord beware of this cold fruit.
Unwholesome, for it much obstructs the spleen,
Thickens the blood, brings melancholy thoughts.
Templar. I'm prone to melancholy and welcome it.
But for this warning's sake you were not sent,
I know, to seek me.
Friar.   No; it was to learn
Something about you, just to sound and probe you.
Templar. And this thou tell'st me boldly to my face?
Friar. Why not?
Templar. [*Aside.*] Crafty brother!   Has the cloister
More of thy kind?
Friar. I know not, my good lord,
I must obey.
Templar.   And there, is it your custom
To listen and obey and never question?
Friar. Were it obedience else, I ask my lord?
Templar. (How near simplicity will come to truth!) ⌉
Confide, to me thou may'st, who is the man
Would know me better; not yourself I'll swear.
Friar. Would it become me or advantage me?
Templar. Then whom becomes it or advantages,
This eager prying?
Friar.   Who's the inquisitor?
The Patriarch, I must believe—he 'twas
That sent me after you.
Templar. Knows he not, then, the red cross on white mantle?
Friar. Even to me 'tis known!
Templar.   Well, Friar, listen;
I am a Templar and a prisoner.
Would you know more?   Ta'en prisoner at Tebnin,
The fort which in the last hour of the truce

We thought to scale and then to rush on Sidon.
Yet more? taken with twenty, me alone
Saladin spared; with this the Patriarch knows
All he need know, and more ev'n than he need.

Friar. But scarcely more than he knew yesterday.
He would learn, too, the reason why my lord
Was pardoned by the Sultan, and he only.

Templar. Do I myself know why? Already I knelt,
My mantle on the ground, and with bared neck
Waited the stroke, when with a searching look
Saladin springs towards me, gives a sign;
They raise me and unfetter; when to thank him
I turn, his cheek is wet with teardrops; dumb
He stands, dumb I; he leaves me there. And now
What this strange story means, there! that's a riddle
The Patriarch may guess at.

Friar.　　　　　　　Thus he reads it—
That God for great things, great things has preserved you.

Templar. Yea, for great things indeed. To save from fire
A Jewish girl; to guide some curious pilgrims
To Sinai's mountain—great things truly!

Friar.　　　　　　　　　　　" Great things "
Will come in time; meanwhile such trifles serve:
Perhaps the Patriarch himself has ready
Affairs of weightier import for my lord.

Templar. What, Friar! Mean you that? Has he said aught?
Whispered? Dropped hint?

Friar.　　　　　　　　Yea, not uncertainly;
Only my lord must first be probed to learn
Whether he's just the man.

Templar.　　　　　　　Oh, merely probed!
(We'll see first how the probing goes!) Well, sir?

Friar. The short way is the best way—that my lord
Be told in plain terms what the Patriarch wills.

Templar. Speak out then plainly.

Friar.　　　　　　　　It would please him much
If by my lord into the proper hands
A letter might be brought.

Templar.　　　　　　　By me? By me?
I am no errand-runner. And was this
The business planned, an employment worthier
Than snatching Jewish maiden from the flames?

Friar. Yea, and with reason. For, the Patriarch says,

That with this missive's import is bound up
Christendom's fortune. Says the Patriarch,
" Carry this letter safe, and earn a crown
Which by and by the King of Heaven will give,
A crown none," says the Patriarch, " is worthier
To wear than thou."

Templar.   None worthier than I?

Friar. " For," says the Patriarch, " no man on earth
Can win this crown more certainly."

Templar.   Than I?

Friar. " He hath full freedom here, goes everywhere,
Well understands how cities may be stormed
And how defended "—says the Patriarch—
" He best can judge the weakness or the strength
Of that new-builded inner battlement
Of Saladin and plainliest describe it "—
So says the Patriarch—" to the host of God."

Templar. Good friar, were it right that I should hear
The content and the intent of the letter?

Friar. That know I not in its entirety.
'Tis for King Philipp's hands. The Patriarch—
Often I wonder how a saint who else
Lives wholly in Heaven can stoop and condescend
To be so intimate with things o' the world.
For they must vex his soul.

Templar.   Well, then, the Patriarch?

Friar. Knows with exactest certainty how, where,
And in what strength and from what quarter Saladin,
In case the truce be broken and strife renewed,
Opens afresh his campaign.

Templar.   This he knows?

Friar. Yea, would be glad King Philipp also knew,
That, with this knowledge fortified, the King
Might judge the risk, whether so terrible
That at all costs the truce must be renewed
With Saladin, the truce your Order bravely
Hath broken already.

Templar.   What a Patriarch !
The dear man wants no common messenger
In me; he wants a spy. Well, good friar,
Tell this your Patriarch : that when you probed me
You found me useless; that I hold myself
A prisoner still; and more, that the one calling

Of Templars ever was to drive the foe
With naked spear, never—to play the spy.
Friar. I thought as much ! and will not blame my lord.
　The best is yet to come.　The Patriarch
　Lately has gathered how the hold is named,
　And where it lies in Lebanon, wherein
　The untold sums are hid that Saladin's
　Provident father stores to pay the army
　And face the war's expense.　Now, Saladin
　From time to time to this stronghold resorts
　By ways remote, with meagre company ;
　Perceiv'st thou ?
Templar.　　　　　No, not I.
Friar.　　　　　　　　　A simple thing
　To ambush then the Sultan, take him captive,
　And give him his quietus ; what were easier ?
　You shudder ?　Two God-fearing Maronites
　Offer the deed, if once some gallant man
　Were found to guide them.
Templar.　　　　　　　And the Patriarch
　Has chosen me to act the gallant man ?
Friar. He thinks King Philipp then from Ptolemais
　Would surely send his aid.
Templar.　　　　　　Friar !　To me ?
　To me ?　Hast thou not heard, or hear'st thou now
　For the first time what debt of obligation
　Binds me to Saladin ?
Friar.　　　　　I've heard the tale.
Templar. And still ?
Friar.　　　　　The Patriarch thinks that's well enough,
　But God's rights and your Order . . .
Templar.　　　　　　　These change nothing !
　Suggest me not a knave's trick.
Friar.　　　　　　　　No, good faith !
　Only the Patriarch thinks a knavish trick
　In man's sight needeth not be so in God's.
Templar. That I might owe my life to Saladin,
　And yet take his ?
Friar.　　　　　O fie !　The Patriarch thinks
　That Saladin were still a foe to Christ,
　Therefore can have no claim to be your friend.
Templar. Friend ?　Since I will not play the villain to him,
　The thankless villain ?

Friar.   Why, of course, of course !
 The Patriarch's mind is, we are quit of thanks,
 Quit before God and man, when service done
 Was not for our sake done, and rumour tells,
 Saladin spared you for that he discerned
 His brother's likeness in your look and ways.
Templar. Ah, this too knows the Patriarch, and still?
 Would it were true !   Ah, Sultan Saladin !
 How?   Nature framed in me one feature only
 After your brother's pattern, should not then
 Something within me answer to the same?
 And shall this something in my soul be shifted
 To please a Patriarch?   No, Nature, no !
 Thou dost not lie !   God does not contradict
 Himself in His own works !   Hence, friar, hence !
 Wake not my anger;   leave me to my thoughts.
Friar. I go;   and I go happier than I came.
 My lord will pardon me.   We cloister people
 Are under rule, we must obey the heads.

SCENE VI

*The Templar and Daja, who has been observing the Templar at a
    distance for some time, and now approaches him.*

Daja. The friar, methinks, left him in no good humour.
 But I must chance my errand.
Templar.   Excellent !
 Who says the proverb lies—that monk and woman,
 Woman and monk, are Beelzebub's two claws?
 To-day he flings me from the one to the other.
Daja. What do I see?   You, my brave knight?   Thank God !
 I thank Him for His grace !   So long a time
 You have been hidden.   You have not been, I'll hope,
 Retired in sickness?
Templar.   No.
Daja.   In health, then?
Templar.   Yes.
Daja. We have been deep in trouble for your sake.
Templar. So?
Daja.   Surely wert on a journey?
Templar.   You have guessed it !
Daja. And art to-day returned?

Templar   No; yesterday.

Daja. To-day, too, Recha's father is returned,
    And surely Recha now dare hope?

Templar.   For what?

Daja. For what she prayed of you so often.   Come;
    Her father now himself most pressingly
    Invites you.   He has come from Babylon,
    A train of richly-laden camels with him,
    And everything that's costliest in spices,
    Jewels and stuffs that only India,
    Persia and Syria or China can provide.

Templar. I'm not a buyer.

Daja.   He's honoured of his people.
    As princes are, and yet, I wonder often
    Their title of honour is " Nathan the Wise,"
    And not " Nathan the Rich."

Templar.   Ah ! to his people
    Are *rich* and *wise* perhaps identical.

Daja. Rather " the Good " should they have named him.   For
    It's not expressible how good he is.
    That moment when he learned what Recha owed you
    What would he not have done for you, or given !

Templar.   Ay !

Daja. But try, but come and see !

Templar.   What then?   How fast
    A moment passes !

Daja.   Think, were it not so,
    Were he not this good man, that I so long
    Had dwelt within his gates?   Think you perhaps
    That I forget my worth as Christian?
    O no, it was not sung beside my cradle
    That I should company my lawful spouse
    Only for this to Palestine, to tend
    A Jewish maiden.   A noble squire my spouse
    In Kaiser Friedrick's host.

Templar.   And was by birth
    A Swiss on whom the honour was bestowed
    With his Imperial Majesty to drown
    I' the self-same river-bed; woman, how often
    Already have you told me this same tale?
    Will you not cease at last, then, to pursue me?

Daja. Pursue?   O gracious God !

Templar.   Yes, yes, pursue.

And once for all I will not see you more,
Nor hear ! nor have recalled thus endlessly
A deed in which my thoughts had never part,
Which when I think of it becomes a riddle
Ev'n to myself.   Regret it I must not—
But see, if such should hap again ; your fault
It were, if I should act less rashly, should
Enquire beforehand—and let burn, what would.

Daja. That, God forbid !

Templar.   I beg you from to-day
Do me at least this favour : know me no longer.
For Jew is Jew.   And keep the father off.
I'm a rough hind.   Long since the maiden's image
Passed from my soul, if it was ever there.

Daja. Ah ! but from her soul yours hath never passed.

Templar. What, then, is one to do ?   Say what.

Daja.   Who knows !
Men are not always what they seem.

Templar.   Yet seldom
Anything better.   [*He turns to go.*

Daja.   But wait a moment.   Why
This haste?

Templar. Woman, these palms I loved and their green shade,
You make them hateful.   [*Exit.*

Daja.   Go then, German bear !
Go !   Yet I follow, not to lose the trail.
                                      [*Follows at a distance*

ACT II—Scene I

Scene : *The Sultan's Palace.   Saladin and Sittah at chess.*

Sittah. Where now, where are you, Saladin ?   You dream.

Saladin. I thought the move a good one.

Sittah.   Good perhaps
For me ; but take it back.

Saladin.   Why, then ?

Sittah.   The knight
Is left uncovered.

Saladin.   True.   Well, then, so !

Sittah. That forks your pieces.

Saladin.   Well, then, I call check !

Sittah. How does that help you?   See, I cover it,
  And you are as you were.
Saladin.   From this dilemma,
  I see no way but sacrifice.   Let be!
  Take you the knight.
Sittah.   I want him not; I pass.
Saladin. Thank you for nothing: better strategy
  Prompts you to leave the knight in place.
Sittah.   May be.
Saladin. Make not your reckoning without the host.
  See!   Do you overlook what you would gain?
Sittah. By no means.   For I could not think you held
  So lightly of your queen.
Saladin.   I, of my queen?
Sittah. I see quite well to-day I shall not win
  My thousand dinars—no, not even a heller.
Saladin. How so?
Sittah.   Canst ask?   Because with all your cunning
  And all your skill you mean to lose.   But that
  I have no mind to, for besides such sport
  Is not quite entertaining, did I not ever
  Win most with you in games that I have lost?
  For then to comfort me for my lost game
  You gave me twice the stake.
Saladin.   Then, sister dear,
  You should have tried with all your might to lose.
Sittah. It well may be, at least, your liberal hand,
  Dear brother, bears the blame if I play ill.
Saladin. We'll stop the game: 'tis late, we'll make an end.
Sittah. And leave it so?   Then check! and double check!
Saladin. Truly I had no thought of such a check—
  That takes my queen as well. . . .
Sittah.   Could it be helped?
  Let's see.
Saladin.   No, no; I must resign the queen.
  Never with this piece was I fortunate.
Sittah. With this piece only?
Saladin.   Take it off?—No good!
  For so all is protected as before.
Sittah. How courteously one must behave to queens
  You've taught me often . . .   [*Lets it stand.*
Saladin.   Take it or take it not.
  I have no move.

Sittah.   But take, what need of that?
  Check! Check!
Saladin.   Proceed.
Sittah.   Well, check! and check! and
    check!
Saladin. And mate!
Sittah.   Not quite; for you can move that man
  Between, or make what move you will; no matter.
Saladin. Right! you have won: Al-Hafi straight will pay,
  Let him be called: Sittah, you guessed the truth;
  My mind was not i' the game: I was distracted.
  Besides, who gives us aye these polished pieces
  Perpetually? all smoothed away to nothing.
  What matter? Losing needs excuse. But not
  The unform'd pieces, Sittah, made me lose;
  Your art, your swift and quiet glance . . .
Sittah.   Even so
  You try to soothe the smart of the lost game.
  Enough! you were distracted; more than I.
Saladin. Than you? What had you to distract you?
Sittah.   Truly
  Not your distractions. O my Saladin,
  When shall we play so eagerly again?
Saladin. All the more eagerly when occasion comes!
  Ah! since the war resumes, you mean. Well, let it!
  On! on! I have not sought it. Willingly
  Had I prolonged anew our armistice, and gladly,
  How gladly first had found a manly spouse
  For my dear Sittah, and that were Richard's brother
  Brother of Richard, think!
Sittah.   Your Richard's praise
  Is ever on your lips!
Saladin.   If brother Melek
  Had, after, Richard's sister for his mate:
  Ha! what a house together! Of the first,
  Best houses in the world the best and first.
  You find I am not slack in my self-praise,
  Deeming me not unworthy of my friends—
  Ah, 'spousals such as these would bring us men!
Sittah. Have I not often laughed at your fair dream?
  You know not Christians, nay, you will not know them.
  Their pride is to be Christians, not to be men;
  For even that which from their Founder's day

Hath seasoned superstition—humanity—
They love, not for its human quality,
But that Christ taught it, that Christ did the like—
Well for them that He was a man so good;
Well for them they can take in utter faith
His virtues! But what virtues? Not His virtues,
No, but His Name, which must be spread world-wide
To cloud with slander and obliterate
The names of all good men. The Name alone
Is everything.

Saladin.   Why else, you mean, should they require
Both you and Melek take the name of Christian
Ere Christians will permit you talk of marriage.

Sittah. Even so! As if by Christians only love
Were to be looked for, love wherewith the Maker
Endowed woman and man.

Saladin.   Christians believe
So many pitiful things that they can swallow
Even this! And yet there you mistake. The Templars—
They are the cause; they, they alone by whom
Our hopes are frustrate: they will not let go
That pleasant town which should be brought to Melek
By Richard's sister as her bridal dower;
They fix their claws on Acre. And not to lose
The privilege of the knight, they play the monk,
The simple monk. And thinking they may shoot
A fortunate arrow at the bird in flight,
They scarce can wait the passing of the truce.
So be it! I'm prepared. On, gentlemen!
If all besides were only as it should be.

Sittah. Ah, what, then, troubles you? What goes not straight?
What makes you tremble?

Saladin.   Even that which for so long
Has made me tremble. I was in Lebanon—
Our father, our good father, is succumbing
To his sore burdens.

Sittah.   O, 'tis pitiful!

Saladin. He can no more. 'Tis pressure everywhere;
Where'er we look is failure.

Sittah.   What, then, fails?
What presses?

Saladin.   What I almost scorn to name;
What when I have it seems superfluous,

And when I want it indispensable.
Where stays Al-Hafi?   Have none gone after him?
This pitiful cursed money!   Ha, Al-Hafi!
'Tis well that you are come.

Scene II

The Dervish Al-Hafi.   Saladin.   Sittah

Al-Hafi.   Th' Egyptian moneys
    Have now, methinks, arrived; and Allah grant
    That they be in great plenty.
Saladin.   Have you news?
Al-Hafi. I?   No; I thought I should receive it here.
Saladin. To Sittah pay the stake—a thousand dinars
                              [*Goes to and fro, in thought.*
Al-Hafi. Pay!   Pay!   and not receive!   O excellent!
    Instead of something—less, still less than nothing.
    To Sittah? evermore to Sittah?   Lost?
    And lost again at chess.   And there's the board!
Sittah. You do not grudge me luck?
Al-Hafi. [*Examining the board.*] What grudge you?—If——
    But you know all.
Sittah. [*Signing to him.*] Hush, Al-Hafi, hush!
Al-Hafi. [*Still examining the board.*] First grudge it not yourself.
Sittah.   Al-Hafi, hush!
Al-Hafi. Were yours the white?   Did you give check to him?
Sittah. Good that he did not hear!
Al-Hafi.   Is it his move?
Sittah. Say out aloud that I can have my money.
Al-Hafi. Why, yes; you'll get it, as you always get it.
Sittah. How?   Are you mad?
Al-Hafi.   The game's not finished yet.
    You have indeed not lost it, Saladin.
Saladin. [*Scarcely attending.*] Still, pay, my good Al-Hafi; we
    must pay.
Al-Hafi. Pay!   Pay!   Your queen still stands.
Saladin. [*Still moody.*]   It makes no odds,
    The piece is taken.
Sittah.   Have done, Al-Hafi, and say
    That I can have my money when I please.
Al-Hafi. [*Still absorbed in the game.*] O that's of course, as
    always—Yet even now

Even if the queen is taken, you are not therefore
Check-mated . . .
Saladin. [*Steps up and throws the pieces down.*]   Yes, I am, and
   wish it so.
Al-Hafi. I see, to play's to win; and payment follows.
Saladin. [*To Sittah.*] What says he?   What?
Sittah. [*From time to time signing to Al-Hafi.*]   You know him:
   how he loves
  To oppose and be petitioned.   Envious too,
  Or I mistake him.
Saladin.   Surely not of you—
  Not of my sister.   What is this, my Hafi?
  Envious?
Al-Hafi.   Maybe, maybe; gladly I'd have
  Myself a brain like hers, and such a heart.
Sittah. And yet he ever pays in honesty,
  And will to-day: leave him alone for that!
  But go, Al-Hafi, go!   Shortly I'll send
  To fetch the money.
Al-Hafi.   No; for further part
  In this mad mummery is not for me.
  Sooner or later he must learn the truth.
Saladin. Learn?   Who? and what?
Sittah.   Is't thus you keep your promise,
  Al-Hafi?   Break not oaths!
Al-Hafi.   How could I think
  That it would go so far?
Saladin.   Well!   What's in hand?
  Am I not to be told?
Sittah. I conjure you, Al-Hafi, be discreet.
Saladin. This is most strange!   This solemn, earnest prayer
  Speaks Sittah to a stranger, to a Dervish,
  And not to me, her brother.   Solve the riddle,
  Al-Hafi, I command you.   Speak out, Dervish!
Sittah. Let not a trifle, brother, trouble your spirit:
  More than its meanness warrants.   Once or twice
  Of late, you know, I won from you at chess
  Just such a stake, and since I have no need
  At present for such moneys; since, besides,
  Al-Hafi's treasure-chest is not too full,
  And posts have not arrived.   But trouble not,
  For I'll not make it a present to you, brother,
  Not yet to Hafi or his treasure-chest.

Al-Hafi. Ah ! were it only that !
Sittah.   And some such trifles.
   That, too, 's untouched which once you set apart
   For me ; for some few months untouched it lies.
Al-Hafi. That is not all.
Saladin.   Not all ?   Then will you tell me ?
Al-Hafi. Since we have waited for the gold from Egypt
   Hath she . . .
Sittah.   Why hear him ?
Al-Hafi.   Hath she not only
   Ta'en nothing . . .
Saladin.   The good girl ! she has besides
   Helped from her own.   Is't so ?
Al-Hafi.   Yea, all the court
   She hath maintained, herself alone hath borne
   Your whole expenditure.
Saladin.   Ha ! that's my sister !
                                        [*Embracing her.*
Sittah. Who made me rich enough for this but you,
   Brother ?
Al-Hafi.   Who'll make you soon as beggar-poor
   As he himself is.
Saladin.   Poor ? the brother poor ?
   When had I more ? or when have I had less ?
   One coat, one sword, one charger, and—one God.
   What want I more ?   And when shall these come short ?
   Yet, Hafi, I could chide you.
Sittah.   Do not chide,
   Brother ; if only I could lighten as much
   Our father's burden—
Saladin.   Ah !   Ah ! there you strike
   My joy again to earth !   Though for myself
   I nothing lack, nor can lack.   Ha, 'tis he
   Whose want is sorest, and with him we suffer.
   What shall I do ?   From Egypt our supplies
   Delay their coming, we may wait them long,
   And why, God knows : for all is quiet there.
   Cut down, draw in, and spare—that will I gladly ;
   Nothing will please me better, if alone
   Thereby I suffer, and none else.   What helps it ?
   I still must have my horse, my coat, my sword.
   And with my God 'tis easy bargaining.
   For He is satisfied with one small gift,

Which is my soul.—Much I had reckoned, Hafi,
Upon the surplus in thy treasure-chest.
Al-Hafi. Surplus? Yourself confess I had been strangled,
  Perhaps impaled had you in vain demanded
  Of bankrupt me this surplus. Fraud, embezzlement,
  Were then my one resource.
Saladin.   Now, what remains?
  But tell me, Hafi, why you turn to Sittah
  And borrow her small store : are there not others?
Sittah. And could I see this privilege torn from me,
  To further you, my brother? No, this joy
  I'll not surrender till I must : my fortunes
  Are not yet foundered quite.
Saladin.   Only not quite !
  It wanted only this ! Hafi, at once
  Contrive, take up from whom you can, nor halt
  On nice considering of means and ways :
  Go, borrow, pledge. Yet, Hafi, borrow not
  Of those whom I made rich. To borrow of them
  Might seem reclaiming. Ask the covetous,
  For they will be the readiest ; they know well
  How fast with me their moneys multiply.
Al-Hafi. I know none such.
Sittah.   Hafi, did I not hear
  Your friend from his far journey had returned
  To his own dwelling?
Al-Hafi.   Friend? My friend? To whom
  Give you that name?
Sittah.   Your much-belauded Jew.
Al-Hafi. Belauded Jew ! Lauded by me?
Sittah.   Whom God—
  Such were the terms that once you used of him—
  Whom God of all the good things of this world,
  With least and greatest in abundancy
  Had crowned.
Al-Hafi.   And said I so? What meant I then
  By that?
Sittah.   The least was, Wealth ; the greatest, Wisdom.
Al-Hafi. How? Of a Jew? I said so of a Jew?
Sittah. What would you not have said of your good Nathan?
Al-Hafi. Oh ! 'tis of him ! of Nathan ! Has he truly
  At last returned again ? If this be so,
  Surely his journey prospered. And 'tis true

The folk call him the Wise, call him the Rich.

Sittah. Yea, more than ever now he's called the Rich.
And the whole city hums of rarities,
The stuffs and jewels in his caravan.

Al-Hafi. So then it is the Rich has come again;
And with him comes, who knows? the Wise as well.

Sittah. What think you, Hafi? Could not you approach
him?

Al-Hafi. For what, suppose you? Not to borrow, surely?
Ah, there you touch him! Nathan lend? His wisdom
Lies just in this: that he will lend to no man.

Sittah. That's not the picture once you drew of him.

Al-Hafi. To men in utmost need he lendeth goods—
But money? money never! Tho' for the rest
He's such a Jew as there be seldom found.
Has brains, knows how to live, can play good chess;
But marks him out in bad points as in good
From other Jews. I warn you, reckon not
On him. 'Tis to the poor he gives; to them
Even with open hand like Saladin,
If not so largely, with as good a will;
Without respect of persons. Christian and Jew,
And Mussulman and Parsee, all is one
To him.

Sittah.   And such a man . . .

Saladin.   How comes it, then,
I have not known this man, nor heard his name?

Sittah. Would he not lend to Saladin? To him,
To him who only cares for others' wants,
Not for his own?

Al-Hafi.   Herein you see the Jew,
The common, vulgar Jew! And yet, believe me,
He envies you the most on score of giving,
So jealous is he; grasping, for himself,
At all God's-hire that offers in the world;
And 'tis for this alone he lends to none:
That he have more to give. His reason, this!
That Charity is in the law commanded,
The law commands not to oblige a neighbour;
So Charity itself has made him quite
The least obliging friend in all the world.
In truth, of late I am in ill accord
With him. Still, think not therefore I will speak

Unjustly of him, good and true-hearted he,
Everyway good, except for only this.
No, not for this.   I'll go at once and knock
At other doors . . . and I have just bethought me
Of a rich Moor, a covetous man—I go !
Sittah. Hafi, what needs your haste?
Saladin.   O, let him !   Let him ِ

SCENE III

Sittah.   Saladin

Sittah. What haste he makes, as though he were rejoiced
      If he could so escape me.   What means that?
      Has he in truth deceived himself in Nathan,
      Or would perhaps deceive us?
Saladin.   How deceive?
      You question me who hardly know of whom
      The talk was, me who never heard until to-day
      Of this your Jew, your Nathan.
Sittah.   Is it possible
      A man remained hid from you who, they say
      Has found the graves of David and Solomon,
      And with a mighty secret word can break
      Their seals? and then bring forth from time to time
      To daylight treasures inexhaustible
      No meaner source could furnish.
Saladin. His wealth if this man finds in graves, 'tis sure
      They're not the graves of Solomon and David.
      Fools lie there buried !
Sittah.   Criminals, mayhap !
      Besides, his wealth's source is more fertile far,
      More inexhaustible than any grave
      Of Mammon.
Saladin.   He's a merchant, so you told me.
Sittah. All highways are his mule-tracks, every waste
      Has seen his caravans, his vessels lie
      In all the havens.   So Al-Hafi to me once
      Declared, and added, with a joyful pride
      How greatly, nobly this his friend employed
      What in his wisdom he did not disdain
      To gather by his diligence ; and added, too,
      How free from prejudice his soul, how open

His heart to every virtue, how attuned
To all things beautiful.   Ah ! how he praised him.
Saladin. Yet Hafi spoke of him uncertainly,
   And coldly . . .
Sittah.   No, not coldly, but perplexed.
   As though he held it dangerous to praise him,
   And could not blame him undeservedly.
   Or might it not be that the noblest Jew
   Cannot deny his kindred, is still Jew;
   That Hafi for this feature is ashamed
   Of his dear friend?   Be't with him as it may,
   The Jew be more Jew or be less, what matter
   If only rich?   This is enough for us !
Saladin. And yet you would not, sister, take from him
   By force what is his own?
Sittah.   What call you force?
   With fire and sword?   No, no, what violence
   But their own weakness need we with the weak?
   But come a moment now into my harem
   And hear a singer-girl whom yesterday
   I bought.   Meantime perhaps a shrewd design
   I have upon this Nathan will grow ripe—
   Come.

SCENE IV

In front of Nathan's house, where it is close to the palm trees.
   Enter Recha and Nathan.   To them Daja

Recha. O, you've tarried long, my father.   Hardly now
   Can we have hope to meet him . . .
Nathan.   Never fear;
   If not among the palms, then otherwhere
   We find him.   Only calm yourself.   And see,
   Is that not Daja this way hastening?
Recha. But she has lost him, that is all too certain.
Nathan. Why so?
Recha.   For then she'd come with speedier foot.
Nathan. She has not seen us yet, perhaps.
Recha.   O now
   She sees us.
Nathan.   Look ! with quicken'd pace she comes.
   Only be calm, be calm !

Recha.   But could you wish
  A daughter who were calm in such a case?
  Untroubled for his weal whose great deed saved
  Her life—her life that's only dear to her
  Because to you she owes it.
Nathan.   O my wish
  Is not to have you other than you are:
  Even if I knew that something new and strange
  Stirred in your loving heart.
Recha.   What, then, my father?
Nathan. What ask you?   Are you then so shy with me?
  What's passing now deep in your inmost soul
  Is innocence and nature.   Let it not
  Trouble your spirit; mine it does not trouble.
  But promise me that when your heart has spoken
  With clearer voice, you will not hide from me
  Your wishes.
Recha.   Nay, the possibility
  Nigh makes me tremble—the thought that I might wish
  To veil my thoughts from you.
Nathan.   No more of this.
  'Tis done with once for all.   And here is Daja—
  Well?
Daja.   Still he walks among the palms, and soon
  Will come by yonder hedge.   Look, there he comes!
Recha. Ah! and appears unsure which path to take.
  Whither? if right? if left? uphill or down?
Daja. No, no; he'll take the footway round the cloister
  Yet once or twice, and then he needs must pass
  Hereby.—What matter?
Recha.   Have you spoken with him
  Already?   How is he to-day?
Daja.   As ever.
Nathan. Carefully!   Warily!   Do not be seen.
  Step back a pace or two: Rather, go in.
Recha. Just one more look! just one, but ah! the hedge.
  It steals him from me.
Daja.   Come! the father's right.
  You run the danger that if he but sees you,
  Upon the spot he'll turn.
Recha.   Ah me! the hedge!
Nathan. If he turn suddenly by it, infallibly
  He'll spy you.   So go in, go in.

Daja.   Come, Recha;
  I know a window where we're safe.
Recha.   So, Daja?

                                    [*The two go in.*

SCENE V

Nathan and presently the Templar

Nathan. Almost I shrink from this strange man.   And almost
  His rugged virtues shake me.   That one man
  Should thus be able to perplex another !
  He comes.   By Heaven !   A stripling like a man.
  I love right well this strong, defiant glance !
  And this brave carriage.   Sure the shell alone
  Is bitter here, and not the kernel.   Where,
  Where have I seen one like him?   Pardon me,
  My noble Frank . . .
Templar.   What say'st thou?
Nathan.   Pardon me . . .
Templar. What, Jew?   Why pardon?
Nathan.   That I venture thus
  To greet you.
Templar.   Can I hinder?   But be brief.
Nathan. Forgive me.   Pass not by so hastily
  And with so scornful brows; slight him not thus
  Whom you have bound to you eternally.
Templar. How bound?   Ah, almost I guess !   You are . . .
Nathan. My name is Nathan, am that maiden's father
  Whom your brave heart delivered from the fire;
  And come to . . .
Templar.   If to thank me—spare your pains !
  I have endured for this mere trifle's sake
  Too heavy a load of thanks.   Assuredly
  You owe me nothing, nothing.   Could I know
  This maiden was your daughter?   'Tis our rule,
  The Templars' duty, thus to run to the aid
  Of whomsoever in the hour of stress.
  Moreover, at that moment to my soul
  My life was burdensome.   How gladly, then,
  I rushed to snatch the opportunity
  Thus for another's life to chance my own,
  Another's, were it but a Jewish girl.
Nathan. Yes, that's the hero's way, to do great deeds

And yet not boast of them, but to hide rather
Behind a modest shame t'avoid applause :
But when he thus disdains the offering
Of grateful praise, tell me what offering then
Will he not scorn?   And, Knight ! were you not here
A stranger and a captive, not thus boldly
I'd put you to the question.   Speak, command :
How can I serve you?

Templar.   Serve me?   In no wise.

Nathan. See !   I am rich.

Templar.   But rich Jew never was
With me the better Jew.

Nathan.   Would you for that
Decline what notwithstanding he possesses
Of good, and take no help of his full hands?

Templar. Nay, as for that, I'll speak no austere vows
Even for my mantle's sake.   When it shall be
Not part, as now, but wholly rags threadbare,
When seam nor stitches longer hold, I'll come
And borrow of you something for a new one,
Money or stuff.—Nay, eye me not so close,
You're still secure, 'tis not yet so far gone.
'Tis still in fair condition ; just one spot
Here on the lappet's foul—where it was singed.
And that it got when out of the fierce flame
I bore your daughter.

Nathan. [*Who seizes the lappet and gazes at it.*]   Now 'tis
    wonderful
That such a foul spot, such a touch of fire
Should bear the man a better testimony
Than his own mouth.   Now would I kiss it straight,
This rusty fleck !   Forgive me ; 'twas not wilful.

Templar. What?

Nathan.   'Twas a tear fell on it.

Templar.   That's no matter !
Has had more drops than that.—(This Jew will soon,
I fear, bewilder me).

Nathan.   Were I too bold
To beg such kindness, that you once would send
Your mantle to my child?

Templar.   Why, for what purpose?

Nathan. That she, too, press her lips upon this fleck.
For she now wishes, though the hope is vain,

F **843**

    Herself to embrace your knees.

Templar.   But, Jew—
    Your name is Nathan?—Truly, Nathan, you have spoken
    To me such words—so kind—so delicate
    You have startled me . . . but certainly . . . I would . . .

Nathan. Pose and disguise you, as you will. Even here
    I find you out. You were too good, too modest,
    To be more courteous. For—the girl, all feeling;
    Her woman-ambassador, all zeal to serve;
    The father far removed—your only care
    Was all for her good name; you fled temptation,
    Fled, that you might not conquer : now I thank you—

Templar. I see you know how Templar Knights should think.

Nathan. And only Templars? only they? and only
    Because the Order's rule commands it so?
    I know how good men think, and I know too
    All lands bear good men.

Templar.   Yet, with difference?

Nathan. O true, difference in colour, dress and form.

Templar. But more or fewer in the different climes.

Nathan. I hold that this distinction is but small.
    Everywhere great men need great spheres, and when
    Too thick they're planted, they then break away
    Their branches. But the medium men like us,
    On the other hand, are everywhere in crowds.
    Only, the one must not abase the other;
    Only, the halt must tolerate the lame;
    Only, the hillock must not vaunt itself,
    Or think it the one summit in the world.

Templar. Most nobly said ! But know you not the people
    That first abased all others? Know you not
    What nation first of all proclaimed itself
    The Chosen Race? How, if I could not cease
    This people, not indeed to hate—not hate—
    But for their pride to dis-esteem? Their pride
    Which they bequeathed to Muslim and to Christian,
    That their God was the true God, and theirs only !
    You start to hear a Christian and a Templar
    Speak thus. But tell me when and where this madness,
    This pious rage to have the better God,
    And to impose this better God as best
    On the whole world, more in its blackest form
    Been shown than here and now? From whose dimmed eyes

The scales fall not? But yet be blind, who will!
Forget what I have said, and let me go. [*Is going.*
Nathan. Ha! know you not with how far firmer grasp
I now would hold you. /Come, we must, we must
Be friends. Despise my people if you will.
Nor I nor you have chosen our people. Are we
Our people? People? What means then the people?/
Are Jew and Christian rather Jew and Christian
Than men? Ah, had I found in you one more
Whom it suffices to be called a Man!
Templar. And so, by God, Nathan, you have, you have
Your hand! am shamed to have mistaken you
Even for a moment.
Nathan. And I'm proud of it.
Only the common rarely is misjudged.
Templar. And what is rare one seldom can forget,
Yes, Nathan, yes; we must, we must be friends.
Nathan. Already are. My Recha will rejoice!
And what a happy future opens up
Before my vision! You must know her first.
Templar. My heart's on fire within.—Who rushes yonder
Forth of your threshold? Is it not your Daja?
Nathan. Yes surely, and in trouble.
Templar. Can it be
Mishap befallen our Recha?

Scene VI

The former, and Daja in haste

Daja. Nathan! Nathan!
Nathan. Well?
Daja. Forgive me, noble Knight, that I break in
Thus on your converse.
Nathan. Well, what is't?
Templar. What is't?
Daja. A message from the Sultan: he would speak
With you. My God! the Sultan!
Nathan. Me? the Sultan?
Curious perhaps to see what novelties
I have brought home. Say only there's but little
Or almost nought unpacked.
Daja. O Nathan, no;

He will see nothing, he will speak with you,—
With you in person, now, with no delay.
Nathan. I come at once.   Do you return to Recha.
Daja. Take it not ill of us, worshipful Knight,—
God, we are troubled, guessing not what means
The Sultan.
Nathan.   That we'll learn.   Go, only go !

SCENE VII

Nathan and the Templar

Templar. You do not know him yet; I mean, in person ?
Nathan. The Sultan ?   No, not yet, though I have never
Avoided him, nor have I sought to meet him,
So loud the general voice spoke in his praise,
That I must rather wish to think it just,
Than see.   But now, even were it otherwise—
He has, by sparing of your life . . .
Templar.   Ah, true;
That certainly is truth; the life I live
It is his gift—
Nathan.   And thereby gave he me
A double, threefold life.   This, I confess,
Has altered all between us; thrown a cord
At once about me, binding me to him,
And to his service.   Scarce now can I wait
To know what he commands me; ready for all
Am I; and ready, too, to tell him what
I do is for your sake.
Templar.   Nor I myself
Have yet had chance to thank him, and have crossed
Ofttimes his path in vain : for that impress
I made on him came like a lightning flash
And vanished even as quickly; who can tell
Whether he has me still in memory ?
And yet he must, once more at least, recall me
To fix my fate.   'Tis not enough that I
Still live at his command, and by his will :
I must await the word, after what rule
And what direction I must spend my days.
Nathan. Doubtless, and therefore I delay no longer.
Perhaps a word will fall may give occasion

To speak of you.   Permit me, pardon me—
I hasten thither.   When, when shall we see you
Within my gates?
Templar.   When may I?
Nathan.   When you will.
Templar. To-day, then.
Nathan.   And your name, if I may ask?
Templar. My name was, sometime, Curd von Stauffen—Curd!
Nathan. Von Stauffen?   Stauffen?   Stauffen?
Templar.   You are startled?
Why start you?
Nathan.   Stauffen?   Branches of this house,
I know, are many.
Templar.   Here in this very soil
Do several rest and rot of this same race.
My uncle—nay, my father as I call him—
Is one—Why turn on me a gaze so keen,
So searching?
Nathan.   Nothing! nothing!   How can I
Grow tired of seeing you?   And for this cause
I leave you.
Templar.   Searcher's eyes not seldom find
More than they seek for.   Nathan, this gives me pause.
Let our acquaintance build on gradual time,
Not prying upon glances.   [*Goes off.*
Nathan.   What said he?
" Searchers find often more than they desire."
As if he read my soul!   'Tis even so.
This might befall me also.—Not alone
Wolf's figure and Wolf's walk; but his voice, too;
The carriage of his head—Wolf to the life;
And how he bare his sword upon the arm
And stroked his eyebrows, as did Wolf, to hide
The ardour of his gaze, so full of fire.
How such sharp-printed pictures yet can sleep
At whiles within, till word or tone recalls them.
Von Stauffen! right, 'tis right; Filnek and Stauffen—
I'll search this soon to the depths, but first must I
To Saladin.   But how?   Is not that Daja
Lurking and listening?   Come, my Daja, come.

Scene VIII

Daja. Nathan

Nathan. What now? Something, to-day, pricks both your hearts
   Quite other news to know than what the Sultan
   Will ask of me.
Daja.   And do you blame her for it?
   You had begun to talk in friendlier mood
   That moment when the Sultan's message came
   And drove us from the window.
Nathan.   Tell her now
   That any moment she may look for him;
   He promised this.
Daja.   For sure? for sure?
Nathan.   My Daja,
   I trust you and will trust. Be on your guard,
   Be dutiful, be true, leave no regrets
   For after conscience—See that you destroy not
   One point of all my plan. Only relate
   And question still with maiden modesty
   And due reserve . . .
Daja.   That you at such an hour
   Could yet remember this! I go; and you
   Must also, for, behold! there comes in haste
   From Saladin a second messenger,
   Al-Hafi, your good Dervish.

Scene IX

Nathan. Al-Hafi

Al-Hafi. Ha, ha! the very man whom I was seeking.
Nathan. Is there such haste? What asks he at my hands?
Al-Hafi. Who?
Nathan.   Saladin. Tell him I come! I come!
Al-Hafi. To whom? To Saladin?
Nathan.   Has he not sent you?
Al-Hafi. Me? No; already has his message come?
Nathan. Yea, verily.
Al-Hafi.   Then everything is right.
Nathan. What? What is right?

Al-Hafi.   That no blame lights on me:
 God knows I'm not to blame. What have I not
 Said, whispered, lied of you to turn it off?
Nathan. To turn what off? What's this that you call right?
Al-Hafi. That you're his right-hand now, his Chancellor.
 I pity you. Yet second thoughts forbid.
 For from this hour I go; go, you have heard
 Already whither, and you know the road.
 Upon the way can I do ought for you?
 Am at your service. It must be only what
 One naked can drag with him. Speak: I go.
Nathan. Bethink you now, Al-Hafi, once bethink you;
 That I as yet know nothing of these things
 Whereof you're voluble. What means it all?
Al-Hafi. But you will bring the sack along with you.
Nathan. Sack?
Al-Hafi.   Well, the gold you'll lend to Saladin.
Nathan. And is this all?
Al-Hafi.   Perhaps I should look on
 And watch him bleed you to the very toes?
 And see the waste of his sweet charity
 Draw from the once-full barns and draw again
 Until the wretched aborigines,
 Ev'n the poor mice, are starved? Perhaps you dream
 That he who's thirsty for your gold will take
 Your counsel also? Ha! he follow counsel!
 Since when has Saladin suffered advice?
 Think rather, Nathan, what's just chanced to me.
Nathan. What, then?
Al-Hafi.   I came on him as he played chess
 With sister Sittah: she's a clever player;
 And the game Saladin imagined lost
 Stood yet upon the board. I gave a glance
 And saw the contest neither lost nor won.
Nathan. For you a find indeed! You trembled then.
Al-Hafi. A move with king on pawn was all required
 To give her check. If I could only show you!
Nathan. I well can trust you there.
Al-Hafi.   For so the rook
 Were freed, and she were done. This I would show him,
 And call him. Think!
Nathan.   He was not of your mind?
Al-Hafi. He would not listen, and contemptuously

He brushed the game down.
Nathan.   Is it possible?
Al-Hafi. Saying, for once at least he'd take checkmate;
  He wished it.   Is that play?
Nathan.   Hardly, in sooth:
  'Tis playing with the play.
Al-Hafi.   Like that, it's worth
  A rotten filbert.
Nathan.   Money here or there!
  That is the least.   But not to listen to you,
  Upon so weighty a point not once to listen,
  Not to admire your eagle vision!   That,
  That cries out, think you not, for its revenge?
Al-Hafi. You jest!   I told you this that you might know
  The kind of brain he is; brief, in one word,
  His whimsies weary me, and I have done.
  Here am I running among filthy Moors
  To ask the use of filthy purses.   I,
  Who never in my days begged for myself,
  Am now for others borrowing.   Borrowing's as bad
  Almost as begging, and the lending so
  At usury as bad almost as theft.
  Amongst my people by the Ganges shore
  I shall need neither, nor need I be
  Of either, instrument.   For by the Ganges,
  The Ganges only you'll find men, but here
  No man save you were worthy of the boon
  To live by Ganges shore.   Come you with me.
  Leave Saladin the plunder, at his will.
  He'll bring you step by step to beggary,
  And all your baggage with you.   For a guide
  And warrantor I'll stand.   I pray you, come.
Nathan. Methinks, indeed, 't might be our last resort.
  Yet, Hafi, I must ponder it.   Wait you . . .
Al-Hafi. Ponder it?   Such things abide no pondering.
Nathan. Only till I return from Saladin;
  Till leave-takings . . .
Al-Hafi.   To hesitate and ponder
  But asks excuses not to dare.   The man
  Who cannot at a wink decide to live
  His self-poised life, must live another's slave
  For ever.   As you will!   Farewell, as seems
  You best.   My way lies yonder: your way here.

Nathan. Hafi ! You'll settle first your treasurership ?
Al-Hafi. A jest. The total of my treasure-chest
  Is not worth reckoning. And for my account
  Yourself or Sittah shall be warranty—
  Farewell !   [*Exit.*
Nathan.   Be warrant for him ! Yes, I know him
  Savage and kind and faithful; the true beggar,
  When all is said, is the one genuine King !

ACT III—Scene I

In Nathan's house. Recha and Daja

Recha. Daja, what were my father's words to-day ?
  " I might expect him any moment now " ?
  Surely that sounds as though he might at once
  Appear. Has not a world of moments gone ?
  Ah, well, who thinks of moments that are fled ?
  In each " next minute " I'm resolved to live ;
  That one will surely come that brings him here.
Daja. O that accursed message of the Sultan !
  But for it Nathan would have brought him straightway.
Recha. And when this longed-for moment has arrived,
  With its fulfilment of my tenderest wish——
  What then ? what then ?
Daja.   What then ? Why, then, I hope
  The tenderest of *my* wishes too shall move
  To its fulfilling.
Recha.   What can take its place
  Then, in my heart, that will have quite unlearned
  To throb without some one o'ermastering wish ?
  If nothing—that were terror !
Daja.   My, my wish
  Will enter then the place of that fulfilled ;
  My wish to know you in safe hands, in Europe,
  In hands all worthy to have *you* in keeping.
Recha. Strangely deceived ! For what makes this wish yours,
  The same forbids it ever should be mine.
  Your country is the magnet which attracts you,
  And shall my own, my own not hold me back ?
  Shall the image of your loved ones vividly
  Rise on your inward vision, and prevail,
    *F 843

More than mine round me, seen and felt and known?
Daja. Struggle you will, but struggle as you will,
The ways of Heaven are still the ways of Heaven.
What if it were then he who rescued you,
Through whom his God for Whom he fights should lead you
Back to the soil whose daughter you were born?
Recha. Daja, you speak most strangely; your wild brain
Does breed the queerest fancies. His? " His God "
" For Whom he fights." Then whom does God belong to?
What kind of God who to one man belongs,
Who needs be fought for by His worshippers?—
Nay; who shall tell for what soil we were born
If just that spot where we were really born
Not claims us? If my father heard you speak!
What would he do to you, who image ever
My happiness removed afar from him?
What do to you, finding you wantonly
Mixing the seed of reason, that in my soul
He sowed so pure, with your land's weeds and flowers?
Daja, dear Daja, no; he will not suffer
Your motley growths to root upon my ground.
And I must tell you I myself have felt
How beautiful so'er these blossoms show,
My ground enfeebled and consumed thereby;
Feel in their soul-sweet fragrance heart and brain
Made giddy and bewildered. Your own head
Can bear it, being used. Nor do I blame
Therefor your stronger nerves, that can support it:
Only it suits me not; and even your angel
Comes little short of quite befooling me.
I am ashamed here in my father's house
Of such a folly.
Daja.   Folly! As if all reason
Had its home here! Folly! Folly! Folly!
O if I dared but speak!
Recha.   And dare you not?
When was I not all ear whene'er you pleased
To tell me of the heroes of your faith?
For their great deeds was I not ever ready
With admiration; from their martyrdoms
Have I withheld the tribute of my tears?
Their faith, indeed, did ne'er appear to me
What's most heroic in them. Yet more welcome

Ever to me the doctrine, that devotion
And piety towards God cannot depend
On our beliefs or fancies about God.
Dear Daja, this my father often said :
And you consented with him to its truth :
Why undermine you what with him you builded?
Daja, this is no talk wherewith to prelude
The meeting with our friend—For me perhaps
'Tis fitting, for to me so much depends—But hark,
A knocking at the gate !   What if 'twere he !

SCENE II

*Recha.   Daja and the Templar, to whom someone outside opens the
    door with the words :*

                    Enter, sir Knight !
Recha.   [Starts back, composes herself, and is about to fall at his feet.]
                              It is ! it is my rescuer !
Templar. This to escape I made my coming tardy
    And yet . . .
Recha.   Before this proud man's feet I kneel
    Only to thank my God and not the man.
    The man refuses thanks, wishes for that
    As little as the water-pail that at the fire
    Did show itself so zealous, filled itself
    And poured itself, and filled, nor cared a whit ;
    So, even so, the man ; he, too, was thrown
    With like indifference upon the flame,
    And there, as chanced, I fell into his arm ;
    And then, by chance, remained, as might a spark
    Upon his mantle, lying on his arms ;
    Till something, what I know not, flung us both
    Out of the burning.   What is here for thanks?
    In Europe wine will urge to other deeds
    Braver than these.   The Templars, too, must ever
    Stand ready for the like, they must, we know,
    Just like to hounds a little better trained,
    Snatch men both from the water and the fire—
Templar. [*Who has looked on surprised and disturbed.*]   O Daja,
        Daja ! if at troubled moments
    My fretted spirit dealt with you unkindly,
    Why every folly that escaped my lips

Brought you to her?   That was too sharp revenge.
Ah, Daja! from this hour in happier light
Set me before her.

Daja.   But, sir Knight, I think
These little thorns you threw against her heart
Did you small damage there.

Recha.   What? you had trouble?
And were more avaricious of your cares
Than of your life?

Templar.   My sweet and gracious child !—
But all my soul's divided between eye
And ear ! Sure this was not the maid; no, no,
This was not she I drew from out the fire
For who that knew her had not dared the same?
Who   would   have   waited   for   me?—True—disguised—the terror
         [*Pause, in which, gazing at her, he seems to lose himself.*

Recha. You are not changed—I find you still the same
[*Pause; until she continues in order to interrupt his astonished gaze.*
Now tell us, Knight, where you have been so long?
Might I not almost ask—where you are now?

Templar. I am,—where mayhap I've no right to be.

Recha. Where you have been, perhaps where you've no right?
That is not well.

Templar.   On—on—what is the mountain?
On Sinai.

Recha.   Ah, upon Sinai?   Beautiful !
Now can I learn at last from trusty lips
Whether 'tis true . . .

Templar.   What? whether it is true
That still the self-same spot is to be seen
Where Moses stood with God, when . . .

Recha.   No, not that
Where'er he stood, 'twas before God; whereof
All that I need I know; but whether true
That this same height is far less hard to climb
Than to descend?   For, with all hills I've scaled,
As yet, 'twas ever just the opposite.
How, Knight, why turn away?   Would you not see me?

Templar. I turn from seeing you to hear you better.

Recha. More that I may not mark you when you laugh
At my simplicity, and how you smile,
When I no weightier questions ask of you

About this holiest of all holy hills.
Is it not so?
Templar.   Then I must look again
Into your eyes.   What? do you shut them fast?
Now stifle you your laughter?   What need I
To read in looks, in questionable looks,
What ears can tell me plainly—audibly
You speak—But silent now?   Ah, Recha!   Recha!
Sure he spoke truly " Know her only first ! "
Recha. Who has—by whom—that told you?
Templar.   " Only know
Her first "; it was your father's word to me,
Spoken of you.
Daja.   And not I, too, by chance?
And not I, too?
Templar.   But he, where is he, then?
Where is your father, then?   Is he perhaps
Still with the Sultan?
Recha.   Doubtless.
Templar.   Still, still there?
O me forgetful !   No, it cannot be
That he's there still.   Down by the cloister wall
He would await my coming; so 'twas fixed,
So settled when we parted.   Pardon me,
I hasten to bring him . . .
Daja.   That is my affair;
Rather, remain.   I bring him instantly.
Templar. Not so, not so.   He looks to meet me there,
Not you.   Besides he might—no man can tell—
So easily with Saladin have fallen
On disaccord—you do not know the Sultan—
Sure he's in danger if I go not.
Recha.   How?
Templar. Danger, danger, for me, for you, for him,
If in all speed I go not.

SCENE III

Recha and Daja

Recha.   What means it, Daja?
All in a moment !   Why?   What's come to him?
What drives him?

Daja.   Patience, let him be.   I think
'Tis no bad sign, perhaps.
Recha.   But sign of what?
Daja. Something takes place within him.   Something boils
Which yet must not boil over.   Leave him only.
'Tis your turn now.
Recha.   My turn; Daja?   You grow,
Like him, past comprehending.
Daja.   Soon you can
Requite him the disquiet he has caused you.
Be only not too hard, or too revengeful.
Recha. Of what you speak, perhaps yourself may know.
Daja. Are you already quite at rest again?
Recha. That am I; yes, that am I . . .
Daja.   Or at least
Confess your unrest gives more joy than pain,
And that you thank his unrest for the rest
That you enjoy.
Recha.   Then all unconsciously!
For what at most I might confess to you,
Were this that it surprises even myself
How such a calm within so suddenly
Can follow in the wake of such a tempest.
This nearer sight of him, his talk, his tone
Have—have . . .
Daja.   Left you quite satiate?
Recha.   No, not quite:
Nay, that I will not say; nay, far from that.
Daja. Only the first fierce hunger stilled.
Recha.   Well, yes.
If so you'll have it.
Daja.   I?   O, not at all.
Recha. To me he must be dear and ever dearer
As the days pass, even if my pulse change not
When I but hear his name; no more my heart
Beat faster, stronger when I think on him—
What am I babbling?   Come, dear Daja, come
Just once more to the window that looks out
Upon the palms.
Daja.   Ah! the fierce hunger, then,
Is not quite stilled.
Recha.   At least I'll see the palms
Yet once again, not only him amongst them.

Daja. This chill begins, I doubt, another fever—
Recha. What chill? I feel no chill. And verily
  See not less gladly what I see in calm.

SCENE IV

An audience chamber in Saladin's palace.   Saladin and Sittah

Saladin. [*In entering, speaks towards door.*]
  Soon as the Jew arrives, let him come here.
  He does not seem to hasten over-much.
Sittah. Perhaps not found at once, or gone abroad.
Saladin. O sister! sister!
Sittah.   Saladin, you act
  As if a battle were in prospect.
Saladin.   Yes;
  And that with weapons I have never practised.
  I have to pose and keep a careful guard;
  To lay traps, too, to stand upon smooth ice.
  When could I so? When studied I such tricks?
  Must do them now. Ay me, for what? for what?
  To fish for money! Money! to extort by dread
  The money of a Jew. To such mean arts
  Am I at last reduced, to gain myself
  The meanest of mean things.
Sittah.   The meanest thing,
  Too much despised, will take revenge, brother.
Saladin. Alas! 'Tis true! And if this Jew of ours
  Be wholly that good man, so wise, humane,
  The dervish painted once?
Sittah.   If such he be,
  Why, then we need no snares. The snare awaits
  Only the fearful, cautious, greedy Jew—
  The good and wise is ours without a snare.
  A pleasure you've before you, even to hear
  How such a man will speak, with what bold strength
  Either he'll snap the cord, or it may be
  With what shy prudence he'll slip past the net:
  This joy's before you.
Saladin.   True, and I await it
  As a new pleasure—
Sittah.   Why, then nothing further
  Can disconcert you. See, 'tis merely one

Out of the multitude; merely a Jew
Like other Jews : would not you be ashamed
To seem to him what he thinks all men are ?
And thinks the better, the humaner, man
The more a fool.

Saladin.   I must do wickedly,
You mean, so that the wicked may not think
Wickedly of me?

Sittah.   True, if wickedness
Be treating things according to their kind.

Saladin. Ah ! let a woman frame what scheme she will,
Trust her to fit it with a fair disguise.
If I but touch a ware so delicate,
It breaks in my coarse hand. For things like that
Whoso invented them must carry through,
With artful sleight and cunning craftiness.
Be it as 'twill ! I dance as best I can—
And think I'd rather do it ill than well.

Sittah. Trust not yourself too little. You will win
If you resolve it. Ever men like you
Would fain convince us 'tis the sword alone,
Only the sword that gained them victory—
The lion who went hunting with the fox,
Of his companion doubtless was ashamed,
Not of his cunning . . .

Saladin.   O, women are so happy
When they seduce men to their level. Go !
Go, Sittah ! I have learned my lesson quite.

Sittah. What, must I go ?

Saladin.   Surely you would not stay ?

Sittah. If not stay with you—in the presence here—
Then in the ante-chamber . . .

Saladin.   There to hearken ?
No, sister, no; if I may once insist.
Away ! the curtain rustles, he is here;
I'll see to it you have not long to wait.

[*While she leaves by one door, Nathan enters by the other ; and
     Saladin sits down.*

SCENE V

Saladin and Nathan

Saladin. Come nearer, Jew ! Approach ! Come closer yet—
  And fear not.
Nathan.   Fear be to your enemies.
Saladin. You are called Nathan ?
Nathan.   Yes.
Saladin.   Nathan the Wise ?
Nathan. No.
Saladin.   By yourself, O no, but by the people.
Nathan. May be ; the people !
Saladin.   Yet you think not, surely,
  I hold in scorn the judgment of the people ?
  Long have I wished that I might know the man
  Whom they call wise.
Nathan.   Ev'n if in mockery
  They named him ? Ev'n if to the people " wise "
  Should mean no more than prudent ? prudent but he
  Who reckons cleverly his own advantage—
Saladin. His true advantage, mean you, his true good ?
Nathan. Then verily were the man of selfish mind
  Most prudent. Then indeed were wise and prudent
  But one.
Saladin.   You seek to prove, what you would contradict.
  Men's true advantages the people know not.
  You know them, or at least have sought to know ;
  Have weighed them, pondered them ; and this itself
  Already makes the wise man.
Nathan.   Which no man
  But thinks he is.
Saladin.   Enough of modesty,
  Too much of that, when one expects dry reason,
  Can make one sick.   [*Springs up.*
                    Let's come to business.
  But—but—uprightly, Jew ! In honesty !
Nathan. I will so serve you, Sultan, to be deemed
  Worthy your constant custom.
Saladin.   Serve me, how ?
Nathan. The best of all I have, be at your service
  And at the lowest price.
Saladin.   Of what speak you ?

    Not, surely, of your wares?   Chaffer and higgle
    My sister may.   (That's for the listener !)
    I have no use for merchants and their goods.
Nathan. Then without doubt you will desire to know
    Whatever on my way I chanced across
    Or marked of your foes' arms—if openly—
Saladin. Even of that I nothing ask of you.
    Of that I know already all I need;
    In short—
Nathan.   Command me, Sultan.
Saladin.   I desire
    Instruction of you in another field,
    Quite other; and to use your wisdom there.
    Since you are wise, tell me as to a friend,
    What faith, what law, have satisfied you best.
Nathan. Sultan, I am a Jew—
Saladin.   A Muslim I.
    The Christian stands between us.   Of these three
    Religions only one can be the true one.
    A man like you will not consent to stay
    Where'er the accident of birth has cast him;
    Or if he stays, 'twill be of 's own election
    As insight, reason, choice of best things, prompt him.
    Come, then, impart to me your insight : let me hear
    The moving reasons : since for this high quest
    Time was not granted me.   Tell me the choice,
    Tell me the grounds—of course, in confidence—
    Which fixed the choice, that I may make it mine.
    How now !   You start, you weigh me with your eye.
    It well may be that of all Sultans yet
    I am the first inspired by such a whim,
    Which yet methinks is no unworthy one
    Even for a Sultan.   Not so?   Then speak out !
    Speak out.   Or would you have a minute's space
    To ponder it?   Good; I will give it you—
    (Has she been listening?   I will catch her out :
    And hear how I have managed.)   Ponder now;
    Ponder it swiftly.   Presently I'm here.
    [*Goes into the ante-chamber, to which Sittah had betaken herself.*

SCENE VI

Nathan, alone

Nathan. Hm ! Hm ! Marvellous ! What's to happen now ?
  What does the Sultan want ? I came prepared
  For money, and he asks for truth—for truth !
  And wants it paid in ready cash, as though
  The truth were coinage. Yea, even as if
  It were old coinage that was told by weight.
  That might pass, truly ! But such new-coined pieces
  That owe the die their value, must be counted.
  As money into sack, does one sweep truth
  Into one's head ? Who, then, is here the Jew,
  I or the Sultan ? Might he not, perhaps,
  Ask for the truth in truth ? 'Twere a mean thing
  Even the suspicion that he used truth
  As a mere trap to catch me. That were mean ?
  Too mean ? What is too mean for great men's use ?
  True, true. See how he drives the door and storms
  The house ! Surely one knocks and listens first
  When one comes as a friend. So, warily
  I'll walk ! But how, but what ? Wholly to be
  The common Jew, that will not serve me here,
  Still less not to be Jew at all. For if
  Not Jew, he well might ask me, Then why not
  A Mussulman ? That's it ! And that can save me !
  Not children only, we can feed men too
  With fables. Ah ! he comes. Well, let him come !

SCENE VII

Saladin and Nathan

Saladin. (The field is clear now.) Not too soon, I hope,
  Do I return to you ? You are at end
  With your deliberation. Come, then, speak !
  Not a soul hears us.
Nathan.   All the world may listen
  And welcome.
Saladin.   Confident, so confident
  Is Nathan of his cause ? Ha ! such I name
  A wise man ! Who dissembles never truth

But stakes all for it—body, life, and soul.
Nathan. Yes, truly, when 'tis needful and availeth.
Saladin. Henceforward I can hope with right to wear
  A title of mine, reformer of the world
  And of the law.
Nathan.   In sooth, a lovely title !
  Yet, Sultan, ere I trust me to your hands,
  Perhaps you will permit me to relate
  An ancient tale?
Saladin.   Why not? I was from childhood
  Lover of tales, well told.
Nathan.   Ah ! ah ! *Well told.*
  That's more than I can claim.
Saladin.   Come, why again
  So proudly modest? Come, the tale ! the tale !
Nathan. There lived a man in a far Eastern clime
  In hoar antiquity, who from the hand
  Of his most dear beloved received a ring
  Of priceless estimate. An opal 'twas
  Which spilt a hundred lovely radiances
  And had a magic power, that whoso wore it,
  Trusting therein, found grace with God and man.
  What wonder therefore that this man o' the East
  Let it not from his finger, and took pains
  To keep it to his household for all time.
  Thus he bequeathed the jewel to the son
  Of all his sons he loved best, and provided
  That he in turn bequeath it to the son
  Who was to him the dearest ; evermore
  The best-beloved, without respect of birth,
  By right o' the ring alone should be the head,
  The house's prince. You understand me, Sultan.
Saladin. I understand : continue !
Nathan.   Well, this ring,
  From son to son descending, came at last
  Unto a father of three sons, who all
  To him, all three, were dutiful alike,
  And whom, all three, in natural consequence,
  He loved alike. Only from time to time
  Now this ; now that one ; now the third, as each
  Might be alone with him, the other twain
  Not sharing his o'erflowing heart, appeared
  Worthiest the ring ; and then, piously weak,

He promised it to each. And so things went
Long as they could. But dying hour drawn near
Brought the good father to perplexity.
It pained him, the two sons, trusting his word,
Should thus be wounded. What was he to do?
Quickly he sends for an artificer,
To make him on the model of his ring
Two others, bidding spare nor cost nor pains
To make them in all points identical;
And this the artist did. When they are brought
Even the father scarcely can distinguish
His pattern-ring. So, full of joy, he calls
His sons, and each one to him separately;
And gives to each son separately his blessing,
Gives each his ring; and dies. Still hear you, Sultan?

Saladin. [*Who has turned away perplexed.*] I hear, I hear—Only
    bring you the tale
To speedy end. Is 't done?

Nathan.   The tale is finished.
For what still follows, any man may guess.
Scarce was the father dead, but each one comes
And shows his ring, and each one claims to be
True prince o' the house. Vainly they search, strive, argue,
The true ring was not proved or provable—
       [*After a pause, during which he waits the Sultan's reply.*
Almost as hard to prove as to us now
What the true creed is.

Saladin.   How? is this to be
The answer to my question?

Nathan.   Nay, it merely
Makes my excuse that I don't trust myself
Exactly to distinguish twixt the rings
The Sire with express purpose had bade make
So that no probing might distinguish them—

Saladin. The rings ! You play with me ! It was my thought
That the religions I have named to you
Were plainly, easily distinguishable,
Down even to clothing, down to meat and drink !

Nathan. Only not so in questions of foundation—
For base not all their creeds on history,
Written or handed down? And history
Must be received in faith implicitly.
Is't not so? Then on whom rest we this faith

Implicit, doubting not?   Surely on our own?
Them from whose blood we spring?   Surely on them
Who from our childhood gave us proofs of love?
Who never have deceived us, saving when
'Twere happier, safer so to be deceived?
How, then, shall I my fathers less believe
Than you your own? or in the other case,
Can I demand that you should give the lie
To your forefathers, that mine be not gainsaid?
And, yet again, the same holds of the Christians.
Is't not so?

Saladin.   (By high God !   The man is right;
I must be dumb.)

Nathan.   Then let us come again
Back to our rings.   As we have said—the sons
Appealed to law; and swore before the Judge
Out of the father's hand, immediately,
To have received the ring—and this was true—
After for long he had the promise sure
One day to enjoy the privilege of the ring—
And this no less was true.   Each cried the father
Could not be false towards him, and ere he might
Let such suspicion stain him, must believe,
Glad as he were to think the best of them,
His brothers played him false, and he should soon
Expose the traitors, justify himself.

Saladin. And now, the Judge?   I'm waiting, fain to hear
What you will make him say.   What was his verdict?

Nathan. Thus spake the Judge : Bring me the father here
To witness; I will hear him; and if not
Leave then my judgment seat.   Think you this chair
Is set for reading of riddles?   Do you wait,
Expecting the true ring to open mouth?
Yet halt !   I hear, the genuine ring possesses
The magic power to bring its wearer love
And grace with God and man.   That must decide;
For never can the false rings have this virtue.
Well, then; say whom do two of you love best?
Come, speak !   What !   silent?   Is the rings' effect
But backward and not outward?   Is it so
That each one loves himself most?   Then I judge
All three of you are traitors and betrayed !

Your rings all three are false.   The genuine ring
Perchance the father lost, and to replace it
And hide the loss, had three rings made for one.
Saladin. O, splendid ! splendid !
Nathan.   So, went on the Judge,
You may not seek my counsel, but my verdict ;
But go !   My counsel is, you take the thing
Exactly as it lies.   If each of you
Received his ring from his good father's hand,
Then each of you believe his ring the true one—
'Tis possible the father would not suffer
Longer the one ring tyrannise in 's house,
Certain, he loved all three, and equal loved,
And would not injure two to favour one.
Well, then, let each one strive most zealously
To show a love untainted by self-care,
Each with his might vie with the rest to bring
Into the day the virtue of the jewel
His finger wears, and help this virtue forth
By gentleness, by spirit tractable,
By kind deeds and true piety towards God ;
And when in days to come the magic powers
Of these fair rings among your children's children
Brighten the world, I call you once again,
After a thousand thousand years are lapsed,
Before this seat of judgment.   On that day
A wiser man shall sit on it and speak.
Depart !   So spake the modest Judge.
Saladin.   God !   God !
Nathan. Saladin, if you feel yourself to be
This wiser promised man . . .
Saladin. [*Who rushes towards him, seizes his hand, which to the
    end he does not release.*] I, dust ?   I, nothing ?
O God !
Nathan.   What would you, Saladin ?
Saladin.   My good Nathan !
The thousand thousand years of the great Judge
Are not yet up.   Not mine His judgment throne.
Go !   but abide my friend.
Nathan.   Had Saladin
Further no word for me ?
Saladin.   Not anything.

Nathan. Nothing?
Saladin.   No, not a jot—Why ask you this?
Nathan. I should have begged an opportunity
    To proffer a petition.
Saladin.   Need you then
    An opportunity?   My friend, speak on !
Nathan. I come from a wide round, whereon my task
    Was gathering in of debts.   Almost I have
    Too much of ready coin.   The time begins
    To assume the look of storm.   I hardly know
    Where safely to bestow it, and have thought,
    Seeing how much this coming war will ask,
    That you, perchance, might use a portion.
Saladin. [*Looking him in the eyes steadily.*]   Nathan !
    I will not ask whether before this hour
    Al-Hafi has been with you, nor enquire
    Whether a suspicion prompts you to this offer
    Of your freewill . . .
Nathan.   What mean you, a suspicion?
Saladin. Yes, I deserve it.   Pardon.   For what helps it?
    I must confess, I had it in my mind—
Nathan. Not surely to request the same of me?
Saladin. Yea, verily.
Nathan.   Thus both of us were helped !
    But that I cannot send you all my means
    The Templar gives occasion : sure you know him.
    A heavy obligation must I meet
    To him before all else.
Saladin.   A Templar, what?
    Surely you will not aid with your good gold
    My worst of enemies?
Nathan.   I speak of one,
    One only, him whose life you spared.
Saladin.   Ah what
    You mind me of—Most strange !   I had forgot
    The stripling.   Know you him?   Where is he lodged?
Nathan. Where lodged?   Why, know you not how much of
    blessing
    Fell to my lot, even through your grace done to him?
    'Twas he, at risk of his new-gifted life,
    That saved my daughter from the flaming walls.
Saladin. He? did he that?   Truly, he looked like that—
    This surely had my brother likewise done,

Whom he so much resembles.   Is he still
In the Holy City?   Bring him here to me.
I've told so many things to my dear sister
Of this her brother, whom she never knew,
That I must needs show her his counterfeit!
Go, fetch him!   See, of one good action, tho'
It was of simple passion born, so many
Other good deeds flow forth!   Go fetch him hither.
Nathan. [*Letting go of Saladin's hand.*] Straightway!   And of
    the rest, the other matter,
  Does it, too, stand?   [*Exit.*
Saladin.   Ah, had my sister stayed
  To hearken!   Quick, to her!   to her!   For how
  Can all be told that now I have to tell?
                                    [*Exit from the other side.*

Scene VIII

*Under the Palms, in neighbourhood of the cloister, where the
        Templar waits for Nathan.*

Templar. [*Walks up and down, struggling with himself, till he
    breaks out.*] Here halts the victim, weary and foredone—
  'Tis well!   I would not know or see more clear
  What in me passes, and would not foresee
  What yet will pass.   Enough!   I've fled in vain,
  In vain!   And yet I could nought else but fly.
  Well, come what will; the stroke fell far too swiftly
  To be escaped; though hard and long I struggled
  To come from under.   To see her, whom yet
  To see I had but small desire, to see her
  And the resolve never to lose her from
  Mine eyes, and yet what speak I of resolve?
  Resolve is plan, is act, while I but suffer,
  Suffer, not act—to see her and to feel
  Bound to her by strong cords, bound up with her,
  Was one; is one: from her to live apart
  Is thought unthinkable and were my death,
  And wheresoever after death we are,
  'Twould be even there my death—Is this, then, love?
  So the Knight Templar loves assuredly,
  The Christian loves the Jewish maid, in truth:

Hm ! what of that ?   In this the Holy Land,
And hereby holy to me evermore,
I have sloughed off a world of prejudices,—
What will my Order say ?   As Templar Knight
I'm dead, was dead to them from that self hour
Which made me prisoner to Saladin,—
The head which Saladin restored to me,
Was it my old ?—'tis new ! and clear of all
The lies and stuff they babbled to it once,
Wherewith 'twas slaved ; and 'tis a better one,
Agreeing more with my paternal clime,
I feel it so in truth.   For it begins
To think even as my father must have thought
Under those skies, unless those tales be false
They tell of him—Tales ? tales, yet credible
Which never seemed to me more credible
Than here they seem where I but run the risk
Of stumbling, where he fell.   Ah, where he fell ?
I'll rather fall with men, than stand with children.
Sure, his example makes me confident
Of his approval.   Whose approval else crave I ?
For Nathan's ?   Furtherance more than approval
Will not be wanting there.   The noble Jew !
Who yet desires not to seem more than Jew !
Here comes he hastening, gladness in his eyes.
Whoe'er came otherwise from Saladin ?
Ho !   Nathan !

Scene IX

Nathan and the Templar

Nathan.   How ?   Is 't you ?
Templar.   It has been long,
Your converse with the Sultan.
Nathan.   Not so long ;
For on my way to him I was much hindered.
Ah, truly, Curd, the man matches his fame.
His fame is his mere shadow.   But now first
I have a thing to say that will not wait.
Templar. What ?
Nathan. He would speak with you and bids you come
Without delay.   Give me your company
Now to my house, where first I must procure

A something for his hand, and then we go.
Templar. Over your threshold, Nathan, willingly
  I pass no more.
Nathan.   Meanwhile you have been there
  Already and spoken with her.   Come then, tell me
  How Recha pleases you?
Templar.   Beyond all speech!
  Only—to see her more—never will I!
  Never, except I have your promise here
  That I may see her ever.
Nathan.   How will you
  I should interpret that?
Templar. [*After a short pause falling on his neck.*] My father!
    father!
Nathan. Young man!
Templar.   Not son?   I pray you, Nathan!
Nathan. Beloved youth!
Templar.   Not son?   I pray you, Nathan!
  Beseech you by the tenderest ties of nature!
  O let not later bonds come in between!
  Let it suffice to be a man!   nor drive
  Me from you!
Nathan.   Dear, dear friend! . . .
Templar.   And son?
  Not son?   Even not then, if gratitude
  Has paved love's way to your loved daughter's heart?
  Not even then, if both hearts only waited
  A father's gracious sign to melt in one?—
  You're silent.
Nathan.   You surprise, you startle me,
  Young knight.
Templar.   Surprise you, Nathan, startle you
  With your own inmost thoughts?   You'll not disown them
  Because my lips have spoke them?   I surprise you?
Nathan. There's something I must know—who was this Stauffen
  You claim as sire?
Templar.   What say you, Nathan? what?
  Is curiosity, then, all you feel
  At such a moment?
Nathan.   Nay, not so, for, look you,
  I myself knew, knew well in earlier years
  A Stauffen, his name Conrad.
Templar.   Well, what think you?

That same name bore my father.
Nathan.   Verily?
Templar. Myself am so called after him; for Curd
    Is Conrad.
Nathan.   Even so, my Conrad could not be
    Your father. For my Conrad was like you,
    A Templar, and unwedded.
Templar.   O, for that!
Nathan. How?
Templar. O, for that he still might be my father.
Nathan. Now you jest.
Templar.   And you, you take it
    Quite too precisely. Say, what were it then?
    Something of bastard or side-blow perhaps!
    Granted, the wound is not to be despised—
    Absolve me of my proof of ancestry,
    And in my turn I will absolve you yours.
    Not truly that I touch with taint of doubt
    Your family tree. That, God forbid! you could
    Uprear it leaf by leaf to Abraham.
    And beyond that I'll build it up myself,
    Attesting it by oath.
Nathan.   Now you grow bitter.
    Have I deserved it? Think you I detracted
    Aught from your worth?—But yet, I will not take
    For a word dropped, offence. No more's to speak.
Templar. Really? No more to speak. O, then, forgive me!
Nathan. Come with me only, come!
Templar.   But tell me whither?
    Not to your house? That never; that I cannot!—
    There's fire there. I will await you here. Go you!
    If I see her again; then many times
    I still shall see her. But if not, why then
    I've seen her far too often . . .
Nathan.   I shall hasten.

Scene X

The Templar, and soon after Daja

Templar. Enough and more. The brain of human-kind
    In grasp is almost limitless, yet often
    Suddenly fills to bursting with a trifle!

It matters nothing, nothing; let it be
Even full of what it will—Let patience work;
The spirit soon compounds the turgid stuff,
Makes itself room; order and light return.
Do I then love for the first time? Or what
I once called love, was it not love at all?
Or is love only what I suffer now?

Daja. [*Who has slipped in from the side.*] Sir Knight!   sir
   Knight!

Templar.   Who calls? Ha, Daja, you?

Daja. I have slipped past him : but where you now stand,
   He still might see us. Come, behind this tree.

Templar. What is it? Why so secret? Tell me why.

Daja. What brings me to you, does concern a secret,
   A secret truly; more, a double one—
   The one only know I, the other you
   Alone can know. How if we made exchange?
   Trust me with yours, then I'll trust you with mine.

Templar. With pleasure, readily; if I may know
   First what you think is mine. But out of yours
   That surely will appear. Only begin.

Daja. O, that would never do; no, no, sir Knight;
   You first; I'll follow; be assured that mine,
   My secret cannot help you by a jot,
   Have I not yours before it. Only quick!
   If I but win it by my questioning,
   Then you've confided nothing. Then my secret
   Remains my secret, and your own escapes.
   Still, you poor soldier! That you men should think,
   O credulous men! that you can keep such secrets
   From us poor women.

Templar.   Secrets we ourselves
   Often don't know we have.

Daja.   That well may be
   Then, to be sure, I'll so far act the friend
   To acquaint you with yourself. Say, what then made you
   So all at once vanish in cloud, and leave
   Your friends deserted? that you do not now
   Return with Nathan? Recha, has she so little
   Worked on you? How? or, should I ask, so much?
   So much! so much! Instruct me how to know
   The fluttering of the poor ensnaréd bird
   Limed to the tree! In brief, confess me here

That you do love her, love her even to madness,
And I will tell——
Templar.   To madness? Verily;
Your insight is astounding.
Daja.   Grant me then
Only the love; I'll let you off the madness.
Templar. Since, I suppose, that may be taken for granted?
A Templar-Knight to love a Jewish girl! . . .
Daja. Truly there seems but little sense in that—
And yet at whiles there's more of sense in things
Than we surmise; nor were 't incredible
The Christ should lead us to Himself by ways
The wise man of himself might never find.
Templar. Your words are solemn. (Well, if Providence
Were put in place of Christ, were she not right?)
You breed in me a curiosity
I never knew before.
Daja.   O, 'tis the land
Of miracles!
Templar.   (Well,—the miraculous.
How can it otherwise? Seeing all the nations
Crowd themselves here together.) My dear Daja,
Consider it confessed—what you desire:
That I do love her, hardly understand
How I shall live without her; that . . .
Daja. Truly, sir Knight? Here pledge your oath to me
To take her for your own, to save my Recha,
Here, while life lasts; yonder, eternally.
Templar. And how? How can I? Can I swear to do
What stands not in my power?
Daja.   But in your power
It stands. For by a single word I bring it
Within your power.
Templar.   So that not even her father
Could hinder or obstruct?
Daja.   Eh, Father—what Father!
Her father *must* agree.
Templar.   Must, Daja? Must?
Sure, he's not fallen amongst robbers yet!
There is no *must* for him.
Daja.   I tell you truth;
He must in the end consent, and gladly too.
Templar. Must, must, and gladly. Daja, how if I say

That I myself already tried to touch
This chord within him?
Daja.   And he would not accord?
Templar. No! No; with such a discord he joined in
As sharply wounded me.
Daja.   What say you? What!
That you had shown him, even in shadow merely,
Your love for her, and he did not leap up
For joy? but frostily withdrew, and muttered
Of difficulties?
Templar.   So it was.
Daja.   Then I
Will not reflect a single moment more—   [*Pause.*
Templar. And yet—you *are* reflecting?
Daja.   All things else
Prove Nathan kind—myself, how much I owe him!
And now he will not listen! O, God knows
My very heart bleeds in me, so to force him.
Templar. I pray you, Daja, free me once for all
From these uncertainties. But if you are
Yourself unsure, whether what you intend
Should good or bad, shameful or worthy praise,
Be called—then, silence! I'll forget
That you have ought to keep unspoken.
Daja.   Rather
That stings me not to speak. Then know—our Recha
Is not a Jewess; is,—she is a Christian.
Templar. So? Wish you joy! Was the delivery hard?
Shrink you not from the travail! O go on,
Go on with zeal to populate the skies,
If you can't earth!
Daja. How, Knight? Deserves my news this mockery?
That Recha is a Christian gives no joy
To you, a Christian and a Templar Knight
Who loves her?
Templar.   Most especially, as she's
A Christian of your making.
Daja.   So you think?
Well, let it be! But no, for I would see
Him who will make her convert! 'Tis her fortune
To have been long, what now she can't become.
Templar. Explain, or—go!
Daja.   She is a Christian child,

And born of Christian parents; is baptized . . .
Templar. [*Abruptly.*] And Nathan?
Daja.   Not her father!
Templar.   Nathan not
  Her father? Know you what you speak?
Daja.   The truth,
  Which many a time has cost me tears of blood.
  No, he is not her father . . .
Templar.   And had her
  Only brought up as a daughter? had the child,
  The Christian child, brought up as Jewish maid?
Daja. 'Tis certain.
Templar.   And she knew not of her birth?
  Had never learnt of him that she a Christian
  Was born and not a Jewess?
Daja.   Never, never!
Templar. And he not merely had brought up the child
  In this delusion, but has left the maiden
  In this deception still?
Daja.   Alas!
Templar.   But—Nathan,
  The wise, good Nathan has allowed himself
  To falsify the voice of nature thus,
  Thus misdirect the outpouring of a heart
  Which, left to itself, would take quite other ways?
  Daja, you have indeed confided here
  A weighty matter—which involves great issues—
  Which quite confounds me—which puts me in doubt
  What I must do. So give me time. Then, go!
  He passes here anon. He might surprise us.
  Therefore, go, Daja!
Daja.   It would be my death!
Templar. Speak with him now I cannot. If you meet him,
  Say only that we two shall presently
  Meet in the Sultan's chamber.
Daja.   But betray not
  To him what you have heard.—This does but give
  The last seal to the matter, takes away
  All scruples from you when you think of Recha—
  And if thereon you carry her to Europe,
  Let me not stay behind. I conjure you—
Templar. I lay that on my heart; but, leave me now.

ACT IV—SCENE I

SCENE : *In the cloisters of the convent*

The Friar and soon thereafter the Templar

Friar. Well, well; of course the Patriarch is right !
  Although as yet no single enterprise
  He laid upon my shoulders has success.
  Why does he choose only such jobs for me ?
  I have no craving for these artful games,
  I am not made for the persuader's part,
  Nor wish to stick my nose in everything
  Or play the meddler. Am I, then, for this,
  Desiring to be separate, for myself
  Alone, only the more by others' will
  To be the more entangled ?
Templar. [*Entering hastily.*] My good friar !
  We meet again. A long time I have sought you.
Friar. Sought me, my lord ?
Templar.   Have you forgotten me ?
Friar. No, no ! I only thought that never in my life
  Should I so come to meet my lord again :
  Prayed the good God I might not. For God knows
  How loathsome was the errand laid on me,
  He knows whether I wished an open ear
  To find for it ; and knows how I rejoiced
  That you so spurned, without a moment's thought,
  What misbecame your knighthood. I was glad ;
  But things go all awry ; we meet once more !
Templar. You know, then, why I come, though I myself
  Can hardly guess.
Friar.   Perhaps, have thought it over,
  Perhaps discovered that the Patriarch
  Was after all i' the right ; that pelf and honour
  His project might ensure you, that a foe
  Remains a foe, even if he seven times
  Had proved our angel. So with flesh and blood
  You have ta'en counsel, and now come again
  To offer service. God !
Templar.   No, my good man !
  Be calm ; for this I come not ; not for this
  Would I consult the Patriarch. What I thought
  G 843

On that point think I still, and would not lose
For anything the world holds that regard
Of which a man so honest, pious, kind
Has deemed me worthy.   No, I have but come
To beg the Patriarch's counsel . . .

Friar.   You—of him
A Knight, consult a—priest.   [*Looking timidly round.*

Templar.   Indeed, the affair
Is rather priestly.

Friar.   Yet you will not find
The priest consult a knight, however knightly
The business be.

Templar.   'Tis a priest's privilege
To go astray, a privilege none of us
Envies him much.   In truth were it myself,
Solely myself in question, and myself
Solely to answer where were need of Patriarchs?
But there be things I would do faultily
By others' counsel rather than do well
By my sole will.   Besides, I now perceive
Religion too is party, and who thinks
Himself therein no partisan, that man
Is in himself a party.   This being so,
'Tis right it should be.

Friar.   That I speak not of,
Not knowing if I understand my lord.

Templar. And yet! (let's see what is 't I really want.
Decree or counsel?   Simple counsel or refined?)
I thank you, friar; thanks for your wise word.
Why Patriarch?   Be you my Patriarch?
I'll rather ask the Christian in the Patriarch
Than Patriarch in Christian.   Now the question—
The matter is . . .

Friar.   No further, sir, no further!
To what good end?   Surely my lord mistakes me.
Who knows too much, has the more care; for me
One care's enough and more.   O good! see yonder,
There comes, for my relief, the priest himself.
Stay where you stand.   He has already seen you.

SCENE II

*The Patriarch, who comes up with priestly pomp by the one cloister ;
and the foregoing*

Templar. I would avoid him.   He's not at all my man !
  A portly, rosy, and most friendly prelate !
  And what a splendour !
Friar.   You should only see him
  Going to court ; comes from a sick man now.
Templar. How Saladin must be abashed before him !
Patriarch. [*Approaching, makes a sign to the friar.*] Here !
    Surely that is the Templar.   What would he ?
Friar. I know not.
Patriarch. [*Approaching him, whilst the friar and retinue retire.*]
              Well, sir Knight !   Am much rejoiced
  To see the brave young man !   Eh, you are still
  A stripling.   Now, by help of God, therefrom
  Something might grow.
Templar.   Scarce more, my reverend lord,
  Than what already is, and mayhap less.
Patriarch. I hope at least that such a pious knight,
  For the good and glory of dear Christendom
  And God's own cause, may flourish many years !
  That surely will not fail, if, as is due,
  Young valour hearken to the ripened wisdom
  Of age ?   How else can I now serve my friend ?
Templar. With what to youth is wanting, that's with counsel.
Patriarch. O willingly !   if counsel but be taken.
Templar. And yet, not blindly ?
Patriarch.   Who could ask it ?   No,
  For verily none should cease to use his reason,
  God-given reason, in its proper sphere.
  Mark you, its proper sphere, not everywhere !
  O no !   As, for example, when God deigns,
  By one of His good angels—that's to say,
  Some servant of His word—suggest to us
  A means, in some uncommon way of action,
  The weal of Christendom and His great Church
  To further and establish, who shall dare
  Question, by reason, the decree of Him
  Who hath created reason, and to test
  The eternal law o' the Glory of the Heavens

By the small rules of what vain men call honour?
Of this enough, enough. What is it, then,
Whereon my lord now seeks our counsel?

Templar.   This :
Suppose, most reverend Father, that a Jew
An only child possessed, a little maid,
Whom he had reared up with the utmost care
And in all kindness, loved as his own soul,
And who most piously returned his love,
And now 'twere whispered unto one of us
This maiden was no daughter of the Jew ;
That he had chosen her in her infancy,—
Bought, stolen—what you will, and that we learned
The maiden was a Christian, and baptized ;
The Jew had only reared her as a Jewess,
Let her remain a Jewess and his daughter ;—
Say, reverend Father, what were here to do?

Patriarch. I shudder. Yet before all else my lord explain
Whether the case he pictures is a fact
Or a hypothesis. That is to say,
Whether my lord has but imagined this
Or whether it has happened, and goes on.

Templar. I thought that were all one; I had but wished
To know your Reverence' mind.

Patriarch.   One ! look you, sir,
⌈How wide the arrogant human intellect
⌊In spiritual things can err—Sir, no, no !
For if the case proposed be but a sport
O' the brain, it is not worth the taking pains
To think it out in earnest. I leave the case
To theatres, where oft such arguments
Of *pro et con* are with the crowd's applause
Handled at large. But if my lord have now
No such stage-trifles in his mind, and if
The case is fact, and in our diocese,
Even in our city of Jerusalem,
This thing has happened—then indeed—

Templar.   What then ?

Patriarch. Then were the Jew without a day's delay
To undergo the penalty which laws
Both Papal and Imperial denounce
For such an outrage, such a heinous crime.

Templar.   And that ?

Patriarch. These laws I speak of for the Jew
   Who leads a Christian to apostasy
   Appoint the stake, the fire . . .
Templar.   What, the dread flame?
Patriarch. And how much more to that most wicked Jew
   Who tears by violence a poor Christian child
   Out of the bond of baptism.   Is not all
   We do to children violence?   That's to say,
   Of course, excepting what the Church may do
   With children.
Templar.   But say only if the child
   Save for the Jew's compassion, were but fallen
   A prey to hunger and to wretchedness?
Patriarch. It matters not !   The Jew must burn.   For better
   It were fallen here to utter misery
   Than be saved thus to its eternal loss.
   Besides, how dares the Jew to forestall God?
   Sure, without him God can save whom He will.
Templar. And also, I should think, in spite of him.
Patriarch. No matter !   He must burn.
Templar.   That touches me
   To the very heart !   The rather that they say
   He has not brought the girl up in his faith
   So much as in no faith, and taught her of God
   No more, no less, than satisfies the reason.
Patriarch. No matter !   He must burn, and were indeed
   On this one count worthy to burn three times.
   What !   Let a child grow up without a faith?
   What !   the great duty of Belief to leave
   Untaught to children?   That is wickedness !
   I wonder much, sir Knight, that you yourself . . .
Templar. Most reverend lord, for what remains, I leave it,
   If God will, to the confessional . . . (*is going*).
Patriarch.   What ! not now
   Render account to me?   The criminal,
   The Jew you'll leave unnamed?   Not now and here
   Produce him?   Well, I think I know the way !
   I'll straightway seek the Sultan.   Saladin,
   In virtue of the sworn Capitulation,
   Which bears his seal, he must, he must protect us ;
   Protect us in all rights and in all rules
   To our most holy faith and Church belonging.
   Praise be to God !   we have th' Original,

We have his hand and seal.   Yes, it is ours !
Easily, too, I'll make him understand
How perilous 'tis even for the State
To believe nothing !   Since all civil bonds
Are loosed, are torn asunder, when men dare
Have no belief . . . Away with such an outrage !
Templar. Pity, I cannot now with better leisure
Enjoy the wise discourse.   I'm called to Saladin.
Patriarch. Indeed? . . . Well,   now. . . . Now   verily. . . .
     Then, then. . . .
Templar. I will prepare the Sultan for your coming
If that be pleasing to your Reverence.
Patriarch. Oh !—ah !—I know my lord enjoys high favour
With Saladin !   I beg but to be named
With my devotion to him.   I am driven
Evermore purely by the zeal of God.
Where I exceed, it is for Him.   But will
My lord yet weigh the matter?   True, is't not,
Sir Knight, that question of the Jew we spoke of
Was nothing but a problem?   That's to say—
Templar. A problem.   [*Exit.*
Patriarch.   Which I notwithstanding mean
To fathom deeper, even to the ground ;
Yet that, again, were really a commission
For Brother Bonafides.   Here, my son !
                         [*He speaks in going off to the friar.*

Scene III

*A room in Saladin's Palace, into which a number of sacks are
brought by slaves, and placed side by side on the floor*

Saladin, and soon thereafter Sittah

Saladin. [*Coming in.*] Well, truly now, there seems no end of
     that.
   Is there still much to come?
A Slave.   Still quite the half.
Saladin. Bear what remains to Sittah.   Where's Al-Hafi?
Let him take charge of these forthwith.   Or shall I
Send them to the old man's stronghold in the hills?
Here 'twill slip through my fingers.   Though indeed
One does grow hard at last, and in the end
'Twill cost some art to extort one coin from me

    Until at least the moneys out of Egypt
    Come to these lands, the destitute must find
    Elsewhere their bread. Alms at the Sepulchre,
    These must go on, or all the Christian pilgrims
    Withdraw with empty hands. If only I . . .
Sittah. What's this? What does this money here with me?
Saladin. Therewith repay yourself; the overplus
    Lay by for after needs.
Sittah.   And is not yet
    Old Nathan with the Templar come to you?
Saladin. He seeks him everywhere.
Sittah.   See what I've found
    In looking through my trinkets.

                    [*Showing him a small picture.*
Saladin.   Ha ! my brother !
    That's he, 'tis he ! *Was* he, *was* he, alas !
    Ah brave young hero, whom I lost so soon !
    My brother dear, wert thou beside me still,
    What had I not accomplished ! Give me, Sittah,
    The picture; look, I know it instantly;
    He gave it to thy elder sister, Lilla,
    One morning when she would not let him go,
    Holding him close embraced. 'Twas the last day,
    The last that he rode out. I let him ride,
    Alone, alas ! And Lilla died of grief,
    And never would forgive me, that alone
    I let him ride away. He came no more.
Sittah. Poor brother !
Saladin.   But let be ! God's will be done !
    Once we shall all ride out and come no more.
    Besides—who knows? It is not death alone
    Frustrates our plans. He had his enemies,
    And many a time the strongest man succumbs
    Like the most weak. Be 't as it may with him ;
    I must compare the picture with this Templar,
    And see perhaps how much my phantasy
    Deceived me.
Sittah.   'Twas for that I brought it. Yet
    Give it to me ! 'Tis for a woman's eye
    To judge such niceties.
Saladin. [*To an usher who enters.*] Speak, who is there?
    The Templar? Let him enter !
Sittah.   I'll sit here,

Out of your way, nor let my questioning looks
Disturb him.

[Sits aside on a sofa and lets her veil fall.

Saladin.　　　　Well, 'tis well! (Now, for his voice!
How will that prove?　The tone of Assad's voice
Sleeps in my memory still, and can awake!)

Scene IV

The Templar and Saladin

Templar. Dare I, thy prisoner, Sultan . . .
Saladin.　　　　　　　Prisoner?
To whom I make the gift of life, shall I
Not also give him freedom?
Templar.　　　　　　What fits thee
To do, befits me best to hear, and not
Presume beforehand.　But yet, Sultan, thanks,
Especial thanks to thee, for granted life
Accords not with my nature or condition.
'Tis at thy service always.
Saladin.　　　　　Only use it
Never against me.　One more pair of hands
Truly I need not grudge my enemy.
But one heart more like thine I cannot spare.
For in no point am I deceived in thee,
Young hero!　Body and soul thou art my Assad.
See! I might ask thee, where this world of time
Thou hast been hiding?　In what cave hast slept?
In what a Guinistan by what kind nurturer
This flower has all this age been kept so fresh?
See!　I might call to your remembrance all
We did long since in company, the woods we roamed,
The gallops o'er the free uncumber'd ground,
I might upbraid thee for that thou hast kept
A secret from me, stolen an adventure from me:
Yes, so I might, if only thee I saw
And not myself as well.　Now, let it be!
Of this sweet dream remains so much of truth
That in my autumn there blooms up again
An Assad here.　Knight, shall we have it so?
Templar. Ay!　Whatsoever comes to me from thee,
Be't what it will, is welcome to my soul.

Saladin. Let us try that forthwith; wilt thou abide
  With me, about me? As Mussulman, as Christian,
  All one! in the white cloak, or gaberdine,
  In turban or in helmet, as thou pleasest,
  All one to me! I never have desired
  That one bark grow on all trees of the wood.
Templar. Else hardly should'st thou be what now thou art,
  The conqueror who would rather by God's grace
  Till his own field.
Saladin.   Well, if thou think'st no worse
  Of me, then surely we are half agreed.
Templar.   Nay, quite!
Saladin. [*Offering him his hand.*] A word?
Templar.   A man! receive herewith
  More than thou could'st take from me. Wholly thine!
Saladin. Too much gain for one day. Too much, sir Knight.
  Came he not with thee?
Templar.   Who?
Saladin.   Thy Nathan.
Templar.   No;
  I came alone.
Saladin.   Ah, what a deed was that of thine!
  And what a happy fortune that the deed
  Fell out to his advantage, that great man,
Templar. [*Coolly.*]   O, yes!
Saladin.   So cold? Not so, young man! When God
  Does a good deed through us, we must not be
  So cold, nor even for modesty appear
  To be.
Templar. Yet everything in this strange world
  Has many sides! Of which 'tis often hard to tell
  How they are reconciled!
Saladin.   Hold to the best,
  Only the best, and praise the Lord who knows
  Best how to reconcile them. But, young man,
  If you are so fastidious, then must I
  Be on my guard with you. Unhappily
  I am myself a thing of many sides
  Hard for me often to bring to harmony.
Templar. That grieves me; for suspicion's not my failing,
  Nor ever was . . .
Saladin.   Well, tell me, then, of whom
  Thou hast it now? It almost seemed, of Nathan.
  *G 843

Mistrust of Nathan? Thou? Explain thyself!
Speak, give me earnest of thy confidence.

Templar. I've nothing against Nathan; 'tis myself
Alone I'm vext with.

Saladin.   And for what?

Templar.   That I
Have dreamt a Jew might once perchance unlearn
To be a Jew, and dreamt it, too, awake.

Saladin. Away with waking dreams—a vain vexation.

Templar. Thou know'st of Nathan's daughter, Sultan.   What
I did for her. I did . . . because I did.
Too proud to reap thanks where I had not sowed,
Day after day, disdainful, I refused
To see the girl again. Her sire was absent;
He came; he heard; he sought me out; he thanked me;
Expressed his hope I might approve his daughter;
Of prospects spoke, of future happy days.
Well, so I was talked over, came, saw, found
A maiden such . . . ah, Sultan, I'm ashamed!

Saladin. Ashamed? Ashamed! Why, that a Jewish girl
Should touch your heart; but that's all past, perhaps?

Templar. That 'gainst this passion my impetuous heart
Stirred by the father's kind inviting words,
Should stand so feebly. Miserable drop,
I fell a second time into the fire.
For now I wooed, and now was I disdained.

Saladin. Disdained?

Templar.   Well, the wise father did not straightway
Bid me begone. But the wise father first
Must make enquiry, must consider first. Of course!
Did I not do the like? Enquired, considered
I too not first, when she shrieked in the fire?
Why, certainly! God! 'tis a pretty thing
To be so wise and thoughtful!

Saladin.   Now, now, come!
Have patience with an old man; thou'rt but young.
How long are these refusals, then, to last?
Will he perhaps demand of thee that thou
Shalt first become a Jew?

Templar.   A Jew? Who knows?

Saladin. Who knows? Why, he who knows what Nathan is.

Templar. The superstition in which we grew up,
Doth not, because we see it as it is,

Lose, therefore, all its power upon our souls.
They are not all free men who mock their chains.
Saladin. Most wisely spoken ! But Nathan verily . . .
Templar. The worst of superstitions is to hold
One's own the most endurable.
Saladin.   May be,
Still Nathan . . .
Templar.   . . . which alone poor purblind men
Must trust, till they can stand the daylight, which
Alone . . .
Saladin.   Yes, good ! But, Nathan ! Nathan's lot
Is no such weakness.
Templar.   So I also thought !
If all the same this paragon of men
Were such a common Jew that he would seek
To seize on Christian babes to bring them up
As Jews—how then?
Saladin. And who thus slanders him?
Templar.   The very girl
With whom he would decoy me, hope of whom
He would hold out as payment for the deed
I am not to have done for her in vain ;
This very girl is not his daughter—no
She is a Christian child, some castaway.
Saladin. Whom notwithstanding he'd withhold from you?
Templar. [*Hotly.*] Will he or will he not? He is found out.
This babbler of equality and tolerance
Found out ! And on the heels of this Jew wolf
In philosophic sheep's wool I shall put
Dogs that will undisguise him.
Saladin. [*Earnestly.*]   Calmly, Christian !
Templar. What, calmly, Christian ! Jew and Mussulman
Will have but Jew and Mussulman ; shall Christian
Alone not dare make Christians ?
Saladin.   Calmly, Christian !
Templar. [*Composedly.*] The weight of this reproach which Saladin
Crams in one word, I feel it, ah, could I
But know how Assad in my place had taken it.
Saladin. Not so much better ! Perhaps with as much rage !
But who so soon has taught thee even like him
To pierce me with a word ? And verily
If these things be exactly as thou sayest,
I cannot find in them my thought of Nathan.

Meanwhile he is my friend, and friends of mine
Must not one with the other come to strife.
Then, be advised, walk warily.   Give him not
A prey to the fanatics of your rabble !
Stir not the pool ; vengeance on him your priests
Would bind on me for duty.   To no Jew,
No Mussulman, be thou in vain a Christian !

Templar. 'Twere soon too late for that ; but I am warned
Even by the bloodthirst of the Patriarch
Who had in fancy chosen me for his tool.

Saladin. How ? cam'st thou first to him and not to me ?

Templar. Yes, in the storm of passion, in the whirl
Of indecision.   Pardon me.   Now no more,
I fear, wilt thou the features of thine Assad
Trace in my countenance.

Saladin.   Was it not
This very fear that hurt !   Methinks, I know
Error and virtue often dwell together.
Go, seek for Nathan as he sought for thee,
And bring him hither.   'Tis my part to bring you
To reconcilement.   For the maiden's sake
Be serious, and be calm, for she is thine.
Perhaps already Nathan understands
That, even swine's flesh withheld, he has brought up
A Christian child !   Go, find him.

> [*The Templar goes out, and Sittah stands up.*

SCENE V

Saladin and Sittah

Sittah.   Strange, how strange !

Saladin. Is it not, Sittah ?   Must not brother Assad
Have been a bright and beauteous boy ?   See here.

> [*Showing the picture.*

Sittah. If he was like this, and the Templar sat not
For this dear picture.   But, my Saladin,
How could'st thou now forget to question him
About his parents ?

Saladin.   And most specially
His mother ? if his mother never came
Into this region ?   What ?

Sittah.   Be sure to ask him !

Saladin. O, nothing were more likely ! Assad was
  With Christian fair ones such a favourite
  And to fair Christians so devoted too,
  That once the story ran—but no, but no ;
  I will not speak of that.   Enough, I have him
  Once more !   And will with all his faults
  And all the fancies of his tender heart,
  Receive him.   Oh, this maiden that he loves
  Nathan must give him.   Think'st thou not ?
Sittah.   Not *give* him,
  Leave him.
Saladin.   Certainly !   What right has Nathan,
  If he is not her father, over her ?
  He who preserved her in her mortal peril
  Alone can take the unknown father's rights.
Sittah. Then, Saladin, how if thou did'st straightway
  Take the girl to thee and withdrew her straightway
  From the illegal holder.
Saladin.   Were that needful ?
Sittah. Not needful, truly.   'Tis my curious heart
  Alone that drives me to th' advice, because
  Of certain men I'm fain to know at once
  What kind of girl they love.
Saladin.   Well, Sittah, send
  And have her brought to us.
Sittah.   O, may I, brother ?
Saladin. Only, spare Nathan !   Nathan must by no means
  Believe that one would part the girl by force
  From him.
Sittah. Be not afraid of that.
Saladin.   And I
  I must myself see where Al-Hafi hides.

Scene VI

SCENE : *The open court in Nathan's house, opposite the palm-tree
  grove, as in Scene 1 of Act I.   Part of the wares and jewels
  lies unpacked, of which they are speaking*

Nathan and Daja

Daja. O, all are splendid ; choicest of the choice !
  O, everything as fits your generous hand.
  Where do they make this lovely silver stuff

Threaded with the gold tendrils? What's its cost?
A wedding dress indeed ! No queen could ask
A better.

Nathan.   Wedding dress? Why call it so?

Daja. Why, yes; of course you did not think of that
In buying it. But, Nathan, verily
That and nought else it is, a wedding dress
As if bespoken. The white ground, an emblem
Of innocence, the heavy golden threads,
That wind about this ground in every part,
Emblem of riches. See you? It is lovely.

Nathan. Why all this wit? A wedding dress for whom
Do you thus emblemize so learnedly?
Are you, then, bride?

Daja.   I?

Nathan.   Who, then?

Daja.   I? Good God !

Nathan. Who, then? Whose wedding dress is this you prate
of?
All this is yours, and for no other.

Daja.   Mine?
Is meant for me? And is it not for Recha?

Nathan. What I have brought for Recha, they have packed
Apart. Come, take your goods and chattels !

Daja.   Templar !
Not I, were they the treasures of the world,
I will not touch them till you swear to me
To use the happy chance that Heaven has given you
And will not give, perhaps, a second time.

Nathan. Make use? Whereof? A happy chance, of what?

Daja. O, this pretence of blindness ! In two words,
The Templar Knight loves Recha. Give her to him;
Therewith at once your sin, your sin whereof
I can no more keep silence, has an end.
So will the girl come once again 'mongst Christians,
Become once more that which she was and is.
And you, for all the goodness you have shown us,
For which our gratitude can never cease,
Shall not have merely heaped up coals of fire
On your own head.

Nathan.   Ah ! the old harp again
But only fitted with another string
That neither can be stilled nor kept in tune.

Daja. How so?

Nathan.   I like this Templar, and would rather
  Recha had him than any in the world.
  But yet . . . have patience with me yet a while.

Daja. Patience! O Patience!—is not this your own
  Old harp again?

Nathan.   Only a few days' patience!
  But look! Who comes along? Is't not a friar?
  Go, ask him what he wants.

Daja.   What can he want?

                    [*Goes up to him and asks.*

Nathan. Give it—before he asks—(*aside:* Could I but come
  Closer the Templar, not exposing him
  The reason of my questions! Which if told
  And the suspicion groundless, then for nothing
  I had staked my fatherhood.) What does he seek?

Daja. He asks to speak with you.

Nathan.   Well, let him come.
  Go you meanwhile.

Scene VII

Nathan and the Friar

Nathan. [*Aside.*] (How glad had I remained
  My Recha's father. And, indeed, can I
  Not yet remain so, tho' I lose the name?
  To her herself I should be so forever
  Did she but know the joy that were to me.)
  [*To Daja.*] Go! What service can I do you, holy friar?

Friar. Really, not much. It gives me joy at least
  To find great Nathan well.

Nathan.   You know me then?

Friar. Why, yes; who does not? For so many men
  You have left your imprint in their hands;
  'T has stood in mine these many, many years.

Nathan. [*Reaching for his purse.*] Come, friar, come; I will
    renew the print.

Friar. Have thanks! I should but steal it from a poorer;
  Nothing for me! Permit me only to refresh
  My own name in your memory. I can boast
  To have laid something also in your hand
  Not quite to be despised.

Nathan.   Forgive me, then—

I am ashamed—say what was that? and take
As my atonement seven times its worth.
Friar. But first of all hear now the reason why
Only to-day is brought to my remembrance
The pledge I trusted to you.
Nathan.   Pledge entrusted?
Friar. Not long ago I lay an eremite
On Quarantana, near to Jericho.
There came a robber-band of Arabs, broke
My little chapel down and my poor cell,
And dragged me off, their prisoner.   By good chance
Escaped, hither I hied me to the Patriarch,
To beg another little resting-place
Where I could worship God in solitude
Until my quiet end.
Nathan.   Be brief, good friar !
I stand on coals.   The pledge !   The pledge entrusted me !
Friar. Forthwith, Sir Nathan.   Well, the Patriarch
Promised to find me settlement on Tabor
So soon as place were vacant, bade meantime
That I should dwell in cloister as lay-brother,
Where now I am, sir Nathan, where I long
A hundred times a day for Tabor.   For
The Patriarch employs me upon things
That fill me with great loathing.   For example :
Nathan. Quick, I beseech you !
Friar.   Well, it comes, it comes !
Some one to-day has whispered in his ear,
That somewhere hereabout there bides a Jew
Who has brought up they say a Christian child
As his own daughter.
Nathan. [*Taken aback.*] How?
Friar.   But hear me out !
As he commissioned me, if possible,
Forthwith to track this Jew ; beside himself
With rage before this horrid sacrilege,
He deemed the sin against the Holy Ghost
Which cannot be forgiven—that is, the sin
That's held the greatest of all sins, altho',
Thanks be to God ! we're not exactly sure
In what the sin consists—there all at once
My conscience woke, and then there came the thought
I might myself sometime have had the chance

   To do th' unpardonable sin. Come, say;
   Did once a groom just eighteen years gone by
   Bring you a little daughter three weeks old?
Nathan. How? what? Well, frankly—it is true.
Friar. Ay, look upon me here. That groom am I.
Nathan. You are?
Friar.   The lord from whom I bro't you her
   Was, 'less I err, one lord Von Filnek. Wolf Von Filnek!
Nathan. Right! Yes; it was so.
Friar.   For the mother died
   In bringing her to birth, and the sad father
   Was called all suddenly to march 'gainst Gaza,
   Where the poor worm could not accompany,
   So sent her unto you. And met I not
   With you in Darun?
Nathan.   Right, quite right!
Friar.   It were
   No wonder if my memory should deceive me.
   I've had so many masters, and with him
   I served so short a term; soon after this
   He dwelt at Ascalon; he was to me
   Ever a gracious master.
Nathan.   A man indeed!
   Whom I have much to thank for; from my head
   Not once but many times he warded off
   The spear's thrust.
Friar.   Beautiful! More gladly, then,
   To your good care you took his little one.
Nathan. That you may well believe.
Friar.   Where is it, then?
   You will not, surely, say the babe is dead?
   O let it not be dead! If only none
   Knows of the matter. There are other ways.
Nathan. What are these ways you mean?
Friar.   Come, Nathan, trust me!
   For see, this is my notion; if the good
   That I intend to do should touch too close
   On what is evil, rather I refrain
   From the good deed; for what is ill we can
   Without much dubitation recognise,
   But not so well what's good. 'Twas natural,
   Quite natural, that if the Christian babe
   You meant to bring up well and happily

It should be as your own; no unjust claim.
Have you then done so, with a faithful love,
With father-care, to be rewarded thus?
That rings not true to me.   Surely more wise,
More prudent had it been, by other's hand
To have reared up the Christian little one
In Christian faith; but then you had not loved
Your friend's dear babe.   And tender babes need love,
Were 't even a wild beast's love, in their first years,
More than they need our Christianity.
For Christianity there's always time
If the girl only sound in body and soul
Grows up before your eyes, then in God's sight
What she was first, remains she.   And has not
The Christian doctrine, after all, been built
Upon the Jewish?   It has often vexed me,
Has often verily cost me tears to think
That Christians could so utterly forget
The Lord of their Redemption was a Jew.

Nathan. Good brother, you must be my advocate
If hatred and hypocrisy should rise
Against me for one act—ah, for one act!
You only, you alone must know of it.
But take the secret with you to your grave!
For never yet did vanity persuade me
To tell it to another.   To you alone
I tell it.   Pious simpleness alone
Shall hear it.   For simplicity alone
Can understand the wondrous recompense
The godly man may earn for loving deeds.

Friar. I see you moved, a tear stands in your eye.

Nathan. You met with me at Darun with the babe,
Perchance you know not that three days before
In Gath the Christians murdered every Jew,
Man, woman, child of them; perchance know not,
That among these my wife, and with her, too,
Seven hopeful sons were numbered, seven sons,
Who in my brother's house had taken refuge,
Were all together burned.

Friar.   My God, my God!

Nathan. And when you came I'd lain three days and nights
In dust and ashes before God and wept.
Wept?   More; had pleaded, argued it with God,

Raged, stormed, and cursed me and the world ;
Sworn to all Christians and their faith a hate
Unquenchable—
Friar.   Ah, I can well believe it !
Nathan. Yet reason by degree came back to me.
  She spoke with gentle voice, " And yet God is !
  This, too, is the decree of God !   Well, then,
  Come, practise what thou long hast understood ;
  Which of a surety is not harder than
  It is to understand, if thou but wilt.
  Rise up."   I rose and cried to God, " I will !
  If thou wilt that I will ! "   And at that moment
  Did you dismount and handed me the babe
  Wrapt in your mantle.   What you told me then
  And what I answered, I've forgotten—quite,
  Only this much I know : I took the child,
  Laid it upon my couch, kissed its soft cheek,
  Kneeled on the ground, and sighed " O God, for seven
  Already one Thou givest ! "
Friar.   Nathan ! Nathan !
  You are a Christian !   By God, you are a Christian !
  No truer ever was !
Nathan.   Happy for us,
  That what to you makes me a Christian, so
  Makes you to me a Jew.   But let us not
  Thus make each other weak.   Here we must act !
  And though a sevenfold love hath bound me fast
  To this lone stranger maiden, though the thought
  Already kills me that once more in her
  I am to lose my sons—if Providence
  Again require her of me—I obey !
Friar. 'Tis finished !   Even the course I have longed
  To prompt you to, your own good heart has chosen.
Nathan. Yet it must be no rash first-comer think
  To tear her from me !
Friar.   No, truly, God forbid !
Nathan. Whoso hath not a greater right than I,
  Must have at least an earlier. . . .
Friar.   Verily !
Nathan. Which blood and Nature warrant.
Friar.   Even so,
  That's my thought, too.
Nathan.   Come, then, name me the man

Who stands to her related, brother or uncle,
Cousin, or by what other tie of blood;
From him I'll not withhold her—her so fit,
Created, reared, to be the ornament
Of any house or any faith on earth.
I hope, of this your master and his kin
That you know more than I.

Friar.   No, hardly that,
Good Nathan, you've already heard how short
My time of service with him.

Nathan.   Yet at least
You surely know of what house or what race
Her mother was? Was she, too, not a Stauffen?

Friar. Quite possible. Indeed, I think 'twas so.

Nathan. Was not her brother, that's Conrad von Stauffen,
    A Templar?

Friar.   Yes, unless my memory cheats me.
But hold! It comes to me I have a book,
A tiny book belonging to my master,
Still in my hands; I drew it from his bosom
When he was laid in earth at Ascalon.

Nathan. Well?

Friar. 'Tis a book of prayers; a breviary, we call it.
This, tho't I, may a Christian man still use
Unshamed—though really I—I cannot read——

Nathan. No matter! Tell me more.

Friar.   In this small book
First leaf and last, written in his own hand,
There are inscribed the names of all his kin.

Nathan. O blessed news! Go! run! fetch me the volume.
I'll buy it from you with its weight in gold,
And add a thousand thanks. O hasten! run!

Friar. Right willingly—But it's in Arabic
All that my master wrote in't.   [*Exit.*

Nathan.   That's all one.
But bring it only. God! if yet I might
Keep the dear child, and such a son-in-law
Win in addition! if I might! But now
Let be what will be. Who can it have been
Played the informer with the Patriarch?
I must not fail to ask. Could it be Daja?

Scene VIII

Daja and Nathan

Daja. [*Entering in haste, agitated.*] Nathan, only think !
Nathan.   Well, what has happened ?
Daja.   The poor child
  Was fearfully alarmed when she was called—
  She has been sent for . . .
Nathan.   Who ?   The Patriarch ?
Daja. The Princess Sittah, sister of the Sultan.
Nathan. And not the Patriarch ?
Daja.   No, Sittah !   Hear you not ?
  The Princess Sittah sends and bids her come.
Nathan. Whom ?   Recha ?   Well, if Sittah sends for her,
  And not the Patriarch . . .
Daja.   Why think of him ?
Nathan. Have you of late not heard from him ?   In truth ?
  Nor whispered to him something ?
Daja.   I ? to him ?
Nathan. Where are the messengers ?
Daja.   They stand without.
Nathan. Then for precaution I myself will see them.
  Come you !   If only nothing lurks behind,
  From him.   [*Exit.*
Daja.   And I—I fear quite other things.
  Forsooth, an only daughter of a Jew
  So rich as Nathan is, were no ill match
  Even for a Mussulman.   It is over,
  All over with the Templar, unless I
  Can dare the second step and to herself
  Discover who she is.   Courage, my heart !
  Let me but use the moment well, when next
  I have her by myself, and that may be
  At once, when I accompany her.   A first hint
  At random dropped can do at least no harm.
  Yes, yes ! 'tis now or never !   Boldly on !   [*Follows Nathan.*

ACT V—Scene I

Room in Saladin's Palace, to which the sacks of money were borne,
where they still lie

Saladin, and soon thereafter several Mamelukes

Saladin. [*In entering.*] There stands the gold then still. And
     none knows where
  To find Al-Hafi, who most probably
  Is somewhere set a fixture at the chess
  Ev'n of himself oblivious, and if so
  Why not of me? But, patience ! Ho, what now?
A Mameluke. The wished-for tidings, Sultan ! Sultan, joy !
  The caravan is come from Kahira;
  Safely arrived, with seven years' tribute drawn
  From plenteous Nile.
Saladin.   Bravo, my Ibrahim !
  Thou art indeed a welcome messenger !
  Ha ! Ha ! at last ! at last ! Your Sultan's thanks
  For the good news.
Mameluke. [*Waiting.*] (Well then, come on with it.)
Saladin. Why waitest? Thou mayst go.
Mameluke.   And nothing more
  By way of welcome?
Saladin.   What?
Mameluke.   To messenger
  No message-fee? Then I should be the first
  Saladin learned i' th' end to pay with words.
  This is itself a name : To be the first
  With whom he played the niggard !
Saladin.   Take thou then
  One of the sacks there.
Mameluke.   No, not now ! Thou might'st
  Wish to bestow them all on me.
Saladin.   What pride !
  Come here ! There hast thou two.—In earnest? Going?
  Out-do me in your magnanimity?
  For sure it costs thee much more to decline
  Than me to give. O Ibrahim ! What evil chance
  Should thus befall me, thus, so short a time
  Before my going hence, to change my nature?
  Will Saladin not die as Saladin?
  Then neither must he live as Saladin.

2nd Mameluke. Ho ! Sultan !

Saladin.   If thou comest to announce . . .

2nd Mameluke. The caravan from Egypt is arrived !

Saladin.   I know it.

2nd Mameluke. Came I then too late ?

Saladin.   Wherefore
   Too late ? Take for good-will one or two sacks.

2nd Mameluke. Say three.

Saladin.   I see that you can reckon ! Take them—

2nd Mameluke. There still will come a third, if come he can !

Saladin. How so ?

2nd Mameluke.   How so ? Most like he broke his neck !
   We three were watching at the water-gate.
   No sooner sighted we the caravan
   Than each man sprang and hasted, sinews strained,
   Up the long road. The foremost fell, and I
   Won to the front and kept it till we reached
   The City, but there Ibrahim, the scamp,
   Knows street and alley better.

Saladin.   O, he fell !
   Was hurt, perhaps ! Go, friend, ride out to meet him.

2nd Mameluke. That certainly I will, and if he live
   Half of these sacks I'll gladly render him.   [*Exit.*

Saladin. See, what a gallant, noble carle even he !
   And who but me can boast such Mamelukes ?
   And were it not permitted me to think
   That my example helps them ? Perish the thought
   That at the last they must accustom them
   To quite another sort.

3rd Mameluke.   Hail to thee, Sultan !

Saladin. Art thou the man who fell ?

3rd Mameluke.   No, lord, I come
   To tell thee Emir Mansor, leader of
   The caravan, has dismounted.

Saladin.   Bring him in !
   Ah, he is here !

Scene II

Emir Mansor and Saladin

Saladin.   Welcome, my Emir ! Well,
   How has all gone ?—Oh, Mansor, Mansor, long
   We've waited thee . . .

Mansor.   This letter will inform you,
  What unrest in Thebais first your captain,
  Your Abdul Kassem, had to quell by battle,
  Ere we could venture to begin the journey,
  The march thereafter I did expedite
  As much as possible—
Saladin.   Trust you for that !
  And now, good Mansor, take without delay . . .
  This, too, thou wilt do gladly . . . wilt collect
  Fresh escort, for at once thou must away
  On further travel, carry the best part
  Of this rich treasure to my father's hold
  On Lebanon.
Mansor.   Most gladly will I do it !
Saladin. And take thou not an escort over weak.
  On Lebanon things are not quite so safe.
  You've heard ?   The Templars are once more afoot.
  Be well upon your guard !   But come—where halts
  The train ? for I must see it, and myself
  Set all in motion.   Then I go to Sittah.

Scene III

*The Palms near Nathan's house, where the Templar is walking up
and down*

Templar. His house I will not enter; I'm resolved—
  He'll show himself at last.   How quickly, gladly,
  They used to notice me at this same spot.
  But I may still survive it, if he cease
  To hunt me as he used when I came near.
  Hm !   I am vexed at heart.   What is the cause
  Of my embitterment ?   Sure, he said " yes ";
  Nor ever yet has he denied me.   Saladin
  Hath promised, too, to bring him to accord.
  Maybe the Christian roots in me more deep
  Than does the Jew in him.   Who knows himself ?
  How otherwise should I so grudge to him
  The little prey he took occasion once
  To stalk down in the Christians' hunting-ground ?
  No little prey, indeed !   That noble creature !
  Creature, but whose ?   O surely not the slave's
  Who set afloat upon life's weary shore

The block, and then made off.   Surely the artist's
Rather, who in the abandoned block perceived
The god-like form within and bro't it forth
By his so potent art?   Recha's true father
Remains, spite of the Christian who begot her,
For evermore this Jew.   So when I think
Of her as merely Christian girl, without
All graces which she only could derive
From such a Jew's upbringing, what, my heart,
Could then in her be found to please thee so?
Nothing, or little!   Even her smile, were that
More than the soft, sweet quivering of a muscle;
Perchance what makes her smile not worth the charm
In which it clothes itself upon her lips;—
No; not her smile even!   For I've seen it spent
In greater charm on idle jest and folly,
On mockery, on flatterer and admirer.
Has it then taken me captive, and inspired
The wish to flutter life away in its
Sweet sunny beams?   In faith, I cannot tell.
And yet I am at odds with him who gave,
Yes, gave alone this higher worth to her,—
How so, and why?   Have I then earned that laugh
Of Saladin at parting?   Bad enough
To think that Saladin conceived me so!
How small he must have thought me, despicable!
And all about a girl.   It must not be,
Curd, Curd, it shall not be.   Then turn and take
Another road.   May it not be that all
That Daja spoke was only idle talk,
And difficult to prove?—See, there at last
He comes, in eager converse, from his house!
Converse, with whom?   With him?   with my old friar?
Ha!   then he knows it all, and is betrayed
Already to the Patriarch.   What have I wrought
In my perversity!   O that one spark,
One little flash of passion, should avail
To burn away our brain's best elements!
Resolve and quickly what must now be done,
And here aside I'll wait them, if perhaps
By happy chance the friar quit his presence.

Scene IV

Nathan and the Friar

Nathan. [*As he approaches.*]   Once more, good friar, take my
    utmost thanks !

Friar. And you the like, sir !

Nathan.   I ? from you ? for what ?
  For my self-will, that I thus push upon you
  What you've no use for ?   Yes, if but your will
  Had yielded to me, but with all your heart
  You strove against being rich, more rich than I.

Friar. The book, besides, does not belong to me,
  But to the daughter :—it is surely hers,
  The daughter's sole paternal heritage.—
  Of course, she has yourself.   And God forbid
  That you should ever rue t' have done so much
  For her.

Nathan.   That I shall never, never !   Fear not that.

Friar. Ah but ! the Templars and the Patriarchs . . .

Nathan. Whatever harm they do me cannot make
  Me rue what I have done : say nought of that !
  And are you then so perfectly assured
  It was a Templar set the Patriarch on ?

Friar. Can hardly be another.   For a Templar
  Shortly before was with him, what I heard
  Seemed to confirm it.

Nathan.   There is only one
  In all Jerusalem, and him I know—
  He is my friend, a frank and noble youth.

Friar. Quite so ; 'tis he !   But what one is, and what
  The world makes of one, are not quite the same.

Nathan. Alas ! 'tis true !—Let whomsoever do
  His worst or best !   For, friar, with your book
  I can defy them all and go straightway
  Therewith to Saladin.

Friar.   Much luck to you,
  And now I'll say farewell.

Nathan.   And even yet
  You have not seen her—Come again and soon.
  If only nought come to the Patriarch's ear—
  Yet what of that ?   To-day tell what you please.

Friar. Not I !   Farewell.   [*Exit.*

Nathan.   Forget us not, my brother !
God ! I could sink down, under open heavens,
Upon my knees ! to see the threatening knot
That often has appalled me of itself
Unloosen ! God ! How light I feel me now
Since there is nothing further in the world
I have to hide ! and even as in Thy sight
Can walk in men's sight too, who judge a man,
Must judge, by deeds alone.

SCENE V

Nathan and the Templar, who comes forward to meet him

Templar. Ho ! wait me, Nathan ; take me with you.
Nathan.   What !
Sir Knight, I thought to meet you at the Sultan's,
Where have you hid yourself ?
Templar.   O, we have missed
Each other ; do not take it ill.
Nathan.   Not I,
But Saladin . . .
Templar.   You had just left his presence . . ,
Nathan. You saw him, then ? 'Tis well.
Templar.   It is his wish
To speak with us together.
Nathan.   All the better,
Come, I was now upon my way to him.
Templar. May I ask, Nathan, who it was that now
Parted with you ?
Nathan.   You do not know the man, then ?
Templar. Was't not that honest father, the lay-brother,
The good retriever that the Patriarch
Likes to make use of ?
Nathan.   Maybe ; he is lodged
Certainly with the Patriarch.
Templar.   No bad trick,
To send simplicity to clear the way
For rascaldom.
Nathan.   Ah, yes, the silly, not the pious.
Templar. No Patriarch believes in piety.
Nathan.   For him
I would go surety.   He will give no aid

To 's Patriarch in any villainy.

Templar. At least he so professes.   But did he
   Say nothing to you about me?

Nathan.   Of you?
   Well, not indeed of you by name; in fact
   He hardly knows your name.

Templar.   Hardly, says he?

Nathan. Of a certain Templar, to be sure, he did
   Say something . . .

Templar.   What was it?

Nathan.   Something by which
   He once for all cannot mean you, my friend.

Templar. Who knows?   But let us hear it.

Nathan.   'Twas that one
   Accused me to the Patriarch.

Templar.   Accused you?
   Accused?   That is, with his good leave, a lie!
   Now hear me, Nathan!   I am not the man
   To shuffle and equivocate.   No, what
   I have done, I have done.   Nor am I either
   One to defend as well done all he does.
   Why should I die for shame of one sole fault,
   Having the firm resolve to make it good?
   And know I not, forsooth, how far repentance
   May yet advance a man?   Hear me, Nathan!
   I am in truth the Templar named by him,
   The friar, am he who did accuse you, doubtless,—
   And you yourself know what it was that vexed me,
   What made the blood boil in my every vein,
   Fool that I am!   I came, my heart aflame
   To throw me in your arms.   How you received me!
   How coldly, how lukewarmly, which is worse,
   Much worse than coldly; and how sedulous
   You were to show me out with formal phrase;
   And how for answer you did stave me off
   With questions all irrelevant, that now,
   Even now I cannot think of and be calm—
   Still hear me, Nathan!   In my yeasty mood
   Came Daja, whispering to my willing ear,
   And threw your cherished secret at my head,
   Which seemed to me to hold the explanation
   Of your mysterious bearing.

Nathan.   How so?   Why?

Templar. Still bear with me !   Yes, I imagined then
   That what one day you captured from the Christians,
   You would not willingly lose to a Christian—
   And the thought came to me to put the knife
   To your throat straightway. . . .
Nathan.   Templar, was it good ?
Templar. Yet hear me, Nathan !   O without a doubt
   I then did wrong ; there was no guilt in you.
   That foolish Daja knows not what she speaks,
   She hates you, and only seeks to entangle you
   In dangerous business—O maybe, maybe !
   But I'm a fool, raving now here, now there,
   Now doing far too much, now far too little—
   And so it maybe now.   Forgive me, Nathan.
Nathan. If this is what you think me.
Templar.   In a word,
   I sought the Patriarch—but have not named you.
   That is a lie, I say again.   I put the case
   Just as a general problem, so to have
   His mind upon it.   Even that, I know,
   I might have left unspoken ; better so !
   For knew I not the Patriarch already,
   The knave he is ? and could I not myself
   Have bro't it home to you ?   How need I, then,
   Bring the defenceless maiden to the danger
   Of losing such a father ?—Well, what next ?
   The Patriarch's knavery, ever the same,
   Has bro't me to myself the shortest way—
   For, hear me, Nathan ; listen, and hear me out !
   Granted, he knew your name—even what of that ?
   He's only able to take the girl from you
   If she be yours alone and not another's ;
   From *your* house only can he drag her off
   Into his cloisters.   So give her to me,
   Give her to me only ; and let him come.
   Ha ! let him try that game, to take my wife
   From me.—Give her to me and quickly.   Whether
   She be your daughter now, or she be not !
   A Jewess, or a Christian or what else !
   All's one !   All's one !   I will not, either now
   Or in my life henceforward, question you
   Upon the matter.   Be it as it will.
Nathan. Perhaps you fancy it were very needful

For me to hide the truth?

Templar.   Be it as 't will!

Nathan. I have not yet to you or any man
  Who had the right to know denied the fact
  That she's a Christian born, and is no more
  Than foster-daughter to me.   Wherefore, then,
  You say, remains it undisclosed to her?
  For that—to her alone need I excuse—

Templar. And such excuse you need not even with her—
  Grant to her yet that she may never look
  With other eyes upon you.   Spare her yet,
  O spare her the disclosure.   You alone,
  You only, have to deal with her as yet.
  Give her to me, I pray you, Nathan, I
  Alone can save you her a second time,
  And will save.

Nathan.   Ah! You could! You could! but now
  No longer can.   It is too late for that.

Templar. How so, too late?

Nathan.   Thanks to the Patriarch . . .

Templar. The Patriarch? Thanks? thank him? For what?
  Does he wish to earn our thanks? For what?

Nathan. That we now know to whom she is related,
  Now know to whose hands she can be delivered.

Templar. He who would thank him for yet further good,
  Thank him for this!

Nathan.   'Tis from those hands that now
You must receive her, not from mine.

Templar.   Poor Recha!
  How all things thrust at you, poor Recha!   What
  Were luck for other orphans still becomes
  Ill-luck for you—and, Nathan, where are they,
  These kinsfolk?

Nathan.   Where they are?

Templar.   And who they are?

Nathan. A brother in especial has been found
  It is to him that you must sue for her.

Templar. A brother!   What is he, this brother?   Soldier
  Or churchman?   Let me hear what 'tis I may
  Promise myself.

Nathan.   Of these two I fancy
  He's both or neither.   As yet I cannot say
  I know him well.

Templar. And otherwise?
Nathan. Most worthy !
  One with whom Recha will agree right well.
Templar. But yet, a Christian ! Now, really at times
  I hardly know what I should think of you :—
  Take it not ill, friend Nathan—Will she not
  Be forced to play the Christian, among Christians ?
  And what for long enough she will have played,
  She will at last become. Will not the tares
  Spring up to choke the pure wheat you have sown ?
  And that scarce troubles you. For, spite of that,
  You still can say that they'll agree right well,
  Sister and brother ?
Nathan. So I think and hope !
  If she miss aught with him, does she not know
  She still has you and me, her friends for ever ?
Templar. What can she miss with him ? Will not this brother
  With food and clothing, finery and sweetmeats
  Richly enough provide her ? What then more
  Can little sister want ? Oh, certainly,
  A husband ! Well, him too, him too will brother
  Find in good time ! One's always to be found.
  The better the more Christian ! Nathan ! Nathan !
  O what a perfect angle you had formed,
  Whom others now will have the chance to spoil !
Nathan. No fear of that : the man will prove himself
  Worthy of all our love.
Templar. O say not that,
  Of *my* love say not that, which fills my soul
  As nothing small or great can share with it :
  But stop ! Doth she suspect already aught
  Of what is coming ?
Nathan. Maybe, although I know not
  Whence she might learn it.
Templar. That's all one ! She shall,
  She must, in either case, know first from me
  What 'tis her fate portends—And so my thought
  Never to see her, or speak with her at all
  Till I could call her mine—that thought is dead.
  I hasten . . .
Nathan. Stop, whither so fast ?
Templar. To her !
  To see whether this maiden soul is not

Yet Man enough, to take the one resolve
Worthy of her.

Nathan.   Which is?

Templar.   This, now no more
To ask of you or of her brother aught—

Nathan. And?

Templar.   Then to follow me, even if she had
Thereby to be wife to a Mussulman.

Nathan. Remain: you will not meet her, she is now
With Sittah, sister of the Sultan.

Templar.   Why?
Since when?

Nathan.   And if you'd find at the same place
The brother that we spoke of,—come with me.

Templar. The brother? which? Sittah's or Recha's, say?

Nathan. Why, both mayhap. Come only: I pray you, come!

SCENE VI

In Sittah's harem. Sittah and Recha engaged in conversation

Sittah. How glad I am to know you, my sweet girl!
But look not so oppressed, so shy and timid!
Be merry. Come, speak freely; I'm your friend.

Recha. O Princess . . .

Sittah.   No! don't call me Princess, call me
Sittah, your friend, your sister, call me rather
Your little mother—That's what I should like
To be to you—so young, so good, so clever!
What you must know, how much you must have read!

Recha. Read? Sittah, now you mock your silly sister;
Why, I can hardly read.

Sittah.   "Hardly." Romancer!

Recha. My father's hand a little. But I thought
You spoke of books.

Sittah.   Why, certainly; of books.

Recha. Now, I find books so really hard to read.

Sittah. In earnest?

Recha.   Quite. My father loves not much
That cold book-learning, which dead letters cram
Into the brain.

Sittah.   What! is it so? Indeed,
He's not far wrong. And yet the thousand things

You know !

Recha.   I only know them from his mouth,
　My father, and of most of them I still could tell
　How, where and why he taught me.
Sittah.   Everything
　Cleaves better so, the whole soul learns at once.
Recha. I'm sure that Sittah, too, has read but little.
Sittah. How so? If so, I am not proud of it.
　Why think you so ? What reason—now speak out !
Recha. You are so genuine, so unaffected, so . . .
　Well, always like yourself. . . .
Sittah.   Well ?
Recha.   Books, you know,
　Too seldom leave us so, my father says—
Sittah. Ah, what a man your father is !
Recha.   Ah, yes !
Sittah. How sure his hand and eye, they never fail.
Recha. 'Tis true, 'tis true, and this my father . . .
Sittah. What ails you, dear one ?
Recha.   O my father !
Sittah.   God !
　You weep !
Recha.   My father—father—it must out !
　My heart is bursting—give me air—I faint !
　　　[*Throws herself, weeping unrestrainedly, at Sittah's feet.*
Sittah. Child, what has happened ? Recha !
Recha.   I must lose him !
Sittah. You ? lose him ? What means this ? Dear child, be
　calm !
　O never, never ! Rise, and tell me all.
Recha. In vain your vow is made to be my friend,
　My sister.
Sittah.   So I am, I am. Only rise up.
　Else must I call for help.
Recha. [*Controlling herself and rising.*] Forgive ! forgive !
　My pain made me forgetful who you are.
　In Sittah's presence no moaning is of use,
　And no despair. Reason calm and cold
　Alone has power upon her spirit. He
　Whose cause has that to aid him will prevail.
Sittah. I understand not.
Recha.   O do not suffer it,
　My friend, my sister, never suffer it—

Another father to be forced upon me !
Sittah. Another father ! forced upon you? Who can
  Do that or even think of doing it, my dear one?
Recha. Who? 'Tis my good, my wicked Daja, thinks
  And more than thinks the deed, can do it. Ah !
  You do not know her, this my good, my wicked Daja.
  Well, God forgive it her—and recompense her !
  She has shown me so much good, and so much evil.
Sittah. Evil to you. Then verily little good
  Can live in her.
Recha.   Oh, yes, much good, much good—
Sittah. Who is she?
Recha.   'Tis a Christian lady who
  Has tended me from childhood, cherished me
  With care so tender that I never missed
  A mother's love. God make it good to her !
  And yet distressed me too, and tortured me !
Sittah. And why, and in what matter? Tell me, how?
Recha. Ah ! the poor lady—let me tell you all—
  She is a Christian—tortures me from love ;
  Is one of those enthusiasts who dream
  They know, they only, the true way to God—
Sittah. I understand . . .
Recha.   And feel themselves compelled
  To lead all others who have missed this way
  Back to the same—and scarcely can do other—
  For be it true this way alone can be
  The way of safety, can they be content
  To see their friends upon another road,
  Which leads to loss, to everlasting loss?
  Thus is it possible, for the self-same people,
  And at the self-same time, to love and hate.
  Yet even this is not what forces from me
  Bitter complaint against her. For her sighs,
  Her warnings and her prayers, her menaces—
  I could have gladly borne—yes, willingly,
  For they have brought ever to my mind such thoughts
  As do one good. And whom does it not flatter
  At heart to find oneself so prized and dear
  To whomsoever that they can't bear the thought
  Of everlasting severance.
Sittah.   That is true !
Recha. But there is something else that goes too far,

For which I have no mental remedy,
Which patience cures not, nor reflection soothes,
Nothing !
Sittah.　　What's that?
Recha.　　　　What she just now disclosed.
Sittah. Disclosed, and now?
Recha.　　　　　　This very moment did.
On our way here we passed a Christian temple,
A ruin.　Suddenly she stood still and seemed
To struggle with herself, with tear-dimmed eyes
She looked up first to Heaven, and then on me.
" Come, dear," she said at last, " the shorter way
Which passes through this temple will we take."
She goes; I follow her; my awe-struck gaze
Fixed on the tottering ruin.　Now again
She stands; I look and find myself with her
On sunken steps of an altar all-decayed. . . .
How think you 'twas with me, when with hot tears
And claspéd hands she fell before me there,
Lying at my feet. . . .
Sittah.　　　　　O Recha, my poor child !
Recha. And by the Almighty, who so many a prayer
Had heard there, and so many a wonder wrought
Besought me to have pity on myself—
At least to pardon, if she must disclose
The claim her church had on me—she went on—
Sittah. O you unhappy one—'twas my foreboding !
Recha. I was of Christian blood; had been baptized;
And was not Nathan's daughter—he not my father !
God ! God ! he not my father ! Sittah ! Sittah !
See me again all prostrate at your feet. . . .
Sittah. Recha ! Not now; rise up.—My brother comes !

SCENE VII

Saladin and the foregoing

Saladin. What's wrong, here, Sittah?
Sittah.　　　　　　She is not herself.
Saladin. Who is it?
Sittah.　　　　Ah, you know . . .
Saladin.　　　　　　　Our Nathan's daughter?

What's wrong?

Sittah.   Come to yourself, my child! The Sultan . . .

Recha. [*Dragging herself on her knees to the Sultan's feet, her head
    bent to the ground.*] I rise not, cannot rise, and cannot see
    The Sultan's countenance, cannot behold
    The bright reflection of eternal justice
    And goodness in his eyes, and on his brow,
    Until . . .

Saladin.   Stand up!

Recha.   Until he promise me . . .

Saladin. Come, then, I promise, be it what it will.

Recha. Not more nor less, to leave to me my father
    And me to him! Nor know I not who else
    Desires to be my father or can desire it.
    I do not want to know. But is 't alone
    The blood that makes the father, only blood?

Saladin. [*Raising her up.*] I see it all! Who was so cruel, then,
    To put such fancies in your head. Is this,
    Then, quite already settled, and proved true?

Recha. O, surely; Daja has it from my nurse.

Saladin. Your nurse?

Recha.   Who dying told to her the secret.

Saladin. Oh, dying. Perhaps drivelling too? And were it
    Even true—You know, the blood, the blood alone
    Can never make the father, hardly makes
    The father of a beast, but gives at best
    The foremost right to earn the name indeed.
    Then be not yet affrighted—cast off fears!
    Hearken, what think you? When the fathers twain
    Contend for you, leave both, and take a third!
    Take me, then, for your father.

Sittah.   Oh. yes, yes!

Saladin. A right good father I will be to you!
    But stop! I've thought of something better still.
    What need have you of fathers, after all?
    Suppose they die? Let's look about in time
    For one who can keep step with us in living!
    Know you of none?

Sittah.   Now, do not make her blush!

Saladin. That is exactly what I want to do:
    For blushing makes the ugliest beautiful,
    And will it not make fairer yet the fair?
    I have your father Nathan here by me

And one besides—bethink you, can you guess?
Hither?   If you'll permit me only, Sittah?
Sittah. My brother !
Saladin.   Will you blush before him now?
Recha. Before whom?   Blushing?
Saladin.   . . . Little Hypocrite !
Well, then, go pale instead !   Even as you will
And can, too.
          [*A female slave steps in and approaches Sittah.*
          What, already are they here?
Sittah. Good; let them enter.—Brother, it is they.

Scene VIII and Last

Nathan and the Templar to the foregoing

Saladin. Welcome, my dear good friends !   Nathan, to you,
To you before all else 'tis duty and joy
To tell you that as soon as pleases you,
Your gold can be restored. . . .
Nathan.   Nay, Sultan, nay !
Saladin. Yea, more, am now prepared to further you—
Nathan. Sultan !
Saladin. My caravan is here, and I am rich
Beyond my hopes, richer than e'er I was.
Come, tell me, is there no fine enterprise
Where I can help you, something great?   I know
Of ready cash you cannot have too much,
You merchant people !
Nathan.   And why speak you first
Of such a trifle?   I see there an eye
In tears;   to dry them touches me more closely,
                              [*Goes to Recha.*
You've wept?   And why—You still are mine?
Recha.   My father !
Nathan. We understand each other : so, enough !
Be cheerful; be composed.   If still your heart
Remains your own !   And if no other loss
Does threaten it; for sure your father is
Still yours, unlost !
Recha.   O no, no other loss !
Templar. No loss besides?   Then I myself have cheated—
What one fears not to lose, one never thought

That one has held or ever wished to hold—
Let be !—let be ! Nathan, this alters all !
O Saladin, we came at your command,
But now I see I have misled you quite,
Trouble yourself no more !

Saladin.   Young man, again
You puzzle me : and are we bound to read
The riddle that you set?

Templar.   Sultan, you see,
You hear, is 't not enough?

Saladin.   Ay, verily ;
'Tis bad enough that you were not more sure
Of what concerns you most.

Templar.   I am sure *now !*

Saladin. He who presumes upon a good deed done,
Takes it all back.   What you have saved is not
Therefore your own possession.   Otherwise
The thief whose greed bade plunge into the fire,
He were your rival here !
                              [*Going to Recha, to lead her to the Templar.*
                                    Come, dear maid,
Come, judge him not so strictly.   He would be
Another, if he were less warm and proud :
He would have let it be, the saving you.
Set one thing 'gainst another.   Make him shamed !
Do that which would become him best to do,
Confess your love to him ! offer yourself !
And if he should disdain you, or forget
How far, far more in this you do for him
Than what he did for you. . . . What has he then
Done for you !   Let himself be scorched a trifle !
Is that so much? . . . then say I he has nothing
Of my dear brother's nature, of my Assad,
He bears about his mask but not his heart.
Come, dear one . . .

Sittah.   Go, my dear one, go !   It is
But little this—to tell your gratitude ;
I call it nought.

Nathan.   Stop, Saladin !   Stop, Sittah !

Saladin. You, too?

Nathan.   Here's one more still to speak a word. ، ، ،

Saladin. Who questions that ?   To such a foster-father
A voice belongs of right ; yea, the first voice—

Hear me; I know the matter through and through.
Nathan. Nay, not yet all. I speak not of myself.
  There is another, whom, O Saladin,
  I beg you first to hear.
Saladin.   And who is he?
Nathan. Her brother.
Saladin.   Brother of Recha?
Nathan.   Yes.
Recha. My brother? Have I indeed a brother?
Templar.   Where?
  Where is this brother? Is he here? 'Tis here
  That I should meet him.
Nathan.   Patience only!
Templar. [*Bitterly.*]   He
  Has found a father to her—will he not
  Contrive to find a brother?
Saladin.   Only that
  Was wanting! Christian, such a low
  Suspicion had not crossed my Assad's lips.
  Good! But continue, Nathan! Pardon him!
Nathan. I do forgive him freely—who can say
  What we in his place, at his age had thought?
                [*Going to him in friendly manner.*
  Suspicion, Knight, must follow on distrust;
  If you had only granted me to know
  Your true name from the first . . .
Templar.   How?
Nathan.   You're no Stauffen!
Templar. Who am I, then?
Nathan.   Your name's not Curd von Stauffen.
Templar. And what, then, is my name?
Nathan.   'Tis Len von Filnek.
Templar. What?
Nathan.   See, you start!
Templar.   With reason! Who says so?
Nathan. I; I, who more, much more, can tell you, but
  Accuse you of no lie.
Templar.   No?
Nathan.   'Twell may be
  The other name is also yours of right.
Templar. That I should think!
          (*Aside :* God gave that word to him.)
Nathan. For, you must hear—your mother was a Stauffen.

Her brother, he who brought you up from childhood,
To whom your parents trusted you in Germany
When, driven from it by the troubled skies,
They landed here for refuge—he was named
Conrad von Stauffen, may have made you child
Of his adoption.   Is it long ago
Since you came hither with him?   Lives he still?
Templar. What shall I say?   It is so, truly, Nathan,
Himself is dead.   I came here with the last
Reinforcement of our Order.   But all this—
What of it—when we speak of Recha's brother?
Nathan. Your father . . .
Templar.   How?   Have you, then, known my father?
Him also?
Nathan.   Yes, my much-loved friend he was—
Templar. He was your friend?   Nathan, is 't possible?
Nathan. Called himself Wolf von Filnek; but was not
A German.
Templar.   Know you that, too?
Nathan.   Yes, he had
A German wife, and only for short time
Accompanied her to Germany. . . .
Templar.   No more,
I beg—but Recha's brother?   Recha's brother?
Nathan. Are you !
Templar.   I?   I her brother?
Recha.   He my brother?
Sittah. Both of one house.
Saladin.   One house !
Recha. [*Going towards him.*] Ah, brother mine !
Templar. [*Drawing back.*] Her brother !
Recha. It can't be, can't be, his heart
Knows nought of it.—We are impostors—God !
Saladin. [*To the Templar.*] Impostors?   How? what think you?
    can you think it ?
Yourself are an impostor—all things false
In you—face, voice, and bearing !   Nothing yours !
Not to know such a sister.   Templar, go !
Templar. [*Approaching him humbly.*]
Misread not, Sultan, my astonishment !
Mistake not in a moment one in whom
You think that nought of Assad can be seen,
Both him and me !   [*Hastening to Nathan.*

You give to me and take;
Both, Nathan, with full hands.   No, no; you give
More than you take ! yes, infinitely more !

[Falling on Recha's neck.

Dear sister, sister mine !

Nathan.   Blanda von Filnek !

Templar. Blanda?   Blanda? and not Recha ! no more
Your Recha?   God !   You disinherit her !
You give her back her Christian name and place,
You cast her off for me—O Nathan, Nathan !
Why should she thus atone—why, Nathan, why?

Nathan. Atone? for what?   My children, O my children !
Shall not my daughter's brother be my child,
He also, when he will?

*[While he surrenders himself to their embrace, Saladin in
restless amazement steps up to his sister.*

Saladin.   What say you, sister?

Sittah. I am so moved to see them—

Saladin.   And I before
Greater emotion still almost recoil—
Brace you against it firmly as you can.

Sittah. How?

Saladin.   Nathan, but one word with you, one word !

*[While Nathan approaches him, Sittah goes to the brother and
sister to express her sympathy, and Nathan and Saladin
whisper.*

Hear me now, Nathan ! have you told them yet?

Nathan. What?   That her father was no German born?

Saladin. What was he, then?   What other land can claim
him?

Nathan. That's what himself would never trust me with :
Out of his lips I know no whit of that.

Saladin. And was he then no Frank, no Westerner?

Nathan. O that he was not that, he freely granted.
He oftenest spoke Persian.

Saladin.   Persian !   Persian !
What need I more assurance?   It was he !

Nathan. Who, then?

Saladin.   My brother—O quite certainly
My Assad, 'twas my Assad, without doubt.

Nathan. Well, since yourself have lighted on the fact,
Take confirmation of it from this book !

[Handing him the breviary.

*H 843

Saladin. [*Examining it eagerly.*] Ah, his own hand ! That, too,
　I know again !

Nathan. They yet know nothing, rests with you alone
　To tell them what this book contains for them.

Saladin. [*Turning the leaves.*] Shall I acknowledge not my
　brother's children ?
　My nephews not acknowledge—not, my children ?
　Not recognise them ? Leave them all to you ? [*Aloud again.*
　'Tis they ! my Sittah, it is they in truth.
　Both of them children of our brother Assad !

　　　　　　　　　　　　　　　　　[*He runs into their embraces.*

Sittah. [*Following him.*] What do I hear ? 'Twere right no other
　way !

Saladin. [*To the Templar.*] And, proud one, you must love me
　after all ! 　　　　　　　　　　　　　　　　[*To Recha.*
　Now I'm in fact what I proposed myself,
　Whether you will, or not !

Sittah. 　　　　　　　　　I too ! I too !

Saladin. [*Turning to Templar again.*] My son ! my Assad's son !
　my son, my son !

Templar. I of your blood ! So were those dreams of old
　With which they rocked my infancy to sleep
　Much more than dreams ! 　　　　　　　[*Falling at his feet.*

Saladin. [*Raising him up.*] Look at the rascal now !
　Somewhat he knew and yet would have allowed
　Even me to be his murderer—Ah, but wait !

　　　　　　　[*Amidst silent renewal of embraces the
　　　　　　　　　　　　CURTAIN
　　　　　　　　　　　　falls.]

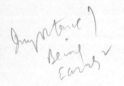

MINNA VON BARNHELM

OR

THE SOLDIER'S FORTUNE

A COMEDY IN FIVE ACTS

BY

GOTTHOLD EPHRAIM LESSING

PERSONS

MAJOR VON TELLHEIM, retired.
MINNA VON BARNHELM.
COUNT VON BRUCHSALL, her uncle.
FRANCISCA, her maid.
JUST, servant to the Major.
PAUL WERNER, formerly Sergeant-Major in the Major's squadron.
THE LANDLORD.
A LADY IN MOURNING.
A COURIER.
RICCAUT DE LA MARLINIÈRE.

The action takes place alternately in the parlour of an inn and in a room adjoining it.

ACT I—SCENE I

Just. [*Sitting dozing in a corner and talking in his sleep.*] Swine of a landlord ! You'll what ? Come on, mate, set about him. [*He puts up his fists and is woken by the action.*] Hullo ! at it again. I can't get a bit of shut-eye but what I find myself fighting him. If only he really got half the back-handers I . . . But it's light now ! It's high time I went to look for the poor old master. He shan't set foot again in this perishing house if I have any say in the matter. I wonder where he spent the night ?

SCENE II

Enter the Landlord

Landlord. Good morning, Mr. Just, good morning ! What, up so early ? Or should I say, not in bed yet ?

Just. Say what you like.

Landlord. All I have to say is Good Morning, and you'd think that would be worth a civil answer ; even from Mr. Just.

Just. Good morning to you.

Landlord. It makes a man touchy, does going without his sleep. I'll lay the Major didn't come home last night and you sat up for him.

Just. The things the man guesses !

Landlord. I speculate, I speculate.

Just. [*Turning to go.*] Your servant, sir.

Landlord. [*Stopping him.*] Oh no, Mr. Just !

Just. Very well, then—not your servant, sir.

Landlord. Oh, Mr. Just ! I do hope you're not still angry about yesterday. You wouldn't bear malice overnight, would you ?

Just. Yes, I would ; and every night to come.

Landlord. Is that a Christian thing to say ?

Just. Just as Christian as running an honest man out of the house because he can't pay on the nail, and throwing him into the street.

Landlord. Who'd do a godless thing like that ?

Just. A Christian landlord—and to my master, such a man, and such an officer !

Landlord. Are you saying that I threw him out ? I threw him on the street ? I've too much respect for an officer to do that, and too much sympathy for a discharged one ! I was simply forced to get him another room. Think no more about it, Mr. Just. [*Shouting off.*] Boy ! I'll make it up in other ways. [*Enter potboy.*] Bring a tot; Mr. Just will take a tot, and good stuff, mind.

Just. Don't trouble yourself, Landlord. May the drop turn to poison that—but I musn't swear—not on an empty stomach.

Landlord. [*To potboy, who enters carrying a bottle of brandy and a glass.*] Give it here. Come. Now, Mr. Just, something first-rate, strong and mild and sound. [*He fills glass and offers it to Just.*] Good for a sleepless stomach.

Just. I really oughn't to—but why should my health pay for his bad manners ? [*Takes glass and drinks.*]

Landlord. Your health, Mr. Just.

Just. [*Returning glass.*] Not bad ! But, Landlord, you're a curmudgeon.

Landlord. No, no, Mr. Just. Have another quick one ; you can't stand on one leg.

Just. [*Having drunk.*] Good, I must say, very good. Your own make, Landlord ?

Landlord. I should say not. That's real Danziger. Genuine double-distilled Salmon brand.

Just. Look here, Landlord, if anything could make me play the hypocrite it's a drop of what you've got there ; but I can't ; I must speak out. And I must say, Landlord, you're a curmudgeon.

Landlord. In all my natural I've never had that said to me. Have another, Mr. Just. Three's the lucky number.

Just. Don't mind if I do. [*Drinks.*] Good stuff, real good stuff. But truth's good stuff, too. Landlord, you're a curmudgeon.

Landlord. If I was, do you think I'd sit and take that from you ?

Just. Oh, yes. That kind don't often have guts.

Landlord. What about another one, Mr. Just ? Four strands make a strong rope.

Just. No. Enough is enough. Anyhow, what's the good ? I'd stick to my word down to the last drop in the bottle. You ought to be ashamed to have such good liquor and such bad manners ! Fancy throwing a gentleman's luggage out of his room while he's out—a man like my officer, that's been in the house by the month and the year, and paid you a pretty penny in his time, and never owed a stiver all his life; just because he's been a bit behind these last few months and not been so free with his money lately.

Landlord. But what if I needed his room urgently? What if I knew well enough the Major would gladly have moved out of his own free will if we'd been able to wait until he came back? Was I to turn away a party that's strange to this place? Was I to hand over that much profit to another landlord? I wasn't even sure anyone else could put her up. All the houses are very full just now. Could I leave a young, charming, pretty young lady like that in the street? Your master is much too polite for that. And he doesn't lose anything by it. Haven't I fixed him up with another room?

Just. Yes: underneath the pigeon-loft, with a view of the neighbours' chimneys——

Landlord. The view was all right until my wretched neighbours built that thing next door. And anyhow the room is very nice, and papered all over——

Just. Was, you mean.

Landlord. No, no, one wall still is. And your room next door, Mr. Just. What's wrong with that? There's a fireplace. It's true the chimney smokes a bit in winter——

Just. But looks all right in summer. I think you're making game of us, sir.

Landlord. Now, now, Mr. Just——

Just. Don't you get Mr. Just's rag out, or——

Landlord. Me get your rag out? The schnapps is doing that.

Just. A gentleman like my officer! Or do you think he's no officer just because he's retired? He can still break your neck for you. Why were you gentlemen in the catering trade so civil while the war was on? Why was every officer a worthy man and every soldier an honest, brave chap? Has a bit of peace made you so saucy already?

Landlord. What are you getting so excited about, Mr. Just?

Just. I'll get excited if I please. . . .

Scene III

Enter von Tellheim

von Tellheim. Just!

Just. [*Supposing the Landlord had spoken.*] "Just!" Getting familiar, aren't we?

von Tellheim. Just.

Just. I was under the impression I was *Mr.* Just to you.

Landlord. [*Noticing the Major.*] Sst! Mr. Just, Mr. Just, why don't you look round? . . . Your master!

von Tellheim. Just, I believe you're quarrelling. What did I tell you about that?

Landlord. Oh, your Honour, quarrelling? God forbid! Would your humble servant presume to quarrel with one of your household?

Just. [*Aside.*] If only I could catch him one on his cringing backside!

Landlord. To tell the truth, Mr. Just was speaking up for his master, and rather heatedly at that. But he was quite right; I esteem him all the more for it; I love him for it.

Just. [*Aside.*] Why aren't I allowed to kick his teeth in?

Landlord. The pity is he is exciting himself about nothing. For I'm convinced your Honour wouldn't have taken it amiss of me because I was forced . . . of necessity . . .

von Tellheim. Enough, sir! I am in your debt; you move my luggage out during my absence; you must be paid, and I must get lodgings elsewhere. Natural enough!

Landlord. Elsewhere? Then you intend to move, sir? What an unlucky man I am! I'm ruined! No, it shan't be. I would rather make the lady move out. The Major can't—won't let her have his room. The room is his. She must leave; I can't help her. I will go now, sir . . .

von Tellheim. Don't be a fool twice over, my friend. The lady must of course keep the room. . . .

Landlord. To think your Honour could suppose that it was out of mistrust and anxiety about getting my money! . . . As if I didn't know you could pay me as soon as it suited you. The sealed purse with five hundred louis-d'or written on it that's in your writing-desk . . . it's in good hands. . . .

von Tellheim. I should hope so. And the rest of my things too. Just will take them over as soon as he's paid you the bill.

Landlord. I promise you, it gave me a shock when I saw that purse. I always considered your Honour a sensible, prudent man, that would never spend himself right out. But still . . . if I'd guessed there was cash in the desk. . . .

von Tellheim. You would have acted more politely towards me. I understand you. Now go, sir, leave me alone. I have something to say to my servant.

Landlord. But, sir . . .

von Tellheim. Come, Just, this gentleman will not permit me to tell you what to do in his house.

Landlord. I'm just going, sir. My whole house is at your service. [*Exit.*]

SCENE IV

Just. Garrh!

von Tellheim. What's the matter?

Just. I'm choking with rage.

von Tellheim. You're more likely to have an apoplexy.

Just. And you, sir. I don't recognize you any more, sir. Strike me dead if you aren't that malicious, hard-hearted devil's guardian angel! I'd have swung for him if I'd been able to get my hands on his windpipe . . . I'd have bitten him to death. . . .

von Tellheim. Bloodthirsty animal!

Just. Better an animal than a man like that!

von Tellheim. What is it you want?

Just. I want you to feel how deeply you're being insulted.

von Tellheim. Well, and what then?

Just. I'd like you to get your own back . . . No, the fellow's beneath your notice.

von Tellheim. But you'd like to get my own back for me? That was what I had in mind from the first. He would never have set eyes on me again and you would have paid our bill. I know you have the knack of throwing down a handful of money pretty contemptuously.

Just. You mean it, sir? That would be a fine come-back! . . .

von Tellheim. But one that we shall have to postpone. I haven't a halfpenny in cash left, and I don't know where to turn for any.

Just. No cash! And what about that purse with five hundred louis-d'or in it that the landlord found in your desk?

von Tellheim. That money was handed to me for safe-keeping.

Just. Well, but that hundred pistoles wasn't, that your old Sergeant-Major brought you four or five weeks ago?

von Tellheim. You mean Paul Werner's money? Why not?

Just. You mean to say you haven't spent that? Sir, you can do what you like with it. On my responsibility. . . .

von Tellheim. Really?

Just. Werner heard from me how the Paymaster-General is holding up your claims. He heard . . .

von Tellheim. That I would certainly become a pauper soon,

even if I were not one already. . . . I am much obliged to you,
Just. . . . This news prompted Werner to share his pittance
with me. . . . I am only too glad to have found it out. . . .
Listen, Just, make out your bill to me at the same time; this
is where we part.

Just. What's that you say, sir?

von Tellheim. Don't speak now; someone's coming.

Scene V

Enter a Lady in mourning

Lady. Excuse me, sir.

von Tellheim. Whom are you seeking, madam?

Lady. None but the honest gentleman whom I have the honour
to address. You do not recognize me? I am the widow of
your former Adjutant.

von Tellheim. But heavens, my dear madam! What a trans-
formation!

Lady. I have but just recovered from the illness caused by the
shock of hearing of the loss of my husband. I am sorry to
trouble you at this early hour, Major. I am going down to the
country, where a kind-hearted friend no more affluent than
myself has offered me a refuge for the time being.

von Tellheim. [*To Just.*] Go; leave us alone.

Scene VI

von Tellheim. Speak freely, madam. You must not be ashamed
to tell me of your misfortune. Can I be of any service to
you?

Lady. My dear sir . . .

von Tellheim. Let me assure you of my sympathy. Can I be of
any service to you? You know your husband was my friend.
I say my friend, and I have always been sparing with that
title.

Lady. Who should know better than myself how very worthy
you were of his friendship, and he of yours. You would have
been his last thought and your name the last on his lips had
not very nature reserved that sad privilege for his unhappy
wife and son.

von Tellheim. Please stop, madam! I would willingly weep with
you; but to-day I have no tears. Spare my feelings. You

find me in an hour when I might be tempted to murmur against
Providence. . . . Oh, poor honest Marloff ! Come, madam,
how can I serve you? If, I say *if*, I am in a position to
help you——

Lady. I must not go away without carrying out his last wish.
Shortly before he died, he remembered he was in your debt, and
implored me to pay it with the first ready money I could lay
hands on. I have sold his kit, and now I come to redeem his
note.

von Tellheim. What, dear lady, is that the reason for your
coming?

Lady. It is. Please allow me to pay you now.

von Tellheim. No, no, madam. Marloff owing me money?
That can hardly be. But let me see. [*Pulling out his pocket-
book and consulting it.*] I cannot find anything.

Lady. I expect you have lost his note of hand, and anyway the
note is of no importance. Allow me . . .

von Tellheim. No; I am not in the habit of forgetting such things.
If I have not got it, that is proof that I never had it, or that it
has been redeemed and returned by me.

Lady. But, Major . . .

von Tellheim. Assuredly, my dear lady, Marloff did not owe me
anything. I cannot even remember his ever having been in
debt to me. On the contrary, it is rather he who has left me
his debtor. I have never been able to do anything to discharge my obligations to a man who for six years shared
honour and danger, good luck and bad with me. I will not
forget that he leaves a son after him. He shall be my son as
soon as I am in a position to be his father. The difficulties in
which I find myself at this moment . . .

Lady. Generous man ! But do not think too meanly of me
either. Take the money, Major. Then at least my mind will
be set at rest.

von Tellheim. And how can that be done better than by the
assurance that the money does not belong to me? Or would
you have me rob my friend's orphan of his schooling? For it
would be robbing him in the fullest sense of the word. It
belongs to him; put it by for him.

Lady. I understand you. Forgive me if I have not yet learned
how to accept charity. But how do you come to know that a
mother would do for her son what she would not do to save her
own life? Now I must go. . . .

von Tellheim. I wish you a good journey ! I do not ask you to send me news of yourself. It might reach me at a time when I could not turn it to account. But one thing more—the most important, and I had almost forgotten it. Marloff still has claims against the Paymaster of our old regiment. His claims are as well-founded as mine. If mine are met, his must be met too. I'll answer for it. . . .

Lady. Oh, Major . . . but I would rather not speak. To plan such charity is, in the sight of Heaven, to have performed it. Accept my tears and the reward of Heaven.   [*Exit.*]

SCENE VII

von Tellheim. Poor, brave woman ! I must not forget to destroy the note. [*Takes papers from his pocket-book and tears them up.*] How can I be sure that my own wants might not at some time tempt me to make use of it ?

SCENE VIII

Enter Just

von Tellheim. You there, Just ?

Just. [*Wiping his eyes.*] Yes.

von Tellheim. Have you been crying ?

Just. I was writing my bill out in the kitchen, and it's full of smoke. Here it is, sir.

von Tellheim. Give it to me.

Just. Have a heart, sir. I know no one has one for you; but . . .

von Tellheim. What do you want ?

Just. It's like a death-sentence, giving you notice.

von Tellheim. I can no longer use your services; I must learn to look after myself without servants. [*Opening and reading out the bill.*] " What the Major owes me : Three and a half months' pay at six dollars a month, 21 dollars. Paid petty cash since the first instant, 1 dollar, 7 groschen, 9 pfennigs. Sum total, 22 dollars, 7 groschen, 9 pfennigs." Well, and it's only fair that I should pay you for the rest of the current month.

Just. About the other side, sir . . .

von Tellheim. What else ? [*Reads.*] " What I owe the Major : Paid the surgeon, 25 dollars. Paid for attendance and nursing while I was sick, 39 dollars. Loaned to my father when his farm was burnt out and looted, 50 dollars, not counting the two captured horses given him. Sum total, 114 dollars. Less 22 dollars, 7 groschen, 9 pfennigs, as above. Remainder owing to the Major, 91 dollars, 16 groschen, 3 pfennigs." My man, you're mad !

Just. I know well enough I've cost you a sight more than that; but it would be a waste of ink to write it down. I can't pay you back. And if you was to take away my livery and all, which I haven't earned yet . . . then I'd rather you'd left me to croak in the infirmary.

von Tellheim. What do you take me for ? You owe me nothing, and I will give you a recommendation to one of my friends who keeps a better house than I do.

Just. I'm not in debt to you, and still you want to send me away ?

von Tellheim. Because *I* don't wish to get in debt to *you.*

Just. Is that all ? Then as sure as I'm in your debt, as sure as you owe me nothing, you shan't get rid of me ! . . . Do what you will, sir, I'll stick by you; I *must* stick by you. . . .

von Tellheim. And your obstinacy, your insolence, your rough and uncouth behaviour towards all those whom you think have no right to give you orders . . . your malicious joy in other people's troubles, your thirst for revenge ? . . .

Just. Paint me as black as you like, sir, you can't make me think worse of myself than I do of my dog. Last winter I was walking in the dusk along the canal and I heard something crying. I climbed down the bank and grabbed at the place where the noise came from, thinking I was rescuing a child, and I pulled a poodle out of the water. That's better than nothing, I thought. The poodle followed me; but I'm no poodle-fancier. I chased him away, but it was no good. I thrashed him away; still no good. I wouldn't let him into my room of a night; he slept on the doorstep. When he got too near I kicked him; he yelped and looked at me and wagged his tail. He's never yet had a bite to eat from my hand. But I'm the only one he'll listen to and let touch him. He jumps about in front of me and does his tricks for me without being told. He's only an ugly poodle, but a very good dog for all that. If he keeps it up much longer I shall finish by giving up poodle-hating.

von Tellheim. [*Aside.*] As I shall do with him ! No, there is no one who is wholly a monster.—Just, we'll stick together.

Just. Of course we will, sir ! How could you manage without a servant ? You forget your wounds and your gammy arm.

Remember you can't even get undressed by yourself. I'm indispensable to you, and though I say it as shouldn't, I'm a man that can beg and steal for his master if it comes to the pinch . . .

von Tellheim. Just, we *won't* stick together.

Just. That's all right, sir !

Scene IX

Enter Servant

Servant. Listen, chum.

Just. What's up ?

Servant. Can you take me to the officer that was staying in that room [*pointing in the direction from which he entered*] yesterday ?

Just. I suppose I could pretty easily. What have you got for him ?

Servant. What we chaps always bring when we come empty-handed—a compliment. My lady has heard that he's been turned out on her account. My lady knows what's right and proper, so I'm to ask his forgiveness for it.

Just. Well, go on, beg his pardon ; that's him.

Servant. Who is he ? What do I call him ?

von Tellheim. My friend, I have already heard your mission. It is a superfluous courtesy of your mistress, which I acknowledge as I should. Give her my compliments. What is her name ?

Servant. Her name ? We have to call her " My Lady ".

von Tellheim. But her surname ?

Servant. I never heard it, sir, and it's none of my business to enquire what it is. I mostly manage things so that I change employment every six weeks. To hell with learning all their names !

Just. Good for you, mate !

Servant. I took on this job a few days ago in Dresden. I think she's looking for her young man . . .

von Tellheim. That's enough, my friend. I asked you about your mistress's name, not about her secrets. Off with you !

Servant. I wouldn't take service with him, mate !

Scene X

von Tellheim. Look alive, Just, we must get out of this house ! I feel more embarrassed by the lady's courtesy than by the

landlord's bad manners. Here, take this ring; it's the only
thing of value I have left, and little did I think that I should
ever put it to such a use. Pawn it. Try and get eighty Fried-
richs on it; our bill here will not be more than thirty. Pay
it and move my luggage. Where to? Wherever you like.
Some inn, the cheaper the better. Meet me at the coffee-
house next door. I'm off now : make a good job of it.

Just. Don't you worry, sir.

[Exit von Tellheim, but returns.]

von Tellheim. Above all, don't forget to pack my pistols that are
hanging behind the bed.

Just. I won't forget anything, sir.

von Tellheim. [*Exit and returns again.*] And another thing : take
your poodle with you. Do you hear, Just?

[Exit.]

Scene XI

Just. The poodle won't stay behind, anyhow. Trust the poodle
for that ! So the Major had this valuable ring put by, had he?
Wearing it in his pocket instead of on his finger. Well, dear
Landlord, we're not so broke as we look. Pretty little ring,
I'll pawn you with the landlord himself. I know he's annoyed
because you weren't frittered away in his house.

Scene XII

Enter Paul Werner

Just. Why, Werner here ! Good morning, Werner. Welcome
to town !

Werner. Blast country life. I can't get used to it again ! Cheer
up, lads, I've got a fresh supply of money. Where's the
Major?

Just. You must have passed him on the way in. He was just
going downstairs.

Werner. I came up the back way. Well, how is he? I'd have
been here last week, but . . .

Just. Oh? What kept you away?

Werner. Just, have you heard about Prince Heraclius?

Just. Heraclius? Can't say I have.

Werner. Don't you know the great heroes of the East?

Just. Well, I know all about the Three Kings of the East that go after the star at Christmas time. . . .

Werner. Man, you don't seem to read the papers any more than you do the Bible. You don't know about Prince Heraclius, that brave man who has conquered all Persia and will soon be taking a swig at the Ottoman Porte? There's still a war going on somewhere, thank God; I was sick of hoping that something would start again in these parts. But they just sit tight and look after their skins. No; once a soldier always a soldier! In short (*looking round carefully in order not to be overheard*], I tell you in confidence, Just, I'm tramping to Persia for the purpose of making a few campaigns against the Turks under His Royal Highness Prince Heraclius.

Just. Not you?

Werner. Myself, no other. Our forefathers used to be great campaigners gainst the Turks, and so should we be too, if we were honest chaps and good Christians. I understand all right that a campaign against the Turks wouldn't be such fun as one against the French; but so much the more profitable, both in this life and the next. I tell you, those Turks have sabres set with diamonds, every man-jack of them.

Just. I wouldn't tramp one mile to get my loaf sliced by a sabre like that. You aren't going to be a fool and leave your nice farm, are you?

Werner. Oh, I'll take it with me. Can you guess how? I've sold it. . . .

Just. Sold it?

Werner. Sh! Here's a hundred ducats that I got on account; I brought them for the Major.

Just. What is he supposed to do with them?

Werner. Do with them? Eat, drink, gamble them away, just as he likes. The man must have money, and it's a shame the way the Paymaster is holding out on him. But I know what I'd do if I was in his place. I'd think, to hell with the lot of you here. I'm off to Persia with Paul Werner. What the hell! Prince Heraclius must have heard of the Major! Even if he hasn't heard of Paul Werner, his old Squadron Sergeant-Major. That brush we had with the Katzenhaeusers . . .

Just. Shall *I* tell *you* about it?

Werner. You tell me? I can see you don't even know what an order of battle means. I won't cast my pearls before swine. Here, take these hundred ducats and give them to the Major. Tell him to keep this lot for me, too. Now I must go to the market. I've brought two loads of rye for sale. What they fetch he can have, too. . . .

Just. Werner, you mean well enough. But we don't need your money. Keep your ducats, and you can have your hundred pistoles back as soon as you like.

Werner. Why? Has the Major still got some money?

Just. No.

Werner. Has he managed to borrow some?

Just. No.

Werner. Then how do you live?

Just. On tick; and when there's no more tick and we get thrown out, then we flog what we've got left and move on. . . . Listen, Paul, we've got to play a trick on the landlord.

Werner. Has he been annoying the Major? I'm on ! . . .

Just. How would it be if we set on him some evening as he was coming out of the smoking-room and gave him a thrashing?

Werner. Set on him two to one at night? That wouldn't do.

Just. Or burn his house over his head?

Werner. Housebreaking and arson? . . . Man, it's easy to see you've been a camp-follower and not a soldier. [*Spits.*] What's up with you? What's going on?

Just. Your eyes'll pop out when I tell you.

Werner. So there's hell to pay here, is there?

Just. There is; listen to this.

Werner. That's fine. All aboard for Persia !

ACT II—Scene I

Minna von Barnhelm's room at the inn

Minna. [*In négligé, looking at her watch.*] Francisca, we got up very early. Time is going to be heavy on our hands.

Francisca. How can one sleep in this horrible great city? What with carts and nightwatchmen and drums and cats and corporals, they never stop rattling and shouting, beating and yowling and cursing. It's as if the night were made for anything but rest. Will you have a cup of tea, my lady?

Minna. I don't care for this tea.

Francisca. Then I'll have some of our chocolate made.

Minna. Yes, have some made for yourself.

Francisca. For myself? I'd as soon talk to myself as drink by myself. Yes, the time is going to hang heavy on our hands.

But when we get bored we must dress up and try on the gown in which we are going to make the first assault.

Minna. Why talk about assaults when I have only come here to demand capitulation?

Francisca. And that gallant officer that we turned out of his room, and sent our apologies to, can't be so very polite, after all, or he would have sent to ask if he might have the honour of waiting on us.

Minna. All officers are not Tellheims. To tell the truth, I only sent our apologies so as to have an excuse for asking about Tellheim. . . . Francisca, my heart tells me that my journey will be successful and that I shall find him.

Francisca. Your heart, my lady? Don't trust the heart too much. It is too ready to say what you want it to say. If the mouth were to speak as the heart does, the fashion of wearing padlocks on the lips would have come in long ago!

Minna. Ha! ha! You and your padlocked lips! That fashion would just suit me.

Francisca. Better hide even the prettiest teeth than have the heart popping out of them every moment!

Minna. Are *you* so reticent, then?

Francisca. No, my lady, but I'd like to be. People don't talk about the virtues they have, but rather of those they haven't.

Minna. Do you know, Francisca, you've made a very apt remark?

Francisca. Have I? Can you say " made " when it just came into my head?

Minna. Do you know why I think it so apt? It applies rather well to my Tellheim.

Francisca. You think everything applies to him.

Minna. Friend or foe alike admit he is the bravest man in the world. But who ever heard him talk of courage? He has the most upright heart, yet honesty and nobility are words he never uses.

Francisca. What virtues does he talk of, then?

Minna. He talks of none, because he lacks none.

Francisca. Just what I thought you'd say.

Minna. Wait a bit, Francisca, I remember now. He does talk a great deal about economy. In confidence, Francisca, I think the man must be a spendthrift.

Francisca. And another thing, my lady. I have often heard him mention his loyalty and truth to you. What if the gentleman were fickle, too?

Minna. Wretched girl! But do you mean it seriously, Francisca?

Francisca. How long is it now since he last wrote?

Minna. Ah me!—he has written only once since the peace.

Francisca. One more grievance against the peace! It's a strange thing how the peace was going to put everything right that the war spoiled, and now it ruins even the few good things that the war brought. Peace has no right to be so contrary. How long have we had it now? It's no use the post running normally again when nobody writes because they have nothing to write about. It's very dull when there's no news.

Minna. "Peace has come," he wrote, "and I approach the fulfilment of my wishes." But that he should only write that one single letter . . .

Francisca. And force *us* to hurry towards that fulfilment! If only we find him we'll make him pay for it! But supposing that meanwhile the man has fulfilled his wishes and we find that . . .

Minna. [*With passionate anxiety.*] That he is dead?

Francisca. Dead to you, my lady, in the arms of Another.

Minna. You little torment! Just you wait, and he'll pay you out for that! . . . But chatter on, or we'll fall asleep again. . . . His regiment was disbanded after the peace. Who knows what confusion of accounts and documents he may be involved in? Who knows but that he may have been posted to some other regiment in some out-of-the-way province? Who knows what circumstances . . .? There's someone knocking.

Francisca. Come in.

SCENE II

Enter Landlord

Landlord. Your ladyship permits? . . .

Francisca. Our Landlord? Please come inside.

Landlord. [*Pen behind ear, sheet of paper, inkhorn and sandbox in hand.*] I have come, my lady, to wish your ladyship a most respectful good morning. [*To Francisca.*] And to you too, my pretty dear. . . .

Francisca. What a polite man!

Minna. We are much obliged to you.

Francisca. We wish you good morning, too.

Landlord. May I presume to enquire how your ladyship slept, this first night under my poor roof?

Francisca. The roof was not so poor, Landlord, but the beds might have been better.

Landlord. Do my ears deceive me? You did not sleep well? But perhaps the over-fatigue caused by your journey . . .

Minna. It may be so.

Landlord. No doubt, no doubt! Otherwise. . . . However, should anything not be to your ladyship's liking, your ladyship has only to command.

Francisca. Certainly, Landlord, certainly! We're not bashful, least of all in an inn. We will tell you soon enough how we like things done.

Landlord. At the same time, I have also come [*taking the pen from behind his ear*] . . .

Francisca. Well?

Landlord. Doubtless your ladyship is aware of the wise ordinances enforced by our police?

Minna. No, I am afraid not.

Landlord. We innkeepers are directed not to entertain any traveller, of any sex or station whatsoever, for twenty-four hours, without reporting in writing to the proper quarter his or her name, place of residence, occupation, immediate business and probable length of stay.

Minna. I understand.

Landlord. If your ladyship will kindly oblige . . .

Minna. Gladly; my name . . .

Landlord. Excuse me one moment. [*Writes.*] " Datem, August 22, anno domini 1763, arrived at the sign of the King of Spain " . . . and the name, my lady?

Minna. Fräulein von Barnhelm.

Landlord. [*Writes.*] " . . . von Barnhelm. Arrived from . . .", whence, my lady?

Minna. From my estates in Saxony.

Landlord. [*Writes.*] " . . . estates in Saxony ". Saxony, my lady, are you from Saxony? Well, well, Saxony!

Francisca. Well, why not? Is it a sin hereabouts to come from Saxony?

Landlord. A sin? God forbid, that would be a new sort of sin! So you come from Saxony! Well, well! Good old Saxony! . . . But as I remember, your ladyship, Saxony is not by any means small, and contains many . . . what shall I say? . . . districts, provinces. Our police are very particular, my lady.

Minna. I see. Well, then, my estates in Thuringia.

Landlord. Thuringia! That's better, my lady, that's more detailed. [*Writes and reads out.*] " Fräulein von Barnhelm, from her estates in Thuringia, together with her chamberwoman and two servants ".

Francisca. Chamberwoman? Would that be me?

Landlord. Yes, my pretty dear. . . .

Francisca. Well, Mr. Landlord, just you put *chambermaid* instead of *chamberwoman*. I hear the police are very particular, there might be a mistake that could make trouble for me when my banns are called. For I am still a maid, and my name is Francisca, surname Willig—Francisca Willig. I'm from Thuringia, too. My father was a miller on one of my lady's estates. The name of the place is Little Rammsdorf. My brother has the mill now. I came up to the Manor when I was very young, and was brought up with her ladyship. We are of the same age—twenty-one come Candlemas. I learnt everything that my lady learnt. I should be glad for the police to know all about me.

Landlord. Very well, my pretty dear, I will take note of all that in case of further enquiries. But now, my lady, the object of your visit?

Minna. The object?

Landlord. Has your ladyship a petition to lay before His Majesty?

Minna. Oh no!

Landlord. Or before our Supreme Court?

Minna. Not that either.

Landlord. Or . . .

Minna. No, no. I'm just here on private business.

Landlord. Certainly, my lady. But how would you describe that private business?

Minna. I would call it . . . Francisca, I think we are being interrogated.

Francisca. Surely, Mr. Landlord, the police won't demand to know a lady's secrets?

Landlord. Certainly, my pretty dear; the police want to know everything, everything—and especially secrets.

Francisca. Now then, my lady, what shall we do? Listen, Mr. Landlord . . . but this is strictly between us and the police alone!

Minna. [*Aside.*] What will the fool tell him?

Francisca. We've come to kidnap one of the King's officers.

Landlord. What's this? My dear girl . . .

Francisca. Or let him kidnap us. It's all one.

Minna. Francisca, are you mad? Landlord, the saucy girl is making fun of you.

Landlord. I should hope not! Or rather, she can have her fun with a nobody like me if she wishes. But with a high police official . . .

Minna. Well, now, Landlord . . . I don't know how to deal with this matter. I think you had better leave all this paper business until my uncle comes. I told you yesterday why he couldn't actually accompany me. His carriage met with an accident nine miles away, and he insisted that it should not mean another night on the road for me. So I had to come on ahead. He will be here in twenty-four hours at the latest.

Landlord. Very good, my lady, let us wait for him.

Minna. He will be able to give a fuller answer to your questions. He will know how much he is obliged to disclose and to whom, and how much he need not divulge.

Landlord. So much the better! Obviously one cannot expect a young girl to talk seriously about serious things to serious people. [*Looking meaningly at Francisca*]. . . .

Minna. Are his rooms ready for him?

Landlord. Completely, my lady, all but one. . . .

Francisca. From which no doubt you'll have to eject some honest man?

Landlord. Saxon chambermaids, my lady, seem to be very compassionate?

Minna. Really, Landlord, that was too bad of you. You ought not to have taken us in at all.

Landlord. May I ask why, my lady?

Minna. I hear that the officer who was dispossessed by us . . .

Landlord. Only a discharged officer, your ladyship.

Minna. What of that?

Landlord. And at the end of his resources.

Minna. So much the worse! He is said to have seen a great deal of service.

Landlord. But, as I told you, he is discharged!

Minna. The King cannot know of everybody's service.

Landlord. Oh yes, indeed, he knows them all.

Minna. Then he cannot reward them all.

Landlord. They would all have been well off if they had lived according to their station. But during the war those gentle-men lived as if there was no longer such a thing as " yours"

and " mine ".   Now all the inns and taverns are full of them,
and a landlord has to be careful.   I didn't do badly with this
one, though.   Even though he had no money left, at least he
had money's worth, and I should have been all right leaving
him in peace for two or three months more.   But it's better to
play safe.   By the way, my lady, no doubt you know something about jewels?

Minna. Not particularly.

Landlord. How could your ladyship not know?   I have a ring
to show you, a valuable one.   Indeed, my lady, there is one
on your finger now that looks very fine, and the more I look
at it, the more I marvel at its likeness to mine.   Look! look!
[*Takes ring from case and hands it to Minna.*] How it sparkles!
The middle diamond alone weighs more than five carats.

Minna. [*Looking at ring.*] Where am I?   What do I see?   This
ring . . .

Landlord. Worth easily a good fifteen hundred dollars.

Minna. Look, Francisca!

Landlord. I didn't hesitate for a moment to lend eighty pistoles
on it.

Minna. Don't you recognize it, Francisca?

Francisca. It *is* the same!   Landlord, where did you get this
ring?

Landlord. Why, my dear, I hope you have no right to it?

Francisca. We have no right to the ring! . . . My lady's
monogram will be on the inside of the case. . . . Show him,
my lady!

Minna. It is he, it is he!   How did you come by the ring?

Landlord. Me?   In the most honest way in the world.   Oh, my
lady, you won't bring trouble and misfortune on me?   How
should I know what is written on it?   During the war there
was many a thing changed hands, with and without the
owner's consent.   All's fair in war, as the saying went.   I
suppose more rings have crossed the border from Saxony
. . . Give it me back, my lady, give it me back.

Minna. Not before you tell me who gave it you.

Landlord. A man I would never have suspected; a good man in
all other respects.

Minna. The best man in the world, if he was the owner.   Bring
him to me quickly.   It must be he, or at least someone who
knows him.

Landlord. But who, my lady?

Francisca. Can't you hear?   Our Major!

Landlord. Major? That's right, he is a Major—the one that had this room before you and gave me the ring.

Minna. Major von Tellheim?

Landlord. Yes, von Tellheim. Do you know him?

Minna. Do I know him! Is he here? Tellheim here? He lived in this room? He pledged you this ring? How did he get into such straits? Where is he? Does he owe you money? . . . Francisca, bring the strong-box! Unlock it. [*Francisca puts strong-box on table and opens it.*] What does he owe you? Does he owe anyone else? Bring me all his creditors. Here's money and notes. All his.

Landlord. What do I hear?

Minna. Where is he? Where is he?

Landlord. He was here only an hour ago.

Minna. Hateful man, how could you be so unfriendly, so hard and cruel to him?

Landlord. Forgive me, your ladyship. . . .

Minna. Quick, bring him here.

Landlord. Perhaps his servant is still here. Would your ladyship like him to fetch him?

Minna. Would I like him to fetch him? Hurry, run; if you do I will forget how badly you treated him. . . .

Francisca. Come, Landlord, make haste! [*Pushes him out.*]

Scene III

Minna. I've found him again, Francisca! You see, I've found him! I don't know where I am for joy. Rejoice with me, dear Francisca! But then, why should you? Yet you must and shall rejoice with me. Come, my dear, I will give you a present to make you glad too. Tell me, Francisca, what shall I give you? Do any of my dresses suit you? Which would you like? Take what you want, only be glad! I see you'll take nothing. Wait! [*Opens her purse.*] There, dear Francisca [*gives her money*], buy what you like. Ask for more if that is not enough. Only rejoice with me. It is so sad to rejoice alone. Come, take it. . . .

Francisca. I'd be robbing your ladyship; you're drunk, drunk with joy. . . .

Minna. And fighting drunk, too, girl; take this, or else [*presses money into her hand*]—and don't dare thank me! . . . One moment [*fumbling for more money in the box*], put this aside, dear Francisca, for the first poor wounded soldier that speaks to us.

SCENE IV

Enter Landlord

Minna. Well, is he coming?

Landlord. The contrary-minded, unmannerly ruffian!

Minna. Who?

Landlord. His servant: he refuses to go and fetch him.

Francisca. Please bring the rascal here. I think I know all the Major's servants. Which one is it?

Minna. Bring him here quickly. When he sees us, I am sure he will go.   [*Exit Landlord.*]

SCENE V

Minna. I can hardly bear waiting for the moment! But, Francisca, you're still so cold. Don't you *want* to share my joy?

Francisca. I would with all my heart: if only . . .

Minna. If only?

Francisca. True, we have found him again; but in what a condition? From all we hear, things must be going badly for him. He must be unhappy; and for that I am sorry.

Minna. Sorry? Let me embrace you for that, dear playfellow. I will never forget that. I am only in love, but you are kind. . . .

SCENE VI

Enter Landlord

Landlord. I've had trouble enough getting him here.

Francisca. A strange face! I don't know him.

Minna. My friend, are you in Major von Tellheim's service?

Just. Yes.

Minna. Where is your master?

Just. Not here.

Minna. But you know where to find him?

Just. Yes.

Minna. Won't you make haste and fetch him?

Just. No.

Minna. It would be doing me a favour.

Just. Would it?

Minna. And your master a service.

I 843

Just. Maybe not.

Minna. What makes you think that?

Just. You're the strange lady that sent him your compliments this morning, aren't you?

Minna. I am.

Just. Then I was right.

Minna. Does your master know my name?

Just. No. But he can't abide ladies that are too polite, any more than landlords that are too rude.

Landlord. That's meant for me, I suppose?

Just. Yes.

Landlord. Then don't let her ladyship suffer for it, but bring him here quickly.

Minna. [*To Francisca.*] Francisca, give him something!

Francisca. [*Trying to press money on Just.*] We do not demand your services for nothing.

Just. Or I your money.

Francisca. Tit for tat.

Just. I can't. My master ordered me to move out. I'm doing that now, and I'll thank you not to hinder me. When I've finished I don't mind telling him he's to come here. He's at the coffee-house next door, and if he has nothing better to do, who knows but what he might come. [*Making to go out.*]

Francisca. Why don't you wait? My lady is the Major's—er—sister.

Minna. That's it; his sister.

Just. I know well enough the Major has no sister. Twice in the last six months he has sent me to his family in Courland. Of course there's more than one kind of sister. . . .

Francisca. How dare you!

Just. I daren't, but you drive me to it.   [*Exit.*]

Francisca. There's a cheeky fellow for you!

Landlord. I told you so. But don't mind him, for I know where his master is. I'll fetch him myself. . . . Only, my lady, I beg of you most humbly to make my excuses to the Major for having acted against my will towards a gentleman of such distinguished service. . . .

Minna. Make haste. I will arrange all that.

                                        [*Exit Landlord.*]

Francisca, go after him; tell him not to mention my name.
                          [*Exit Francisca, following Landlord.*]

SCENE VII

Minna. I've found him again! Am I alone? I must not waste the opportunity [*she folds her hands*]. And I am not alone, either [*looking upwards*]. One thought of gratitude to Heaven is the most perfect prayer! He is mine, mine! [*Stretching out her arms.*] I am happy. And joyful. What sight can be more pleasing to the Creator than a happy creature! [*Enter Francisca.*] Back again, Francisca? Are you sorry for him? I am not. Misfortune may be also a blessing. Perhaps Heaven took everything from him in order to restore everything—in me!

Francisca. He'll be here any minute. You're still in your *négligé*, my lady. What about dressing quickly?

Minna. Oh no. From now he will see me oftener like this than in full dress.

Francisca. Well, you know best yourself, my lady.

Minna. [*Short pause.*] Really, girl, you've hit the nail on the head again.

Francisca. If we are pretty, we are all the prettier unadorned.

Minna. After all, must we be beautiful? But perhaps it is necessary for us to think ourselves beautiful. No, it is enough if I am beautiful only in his eyes. . . . Francisca, if all girls are as I feel now, then we are strange creatures : tender and proud, virtuous and vain, voluptuous and pious—there, you don't understand me. I hardly understand myself. Joy makes one giddy, light-headed.

Francisca. Compose yourself, my lady, I hear him coming.

Minna. Compose myself! Am I to receive him calmly?

SCENE VIII

Enter Landlord and von Tellheim

von Tellheim. [*Sees Minna and hastens to her.*] Minna! My Minna!

Minna. Oh, my Tellheim!

von Tellheim. [*Suddenly hesitating and retiring.*] Excuse me, madam, I never expected . . .

Minna. To find Minna von Barnhelm here? Surely not! [*Advancing towards him as he draws back.*] Am I to excuse you because I am still your Minna? May Heaven forgive you for leaving me still Fräulein von Barnhelm!

von Tellheim. [*With a stony stare at the landlord and a shrug of the shoulders.*] Madam . . .

Minna. [*Becoming aware of the landlord and signalling to Francisca.*] Sir . . .

von Tellheim. If neither of us is mistaken . . .

Francisca. Oh, Lord, whom have you brought to see us? Come quick and find the right man with me. . . .

Landlord. Isn't this the right man? Of course he is!

Francisca. Of course he is not! Come, quick. I haven't said good morning to your daughter yet.

Landlord. Very civil of you, I'm sure. [*Without moving.*]

Francisca. [*Taking him by the arm.*] Come, let's go and make out the menu. Let's see what we can have to-day. . . .

Landlord. Well, to begin with, there's . . .

Francisca. Sh! quiet! If my lady were to hear now what she is to have for dinner it would ruin her appetite. Come, we must talk this over alone. [*Forcibly leads him off.*]

Scene IX

Minna. Well? Are we still mistaken?

von Tellheim. I wish to Heaven we were! . . . But only one of us is, and you are she. . . .

Minna. What formality! Anyone may hear what we have to say to one another.

von Tellheim. And you are here! What are you seeking here, madam?

Minna. I want nothing now. I have found all that I ever wanted.

von Tellheim. [*Drawing back.*] You were seeking a happy man, worthy of your love, and you find . . . a most wretched one.

Minna. So you love me no longer? You love another woman?

von Tellheim. Ah, madam, he never loved you who could love another after you.

Minna. You pluck but *one* thorn from my heart. If I have lost your love, what is it to me whether a greater attraction or mere indifference has lost it me? You have ceased to love me and yet love no one else? Unhappy man, to love no one!

von Tellheim. You are right there, madam; he who is unfortunate must not love. He deserves his misfortune if he is unable so far to conquer himself; if he can be content to let her whom he loves share his unhappiness. How hard a victory is this! Since the day when reason and necessity enjoined me to forget Minna von Barnhelm, what labour has it cost me ! I was beginning to hope that my effort would not be ever in vain . . . and now you come, madam ! . . .

Minna. Do I understand you aright? One moment, sir; let us see where we are before we go farther astray. Will you answer me one question?

von Tellheim. Any question, madam. . . .

Minna. Will you answer me without evasion or prevarication? With nothing but a sober " yes " or " no " ?

von Tellheim. I will . . . if I can.

Minna. You can. Very well : notwithstanding the effort it cost you to forget me, do you still love me, Tellheim ?

von Tellheim. Madam, that question . . .

Minna. You promised to answer yes or no.

von Tellheim. But I added, if I could.

Minna. You can—you must know what is going on in your heart. Do you still love me, Tellheim . . . yes or no ?

von Tellheim. If my heart . . .

Minna. Yes or no !

von Tellheim. Well, then, yes !

Minna. Yes?

von Tellheim. Yes, yes . . . but . . .

Minna. Patience. You love me still. That is enough for me. What a tone I've fallen into with you ! A hostile, gloomy, poisonous tone ! I'll find my own again ! Now, my unhappy darling, you still love me, you still have your Minna, and yet you are unhappy ? Listen while I tell you what a conceited, foolish thing your Minna was; and is. She dreamt, she dreams, that she is your only happiness. Quick, unburden your unhappiness to her. Let her see how much it weighs against her. Well?

von Tellheim. Madam, I am not accustomed to complain.

Minna. Good. I know nothing I admire less in a soldier, after bragging, than complaining. But there is a certain cold, indifferent manner of referring to one's bravery, and to one's misfortunes . . .

von Tellheim. Which is, at bottom, bragging and complaining?

Minna. O you sophist ! In that case you should not have called yourself unhappy. Either keep silent or out with it. A reason, a necessity, that made you forget me? I am a great lover of reason, and I have much respect for necessity. But let me hear how reasonable is this reason, how necessary this necessity.

von Tellheim. Listen, then, madam. You call me Tellheim; the name fits me. But you take me for the Tellheim you knew in your own country, the man in his prime, full of purpose, full of the thirst for glory, master of a whole body and soul, to whom the lists of honour and of fortune stood open, who, though not worthy of your heart and hand, might hope daily to become more worthy of them. I am no more that Tellheim— than I am my own father. Both are of the past. I am a Tellheim discharged, a Tellheim wounded in honour, a cripple and a beggar. You promised yourself to the first, madam; will you hold by your word to the second?

Minna. That sounds very tragic. But, sir, until I find the first again, I am so enamoured of all these Tellheims that I must even make the best of the second. Your hand, dear beggar ! [*Taking him by the hand.*]

von Tellheim. [*Covering his face, with his hat in his other hand, and turning away.*] This is too much. Where am I? Leave me, madam. Your kindness tortures me. Leave me.

Minna. What is the matter? Where are you going?

von Tellheim. Away from you !

Minna. Away from me? [*Drawing his hand to her breast.*] Dreamer !

von Tellheim. Despair will strike me dead at your feet.

Minna. Away from me?

von Tellheim. Away from you. Never to see you again. Or at least so determined, so firmly determined, to commit no base action, nor to let you commit any indiscretion. . . . Let me go, Minna ! [*Tears himself loose and exit.*]

Minna. [*Following him.*] Minna let you go? Tellheim ! Tellheim !

ACT III—SCENE I

The parlour of the " King of Spain "

[*Enter Just, a letter in his hand.*]

Just. I've had to come to this blasted house again ! A letter from my master to the lady that calls herself his sister. I hope nothing comes of this. Otherwise there'll be no end to message-carrying. I'd be glad to get rid of this thing, but I don't want to go into the room. These women ask so many questions, and I hate answering them. Ah ! the door's opening. Just what I wanted—the little chambermaid !

SCENE II

Enter Francisca

Francisca. [*Calling back through the door.*] Don't worry, I'll keep
a look-out. [*Seeing Just.*] Well! Look what's here! But
you can't deal with a brute like that.

Just. Your servant. . . .

Francisca. I wouldn't want a servant like you. . . .

Just. Now, now, it's just a manner of speaking. I've brought a
note from my master to your young lady, his sister . . . it
was his sister, wasn't it? Yes, sister.

Francisca. [*Snatching.*] Give it me!

Just. You're to be so good, he says, as to deliver it. After that
you're to be so good, says my master . . . I'd not have you
think it's me that's asking . . .

Francisca. Well, what is it?

Just. My master has rumbled you. I've a notion he knows that
the way to a young lady lies through her chambermaid. As
I was saying, my master asks you to be so good as to let him
know if he can speak to you for a few minutes.

Francisca. To me?

Just. Excuse me if I've addressed you wrong. Yes, you.
Only for a few minutes, but alone, quite alone, privately—
tête à tête, as they say. It seems he has something out of the
ordinary to tell you.

Francisca. All right: I've plenty to tell him too. Just let him
come. I'm at his orders.

Just. Yes, but when can he come? What time would be most
convenient to you, miss? About dusk?

Francisca. What do you mean by that? Your master can
come when he likes. And now be off!

Just. [*Going.*] With pleasure!

Francisca. Listen! One other thing. Where have the Major's
other servants got to?

Just. The others? Oh, here, there and everywhere.

Francisca. Where's Wilhelm?

Just. The valet? The Major sent him on a trip.

Francisca. Oh? And where's Philip?

Just. The gamekeeper? He's in good hands, where the Major
left him.

Francisca. Because he hasn't any shooting left, no doubt.
What about Martin?

Just. The coachman?   He's gone out for a ride.

Francisca. Fritz, then?

Just. The footman?   He's been promoted.

Francisca. Where were *you* when the Major was billeted on us in
Thuringia?   You weren't with him then, were you?

Just. Oh, yes, I was his groom.   But I was in hospital.

Francisca. Groom, eh?   And what are you now?

Just. Valet, keeper, footman and groom, all in one.

Francisca. Well, I must say!   Fancy letting so many good,
honest men go, and keeping the worst of the lot!   I'd like to
know what your master sees in you.

Just. Maybe he sees an honourable man.

Francisca. That's precious little, just honourable and no more.
Wilhelm was a different kind of man.   So the Major sent him
on a trip?

Just. You might say he sent him; he couldn't stop him.

Francisca. Meaning?

Just. Oh, Wilhelm did himself proud on that trip.   He took all
the Major's clothes with him.

Francisca. What?   You don't tell me he skipped with the
lot?

Just. No, I wouldn't exactly say that.   Only that when we left
Nuremberg he didn't come after us with them. . . .

Francisca. The dirty dog!

Just. He was a lad, he was!   He was the boy for hairdressing
and shaving and telling the tale and getting round the girls—
wasn't he?

Francisca. Then the gamekeeper—I wouldn't have given him
up if I'd been in the Major's place.   Even if he couldn't use
him as a gamekeeper, still he was a steady chap.   Where did
you leave him?   In good hands, you said?

Just. With the Governor of Spandau.

Francisca. The jail?   The shooting can't be so good in the
exercise yard.

Just. Oh, Philip doesn't do any shooting there either.

Francisca. Then what does he do?

Just. Wheelbarrowing.

Francisca. Wheelbarrowing?

Just. But only for three years.   He made a little arrangement
among the Major's command to guide six of the lads past the
sentries.

Francisca. I'm surprised at him.   The scoundrel!

Just. Oh, he's a steady chap!   A gamekeeper that knows every

track and footpath for fifty miles round, woods and bogs and
all ! And what a shot !

Francisca. What a good thing the Major still has that fine
coachman !

Just. Has he still got him ?

Francisca. I thought you said Martin was out for a ride ? I
suppose he's coming back ?

Just. You suppose so ?

Francisca. Which way did he go ?

Just. To the horse-pond, on the Major's one and only saddle-
horse ; going on ten weeks ago now.

Francisca. And not back yet ? Oh, the gallows-bird !

Just. Of course, he might have got drowned. He was such a
good coachman. He'd been driving ten years in Vienna.
We'll never get another like him. If the horses were going full
gallop he had only to say " Brrr ", like that, and they would
stand like rocks. He was a good horse-doctor as well.

Francisca. Now I'm worried about the footman's promotion !

Just. No, no ; he's got his deserts. He's a drummer in a garrison
regiment.

Francisca. I might have known it !

Just. Fritz got into low company, and came home at all hours,
ran up debts in the Major's name and was up to all sorts of
disreputable tricks. To cut a long story short, the Major saw
he wanted to get to the top of the tree by hook or crook
[*imitating the hangman*]; so he put him on the right road to
do it.

Francisca. The low fellow !

Just. But for a footman he was nippy on his feet, I will say. If
the Major gave him fifty yards' start he couldn't catch up with
him on his best charger. But, on the other hand, Fritz could
give the gallows a thousand yards' start, and I'd stake my life
he'd catch up with it. So they were all good friends of yours,
miss ? Wilhelm and Philip and Martin and Fritz ? Well,
well, Just bids you good day.   [*Exit.*]

SCENE III

Francisca. [*Looking thoughtfully after him.*] I deserved that.
Thank you, Just ! I rated honesty too low. I shan't forget
the lesson. . . . Oh, poor man ! [*Turns to go into M. von B.'s
room, as landlord enters.*]

Landlord. Wait a minute, my pretty dear!

Francisca. I've no time just now. . . .

Landlord. Just a second! Still no news of the Major? I'm certain that can't really have been his leave-taking.

Francisca. Why?

Landlord. Didn't her ladyship tell you? When I left you in the kitchen, my dear, I happened to come up to the parlour . . .

Francisca. Just by chance, to try and overhear something.

Landlord. My dear, how can you think such a thing of me? Nothing becomes a landlord less than curiosity. . . . I hadn't been here long when the door of her ladyship's room flew open. The Major rushed out and her ladyship after him. Both at once, and looking and acting—you should have seen them! She caught hold of him; he tore himself loose; she caught hold of him again. "Tellheim!" "Leave me, madam." "Where are you going?" He dragged her as far as the staircase. I was afraid he'd sweep her down with him. But he managed to break away from her. She stopped at the top of the stairs, looking and calling after him and wringing her hands. Suddenly she turned round and ran to the window, from there back to the stairs and then into the parlour, up and down. I was standing just here. Three times she went past me without seeing me. Then she seemed to see me. But Lord love you, I think she thought I was you, my dear. "Francisca," she cried, looking full at me. "Am I happy now?" Then she stared up at the ceiling, and again she says, "Am I happy now?" Then she wiped the tears from her eyes and smiled and asked me again, "Francisca, am I happy?" To tell you the truth, I didn't know how I felt. At last she ran to her door; then she turned round again and faced me: "Why don't you come, Francisca?" she says. "What is the matter with you?" And with that she went into her room.

Francisca. Oh, Mr. Landlord, you must have dreamed it!

Landlord. Dreamed? No, my pretty dear, you don't get all that detail in dreams. . . . I'd give a lot—and I'm not inquisitive—but I'd give a lot to have the key to that.

Francisca. The key to our door? It's on the inside. We changed it round in the night because we were nervous.

Landlord. Not that sort of key. I meant, my dear, the key, the explanation, as it were, the meaning of what I saw.

Francisca. Oh, I see! Well, good-bye now. When do we have luncheon, Landlord?

Landlord. I was forgetting what I was really going to say, my dear . . .

Francisca. Well, be quick. . . .

Landlord. Her ladyship still has my ring; I call it mine because . . .

Francisca. You won't lose it.

Landlord. I wasn't worrying about that; I only wanted to remind you. You see, I don't even want it back. I know well enough how she came to recognize the ring and why it looks so like her own. It is better in her keeping. I don't want it any more, and in the meantime I'll put the hundred pistoles I lent on it on her ladyship's bill. Will that be all right, my dear?

SCENE IV

Enter Paul Werner

Werner. There he is !

Francisca. A hundred pistoles? I thought it was only eighty.

Landlord. That's right, only ninety, only ninety. I'll do it, my dear, I'll do it.

Francisca. We'll see about that.

Werner. [*Coming up behind her and suddenly clapping her on the shoulder.*] Little girl, little girl.

Francisca. [*Startled.*] Eh !

Werner. Don't be afraid, little girl. Little girl, I see you are pretty, and I think you must be a stranger here—and pretty strangers must be warned. Little girl, beware of that man ! [*Pointing to the landlord.*]

Landlord. Ah, what an unexpected pleasure ! Mr. Paul Werner ! Welcome to our house, welcome indeed ! Still the same jolly, jovial, honest Werner ! Beware of me indeed, my pretty dear ! Ha, ha, ha !

Werner. Avoid him at every turn !

Landlord. Avoid me? Am I so dangerous?—Ha, ha, ha !— Listen to him, my dear ! Isn't he a one !

Werner. Isn't it funny how people like him always treat it as a joke when anyone tells the truth?

Landlord. The truth ! That's even funnier, isn't it, my dear? He *is* a comic ! Me dangerous? Me? That might have been so twenty years ago. Yes, my pretty dear, I was a menace then; there's many a girl could tell you about that; but now . . .

Werner. There's no fool like an old fool.

Landlord. You've hit it.   When we're old we're not dangerous
any longer.   You'll fare no better yourself, Mr. Werner !

Werner. Have done chattering, you fool !—Little girl, you will
credit me with enough sense to know that I am not talking
about that kind of danger.   One devil has gone out of him,
but the seven worse than the first have nipped in . . .

Landlord. Listen to him, listen !   How he can twist things
round !—Joke upon joke, and never repeats himself !   Oh,
he's a splendid chap, Mr. Paul Werner !   [*Whispering in
Francisca's ear.*]   Well off too, and still single.   He has a
nice freehold property about ten miles away.   He made a bit
out of the war !—and he used to be Sergeant-Major under our
Major !   He's a good friend of our Major's, a good friend
indeed, that would lay down his life for him ! . . .

Werner. Yes, and you're a nice friend of my Major's !   A nice
friend indeed.   The Major ought to have his blood !

Landlord. What's that you say ?—No, Mr. Werner, that's not a
good joke.   Me, no friend of the Major ?   I don't understand
that one.

Werner. Just has been telling me a fine story.

Landlord. Just ?   I thought as much, I thought that was Just
talking.   Just is a nasty, mean-minded man.   But look at this
pretty child here ; she can speak and bear witness whether I
am a friend of the Major's, and whether I have been of service
to him.   And why shouldn't I be his friend ?   Hasn't he done
a lot of service ?   It's true he has been unlucky enough to be
discharged, but what of it ?   The King can't know about
everybody's service :   and if he did, he couldn't reward them
all.

Werner. Your good angel must have prompted you to say that !
But Just—well, granted there's not much to him : but whatever he is, Just is not a liar, and if it's true what he has been
telling me . . .

Landlord. I don't want to hear about Just.   As I was saying,
this pretty child can speak for me.   [*Whispering in her ear.*]
You know, my dear, the ring !   Tell Mr. Werner about it.
That will show him the kind of man I am.   And just so as
not to let it seem as if you were doing it to please me, I won't
be present.   I won't be present, I'll go away ; but you must
tell me again, Mr. Werner, you must tell me some other time
whether Just isn't a nasty slanderer.   [*Exit.*]

SCENE V

Werner. Do you know my Major, little girl?

Francisca. Major von Tellheim? Indeed I know him, and a fine man he is.

Werner. Isn't he a fine man? I suppose you wish him well?

Francisca. From the bottom of my heart.

Werner. Truly? Look here, little girl. I now see you are twice as pretty as I thought. But what are the services that mine host says he has done for our Major?

Francisca. I've no idea. It might be that he is writing up to his own credit the good things that, luckily, have come out of his dishonest goings-on.

Werner. So it's really true what Just has been telling me? [*Calling in to the wings after the landlord.*] Lucky for you you've gone! So he really did turn his luggage out? To play such a trick on a man like that because the blockhead believes he had no money left! Fancy the Major having no money!

Francisca. Oh, has the Major any money?

Werner. And to spare! He doesn't know how much he has. He doesn't know who owes him money. I am in debt to him myself, and I'm paying some of it now. Look here, little girl, in this purse [*pulling it out of his pocket*] are a hundred gold louis, and in this little roll [*pulling roll out of another pocket*] a hundred ducats. All his money.

Francisca. Really? Then why is he pawning things? He did pawn a ring. . . .

Werner. Pawned it! Don't you believe it! Perhaps he wanted to get rid of the rubbish.

Francisca. It isn't rubbish! It's a very valuable ring, and besides it has a sentimental value.

Werner. That explains it—sentimental value. Oh, yes, that sort of thing often reminds you of something you don't want to be reminded of. So you get it out of your sight.

Francisca. What do you mean?

Werner. Funny things happen to soldiers when they're billeted for the winter. They have nothing to do, so they set to, and out of boredom they strike up acquaintances which they only mean to last for the winter, and which the good souls with whom they get acquainted intend to last for a lifetime. And before you can say Jack Robinson a ring appears on your finger, and you don't know yourself how it gets there. Often enough you'd let the finger itself go, just to be rid of it.

Francisca. And might something like that have happened to the Major?

Werner. Certainly it might. Especially in Saxony. If he had ten fingers on each hand he'd have got all twenty covered with rings.

Francisca. [*Aside.*] That sounds rather strange. It's worth looking into. . . . . Farmer Werner—or should I say Sergeant-Major? . . .

Werner. Little girl, if it's all the same to you, I prefer Sergeant-Major.

Francisca. Well then, Sergeant-Major, I have a note here from the Major to her ladyship. I'm just going to take it in, and I'll be back in a minute. Will you be so kind as to wait for me? I should very much like to have a little chat with you.

Werner. Do you like chatting, little girl? Well, I'm willing: go on, I like chatting too; I'll wait for you.

Francisca. Oh, yes, please do wait.   [*Exit.*]

Scene VI

Werner. Quite a nice little girl! But I shouldn't have promised her to wait. The most important thing is to look up the Major. So he's pawning things rather than take my money. That's just like him. I have an idea. When I was in town yesterday I called on Captain Marloff's widow. The poor woman was sick in bed and bemoaning that her husband owed the Major four hundred dollars that she didn't know how to pay him. To-day I was going to see her again to tell her that if I could get the money paid down on my farm I could lend her five hundred dollars—for I suppose I had better have something put away in case the Persian business doesn't come off. But she was up and away, and I'm certain she can't have paid the Major. Yes, that's how I'll do it, and the sooner the better. The little girl mustn't take it unkindly of me, but I can't stay. [*He turns to go, absorbed in thought, and almost runs into the Major, who enters from the opposite direction.*]

Scene VII

von Tellheim. Hallo, Werner! In a brown study?

Werner. Why, it is you, sir! I was just coming to see you in your new quarters.

von Tellheim. And have a good curse about the landlord of the old ones? But I'd rather you didn't.

Werner. I'd have done that as well. But actually I intended to thank you for being so kind as to take care of my hundred gold louis. Just has given them back to me, though I must say I'd be glad if you'd keep them a bit longer. However, you're moving to new quarters that neither you nor I know anything about. Who knows what they're like? You might be robbed there and have to pay me back notwithstanding. So I can't ask you to do it.

von Tellheim. [*Smiling.*] Since when have you come to be so cautious, Werner?

Werner. Oh, one learns as time goes on. You can't be too careful with money nowadays. Then I had another message for you, sir, from Captain Marloff's widow; I've just left her. You remember her husband owed you four hundred dollars? She sends you a hundred ducats on account. She will send the rest next week. Probably I'm the reason why she didn't send the lot. She owed me one dollar eighty; and because she thought I'd come to claim it—which was more or less true —she gave it me out of the roll she'd just made up for you. You'll feel the need of your hundred dollars a week or so before I miss my few groschen. Here you are, sir. [*Handing him the roll of money.*]

von Tellheim. Werner !

Werner. Why are you staring at me like that, sir? Take it, sir.

von Tellheim. Werner !

Werner. What's the matter, sir? Why are you angry?

von Tellheim. [*Bitterly, striking his forehead and stamping his foot.*] Because the four hundred . . . aren't complete.

Werner. Now, now, sir, didn't you understand me?

von Tellheim. I understood you all too well ! Why must it be that the best of mankind torture me most to-day?

Werner. What's that you say?

von Tellheim. Only half of it applies to you. Leave me, Werner ! [*Pushing aside the hand with which Werner is pressing the money on him.*]

Werner. Not till I have got rid of this.

von Tellheim. Werner, what if I told you that Captain Marloff's widow was here first thing this morning?

Werner. Was she?

von Tellheim. And that she doesn't owe me anything?

Werner. Really?

von Tellheim. That she has paid me every penny? What would you say?

Werner. [*After a moment's thought.*] I'd say I had lied to you, and that lying is a hell of a business if you get found out.

von Tellheim. Aren't you ashamed?

Werner. And what about the man that forced me to lie like that? Oughtn't he to be ashamed too? Look here, sir. If I was to say that your behaviour didn't annoy me, I'd be lying again, and I don't want to tell any more lies. . . .

von Tellheim. Don't be annoyed, Werner. I know how kind and how fond of me you are. But I don't need your money.

Werner. Don't need it ! You'd rather pawn and sell things and get yourself talked about?

von Tellheim. I don't care who knows that I've no money left. It is not right to seem richer than one really is.

Werner. But why seem poorer? We've all got something as long as our friends have.

von Tellheim. It is not right for me to be your debtor.

Werner. Not right? That scorching day when the sun and the enemy together were making it hot for us, your groom lost himself and your canteen too. And you came to me and said, " Got a drink, Sergeant-Major ? " When I handed you my water-bottle, you took it and drank, didn't you? Was that right? Strike me dead if a swig of dirty water wasn't worth more then than all that muck [*pointing to the purse of louis-d'or and offering it together with the roll*]. Take it, my dear Major ! Think to yourself it's just water. God made them both for everybody.

von Tellheim. You torture me. You heard me say I'll not be your debtor.

Werner. First you say it isn't right, and now you say you don't want to. Well, that's another thing. [*Rather angrily.*] You don't want to be my debtor? What if you are that already, sir? Or do you owe nothing to the man that once parried a blow that would have split your skull, and another time cut off the arm of a man that would have shot you through the heart? . . . What more can you owe a man than that? Or is my neck worth less than my purse? . . . That may be a gentlemanly way of thinking, but by God it's a silly one.

von Tellheim. How can you say that, Werner? We are alone, so I can say it, but if any one else were to hear me, he'd call me a windbag. I'm glad to think you saved my life twice.

But, old friend, wouldn't I have done the same for you, given the chance? Eh?

Werner. Only lack of the chance! Who doubts that, sir? Haven't I seen you again and again risk your life for the sake of the lowest trooper, when he was hard-pressed?

von Tellheim. There you are!

Werner. But . . .

von Tellheim. Why can't you understand me? I say it isn't right that you should lend me money; I do not want to be your debtor. That's to say, in the circumstances in which I am now.

Werner. Oh, I see! You want to put it off for better times. You want to borrow off me some other time when you don't need any money, when you have some yourself and I have none, maybe.

von Tellheim. It is wrong to borrow when one sees no way of paying back.

Werner. A man like you can't be down on his luck all the time.

von Tellheim. A lot you know about the world! Least of all ought one to borrow from a man that needs his money himself.

Werner. Such as me? What do I want with money? Anyone that needs a sergeant-major will pay me a living wage.

von Tellheim. You need to be more than a sergeant-major to get along in a career where even the best men get left behind without money.

Werner. More than a sergeant-major? I'm a good sergeant-major, and I might very likely be a bad captain and a worse general. I wouldn't be the first.

von Tellheim. Don't force me to think ill of you, Werner. I didn't like what just told me about you. You've sold your farm and you're on the tramp again. Don't make me think that it's not so much the profession you love as the wild, unruly life that goes with it, more's the pity. A man should soldier for his country or for love of the cause that's being fought for. A man that serves here to-day and there to-morrow is no better than a journeyman butcher.

Werner. Well, all right, sir, I'll take your advice. You know better what's right. I'll abide by your choice. But, my dear Major, please take this money off me. In a day or two your claim will be settled, and then you'll have bushels of money. Then you can pay me back with interest. I'm only doing it on account of the interest.

von Tellheim. Enough of that, now.

Werner. By God, I tell you it's only on account of the interest !
How often I've said to myself, What will become of you in
your old age ? What if you get carved up ? What if you
have no money left, and have to beg for your living ? And
then again I think to myself, No, you won't have to beg;
you'll go to Major von Tellheim and he'll share his last penny
with you; he'll stuff you with grub till your dying day;
you'll die decent with the Major.

von Tellheim. [*Taking his hand.*] And you don't think so still ?

Werner. No, I don't think so now. A man that won't take
anything from me when he needs it and I have it won't give
me anything when I need it and he has it. All right ! [*Going.*]

von Tellheim. Man, you'll drive me mad ! Where are you
going ? [*Holding him back.*] If I promise you now, on my
honour, that I still have money ? If I promise you on my
honour to tell you when it is all gone that you shall be the first
and only one to lend me money . . . will that satisfy you ?

Werner. I suppose it must. Give me your hand on that, sir.

von Tellheim. There you are, Paul. And that's enough of that.
I came here to speak to a certain lady's maid. . . .

Scene VIII

Enter Francisca from M. von B.'s room

Francisca. [*Entering.*] Still here, Sergeant-Major ? [*Seeing v. T.*]
You too, sir ? I'll be at your service in a moment.
[*Exit quickly to M. von B.'s room.*]

Scene IX

von Tellheim. That was the girl. But I see you know her,
Werner ?

Werner. Yes, I know that little girl. . . .

von Tellheim. All the same, if I remember rightly, you weren't
with us when I was billeted in Thuringia that winter ?

Werner. No, I was seeing after some equipment in Leipzıg.

von Tellheim. Then how do you come to know her ?

Werner. Well, our acquaintance is very recent. Not a day old.
But all the warmer for that.

von Tellheim. Have you seen her young mistress too ? I suppose
you have.

Werner. Is she with a young lady ?   She told me you knew her mistress.

von Tellheim. Didn't I tell you ?   I met her in Thuringia.

Werner. Young, is she ?

von Tellheim. Yes.

Werner. Pretty ?

von Tellheim. Beautiful.

Werner. Rich ?

von Tellheim. Very rich.

Werner. Is the mistress as nice as the maid ?   That would be absolutely splendid !

von Tellheim. What did you say ?

SCENE X

Enter Francisca, carrying letter

Francisca. Major Tellheim . . .

von Tellheim. My dear Francisca, I haven't had a chance of welcoming you here yet.

Francisca. Well, I dare say you've done it in your mind already. I know you think well of me.   So do I of you.   But it's not kind to frighten people who wish you well.

Werner. [*Aside.*] Ah, now I see !   It really is so !

von Tellheim. That's my fate, Francisca !   Have you given her the letter ?

Francisca. Yes, and here's . . . [*Handing over letter.*]

von Tellheim. Her answer ?

Francisca. No, your own letter back again.

von Tellheim. Won't she read it ?

Francisca. She would like to, but we can't read handwriting very well.

von Tellheim. Little fibber !

Francisca. And we don't think writing letters was meant for people that can talk to each other face to face if they want to.

von Tellheim. What a pretext !   She must read it !   It contains my apology . . . all the reasons and causes . . .

Francisca. My lady wants to hear them from yourself, not read them.

von Tellheim. Hear them from me ?   So that I shall be driven desperate by every word, every gesture of hers, so that I shall feel the whole weight of my loss at every glance ?

Francisca. You'll get no pity !   Take this. [*Giving letter.*] She expects you at three o'clock. She intends to drive round and have a look at the town, and she wants you to go with her.

von Tellheim. Go with her?

Francisca. And what will you give me to let the pair of you go alone? I'll stay at home.

von Tellheim. Alone?

Francisca. Yes, in a nice closed carriage.

von Tellheim. Impossible !

Francisca. Oh, yes. In the carriage Major von Tellheim will have to face the music. He can't escape us there. That's just the reason. In short, sir, you are to come on the stroke of three. And now, you wanted to talk to me alone. What have you got to say? Oh, I see, we are not alone [*looking at Werner*].

von Tellheim. Oh, yes, Francisca, we are as good as alone. But since her ladyship has not yet read the letter, I cannot as yet say anything to you.

Francisca. So this is what you call as good as alone? You have no secrets from the Sergeant-Major?

von Tellheim. None at all.

Francisca. All the same, I think you should have.

von Tellheim. Why so?

Werner. Why, little girl?

Francisca. Especially secrets of a certain kind. All twenty of them, Mr. Sergeant-Major? [*Holding up both hands with out-spread fingers.*]

Werner. Ssh !   Little girl, little girl !

von Tellheim. What is all this about?

Francisca. Before you can say Jack Robinson, eh, Sergeant-Major? [*Making as if to slip a ring on a finger.*]

von Tellheim. What is the matter with you two?

Werner. Little girl, little girl, surely you can take a joke?

von Tellheim. Werner, have you forgotten what I have so often told you, about never joking with women on certain subjects?

Werner. God bless my soul, I must have done. Little girl, I beg of you . . .

Francisca. Well, seeing it was a joke, I will forgive you this time.

von Tellheim. If I really must come, Francisca, contrive for her ladyship to read my letter beforehand ! That will save me the torture of thinking and saying over again things that I would so much rather forget. Here, give her this ! [*Turning the letter over in his hand and offering it to F., when he notices that it has been opened.*] Am I mistaken? Why, look, Francisca, the letter has been opened !

Francisca. Maybe. [*Looking at it.*] Why, yes, it has been
opened ! Who can have done that? But really and truly,
sir, we didn't read it. We don't wish to read it either, for the
writer is coming himself. Do come; but I'll tell you what,
sir. Don't come as you are in those great boots, and your hair
not dressed, though you can be excused because you weren't
expecting us. But come in shoes, and have your hair dressed.
As you are now you look much too soldierly and Prussian for
my taste.

von Tellheim. Thank you, Francisca.

Francisca. You look as if you had slept out of doors last night.

von Tellheim. That's not a bad guess.

Francisca. We are going to dress now, and then dine. We
would like to ask you to dinner, but your presence might
hinder our eating. And you see we are not so much in love
that we've lost our appetites.

von Tellheim. I must go. Francisca, prepare her a little beforehand, so that I don't seem so contemptible in her eyes or my
own. Come and dine with me, Werner.

Werner. What, at the ordinary here? I couldn't fancy it.

von Tellheim. No, up in my rooms.

Werner. In that case I'll be with you directly. After I've had a
word with this little girl.

von Tellheim. A very good idea !   [*Exit.*]

SCENE XI

Francisca. Well, Sergeant-Major? . . .

Werner. When I come back, little girl, shall I smarten up a bit
too?

Francisca. Come just as you like, Sergeant-Major. My eyes will
have nothing against you. But my ears will have to be all
the more on their guard. Twenty fingers all over rings
indeed ! I'm surprised at you.

Werner. No, little girl, I was just going to tell you about that;
the joke slipped out somehow. There's nothing to it. There's
quite enough bother over *one* ring. And many's the score of
times I've heard the Major say that only a worthless kind of
soldier would lead a girl on. I think so too, little girl. You
can depend on that. I must hurry up and go after him.
Good-bye for now, little girl !   [*Exit.*]

Francisca. Good-bye, Sergeant-Major. . . . I believe I like that
man !   [*As she is about to leave the room, enter M. v. B.*]

Scene XII

Minna. Has the Major gone already? Francisca, I believe I'm calm enough by now to have let him stay.

Francisca. And I'll make you calmer still.

Minna. Good. His letter, oh, his letter! Every line bespoke the noble, honourable man. His every refusal to have me made his love more precious to me. He must have realized that we had read the letter. Well, let him, if only he comes! He *is* coming, isn't he? Only it seems to me, Francisca, that there is a little too much pride in his attitude. For not to want to owe one's happiness even to one's sweetheart, *is* pride, unpardonable pride. If he rubs that in too much, Francisca . . .

Francisca. Then you'll give him up?

Minna. Oh, don't say that! Aren't you sorry for him all over again? No, foolish Francisca, no one gives a man up just on account of *one* fault. No: but I have thought of a way to plague him a little for his pride by means of a pride to match.

Francisca. Well, you must be quite calm again, my lady, if you're already thinking of more strategems.

Minna. Indeed, I am. Come along; you will have your part to play too.   [*Exeunt.*]

ACT IV—Scene I

Minna's Room

[*Minna and Francisca discovered rising from table. Minna is elaborately and richly but tastefully dressed. A servant clears the table.*]

Francisca. Surely, my lady, you have not had enough?

Minna. Do you think not, Francisca? Perhaps I wasn't hungry when I sat down.

Francisca. We agreed not to talk of him during the meal. But we ought to have determined not to think of him either!

Minna. Really, I thought of nothing but him the whole time.

Francisca. I noticed that. I began all kinds of subjects, and you gave me the wrong answers every time. [*Another servant brings coffee.*] Here comes something better suited to the megrims. Dear old melancholy coffee!

Minna. Melancholy? Not I. I'm only thinking over the lesson

I mean to teach him. Do you understand your part, Francisca?

Francisca. Oh yes. But I think it would be better if he spared us the trouble.

Minna. This will show you that I know him like the palm of my hand. The very man who refuses me and all my fortune will stand up to the world for me as soon as he hears I'm unlucky and forlorn.

Francisca. [*Very gravely.*] Yes, such a situation would flatter the most delicate kind of self-love.

Minna. Oh, you moralist ! Look at her—first she accuses me of levity and now of vanity ! Let me go my own way, Francisca dear. You can do what you like with your Sergeant-Major.

Francisca. *My* Sergeant-Major ?

Minna. Yes, it's true, however you deny it. Although I've not seen him yet, every word you've said to me about him foretells a husband for you.

Scene II

Enter Riccaut de la Marlinière

Riccaut. [*Speaking without.*] *Est-il permis, Monsieur le Major ?*

Francisca. What's this ? Does somebody want us ? [*Going to the door.*]

Riccaut. Parbleu I am mistook. *Mais non,* I am unmistook . . . *C'est sa chambre.*

Francisca. My lady, I believe the gentleman thinks Major von Tellheim still lives here.

Riccaut. But yes ! *Le Major de Tellheim ; justement, ma belle enfant, c'est lui que je cherche. Ou est-il ?*

Francisca. He does not live here any longer.

Riccaut. Comment ? Twenty-four hours ago he stay here. And now no more. Where does he stay ?

Minna. [*Coming forward.*] Sir . . .

Riccaut. Ah, *madame, mademoiselle,* excuse, please. . . .

Minna. A pardonable mistake, sir, and a very natural surprise. The Major has been good enough to give up his room to me, as I was a stranger and unable to find lodging elsewhere.

Riccaut. Ah, *voilà de ses politesses ! C'est un homme très galant que ce Major.*

Minna. I am ashamed to say I cannot tell you where he has moved since.

Riccaut. Your ladyship not know? *C'est dommage : j'en suis fâché.*

Minna. I really ought to have found out about that; for of course his friends will keep calling for him here.

Riccaut. I am of his best friends, *mademoiselle.* . .

Minna. Francisca, do you know where he is?

Francisca. No, my lady.

Riccaut. It is most necessary that I speak with him. I bring him news that will make him most glad.

Minna. I am all the more sorry I cannot direct you. Yet I hope to see him myself soon. Does it matter from whom he hears this good news? If not, I should be glad to. . . .

Riccaut. I understand . . . *Mademoiselle parle français ? Mais sans doute ; telle que je la vois ! La demande était bien impolie ; vous me pardonnerez, mademoiselle.* . . .

Minna. Sir . . .

Riccaut. No? You speak not French, *mademoiselle?*

Minna. Sir, in France I would do my best to speak it. But why here? I can see that you understand me, sir. And I shall certainly be able to understand you. So speak as you please.

Riccaut. Good! I too can explain myself in German. *Sachez donc, mademoiselle.* You must know that I come from to dine at the Minister of—of—how does he call himself, that Minister outside? In the long street by the so large place?

Minna. I do not know anyone here yet.

Riccaut. Well, the Minister of the War *département.* I have dine with him, as I do in general. One has spoken of the Major de Tellheim. *Et le ministre m'a dit en confiance, car son Excellence est de mes amis, et il n'y a pas de mystères entre nous.* His Excellency, I say, has confided in me that the cause of our Major is approaching to an end, and a happy end. He has made a report to the King, and the King has decided *tout-à-fait en faveur du Major. Monsieur, m'a dit son Excellence, vous comprenez bien que tout dépend de la manière dont on fait envisager les choses au roi, et vous me connaissez. Cel fait un très joli garçon que ce Tellheim, et ne sais-je pas que vous l'aimez ? Les amis de mes amis sont aussi les miens. Il coûte un peu cher au roi ce Tellheim, mais est-ce que' on sert les rois pour rien ? Il faut s'entr'aider en ce monde ; et quand il s'agit de pertes, que ce soit le roi qui en fasse, et non pas un honnête homme de nous autres. Voilà le principe dont je ne me dépars jamais.* What does your ladyship say to that? A good man, is it not? *Ah, que son Excellence a le cœur bien placé. Au reste,* he tells me that if

the Major has not already received *une lettre de la main*—a
royal patent—he will without doubt receive one today.

Minna. Indeed, sir, this news will be most welcome to Major von
Tellheim. I only wish I might tell him the name of the friend
who has taken such an interest in his fortunes. . . .

Riccaut. My name? *Vous voyes en moi*, your ladyship, *le
Chevalier Riccaut de la Marlinière, Siegneur de Pret-au-Val, de
la Branche de Prens-d'Or. Mademoiselle* marvels to hear that
I am of a so great family? *Elle est véritablement du sang
royal. Il faut le dire ; je suis sans doute le cadet le plus aventu-
reux que la maison n'a jamais eu.* I am since my eleventh year
a soldier. An affair of honour caused me to flee. Since then
I have served His Holiness the Pope, the Republic of San
Marino, the crown of Poland and the States-General, until
finally I was called here. Ah, *mademoiselle, que je voudrais
n'avoir jamais vu ce pays-là !* Had I not disengaged myself
from the service of the States-General, I should have become
at least colonel. But to remain here ever and always a
captain, and now only a retired captain . . .

Minna. That is very bad luck.

*Riccaut. Oui, mademoiselle, me voilà réformé et par là mis sur le
pavé !*

Minna. I am so very sorry.

Riccaut. Vous êtes bien bonne, mademoiselle. No, they do not
recognize the merit here. To discharge a man like me ! And
a man too that has ruined himself in their service ! I have
lost more than twenty thousand livres since I engaged myself.
And what have I now? *Tranchons le mot, je n'ai pas le sou,
et me voilà exactement vis-à-vis du rien.*

Minna. This is very sad indeed !

Riccaut. Vous êtes bien bonne, mademoiselle. But as one says,
each misfortune brings with it its brothers; *qu'un malheur ne
vient jamais seul.* So it is with me. What can a gentleman of
my origins have to fall back on but the cards? Now always
I have won with good fortune so long as I do not have need of
the good fortune. Now that I do need her, *mademoiselle, je
joue avec un guignon qui surpasse toute croyance.* Since
fifteen days is not one day gone by that I have not gone broke.
And yesterday three times running. *Je sais bien qu'il y avait
quelquechose de plus que le jeu. Car parmi mes pontes se
trouvaient certaines dames.* I will not say more. One must
be gallant towards the ladies. They have invited me to take
my revenge today; but you understand, *mademoiselle.*

First one must have the means to live before having the means
to gamble.

Minna. I hope, sir, you are not . . .

Riccaut. Vous êtes bien bonne, mademoiselle.

Minna. [*Taking Francisca aside.*] Francisca, I am truly sorry
for him.   Do you think he would take it ill of me if I offered
him help?

Francisca. He doesn't look to me as if he would.

Minna. Very well, then.   I hear, sir, that you play and hold
the bank at places where something is to be won.   I must
confess that I likewise am very fond of gaming . . .

*Riccaut. Tant mieux, mademoiselle, tant mieux.   Tous les gens
d'esprit aiment le jeu à la fureur.*

Minna. I am very fond of winning, too, and I like to stake my
money through a man who—knows how to gamble.   Would
you consider taking me into partnership?   Giving me a share
in your bank?

*Riccaut. Comment, mademoiselle, vous voulez être de moitié avec
moi ?   De tout mon cœur.*

Minna. Only for a trifle at first.   [*Taking money out of the strong-
box.*]

Riccaut. Ah, mademoiselle, que vous êtes charmante !

Minna. Here are my last winnings . . . only ten pistoles.
Indeed, I should be ashamed to have so little. . . .

Riccaut. Donnez toujours, mademoiselle, donnez. [*Taking money.*]

Minna. Doubtless, sir, your bank is pretty large?

Riccaut. Yes, very large.   Ten pistole?   Your interest, your
ladyship, shall be for one-third of the profits.   True, I ought
to get a little more to offer you one-third.   But with a fair
lady one should not be so exact.   I felicitate myself of having
come into contact with your ladyship through this affair, *et de
ce moment je recommence à bien augurer de ma fortune.*

Minna. But I cannot be present at the tables with you.

Riccaut. What necessity is there for your ladyship?   We other
gamblers are honest among ourselves.

Minna. If we are lucky, sir, you will bring me my share soon
enough.   But if not . . .

Riccaut. Then I will come to fetch reinforcements, is it not?

Minna. Reinforcements are likely to give out in the long run.
So defend our money stoutly, sir.

Riccaut. For what do you take me, *mademoiselle?*   For a
simpleton?   For a booby?

Minna. Forgive my . . .

Riccaut. Je suis des bons, mademoiselle. Savez-vous ce que cela veut dire ?

Minna. But surely . . .

Riccaut. Je sais monter un coup. . . .

Minna. [*Amazed.*] Do you mean to say . . .

Riccaut. Je file la carte avec une adresse. . . .

Minna. No, no !

Riccaut. Je fais sauter la coupe avec une dexterité . . .

Minna. But I do hope you'll do nothing of the kind, sir !

Riccaut. Why not, *mademoiselle*, why not? *Donnez-moi un pigeonneau a plumer, et . . .*

Minna. You play false? You cheat?

Riccaut. Comment, mademoiselle, vous appelez cela cheat ? Corriger la fortune, lénchaîner sous ses doigts, être sur de son fait, the Germans call that to cheat? Cheat? What a poor language ! What a dull language !

Minna. No, no, sir; if you think that . . .

Riccaut. Laissez-moi faire, mademoiselle, and please to be calm ! What makes it to you how I play? *Bien,* either you see me to-morrow with hundred pistole, or never no more. . . . *Votre très humble, mademoiselle, votre très humble.* [*Exit in haste.*]

Minna. [*Looking after him with astonishment and disgust.*] May it be the latter, sir; may it be the latter !

Scene III

Francisca. [*Bitterly.*] And now may I speak? A fine business ! A fine business !

Minna. Laugh away ! I deserve it. [*After a pause, more composedly.*] No, don't laugh, Francisca, I don't deserve it.

Francisca. Splendid. You have done a kind action ! Put a down-and-out trickster on his feet again.

Minna. My help was meant for an unfortunate man.

Francisca. And the best of it is that the fellow takes you for one of his own sort. Oh, I must go after him and take the money from him. [*Going.*]

Minna. Francisca, don't let the coffee go stone cold. Pour some out.

Francisca. He must give it you back. I'll tell him you have thought better of it. You don't want to go in with him. Ten pistoles ! You could tell, my lady, from his way of talking that he is just a beggar. [*Minna pours out coffee for herself.*]

Who'd give all that to a beggar? And to try to spare him
the shame of having begged it, too! Those that will misjudge beggars out of the kindness of their hearts, will find the
beggar misjudging them. Well, it serves your ladyship right
if he uses your gift for I don't know what. [*Minna hands her
a cup of coffee.*] Do you want to bring my blood to the boil
again? I want no coffee. [*Minna puts the cup aside.*] *Parbleu,*
they do not recognize the merit here. [*Mimicking the Frenchman.*] No, they don't, if they let tricksters like that run about
unhung.

Minna. [*Coldly and deliberately, as she drinks.*] My dear, you
get on so well with good people. But when will you learn how
to put up with bad ones? For they are people too. And
often not nearly so bad as they seem. One should search for
their good side. I imagine this Frenchman is no more than
conceited. Out of sheer conceit he makes himself out to be a
sharper. He doesn't want to seem under an obligation to me.
He doesn't want to thank me. Perhaps he'll go away now
and pay his little debts, and live quietly and thriftily on the
rest as long as it lasts, without a thought of gambling. If
that is so, Francisca dear, he may come and fetch reinforcements as soon as he likes. [*Giving her the cup.*] There, put it
away! But ought not Tellheim to be here by now?

Francisca. No, my lady, I can't do either—look for the good
side of a bad man or the bad side of a good man.

Minna. You think he will be sure to come?

Francisca. I wish he'd stay away! You see a little pride in
him, the best of men, and just for that you mean to tease him
so cruelly?

Minna. Harping on that again, Francisca? That's enough. I
do mean to, and that's all. Don't dare to try to spoil this for
me, or not say and do as we have agreed. We will arrange
that you are left alone with him, and then—— That must
be he now!

SCENE IV

Enter Paul Werner, marching as if on parade.

Francisca. No, it's only his dear Sergeant-Major.
Minna. Dear Sergeant-Major! Dear to whom?
Francisca. Please don't bewilder the man, my lady. At your
service, Sergeant-Major. What news have you for us?
Werner. [*Going up to Minna without noticing Francisca.*] Regi-

mental Sergeant-Major Werner begs to report on behalf of Major von Tellheim that he sends his most respectful compliments to her ladyship and that he will soon be present.

Minna. Where is he now?

Werner. Begging your ladyship's pardon, we left billets at three o'clock or a little before; but the Paymaster intercepted us on the way: and as there is no end to the conversation of those gentlemen, the Major signalled to me to report the incident to your ladyship.

Minna. Thank you, Sergeant-Major.   I only hope the Paymaster has some good news for the Major.

Werner. It's seldom enough those gentlemen have such news for the officers.   Has your ladyship any orders?   [*Preparing to go.*]

Francisca. Why go so soon, Sergeant-Major?   Hadn't we something to talk about?

Werner. [*In an earnest whisper.*] Not here, little girl.   It's against all respect and discipline. . . . My lady . . .

Minna. I thank you for your trouble, Sergeant-Major.   I am glad to have made your acquaintance.   Francisca has spoken to me very well of you.   [*Werner bows stiffly and exit.*]

Scene V

Minna. So that's your Sergeant-Major, Francisca?

Francisca. You are so teasing about him I can't haggle about that " your " again.   Yes, my lady, that's " my " Sergeant-Major.   No doubt you find him a bit stiff and wooden.   I thought so too just now.   But I know he thought he had to be on parade in front of your ladyship.   And when soldiers are on parade, to be sure they look more like marionettes than men. But you should see him and hear him talk when he is off duty.

Minna. Yes, I suppose I should.

Francisca. He'll be in the parlour still.   Mayn't I go and have a little chat with him?

Minna. I don't like denying you that pleasure, but you must stay here, Francisca.   You must be present at our interview ! I have a new idea. [*Takes ring from her finger.*] Here, take this ring, keep it, and give me the Major's instead.

Francisca. Why?

Minna. [*While Francisca is getting the other ring.*] I hardly know myself.   But I think I foresee an occasion when I might need it.   There's someone knocking.   Quick, give it to me.   It's he ! [*Putting on ring.*]

Scene VI

*Enter von Tellheim, in the same coat, but otherwise
dressed as Francisca advised.*

von Tellheim. Madam, you will excuse my lateness . . .

Minna. Oh, Major, let's not behave in such a military manner
to one another ! The main thing is that you are here. And
the anticipation of pleasure is a pleasure in itself. Now
[*smiling into his face*], dear Tellheim, have we not been behaving like children ?

von Tellheim. Yes, madam, like children who struggle when they
ought meekly to submit.

Minna. Let us go for a drive round the town, my dear Major,
and then go to meet my uncle.

von Tellheim. Your uncle ?

Minna. There, you see, we haven't yet had time to tell one
another the most important things ! Yes, he is arriving some
time to-day. It was only because of an accident that I got
here a day before him.

von Tellheim. Has Count von Bruchsall returned then ?

Minna. The war troubles made him flee to Italy, but the peace
brings him back. Do not worry, Tellheim. Even though
we feared at one time the strongest opposition to our union
on his part . . .

von Tellheim. To our union ?

Minna. He is friendly to you. Too many people have spoken
well of you to him for him to be otherwise. He is most
anxious to come face to face with the man whom his sole
heiress has chosen. He is coming as my uncle, my guardian,
my father, to give you my hand.

von Tellheim. Oh, madam, why did you not read my letter ?
Why did you refuse to read it ?

Minna. Your letter ? Oh yes, I remember you sent me one.
What happened to the letter, Francisca ? Did we read it or
not ? What did you write to me about, my dear Tellheim ?

von Tellheim. Nothing but what my honour dictated.

Minna. And that would be not to jilt an honest girl who loves
you. I'm sure that's what honour would say ! I really
ought to have read the letter. But of course I am hearing
now what I did not read.

von Tellheim. Yes, you shall hear it. . . .

Minna. No, I do not need to hear it. It's self-evident. Could *you* be capable of so vile an act as to give me up now? Do you realize that I should be laughed at for the rest of my life? My countrywomen would point their fingers at me. " There she is," they would say. " That's the Fräulein von Barnhelm who thought she could get that fine man, Major von Tellheim, just because she was rich; as if good men were to be had for money ! " That's what they would say because they are all jealous of me. They can't deny that I am rich. But they don't want to admit that, apart from that, I am a nice enough girl and deserve a good husband. Isn't that true, Tellheim?

von Tellheim. Yes, yes, madam, it would be just like your countrywomen to envy you bitterly your half-pay officer, sullied in his honour, a cripple, a beggar.

Minna. So that is what you claim to be? I seem to have heard something like that already this morning. The good and bad are rather mixed, Major, if we look a little closer at each? You are discharged? I was told so. But I thought your regiment had only been incorporated with another. How is it that a man with a record of service like yours was not retained?

von Tellheim. It was just the way of it. Those in high places have convinced themselves that no soldier does much for their sake and very little out of a sense of duty, but everything for his own honour. What in their own estimation can they owe him then? The peace has rendered many, like myself, superfluous to them—and in the long run no one is indispensable.

Minna. You speak as a man must who in his turn finds the great superfluous. And never more so than now. I'm grateful to these great ones for having waived their claims to a man whom I would have been very loath to share with them. You're under my command now, Tellheim, and you need no other master. I could not in my happiest dreams have thought to find you discharged ! But that was not the only thing. What else were you besides? Crippled, you said? Well [*looking him up and down*], the cripple is pretty straight and sturdy and seems fairly sound and healthy. Dear Tellheim, if you were to go begging on the strength of having lost the use of your arm, I prophesy that very few doors would open to you, except those of kind-hearted girls like myself.

von Tellheim. Now I hear only a wilful girl talking, my dear
  Minna.

Minna. And in your reproach I hear only the words " dear
  Minna ". I won't be wilful any more. For I remember that
  you are a little crippled. You got a slight bullet wound in the
  right arm. But, all things considered, that is no bad thing.
  You won't be able to beat me !

von Tellheim. Madam !

Minna. You're going to say that you'll be so much the more
  exposed to violence from me. Now, now, dear Tellheim, I
  hope you won't let it come to that point.

von Tellheim. You are pleased to laugh, madam. I regret I am
  not able to laugh with you.

Minna. Why not ? What have you against laughing ? Can't
  one be in earnest and laugh too ? Laughter, dear Major,
  keeps us saner than anger. The proof is before you. Your
  laughing lover assesses your circumstances far more justly
  than you do yourself. Because you have been discharged
  you describe yourself as sullied in honour. Because you have
  been shot in the arm you see yourself a cripple. Is that fair ?
  Is there no exaggeration ? Is it my fault if all exaggerations
  are so open to ridicule ? I wager if I were to take your term
  " beggar " it too would prove to have little sting in it. You
  may have lost your kit two or three times. Your credit with
  this or that banker may have disappeared like that of other
  people. You may have lost all hope of recovering loans
  which you have made here and there on service. But does
  that make you a beggar ? Even if you had nothing left but
  what my uncle is bringing you . . .

von Tellheim. Your uncle, madam, is bringing me nothing.

Minna. Nothing but twenty thousand pistoles that you were
  generous enough to lend to our Saxon Estates.

von Tellheim. If only you had read my letter, madam !

Minna. Well, then, I *have* read it ! But what you wrote on that
  subject is indeed a mystery to me. It is impossible that
  anyone should construe your noble action as a crime. Explain
  it to me, dear Major Tellheim.

von Tellheim. You will remember, madam, that I had orders to
  collect contributions from your local authorities with the
  utmost rigour, and in cash. I wanted to spare myself that
  rigour, and so I advanced the balance myself.

Minna. Of course I remember. I would have loved you for that
  deed, if for nothing else.

von Tellheim. The Estates gave me their note of hand, which I was to cash together with all debts to be acknowledged at the ratification of the peace. The note was declared valid, but my title to it was disputed, and they sneered at me when I told them I had advanced cash down. They called it a bribe, a bonus to me from the Estates for having been so ready to accept from them the least sum I had authority to settle for in case of emergency. So the note passed out of my hands, and when it is met, it is certainly not I who will be paid. It is in this matter, madam, that I feel my honour has been impugned, not on account of my discharge, for which I should have applied had it not been ordered. That makes you grave, madam? Why don't you laugh? Look, I'm laughing. Ha, ha!

Minna. Tellheim, I beg you to stop laughing! I implore you! It is the dreadful laughter of misanthropy. No, you are not the man to regret a good deed because it brings ill for you. And these consequences cannot last. Truth must come to light. The testimony of my uncle and of all the Estates . . .

von Tellheim. Oh, your uncle? Your Estates? Ha, ha, ha!

Minna. Your laughter is killing me, Tellheim. If you believe in goodness and Providence, Tellheim, do not laugh like that! I have never heard anyone curse more horribly than you laugh. Let us put it at its worst. If they persist in misjudging you here, no one will do so at home. No, we cannot and will not misjudge you, Tellheim. If our Estates have the least smattering of honour they will do as I think they must. But what am I saying? Why should that be necessary? Imagine, Tellheim, that you had lost twenty thousand pistoles in a night at the tables. The king was an unlucky card for you; the queen [*pointing to herself*] will be all the luckier. Providence, believe me, always holds the honourable man blameless, and often saves him beforehand. The very act that was eventually to lose you twenty thousand pistoles, gave me you. Had it not been for that action, I should never have desired to know you. You know I came uninvited to the first party where I could hope to meet you. I came only because of you. I came firmly resolved to love you . . . I loved you already . . . resolved to have you, even if you should turn out as black and ugly as the Moor of Venice. You are not as black or as ugly as that, and perhaps not so jealous. But, Tellheim, Tellheim, you still have much in common with him. Oh these fierce, inflexible men, with their eyes fixed immovably on the spectre of honour, who harden themselves against all

K 843

other feeling ! Look, Tellheim, here, at me ! [*Tellheim stares fixedly at one spot.*] What are you thinking about? You aren't listening to me?

von Tellheim. [*Absently.*] Oh yes ! But tell me, madam, how did Othello come to be in the Venetian service? Had he no country of his own? Why did he hire his sword and his blood to a foreign State?

Minna. [*Frightened.*] Tellheim, where are you? It is time for us to stop. Come with me. [*Taking him by the hand.*] Francisca, have the coach brought round.

von Tellheim. [*Wrenching himself free and following Francisca.*] No, Francisca, I cannot have the honour of escorting her ladyship. Madam, let me keep my senses for to-day at least and give me leave to go. You are in a fair way to drive me mad. I am trying to control myself as well as I can. But while I am still in my right mind let me tell you, madam, what I have resolved to do, and what nothing in the world shall prevent my doing. Unless I throw a lucky number next time, unless I meet a complete reversal of fortune . . . unless . . .

Minna. I must interrupt you, Major. We should have told him at once, Francisca. Really, you never remind me about anything. This conversation would have gone quite another way, Tellheim, if I had begun it with the good news which the Chevalier de la Marlinière has just brought.

von Tellheim. The Chevalier de la Marlinière? Who is he?

Francisca. A good enough man, most likely, sir, but for . . .

Minna. Be silent, Francisca. Another discharged officer, I think he said from the Dutch service. . . .

von Tellheim. Ah, Lieutenant Riccaut !

Minna. He assured us he was a friend of yours.

von Tellheim. And I assure you I am none of his.

Minna. He said some Minister or other had told him that your case was about to reach a favourable solution. He said there must be a letter from the King on its way to you.

von Tellheim. How did Riccaut come to be talking to a Minister? But something must have happened about my case. For just now the Paymaster said that the King had quashed all the charges against me, and that I could recover my written parole not to leave this place until I was fully exonerated. But that is most likely all. They propose to let me off. But they are wrong; I won't be let off ! I would rather stay here, devoured by the most grinding poverty under the eyes of my traducers . . .

Minna. Obstinate man !

von Tellheim. I need no pity. I want justice. My honour . . .

Minna. The honour of such a man as you . . .

von Tellheim. [*Heatedly.*] No, madam, you may be a good judge
of everything else, but not of that.   Honour is not the voice
of our conscience, not the testimony of others less upright . . .

Minna. No, no—I know. Honour is—honour.

von Tellheim. In short, madam—you do not let me finish. I
was about to say that if they so disgracefully hold back my
due, if the fullest satisfaction is not accorded to my honour,
then, madam, I cannot be yours.   For in the eyes of the world
I should not be worthy of you. The Fräulein von Barnhelm
deserves a husband without reproach. It is a worthless love
that does not scruple to expose its object to contempt.   It is a
worthless man that does not think shame to owe his whole
happiness to a woman whose blind tenderness . . .

Minna. You really mean that, Major? [*Suddenly turning her
back on him.*] Francisca !

von Tellheim. Don't be so impetuous, madam. . . .

Minna. [*Aside to Francisca.*] Now's the time, it seems to me.
What would you advise me to do, Francisca?

Francisca. Nothing : but I do think he is going too far.

von Tellheim. [*Interrupting them.*] You are too hasty, madam . . .

Minna. [*Scornfully.*] I ? Not in the least.

von Tellheim. If I loved you less, madam . . .

Minna. [*As before.*] Oh, of course, that would be my misfortune !
And be assured, sir, I do not desire your misfortune, either.
One should love unselfishly.   It is as well that I have not been
franker ! Perhaps your pity would have granted me what your
love has denied me. [*Slowly drawing the ring from her finger.*]

von Tellheim. What is the meaning of this, madam?

Minna. No, neither of us must make the other either more or less
happy.   That is the way of true love ! I take your word for
it, sir.   And you are too full of honour to misjudge love.

von Tellheim. Are you jesting with me, madam?

Minna. Here, sir, take back this ring with which you pledged
me your troth. [*Handing him ring.*] What must be, must be.
Let us pretend we never knew one another.

von Tellheim. What are you saying?

Minna. Does it astonish you? Take it, sir. You have not, I
hope, been pretending?

von Tellheim. [*Taking the ring from her hand.*] My God, can Minna
speak like this?

Minna. In *one* contingency you cannot be mine. I cannot be yours in *any*. Your unhappiness is probable, but mine is certain. Farewell! [*Going.*]

von Tellheim. Where are you going, Minna dearest?

Minna. Sir, you insult me by using that intimate name now.

von Tellheim. What is the matter, madam? Where are you going?

Minna. Let me go, and hide my tears from you—traitor!
[*Exit.*]

Scene VII

von Tellheim. Her tears? And I was leaving her thus! [*About to follow.*]

Francisca. [*Holding him back.*] Stay, sir. You wouldn't follow her to her bedroom?

von Tellheim. Unhappiness? Did she speak of unhappiness?

Francisca. Yes, to be sure, sir: the unhappiness of losing you after . . .

von Tellheim. After what? There's more behind this. What is it, Francisca? Tell me.

Francisca. I was going to say, after she had sacrificed so much for you.

von Tellheim. Sacrificed?

Francisca. Listen, I'll tell you quickly. It is well for you, sir, that you have got free of her like this. Why shouldn't I tell you? It can't remain secret much longer. We have run away! Count von Bruchsall disinherited her because she would not accept a husband of his choosing. Everyone forsook and despised her because of it. What could we do? We resolved to go to the man we . . .

von Tellheim. I've heard enough. Come, let me go and throw myself at her feet.

Francisca. Don't think of such a thing. Go away and thank your lucky stars . . .

von Tellheim. Wretched girl! What do you take me for? No, my dear, that advice did not come from your heart. Forgive my severity.

Francisca. Don't keep me any longer. I must go and see how she is. Something might have happened to her.—Go away now and come back later, if you *want* to come.
[*Exit, after Minna.*]

Scene VIII

von Tellheim. Francisca !—Oh, I'll wait for you here.—No, the other is more urgent.—When she sees that I am in earnest, she will not deny me her forgiveness. Now I need you, honest Werner ! No, Minna, I am no traitor !

[*Exit hastily.*]

ACT V—Scene I

The Parlour as in Act III

Enter von Tellheim and Werner from opposite sides.

von Tellheim. There you are, Werner. I have been looking for you everywhere. Where have you been ?

Werner. Looking for you, sir—it's always the way. I have good news for you.

von Tellheim. It's not your news I need now, it's your money. Quick, Werner, give me what you have, and then go and fetch as much more as you can raise.

Werner. Beg pardon, sir ? By God, it's just as I said ! He'll borrow money off me when he has it to spare himself !

von Tellheim. You're not trying to back out ?

Werner. Just so that I shan't have anything to reproach him with, he takes with his right hand and gives with his left.

von Tellheim. Don't keep me waiting, Werner. I intend honestly to pay you back; but when and how, God alone knows.

Werner. So you don't know that the Treasury has orders to pay you your money back ? I've just heard about it from . . .

von Tellheim. What are you chattering about ? Are you letting people tell you the tale ? Don't you see that, if it were true, I should be the first to hear about it ? Come on, Werner, I want money !

Werner. Why, of course, with pleasure ! Here's the hundred gold louis, and here's the hundred ducats. [*Giving him both.*]

von Tellheim. Give the hundred louis to Just. Tell him to redeem the ring he pawned this morning. But where will you get more from, Werner ? I need a lot more.

Werner. Trust me to find that. The man that bought my farm lives in this town. True, he's not due to pay for a fortnight,

but the money's ready, and a little discount of a half per
cent. . . .

von Tellheim. Well and good, Werner, my dear fellow. You
see, you are my only resource, and I really must tell you
everything. The young lady here—you've seen her—has
had some ill luck . . .

Werner. What a pity !

von Tellheim. But to-morrow she will be my wife.

Werner. Well, that's fine !

von Tellheim. And the day after to-morrow we leave together.
I am free to go, and go I will. I'll leave everything here to
take care of itself. Who knows whether there may be a bit of
good luck in store for me elsewhere ! Come too, if you will.
We'll take service again.

Werner. Do you really mean that ? But some place where there's
a war, sir ?

von Tellheim. Where else ? Be off, now, Werner, we'll talk about
it later.

Werner. Good old Major ! The day after to-morrow ? Why not
to-morrow ? I'll raise the lot all right. There's a grand war in
Persia, sir. What do you say ?

von Tellheim. We'll think it over. But go now, Werner.

Werner. Hooray ! God save Prince Heraclius !

Scene II

✳ *von Tellheim.* What has come over me ? My very soul is filled
with new life ! My own misfortunes cast me down, made me
fractious, blind, inert. Hers lift me up. Now I can look
around me freely. I feel willing and able to undertake anything for her sake. But why do I dawdle here ? [*Goes towards
Minna's room, but meets Francisca as she comes out.*]

Scene III

Francisca. So it *is* really you ? I fancied I heard your voice.
What can I do for you, sir ?

von Tellheim. What can you do for me ? What is her ladyship
doing ? Tell me that.

Francisca. She's just going out.

von Tellheim. Alone ? Without me ? Where ?

Francisca. Have you forgotten, sir . . .

von Tellheim. Are you mad, Francisca ? I provoked her and

she was offended. I have come to ask her pardon, and she will forgive me.

Francisca. What, after you have taken the ring back, sir?

von Tellheim. Ha, I did that in a stupor. I never thought of it till now. Where did I put it? [*Looking for it.*] Here it is.

Francisca. Is that it? [*Aside, as he pockets it again.*] If only he'd look closer at it!

von Tellheim. She forced it on me, with such bitterness . . . but I have forgotten her bitterness already. A full heart cannot weigh words. . . . But she'll not refuse for a moment to take it back. . . . And have I not hers still?

Francisca. She is expecting you to return hers. But where is it, sir? Please show it me.

von Tellheim. [*Rather embarrassed.*] I—forgot to put it on. Just . . . Just is fetching it.

Francisca. I suppose it is much like the other? Let me look at this one. I love looking at such things.

von Tellheim. Some other time, Francisca. Now come. . . .

Francisca. [*Aside.*] He just won't be undeceived.

von Tellheim. What's that? Deceived?

Francisca. I say you are deceived if you think my lady is still a good match. Her own property is nothing considerable. By a bit of self-seeking accountancy her guardians could whittle it down to nothing. She had good expectations of her uncle. But that cruel uncle . . .

von Tellheim. Never mind about him. Am I not man enough to make everything up to her?

Francisca. Listen—she's ringing for me. I must go to her.

von Tellheim. I'll go with you.

Francisca. Don't, for heaven's sake! She has expressly forbidden me to speak to you. At least come in a little after me.

Scene IV

von Tellheim. [*Calling after her.*] Tell her I'm here. Speak for me, Francisca. I'll follow at once. What shall I tell her? When the heart dares to speak no preparations are needed. Only one thing might need reflection—her hesitation, her scruples about throwing herself into my arms in her misfortune, her efforts to pretend to me a happiness that she has lost on my account; to excuse to herself the lack of faith in my honour and in her own worth. Well? I have excused it already! Ah, here she comes!

Scene V

Enter Minna, as if unaware of the Major's presence.

Minna. Hasn't the carriage come, Francisca? Bring my fan.

von Tellheim. [*Stepping towards her.*] Where are you going, madam?

Minna. [*With an assumed coldness.*] I am going out, Major Tellheim. I think I can guess why you have been at pains to come here again—to return me my ring. Very well, Major Tellheim, be so good as to give it to Francisca. Francisca, take the ring from the Major. I have no time to lose. [*Going.*]

von Tellheim. [*Barring her way.*] Ah, the news I have just heard, madam! I was unworthy of so much love.

Minna. What, Francisca? Have you . . .?

Francisca. I have told the Major everything.

von Tellheim. Do not be angry with me, madam! I am no traitor. For my sake you have lost much in the eyes of the world, but not in mine. In mine you have gained immeasurably by this loss. But it was too sudden for you. You were afraid it would make an unfavourable impression on me. At first you sought to conceal it from me. I do not complain of your misgiving; it sprang from an impulse not to lose me. I am proud of that impulse! You found me also unfortunate, and you did not wish to heap sorrow on sorrow. You could not know how much more important your unhappiness would seem to me than my own.

Minna. Very well, sir. But what is done is done. I have released you from your obligation. By taking back your ring . . .

von Tellheim. I did not do it willingly! I feel myself now even more bound than before. You are mine now, Minna, for ever more. [*Taking the ring from his pocket.*] Here, take this for the second time, the pledge of my loyalty.

Minna. Am I to take this ring back? *This* ring?

von Tellheim. Yes, yes, dearest Minna!

Minna. Do you expect me to take *this* one back?

von Tellheim. The first time you took this ring from my hand our circumstances were both equally fortunate. Now they are no longer fortunate, but they are still equal. Equality is ever the surest bond of love. Allow me, dearest Minna. [*Takes her hand to put on the ring.*]

Minna. What? You use force, Major? No, there's no force in this world that can compel me to accept this ring again.

Do you think I am in need of a ring? You see as well as I do that I have here a ring in no way inferior to yours. [*Indicating her own ring.*]

Francisca. Well, if he doesn't notice now. . . .

von Tellheim. [*Letting go her hand.*] What's that? I see Fräulein von Barnhelm before me, but I do not hear her. You are pretending, madam. Forgive me for using your own expression.

Minna. [*In her natural voice.*] Are you insulted by that word, Major?

von Tellheim. It hurt me.

Minna. [*Touched.*] It was not meant to; forgive me, Tellheim.

von Tellheim. Ah, this warm tone tells me that you are coming to yourself, madam, that you still love me, Minna. . . .

Francisca. [*Breaking in.*] A little more and the joke would have gone too far. . . .

Minna. [*Imperiously.*] Pray mind your own business, Francisca.

Francisca. [*Aside, surprised.*] Hasn't she had enough yet?

Minna. Yes, sir, it was feminine vanity that made me cold and contemptuous. Away with it! You deserve to find me as straightforward as you are yourself. I love you, Tellheim, I love you still, nevertheless . . .

von Tellheim. No more of that, dearest Minna, no more of that. [*Taking her hand again to put on the ring.*]

Minna. [*Withdrawing her hand.*] In spite of that, or rather because of that, I will never permit this—never! How can you think of such a thing, sir? I should have thought your own troubles were enough. You must stay here and by truculence—truculence is the only word that occurs to me at the moment—obtain the fullest satisfaction for your honour, even if while you do so you perish in the extreme of poverty under the eyes of your slanderers!

von Tellheim. So I thought, so I said at a time when I did not know what I was thinking or saying. Anger and suppressed rage had clouded my mind. Love itself, in all its blissful power, could not then disperse those clouds. But Love sent her daughter, pity, who, more familiar with darkness and pain, pierced the mists and opened every gateway of my soul to tender feelings. The motive of self-preservation awoke now, when I had something more precious than myself to preserve, something that I alone could save. Do not be offended by the word pity, madam. We may hear it without humiliation from the innocent cause of our misfortune. I am that cause.

* ₭ 843

Through me, Minna, you have lost friends and family, home
and possessions.   In me, through me, you must find all these
again, or else I shall have on my conscience the destruction of
the sweetest of her sex.   Let me not face a future of self-
hatred !   No, nothing shall keep me longer here.   From this
moment I will answer with nothing but contempt the injustice
that has been shown me here.   Is this country the world?
Does the sun rise on Prussia alone?   Where can I not travel?
What country will refuse my services?   Even if I had to seek
service under the most distant skies, you may follow me with
confidence, dearest Minna, we shall want for nothing.   I have
a friend who will gladly help us. . . .

SCENE VI

Enter a courier

Minna. [*Seeing the courier.*] Sh ! sir !
von Tellheim. [*To the courier.*] For whom are you looking?
Courier. For Major von Tellheim.   Ah ! I see you are the officer
   himself.   Sir, I am commanded to deliver you [*taking docu-
   ment from a portfolio*] this royal letter.
von Tellheim. To me?
Courier. According to the address . . .
Minna. Do you hear that, Francisca?   The Chevalier spoke
   truth after all !
Courier. [*As Tellheim takes letter.*] I beg your pardon, sir.   You
   should have received it yesterday, but I was unable to find
   you.   It was not until to-day that Lieutenant Riccaut told
   me of your new address when I met him on the Parade.
Francisca. Do you hear that, my lady?   That's his " Minister "
   —" How does he call himself, the Minister out there on the
   so large place ? "
von Tellheim. I am deeply obliged to you for your efforts.
Courier. It is my duty, Major Tellheim, sir.   [*Exit.*]

SCENE VII

von Tellheim. Ah, madam, what is this?   What does this letter
   contain?
Minna. I have no right to extend my curiosity so far.
von Tellheim. No right?   You still separate my fate from yours?
   But why do I hesitate to unseal it?   It cannot make me more

unfortunate than I am—no, dearest Minna, it cannot make *us* more unfortunate; but perhaps more fortunate! Permit me, madam. [*Opens and reads letter while the Landlord steals in.*]

SCENE VIII

Landlord. [*To Francisca.*] Hist! my pretty dear, a word with you, please.

Francisca. [*Going to him.*] Our landlord? Indeed, we don't ourselves know yet what's in the letter.

Landlord. Who cares about the letter? I've come about the ring. Her ladyship must give it me back at once. Just has come to redeem it.

Minna. [*Also going to him.*] Tell him it's already redeemed. And tell him I redeemed it.

Landlord. But . . .

Minna. I'll take the responsibility. Be off, now!

[*Exit Landlord.*]

SCENE IX

Francisca. Now, my lady, stop tormenting the poor Major.

Minna. Little intercessor! Can't you see that the knots will soon untangle themselves?

von Tellheim. [*Having read the letter, with lively emotion.*] Ha! Again he has not disappointed me! Oh, madam, what justice! What graciousness! It is more than I had expected! More than I deserved! My fortune, my honour—all restored! Is it indeed no dream? [*Looking at the letter again, as if to reassure himself.*] No, it is no mirage of desire. Read it yourself, madam, read it yourself!

Minna. I am not so intrusive, sir!

von Tellheim. Intrusive? The letter is to me, to your Tellheim, Minna. It contains something your uncle cannot take from you. You must read it; do, please, read it!

Minna. Well, if it would please you . . . [*Takes letter and reads.*]

" MY DEAR MAJOR VON TELLHEIM,—

" This is to inform you that the business concerning your honour that caused me so much anxiety has been cleared up to your advantage. My brother was informed of the details, and his testimony has proved you more than innocent. The

Treasury has orders to return to you the bill of exchange in
question, and to repay you the sums advanced. I have also
directed that the queries raised by the Field Cashier's Office in
regard to your account be disallowed. Let me hear from you
as soon as your health allows you to take up your commission
again. I would not willingly dispense with the services of a
man of your gallantry and sentiments.

" FREDERICK OF PRUSSIA."

von Tellheim. Well, what do you say to that, madam?
Minna. [*Folding and returning letter.*] I? Nothing.
von Tellheim. Nothing?
Minna. Well yes, this—that your King, who is a great man, may
also be a good man. But what is that to me? He is not my
King.
von Tellheim. And you have nothing else to say? Nothing
about ourselves?
Minna. You are entering his service again. You will be promoted Lieutenant-Colonel, perhaps Colonel! I congratulate
you most sincerely.
von Tellheim. Do you know me no better than that? No;
since fortune has restored me enough to satisfy the wishes of
any sensible man, it shall depend on my Minna alone whether
I ever again belong to anyone but herself. My whole life
shall be dedicated to your service alone! The service of the
great is dangerous and not worth the effort, the servitude, the
humiliations it entails. Minna is not one of those vain women
who love in their husbands nothing but title and rank. She
will love me for my own sake, and for her I will forget the whole
world. I became a soldier from partiality—I myself do not
know for what political cause, and from a notion that it was
good for a man of honour to try his hand at that calling for a
time, to familiarize himself with all that danger implies, and to
learn coolness and resolution. Only utter necessity could have
forced me to make a profession of this experiment, a trade out
of this casual occupation. But now that I am no longer under
any such compulsion, my sole ambition is to be once again a
calm and contented man. I cannot fail to realize that ambition with you, dearest Minna; and in your company I shall
continue unshaken in that state. Let us be united to-morrow
in the holiest of bonds. After that we will look over the whole
wide inhabited world and choose the quietest, happiest,
brightest corner that only lacks a happy pair to make it a

paradise. There we will live. There every day of our lives.
. . . What is the matter, dear madam?

[*Minna turns uneasily from side to side, trying to conceal her
emotion.*]

Minna. [*Composing herself.*] You are very cruel, Tellheim, to
paint so charmingly a happiness I must renounce. My
loss . . .

von Tellheim. Your loss? What do you mean by your loss?
Whatever Minna can lose is not Minna. You are still the
sweetest, dearest, most charming, best creature under the
sun, all kindness and magnanimity, all innocence and joy!
—Here and there a little frivolity; now and then a little
obstinacy—so much the better! So much the better! Otherwise, Minna were an angel whom I could only revere with awe,
whom I could not love. [*Seizes and attempts to kiss her
hand.*]

Minna. [*Withdrawing her hand.*] No, no, sir! Why this sudden
change? Is this flattering, violent lover the cold Tellheim?
Could nothing but his returning good fortune so kindle his
ardour? He must allow me to reason for us both during the
transient heat of passion. While he could still think clearly
I heard him tell me it was but a worthless love that would
not scruple to expose its object to contempt. True: but I
aspire to a love as pure and as noble as his own. Now that
honour calls him, now that a great Monarch courts his alle-
giance, shall I allow him to give himself up to sentimental
dreams with me? Shall I permit the famous soldier to de-
generate into a love-sick shepherd? No, Major Tellheim,
follow the beckoning of your improving fortunes. . . .

von Tellheim. Very well! If the great world attracts you more,
Minna, then let the great world have us! How small, how
petty, is this great world! So far you know it only on its
gilded side. But, Minna, I am sure you will—— Let it be.
So far so good. Your perfections will not lack admirers, nor
my happiness many to envy me.

Minna. No, Tellheim, I did not mean that. I point you back
to the great world by the path of honour, without offering to
follow you. There Tellheim would need a wife above reproach.
A runaway Saxon miss who threw herself at his head . . .

von Tellheim. [*Starting up and looking fiercely about him.*] Who
dares speak so? Ah, Minna, I fear myself when I imagine
anyone saying that but you. My fury against him would
break all bounds.

Minna. There you are! That is what appals me. You
wouldn't endure the slightest taunt against me, and yet day
by day you would have to swallow very bitter ones. Now
listen, Tellheim, this is what I have decided on, and nothing
in the world shall change me . . .

von Tellheim. Before you finish, madam, I implore you, Minna—
remember for a moment that you are pronouncing a life or
death sentence on me!

Minna. I need no further consideration! As surely as I have
returned you the ring with which once you pledged me your
troth, as surely as you accepted that ring, so surely will the
unhappy Minna never be the wife of the more fortunate
Tellheim!

von Tellheim. Are you condemning me to death, madam?

Minna. Equality is the only firm bond of love. If I were happy
I should want to live only for your happiness. Even were I
unhappy I could have been persuaded to share your unhappiness, be it to increase or to alleviate it. You no doubt will
have noticed, before this letter came to put an end again to our
equality, that I was only making a pretence of refusing?

von Tellheim. Is that true, madam? My thanks, Minna, that
you have not yet pronounced sentence! You want only an
unhappy Tellheim? You may have him. [*Coldly.*] It seems to
me now that to accept this tardy rehabilitation does not become
me; it would be better not to reclaim what has been dishonoured by such a shameful suspicion. Yes, I will behave as
if I had not received the letter. This shall be my sole answer
to it. [*About to tear up letter.*]

Minna. [*Seizing his hands.*] What are you thinking of, Tellheim?

von Tellheim. Making you my wife.

Minna. Stop!

von Tellheim. Madam, it will irrevocably be torn if you do not
quickly change your mind. Then we shall see what *else* you
have against me.

Minna. What? You speak to me so? Then shall I, must I,
become despicable in my own eyes? Never! She is a
worthless creature who is not ashamed to owe all her happiness
to the blind tenderness of a man!

von Tellheim. It is false, utterly false!

Minna. Do you dare deny your own words when they come from
my mouth?

von Tellheim. Sophistry! Is the weaker sex dishonoured by all that does not become the stronger? May a man allow himself everything that beseems a woman? Which of us did Nature ordain to be the prop of the other?

Minna. Do not be alarmed, Tellheim. I shall not be quite without support, even if I must decline the honour of yours. I shall still have as much as the occasion requires. I reported to our Ambassador. He has granted me an interview for to-day. I hope he will take up my case. Time passes. Excuse me, sir . . .

von Tellheim. I'll go with you, madam.

Minna. No, no, Major. Let me go alone.

von Tellheim. As soon bid your shadow let you go! Come, madam, let us go wherever you will, to whomsoever you will. I will tell all, friend and stranger alike, a hundred times a day in your presence, with what bonds you have bound me, and with what cruel obstinacy you are trying to sever them. . . .

Scene X

Enter Just

Just. [*Hurrying in.*] Major von Tellheim, sir!

von Tellheim. What is it?

Just. Come quick, sir!

von Tellheim. What do you want? Come over here to me. Tell me what's the matter.

Just. Listen! [*Whispers in his ear.*]

Minna. [*Aside to Francisca.*] Do you see what that means, Francisca?

Francisca. Oh, you were cruel! I've been on tenterhooks!

von Tellheim. [*To Just.*] What do you say? It's not possible! . . . She? [*Looking wildly at Minna.*] Say it aloud; say it to her face! Listen to this, madam.

Just. The Landlord says her ladyship has in her possession the ring I pawned with him, saying it was hers, that she recognized it, and she wouldn't part with it. . . .

von Tellheim. Is that true, madam? No, it cannot be!

Minna. [*Smiling.*] And why not, Tellheim? Why cannot it be true?

von Tellheim. Well, suppose it is true. What a fearful light dawns on me! Now I recognize you—false and faithless!

Minna. [*Startled.*] Who is faithless?

von Tellheim. She whom I will no longer name.

Minna. TELLHEIM !

von Tellheim. Forget my name ! You came here to break with me. That's clear. How strange that fate should so often aid the disloyal ! It brought your ring into your hands again. Your cunning succeeded in exchanging it for mine.

Minna. Tellheim, what spectres are you seeing ? Be calm and listen to me.

Francisca. [*Aside.*] It serves her right.

SCENE XI

Enter Werner with a purse of money.

Werner. Here I am again, sir.

von Tellheim. [*Not looking at him.*] Who wants you ?

Werner. Here's money—a thousand pistoles.

von Tellheim. I don't want it.

Werner. To-morrow, sir, you can have as much again.

von Tellheim. Keep your money.

Werner. But it's *your* money, sir. I don't think you see who you're talking to.

von Tellheim. Take it away, I say.

Werner. What's the matter ? I'm Werner.

von Tellheim. All kindness is hypocrisy ; all service is deceit.

Werner. Is that meant for me ?

von Tellheim. If you like.

Werner. Why, I only carried out your orders. . . .

von Tellheim. Then obey this one—and get out !

Werner. Major von Tellheim ! [*Angrily.*] Sir, I'm a man . . .

von Tellheim. Then you are something indeed marvellous !

Werner. A man with a temper, too !

von Tellheim. Good ! After all, temper is the best thing about us.

Werner. I beg you, Major . . .

von Tellheim. How many times must I tell you ? I don't need your money.

Werner. [*Angrily.*] Then let anyone have it that wants it ! [*Throwing down the purse at his feet and going upstage.*]

Minna. Ah, dear Francisca, I should have taken your advice. I've carried the jest too far. Yet if only he would listen to me ! [*Going to Tellheim.*]

Francisca. [*Not answering Minna, and going to Werner.*] Sergeant-Major . . .
Werner. [*Sullenly.*] Go away !
Francisca. Ugh ! What nice men !
Minna. Tellheim, Tellheim [*von Tellheim bites his nails with rage
  and turns his face away, refusing to listen.*] Oh, it's too much !
  Listen to me.   You are mistaken !   It's all a misunderstanding.   Tellheim !   Won't you listen to your Minna?—How
  could you suspect me so?   *I* break with you?   *I* come here
  for that ?   Tellheim !

SCENE XII

Enter two servants, one after the other, from opposite sides of stage.

First servant. Madam, his Excellency the Count ! . . .
Second servant. He's here, my lady.
Francisca. [*Running to the window.*] It is he !   It is he !
Minna. Is it he?   Oh ! now quickly, Tellheim! . . .
von Tellheim. [*Suddenly coming to himself.*] Who?   Who is
  coming?   Your uncle, madam?   Your cruel uncle?   Let him
  come !   Have no fear !   Let him dare offend you, by as much
  as a look.   He will have me to reckon with. . . . Indeed you
  don't deserve it of me. . . .
Minna. Quickly, Tellheim, embrace me and forget everything . . .
von Tellheim. Oh, if I could be sure you could be sorry for it
  all !
Minna. No, I cannot be sorry for having obtained this insight
  into your whole heart.   What a man you are !   Embrace
  your Minna, your happy Minna !   But happier, in nothing
  happier, than in you. [*Falls into his arms.*] And now let's go
  to meet him.
von Tellheim. Meet whom?
Minna. The best of your unknown friends.
von Tellheim. What?   Whom?
Minna. The Count, my uncle, my father, your father.—My flight,
  his enmity, my disinheritance—didn't you understand it was
  all invented?   O credulous knight !
von Tellheim. Invented?   But what about the ring—the ring?
Minna. Where is the ring I gave back to you?
von Tellheim. Do you want it back?   Oh, how happy I am !
  Here, Minna. [*Taking it from his pocket.*]
Minna. Look at it first.—Oh, there's none so blind as those that

won't see ! Which ring is it? The one you had from me, or
the one I had from you? Is it not the very one I did not want
to leave with the landlord?

von Tellheim. My God, what's this I hear? What do I see?

Minna. Shall I take it back? Tell me? Give it to me, give it
to me. [*Takes it from his hand and herself puts it on his finger.*]
Now, is all well?

von Tellheim. Where am I? [*Kissing her hand.*] You malicious
angel—to torment me so !

Minna. This is for a pledge, my dear husband, that you shall
never play a trick on me but I'll play one on you ! Do you
suppose you did not torment me too?

von Tellheim. O you comedians ! I ought to have found you out !

Francisca. That we are not. I'm not cut out for an actress. I
shook and shivered and had to put my hand over my mouth.

Minna. I did not find my part easy, either. But will you not
come with me?

von Tellheim. I am still not recovered. How relieved and yet
afraid I feel ! As if I had awakened from a dreadful dream !

Minna. We must not delay. I hear him coming.

Scene XIII

*Enter Count von Bruchsall, accompanied by several Servants
and the Landlord.*

Count. So she got here safely?

Minna. [*Running to him.*] Ah, my father !

Count. Here I am, Minna dear. [*Kissing her.*] But what's this,
my dear? Here only four-and-twenty hours and already
entertaining friends?

Minna. Guess who it is?

Count. Could it be your friend Tellheim?

Minna. Who else? Come, Tellheim. [*Leading him towards the
Count.*]

Count. Sir, we have never met; but I thought I recognized you
at sight. I hoped it might be you. Embrace me. You have
my highest regard. I would welcome your friendship. My
niece, my daughter, loves you . . .

Minna. You know it, father ! And is my love blind?

Count. No, Minna, your love is not blind. But your lover—is
dumb.

von Tellheim. [*Embracing the Count.*] Let me recover from my surprise, my father.

Count. That's the way, my son ! I see that if your tongue is unready your heart can speak. I don't usually much care for officers wearing tunics that colour. [*Pointing to his uniform.*] But you're an honourable man, Tellheim, and an honourable man may wear what cloth he chooses and still be loved.

Minna. Oh, if you knew everything ! . . .

Count. What's to prevent me knowing everything? Where are my rooms, Landlord?

Landlord. Will your Excellency be so kind as to step this way?

Count. Come, Minna, come Major.

[*Exit with Landlord and Servants.*]

Minna. Come, Tellheim.

von Tellheim. I'll follow you in a moment, madam. I want a word with this man. [*Turning to Werner.*]

Minna. Let it be a very kind one. I think you owe it him— doesn't he, Francisca? [*Exit, following the Count.*]

SCENE XIV

von Tellheim. [*Pointing to the purse that Werner had thrown down.*] Here, Just, take up that purse and be off home with it. Go on ! [*Exit Just.*]

Werner. [*Still standing sullenly in the corner and seeming to pay no attention.*] Well?

von Tellheim. [*Approaching him in friendly manner.*] Werner, when can I have the other thousand pistoles?

Werner. [*Suddenly relapsing into a good humour.*] To-morrow, sir, to-morrow.

von Tellheim. I have no need to be your debtor, but I would like to be your treasurer. There should be a guardian for all such generous people as you. You are a kind of spend-thrift !—I annoyed you just now, Werner?

Werner. By God, you did, sir !—But still, I ought not to have been such a blockhead. Now I realize it. I deserve a hundred lashes, and I don't care if I get them either. Only no more hard feelings, Major Tellheim, sir !

von Tellheim. Hard feelings? [*Taking his hand.*] You may read in my eyes all that I cannot tell you—I should like to see the man that has a better girl and a stouter friend than I.— Wouldn't you, Francisca? [*Exit.*]

SCENE XV

Francisca. [*Aside.*] Yes. Indeed, he is a wonderful man ! I shall never see his like again.—I must say it. [*Shyly, and shamefacedly going up to Werner.*] Sergeant-Major . . .

Werner. [*Wiping his eyes.*] Well?

Francisca. Sergeant-Major . . .

Werner. What is it, little girl?

Francisca. Please look at me, Sergeant-Major. . . .

Werner. I can't yet; I don't know what's got into my eye.

Francisca. Oh, but do look at me, please !

Werner. I'm afraid I have been looking at you too much already, little girl—there, now I can see you, what's up, then?

Francisca. Sergeant-Major—don't you want a *Mrs.* Sergeant-Major?

Werner. Do you really *mean* that, little girl?

Francisca. I do indeed. . . .

Werner. Would you go to Persia with me?

Francisca. Wherever you like.

Werner. Would you really? Hallo, Major, don't you boast ! Now I have at least as good a girl and as stout a friend as you ! Give me your hand, little girl. Done with you ! In ten years time you'll be either the General's Lady or a widow.

EVERYMAN'S LIBRARY: A Selected List

BIOGRAPHY

ESSAYS AND CRITICISM

1

FICTION

3

4

POETRY AND DRAMA

REFERENCE

Reader's Guide to Everyman's Library. Compiled by *A. J. Hoppé*. This volume is a new compilation and gives in one alphabetical sequence the names of all the authors, titles and subjects in Everyman's Library. (An Everyman Paperback, 1889.)
Many volumes formerly included in Everyman's Library reference section are now included in Everyman's Reference Library and are bound in larger format.

RELIGION AND PHILOSOPHY